RED GRANITE

The Grains of Truth
Beneath the Sands of Egypt

ALEXANDER RETROV

III

DENDERA - DAHSHUR

RED GRANITE

The Grains of Truth Beneath the Sands of Egypt
III
Dendera - Dahshur

Alexander Retrov

Editor: Alexander Retrov
Graphic Design: Goran Djcinovic
Publisher: Renaissance Entertainment Pty Ltd
Printer: Amazon books

This work is 90% fact and 10% fiction.
It's up to you to determine which is which.

To see the truth for yourself and join Krystal or Alex
on one of the Red Granite or Goddess Reawakening Tours
go to the website for more details on the next tour.

www.alexanderretrov.com

© 2018 Renaissance Entertainment Ltd Pty
Second edition
First edition printed in Australia by Eureka Printing
ISBN: 978-0-9943146-5-9

www.alexanderretrov.com

RED GRANITE

The Grains of Truth
Beneath the Sands of Egypt

III

Dendera - Dahshur

ACKNOWLEDGEMENTS

My deep gratitude goes to Krystal,
without whose support and patience
this book would never have been written.

I also want to acknowledge Source
for choosing me as the conduit for this work

To my brother in Egypt, Abdou Ashour

This book is dedicated to the truth.

CHAPTER 21 – ITS ALL IN THE STARS

The air was pregnant with the balmy scent of morning as I made my way out of the undergrowth of the jungle and into the clearing; the first throws of sunlight illuminating the gently undulating surface of the waterhole. Around the perimeter, a herd of apprehensive antelope twitched as they gathered to partake of their morning drinks from the cool waters.

Above, from an outcrop of boulders, the crystal clear waters cascaded down over the rocks forming a sparkling waterfall. Caressed by the water, the silken strands of hair and svelte skin of a naked woman glistened in the fervent embrace of the flow, which hugged her undulating figure like an over-zealous admirer.

Enveloped in her aquatic cocoon, the woman sensuously stroked her breasts, stomach, buttocks and legs. In contrast to the fluid motion of the water, the initial stirrings in my groin suddenly became rock hard and rigid, drawing me towards her like a bee to an open blossom. I drifted ever closer, the pressure in my groin intensifying with each caress, each stroke of her dripping skin and moist body. Pausing at the edge of the pool, I cast my gaze across the water, an ominous ripple catching my attention. On closer inspection, I made out a dark shape moving undetected below the surface and towards the woman. Suddenly I was frozen, not only unable to move, but unable to call out, powerless to prevent the sinister shape from closing in on its target.

Oblivious of the danger closing in on her, the women turned away, her back to the pool, and bent over, her hands drifting erotically between her soaking thighs. I was on the point of exploding, but immobilized, incapable of any action.

As the submerged spectre lunged from the water, the flow of the waterfall suddenly ceased and I was jolted into the now, realizing it was just a dream and I was lying in bed with a rather pressing erection. I lay there momentarily reviewing the scenario then rolled over on to my back, my erection like a telescopic tent-pole under the sheet.

'Oh I was just about to suggest you get up, but I see you already are.'

Shit, suddenly I realized and remembered where I was, or rather where I wasn't; back at the Nubian Oasis. I was at the Nefertiti and in Crystal's bed wearing just my top and my Calvins; somehow Crystal had removed my shoes, socks and pants, without me even stirring.

Caught literally with my pants down, I rolled back over towards her voice and, as nonchalantly as possible, opened an eye. There she was, having just stepped out of the shower, as naked as the day she was born, drying her hair with a towel. This time I wasn't going to be so shy.

'Now that's a sight I could get used to waking up to.'

'Then you had better get a move on, or we shall have to leave you behind.'

And what a behind it was! I followed her every move as she sauntered out of the ensuite and into the main room.

'What's the time?'

'Just after 7:00.'

'And what time do we have to go?'
'Bill and Pernille will be here around 7:45.'

I had to admit, at the time, the thought of forty-five minutes of passionate morning-sex sounded pretty appealing; especially if it involved the walking embodiment of sexuality that was parading before me. Somehow though, as Crystal slowly dressed, I don't think a little morning glory was on her agenda; perhaps, if I played my cards right, the evening may present another opportunity.

I slithered out of bed, took off my shirt and Calvins and hopped in the shower. It felt great, refreshing, though my mind was filled with images of the naked woman in the waterfall, and of course that woman was Crystal. That wasn't helping me avoid an erection, and rubbing soap over my body, including my groin was making me as horny as a rampant gerbil on Viagra.

Contemplating taking matters a little more earnestly in hand, I glanced over my shoulder towards the door to check the coast was clear. To my surprise Crystal calmly stood in the doorway.
'Is everything…OK?'
'Yeah, perfect, why?'
She gave me the once over: down, then back up.
'Oh, nothing, I'm just sizing up what *my* options might be for sights to wake up to every morning.'
'And...?
'They might be too much of a distraction, I mean, I might be tempted never to get out of bed again. I will see you at breakfast; it's just down the hall, along from the meeting room. Don't take … *too long...*'
She grinned, raised and eyebrow then took one definite prolonged appraisal of my groin.
'…Yes, a big distraction in deed.'

I think I had my hands on the soap before the latch on the door even closed behind her. It had been a few days since Candy took a load off my mind, and in the ensuing days I'd had several alluring and erotic episodes where the spitting cobra was poised to strike but reined in before he was even unleashed. After this morning's visions and dialogue, the beast could no longer be restrained.

The past three or four days built up within me faster than the imminent eruption of Thera. To say that within minutes I had sprayed a mural half way up the shower wall that would have made Pro Hart or Jackson Pollock proud would have been an understatement.

Clean and refreshed, the room and shower similarly taken care of, I arrived at breakfast to be greeted by Diane and the rest of the ladies. They were all genuinely interested in my welfare without directly probing into the details of my previous night's experience, which was fine by me, as I really hadn't even had a chance to process it myself.

Obviously the breakfast table was not the appropriate place to follow up with Crystal on the morning or evening's events. Even when 7:30 arrived, and Diane led all the ladies off to their awaiting bus, I still didn't get a chance, because by the time they'd said their goodbyes, all made last minute dashes to their rooms for hats, sunscreen, and other 'personal effects', it was 7:40 and Bill and Pernille had arrived.
'Hey, Alex, good to see you; we thought we'd lost you to the infinite ether.'
'No chance of that, Bill, we've still got work to do; I'm not sure what it is

exactly, or how we're supposed to do it, but we certainly ain't here to watch the flowers grow or the paint dry.'

Bill and Pernille joined us as Crystal and I finished off our breakfast.

'That must have been some trip you were on last night.'

'It was.'

I filled them in on my encounter with Hesat and the mission of the Hathors to offer advice through their own experiences and perspectives to assist the ascension of human consciousness and the possibility of a new age on the earth.

'I can't believe I'm telling you this, you must think I'm crazy.'

'No crazier than the rest of us…'

After Bill's experience the day before, it was no wonder he was the most vocal, and most curious.

'…what else did she say?'

'That if the human race is ready to build a new world, then they must take responsibility for their own words and action and that the Hathors will share their experiences and wisdom, but that in the end, the human race can take it or leave it.'

'So they're here to help the human race ascend.'

'Sort of; but rather than see ascension as a pathway, they see it as a process of self-awareness and mastery on all levels of space/time.'

'So what advice do they have?'

'It's not so much advice, as the use of sacred geometry and vibration.'

'Such as?'

'Through things like crop circles they stimulate the retinal receptors and trigger the sub-atomic neural pathways of the brain.'

'Why don't they just beam down and tell us directly?'

'I'm not sure; maybe they're not allowed. But they did say, contrary to popular belief, that no advanced alien race, no messiah or ascended master, was going to come down to save mankind and save the planet.'

'Well that blasts the major religions out of the ballpark; I don't think they'll be taking much heed of what the Hathors have to say. Anything else?'

I hesitated, then decided, 'what the hell, in for a penny, in for a pound'.

'That I may have incarnated into a human form, but that's just what I *appear to be,* not what I am; like the driver of a car is not the car, or an actor is not the costume he wears or the character he plays. That my purpose, that *our* purpose, is to assist humans to raise their vibrational existence.'

'And how do we do that?

'She wouldn't say; just that sometimes the script must be left to unfold by itself.'

Bill slapped the table.

'Right then, we'd better get unfolding.'

'We need to call in at my hotel first to pick up my backpack and hopefully my hat.'

'No problem; we have to get Pieter and Yuko anyway.'

As we headed out to the minibus, I suddenly realized that everything Hesat had said, I'd heard before, from Crystal. Was she a Hathor incarnate? It wouldn't surprise me.

A familiar face greeted us at the minibus, Saleem, whom it turned out was yet another of Saeed's cousins. It turned out Bill had teed the trip up with him the day we arrived in Luxor, though at the time he wasn't sure who, or how many, would be travelling with him. So far there were four of us on board and, a few minutes later, we arrived at the Nubian Oasis to extend that to our full compliment of six.

'Wait here, I'll go in.'

I leaped out of the magic bus and hustled inside to where Pieter and Yuko were waiting in the lobby. Ready and eager to go, they greeted me then moved straight out and into the bus. Thankfully the shop owner from the day before was also waiting in the lobby with my trusty dusty akubra and, as soon as I stepped through the door, he made a beeline for me. And I don't blame him either, two hundred Egyptian Pounds was nothing to be sneeze at. I took a wad of notes out of my pocket, counted out four fifties and held them out for him.

'Please, but the dress for the lady, three-hundred, very good quality.'

Fair enough, and I counted out another hundred.

'Three hundred for dress, two hundred for hat.'

Damn, I was being shafted again. I felt like telling him to find Ahmed and sort it out with him, but before I could launch into the next round of negotiations, Seleh called out from behind the reception desk.

'Mr. Alex, before you go, Mr. Dwight he leave it the message for you.'

He held out a single sheet of A4 folded in half and I leaned over to take it.

"The grains of truth are buried beneath the sands of the oasis."

What the hell did that mean? My mind started ticking over.

'Seleh, were the police here yesterday?'

'Yes, they come about 3:30 and ask to check it the hotel list, and to see it the passport. Then they ask to see it your room. I remember Mr. Dwight he is up on roof read it the paper you give him. At breakfast I see the paper he read: very dangerous. I have Mustaphe take police to it your room, and while they are being there I go up to Mr. Dwight. I tell him it not good to be find with these paper. He and Mr. Randy decide it best to go straight away to airport so I take it them myself. That is when Mr. Dwight he hand it me the note and say to give it you, that it very important.'

'What happened to the folder of papers?'

'This I do not know.'

'Did he take them with him?'

'This he must have.'

I was concerned and confused.

'Then why leave this message?'

Like a blue-heeler pup persistently annoying its nursing mother, the shop-owner continued to nibble at my ankles, adding to my concerns.

'Three-hundred.'

'One-fifty.'

'No, please, it worth five hundred. Three-hundred.'

I was cornered; if I wanted my hat back, I *had* to negotiate. Sure I could just walk away and buy another hat for thirty or forty Egyptian pounds, but the problem was, I'd become very attached to my akubra and wasn't going to part with it without a fight. At that moment, sensing things had been delayed, Bill swaggered into the lobby.

'What's the hold up?'

'Hold up's the word; Ned Kelly over here wants three-hundred for the dress I had on last night, that's three-hundred *on top* of the two-hundred I promised him for returning my hat.'

'You know, Alex, I wouldn't have picked you for a cross-dresser.'

8

'Very funny. There's also this.'

I handed him Dwight's note.

'"The grains of truth are buried beneath the sands of the oasis." What's it mean?'

'I don't know.'

'Have you focused on the underlined words; grains, truth, buried, beneath the sands, the oasis. I mean, this is the oasis, here, the Nubian Oasis.'

Then it hit me.

'Of course! They're here, upstairs on the roof.'

I took off up the stairs as Bill called out after me.

'What are?'

'Kareem's papers.'

Reaching the rooftop I headed straight for the beach, dropped to my knees and started feeling around in the sand. As I moved to the hammock that Randy spent most of his time reclining and recovering in, right underneath I uncovered a scrap of plastic. Brushing away the surrounding sand I quickly unearthed 'the bag'.

'Shit, what do I do now?'

I couldn't just leave them there; Kareem had entrusted them to me, and if the police got hold of them, Kareem was history. On the off chance someone was watching, I stuffed the papers under my shirt and hustled down the stairs to my room. The door securely closed, I grabbed my laptop from under the bed, grabbed my backpack, and stuffed both my laptop and the papers into it. Taking a few deep breaths, I headed back downstairs to the lobby where Bill was waiting on his 'pat malone', my akubra in his hand.

'Where's the shop-owner?'

He tossed me my hat.

'Gone. I took care of it.'

'How much do I owe you?'

'Don't worry about it, he went away happy.'

I was sure Bill probably gave him the five-hundred but I didn't want to hang around here sorting it out.

'Quick, let's get going.'

'What's up?'

'I'll tell you about it, once we're out of Luxor.'

Drowning in the desert

I spent the first fifteen minutes or so of the trip hugging my backpack like a stressed-out two-year-old clutching his favourite teddy bear, watching the traffic behind us to see if we were followed. Sitting in the back seat, Pernille and Crystal had quickly resumed their in-depth conversations and were clearly becoming close friends, like sisters; they probably were in another life. Beside them, Bill politely sat and listened; only contributing when asked. He was obviously besotted with Pernille, and why not, since she had dumped Jacques she was literally glowing.

In contrast Pieter and Yuko stayed fairly quiet and pensive; content with watching the abject poverty of the Egyptian villagers roll passed mile after mile, only to be interrupted by the multitude of speed bumps that adorned the roads. Every intersecting road or village had speed bumps, not your basic conventional speed bump but mutated ones large enough to bring even the biggest buses and trucks to a virtual standstill.

Given how prone the Egyptians were to speeding, clearly this was the local villages response to creating safe roads. It meant that instead of taking less than an hour to cover the sixty kilometres to Dendera, the trip was going to take nearly two hours.

Eventually satisfied we were not being followed, I pulled out my iphone and called Saeed.

'Saeed, it's Alex.'

'Indy, where have you been, I have been trying to warn you, the Secret Police they have arrested Kareem, they know it about the paper.'

'No shit, Sherlock. Why didn't you call me?'

'Indy, I did not have it your number, this is why I send him my nephew to your hotel. Why was it you did run away from him?'

'I thought he was the Secret Police.'

'OK, never to mind, do you still have it the paper?'

I looked at my backpack.

'Well, yes I do, that's the problem.'

'Where are you?'

'On my way to Dendera and Abydos with Bill, Pernille, Pieter, Yuko and Crystal.'

'Very good, stay calm; the Secret Police they have already searched your room so they do not think you are have them. I think it our little stunt the other night it must have fooled them.'

'You think so?'

He laughed.

'Yes, they think it that I am have them.'

'Are you OK?'

'So long as I do *not* have them, yes.'

'So what should I do with them?'

'Please to keep them somewhere safe. I will meet it you at your hotel when you get back tonight from Abydos and we shall work it something out. In the meantime enjoy your visit to Dendera and Abydos; everything it will be fine.'

'Inshallah!'

He chuckled.

'Yes, Inshallah.'

As I put my iphone away, Bill, who had overheard his name and made his way to the front of the minibus, stated the bleeding obvious.

'Let me guess, the pellet with the poison's in the vessel with the pestle.'

'Huh?'

As he pointed to the backpack, I got the reference to Danny Kaye's 'Court Jester'.

'The poisoned papers are in the backpack, right?'

'Yep.'

'Sort of like a pharaoh's curse, or a bad case of herpes, no matter what you do with them, or who you give them away to, they always find a way of coming back.'

'Very funny.'

'Do you mind if I take a look?'

'You sure you want to touch them, the curse might be contagious?'

'I'll take my chances.'

'Can you read Arabic?'

'No, but I've never let that hold me back.'

I took the plastic bag of papers from my backpack, handed them over, then, deciding I needed to liven up the 'magic bus' with a little music, took out my laptop as well and fired it up. For some reason I chose Beethoven's 3rd Symphony.

I made brief notes on my further discussions with Dwight and Randy on the roof about Muburak, Hawass's corruption and connection to the CIA, and about leaving the papers with Dwight and heading to Karnak. How, once there, the spirits of the Amun Priests harassed me, my experience at the alabaster altar and my feeling I was Akhenaten.

I noted Bill's channelling, and my connection with Sekhmet, in the Temple of Ptah, as well as my experiences in the inner sanctum, and the alabaster 'barque shrines' of Amenhotep I and II and the red-granite shrine of Hatshepsut in the open museum. How I believed, because of their dimensions, and the vibrational nature of the stone, that they were connected with the obelisks, which acted as antennae, and formed some type of molecular accelerators. That Khepri was more a symbol of recycling, of rejuvenation, rather than rebirth.

Then there were the constant examples of worn and weathered red granite in both the Amun Precinct and the Mut Precinct and, in particular, the statues and altars made of alabaster, which I believed belonged to the Middle Kingdom or even earlier. In addition, I was still contemplating the broken statue fragment with the reptilian claw on both sides, and the crypts under the Temple of Opet.

It was slightly embarrassing recalling my 'escape' from Saeed's nephew, and the subsequent chase through the bazaar, though by the time I'd arrived at the Winter Palace again for drinks, and noting Bill's American Indian awakening, and the discussion of the concept of 'change', I felt more relaxed.

Finally I detailed my encounter with Hesat and that I may well not be of human consciousness; that I have a definite purpose here on earth. Oh, and of course there was the gorgeous vision of Crystal I awoke to, hmmm, only to be tempered somewhat with the unearthing of Kareem's papers, that ominously presented before me in Bill's hands.

'Well, they look official enough.'

'Yeah, so is a death certificate.'

'Why don't you just mail them to yourself?'

'That's not a bad idea, I don't know why I didn't think of it earlier.'

'You can do it when we get back to Luxor.'

'But what if they get lost in the mail, I'd never forgive myself if something happened to them; I promised Kareem.'

'Then make a copy first; scan them, photocopy them, even take some snaps with your iphone...'

Bill was right, I had heaps of options, and he handed them back.

'...just don't get caught with them.'

'Don't worry, I don't intend to.'

And with that I went to stash them in the cooler of the mini bus.

'Whoa, I wouldn't do that, bucko; if those papers get wet, the ink will run faster than Usain Bolt with a rocket up his ass.'

'Even though they're in the plastic bag?'

'I wouldn't take the risk, even if they were hermetically sealed and in the middle of the White Desert.'

I got the point and stuffed them back in my backpack, but I was also curious.

'The White Desert? Where's that?'

'About five or six hours drive south-west of Cairo, near the Bahariya Oasis;

amazing place, an area of nearly six-thousand square kilometres in the middle of nowhere. Miles and miles of massive chalk rock formations for as far as the eye can see, all sculptured out of the ground by swirling sandstorms.'

'Sounds amazing.'

'It's one of the most extraordinary places on the planet. Hang on; I think I've still got a few snaps on my camera.'

Bill dived into his bag, pulled out his camera, flicked through the files until he found what he was looking for, then handed me the camera.

'Here you go, scroll through these...'

As I perused the images, Bill continued his geology lecture.

'...When an asteroid hit the earth and ended the Cretaceous period sixty-five-million years ago, the area became a shallow sea that covered layers of sandstone formed one-hundred-million years ago during the Cenomanian age. During the next thirty-million years, three-hundred metres of limestone and chalk collected at the bottom of the sea.

Then, around the Oligocene epoch thirty-million years ago, an ice formation in the Atlantic caused the sea to recede and the interesting shapes were formed as the result of millions of years of erosion of the limestone and chalk by wind and sand.'

'These look like icebergs.'

'I know; if it wasn't for the heat, you'd think you were in the Antarctic somewhere.'

'And you say this erosion was cause by sandstorms?'

'That's the thinking.'

'It looks more like water erosion to me. Sure sandstorms may have had *some* effect, but how high did you say these were?'

'Up to thirty to forty metres.'

'No way; had to be water erosion.'

'Give me a look again.'

I handed the camera back, then had a brainwave.

'Do you think it could have been the tsunami from the Thera eruption in 1600 BC?'

'I don't know, I suppose it's possible, but the desert's maybe a thousand kilometres inland, and the wave would've had to have been maybe fifty metres high at least.'

'Well, if the Thera eruption was as big as they say it was, then the wave that hit the Nile Delta could have been at least a *hundred* metres high, possibly more.'

Bill handed me back the camera.

'You know what, I think you may be right.'

Yuko, who had been silently witnessing the conversation, chipped in her thoughts.

'Actually, scientists have calculated that the Thera eruption would have produced a tsunami around *two* hundred metres high.'

'Jesus!'

Bill and I looked at each other, both trying to visualize what the impact would have been like.

'I think that definitely answers your tsunami theory; it's a wonder anything survived.'

'The Valley of the Golden Mummies did.'

'Whoa, what and where is the Valley of the Golden Mummies?'

Yuko had suddenly thrown in a location I hadn't even heard of, and I wasn't going to let it slip by without hearing the details.

'It is a huge burial site in the Bahariya Oasis. The story goes that, in 1996, an antiquities guard was riding his donkey, when the donkey's foot fell into a hole.'

That didn't add up.

'What was an antiquities guard doing in the middle of nowhere?'

'That's a good point.'

Bill had the answer.

'There's actually the ruins of a temple to Alexander the Great there, and some Egyptologists believe he passed through Bahariya while returning from visiting the oracle at the Siwa Oasis, so the site actually dates to the Ptolemaic and Roman Period of Egypt, which means it post-dates the Thera tsunami anyway, though I guess it doesn't fully account for its subsequent demise.'

'Have you been there?'

Bill shook his head.

'No, I was really only interested in the geological aspects of the area.'

Yuko gave it more prominence.

'Pieter and I are planning to visit it when we head out to the Western Desert.'

'What's the big attraction?'

'The hole led to the discovery of about thirty-four tombs and around two-hundred-and-fifty mummies, many with coffins covered in gold. It's turned out to be a massive burial site, and they're still digging. The archaeologists think there could be as many as ten-thousand mummies in the area.'

'Ten thousand!'

It meant there must have been quite a large population out there in 'the middle of nowhere' as well, at least until the early years AD. So, what happened to them? Was this more evidence of another natural disaster, another tsunami? Or could it just be fobbed off with the explanation of successive invasions? I guess the answers are all out there in the desert, but you'd have to have more than just a bucket and spade to find them. I kept flicking through the images.

'What are these others photos of; these black mountains scattered across the desert?'

'That's the Black Desert, it's just down the road from the white desert, maybe an hour or so further north and about fifty kilometres south of Bawiti.'

'They look like mini volcanoes.'

'They are, they're volcanic plumes; long ago there was a volcano in this region that erupted covering the ground in magma. Over thousands of years the wind has eroded the mountains leaving the ground covered in millions of pieces of small igneous rocks of ferruginous quartzite and dolorite; that's what makes the Black Desert black.'

'Come on, Bill, mountains of igneous rock eroded by the wind? Do you really buy that?'

'Now that I think of it, millions of tons of surging water from a tsunami does sound a more logical proposition.'

Then an idea hit me.

'Bill, you can't date rock through carbon-dating can you?'

'No, it has to be organic material.'

'So these little volcanoes, these plumes, *could* have erupted just *before* the tsunami, as a reaction to the passing of Nibiru?'

Bill went into deep thought.

13

'I guess it's possible; there *is* a fault line that runs through the Bahariya Oasis.'

By now Pieter had joined in the discussion.

'I think it probably happened earlier.'

'What makes you say that?'

'According to Albert Slosman, it probably happened as a result of the pole shift and the final sinking of Atlantis in 9792 BC.'

'Slosman? Never heard of him?'

Albert Slosman

'Albert Slosman was a French professor of mathematics and an expert in computer science who travelled to Egypt to study hieroglyphics and the Zodiac at Dendera.

'Isn't that where we're going today?'

'Exactly.'

'What did he find?'

'He came to the conclusion that chapters seventeen to sixty-three of the Book of the Dead dealt with explanations of the mythic origin of the gods and included evidence the Earth previously underwent a pole-shift in 9792 BC which caused the "sun to rise at a new horizon" and the last parts of Atlantis to disappear under the ocean.'

'When was he writing?'

'He died in 1981, although he did manage to publish ten books before his death, at least two related to Atlantis.'

'I've never heard of him.'

'That's probably because his books are in French and, as far as I know, have not been translated into English yet.'

As usual, Bill was intrigued.

'9792 BC, that correlates with all the geological evidence, as well as the disappearance of the sabre-toothed tigers and woolly mammoths, which all suggest a pole-shift happened sometime about 10,000 BC.'

'And if that correlates to the effects of a passing of Nibiru, then it explains why the period from 9,000 to 6,000 BC, which would have been around the next passing of Nibiru, has left very little in the way of archaeological evidence.'

Bill began pondering it deeper.

'What we geologists *do* know, is that the Nile Valley of the Palaeolithic era was much larger than it is today, supposed because the annual flooding of the Nile made permanent habitation of its floodplain impossible. But that assumes it was in fact a floodplain and not perhaps something else, like a part of the Mediterranean Sea due to a pole shift.'

I was a step ahead of his thinking.

'Would that explain the White and Black Deserts?'

He was weighing up the possibilities.

'It would, but so would a passing of Nibiru and an eruption and tsunami in 1600 BC.'

I did some quick math in my head; 9792 BC, add 3600 makes 6192 BC, then 4592 BC, 992 BC, and 2592 AD. No, it didn't correlate with either the 1600 BC date *or* the supposed beginning of the last Mayan cycle in 3114 BC; something was missing. There were so many variables; a ten percent error in any or all of the dates would need some mathematical genius in algorithms to spot the pattern. Or perhaps there was some complex aspect to the orbit of Nibiru around our sun? There had to be more concrete, unshifting evidence, something like references to the positions of the stars. I probed Pieter for more information.

'What else does Slosman say, anything about the stars?'

'Yes, he says that Osiris, who was represented in the sky by the Orion constellation, had something to do with it, and we all know that the constellation of Orion has something to do with the three pyramids at Giza, right?'

'Maybe that's why this Slosman guy was in Dendera; he knew something about the constellations, and about the Zodiac, that we don't?'

'I guess we'll soon find out.'

The 'Eroica' Symphony came to its rousing conclusion and the hero's journey came to an end, though, for me I was somewhere back between the second and third movements; the funeral march and the scherzo, somewhere between a rock and a hard place, the devil and the deep blue sea. From the back of the bus, Pernille broke the contemplative nature of the moment.

'Alex, can we please have something a little more modern, perhaps at least in the last fifty years.'

I think she was looking for a repeat of The Beatles and the Magical Mystery Tour that had been a part of bringing her and Bill together.

'More Beatles?'

'Perhaps. What else do you have?'

'Opera, Classical, Jazz, Blues, Rock, Popular.'

'No opera; something popular.'

I flicked through the files, calling out options.

'Journey (which seemed appropriate to me), Boz Scaggs, Shirley Bassey, Abba, Or maybe a musical, Avenue Q, Chicago, Jesus Christ Superstar, The Producers, Stop The World I want to Get off.'

'No musicals either; something popular.'

Geez; tough audience.

'The Corrs…'

'Oh yes, can we have The Corrs please, I love them.'

Everyone was in agreement with Pernille so I clicked the album and away we went. As the fiddle and piano set the Irish flavour for the rest of the journey and the first strains of 'Forgiven not Forgotten' rang out, it took me back to something Bill had said a few days before.

'Hey, Bill, since we're in an Irish state of mind, remember the other day at Edfu you were saying about the Hyksos princess, Scota, who fled Egypt, survived the tsunami and made her way to Spain then to Ireland. Can you tell me more about the evidence of the ancient Egyptians in Ireland and Scotland?'

Most of the others pricked up their ears; actually all of them except Crystal took an interest. I presumed Crystal must have already been aware of it, and that didn't surprise me one bit, there was very little she *didn't* seem to know about, or as she would put it, 'was fully aware of'. But it was Pernille who was the spokesperson.

'The ancient Egyptians were in Ireland and Scotland?'

'Sure. According to the ancient Scots Chronicles and old Irish Annals, the origin of the Scottish and Irish people derives in part from an Egyptian Princess of the Hyksos Dynasty named Scota, who made her way to Ireland from Egypt via Spain around the time of Moses.'

'How?'

'By boat; they've even found ancient Egyptian sea-going boats buried in a bog somewhere in Northern England, though I don't know if they were the *actual* boats they set forth in; I certainly don't think she flew Ryanair.'

'Is there any other evidence; any ruins or artefacts?'

Pernille was probing for facts, and, though Bill had nothing concrete, as the words of 'Heaven Knows' filled the bus, almost as if mocking or commenting on our journey...

'No more, no more a life without meaning....only Heaven knows.'

... he did have some tempting morsels.

'Not really, they have found some Egyptian faience beads, dating from around the same period, in Scotland and other parts of the British Isles, but, apart from the boats, most of the evidence, if that's what you would call it, is circumstantial.'

'Such as?'

'Well, I haven't been there myself, but I believe there's a place called Glen Scota, or Glenscoheen, near Tralee in the county of Kerry, where Scota is supposedly buried. There was apparently a long bloody battle about three miles from Tralee and not only were the Danaan princes killed in the battle but also Scota, the warrior Queen of the invaders.

The burial site is apparently in a site of woodland and natural rocks, somewhere on the sloped mountains between Sliabh Mis and the sea, in view of Tralee Bay, and marked by a dubious inscription and flagstone. The Ordnance Survey of Ireland has shown the actual location, but as far as I know, Irish archaeologists haven't carried out any investigation on the site.'

The answer seemed pretty obvious to me.

'Let's see, dig up a pile of old bones, or have a nip of whisky and a pint of Guinness? No-brainer; your shout Paddy. Seriously though, if they dug her up and did a DNA test, surely that might answer a few questions.'

'It might also raise a few more that they *don't* want answered.'

'Such as?'

Bill frowned.

'There's already enough fighting between the Protestants and the Catholics in Ireland. Imagine what would happen if you threw an Egyptian Hyksos princess and her religion into the mix. Who knows, the next thing you might have the Jews claiming Ireland as theirs, just like they did in Palestine; that Ireland is yet another "chosen" land.

Did you know, the irony is, for a long time it was Egypt that was regarded as the 'Holy Land', not Palestine, and the monastic life of the Egyptian Coptic monks was renowned throughout the whole Christian Church.'

Pernille was still curious.

'So why would Scota sail all the way to Ireland?'

Bill scratched his head.

'I guess to escape Egypt.'

The contorted aspects of confusion crept over Pernille's face.

'Why would an Egyptian princess need to escape her own country?'

I started wondering if Pernille may have also had an incarnation as Scota, but, before I could explore the option, Bill answered her question.

'Alex and I figured out that Scota was more than likely Herit, daughter of the Hyksos pharaoh, Apopi, and that Moses was most probably Joseph of the amazing technicolour dreamcoat fame. So when Joseph caused the death of Seqenenre Tao at the end of the 17th Dynasty, and the subsequent civil war between the true Egyptians in the south and the Hyksos dynasty in the north, Scota was forced to flee the advancing armies of Seqenenre's son, Kamose.'

As the lyrics to the next song unfolded…

'Someday you'll forget me.'

… I couldn't help but think 'Yes we had forgotten Herit, even under her anglicised name of Scota', but now she was being remembered and Pernille wanted to know all about her.

'That explains why she left, but not why she sailed all the way to Ireland?'

Bill shook his head.

'It certainly wasn't for the weather, and I don't think Guinness had been invented then, so it's got me beat.'

To my surprise it was Yuko that knew more than anyone.

'She didn't sail straight to Ireland, she went via Spain.'

'Spain?'

'Scota apparently married a Spaniard called Milesius.'

Now it was Bill's turn to probe for answers.

'Milesius? He sounds more Roman that Spanish.'

'Or Greek….'

I was starting to put the pieces together in my mind.

'…Do you think he could have been Minoan?'

Yuko took a moment to contemplate the idea, then nodded her head.

'It would make sense; the Minoans were a dominant civilization at the time and sailed extensively throughout the Mediterranean and beyond. Milesius is reported to have led a fleet of a hundred ships all the way to the island of Taprobane, which is modern day Sri Lanka, then back via the Red Sea to the Caspian Sea to Scythia and then via the Black Sea to Egypt where he met and married Scota.'

In my head, red flags started waving and alarm bells going off, especially as the next song coincidently was "Runaway";…

'And I would run away… with you.
'cause I have fallen in love with you '

We were all feeling it, Bill and Pernille, Pieter and Yuko, even Crystal was reacting to the sensual undercurrent and atmosphere within the bus; was it possible we were all on this sea trip with Scota? This was just getting too freaky and I called a timeout.

'Whoa, hold the phones. Do these chronicles actually say he sailed from Sri Lanka, up through the Red Sea into the Caspian Sea to Scythia and then via the Black Sea to Egypt?'

'Yes.'

'That means they must have all been connected by water in some way, be it rivers or straits, and that paints a very different geographical picture of the world at the time.'

'I guess it does.'

'So are you suggesting Milesius was a trader?'

'It's possible, but it's more likely, that as he had a fleet of a hundred ships at his disposal, he was the warrior son of the King of Greece.'

'How can you be so sure?'

'When he arrived in Egypt, Milesius stayed for eight years with the Hyksos Pharaoh; a simple trader would not be extended that courtesy. Nor would a trader be permitted to marry the daughter of a Pharaoh. The Hyksos were invaders from the east;

17

they knew how important it was to protect your boundaries. Marrying his daughter to the son of the Minoans would have provided the Hyksos pharaoh with an alliance to the north, and a certain amount of security.'

'Well, Alex, I think that confirms who Scota really was, don't you?'

I looked back at Bill.

'Indubitably!'

It also confirmed my thoughts about higher water levels, though not just after the tsunami, even before. This truly was the "*Right Time*".

'*Once in a lifetime.*'

This trip certain was a once in a lifetime trip, though it seemed we had all had many trips together in many alternate lives. I even contemplated if we'd all been on the boats alongside Scota, fellow escapees with Herit?

Meanwhile we'd arrived at Qena, so didn't have much further to go, at least on this part of our journey. Perched on the precipice of the back seat, Pernille was still looking for the answer to her question.

'So, Scota was Herit, but it doesn't explain why or how it was that she finished up in Ireland.'

I explained my thoughts about the Thera eruption and its subsequent tsunami then Yuko quickly took up the reins.

'Milesius and Scota may have left well before the tsunami, and perhaps even been as far away as Sri Lanka when it happened, for the chronicles say they went on the great sea past the island of Taprobane. After staying a month there, they went to Scythia via the Caspian Sea then on to Daci, which is part of modern day Romania and Bulgaria, where they stayed for a month.'

'They could hardly have return to Greece, as it was obliterated.'

'Perhaps they sailed past it, and past the Rif Mountains in northern Morocco, until they landed in Spain where they remained for thirty years, fighting over fifty battles against Frisians, a Germanic group native to the coastal parts of the Netherlands and Germany, and Longobards, the Northern Italians.'

My mind was putting pieces together like a teenager with a child's jigsaw.

'That would make perfect sense, as those areas wouldn't have been directly affected by the tsunami. The Frisians and Longobards would surely would have taken the opportunity created by the confusion to invade the affected areas.'

Bill was right with me.

'And though the south-east of Spain may have been sheltered to some extent by the islands of Sardinia and Sicily, as well as by Southern Italy and Tunisia, there would surely have been some effect on Spain given the wave that hit Egypt was probably around six hundred feet high.'

Pernille was patient, yet persistent.

'Ireland?'

We all looked to Yuko.

'Following his victories in battle, Milesius was then known as "Milidh of Spain", however Milesius died of plague, and, soon after, Scota, with her eight sons, sailed to Ireland in a fleet of about a hundred boats, each containing around fifteen families plus soldiers, apparently to conquer the ancient tribes and take the kingdoms from Tuatha-De-Danaans.'

It was Bill's turn to play devil's advocate.

'There are, however, two problems with that deduction in the chronicles; firstly, how did Scota know Ireland existed, and secondly, how did she know there were people living there that had to be conquered? It makes much more sense that, without Milesius to lead them they felt vulnerable, that rather than continue their battles against the Germans and Italians of the time, they fled the plague and, knowing they couldn't go back east to Egypt or Greece, headed north in search of new lands.'

Yuko was nodding her head in approval.

'The plague, yes, because apparently they circled Ireland three times before landing.'

'And I don't think the locals would have been keen to permit a fleet of plague-laden foreigners to land. It's no wonder Scota had to "conquer" them.'

Pernille was hanging on every word, especially Bill's.

'Wow, it really gets you thinking?'

Crossing one of the few bridges that spanned the Nile, to the western bank, I was putting more pieces together.

'So you think the history writers simply mistook Scota's Greek husband for Spanish just because they'd come from Spain?'

'It looks that way.'

I looked at Crystal to check how I was doing and she gazed back at me with the most sensual erotic smile; it was like she was basking in my awakening.

'I would love to love like you do me.'

How is it that songs always seem to happen exactly at the right moment? Or is it that we only notice when they *do* happen at exactly the right moment? Or is it that we are actually not noticing the majority of times when the messages of the words are right in front of us?

'There's a pillar in my way you see.'

OK, what was the pillar? Or was I the pillar; was I getting in my own way? Or was I in the process of getting *out* of my own way?

Pernille was appreciating the song as well, singing along with the lyrics and clearly directing them towards Bill.

'I met you on a sunny Autumn day. You visually attracted me when asking for the way.'

There was a great feeling in the bus and I was riding on the crest of the wave. Did I love Crystal? Did she love me? There was certainly a strong connection between us.

'Oh if you should leave me. Time make it be alright.'

Suddenly Pernille got a little choked up and teary, so Bill reached out and took her hand. She gathered instant strength from him and switched us back to the main topic.

'So, when did Scota's descendants migrate to Scotland again?'

Aware of Pernille's emotional pendulum, and wishing to help, Yuko was quick to answer

'Around 300 BC...'

I wondered if it was actually around the time that Alexander the Great went back to Egypt and ordered the temples rebuilt. Something happened around that time; that was for sure.

'...and from then they formed the foundation of the Scottish Royal lineage.'

Bill helped to settle the mood.

'You know, it's interesting that there's a little distillery called Glen Scotia in

Campbelltown, in south west Scotland, just across the waters from Northern Ireland. Coincidence? Nah.'

In the meantime, I was scratching my head about the Scots and their history. I knew about Robert the Bruce, and how he routed the English, led by Edward II, in 1314, and gave Scotland Independence.

'It's no wonder the Scots were so keen to fight against the English; the Scots probably knew they were descended from the Egyptian pharaohs and would never let the peasants from the south rule over them.'

Wait a minute, what did I just say? Pernille was Isabella, who had been traded off by her father Phillip IV, to Edward II when she was only thirteen, as a ruse to resolve the conflict between France and England, and Bill was Roger Mortimer, who led a successful rebellion against Edward. In effect they were replaying the same battle of the lineages out in Scotland as they had in ancient Egypt; history was merely repeating itself, with the same characters, just different costumes.

So could Bill have been Robert the Bruce, or part of the Templar Knights that supported him? No, that's right, he was Roger Mortimer; looking at his squat little figure, it was hard to see him as the legendary figure of Robert the Bruce painted by the history books, but, as they say, 'it's not the size of the man in the fight, but the fight in the man'.

So who could have been Robert the …Oh, oh, someone of the bloodline, fighting for justice? Surely not? No way! Could Robert have been …me?

It hadn't just got *me* thinking; Bill was heading off on a parallel tangent as well.

'Yes, it's weird that. Leading up to the "Battle of Bannockburn", as it's known, there was an Auld Alliance between Scotland and France in 1295, France of course being in continual conflict with England at the time. Then, the following year, Scotland was 'annexed' by England, no doubt increasing the conflict.

We know the reality is the Church were controlling the state in both France and England, not the other way around; so maybe the Catholic Church influenced Phillip IV to marry his daughter off to Edward II? Several years later, after the routing of the Knights of Templar in 1307, the Church knew many of the Templar Knights had not only escaped, but taken refuge in Scotland, and the Church didn't want the Templars' knowledge to survive, let alone spread, so they used the English as a tool to try to eradicate the Templars and their knowledge by overthrowing the Scots.'

'It sounds like the sort of conspiracy theory Randy would salivate over, but totally plausible.'

'Break those pillars down. Take those pillars down.'

There it was again, that subliminal message, and I got it loud and clear. That's why I had Kareem's papers in my backpack; each page was a sledgehammer on the Berlin Wall of truth. I *was* Robert the Bruce; I had to be. It seemed this journey I was on wasn't just about breaking down my own personal pillars, but the pillars of 'truth' that had been falsely erected on the history of the world.

They say 'History is written by the victors'. OK, that may well be true, but if The Illuminati were behind everything, orchestrating all the conflicts, wars, and financial markets, then though the history may have been written by the victors, the truth often lies not with the victors, but within the anguished cries and screams of the vanquished.

'Break those pillars down. Take those pillars down.'

And with each blow I knew I would be closer to finding my true self, my true purpose. By the time 'Secret life' started, I was totally tuned in.

'You're all alone and it doesn't seem quite fair.
Why we're all left in ignorance turning to despair.
Philosophy, theology, offer us a glimpse
At something more incredible than you or I'

Hell, I even had Irish *and* Scottish ancestry!

'Call on the secret life.'

Heading to the outskirts of the village, we turned a corner, past a few lush fields of banana and date plantations, past a couple of fully-laden donkeys, and lo and behold, about four kilometres from the Nile, we had arrived at our first destination for the day.

Dendera

The village of Dendera sits about sixty-kilometres north of Luxor, on the west bank of the Nile, opposite the provincial town of Qena, where the Nile does a big loop to the left towards Dendera and the road branches off to the right towards the Red Sea and the seaside resorts of Hurghada. And that's where I thought Bill was headed, Hurghada. But it seemed Bill had modified his trip somewhat and was now intending to go there tomorrow, taking Pernille with him.

He'd decided to continue on with us to Abydos after Dendera, then get dropped off with Pernille in Qena on the way back, leaving the rest of us to take the minibus back to Luxor while he and Pernille headed off to Hurghada from Qena the next morning for some well deserved R&R. I was going to miss him in so many ways that was for sure: his knowledge, his sense of humour, his warmth and generosity.

As he stepped from the minibus, I shut down my laptop, but not before the first strains of "Closer" had filled my brain-space…

'I see you, walking every day, with a smile beneath a frown
But I won't look away, yeah. What does it mean?
What's there to see if I look closer, closer

…then, as the others hopped off and joined the procession to the ticket office, stuffed my laptop into my backpack alongside Kareem's papers. I briefly considered taking it with me, but, since Saleem was related to Saeed, I figured he was hardly likely to let my backpack be stolen, so I stashed it away under the seat, jumped off the minibus and tagged on at the end of the line.

Crystal's ripe peach of a bottom jiggled seductively before me in her now-familiar white temple attire. The words of the song continued in my head.

'Where are you going, and what are you thinking at all
Your eyes show nothing more than a dazed oblivion
What does it mean?
What will I see when I look closer, closer.'

Hell, I must have looked like one of the Pied Piper's rats; like one of the dazed Eloi in the original 1960 film version of 'The Time Machine', mindlessly trekking into the underground mines of the Morlock.

'There's more to me than what you see, when you look closer, closer.'

Thankfully, as we walked towards the entrance, Pernille looked back and jolted me into the now.

'Hey, Alex, do you have any notes on Dendera?'
'Sure do.'

I pulled up the notes on my iphone and went into tour-guide mode.

'Once the capital of the 6th nome of Upper Egypt and a town of some importance, Dendera has a long history; in Ancient Egyptian times it was known as Iunet, or Tantere, and during the classical to Ptolemaic era was known to the Greeks as Tentyris.

Apart from the Ptolemaic period temples, there's also a necropolis that includes tombs from the Early Dynastic Period. Some of the other important periods identified here include; the end of the Old Kingdom, with many remains of Old Kingdom tombs scattered in the desert behind the forty-thousand square metre mud-brick enclosure, and the First Intermediate Period, notable for the building of a number of substantial mastabas, though only one has any decoration apart from stelae and false doors.

On the west end of the site are brick-vaulted catacombs from the Late Period, of animal burials, primarily birds and dogs, while cow burials have been found at various points in the necropolis.'

By the end of my discourse we all had our entrance tickets, only twenty-five Egyptian pounds, and were ushered into a small 'viewing' room where, along with a handful of other tourists, we were shown a ten-minute introductory film about Dendera. There was nothing particularly mind-blowing about it, although the presence of Zahi Hawass on the film sent shivers down my spine and I found myself reaching back over my shoulder like a frightened two-year-old searching for his favourite teddy, or like it was my last canteen of water and I was about to be abandoned in the middle of the Sahara Desert. Of course the backpack was back under the seat in the bus and nothing happened so we all filed out of the visitors' centre and towards the Dendera complex.

Straight away, the paved path led to a grassy area filled with bits and pieces of columns, walls, and who knows what else. I looked back away from the complex, 'Hell, we were about four kilometres from the river, that's a lot of land to make up considering this temple would surely have nestled on the bank of the river.' It would be interesting to know what these ruins entailed; a Roman quay perhaps, or maybe something that would reveal even greater information about the water levels at the various times. But there was nothing in my notes about it, and no one seemed in a rush to excavate and restore it, and the rest of the group had just walked on past it, so I decided I might as well focus my attention on the main complex and on Crystal's undulating derriere.

Turning towards the complex, the next ruin was not so easy to ignore. A massive mud-brick enclosure wall, similar in size to the one at El Kab, but much more structured, still survived and encircled the whole temple complex. I took special note of the angled sections, perhaps not only built for structural strength, but also to deflect surges of water.

The scant remains of a Roman colonnaded street flanked both side of the approach; this would possibly have extended back as far as the ruins outside the visitors' entrance and given support to it possibly being a quay. Still, it was at least a hundred and fifty metres to the entrance proper and, until extensive excavations were done, it was anyone's guess what buildings once lined the path.

As Pernille and Crystal continued their discussions up ahead, Bill dropped back to keep me company.

'Hey, Bill, I don't remember much about Scottish history, what else do you know about Robert the Bruce?'

'He was one of Scotland's greatest kings, ruling from just before the Templars were all arrested in 1307, until his death in 1329. I guess he was most famous for leading Scotland to victory against England at the "Battle of Bannockburn" and during the Wars of Scottish Independence.'

'Do you know anything about his lineage?

Bill gave his noggin a scratch.

'I think his father was Scottish-Norman and his mother was French-Irish.'

'Do you think he was of the *sang réal*?'

'Ooh, I think your pushing it, I know he was the fourth great-grandson of David the First, but the history of the Scottish kings only goes back to the 9th Century AD.'

'I can go back as far as Macbeth; but only because I know him from my studies of Shakespeare and, from memory I think Macbeth was around 1060AD, but before that it's all a bit of a blank.'

'Well, there's not much to tell; the written history of the lineage of the Scottish Kings only started just over a hundred years earlier in 843, and, before that, the only real mentions are in 503 AD, when the Gaelic Kingdom of Dal Rialen was founded in Argyll when the Irish warring tribe known as the Scots left Ireland and built their kingdom on the west coast of Scotland, and the Romans recording resistance from local savages in 79AD and the subsequent building of Hadrian's Wall in 122 AD.

But if you want to trace Robert the Bruce's maternal lineage back to the *sang réal* through his Irish side all the way back to Scota, or more correctly, Herit, then I'm sorry to say you'd have an almost impossible task, because the records just don't exist. And even if you could find the connection, then you'd have to prove *Scota's* mother was not Hyksos, but from the lineage of Upper Egypt.'

'Like trying to find a needle in a haystack.'

'You'd have more chance of finding an atheistic homophobic brickies labourer in a vegetarian cooking class for gay nuclear-free Seventh Day Adventists.'

'But what if we dug up the bones of Robert the Bruce, and those of Scota, did a DNA match, and found they were related?'

'Well, his bones were ceremonially re-interred in Dunfermline Abbey in 1819 in a new lead coffin, into which they poured fifteen-hundred pounds of molten pitch to preserve the remains, before the coffin was sealed, so I don't think the authorities would be too keen on approving you exhuming him on the off chance he may be related to the pharaohs of ancient Egypt. I think they'd be more likely to fit you in a reverse jacket with oversized sleeves, cart you off in a wagon, and hide you away in a padded cell never to been seen or heard from again.'

'You mean like they do with most conspiracy theorist who get too close to the truth?'

Bill looked at me with a raised eyebrow and patted me on the back.

'Haven't you got enough 'truths' to carry already?'

Bill was right.

'I guess Bobby will remain one of those dead man that tell no tales.'

As we reached the end of the approach, on either side of the street, were the ruins of two colonnaded Roman Nymphaea; monuments consecrated to the nymphs, which traditionally served the threefold purpose of sanctuaries, reservoirs and assembly-rooms. Once adorned with statues and paintings, small holes for drainage still spanned the façade. The nymphaea would probably have been preliminary meeting places to wash or refresh after a long trek, before entering the main complex.

Next, was the northern access to the temple complex, the Gateway of Domitian; built by the Roman Emperor Domitian in 80 A.D. To either side, strewn along the walls were various bits and pieces of walls, columns, statues, stone sarcophagi, and stelae.

Two incomplete sphinxes, one just having the rear haunches, the other headless, stood guard facing each other at the gateway. Above them were reliefs of the pharaoh, probably Domitian, before the figures of Horus, and Isis with her Hathor head-piece.

'I feel strange.'

Pernille was frozen; poised to enter, yet hesitant. We all gravitated towards her, Bill, her knight in shining armour, showing the most concern.

'Is it like at Luxor?'

She took a moment to assess her reactions.

'Yes, … no, it's different; I feel like something is going to happen, like I've been here before, but this time I feel like I want to cry, but cry tears of joy.'

'Are you OK to go on, or do you want to go back?'

She took Bill by the hand…

'Oh, definitely go on.'

…and led us forward. I followed the others through the massive gateway, which was at least twenty-metres high and made humans seem like mere dwarves.

'Hey, Alex, red granite.'

Bill was right. An enormous block of red granite formed the foundation of the gateway; and it was old, much older than the gateway that towered over it. I just knew there would be some hidden treasure here, and that it would probably be in plain site of everyone, yet totally ignored.

I looked up to the lintel of the gateway, half expecting to see the usual winged disc, or the vulture. They were there, but to my surprise there was an unexpected carving of a winged scarab dominating the underside of the lintel, holding the red disc in its forelegs; not that the image was unusual, but certainly in such a prominent position, and particularly on what was supposedly a Roman edifice.

Given my experiences with the Khepri plinth at Karnak, and my understanding that the scarab was an image about the recycling nature of the universe and *not* the rebirth of the sun each morning, I started pondering the presence of the image here, right at the entrance to the Dendera complex. If the red disc represented Nibiru, what part did it play in the recycling of life on earth? I was pretty sure the answers were somewhere inside the main temple.

I was keen to head straight inside and get to the heart of the temple, but glancing towards the main temple I quickly had second thoughts. Not only were Diane's group just ahead of us and about to enter, but a second, larger group, of Chinese tourists were pouring in. God, I'd been so lucky in not having to deal with them for most of the West Bank at Luxor and in getting off the beaten track in Karnak, that I'd almost forgotten about them. I thought Crystal and the others were prepared to endure the onslaught as they all stepped off towards the main temple, everyone that is except Pernille, who pointed right, towards a Mammasi.

'I think I'll start over here, then work my way around the complex and save the main temple until last. Besides, the main temple looks a little crowded at the moment.'

'Sounds like a plan to me.'

Understandably, Bill, was quick to follow and the two of them drifted towards the Mammasi. But, not everyone was of the one mind.

'I think we'll continue on.'

Yuko had thrown down the gauntlet, and in that moment we all saw who really wore the pants in her and Pieter's relationship. As they headed off, it left Crystal and me to make our decision. She looked straight at me with a raised eyebrow and a wry grin on her face, then indicated towards Pernille, Bill and the Mammasi.

'Well, what are we waiting for, lead on Macduff.'

Clearly Crystal had not only overheard my reference to Shakespeare and Macbeth, but she was well versed with the play enough to make a poignant quote. Hang on, was she Lady Macbeth, or perhaps Hecate? She had certainly bewitched me.

I detoured slightly, scanning the flotsam and jetsam cast against the inner side of the outer mud-brick wall. Pieces of black granite columns and statue fragments were interspersed amongst worn red-granite blocks and sandstone sarcophagi, relief-covered wall stones and Hathor-headed capitols. I'd seen this so many times; thousands of years of history and juxtapositions of Kingdoms and Dynasties. Whilst it pissed me off, as I made my way to join the others at the birth-house, it also confirmed there were older temples here at some time.

The Mammasis

Checking the notes on my iphone, I expected the Mammasi, built by the Roman Emperor Augustus, with later reliefs by Trajan and Hadrian, to be dedicated to Horus, however, instead, it was dedicated to Horus's son, Ihy.

'Ihy was the son of Hathor and Horus, although Ihy was also known as the son of several other gods including Isis, Nehptys and Sekhmet, and though Horus was most often seen as his father, even Re had this position.

Initially I failed to see the significance, so I dug a little deeper.

'Dendera was the ritual location where Hathor gave birth to Ihy, the youthful representation of the creator gods associated with both music and sometimes with the afterlife. Though he is rarely mentioned outside of Dendera, worship of Ihy goes back to the Old Kingdom when Khufu built a shrine to him and to Hathor at Dendera during the 4th Dynasty.'

OK, so there *were* old temples here as well, that was not a surprise, but it was relevant, extremely relevant; I just had to keep a look out for evidence.

In the forecourt just before the Mammasi, two dismembered torsos of black granite, or diorite, lay prostrate on the ground as if they were the victims of a bloody battle. They looked either Roman or Greek, and perhaps they were symbolic in some way of how the Egyptologists had treated the ruins. At first I contemplated that maybe they'd been discovered and dug up there, but clearly that was not the case. Rather, they'd been placed there, or rather left there to fill an empty space or two.

As for the Mammasi itself, what first struck me was that it was on a raised platform, which, comparing it to that of the main temple, was possibly to position it on an even keel.

The colonnade, rather than running around the inside of a courtyard, here, like at Philae, travelled around the exterior of the building, creating a covered walkway. As the others headed inside the Mammasi, I decided to do a lap of honour first.

Walking around the perimeter, the exterior of the screen walls was dominated by reliefs. It seemed to be a story; first Hathor and Horus receiving the creative egg, then

Ihy being suckled by Hathor as they are presented various offerings, such as the menat necklace. Apart from lacking colour they were superbly preserved, and clearly portrayed the divine birth and childhood of Ihy.

Beside the Mammasi, I couldn't help but notice a small field of ruins that contained rows of building fragments, including numerous long stretches of columns. As I drew closer, I quickly confirmed they were red granite; again heavily worn. I guessed they probably belonged to the ruins of the structure beside the Mammasi, but I would get to that soon enough. I snapped a quick photo and hurried to catch up with the others, circling back through the corridor and walkway created by the colonnade and the inner chambers. The walls were again covered in reliefs of Ihy, depicted as a naked boy with the sidelocks of youth, his finger in his mouth, sometimes holding a sistrum, and at other times with the menat necklace. From within the Mammasi I could hear Crystal and Pernille toning, the dulcet sounds somehow drifting out and into the surrounding walkway.

Arriving back at the entrance, I noticed the front section of the Mammasi had been extended through the addition of several rooms, some on a higher level, plus three pairs of extra columns to form a kind of kiosk, which would once have had a timbered roof. I surmised the kiosk was an addition attributable to Trajan, as kiosks seemed to be his trademark. Each of the columns had a different capital and was decorated with reliefs of Bes, protector of women during childbirth, his grotesque appearance, big stomach and long whiskers thought to ward off evil spirits at the moment of birth.

Inside, the birth-house followed the standard Ptolemaic model of a sequence of three rooms surrounded by two narrow corridors, although here they seemed too narrow to be practical and must have been added purely for some symbolic or aesthetic effect. The walls were covered in dedications, inscriptions and scenes of Trajan, making offerings to Hathor. They were magnificent and possibly the finest I'd seen so far.

At the rear of the sanctuary, 'guarded' by Bill, Crystal and Pernille stood in an embrace, Pernille sobbing and saying 'thank you' over and over. It wasn't the sort of sensual and sexual embrace I'd been privy to in the waters of the Nile a few days earlier, but it was certainly as powerful. Not wanting to interrupt, I focused my attention on the inner walls, the rear wall of which being dominated by an enormous false door. Crystal and Pernille seemed framed by the door, which was in turn framed by a double cavetto moulding on slender columns and topped by a uraeus frieze. High up in the wall was a niche for a statue, most probably of Hathor, and I wondered if it, and/or the door, had something to do with their present embrace. Bill and I telepathically decided to move on, leaving the girls to have a few moments to themselves.

Next to the birth-house, according to my notes, were the remains of a Christian Coptic Basilica from the 5th Century AD; supposedly 'an excellent example of early Coptic Church architecture'. I don't know how they deduced that from what remained; it looked like it had recently been, or was currently being, excavated, as there was a great deal of restoration work done, and needed, but surely not enough to claim it as 'an excellent example'.

I wasn't really interested in anything that late, I mean 5th Century AD was way past my target zones. Bill, on the other hand, with his own personal history with the Catholic Church, was in his element. But, as he explored the heart of church, a now familiar battlecry changed my interest dramatically.

'Hey, Alex, more red granite!'

He was pointing to the worn remains of several column bases regularly positioned around the inside of the church; this is where the columns from beside the

Mammasi obviously belonged. But that didn't make sense to me; maybe Bill had a clue.

'Hey, Bill, do you know much about the Coptic Churches?'

'A little.'

'Would they have built them out of red granite?'

Bill took a second look, then figured it out.

'Here in Egypt? Actually, no, they usually just took over the existing temples, like they did at Luxor and Philae.'

'There's one on Elephantine Island as well. So, why the red-granite columns?'

Before Bill could answer, Crystal gave us a hurry up.

'Can you boys multitask, walk and talk at the same time, or do you want us to go on ahead without you?'

The girls were standing outside the church ready to move on.

'Right behind you ladies.'

They took off and, as we slowly tagged in behind, Bill picked up where we'd left off.

'Logic dictates that the Copts took over a pre-existing structure here, one with very old granite inside.'

'That's just it, supposedly this is 'an excellent example of early Coptic Church architecture', but if the supporting columns are all of worn old red granite, then ...'

'Then that blows *that* theory out of the water.'

'Indeed it does. But I remember seeing the Coptic cross on the columns at Elephantine, but I figured they must have been carved in much later, during the Coptic period'.

'Well the Coptic cross has been around a lot longer than that, it doesn't belong to them.'

'You mean they took it on just like they took on the temples?'

'Probably, but the cross comes from way before then.'

'What do you mean?'

'Well, for a start, it appears in Scotland.'

'Scotland again?'

'Yep, in fact, the Egyptian Coptic wheel cross is the earliest type of monumental cross in Scotland.'

'What's the evidence?'

'It's on several stones at Kirkmadrine in Wigtonshire, along with the Crux Ansata,'

'The what?'

'The Crux Ansata, the Egyptian ankh; the emblem of life in Egyptian hieroglyphics.'

'The ankh is in Scotland as well?'

'It's on a stone at Nigg in Ross-shire, and there's another one at Ardboe, in Ireland, which confirms the Irish pathway.'

'Jesus!'

'That's not the half of it, there's actually lots of symbols on the Celtic stones of Scotland which are still unexplained; The Crescent, the Serpent, and the Elephant which must all have originated in either Africa or the far East.'

'So if the Scots came from Ireland in 300 BC, then the cross had to have come via Ireland with them, which means it had to have come via Scota from Egypt around 1600 BC. And that totally predates the Copts by over a thousand years.'

'Not necessarily, the old Scots Chronicles also record that during the 2nd Century BC certain "Egyptian philosophers", who were probably High Priests from the

Egyptian temples, came to Scotland to advise the Scots King of the period. They would definitely have brought their symbols with them.'

'Perhaps they were even underground members of the Tat Brotherhood?'

'I'm sure they were; these "Egyptian philosophers" would certainly have associated with the Druid magi who were advisors to the ancient Scottish Royal families.'

As I mulled it over, putting the pieces into place, the girls had already arrived at the next structure and were exploring the ruins. It was a second, earlier Mammasi, further south, built by Nectanebo I.

About seventeen metres by twenty metres, the Nectanebo birth-house was built mainly of brick but with an interior stone casing. That made me think the inner section may well have been older than the mud-brick casing that surrounded it. What was left of the temple indicated the internal structure consisted of a transverse hall leading to three shrines, somewhat similar to the Hatshepsut shrine in the Luxor temple, and that made it considerably different to the previous Roman Mammasi.

The decorations were varied as well; the inner walls of the wide hall depicting the Ptolemaic kings offering to Hathor. This confirmed the other mud-brick section was, at the least, a post-Ptolemaic addition. Further in were other scenes, again celebrating the birth of Ihy and the pharaohs, seemingly enacted in the form of a mystery play in thirteen acts, and including a scene on the north wall showing Khnum, the creator god, fashioning Ihy, with Hekat, goddess of childbirth in her image of a frog, looking on.

Then Bill pointed it out; in fact they were so worn, crumbling and faded I almost missed them. There, as the foundations, were red-granite blocks: worn red-granite, *very worn red-granite blocks*, much much older than the sandstone that sat atop it. They were in almost exactly the same state as the red-granite blocks at El-Kab. Something else had been built here before the time of Nectanebo I, the question was, 'were the red-granite blocks part of the older temple's foundations, or part of its upper structure?'

Looking around, I noticed this earlier Mammasi had been dissected by the foundations of the wall of the first court of the main Temple of Hathor, which probably explained the need to build a second birth-house further out from the main temple. I could trace the foundations of an original stone wall, that enclosed the main temple on three sides with an entrance through a gateway built by Domitian, the remains forming the modern temple entrance. But was the Domitian Gateway, that now stood in place, a later construction of various other entrance elements. It now appeared that way, especially with the red-granite foundations and the image of Khepri on the lintel.

Continuing south, arm in arm, towards the mud-brick remains of a Sanatorium, and chatting away like two best friends on a Sunday stroll through the park, the girls clearly weren't as interested in the details of the buildings as Bill and I were. However, if Bill and I wanted to keep up with them, and why wouldn't we, then we would have to discuss things as we explored. Quickly checking my notes about the Sanatorium, I also discovered;

> 'To the west of the Sanatorium was once a small chapel of Montuhotep Nebhepetre dating to the 11th Dynasty. It was recovered from the site and re-erected in the Cairo Museum. The building, which has secondary inscriptions of Merneptah, was as much for the pharaoh as for the goddess, and probably ancillary to the lost main temple of its time.'

Shit, I didn't see any 11th Dynasty chapel to Montuhotep in the Cairo Museum. I wondered if it was made of alabaster and resembled the Amenhotep ones at Karnak. Damn these bloody Egyptologists, why can't they just leave things where they belong?

But the fact it *was* here reinforced there was once a main temple dating back to the Middle Kingdom at least. Whether I could find any traces of it was another question. Looking around I realized the answers were probably on the main temple site, or, rather, *under* it.

Returning to my examination of the ruins of the Sanatorium, I quickly checked my notes and discovered it was the only one of its type known in association with an ancient Egyptian temple. In addition, that;

'Dendera was once an ancient healing centre, comparable to Lourdes.'

There were benches around the sides, most likely where the sick would have rested, waiting for cures provided by the priests, and basins at the western end, mostly likely used to collect the holy water. Here, pilgrims would have bathed in the sacred waters, or slept overnight in order to have a healing dream of the goddess.

'An inscription on a statue base found here suggests that water was poured over magical texts on the statues, causing it to become holy and to cure all sorts of diseases and illnesses.'

That reminded me of Jesus, and the ritual of washing the feet, certainly the Sanatorium would have been around in Jesus' time; and that got me thinking even more.

'So, let me get this right, there are definite connections between the Druids of Scotland and the ancient Egyptian Coptic Church, right?'

'Yep.'

'Are there any connections between them and any *other* Middle Eastern monastic or religious traditions?'

'Sure, they're both connected to the Essenes.'

'The Essenes! Hang on, aren't they the Qumran group supposedly responsible for the Dead Sea Scrolls, and supposedly consisting of Jesus and the apostles?'

'That's them.'

'How are the Druids and Copts connected to the Essenes?'

I wash my hands

'There was an Irish monastic group called the Culdees, who date back to the early centuries A.D. They were a group of Pythagorean Druidical monks; the last of the Druids, and often referred to as the "Christian heirs of the Druids".'

'Where are these connections documented, in the ancient Scots Chronicles?'

'Actually, no, they're in an early Irish version of the gospel of St. Matthew.'

'In *'The Bible'*?'

'Yep, but in the Irish version; the phrase "there came wise men from the east" is rewritten as "the Druids came from the east" and similarly, in the Old Testament, in Exodus, the "magicians of Egypt" are referred to as the "Druids of Egypt".'

'So the Druids are actually connected to *'The Bible'*?'

'More than connected, they claimed that the doctrine of their teaching is derived directly from the disciples of St. John.'

'John the apostle; author of the Book of Revelation?'

'That's him.'

This was all getting very interesting. I didn't know where it was heading, but it had to be going somewhere, like us I guess, we were going to the main temple but heading on an alternate path to the one we would have originally taken.

As we moved further south, we passed a well, with rock-cut steps that led downwards giving access to the priests for their morning ablutions, as well as to the water for daily use in the temple.

'Do you think the Culdees might have been part of the Tat Brotherhood?'

'They certainly weren't part of the Amun Priests.'

'So it's possible they could have come either directly, or indirectly, from the Tat Brotherhood via the Essenes?'

'Possible? I think it's highly likely. They could even have been Essenes; they wore long white gowns, just like the Druids, just like the Essenes, and they occupied places connected to the Druids. And it would totally account for the easy way in which they embraced Christianity; way before the Roman Church got any footing in Britain.'

'I guess all we really need then, is some absolute concrete link between the Tat Brotherhood and the Essenes?'

'That would certainly be a clincher.'

There were tunnels leading to and from the well, as well as a small shaft, next to the adjoining lake, which, according to my iphone files;

'... was discovered in 1917 and once contained valuable treasures from Cleopatra's era that are now displayed in the Egyptian Museum.'

Oh hell, I hadn't seen those either, whatever they were. Maybe it was a cache of jewellery, mini statues or assorted icons. I started to wonder if I had spent most of my time in the Cairo museum wandering around like a catatonic Zombie. It made me pause for a moment to stop and take in what was around me.

Beyond the immediate ruins were mounds and mounds of dirt and sand that, upon closer scrutiny, were actually heaps of debris created from the many years of excavations carried on at the complex. They were scattered around, stretching from the edge of the main buildings to the inner part of the mud-brick outer wall and around the perimeter.

But, had they dug deep enough, or had they merely scratched the surface to reveal the 'post-tsunami' layers? It was a metaphor for the whole history of Egypt.

Ahead, Pernille and Crystal suddenly got all excited and disappeared behind a stone wall and down into the ground. Beyond the well, and probably connected to it by one of the subterranean passages, was a massive rectangular stone-lined ceremonial basin about sixty metres long by forty metres wide with numerous palm trees sprouting from its floor; this was the famous sacred lake, this was Cleopatra's Oasis. It reminded me of one of those glamorous Hollywood movie sets, or parties, where all the celebrities lazed by the pool sipping Pina Coladas or Long Island Teas.

The best preserved of its type in any Egyptian temple, at each corner of the oasis were flights of stone steps leading down to a terrace, there were other flights of stairs concealed in the walls at either end that probably connected to underground tunnels connected to the main temple and would have given private access for Cleopatra to the Oasis as well as access for the priests and priestesses to water when it was at a lower level. I couldn't trace them back as they were flooded or filled in with wet sand. That told me there was some underground water table or source of water, most likely from the Nile, as the oasis itself was empty apart from a grove of tall palm trees growing inside its walls.

Pernille and Crystal were strolling around as if reminiscing. I knew Crystal hadn't been Cleopatra, she'd told me so, but did say she had been Cleopatra's daughter, she must have spent numerous sunny days relaxing here in the water.

But what about Pernille? Maybe *she* had been Cleopatra? Maybe this was a mother and daughter moment. And if Pernille *was* Cleopatra, did that mean that Jacques was possibly Julius Caesar, he certainly had a high opinion of himself, and it certainly set himself up to be assassinated by those most close to him. And where did that leave Bill? Was he Marc Antony?

OK, I was letting my imagination go wild. No, maybe it wasn't my imagination, maybe it was my memory; maybe it was part of my re-membering. Anyway, to try and keep things in perspective, I left the girls to wander and reminisce and moved on from Cleopatra's oasis, focusing instead on my previous discussion with Bill.

'So, do you think any of the Essenes actually went to Ireland?'

'Sure, there's an Arthurian legend that Jesus, during his "lost" years between the ages of thirteen to thirty, travelled to Britain with his uncle, Joseph of Arimathea, to study with the Druids. There are also legends and folklore that associate Joseph of Arimathea with the Scottish Isle of Skye.'

'Yeah, but that could just be myths or here-say.'

'True, they could, but I don't think they are.'

We headed behind the main temple, to the south, to an Iseum; a small temple dedicated to the goddess Isis, dating from the time of the Roman emperor Augustus. As we gave it the once over, Bill continued his exploration of ancient Scotland.

'I remember reading about an article published in the 1930's by a former keeper of the manuscripts department at the British Museum in London, who wrote about finding a whole set of legends from the late 19th Century of the wanderings of the Holy Mother and Son in the Catholic part of the outer Scottish Hebridean Islands.'

Heading inside the remains of the outer walls of the Iseum, this time it was my turn to play the Devil's advocate.

'Still could be just a lot of myths.'

I instantly noted the main part of the structure, the outer court and small four-columned hypostyle hall, faced east, towards the Eastern Gateway in the distance, which clearly led directly to *this* temple and not to the main temple. Meanwhile Bill was not so distracted.

'OK, but we know that during the early centuries AD, a place was often named to record the actual presence and consecration of that place by the early Celtic Christian monastic saints. You see, there's a small island off the Scottish Isle of Skye called Eilean Isa, or the "Island of Jesus". There are no religious sites on the island, or anything to suggest that its name was conceived from a religious dedication, so it could be speculated quite strongly that the "Island of Jesus" was named as a result of it being sanctified by the presence of Jesus himself.'

'I'd like to believe it, but I'm not convinced. You could use that argument to say that Phillip Island in Victoria was named because of the presence of Arthur Phillip, first Governor of New South Wales, or that Churchill Island got *its* name from a visit by Winston Churchill.'

Bill reluctantly conceded the point.

'I hear what you're saying!'

We had a chuckle and returned our attention to the Iseum. What I found even more interesting than its outer orientation, were the black-granite steps at the entrance to both the outer courtyard and to the hypostyle hall. They apparently were part of the Ptolemaic rebuilding, probably Ptolemy X and VI, but they'd been rather poorly restored, either because they didn't belong there, or the sandstone blocks around them were not contemporary with them. It was just more evidence of an earlier structure and the shoddy slap-dash restoration work done by the modern Egyptologists. My iphone notes shed a little more light on the situation.

'The Iseum used the foundation blocks from a previously destroyed Ptolemaic building.'

But I wasn't so convinced; there was at the very least a structure attributable to Nectanebo I, but it seemed even more logical to me, that like so many other structures in Egypt, the foundation stones of the Iseum belonged to an even older structure.

At the rear of the hypostyle hall, stood the remaining part of the Iseum, supposedly attributable to the Roman Emperor Augustus. Rather than it opening into the inner sanctum, there was a false door in the centre of the wall; the actual entrance to the inner sanctum was bizarrely via a short inner staircase to the right and in from the north.

Following the stairs into the inner sanctum, I discovered not only a sanctuary with two side chambers, but that the inner rooms faced north, towards the main Temple of Hathor. This was a clear indication to me that the building of the inner rooms was not connected to the Ptolemaic parts of the ruins beneath, that they had been built later, most likely by Augustus, on top of the older ruins, and without any connection to either them, or the eastern gate.

The inner walls depicted scenes of Hathor suckling Horus as a child, with further depictions of Hathor as a cow-goddess on the east and west walls. The central high relief in the sanctuary, which showed Isis giving birth, had been badly vandalized, probably by some fanatical religious prude, whilst the rear wall of the sanctuary contained a niche which would once have contained a statue of Osiris, now destroyed, supported by the arms of Isis and Nepthys. There was also, logically and understandably, a figure in high relief of the god Bes.

Eager to move on, Bill and I left the Iseum and stood before the exterior of the rear wall of the main temple.

'It's not quite as impressive as the one at Edfu; close, but not quite.'

Bill was right, it wasn't. But it did have a few differences worth noting. Spanning the back were duplicate mirror-imaged scenes showing the massive figure of Cleopatra VII at each extremity, with her son, Caesarion, standing in front of her. Cleopatra was presenting him to Hathor, Ihy and a line of four other gods. I knew all about Cleopatra: well I thought I did. After all, I'd seen the movie with Elizabeth Taylor and Richard Burton numerous times: who hadn't? I knew how she had herself smuggled secretly into Julius Caesar's palace rolled up in a carpet, seduced him, then convinced him to abandoned his plans to annex Egypt and back her claim to the Egyptian throne over her younger brother, Ptolemy XIII. Caesar's army then overthrew Ptolemy XIII and Cleopatra was reinstated as pharaoh of Egypt. But, when Caesar was assassinated on the Ides of March, Cleopatra returned to the relative safety of Egypt.

Soon after, Marc Antony called her to see him, and Cleopatra stamped her position as ruler of Egypt by making a grand entrance into Tarsus. That done, she set about, and succeeded in, seducing Marc Antony as well. All I can say is that she must have been amazing in the cot.

However, when Marc Antony and Octavian, or as he was later known, Augustus, had a big falling out, Augustus turned on Marc Antony and Cleopatra, and, shortly after, Marc Antony fell on his own sword and Cleopatra took her life by coercing an Egyptian cobra to inflict a fatal bite. What I wasn't up to speed on, were the details about Cleopatra's son, Caesarion. As I went for the iphone, I pointed to Caesarion's image on the wall.

'Hey, Bill, do you know much about Caesarion?'

'Caesarion? A little. I know he was the son of Julius Caesar and Cleopatra, but that Caesar refused to accept he was the father, and named his grandnephew Octavian as heir to the Roman Empire instead of Caesarion. Then, when Caesar was assassinated, Cleopatra made Caesarion co-regent of Egypt and her successor, even though he was only a few years old.

It was formalized about ten years later, in late 34 BC, at the Donations of Alexandria, when Marc Antony named Cleopatra and Caesarion co-rulers of Egypt. Consequently Caesarion was proclaimed with all sorts of titles including 'god', 'son of god' and 'king of kings'.'

'Hang on, I thought those titles were reserved for Jesus?'

'That's the general belief, but it seems they weren't.'

'A coincidence, or a *co*-incident?'

'No matter what the answer, the titles were clearly an obvious threat to Octavian, as he invaded Egypt. Cleopatra, fearing Caesarion's safety, supposedly sent him away to the Red Sea port of Berenice, with plans for him to escape to India should Octavian's invasion prove successful. It was, and when Marc Antony and Cleopatra each committed suicide, Octavian ordered the death of Caesarion, and *that's* where the stories begin to differ.'

'What do you mean?'

'Well, one story goes, that Caesarion was lured back to Alexandria and strangled to death, the other, that he escaped to India.'

'Which do you believe?'

'As far as I know, there's no evidence supporting the later, so I guess he was killed.'

To be sure, I flicked through the file on the iphone.

'Ptolemy XV Philopator Philometor Caesar, (June 23, 47 BC – August 23, 30 BC), sometimes referred to as "Ptolemy Caesar", most commonly known by his nickname *Caesarion*, (little Caesar) was the last king of the Ptolemaic dynasty of Egypt. He also had a full set of Egyptian royal names; Iwapanetjer entynehem, Setepenptah, Irmaatenre, Sekhemankhamun, usually translated as: "Heir of the God who saves", "Chosen of Ptah", "Sun of Righteousness" and "Living Image of Amun".

Proclaimed a god, son of god and "King of Kings", it caused a fatal breach in Antony's relations with Octavian, who is supposed to have had Caesarion executed in Alexandria, although the exact circumstances of his death have not been documented.'

It didn't really throw any more light on the subject, but sometimes nothing can mean something.

'I guess Caesarion *must* have been murdered, because nothing was ever heard of or from him again. And, with *his* ancestry, disappearing into obscurity wasn't really an option, unless he *did* go to India and changed his name.'

Suddenly an idea flashed through my mind.

'Hey, Bill, do you think there's any link between Caesarion and Jesus?'

'Now *that's* an interesting question; hmm, there was only about forty years or so between the two, both called the "son of god", both called the "king of kings".'

Then I took a leaf out of Randy's book.

'You know what Randy would say if he was here; he would say they were one and the same person.'

That amused Bill no end.

'Good old Randy; now wouldn't that send a skyrocket up the backside of all the major religions?'

'At *least* a Saturn V.'

We both laughed aloud at the audacity and ludicrousness of the suggestion, then, once I'd regained my composure, I returned to scanning the rest of the wall. Stretching across the width, just under the cornice, was a series of reliefs which, according to my notes,

'It depicts the festival of "Raising the Sky".'

'A festival dedicated to "Raising the Sky", what do you think that's all about, Bill?'

He took a deep breath and scratched his head.

'Well, Dendera *is* all about the zodiac and the constellations, so the first thing I would say is that it's to do with something extra-terrestrial. However I don't think it could just be the rising of a particular constellation on the horizon, that would be fairly innocuous, *but* ...'

We both squinted trying to make out the reliefs, but they were too high and harder to see than the larger images that stretched across the span of the temple.

'Yes?'

'... well, if the sky had *"fallen"* due to some catastrophe, then it would explain a need to have a festival celebrating the *raising* of the sky.'

'The tsunami?'

'No, that wouldn't have affected the position of the stars.'

I got it!

'A pole shift!'

'It *would* fit the bill perfectly.'

'I guess the answer must be somewhere inside the main temple.'

'Yep, probably on the ceiling or in the chapel on the roof.'

Below that, dividing the wall into thirds, were two lion-headed waterspouts just below the cornice, clearly there to drain rainwater from the roof. Rainwater? That was optimistic. But why lion heads? Was there some significance to that? Did it have something to do with Sekhmet? I knew from Karnak that Sekhmet was connected in some way to the Hathors. But there's no way you could confuse a being with cow's ears for a lion, so not even Randy would suggest they were the same being.

The other point of difference was at the centre of the wall where there was a large false door containing a gigantic emblem of Hathor. Similar to the one at Kom Ombo, it would have been the location of a 'hearing ear' shrine, which allowed the goddess to 'hear' the prayers of pilgrims and other common folk not otherwise allowed into the main temple to submit their prayers directly to the goddess. It was heavily worn, no doubt from countless hands over numerous centuries rubbing the image and scraping at it to obtain a little of the sacred stone so they could get as close to Hathor as possible; much like modern teenagers ripping at the clothes of pop idols.

Speaking of goddesses, out of the corner of my eye I saw Pernille and Crystal approaching from Cleopatra's Oasis, arm in arm and smiling like two teenage girls.

34

Keen to reconnect with Crystal, I fired off what I thought was a mildly humorous greeting.

Well, stone the crows!

'Welcome back, Bill and I were just admiring the image of your mother.'

Crystal gave a quick look at the image of Cleopatra on the back wall, then looked to Pernille.

'Of my sister.'

The two of them laughed and embraced once more. Had I missed something?

'Sister, I didn't even know Cleopatra had a sister? I thought you were Cleopatra's daughter; what was her name again?'

'You don't remember? Cleopatra Selene II.'

'That's right, I thought you were her?'

'I was.'

'But, you just said you were her sister.'

'I was.'

I scratched my head.

'I'm confused.'

Thankfully Pernille took over the story.

'Yes, Cleopatra had a younger half-sister, Arsinoe IV, who was a high priestess in the Temple of Artemis in Ephesus, which was under Roman control.'

That sparked a remembrance from Bill.

'I remember; Arsinoe and her younger brother, Ptolemy XIV, tried to seize the Egyptian throne back from Roman hands, from Cleopatra and Julius Caesar. But they failed, and though they released Ptolemy, Arsinoe was captured and held in the Temple of Artemis in Ephesus as insurance against further attacks. But then, to avoid any further challenges to the throne, Cleopatra poisoned her younger brother, and had Marc Antony order the death of Arsinoe. And, if my memory serves me correctly, the execution was carried out on the steps of the temple, which was a violation of the temple sanctuary and caused a scandal in Rome.'

It was all spinning in my head faster than a Roman Candle, so I turned to Crystal to sort it out.

'So you were Cleopatra's sister, Arsinoe, Cleopatra had you killed, but you reincarnated as her daughter, Cleopatra Selene II, the daughter of Marc Antony, the man who had you killed, right?'

'You shouldn't believe everything you read. Yes I was Cleopatra's sister, Arsinoe IV, but I was murdered by order of Augustus, who feared the royal blood of Egypt. What better way for everyone to play out and resolve their "karma".'

'Everyone?'

She raised her eyebrows.

'Everyone!'

I looked around at the others.

'Wait a minute, if Crystal was Cleopatra's sister, Arsinoe, and was also her daughter, Cleopatra Selene II, then, that means that Pernille was ....'

'Yes, Cleopatra VII.'

Crystal took off along the back of the temple with Pernille, leaving Bill and I gawking at the image on the back wall with renewed interest.

'Well, she's certainly maintained her figure.'

We both took the opportunity to appreciate the sumptuous curves of the two goddesses leading the way before us. For me, Pernille being Cleopatra was a major confirmation of 'stuff' that had been buzzing around inside my head.

'You know, Bill, it means Jacques was not only Ramses II, not only Phillip IV, but he must have been Julius Caesar as well.'

'Some guys never learn.'

'Yeah, talk about type-casting.'

Bill chuckled away as he patted his rounded little pot-belly.

'Well, I don't think I was Caesarion, so I guess that makes me Marc Antony.'

'You and Richard Burton that is. And that leaves me, which means I was …? Do you think I was Caesarion?'

'That would make you Jacques' son; how does *that* fit with you?'

I shuddered.

'Like Stan Laurel's pants on Oliver Hardy, like a training bra on Maria Venutti, like a pair of Twiggy's knickers on Mama Cass.'

'Enough; a little *too* much information. Maybe you're one of Marc Antony and Cleopatra's sons? That would make you my son, and Crystal's brother.'

'That sounds more like it; how many sons did they have?'

'Two; about a year after Arsinoe's assassination, coincidentally on 25th December, Cleopatra gave birth to twins, Cleopatra Selene II and Alexander Helios, and four years later to Ptolemy Philadelphus. So, take your pick, Alexander Helios, or Ptolemy Philadelphus.'

It was pretty obvious really; I've never related to the Ptolemy name, it sounded like a nasty disease, and my own name was actually Alexander.

'I guess it's a fait accompli; I was Crystal's twin brother, Alexander Helios.'

The girls rounded the corner and headed down along the side of the temple. Bill followed closely behind, but I wanted to make sure I didn't leave any stones unturned.

'You three go on ahead, I'll catch up with you, I want to quickly check out the eastern wall and gateway.'

'No worries, *son*, we'll see you inside.'

He chuckled away as he caught up with Crystal and Pernille, no doubt having a family reunion of sorts, leaving me to explore the eastern part of the complex and absorb the latest developments. Explore the east, it sounded like a spiritual pilgrimage to Nepal to find my inner self. Oh, what would my ex-wife say now?

Go East, young man

I headed past another set of steps that led underground to a tunnel: to where, I had no idea. I couldn't believe it was filled in with dirt and sand; how difficult would it be to excavate it? It had to lead somewhere? Or maybe they already *had* excavated it, decided they didn't want people to know what was underground, and subsequently filled it in again. Good one guys, let's bury the truth. Moving on, I flicked through my files for more information of Cleopatra and her family.

'Cleopatra's father, Ptolemy XII Neos Dionysos Theos Philopater Theos Philadeplos, or Auletes, was a direct descendant of Alexander the Great's general, Ptolemy I Soter, son of Arsinoe and Lacus, both of Macedonia.'

There was that Greek-Macedonian connection again.

'The identity of her mother is unknown, but generally

believed to be Cleopatra V Tryphaena of Egypt, the sister or cousin of Ptolemy XII, or possibly another Ptolemaic family member, who was the daughter of Ptolemy X and Cleopatra Berenice III Philopator if Cleopatra V was not the daughter of Ptolemy X and Berenice III.'

Which is basically a way of saying, 'We haven't really got a clue'. But let's suppose that Cleopatra knew she was descended from the bloodline of the gods, part of the *sang réal* lineage. Her ancestry all married each other, so they would have kept the bloodline of the Ptolemy's. The only question is whether the Ptolemy bloodline was connected to Alexander the Great, and, whether it was through the women, not the men. So not knowing who Cleopatra VII's mother was would make it harder to trace. The only saving grace was the names, like the Nefer suffix, Cleopatra may have been a family name.

'When her mother died, Cleopatra briefly ruled jointly with her father Ptolemy XII Auletes, but, when he died, the 18-year-old Cleopatra was made joint monarch with her 10-year-old brother Ptolemy XIII. Although Cleopatra was married to her brother, she had no intention of sharing power with him.'

There may have been more to it, maybe he was a half-brother; it could have been a Hatshepsut and Thutmoses III thing all over again.

'As he grew older, relations between Ptolemy and Cleopatra completely broke down and eventually Cleopatra was removed from power and Ptolemy made sole ruler. She tried to raise a rebellion, but was soon forced to flee to Rome, with her only remaining sister, Arsinoë.'

No doubt the priests would have been in the young regent's ear, as they had been with Thutmoses III and Tutankhamen, manipulating him and regaining power. But she did manage to manipulate Caesar, something no one else had been able to do, and eventually she and Caesarion were crowned co-regents of Egypt.

When Octavian eventually overthrew them, and Marc Antony, Cleopatra and Caesarion were dead, it ended not just the Hellenistic line of Egyptian pharaohs, but the line of all Egyptian pharaohs. As for her children...

'The three children of Cleopatra and Antony were taken back to Rome where they were taken care of by Antony's Roman wife, Octavia Minor. Cleopatra Selene, was soon married, by arrangement by Octavian, to Juba II of Numidia, where she became queen.'

There was no mention of what happened to Alexander Helios, but at least it was a happy ending for Cleopatra Selene II, for Crystal. As I approached the eastern gate I suddenly realized that the reason history repeated itself was probably because the incarnating souls were repeating themselves. Did that mean there was a happy ending ahead for Crystal? If I had anything to do with it there would be.

Speaking of things repeating themselves, the first thing I noticed were the two massive red-granite blocks forming the foundation of the gateway. This was exactly what I was finding in almost every single temple, there had to be some significance to it. I mean, why quarry massive blocks of red granite hundreds of miles away, then transport them to these sacred sites just for people to walk over them, especially when other paths are constructed of simple sandstone?

The walls certainly held clues, but not to the foundations. I spotted a number of cartouches at several levels up the inner wall, one of which was high up and belonged to Alexander the Great. There was another, at eye level, that I thought I'd be able to cross-reference.

I couldn't match it exactly, but it seemed similar to that of Ptolemy XII Neos Dionysos, Cleopatra's father, which would be consistent with the complex.

Then I spotted a row of ankhs, in fact it was a row of ornamental reliefs comprising a repeated motif of an ankh in a shallow bowl, framed on either side by a staff of Ptah. I knew the Egyptians didn't just make up interesting patterns for aesthetic reasons, there had to be some specific meaning to the image, especially as it repeated the pattern, row after row, running up the inside of the gateway.

There were three elements: the ankh itself, the two staffs of Ptah looking inwards towards the ankh, and the shallow bowl in which they sat. There had to be more to the ankh than it just being the 'breath of life'; it was such a strong symbol it was carried all the way to Ireland and Scotland and had survived thousands of years. Similarly the staff of Ptah had to have deeper meaning, especially as it related to the ankh. As for the bowl, well, the only thing I could think of that was bowls held things. I took a photo of it, for reference and to contemplate at some time down the track, and headed out through the gate.

Imagine my surprise when I encountered a tiny enclosure, formed from mud-brick walls about twelve feet high, that prevented me going any further. Or was it to prevent entrance from outside? This made no sense in the scheme of the complex; gateways led *from* somewhere *to* somewhere else. There was no way to climb up and look at what lay beyond; I thought maybe my notes would reveal something.

'East of the temple was a part of the town, which the temple texts mention as having a Temple of Horus of Edfu in its midst. There was also a temple to Ihy. This may be the same as some remains of the Roman Period about 500 metres from the main enclosure.'

OK, so there was, or even possibly is, the remains of another huge temple beyond the mud-brick walls: another Temple of Horus. *That* would be impressive, but it would hardly be Roman, more than likely Ptolemaic, unless of course it was built on top of an even older New Kingdom, Middle Kingdom, or even Old Kingdom temple. Now that *would* be impressive. That said, if it was totally gone, or even mostly gone, then that would be the most impressive of all, for how would a temple that size just disappear? So, maybe it's still there, just buried under metres of mud?

It seems the answers would escape me, as there was little chance of me retracing my steps, exiting the complex, circling back and exploring the wilderness to find any trace of the Temple of Horus. I certainly couldn't do that *and* explore the main temple; there just wasn't the time. All I could conclude was that though the eastern gateway may well have hailed from the Ptolemaic era, its foundations certainly didn't.

I hightailed back to the main temple: back through the gateway, following the path that led directly to the Iseum at the rear of the main temple. To the right, the piles of dirt and debris indicated there was probably much more to discover beneath the surface, and that perhaps the exploration here at Dendera had been as superficial as the stories about the history of Egypt.

Turning right at the temple, I made my way along the side of the building, eager to join the others inside. Lined up along and on the remains of the outer stone wall, that ran down alongside the temple, the opposite wall to the one that cut through Nectanebo's Mammasi, were numerous pieces of red and black granite.

Many of the pieces were curved or rounded, possibly being large sinks, wheels, or parts of ceremonial fountains or rituals. They didn't belong to the main temple that was for sure. You only had to compare the wear and tear on the granite to that of the sandstone wall upon which they leaned and the building alongside to realize these pieces of granite had to have been thousands of years older, and that meant they must have been dug up from the surrounds.

There was even a red-granite floor-block in a gateway that existed about half way along the side of the main temple between the temple and the outer wall. In addition, the side entrance to the temple also had a red-granite footer. As far as I knew, not one single Egyptologist had even noticed this consistent inconsistency: were they all blind, or was it that they couldn't see the forest for the trees?

Similar to the mud-brick walls outside the east gate, a twelve-foot mud-brick wall had been erected inside the actual thirty-foot remains of the original mud-brick walls of the complex. Clearly this was a modern addition, more than likely built to protect some unsuspecting tourist from the unstable walls of the original thirty-foot wall collapsing onto them.

I followed the trail of breadcrumbs as it led north along the outer wall of the compound back to the main entrance. Along the wall were rows of bric-a-brac and architectural fragments; columns, statues; capitols, all from a variety of eras. In the corner were two magnificent Hathor-headed capitols.

Capitols meant columns and columns meant a temple. Were they part of the Roman mammasi, I doubted it. Maybe they were the capitols of the columns of the Trajan kiosk before it, or perhaps they were part of the Nectanebo mammasi? That was my guess, but then they could have belonged to even another structure, a much older structure.

Just along from the Hathor heads, I took notice of one section that had a very worn red-granite stela covered in reliefs, a black-granite wheel fully etched with images, and, behind, a small red-granite sarcophagus decorated with lotus flowers. Lotus flowers? Interesting!

The Egyptologists had placed them together implying they were contemporary with each other. But several questions arose; where did they come from, what were they used for, and where did they belong?

Just prior to arriving back at the Domitian Gateway was another squared-column section, this one with a fantastic raised relief of Bes. Come on, guys, you really think the ancient Egyptians made up such a troll for a god? Look at all the other mythologies, they all have some sort of bearded-dwarf-creature. Or are they suggesting it was some dark aspect buried deep within the human psyche?

Apart from excavating and searching below the surface of the compound, there was only one place left to look for answers, the main temple of Hathor. Hathor? Just who was Hathor? I thought about my encounter with Hesat, emissary of the Hathors to earth. Maybe Hesat was Hathor?

Hathor

As I headed towards the temple entrance, I opened the file on Hathor on my iphone.

'Hathor, also known as Het-Hert, wife of Horus, was the goddess of the sky, fertility and healing. 'Lady in the Sky' whose womb protected the hawk god, she was the 'Celestial Cow' or 'Lady of the Southern Sycamore'.'

"Het-hert", Hesat; the similarity was notable. And "Lady in the Sky"; a sudden idea hit me, what if the references were celestial? What if the 'Celestial Cow' was not just a reference to her appearance, but maybe she came from a place in the heavens later identified by that image, which would possibly be the constellation of Taurus. Hmmm, I didn't know much more than that, I'd have to check with Yuko later on, she seemed the astronomy expert.

'The ancient Egyptians often chose animals to symbolize a god's properties, and as the wild cow was very protective about its calves, it was therefore a perfect ideal for maternal protectiveness.'

So was a crocodile, or a lion; no, that didn't wash, I was still in favour of Hathor actually looking as Hesat had appeared to me, as she was shown on the capitals of columns, with a woman's head and a cow's ears.

'Her full image, smiling and naked, is often found decorating mirrors, whilst in reliefs she is often seen depicted with a sun-disc surrounded by cow's horns on her head, but also sometimes with a cow's head, or in later periods in full bovine form.'

OK, why mirrors, was it something to do with reflecting on yourself? Of course it was, mirrors enable you to see things from a different perspective, but mainly to see yourself as others see you. Expanding self-perception is the first step in the process of self-awareness, and mirrors give you a perception that is not yours.

'The earliest representations of Het-Hert are from the 4th Dynasty where she is described in the Pyramid Texts as the "Eye of Ra", foremost of goddesses, and Divine Mother of the King, a title she shares with Bast, Sekhmet, Aset and Mut.'

"The eye of the sun, daughter of Ra"? Not sure about that: mental note to explore it later.

'A patron of beauty, love, sexuality, joy, dance and music, her greatest influence was as a protector of pregnant women and children. At various periods she had a large number of priestesses who acted as singers, musicians and dancers in temple rituals and processions, which included the use of a sistrum, or rattle.'

That made total sense; Hesat said the Hathors used supersonic, subsonic and audible sounds to stimulate psycho-spiritual experiences. Many primitive cultures used drumbeats and trance-like dances to much the same effect, though I don't think that would include the mindless duff-duff 'music' that some modern kids listened to.

I paused outside the entrance, not so much to gather my thoughts, but because I found random well-worn red-granite stones emerging from the sandstone paved forecourt. Oh, I bet there was so much to discover under the ground here.

The Temple of Hathor

One of the latest and possibly the best preserved of the Egyptian temples, the Temple of Hathor is largely a Ptolemaic structure, begun before the reign of Ptolemy VIII Euergetes II, continued through the Ptolemaic kings, and completed during Roman times around 14 AD. How it survived when the temples of Hathor's consort, Horus, and their child, Ihy, which both originally stood close by, didn't, is anybodies guess. Perhaps it had something to do with the massive mud-brick wall surrounding the complex. If the other two temples were outside the walls, then they may well have been razed to the ground by an event such as a tsunami.

'Oriented towards the Nile, the present temple was built on top of an older temple dating back possibly to the Old Kingdom. There are texts that refer to earlier shrines on the site sometime from the Old Kingdom onwards.'

That was it; there were other temples here before this one, and they were somewhere underneath the present structures.

'Other texts refer to an Old Kingdom temple on the site that was rebuilt during the Old or Middle Kingdom, with several New Kingdom monarchs, including Thutmoses III, Amenhotep III and Ramses II and III, known to have embellished the structure. Pepi I, from the Old Kingdom, and Thutmoses III in particular, were recalled in the new temple's inscriptions. However, while fragments of those earlier periods have been found on the site, there have been no earlier buildings unearthed.'

It totally reinforced my tsunami theory. If I could find any evidence of alabaster, then that would be a definite sign of the Middle or even Old Kingdom, and if I found any more red granite, then that would indicate to something that went back way even before then.

'It is probable that the design of the later temple is based on that of the older one, and that the massive foundations probably contain many blocks from the earlier structure it replaced.'

My only point of difference was that I believed the massive foundations of *this*, current temple were not the foundations of the previous temple, but more than likely the roof beams of the previous structure. Hopefully I was about to find some evidence.

About forty-metres wide, sixty-metres long and maybe fifteen-metres high, the temple façade consisted of an imposing low screen, inter-columnar wall divided by six massive Hathor-headed columns and a huge curved cornice with a winged sun-disc over the entrance. On the screens between the columns were scenes of the Roman Emperor Tiberius and other Roman rulers making offerings to Hathor, who was mostly represented with the horns of the sacred cow protruding from her head and supporting the solar disc of the sun.

I'd started to look at the image of Hathor somewhat differently to the Egyptologists; to me the horns represented something else, possibly antennae or some psycho-cerebral communicative device, and the disc, maybe not just the sun, but something *about* the sun, or maybe it referred to the second sun. In her hands, Hathor held an ankh, the symbol of life, and a sceptre.

Standing before the entrance, I looked up at the huge opening. According to the inscribed dedication on the cornice thickness above the entrance, this part of the temple was built during the reign of Tiberius between 34 and 35 AD. I looked back down and couldn't believe my luck, somehow I'd avoided kissing a Chinaman: well, not just one, but a couple of busloads of them. Thankfully they filed past me much as the group had at the obelisk in Aswan, oblivious of anyone or anything in their path. They bounced off me like those little metal balls in that Japanese game.

Once they were all downstream, I crossed the now familiar red-granite threshold and entered the Hypostyle hall; about eighteen-metres high, twenty-five metres deep and spanning the full forty-metres of the temple. Just inside and to the right was the remains of what looked like a footbath imbedded as part of the floor.

On the inner walls of the screen, Horus, and the Ibis headed god Thoth, were anointing the pharaoh by pouring drops of holy water over him. I wondered if this wasn't just a scene symbolizing life and happiness, but also possibly the first representation or reference to a baptism. The interior walls had even more remarkable scenes of various Roman emperors ranging from Augustus to Nero all depicted as pharaohs alongside Egyptian gods, making offerings to Hathor.

Dominating the main space of the hall was a forest of eighteen Hathor-headed columns similar to those in the façade. Despite the fact that every one of the faces had been vandalized in antiquity, probably during the early Christian Period, or later Islamic occupation, the columns were all still in remarkable condition. Each column had a four-sided capital, occupying about a quarter of the column height, with each side carved with the face of the cow-eared goddess. The circular shafts upon which they sat were decorated with numerous colourful scenes, most of which were dominated by the blue paint of Hathor's hair. Was it representative of the "Lady in the Sky"?

As I stood there looking up at the imposing image, the face of Hathor came to life and I found myself drawn back to my experience the previous night.

'We come in love, to assist humans in raising their vibrational existence, heralding the possibility of a new age for the earth.'

Suddenly it was Hesat looking down over me, much as the Hathors had done over the entire human race.

'Remember, ascension is not a pathway, it is a process of self-awareness and mastery of all levels of the moment that is the Oneness.'

I got the message, just not the game plan.

'How do you hook into the process, how do you get things started?

Hesat smiled.

'Look for the sacred geometry, for it is present in all things; all things contain it, all things exist because of it.'

And then she faded away. "*Look for the sacred geometry.*" My eyes were instantly drawn towards the ceiling where, arranged between the columns, seven bands of well-preserved reliefs stretched along the depth of the temple.

Much like the ceiling at Esna, it was no big surprise to see that all sorts of astronomical figures dominated the decorations; including an alternating row of vultures and winged sun-discs running down the centre of the hall towards the inner sanctum, much of it restored to its original blue colour. Where to start? In the east of course; after all, isn't that where the sun rises?

The first section on the eastern side depicted the Goddess Nut, Goddess of the sky, bending herself towards the earth, with the moon coming from her mouth and a wing shining down from it. At the other end of the row, as if emerging from Nut's womb, was the sun, shining down on the Temple and a weird image of Hathor's head.

There was something about it that didn't quite look right. Perhaps it was the fact Hathor's head was recessed into the stone; it looked like an after-thought. Then it was the position, right under the rays of the sun. Surely it meant more than just Hathor getting a good sun tan. Was it something to do with 'life' coming from the sun? Somehow that seemed too trite.

Running beneath the stretched out image of Nut was a series of figures, including the first six signs of the modern zodiac from Aquarius through to Cancer; they were easy to understand. What I couldn't work out were the male and female figures that were interspersed amongst them, including a headless man before Aquarius, a male holding a dog by the tail surrounded by a large disc, and a baboon with a falcon on its head between the ram of Aries and the bull of Taurus.

Perhaps they were related to some of the eighty-eight zodiac signs of Ptolemaic and Roman times? Many of the other figures had single stars above their heads, and I wondered if that meant they were beings associated with those particular constellations. Beneath was a row of single figures, probably gods, in single barques.

The next row looked like a procession of mainly animal-headed creatures, mostly lions and snakes, walking serpents, mermen, several gods seated on thrones, most seemingly making offerings to, one would assume, Hathor. The lower tier had many beings, including gods in barques and spiting cobras, some with red discs above their heads. That red disc got me wondering if those beings were somehow associated with Nibiru; clearly there was some significance to the difference between the white disc and the red disc.

Approaching the centre aisle, the third row contained a series of long barques with multiple beings on board.

These were no random decorations, but, like a cosmic comic strip, they clearly told a story; a story of the heavens and the journeys of the gods through them. As I crossed the centre and, like the sun, traversed into the west, I moved from section to section, looking for signs, messages, clues, looking for evidence of sacred geometry.

Across the central line of the hall, covered in winged discs, the first row in the western half was nothing less than amazing. Cranking my head back to see the images on the ceiling was proving more than a little uncomfortable; I was starting to get a crick in my neck and feel a little dizzy. There was only one way to see it properly, lie down on my back and star gaze.

To the right was the all-seeing eye of Horus, attended by fourteen squatting figures, all in a large disc that sat on a solar barque along with several gods onboard as well. If the disc was the sun, which would make sense, then it implied that the eye of awareness, and all people, originated with the sun. The only way I could make sense of that, was if all *consciousness* originated from the sun, that the sun was, in itself, a consciousness, and something about that sounded very familiar. Or, and the idea was very science fiction, was the sun some sort of portal, a wormhole. Did the gods use it to visit our part of the galaxy? If so, why? Who knows, maybe it was both?

Further left, the eye appeared again, once again in the disc, but this time supported by a sort of cup on a pedestal, like a champagne glass. It was difficult to make them out but, to the right was Thoth, and leading up a series of steps to it from the left was a procession of fourteen gods, led by Horus, Osiris, Maat, Sekhmet, then further down the line, Isis and Nepthys.

I spent five or so minutes taking photos, trying to absorb the true meaning of the images, other tourists navigating around me as if I was a rotting corpse, almost stunned as to the concept of someone lying on the floor to avoid severe dislocation of their neck. This row really meant something; every part of it, the eye, the disc, the pedestal, Thoth, the rising staircase, even the order of the gods. But what did it actually mean, that was the question?

Eventually I moved on to the penultimate row, poorly preserved and difficult to make out, and then the final row, to the west, another setting of Nut, this time embracing the second six constellations of the zodiac, Leo through to Capricorn. These ceilings definitely weren't just a series of unrelated images. Just like the ceiling at Esna, they were a complex and carefully aligned symbolic chart of the heavens, which included the majority of the signs of the Ptolemaic and Roman eras along with the much older images of the sky goddess, Nut. It was time to delve deeper into Dendera.

The rear wall of the first hypostyle was once the façade of the original temple, and a central doorway led through it into a second, smaller hypostyle known as the 'hall of appearances'. This would have been the outer hall of the previous temple. From here I could see into the depth of the inner sanctuary and hear Crystal and Pernille holding hands and toning.

I decided to take my time and explore the rooms around the sanctuary to give the ladies as much undisturbed time there as possible. The walls of the 'hall of appearances' depicted scenes of the pharaoh participating in the foundation ceremonies for the construction of the temple, though which temple I couldn't be sure, as the cartouches were blank, possibly due to the rapid turn over of pharaohs during the later periods. The ceiling had several small square apertures that admitted light into the hall, and was supported by six, smaller Hathor columns, in two rows of three, each adorned with decorative capitals. Looking down the columns, I saw a major piece of evidence; while the upper parts of the columns, like the walls around them, were made of sandstone, the bases and lower parts of the columns were made of granite. That showed not only that the previous structure was made of red granite, but more so that something had literally swept away the top part of the temple. Dendera was revealing its secrets.

As with many of the other temples, on each side of the hall were three chambers. On the east side was a room that opened to the outside, probably for the receiving of offerings, next to it a storeroom used to store the offerings, and the third a laboratory for preparation of ointments and libations. On the western side was possibly a treasury, a central western room with access to the well outside the temple, and in the next room along, to a staircase leading to the roof.

Beyond the second hypostyle was the rear part of the temple, most likely built first, probably in the early 1st Century BC. The earliest king named was Ptolemy XII Auletes, but mostly the cartouches were blank, probably because of the rapid dynastic struggles at the time.

The first part of this inner core was a 'hall of offerings' where daily rituals and sacrifices were carried out by the priests and priestesses of Hathor. To the right was a squared staircase that ran presumably up to the roof, to the left, an entrance that led to another staircase that ran up along the inside of the wall. I would come back to them after exploring the inner sanctuary.

More red granite, this time in the floor, greeted me as I moved across the threshold and into the next part of the temple, the "hall of the ennead", also known as the "hall of the cycle of the gods", where statues of other deities and associated divinities were assembled on feast days with Hathor before a procession began. Beyond that was the inner sanctuary, surrounded, as it was at Edfu and Philae, by a corridor and numerous rooms. Bill was hovering outside while within Pernille and Crystal were still standing face-to-face, eyes closed and softly toning.

Bill gravitated to me and we headed left, giving the girls more time to themselves. First thing we both noticed was the entrance to the corridor, again it comprised a red-granite threshold. Beyond it four small rooms ran along the eastern side.

'The Shrine of the Nome of Dendera, the Shrine of Isis, the Shrine of Sokar, and the Shrine of Harsomtus.'

The first ante-room had no granite threshold, although the one after that, the Shrine of Isis, did. The next was sans granite, the fourth, with granite. Bill and I mused over the inconsistency.

'Surely, if the temple was built from scratch, there would be a red granite threshold at each doorway?'

'And yet here are rooms without them.'

As some rooms didn't have granite thresholds, it took away the notion that the granite was used for any functional purpose related to wear and tear. So, there had to be some other explanation.

'If my theory, about the previous temple being washed away is true, then the new builders may not have been able to find all the pieces they needed, or they just built on top of the previous structure. One thing's certain, there's probably more evidence below the ground.'

Each of the side rooms was extensively decorated, including ceilings adorned with stars, although soot from previous flame torches had left considerable soot muting the colour.

'So, Pernille and Crystal were sisters?'

'Yeah, it seems so. They spent a bit a time in the birth-house, remembering they were both born there, and then at the oasis remembering they'd spent much of their youth lazing in the water around the palm trees like movie stars.'

I had a sudden flash that amused Bill no end.

'Like Bette Davis and Joan Crawford in "Whatever happened to Baby Jane?"'

We crossed along the rear corridor of the temple, which contained five chambers;

'The Shrine of Hathor's Sistrum, the Shrine of Gods of Lower Egypt, the Shrine of Hathor, the Shrine of Re, the Shrine of the Throne of Re.'

Outside the first room was a piece of alabaster poking up through the flooring. Most people probably didn't even notice it, not even Bill, but to me it was like an iceberg to the Titanic; there was no way you could miss it. I pointed down to the floor.

'Hey Bill, check it out.'

Bill, was slightly confused, obviously looking at the red-granite threshold of the first room.

'What?'

'Alabaster.'

'Yeah?'

'It confirms the previous structure must have comprised a considerable amount of not only red granite, but also alabaster, and that takes the previous temple here definitely back to the Middle Kingdom at the very least.'

He did an impersonation of Arty Johnson from the sixties TV show 'Laugh In'.

'Ah, very interesting, I'll keep my eyes peeled.'

The most important of the back rooms was obviously the chamber directly behind the sanctuary, which also had a red-granite threshold. The room would have held a shrine with images and symbols of Hathor. High up in the wall of the chamber, just like in the first birth-house, was a niche, this one containing a relief of Hathor. It probably corresponded with the shrine of the 'hearing ear' on the outside of the rear of the temple where prayers to the goddess by the masses would have been offered.

The next room, the Shrine of Re, really sparked my interest, well, not just because it had a red-granite threshold, and not so much the decorations in the room, it was what lay beneath it. Sitting against the wall was one of the local guardians and, beside him, a grill in the floor that led to one of the fourteen crypts that apparently existed beneath the floor and walls. As I approached the guardian I wondered if there was any correlation between the fourteen gods, represented at various places on the hypostyle hall ceiling, and the fourteen crypts?

'We go down?'

He looked around to check that the coast was clear, then began opening the grill.

'Yes, come you go.'

That was easy, too easy; no doubt he would sting us for some baksheesh before we could climb back out.

Hidden secrets

Removing my akubra, I made my way down the steep narrow access, ducking considerably to squeeze through the tiny opening leading to the crypt. My difficulty was height; Bill's, width.

The crypt was hot, humid, narrow, and had a low roof, not the most comfortable of places to explore; I headed right, Bill to the left. It was here where the priests and priestesses would have stored the treasures of the temple. I pulled out my iphone to see what other treasures I might discover.

'The crypts are suites of rooms on three (and sometimes even four) stories, set in the thickness of the outside wall, and beneath the floors of the chambers in the rear part of the temple.

The walls? I wondered about the outer wall that surrounded the temple itself. Were there crypts contained in the foundations of it as well? Most probably, after all, this was just one of the fourteen crypts discovered here. Maybe there were even more.

'Eleven of the crypts are decorated and painted and it is presumed that some of the most secret rituals of the goddess were associated with these small chambers.'

I looked around at the walls, covered in rows of unusual decorations.

'The main use of the crypts was for keeping cult equipment, archives and magical emblems for the temple's protection, though the most important cult object kept in the crypts was a statue of the ba of Hathor, which was taken in its shrine to the roof of the temple at each New Year's festival.'

I expected the images to relate to the objects, but I suppose without actual examples of the objects it was going to be hard to figure out what some of the more bizarre images actually referred to. One thing was for sure, it was bloody claustrophobic down there.

'The elongated, narrow chambers and passages are arranged one above the other, with the lowermost laid deep within the temple foundations. Access is gained through trapdoors in the pavement and behind hidden sliding wall blocks.'

So, there were probably other crypts below this one.

Looking down at the floor, I got my first confirmation; alabaster, many parts of the floor were made of marbleised alabaster. Was it the floor, or was it the ceiling of yet another chamber that lay beneath, a chamber that not only belonged to an older temple, but may well still be unopened.

'Hey, Bill, did you check out the floor?'

'Yep, alabaster, but forget the floor, wait until you see the images on the wall here.'

I made my way along the tight corridor to the other end of the crypt, making certain I didn't crack my sconce on a lower stone beam. Along the way I saw an image that made absolutely no sense what-so-ever. It was of what I considered to be a menat necklace, with four Hathor-headed columns on it, and, on top of each column, a container, with liquid flowing from it into, or into it from, what looked to me like a giant yard-glass. I paused for a second, scratched my head, then snapped a pic and joined Bill at the far end of the crypt.

'What the f…?'

'What do you make of that?'

'My guess it's either a giant condom for a man with a penis like an anaconda, or it's a type of cathode tube.'

'You know, these crypts were supposed to contain the magical cult equipment used in the temple.'

'Then my money is on the latter.'

'So it appears the ancient Egyptians not only had electricity, but glass as well.'

'Not as technologically primitive as we have been led to believe.'

'I'm pretty sure that giant electrical tubes spitting electricity and light would appear pretty magical to the masses.'

'Ah, yes, but where did they get the technology from, or rather from *whom* did they get it? And more importantly, why have they never found any evidence of them?'

'Maybe have they, and they've just withheld it?'

'But, why?'

'Well, the tube doesn't appear to have a power source, it seems to be connected directly to the earth. To me, that sounds like free energy.'

'Well, we couldn't possibly have that, now could we!'

Feeling time pressing on, we snapped a few more photos and hustled back up above ground before we both sweated away completely. Naturally the guardian wanted a handout, although this time it was well worth it, and we each gave him fifty pound. Bill's generosity was obviously rubbing off on me, a few days ago I would have beaten him down to maybe ten or fifteen, tops.

Heading back up the western corridor we noticed three more red-granite thresholds, at the entrances to the Shrine of the Menat Collar, the Shrine of Ihy, and the entrance to the corridor itself. We also connected up with Crystal and Pernille, who had just exited the inner sanctuary and were heading west presumably to go up the staircase to the roof.

To the west of the 'hall of the ennead' was a passage leading on one side to a staircase, to the other a small open-air courtyard within the temple, the Court of the First Feast. That in turn led up a short staircase to another small chapel known as the 'Pure Place'.

Checking my iphone files I quickly ascertained:

'It was here that sacrifices were performed during the New Year's feast.'

I cast a cursive glance towards the ceiling; there it was again, the beautiful image of Nut stretched across the sky, with the moon shimmering from her mouth and, more importantly, the sun being birthed by Nut and shining down on an image of Hathor in a square, which I guessed represented the temple.

Here was even more evidence of the connection of Hathor, or rather *the* Hathors, to the consciousness of the sun. It was as if the consciousness of the universe was birthed through the sun, into the Hathors, and ultimately to oversee the development of the human race.

The girls gave the room little more that a passing glance, instead heading up the staircase. Bill followed, then, realizing I was lagging behind, stopped to wait. But I had other things to see first.

'You go ahead, I just want to check out the inner sanctum and I'll be right behind you.'

He nodded and joined the others as they made their way up to the roof. Meanwhile, I doubled back to examine the inner sanctuary.

Having a splendid, temple-like facade topped by a cavetto with a uraeus frieze, the central chapel measured just under six-metres by twelve-metres. Once again I was greeted by red granite, the threshold and also the door jambs; this was clearly part of a much older structure. On either side of the door, the king was depicted offering a copper mirror, one of Hathor's sacred emblems, to the goddess.

Inside, the beautifully sculptured reliefs of the pharaohs, dancing and making offerings to Hathor and Horus, continued. Yes, they were beautiful, but nowhere near as interesting to me as the reliefs down in the crypt. Mission accomplished, I followed the others up the western staircase.

Lit only by small apertures in its walls, the western staircase had carved images of the pharaoh and a procession of priests, carrying standards and symbols of Hathor, ascending on the right wall, and descending on the left, as it wound around, encompassing rooms at several different levels. It also depicted other symbols representing the twelve months of the year and various aspects of the New Year's festival. Reaching the top, it was time to explore the roof!

Cast your eyes to the skies

The roof contained several chambers, split on each side of the temple, known as the 'Osiris suite'. They are dedicated to the death and resurrection myth of Osiris, which also reflects the mysteries of the divine birth of Hathor's son, Ihy.

'Dendera was considered one of Osiris's many tombs, and the shrines, which have no link with Hathor, were used to celebrate his death and resurrection.'

So, part of Osiris was originally buried here, possibly in one of the crypts, just like in Karnak under the Temple of Opet. And, just like there, the temple built on top was dedicated to someone else; Opet there, Hathor here. I wondered what was so compelling about the resurrection of Osiris? The only other figure in history who fitted being resurrected was Jesus Christ, and no matter what Randy would have thought or said, there was no way to suggest Jesus and Osiris were the same person. However I had this gut instinct there was some sort of connection, somewhere.

I headed into the western half of the suite, concealed in a kind of mezzanine floor and consisting of an open court leading into a single chamber divided into two rooms. I caught up with Bill, Crystal and Pernille in the inner of the two rooms, examining several reliefs. In one, Isis and Nephthys were mourning the death of Osiris, who was lying on his funeral bier awaiting resurrection. Further along, Crystal and Pernille were taking particular note of an image of Isis being magically impregnated with the seed of her son, Horus.

Now, *that* was interesting; not so much the relief, but the concept, so I joined back in with the group and in the discussion.

'Where would the ancient Egyptians get the concept of artificial insemination? Unless, of course, Isis *was* actually artificially inseminated?'

Crystal looked at me with that 'Wake up, Norbert' sort of look.

'In a way, she was.'

I screwed up my face; that didn't make sense.

'But why, if it was no big deal for the ancient pharaohs to marry their sisters, nieces etcetera, I doubt there would have been any taboo associated with Horus actually copulating with his mother...'

Bill was in fine form and fired out a razor sharp quip.

'Hey, that'll make Oedipus Rex feel better; the ultimate mummy's boy, the concept was around thousands of years before he came along.'

'...so why the need for artificial insemination?'

'If you look closer you will notice it's not actually artificial insemination.'

Crystal was right, the insemination was not vaginal, but through the abdomen. That opened up the possibility that it was not so much insemination, but more than likely the harvesting of Isis's ova.

'Are you suggesting Isis either donated her ova, or received a fertilized embryo?'

'I am not *suggesting* anything; when Osiris was dismembered and his body parts scattered across the country, Aset set about recovering the numerous parts of the body. Then, with the aid of her sister, Nephthys, she extracted his DNA and implanted it into one of her own eggs. The embryo was then implanted back in her womb and soon after she gave birth to Horus.'

Now we were definitely in the realm of genetic engineering.

'So it wasn't so much Horus's seed, as Horus being seeded; that Horus was a clone of his father?'

'In mind, body, *and* spirit.'

And she walked out of the chamber, closely followed by Pernille. Bill looked at me and shrugged his shoulders.

'What do you think?'

'After everything I've experienced in the past few days, it's crazy enough to be true.'

'But Crystal said "In mind, body, *and* spirit", and to my thinking, that means Osiris reincarnated in his own cloned body as his own son.'

'And how does that make you feel?'

'To tell you the truth, a little freaked out.'

'Yeah, me too.'

As Bill and I exited the suite, I noticed Crystal and Pernille were heading into a small kiosk that sat in the southwest corner of the roof. Known as the 'Chapel of the Disc' it comprised twelve Hathor-headed columns, four on each side. The girls didn't even give it a second glance, just turned right and exited the chapel through the eastern doorway. Bill and I were about ten paces behind them and entered the kiosk from the north. As we did, I noticed an opening in the floor to allow light into the Ihy chapel below. There were also regular openings in the architraves suggesting the kiosk once had a barrel-shaped timber roof with windows to let in the sun's rays.

" According to the texts on the walls, the kiosk consisted of a gold base surmounted by a gold roof supported by four gold posts, covered on all four sides by linen curtains hung from copper rods.'

The space was small and obviously there was no gold now, but once it must have been quite a sight and clearly had an important function.

'It was here that the ritual of the goddess's union with the sun disc was performed. On the evening of the New Year, the gold statuette of the ba of Hathor, represented as a bird with a human head capped with a horned disc, was taken from its hiding place in the crypts and carried up the staircase to the kiosk prior to being brought out on New Year's morning to be symbolically reunited with the sun's first rays.'

No alabaster, no red granite, maybe because we were up on the roof, hence Bill and I quickly hightailed it after the girls, heading up the eastern side of the temple towards the eastern part of the Osiris suites. As we did, I noticed the roof of the hypostyle hall was reached by another two flights of steps, built into the outer wall and ascending from either side towards the centre. Along each path were carved various gods ascending to the stars. The view would have been spectacular from up there; alas it was roped off for safety reasons. I contemplated bribing the guards, but time was a wasting and I wanted to get back to Crystal and the life of Osiris.

The corresponding Osiris suite on the eastern side of the roof similarly had a courtyard, but here it led to two chambers, the first of which, unlike the equivalent room on the western side, had a window to either side of the door.

'It celebrated the lunar festival of Khoiakh, in which an 'Osiris bed' was filled with earth and grain as part of an important fertility rite.'

Entering the first room, the walls were covered in rows of figures in boxes. Of course it was different, but it looked just like the reliefs I had seen in the ante-chamber of the tomb of Thutmoses III in Luxor. I was sure they had some sort of connection to the stars, but, without spending hours identifying and deciphering them, they just reminded me of Elvis Presley's film clip of 'Jailhouse Rock'; the one where all the inmates are in their cells on several different levels.

I took a moment to wonder who Elvis might have been in ancient Egypt, if in fact he had been anyone at all? Would he have been a pharaoh, or a high priest? There is no doubt he was worshipped as a god; maybe he was Imhotep? No, if he was Imhotep, then he was all the others, including me, and that didn't add up, for one, though I could sing, I couldn't sneer, and my dance moves were more akin to those of an epileptic orang-utan.

However, the most fascinating sight, apart from the glimpse of Crystal in her figure-hugging white outfit, was the ceiling, which contained a circular zodiac that apparently represented the cosmic aspect of the Osiris mysteries. Actually, on first inspection, it wasn't that exciting; all blackened and difficult to discern. It was even less exciting when I discovered this was actually a replica, that the original had been removed and now sat in the Louvre in Paris. That meant the replica I was looking at had been deliberately made to look as it had been when they removed the original, all covered in centuries of soot; how stupid is that?

Why couldn't the French have replaced it with a replica in the full colours it would have had in its prime? I suddenly had images of Jacques as Napoleon Bonaparte, one hand stuffed in his jacket, probably firmly grasping his massive ego; 'Oh, no, mais oui, Pierre, we cannot do anything *that* radical.' Thankfully I had a few images on my iphone to compare and correlate.

The first was a grey image with the constellations in a lighter shade; making them easier to define. The second was a colour representation, probably of how it would have looked in its heyday. The final image was in sketch form, highlighting the modern zodiacs in pink.

That annoyed me, if we were to truly understand the ancient Egyptians, then we had to take in the significance of *all* of their constellations, not just those twelve that have survived into modern times and conditioned our thinking and beliefs.

Continuously chatting and intermittently checking out the decorations, Crystal and Pernille were less interested in the ceiling than I was, actually it would be more correct to say they were massively *dis*interested, or rather, preoccupied with other matters, those being their own personal awakenings and re-membering. And the ceiling didn't trigger them at all; so they 'escaped' and meandered straight into the adjoining second room. With two perfectly shaped backsides leading the way, we were easily distracted from the ceiling and followed them in.

Here, like in the western room, the walls contained scenes of Osiris rising from the dead and becoming the God of the underworld. They included images of the burial goods of Osiris, as well as his canopic jars. On the ceiling, Nut was again portrayed with other astronomical figures.

Bill was clearly in a musing sort of frame of mind.

'You know, I've been thinking, the story of Osiris is a very interesting one.'

'In what way?'

'For starters, most Christians, in fact *all* Christians know about it, without being aware they know about it.'

'Bill, if you're going to talk in riddles, I may just have to entomb you back down in the crypts.'

'OK, well, Osiris was the leader of twelve Egyptian gods, right?'

51

'Just like the twelve apostles.'

'One of those gods, Seth, convinced the others to betray Osiris by locking him in a box.'

'For Seth, read Judas.'

'Right! Then they killed Osiris by knocking nails in the box.'

'You're pushing it a bit, but I see the bizarre similarity to crucifixion.'

'Perhaps the Romans were more masochistic than the ancient Egyptians and just embellished the story?'

'Perhaps. Go on.'

'Then Osiris was resurrected, thanks to the assistance of Isis.'

'OK, Jesus was resurrected, but it wasn't Mary-Magdalene who did it, though she does play a significant, albeit passive, part in it.'

'Finally, though the Osirian myth has several versions, one version includes a crucifixion between two thieves, as well as Osiris walking on water.'

'OK, let me get this straight, what you're saying is that Osiris reincarnated as Jesus?'

'Noooo, ….hmmm, but I hadn't considered that. Now that *IS* an interesting concept.'

'So what *are* you saying?'

'That basically the whole story of Jesus is made up from pre-existing Egyptian stories.'

'No way, there has to be some truth to it, I mean the guy had to actually exist, right?'

'Well, there seems to be lots of corroborative evidence that *someone* existed, but actual details about him are pretty sketchy.'

'So why make up a whole lot of lies about him, why not just tell the truth?'

'I don't know, maybe to make him more than he was.'

'Or maybe to make him *less* than he was, to suppress his true identity.'

'Turn him into Clark Kent, or Bruce Wayne, or Peter Parker?'

'It's possible.'

'That would mean that whoever he was, or whoever made up the stories about him, had to have a knowledge of Egyptian history.'

Bill scratched his chin.

'Yes, the plot thickens!'

In the meantime, while Bill and I were pontificating, the girls had exited the Osiris suite and were heading back downstairs. Knowing they would probably take their time, and that they still had to run the gauntlet of the local stall owners, I excused myself and refocused back on the Dendera zodiac. Bill slapped me on the shoulder.

'I'll leave you to your star gazing, and see you somewhere on the way back to the bus.'

'No dramas, I don't think I'll be that far behind you.'

Just then, Pieter and Yuko entered. I don't know where they'd been, but somehow we'd managed to totally miss running into each other since we left them at the birth-house. We all synchronized our watches to meet back at the bus in twenty minutes and Bill exited, leaving me to turn my attention back to the heavens.

'So this is what that Slosman guy was so excited about.'

'Yes, it shows the twelve signs of the zodiac, plus Ophiucus, the Snake Handler, but without the snake, several other constellations, the five visible planets, the thirty-six decans...'

'What, or who, are the decans?'

'The decans are thirty-six small constellations that rise consecutively on the horizon throughout each rotation of the earth. Beginning at least by the 9th or 10th Dynasty, the ancient Egyptians used them as a sort of star clock.'

I looked back at the ceiling and quickly realized not only that the figures running around the perimeter of the circle were the decans, but they explained those extra figures I had seen between the main zodiac images in the rows on the ceiling of the hypostyle hall. That said, I alternated between looking at the ceiling and examining my iphone.

'It says here, *"The ceiling consists of two superimposed constellations, one centred on the geographical north pole, the other on the true north pole. An axis passes through Pisces, confirming what we know from archaeological evidence, that it was built in the age of Pisces, just over 2,000 years ago."* Do you think it's a clue to when the first temple was built here?'

'Possibly.'

If it was, then there had to be more red-granite blocks deep below the current temple. Meanwhile, I was having trouble finding Pisces amid the blackened images. Thankfully Pieter pointed it out.

'The axis runs from the four rams' heads, through Pisces, and across the pole to the star Spica, being held by Virgo. This is the position of today's vernal equinox, and if you draw another line at exactly 90 degrees to that axis, it passes through the tip of the arrow of Sagittarius and points to Galactic Centre.'

Right, I could see the Pisces axis now; once pointed out it was pretty obvious, but to me what it didn't account for were reports of the current magnetic pole shifting, though it did give a frame of reference for both the ceiling, and thus the current temple. Then I noticed a few hieroglyphs further around the circle.

'Two hieroglyphs on the edge of the zodiac appear to indicate that another axis passed through the beginning of the age of Taurus.'

They weren't at right angles to the Pisces axis, so they had to mean something else.

'Hey Pieter, do you know when the Age of Taurus began?'

'The Age of Taurus, that was around 4,200 BC.'

'4,200 BC! That's a thousand years before dynastic Egypt supposedly even started!'

'What about it?'

'Well, the zodiac on the ceiling here apparently goes back to then.'

'Slosman says it goes back further than that.'

'That's right, you said Slosman worked out from this ceiling that there'd been a pole shift around 10,000 BC?'

'Three actually, the one in 9792 BC was just the last one, the one responsible for the last parts of Atlantis to disappear under the ocean and the "sun to rise at a new horizon".'

'When were the other two?'

'In Slosman's second book, *"Le Grand Cataclysme"*, he says there was a previous cataclysm in 21,312 BC, and a third one back in 29,808 BC.'

'Didn't you say Slosman said something about the Orion constellation having something to do with it all?'

'He said that there was an astronomical phenomenon, which he referred to as "Mathematical Combinations of the starry vault", that occurred on a lengthy but regular basis near Gemini, or the Twins as he called it, and Orion, and that this phenomenon was a augury of imminent global destruction, following which, "the old Lion turned around".'

'What does that mean?'

'That a catastrophe, which came from heaven during the age of Leo, caused the Earth's magnetic poles to reverse, the core to disconnected from the mantle causing crustal slip, all of which was accompanied by massive earthquakes, volcanic eruptions and tidal waves.'

'A pole shift.'

'Yes.'

I looked back up at the blackened images.

'He got all that from this?'

'This, and studying the writings of Herodotus.'

'What did *he* have to say?'

'There is a quote from Herodotus, who, when reporting the wisdom of the ancient Egyptian priests, said that "The Sun fell into the sea", and that the sun had, within a period of three-hundred-and-forty-one generations, moved from its course on four occasions, twice rising where it now sets and twice setting where it now rises.'

'How long is three-hundred-and-forty-one generations?'

'According to Herodotus it's eleven-thousand, three-hundred-and-forty years.'

I did some quick math; 3600 x 3 = 10,800; and, given a ten percent error, that made it 11,880, and that was well within the acceptable feasibilities of two passings of Nibiru and consequently two pole shifts, every thirty-six-hundred years.

'So you think these pole shifts were caused by the return of the sun's companion star, the brown dwarf, Nibiru?'

'Yes.'

Yuko took the pregnant pause as her chance to speak up.

'I hate to interrupt you two, but we had better be heading back; you can keep chatting on the way.'

We exited the Osiris suite, deciding to head down the eastern stairs, which led off from the south-eastern corner of the roof. The dimly lit staircase had small slits in the walls admitting the barest of light. Gently descending along the eastern side, towards the front of the temple, on the walls were images of priests journeying back from the roof as if coming from some ritual of great importance. This was no ordinary staircase, but clearly a ceremonial one.

The staircase arrived back at the 'hall of appearances' and within seconds we were heading out of the temple through the Hypostyle hall. Leaving the hall, I took once last look at the images on the ceiling.

'To think that all that information, covering tens-of-thousands of years, is encoded into the reliefs on the ceiling here.'

'That's nothing, apparently the star charts in the labyrinth went back hundreds-of-thousands of years, past the Atlanteans and way back to the historical records of the Annunaki.'

'The labyrinth in Hawarra?'

'Yes, for thousands of years various historical sources have spoken about a forgotten time-capsule of ancient wisdom, a "Hall of Records", created by an antediluvian race who wanted to preserve their accomplishments and wisdom for posterity. The sources speak of hundreds of secret chambers filled with ancient technologies, artefacts and documents from before the great flood. But it's long been razed to the ground, which is a pity; imagine what secrets might have been there.'

'It's still there.'

54

'No, Flinders Petrie discovered the site a hundred years ago, but all he found was the remains of the floor.'

'No, he *thought* it was the floor, so he abandoned it, but I think he actually found the roof.'

'What makes you think that?'

'I met this Australian lawyer once, at a party back in Melbourne, who was part of an organization called "The Horus Foundation". They'd done some ground scans at Hawarra and are convinced the labyrinth is still there.'

'Now that would be something!'

Back on the bus

We made our way back through 'hawkers alley' relatively unhindered and joined Crystal and Pernille, who had boarded the bus just ahead of us. It was hot, damned hot, and we all dived into the onboard fridge for bottles of water and some fruit for lunch.

'So, Bill, how come the change of plans, I thought you were going on to Hurghada?'

'No rush. Pernille feels she needs to go back to the island of P'aleeq with Diane and the others so I'll join her on the cruise and escort her, then we'll make our way to Hurghada after that.'

'Going with the flow, hey?'

'If it's one thing I've learned from my time on the felucca, it's that there is only *this* moment, and if you don't seize it, it may wash away like grains of sand through your fingers.'

Pernille, as if to reward his decision, handed Bill an apple, then politely made an enquiry of the trip ahead.

'Saleem, how far to Abydos?'

Saleem was keen to oblige.

'Yes, please, it is just over one hour, Inshallah.'

'Is that western time or Egyptian time?'

Saleem understandably looked confused.

'It's OK, Saleem, just kidding.'

He nodded, then clearly remembered something of some import.

'Mister Alex, Saeed, he call, he say he see you after Abydos.'

'OK, thanks.

I wondered what it might have been about, but guessed it just meant Saeed was actually going to meet me at the Nubian Oasis when we returned. Still, it made me check the backpack was still under the seat, which it was. No thoughts of music this time around though, there was too much to discuss, and, as Saleem got us going on the road to Abydos, Bill got the ball rolling.

'So, what was everyone's best bit? Alex?'

'Gosh, there was so much to see, so many examples of red and black granite everywhere, but I think it had to be the rows of blue hieroglyphs on the ceiling in the Hypostyle hall, particularly the row with the all-seeing eye of Horus, and the images in the crypts, especially the one Bill spotted of the man with a condom on his anaconda penis.'

'What?'

'What crypts?'

'Anaconda penis?'

Bill explained the image of the 'cathode ray tube' and showed them a few of the photos he'd snapped while we were down there. Pieter and Yuko were amazed, yet at the same time disappointed.

'Wow, where *was* this crypt?'

'In the room to the west of the very back central chapel; there was a grill in the floor and you just had to ask the guardian to let you in.'

'For a small fee of course.'

'Of course.'

'What was it like?'

'Cool!'

I qualified Bill's appraisal.

'Actually it was hot, stuffy and cramped, but well worth the fifty pounds for the five minutes or so it took to check it out.'

'Fifty pounds, I don't think we would have been prepared to pay that much, but I'm sorry we missed it.'

I turned the tables on Bill.

'What about you, Bill, favourite bit?'

'Hmmm, I think the Basilica and the Sanatorium were interesting for obvious reasons, and, yes, the ceiling in the main hall was pretty funky, but, I agree with you, Alex, the crypt was awesome.'

'Pernille?'

'Easy, but not so much where we went, as what we did there. So, for me it was definitely Crystal helping me reconnect in the birth-house and remember who I was, then reminiscing as we walked around in the sacred lake.'

Yuko was more than curious.

'And who were you?'

I'd forgotten; she and Pieter weren't there with us, they'd gone off straight into the temple. Bill, Crystal and I looked to Pernille, I'm sure all feeling it was her right to divulge the truth. She sat tall and regal.

'I was Cleopatra VII, last of the true pharaohs to rule Egypt.'

In response, Yuko suddenly lit up like a Christmas tree.

'Oh, how interesting.'

'And Crystal was both my sister, Arsinoe, and then my daughter, Cleopatra Selene.'

Yuko slapped Pieter on the arm.

'I knew it.'

I thought she was referring to Crystal being related to Pernille, but I was soon to find out Yuko was on a totally different wavelength. In the meantime Bill asked Crystal what was *her* favourite part of Dendera.

'Reconnecting with my sister.'

'What about your mother, wasn't Pernille your mother as well?'

As I said it, a strange shiver went up my spine; of course, she was my mother as well. In contrast Crystal remained calm and composed.

'My mother died when I was young, my strongest memories of that time are therefore of, and with, my sister.'

'What about your brother, do you have fond memories of him as well?'

She knew exactly what I was talking about and looked me straight in the eye.

'How could I ever forget him, he was my closest companion, but he used to drive me crazy with his naïve lack of awareness.'

Was she pushing my buttons deliberately? Hell, yes, of course she was. I took a deep breath and played right along.

'I have absolutely no idea what you're talking about.'

Yuko laughed.

'Oh how awesome, of course, you two were brother and sister.'

'Yep, you can pick your friends, but you can't pick your family.'

Crystal was right on form.

'Oh, your family is the first thing you pick.'

I quickly figured out I was on the losing end of the exchange of wit and quickly shifted the focus.

'What about you, Pieter, what was your *piece de resistance*?'

'I am with you guys about the hieroglyphs on the ceiling of Hypostyle hall, they were quite remarkable, those, and the circle on the ceiling of the chamber on the roof.'

The Dendera circle still had me thinking too.

'I still don't understand what the axis of Pisces and axis of Taurus are all about though.'

Bill's brain was churning over as well.

'We're in the Age of Pisces right now, right?'

He paused momentarily, awaiting Pieter's reply.

'Yes, about to transit into Aquarius.'

'And before Pisces we were in Aries, and before that, in Taurus, yes?'

'Yes.'

Bill started connecting the Ages of Precession to religions.

'Let's see, Christianity is represented by the fish, by Pisces, starting around 1 AD, with Jesus who was the fisherman, or rather "fisher of men". Worshiping the ram relates to the Age of Aries, which was …'

Pieter had the answer.

'From around 1900 BC.'

'And the ram correlates with Moses worshipping the Lamb of God around 1600 BC, and explains the symbolic references in the Jewish Religion he created. As for the bull, it's associated with the age of Taurus, which was from around…?'

'4500 BC.'

'Which would encompass all of the early and predynastic Egyptian cultures up until at least the Middle Kingdom, possibly even until the end of the 17th Dynasty. And the bull was …?'

We all took turns proposing a candidate.

'The Apis bull?'

'The craven image that Moses got so pissed off about?'

'What about Hathor? The religion of the Hathors?'

Pieter nodded in agreement.

'I don't see why not, the imagery fits. It even fits with the sacred cows in India, and that would be consistent with the cow being sacred back in the Vedic times of the Hindi religions.'

Sensing there was something more to be discovered about where the Hathors originated, my mouth flapped in the breeze like a bull at a gate.

'What's the constellation for the bull?'

Not only was I stunned that I had just mixed my metaphors, I couldn't believe

I'd actually said what I'd said, after all, I *was* a Taurean. They all looked at me with wry smiles of disbelief, but it was left to Crystal to rub salt into the wounds of my exposed ego.

'Alex, Taurus, the bull, *is* a constellation, a very important one. It's a binary star system, just like ours, sitting between Orion's belt and the Pleiades, with Aldebran being the eye of the bull.'

'Of course.'

Thankfully Pernille threw my humility a lifeline.

'There is another possibility, Berengaria, the cow. It's a constellation of seventeen stars that rises in the pre-dawn autumn skies.'

'Berengaria?'

'She was the finder of lost children and bringer of dawn, the first light that shatters the darkness.'

I couldn't help but return the dig to Crystal.

'A cow hey? She sounds just like someone who would be responsible for illuminating your consciousness.'

'If there were anything to illuminate.'

Damn it, she was good. And I think the others were enjoying my and Crystal's pre-copulatory ritual of intellectual foreplay, especially Bill and Pernille. However, as it was looking like the rooster may well have his wings clipped, I decided it was time to get back to the main topic.

'I guess it depends how far back you go. Before Taurus was the Age of Gemini, next was Cancer and then we get to Leo.'

'But we have no archaeological evidence indicating anything from the Ages of Gemini or Cancer.'

He may not have known where I was heading, actually, neither did I, however Bill was filling in the blanks superbly.

'When were they?'

Pieter knew.

'Gemini was from 6500 BC, Cancer from 7900 BC.'

'Well then, they would have been straight after the pole shift that happened sometime in Leo, sometime around 10,000 BC, and civilization would have probably barely recovered.'

A thought suddenly hit me.

'Hey Pieter, maybe you can tell me, why does the Dendera zodiac, and the Hypostyle hall hieroglyphs go Pisces, Aries, Taurus, etc, when the Ages are going in the other direction, Taurus, Aries, Pisces?'

'I.. er, wow, that's a good point. I don't know.'

It hit Bill as well.

'Yeah, they're back-to-front.'

Surprisingly, it was Pernille who came up with the first possibility.

'Maybe the zodiac originally ran in the other direction, and in the age of Leo it got swapped around, the precession of the equinoxes was reversed, so that the equinox sun slowly precessed back out of Leo into Cancer?'

'Maybe it did, but why, there must have been a good reason.'

Feeling more in his area of expertise, Pieter picked up the baton.

'I guess it's all to do with precession; the wobble of the earth. Because the earth slowly wobbles as it travels through space, …'

'And why does it wobble again?'

'Another good question. My own thoughts are that it's because of the impact of the asteroid that wiped out the dinosaurs sixty-five million years ago. I think the asteroid hit at such an angle, and with sufficient mass and momentum, that it not only pushed the planet off its normal perpendicular angle by around twenty-three degrees, but pushed the earth out of its circular orbit into a slightly elliptical one.'

'That would mean the dinosaurs had a more consistent environment before that; no seasons?'

'I think it's possible, yes. Of course I'm sure the botanists would be better versed to explore *that* theory.'

Bill joined in the conversation.

'You know, as a kid I was fascinated by dinosaurs, I mean what kid wasn't, but I've always wondered how most of these massive dinosaurs supposedly raced around like gazelles. Surely if they were alive today, they wouldn't be able to move with such agility?'

That got Pieter thinking.

'Interesting, I've never thought of that.'

I had an idea.

'Maybe the gravity was less.'

It didn't float Pieter's boat though.

'No, gravity is linked to mass, I don't see how it could be; the earth's mass was pretty much the same as it is now.'

'Then maybe the planet rotated faster back then, which would reduce the effect of gravity, of the centripetal force, due to an increased centrifugal force, or maybe the air pressure was less.'

Bill chipped in.

'No, not the air pressure, I think they say the air was saturated with oxygen then, so I think that would increase the air pressure, wouldn't it?'

We looked to Pieter for an answer.

'I've got no idea, but I do like the earth spinning faster theory. If the earth *was* spinning faster then, and the angle of the impact was contrary to the direction of spin, then it may well have slowed the rotation of the planet.'

I momentarily went off on a tangent.

'How would that effect time?'

Bill tried to answer it.

'I guess if the earth rotates faster, time appears to go faster, or is it slower?'

Thankfully Crystal put it into perspective.

'Time is an illusion, and in this respect it's all relative; if you were on the planet it would still feel the same. A year would still be a year; it's just there would be more days of shorter length. So days would feel shorter, but years longer, though "time" would not have changed at all.'

There's something genetic about a group of men caught up in testosterone-induced problem-solving and having a women come in uninvited and find the solution; we may appear to acknowledge it, but in reality we just plough on regardless, as if her words went in one ear and straight out the other – especially when they're profound and right. And that's exactly what we did; me leading the way.

'So, if each Age is around 2,200 years, then the age of Leo would have started around 10,800 BC.'

'Which matches perfectly with the last pole shift.'

'*And* when the Sphinx was built.'

'So Slosman was right.'

'Maybe that's why the Sphinx was a Lion, to tell the world the next pole shift was in the age of Leo?'

'And that's what Hancock, Bauval and West say, that the Sphinx was built in the age of Leo around 10,000 BC.'

'They're wrong.'

'What?'

They all looked at me with a variety of looks ranging from incredulous to confusion, but I'd read all the books about the Sphinx, and it still didn't completely add up.

'Well, if you knew some great catastrophe was going to befall the planet, and you were going to warn the world, you would hardly wait until it was about to happen, until the age of Leo to tell anyone, you'd build it way before that, so that people could never forget.'

Bill was all ears.

'So you're saying the Sphinx was built before 10,800 BC?'

'Way before then, sometime between 21,000 BC and 10,800 BC.'

Pieter was similarly excited.

'And what better place to keep all the calculations and information about it, than in a secret chamber beneath the feet of the Sphinx.'

'That means the Hall of Records must not only contain all the star charts of the Atlanteans, of the Annunaki, but also their calculations for the dates of the pole shifts, for the passings of Nibiru.'

'So if we can find and open the Hall of Records, we can figure out when the next passing is.'

'And be able to save millions of lives.'

I wasn't so easily drawn in.

'It's a noble thought, but people have been searching for the Hall of Records for hundreds of years, even Zahi Hawass has had a look for it, but they haven't found anything.'

Crystal chipped in.

'Or they *have* found it, and couldn't get in. Or they *have* got in, but haven't told anyone.'

'Why wouldn't they tell anyone?'

'Knowledge is power; why would you give your power away when you can use the knowledge to control people.'

'But that's not right.'

'I didn't say it was right, I simply said what it is.'

Crystal had a way of staying calm and detached no matter what was thrown at her. As for me, I still needed clarity and pulled Pieter back to the topic.

'So precession explains how the earth slowly turns, and that means that as it rotates, it slowly changes the point at which the stars line up at dawn, right?'

'That's it exactly.'

'But I'm still not clear *how* the sun rises in a different location after a pole shift if the polarity simply reverses?'

'According to the ancient Egyptians and some modern theorists, the Earth slows in its axial rotation until it stops, then begins to rotate in the opposite direction, and thus the Sun was reborn from a new horizon.'

'So the polarity doesn't so much shift, as the earth spins in the opposite direction?'

'Yes.'

'Which then causes the polarity to shift?'

'I guess so.'

'OK, that's fine, it seems the wrong way around, but I got that, that's what it does, but *how*; what causes it? I don't see how the earth could stop rotating and then start spinning in the other direction? Something has to *make* it change; effect has to have a cause.'

'The passing of Nibiru causes the pole shifts.'

'OK, but *HOW?* And why is the precession 'back-to-front to the zodiac.'

There was a pregnant pause from everyone, searching for answers, until once again it was Crystal who broke the silence.

'It wouldn't be back-to-front if you were looking at it from the southern hemisphere.'

'What do you mean?'

'Well if you look at the earth from above the north pole, it rotates anti-clockwise, but if you look at it from below the south pole, it rotates clockwise.'

I pictured it in my mind, then got the geography of the rotation.

'So you're saying the ancient Egyptians looked at it from the south pole?'

'Exactly.'

'Why would they go there?'

Bill was catching on.

'Maybe they didn't, maybe they were already there?'

Then I got it and turned to Crystal.

'You mean Egypt was once in the southern hemisphere, don't you?'

'There you go, making a statement and then questioning it.'

It made me think about what I had just said, and even more so as I said it again.

'Egypt was once in the southern hemisphere.'

'Exactly.'

'That's what the pole shift means.'

For once, Pieter was lost.

'I don't understand.'

I took my time, thinking it through as I said it.

'If the crust separated from the core completely, then crustal slip would be at its maximum, and when the crust shifts, it flips, it does a complete one-hundred-and-eighty degree rotation and turns upside down. But the core stays where it is, rotating in the same direction it used to.

Then, when the crust reattaches, to all those on the surface, the earth is now rotating in the other direction, the sun rising in what was the west, and setting in what was the east. That's the "how", but it doesn't solve the "why". What would cause the crust to flip?'

Bill was right on it.

'It's very simple actually, magnetism.'

'Magnetism?'

'Yep.'

He reached into the cooler and grabbed an apple.

'If an object like a brown dwarf passed close to the earth, then its gravitational pull would tug at the earth, and, just like the moon tugs at the water on the planet causes

61

the tides, anything even slightly unstable would be subject to the red dwarf's massive gravitational field.

Now, the crust on the earth is very thin in comparison to the core, even thinner in comparison to the peel on an apple. The brown dwarf star would pull at the crust of the planet and pull it away and apart from the core. When the crust is attached to the core you have one north pole and one south pole, but as soon as the crust separates, then you have two north poles, one on the crust and one on the core, and two south poles, the crust and the core.

Poles with like polarity repel each other, so the massive core pole pushes the tiny crust pole and the crust pivots to line up south core to north crust and north core to south core, then reattach.'

'So how do you explain the pole shifts of only five to twenty degrees?'

'Elementary, my dear Watson, if the brown dwarf star passes far enough away from the earth, say on the other side of the sun, so that the crust is not completely separated, then the pivot will only travel as far as it can until it literally "runs aground".'

'My friend I think you have just explained how the poles shift to a tee…'

I took the apple out of Bill's hand and took a large bite.

'… We know what role the Sphinx has in things, now all we have to do is figure out what the pyramids and the temples have to do with the pole shifts.'

It was Pieter who picked up the story.

'According to the ancient Sumerian Clay Tablets, the Lost Book of Enki describes how the Annunaki built pyramids all over Earth to demonstrate which Zodiac Age they were actually in.'

'Like a big celestial clock.'

'Sort of, more like astronomical markers, but mainly because their laws decreed a change of ruler with each Zodiac Age and there was a dispute between the two half-brothers and rulers, Enki and Enlil, as to who should rule and when. It actually caused one of them to leave Sumer and set up his own kingdom in Egypt.'

'Hence the story of Seth and Osiris.'

'I think you're right.'

'So it's not so much the temples that are relevant, but the pyramids associated with them?'

'Yes, all the pyramids along the Nile correspond to constellations and stars within the Milky Way; Giza is Orion's belt, Saqqara is Andromeda, Dendera is Deneb in the constellation Cygnus, there's even the turn in the Nile near here that corresponds exactly with a curve in the Milky Way.'

'So the Nile is not so much a clock, as one big galactic calendar.'

'That's a better analogy.'

Then Bill had a brain-buster of an idea.

'Hang on. I just had a thought. Do you think that each location could have been built chronologically in alignment with the rise of each constellation through precession?'

'Wow, big question, let's see…'

I counted them off on my fingers as I pictured the Nile in my mind.

'…Giza, Saqarra, Dahshur, Meidum, Hawarra, Abydos, Dendera, nah, you certainly couldn't say that was the case based on the current temples, you could only know for sure based on when the first temples were built, and I reckon what remains of most of them is buried under at least twenty-five metres of silt and sand. Mind you, it's still a great idea.'

We were flying along, not just in the discussion, but time as well. Although we had been on the road for well over an hour, it had zipped past faster than an ice-cold beer down your throat after a full-on day out in the desert. We'd covered so much ground, but I still felt there was more awaiting down the track, and no way was I going to leave any stone unturned.

'So, Pieter, what else do these Sumerian Tablets have to say?'

'The Sumerians were the oldest known civilization on earth, dating to around 5,000 BC, but the tablets tell a story about how, starting about four-hundred thousand years ago, not only the earth was being mined by the Annunaki, but also Mars. They speak of how the human race, as we know it, was created by the gods by mixing Annunaki genes with early Neanderthal man to provide a labour force particular for the mining of the planets.'

Bill was totally up to speed.

'That's pretty much exactly what we were talking about on the felucca, only it appears it was happening on Mars as well.'

'There's more, they go on to describe how Alulu, who was once the King of Niburu, was exiled to Mars, where he later died.'

'So there was already political conflict within the Annunaki before they even came here.'

I tried a humorous and quasi-sarcastic aside...

'Maybe the political mess on the earth is not man's fault after all, maybe it's simply genetic?'

...and Crystal couldn't resist an equally quick, but vastly superior retort.

'Just because you're born an idiot, doesn't mean you have to act or speak like one for the rest of your life.'

There was nothing malicious or aggressive about it, on the contrary it was calmly delivered with a subtle edge of sexual teasing. But, boy, was I taking a pasting. You would think I would have realized by now that when it came to Crystal, I had not only met my match in every way, but needed to get down on my knees and grovel in abject submission.

Chuckling under his breath, Bill let me suffer in silence for a few seconds before coming to the rescue.

'So, with all its mining, do you think Mars might have been a type of prison planet?'

'It's a possibility. The tablets say Alulu's body was found by the Annunaki inside a mountainside cave and buried there on Mars. And to honour the first King to die outside of Niburu, and on another planet, they carved his likeness into the stone of the mountain to forever enshrine his image.'

I got it straight away.

'Hell, I've seen pictures of that; the face on Mars at Cydonia.'

Bill was chuckling away.

'I bet Randy wishes he was here now.'

'Yeah, he'd be right in his element.'

'Hmmm, and interesting how NASA have just sent probes back to Mars. I wonder why, and what they're not telling us.'

Suddenly Pernille joined the conversation.

'I know what they're not telling us.'

We three guys spoke almost in unison.

'What?'

'The truth!'

As we were all musing over Pernille's comment, all of a sudden, the bus came to a stop.

'Abydos.'

I looked out of the windows trying to see the temple.
'Where?'

Saleem pointed ahead.
'Just here.'

I could see the ticket box and expected to see an imposing pylon or at least a Hypostyle hall like the one at Dendera or Karnak, but, instead, all I could see was the uninspiring squared frontage of a reconstructed edifice. I tried to wind everything up.

'Well then, I think we've certainly exhausted everything about Dendera, maybe Abydos has some hidden secrets?'

It seemed Crystal wasn't so sure, as, while everyone started filing off the bus, she posed the opener on yet an even bigger can of worms.

'Perhaps not *everything* about Dendera has been exhausted, after all, we haven't asked Yuko about her experiences there.'

Bill and Pernille led the way as we all headed to the ticket box and queued up to get our tickets.

'So, Yuko, what about you, what was your Dendera highlight?'
'Oh, definitely seeing the only real original images of Jesus.'

I did a double take; did I hear her correctly?
'Jesus? Jesus Christ?'
'Yes.'

I ran through the building to see how I could have missed them.
'Where were they, the Basilica, the Sanatorium?'
'No, on the outside back wall of the main temple; you didn't see them?'

I scratched my head, wildly trying to recall the images.
'No, the only images I saw on the back wall were the gods receiving Cleopatra and her son Caesarion.'

'Yes, that's right, that's them; Jesus Christ and Caesarion were the same person.'

It nearly floored me.

'Shit, Bill and I were only kidding, but if it's true, I mean if you can prove it, then you may have just opened the biggest Pandora's box of all time.'

Bill had just bought his and Pernille's ticket, and, being our resident Catholic and religious expert, I *had* to bring him in straight away.

'Hey, Bill, you'll never guess what Yuko just said?'
'What?'

I indicated for Yuko to tell Bill herself, which she did.
'Caesarion and Jesus Christ were the same person.'

He chuckled away and lifted up Yuko's hat.

'Are you sure it's not Randy under there? Or maybe you've been drinking too many of Randy's beers? But seriously, wow, I can't wait to hear what your evidence is, because if you're right, then it would be like letting a hungry fox loose in the chicken coop of religions.'

CHAPTER 22 - RED GRANITE

A couple of hours drive north of Luxor, Abydos, or Abdju as it was known in ancient times, encompasses the modern village of Beni Mansur to the north and el-Araba el-Madfuna, now called Arabet Abydos, to the south. It dates back to the very beginnings of Egyptian history, from the Early Dynastic Period, right through to Christian times, and was a popular place of pilgrimage and burial as the ancient Egyptians believed the head of Osiris was buried here. Hence the location became a cult centre, gateway to the underworld, and one of the holiest sites in the world.

As I had spontaneously stepped into the role of 'Tour guide' at several of the other temples, while the rest of us waited to get our tickets, I felt somewhat obliged to do so again, and pulled up the file on Abydos.

'*The site of Abydos is huge, and includes a number of ruins and mounds to the north and south and stretching westwards into the desert. Successively, from the 1st Dynasty to the 26th Dynasty, nine or ten temples were built on one site at Abydos.*

The first temple was an enclosure, about nine metres by fifteen metres, surrounded by a thin wall of unbaked bricks. Incorporating one wall of the first structure, a second temple, about twelve metres square, was built within a wall about three metres thick, with an additional, enclosure wall surrounding it. This outer wall was thickened around the 2nd or 3rd Dynasty but the old temple entirely vanished in the 4th Dynasty, and a smaller building was erected behind it, enclosing a wide hearth of black ashes.'

I wondered if that was that some obscure reference to the ash of a volcanic eruption sometime before 2400 BC? Perhaps it was a reason for the demise of the old temples, or perhaps I was just making mountains out of molehills. If I was lucky, I might just find some evidence, like an excavation showing the layers of mud just like at Edfu and Esna.

'*The temple was entirely rebuilt, on a larger scale, by Pepi I in the 6th Dynasty. He built a great stone gateway leading to the designated land, an outer enclosure wall and gateway, with a colonnade between the gates. The inside of the temple was around twelve metres by fifteen metres, with stone gateways front and back.*

In the 11th Dynasty, Montuhotep I added a colonnade and altars, but, soon after, Montuhotep II entirely rebuilt the temple, adding subsidiary chambers and laying a stone pavement over the area of about fourteen square metres. Not long after, in the 12th Dynasty, Senwroset III laid massive foundations of stone over the pavement of his predecessors, a great tract of land was laid out enclosing a much larger area, and the new temple itself was expanded to about three times the earlier size.'

What that showed, was exactly what I thought, that location was important, and that new temples were usually built on the exact locations of previous temples, and not somewhere alongside.

'*The building during the 18th Dynasty began with a large terraced chapel by Ahmose I, who also built a small shrine for his grandmother, Queen Teti-sheri. That was followed by a larger temple, about forty metres by sixty metres, by Thutmose III who also built a processional way, featuring a great gateway of granite, that led past the side of the temple to the cemetery beyond. The 19th Dynasty saw a small temple to Ramses I, now totally gone, and temples to Seti I, and Ramses II. The temple of Seti I, which* *currently dominates the site, was built on entirely new ground, half a mile to the south of the earlier temples and half a mile north of the Thutmoses III temple.'*

Well that was a fly in the ointment! That was until I realized that Seti I and Ramses I & II were not really part of the true pharaonic bloodline, rather, part of the military usurpers. If the Amun priests withheld crucial information about the location of the temples, then Seti may well have just decided to build somewhere new.

'The latest building was a new temple of Nectanebo I, built in the 30th Dynasty, although various additions to the site were made through the Ptolemaic and Roman periods. However it is the New Kingdom temples of Seti I, built around 1300 BC by Seti I, and later finished by his son, Ramses II, and Ramses' son, Merenptah, and Ramses II's own temple, further north, that dominate the current site.'

'Right then, let's go.'

It didn't look much from the ticket office, which may have explained why the entrance fee was only forty pounds; still, once we all had our tickets in our hot little hands, we quickly entered the complex. No flash-bang tourist centre here, they hadn't even bothered to man the metal scanner, which was set up in what looked like nothing more than a makeshift bus shelter.

Speaking of buses, we were fortunate to have arrived just as the busload of Chinese tourists we'd seen at Dendera was exiting. They flooded down the ramp-like staircase like a flock of waddling penguins. Is it a flock, or a pod, or...? No, a chill, that's what I'd call them, a chill of penguins. I'd never really noticed it before, but they all walked funny, not the penguins, the Chinese, as if they all had arthritis of the hips.

Once through the scanner, and having navigated the Asiatic sea, we made our way up the staircase with all attention straight back on Yuko. I was the first to speak as I saw a major flaw in her theory.

'The first problem I see with Caesarion and Jesus being one and the same person, is that Caesarion was born in 47 BC.'

Surprisingly, it was Bill who replied.

'Actually, now that I think about it, maybe that's not such a problem after all, as there is, at the very *least*, a marginal error of about thirty years between BC and AD.'

'How do you figure that?'

'Well, in 46 BC, just after Caesarion was born, Julius Caesar reformed the Roman calendar and introduced what is now known as the Julian Calendar in 45 BC.'

'So we're currently in the Julian Calendar?'

'No, that ended in 1582, when further reform was needed because there were too many leap days added with respect to the astronomical seasons of the Julian Calendar. By 1582, it was ten days out of alignment from where it supposedly was in 325 during the Council of Nicaea, so Pope Gregory XIII announced a new, Gregorian Calendar.'

'And that's the calendar we have now?'

'Yep, but what *is* interesting is that it continues the previous year-numbering system based on the AD, the Anno Domini system, which counts years from the traditional Incarnation of Jesus.'

'Wait a minute, isn't it possible that with over fifteen-hundred years having passed, Pope Gregory could have forgotten that Year 1 actually started around 47 BC with the birth of Caesarion, because, if that's the case, then Caesarion would have been born in the exact year that Jesus was supposedly born.'

'I think it's highly probably, in fact BC could really mean "Before Caesar", but I don't think it's enough evidence to turn the church on its ass.'

We reached the top of the staircase and entered the first courtyard, through the now totally ruined first pylon that would have fronted a quay linking the temple with the River Nile, which now sat about ten kilometres to the east. Basically nothing remained, which, according to the experts, was because the locals had pilfered all the stone to build their houses. OK, braniacs, how did they remove the first stones, the ones from the very tops of the pylons, and lower them down to the ground? Doesn't it make more sense that the pylons were bowled over by a massive tsunami, and *then* the locals used the rubble to rebuild? It does to me.

The following forecourt, like the first pylon, was originally built and decorated by your favourite megalomaniac and mine, none other than Ramses II, son of Seti I. It was Seti's temple that lay beyond, looking more like the façade of a community library from the 1960's, but Ramses II had supposedly completed it following his father's death. As with the pylon, the courtyard was mostly destroyed, however it still contained the foundations of two 'wells', or ablution pools, used for the ritual purification of the peasants and priests. These were surrounded by gravel, which 'filled in' the courtyard but was clearly a modern 'restoration'. On what remained of the walls, were some partial reliefs, including, on the left side of the forecourt, the now familiar battle scenes of Ramses II defeating enemies at Kadesh. As we wandered around, giving it all the once-over, I hit Yuko with my second fly in the ointment.

'OK, so it's *possible* Jesus and Caesarion were born at the same time, *BUT*, Caesarion was assassinated when he was thirteen or fourteen.'

Bill jumped in again.

'Hang on, Alex, remember, Octavian may have *ordered* the death of Caesarion, but that doesn't mean it was actually carried out.'

'But wasn't it reported that Caesarion was killed?'

'Let's say that Octavian gave you an order to go to Alexandria, find Caesarion, and kill him. When you get there, you discover Caesarion has vanished, can't be found, and you know you can't go back and tell Octavian you didn't kill him, that Caesarion is still alive, because, if you do, Octavian will probably order that you be killed for failing your mission, especially a mission with such important repercussions. Remember, Caesarion was actually the legitimate heir to not only the Egyptian Kingdom, but the entire Roman Empire as well, and Octavian was adopted. What would you do?'

'Snow White and the woodsman, hey?

'Yep, so what would you do?'

'I see your point. I guess I'd give him the deer's heart in a box; I'd tell Octavian that I'd been successful, and Caesarion was not only dead, but that I personally strangled him to death with my own bare hands.'

'Suddenly the possibility that Caesarion escaped to India becomes more than plausible.'

'But how?'

'I'm sure Cleopatra had her finger on the political pulse of her world, and, as soon as she heard word of Caesar's assassination, she took Caesarion and retreated back to the relative safety of Egypt, but she knew she had to built new alliances.'

'Hence her seduction of Marc Antony.'

'But when Antony named Caesarion co-ruler of Egypt and Cyprus in 34 BC, Octavian realized the writing was on the wall and that at sometime in the future, the now thirteen-year old Caesarion would eventually challenge his claim to the Roman Empire.'

'So he ordered Caesarion's assassination.'

'And Cleopatra, knowing Caesarion was now in danger, probably sent him away to Taprobane, modern-day Sri Lanka, maybe via Ethiopia. From there, he could have gone anywhere.'

'But he was only thirteen.'

'So she probably sent him away accompanied by members of her own family, or her most trusted servants, more than likely Caesarion's wet-nurse and her husband.'

'Which is where Mary and Joseph may come into the picture.'

Another set of sloping stairs led from the first courtyard through the almost scant remains of what would have been the second pylon; at least there was more left than the first pylon. Originally built by Ramses II, and fronted by the remains of a portico with niches that would once have contained Osirid statues of Mr. Megalomania, what remained of the walls depicted several of Ramses II's children, sons on the left, daughters to the right.

What caught my eye was the white telltale signs of an alabaster or marble floor in the doorway and surrounds. The marbled stones were much older than the sandstone walls and doorjambs; it looked to me like Abydos may have even more secrets than Dendera.

The second courtyard, also decorated by Ramses II, had a doorway in the southwest corner that led to a complex of administration buildings. Near the entrance was a stela of Ramses II making offerings to Ptah.

Also in the second courtyard were several damaged statues including an alabaster statue of a king sitting in a shrine, apparently from the Middle Kingdom, and supposedly brought here from elsewhere in the Abydos area.

As we perused them, I kept probing Bill for more answers.

'So what about the differences in their births? Jesus was born in a stable, Caesarion was probably born in a palace in Rome, or back at Dendera. Mary was a virgin, Cleopatra was a pharaoh.'

That was Pernille's cue to join the discussion.

'Cleopatra was the reincarnation of Isis, virgin mother of Horus, and Caesarion was raised knowing this, and knowing his father, Caesar, *was* a god. So you have his mother, who in her role as Isis is very similar to Mother Mary, and his father was god. That's exactly the same as Jesus.'

For some reason I directed my reply to Bill.

'Well if Horus *was* cloned, and Isis implanted with the embryo, then that could quite easily be interpreted as a virgin birth, but I doubt Julius Caesar sat back and took a spectator's role in the impregnation of Cleopatra.'

Bill gave Pernille a wink.

'Damned fool if he did.'

I was right with them, but playing the 'devil's advocate' roll.

'What about the other things associated with Jesus' birth; the three wise men for instance? According to the story in *'The Bible'*, the three kings follow the eastern star that leads them directly to the miracle birth of the messiah.'

'That's what everyone has been led to believe.'

'Hell, if you could invent a Sat-Nav for your car like that you'd make a fortune. Wait a minute, if you were already in the east, wouldn't it be more logical to follow a western star?'

'I think they mean the star arose in the east in the night sky and they followed it as it transited towards the west.'

'But the stars don't go east to west through the night, the moon does, but not the stars, they go in a circular motion.'

'Then maybe it was a comet, some people have even suggested it was Halley's Comet.'

Pieter had another interpretation.

'Surely the three kings are just a reference to the three stars of Orion, which point to the brightest star in the sky, Sirius. In ancient Egyptian times, Sirius was known as Isis and basically the belt of Orion and the star Sirius pointed to where the sun would rise on Christmas day.'

'Sirius arose on Christmas day?'

'It wasn't Christmas day *then*, that was a later label tagged on. Back then, because of the tilt of the earth as it orbited the sun, Sirius would drop below the horizon about a day before the winter solstice and re-emerge three days later, signifying the re-birthing of the gods as well as the beginning of the new year and the imminent arrival of the annual floods that brought life to the Nile.'

'Jesus! Even the resurrection concept belongs to the ancient Egyptians?'

'Almost everything about the Jesus story has its origins thousands of years beforehand in ancient Egyptian or ancient Sumerian history and folklore.'

'OK, what about the gifts; the frankincense, myrrh and gold? Stars don't bring gifts to people.'

As we all approached the main temple, Bill mulled it over.

'Yes, strange gifts those when you think about it; there's no doubt they came from the east, as frankincense and myrrh were pretty much confined to the south-eastern part of the Arabian Peninsula, but myrrh was used for embalming, and frankincense for mourning the dead, although it was also used for healing, in particular the female hormone system, and would be especially relevant just after a birth. As for the gold, if it was mono-atomic gold then it would all make sense if the gifts were for an Egyptian heir to the throne. But for the son of a carpenter, I don't think so.'

That sparked an idea.

'So, what if the three kings actually were three rulers from Asia and Arabia, who all travelled to Rome to pay homage to the birth of Caesarion, either because he was the heir to the Egyptian throne, or because he was heir to the Roman Empire, or both. That would make total political sense in every aspect.'

'Yes it would, and it makes a lot more sense than the biblical version.'

'And it's easy to see how the original story could be so easily distorted by the church.'

'Enough evidence?'

'No, not for me.'

'OK, what about those titles Jesus was known by, the "son of God", a title reserved for the pharaoh of Egypt, and the "King of Kings", created by Julius Caesar and reserved for the ruler of the Roman Empire, they fit Caesarion like hand in glove.'

'True, there's no one else in history they *do* fit. But it's still not enough to change the tide of public opinion.'

Overlooking the second courtyard, the façade of Seti I's temple comprised a colonnade of twelve square pillars, the lower parts of which were covered with reliefs of Ramses II greeting Osiris, Isis and Horus. Whilst the lower parts were still intact, the tops of the columns and the ceiling had been reconstructed using concrete; it was what made it look like some derelict leftover from the sixties.

If you could image a row of twelve square candlesticks, and one of the three musketeers coming along and with one swish of his sword cutting off the tops, then that's what it looked like had happened. The only two explanations the Egyptologists have proposed are; an earthquake, or, that they had been appropriated by the locals to build houses, or a combination of both. Common sense tells you that if you were to appropriate the stones you would remove a complete column rather than make life difficult and remove just the tops; it would be much easier removing the bases.

The entrance to the outer hypostyle hall was at the top of another shallow ramp-like staircase and through a central doorway, but apparently, in the time of Seti I, there were once seven doorways through the façade, each leading from the courtyard directly to one of the seven chapels within. God knows why, but Ramses supposedly filled them all in except for the central doorway and a smaller doorway at the north end of the portico. In any case, it had to be the most uninspiring temple so far, and it didn't bode well for what may await inside.

The Temple of Seti I

As we slowly walked up the long shallow steps, Bill turned to Yuko.

'I'm sorry, but the only convincing evidence that Caesarion was Jesus, or vica versa, would be if you could account for the missing years of Jesus, between the age of thirteen and when he return to Jerusalem, and somehow they correlated to Caesarion.'

'Not a problem.'

Stepping into the temple, we were all primed to hear what Yuko had to say but, before we could, Bill threw in a decoy.

'Hey, Alex, marble floors.'

I looked down; Bill was spot on. The entire floor was made of white marbled limestone; not the walls mind you, or the twenty-four papyrus-capitaled columns that each showed Ramses II in the presence of the god of the shrine at the end of the aisle, just the floor, and the round bases of the columns. I smelled the indicators of an older temple. Not only that, but there were pieces of black granite incorporated in the floor as well.

Hell, I don't know where the nearest limestone deposits were, but this definitely didn't look as if it was part of the original landscape. But what was even more exciting to me was that the floor was not made of a series of smooth tiles, but large heavily-weathered marble blocks, clearly water-damaged, as if large quantities of water had washed over it and eroded the limestone. Over the top had been laid smaller quasi-regular tiles of marble in an attempt to 'repair' the original floor.

Several questions immediately raced to mind; was the black granite part of an even earlier structure, and the large marble block laid subsequent, and, if the water damage *was* caused by the Thera tsunami, was Seti I responsible for the smaller marble tiles, or were they too from an earlier time?

According to the experts, the Temple of Seti I was begun during the 19th Dynasty of the New Kingdom in the reign of Seti I (1318-1304 BC) and represented an attempt by Seti to identify himself directly with the gods, and to add legitimacy to a ruling family that had been nothing more than mere spear-chucking militia less than three generations, or twenty years, earlier.

After Seti's death, the temple was completed by his son, Ramses II (1304-1237 BC), and *his* son, Merenptah. The sunken reliefs on the walls, like those in the courtyards, had been completed by Ramses II, and showed Ramses II before several gods. Compared to other reliefs I'd seen, they weren't very impressive, suggesting that Ramses redeployed Seti's best craftsmen to work on his own temples. Clearly neither pharaoh had repaired the floor; one look at it was enough to tell me this marbled "floor" belonged to, at the very least, the Middle Kingdom or earlier.

Then a thought hit me like a four-by-two to the head, 'Is this actually the floor, or is it really the roof of another temple? Maybe there's an original temple right beneath my feet, totally undiscovered. Maybe Seti, like everyone else, built his temple on the site of a much earlier, yet tsunami-buried, temple.' The marble column bases and sandstone shafts clearly indicated a post-tsunami restoration of an earlier structure, but, was there more evidence? I'd have to keep my eyes peeled.

'So, Yuko, you think you can link the missing years of Jesus to Caesarion?'

'I don't think I can, I *know* I can.'

'We're all ears.'

As we strolled along, casting a wandering eye over each wall, each column, we all carefully listened to Yuko's explanation.

'There is a place in India, in Kashmir, called Srinagar, where there is a shrine called Roza Bal, which is the tomb of Yuz Asaf, the leader of the healed, also known as "Isa". "Isa" is an Arabic name used in the Koran to refer to Jesus and in Sanskrit "Īśa" means "the Lord".'

'Are you saying Jesus is in some mausoleum in India?'

'Yes.'

That amused Bill.

'That's going to be interesting to prove, though it would possibly explain what the real fighting is over Kashmir if it's true, it's certain not for the ownership of the trademarks to sweaters.'

I was more pragmatic.

'That takes you even more off the path, now not only do you have to connect Caesarion to Jesus, but to someone called "Isa" and also how Jesus finished up being entombed in northern India after he was supposedly crucified in Jerusalem.'

Yuko remained unflustered.

'The name "Isa" is also almost identical to the name "Issa", the name of a young man who, during the missing years of Jesus, fled a middle-eastern country to the area around Tibet around the same time that Caesarion fled Egypt.'

'Hardly concrete evidence.'

'What about the name "Esau", it's a Hebrew name meaning "son of Isis", or how Horus is called Iessus in some languages, and it's not hard to see how Iessus gets turned into Jesus after time, and how the name, Issa or Iessus is "Christ" in Greek. That's all pretty compelling.'

Bill wasn't convinced either.

'It's all very *interesting*, but unless there's some hard evidence, it's really nothing more than conjecture.'

'Well, in 1887, a Russian aristocrat called Nicolas Notovitch, who was also a Cossack officer, spy and war correspondent, visited India and then Tibet. He left Srinagar shortly after visiting Roz Bal, and crossed the Himalayas to the remote Ladakh region. Notovitch claimed that, at the monastery of Hemis in Ladakh, he learned about a text with the title *"Life of Saint Issa, Best of the Sons of Men"*.

Notovitch's asked the chief lama, who had told him about the work, to read it to him, through a translator. According to Notovitch the work consists of two-hundred-and-forty-four short paragraphs, arranged in fourteen chapters, that detailed how, during the years of Jesus Christ's life missing from '*The Bible*', he followed travelling merchants abroad into India and the Hemis Monastery in Ladakh, India, where he studied Buddhism.'

Bill was open to the possibility, but still somewhat diplomatically reserved.

'There are, I concede you, many parallels in the teachings of Jesus and eastern

71

philosophies, which could well account for where he picked them up, but he may well have learned them anywhere. Of course, it would depend on the details in this text you speak of.'

'The *"Life of Issa"* begins with an account of Israel in Egypt, its deliverance by Moses, its neglect of religion, and its conquest by the Romans.'

I had my doubts straight away.

'That sounds like a very pro-Judaic and possibly even a pro-Christian perspective to me.'

'After that is an account of his incarnation and how, at the age of thirteen, the divine youth, rather than take a wife, leaves his home to wander with a caravan of merchants to India, to study the laws of the great Buddhas.'

'True, it might fit the life of Jesus, but it hardly fits the situation of Caesarion escaping assassination.'

Trust Bill to have an alternative.

'Assuming Caesarion was only thirteen, Cleopatra would hardly have told him the real reason she was sending him away was to save his life. It's totally plausible however that she would say she was sending him to another country "incognito" as a humble merchant's son, for "political" reasons, to learn the language and culture. Given the political climate at the time, Caesarion would have bought that hook, line, and sinker.'

'So what did Jesus, stroke Issa, stroke Caesarion, do for the sixteen-odd years he was there?'

'He was welcomed by the Buddhists and spent the first six years amongst them mastering the Vedas, their religious texts. The next six years were spent studying and teaching at several holy cities until he became mixed up in a conflict between the Kshatriyas, who were the warrior class, and the Brahmins, the priestly class, for teaching the holy scriptures to the lower castes, namely the Vaisyas and Sudras, the farmers and labourers, who weren't even allowed to look at religious texts.'

'Well, that's very "Jesus-like" I must say.'

'Then, rather than abide by the Brahmin and Kshatriya commands, Issa preached against their wishes, so they plotted his death.'

Bill and I batted it back and forth like a political ping-pong ball.

'Hardly an enlightened Buddhist approach.'

'It sounds exactly like what happened to him later on in Jerusalem.'

'You'd think he would have learned by then.'

'As Randy would say, "Same shit, different shovel".'

'So, did the Brahmins nail him to a couple of chopsticks during Chinese New Year?'

I'd said it before realizing that Yuko might have considered it a racist comment. Fortunately, she saw the humour in it.

'No, Issa was warned by the Sudras and left, travelling to the birthplace of Buddha in the foothills of the Himalayas in Southern Nepal.'

'So how did Issa, stroke Jesus, stroke Caesarion, get from the Himalayas to Jerusalem?'

'Maybe he took a helicopter.'

'What?'

I looked at Bill thinking he was just being stupid, but he was standing in the centre of the hall, dead serious, pointing up at the ceiling.

'It seems the archangels may have had alternative means of transport.'

We'd done a complete circuit of the outer hall and had wound our way back to the centre. I had no idea what Bill was looking at until he directed me to it.

'There, on the roof lintel and to the right.'

'Shit, it's a helicopter, and not just any old helicopter, it even looks like a blackhawk attack-helicopter. And that looks like a jet fighter.'

'You know the archaeologists explain the shapes away as the result of erosion and the layering of one cartouche over another.'

'Yeah, good one guys, erosion at the top of the roof? Erosion from what – fairy dust? Seriously though, are they blind, or just plain stupid?'

'Maybe they've all been religious conditioned so much that anything outside of their belief structures just can't be possible.'

'Yeah, that's what I said, Bill, blind and stupid.'

As ever, Crystal picked her moments and her words to perfection.

'It seems that being blind and stupid is not restricted to the archaeologists.'

I quickly leapt to Bill and my defence.

'We're just being sceptical, after all, it's a pretty big call don't you think, that Jesus Christ was actually the son of Julius Caesar and Cleopatra?'

'Just as it's a big call to suggest there were helicopters in ancient Egypt.'

Surprisingly, Yuko fuelled the scepticism.

'If it makes you feel any better, most recognized scholars think the entire story was invented by Notovitch.'

That seemed to placate Bill.

'My point exactly.'

As always, like the asp coiled around Cleopatra's arm, Crystal was poised to strike.

'However, just because the supposedly learned scholars choose not to believe it, doesn't mean it didn't happen. After all, haven't I heard you both say on numerous occasions on this trip, that most scholars are either running religious filters or protecting the letters after their name?'

She had nailed us both, and Bill got the point straight away.

'True, you're right, I mean, here I am looking at a hieroglyph of a helicopter, that dates from at least 1300 BC. If someone had told me about it, even shown me a photo, I would still have had major doubts, but here I am, standing here, and it's right before my eyes.'

'So how much evidence do you need?'

'I guess I'm with Alex, I need to know how Caesarion got from being Issa in the Himalayas to being Jesus in Jerusalem?'

'Then perhaps it's time to move on, to shift your perspective.'

Having said that, Crystal deferred to Yuko, then reinforced her metaphor by heading directly into the inner hypostyle hall. As we all followed like sheep, Yuko gladly took up the story.

'The *"Life of Issa"* apparently says that Issa returned to his own country at the age of twenty-nine, and began to preach...'

'Which is consistent with the reappearance of Jesus from the wilderness, but when you say he returned to his own country, do you mean to Egypt, Rome, or the Middle East in general?'

Bill was not so much shifting his perspective as attempting to broaden his awareness. Still, it put Yuko a little on the spot, and she was suddenly less secure.

'I'm not sure, Egypt I think, because he went to Jerusalem *after* that, which is where the Jewish leaders and Pilate all became very apprehensive about his teachings.

And yet he was still able to keep preaching for three years before he was finally arrested and put to death for claiming to be the "son of God".'

'But he was Caesarion, he *was* the "son of God".'

Pernille had suddenly, and understandably, rushed to his defence, after all, she *was* his mother. Bill put his arm around her, comforting her, but it was clear his head was in another space and he was deep in thought.

'I know "*The Bible*" says it was the Jews who set him up and betrayed him, the Pharisees and Sadducees who wanted him dead, but I think the Romans, especially Tiberius, stood to lose more; I think the Romans killed Jesus and, because they got to write "*The Bible*", simply shifted the blame to the Jews.'

'It's interesting you say that, because in Notovich's translation of the book, the section about Pontius Pilate and the events around the death of Jesus, says something similar. In it, the Sanhedrin go to Pilate and argue to *save* the life of Jesus, and *they* are the ones who "wash their hands" of his death, of Pilate's decision.'

'Interesting.'

Bill was shifting.

We passed through the central of seven doorways that led into the inner hypostyle hall, which was made of sandstone on the east and west sides and limestone to the north and south. That was huge; if my theory was right, then Seti didn't build the temple at all, rather he *rebuilt it* from the alabaster remains of a previous temple, more than likely one from the Middle Kingdom or earlier.

Once inside the second hypostyle hall, Bill continued his inquiries of Yuko.

'Has anyone actually taken the trouble to go to Nepal and investigate, to see if the *"Life of Issa"* actually exists?'

'Yes, Swami Abhedananda. He was a devotee of Sri Ramakrishna, one of the sceptics who initially doubted Notovitch's story. Abhedananda was determined to either discover a copy of the manuscript or expose it as a fraud, so, in 1922, he travelled to Tibet, to the monastery, to investigate Notovich's claim.'

'And? What did he find?'

'He wrote a book about his travels, including his visit to the Hemis monastery where he was shown the manuscript of the *"Life of Issa"* by the lama.'

'And what did it say?'

'Part of the document contained a Bengali translation of two-hundred-and-twenty-four verses, which were basically exactly the same as the Notovitch's book.'

Bill and I looked at each other.

'What do you think?'

'It's pretty compelling I must say.'

I could see Bill was mulling things over as we explored the inner hall, which contained thirty-six columns, mostly made of sandstone, in twelve rows of three, the first two rows having lotus bud capitals, while the last row was without capitals but sat upon a raised platform. The hall itself was decorated with beautifully painted images of Seti I worshipping and performing rituals before various deities including Osiris, Horus, Maat, Isis, and Nepthys.

Bill emerged from his musing.

'The only missing piece is, how did Jesus' body get from the cave in Jerusalem to Srinagar?'

As we checked out the images, Yuko gave us even more to contemplate.

'You must have misunderstood me, Jesus didn't die on the cross, according to the Ahmadis, Jesus died in Kashmir at the age of one-hundred-and-twenty.'

That really surprised me.

'One-hundred-and-twenty! Who are these Ahmadis?'

'They're a Muslim sect in the Punjab region of Pakistan founded in 1889 by Mirza Ahmad.'

'So, for over a hundred years, they've been saying Jesus didn't die on the cross.'

'Yes.'

Bill chuckled again.

'Wow, I bet the Vatican love that!'

The rear quarter of the hall, the raised section, served as a sort of a reception area or foyer for not the usual one, or three, but seven cult chapels in the rear, or western, wall. From left to right the shrines belonged to; Seti I as a deified King, Ptah, Ra HorAkhty, Amun Ra, Osiris, Isis and Horus.

Then I realized two things; firstly, that the order of ascension of the gods was right to left and that Seti I had put his shrine at the 'top of the list', above that of Ptah, creator of the universe, secondly, that as the 'order of ascension' was right to left, not left to right as it had been with the images I'd seen on the ceilings at Dendera, and, from memory, at Esna; that it went in the opposite direction to images of the gods normally portrayed.

I instantly thought it was because the Amun priests, as a rebellion against the military dynasties, had withheld their sacred knowledge, or perhaps even deliberately built and decorated the temples in the reverse order, to symbolize the decline of Seti, rather than his ascension. Seti probably didn't have a clue what the direction of the hierarchical order should have been, from left to right; Horus, Isis, Osiris, etcetera, just that he had to be top dog.

All of that raised some really important question; should Hieroglyphs be read right to left, or left to right, and does the direction of reading depend upon the Dynasty or Kingdom? And then another idea struck me; do they also read from top to bottom as a direct reflection of messages from heaven coming down? That part seemed easy.

Between several of the doorways were recessed niches, beautifully decorated with scenes of Seti making offerings to the gods. It's possible the niches were used to hold statuettes of the gods, or to receive offerings. In either case they were meticulously decorated.

In fact, the reliefs in this part of the hall were brightly coloured, and possibly the best of the New Kingdom. They showed Seti making offerings before the shrine of Osiris, and being anointed with holy water from garlanded vases by Osiris and Horus, attended by other gods including Maat, Isis and Nepthys.

There was an especially beautiful relief high on the left, between the sanctuaries of Ptah and Ra HorAkhty, where Seti knelt before Osiris and Horus with the sacred 'persea', a smallish evergreen tree with small yellow fruit, in the background. The 'Persea' is often mentioned in Egyptian mythology and was common in Upper Egypt, its fruit symbolizing the 'Sacred Heart' of Horus.

We split up and headed into different shrines, Pieter and Yuko in the central shrine of Amun, Bill made a beeline, not surprisingly, for Ptah, whilst Crystal and Pernille opted for the shrine of Isis. Being my usual methodical self, I decided to head left and start with the shrine of Seti and move my way 'down' the pecking order.

The first thing I noticed was the soot-covered vaulted ceiling, consisting of uniform pieces of curved stone, which were obviously carved from massive individual blocks. The marbled alabaster floors beneath them continued from the foyer, showing mostly smaller irregularly paved sections.

The presence of alabaster possibly included the walls, which were decorated with probably the best reliefs I had seen, not only in the temple, but in all of Egypt. And why not, if you're going to make a statement, call in your best artists. They emphasized the pharaoh's sovereignty and recognition by the other gods. Along the northern wall they showed the gods leading Seti into the temple and him ceremonially uniting the Two Lands of Upper and Lower Egypt.

In the centre of the rear wall was a massive false door, or pair of doors; perhaps they represented 'in' and 'out', a bit like the doors in a five-star restaurant. I wondered what they were for, were they just ornamental, just ceremonial, or did they have some greater function and meaning. No time to ponder them now, I still had six others to check out.

Near the back of the left wall, Seti was receiving a list of offerings from Thoth and a leopardskin-wearing High Priest, while Seshat, Thoth's consort, wearing her seven-petalled headdress, wrote the king's name for all eternity. Lastly, Seti was shown exiting the temple, carried on a bier borne by jackal-headed and hawk-headed gods. No bier for me, just time to move on.

The next shrine, that of Ptah, was structurally identical to Seti's, having an arched ceiling, and a false door at the rear. Bill was standing centre, facing the false door, mumbling away in his new-found American-Indian alter-ego. Clearly he was having another 'moment' and I didn't want to disturb him, so I took a short silent scope of the reliefs. Unlike the walls in Seti's shrine, the walls here were unpainted, yet covered in beautifully rendered accounts of the rituals associated with the festivals associated with Ptah.

I left Bill to chew the fat with the almighty creator and moved on, through to the next shrine of Ra horAkthy, which was similarly structured and decorated yet completely bereft of paint. That, together with the fact the Ptah shrine was unpainted was consistent with Seti dying before they were finished; that while he was alive all the detail work was done on his shrine, and that once he died, Ramses II took all the best artists away to work on his own temples.

Moving quickly on, I couldn't help but notice a white glow emanating from the central shrine, that of Amun Ra, and Akhenaten 'making his presence known'. Entering the shrine, I was also surprised to see the colour had returned to the reliefs; that didn't really blow my theory out of the water it just took the wind out of its sails. I paused to contemplate that it was plausible Seti's shrine was finished first, then Amun Ra's and *then* Seti died, but within seconds I found myself standing before the origin of the glow, the false door, and, as Bill had been, going into an altered state.

My eyes were closed, but I could still see the door before me; in many ways it was just like my experience in the shrine of Amenhotep at Karnak, only this time it was the other way around, instead of having open eyes and seeing through the stone, now my eyes were closed, and yet I could still see the full image of the false door before me as clear as day. Then, just like at Karnak, I began humming: well, actually *he* started humming, and boy was it low; it was as if my voice box had been turned upside down and grown the testicles of a fully-grown Argentinosaurus.

This isn't Kansas

As the rumbling tones filled the room, the false door began to fade, to become transparent, just as the shrine at Karnak had done. This time though, something *very* different happened; the doorway opened to a blackness deeper than a black hole. Actually that wasn't far from the truth, because I felt drawn, sucked in through the opening to some distant place in the universe. This wasn't a false door; this was a portal, but a portal to where?

At first I hesitated, resisted the pull, concerned I might actually physically be sucked off the planet, but then I surrendered and was quickly whisked into the void. Like a back-seat passenger, in a seemingly out-of-control vehicle being driven by a maniac on speed, I was drawn past the moon, seeing it covered in structures, alive, teeming with life forms, though they were definitely not human.

Shooting on, I was rapidly whizzing through the solar system, ticking off the planets like train stations on an express. First there was Mars, and not only did I see the face at Cydonia, but also massive cities and five-sided pyramids. I wanted to stop and explore the 'red' planet further, but Akhenaten would have nothing of it and propelled me onwards.

On to Jupiter, then to Saturn, both of which had extraordinary cloud patterns at their poles, and I could 'see' the planets teeming with higher consciousnesses. The same happened with Uranus, and Neptune, then past Pluto, and, before I realised, I was out beyond the Kuiper belt and the Oort Cloud within seconds.

Then we did a strange curved about-face and headed back into the solar system, where, in the rapidly approaching distance, an intense dark star ominously loomed. I instantly knew, *this* was the brown dwarf; this was Nibiru. Surrounding it were several massive planets and Akhenaten diverted directly to one of them and I had instant feelings of belonging, of home. Advanced cities with extraordinary technologies dotted the surface, but I knew there was even more below the ground, where the surface conditions had no effect. Then, with no warning, and like a giant elastic band, I was snapped back into the shrine of Amun Ra, and the false door fully materialized and 'slammed shut'.

That was freaky; yes I'd had some pretty far-out stuff happen in the last week or so, but that took the cake. It was as if everything I had become aware of in the last week had come together like a giant jigsaw puzzle. I took a moment to clear my head, absorb what I could, and moved on to the next shrine, the shrine of Osiris.

Before I entered, I heard Pernille and Crystal toning in the next chamber, the shrine of Isis, and stuck my head around the corner. The two girls were standing, as they had at Dendera, face-to-face, holding hands, eyes closed, and toning. As I had with Bill, I had a quick survey of the shrine, which, like most of the others, had an arched ceiling, false door, and unpainted rituals, this time related to Isis, on the walls. I left Pernille and Crystal to their 're-membering', and moved on to the final shrine, that of Horus. It too followed the common pattern of arched ceiling, false-door, and unpainted reliefs so I returned to the Osiris shrine.

Devoted almost exclusively to the different forms of Osiris, each distinguished by a different headdress, as well as by different ceremonial costumes and apparatus, colour had returned in abundance to the chapel. Predictably, there were scenes of the pharaoh making offerings of incense and libations to Osiris, and anointing his image. To the left, Seti offered various cloths and the menat necklace to Osiris in the presence of numerous other gods. What *was* different, was that, unlike the other shrines, the shrine of Osiris didn't have a false door; instead there was a real doorway that led to an inner suite of rooms behind.

First, was another transverse hypostyle hall, this one with ten capital-less columns in pairs running down the length of the hall. Everywhere within the room were exquisite colourful reliefs of ceremonies related to the resurrection of Osiris in the form of Horus, and symbols of resurrection and rebirth, including scenes of Isis offering eggs, an offering made to the Benu bird, and a depiction of the Egyptian phoenix.

Was this a representation of Isis offering her own ova, her own genetic material, to the most intellectual of the 'reptilians' as some sort of deal, an exchange? Or perhaps it was symbolic of something else? But, why would Isis be offering anything to a bird? Other images depicted the pharaoh making offerings and enacting various other rituals to Osiris.

Immediately upon entering, to the right of the hall, were three sanctuaries, dedicated to Horus, Seti I, and Isis respectively. The reliefs in each of the three chapels were of Seti before the respective gods and were exquisite, retaining almost all of their colour. I also discovered from my iphone that;

'Behind these chambers is a secret room that appears to have no entrance. It is thought to have been a crypt where the most sacred temple treasures were stored.'

I groped around the walls a little but I couldn't find any evidence of a secret panel, and believe me I looked. However, apparently the crypt had lost its roof and was now open to the sky, which means it could be viewed from the roof of the temple, *with* permission of course. I wasn't sure we would have the time, or if it was going to be worth forking out fifty-odd pounds, but I'd keep it open as an option.

Beyond the chapels, on the rear, or south-western, wall, was a magnificent representation of the *Djed* pillar; the pillar of Osiris. This was extraordinary, not just because of the detail, but more importantly the subject. It looked like Seti, wearing the combined crown of Upper and Lower Egypt, was holding a giant electrical transformer and presenting it to Isis. Or maybe Seti was receiving it *from* Isis. If that were the case, then it gave Isis the role of providing the pharaohs with some sort of free-energy technology.

As far as I knew, there had never been any such object recovered from any archaeological site in Egypt. Of course there was the possibility they had, but that the rest of the world had never been told about it. But, here it was, painted in exquisite detail.

My mind instantly went underground; was it possible there was still a *Djed* column awaiting discovery in one of the older temples buried by the Thera tsunami? *That* really got me excited. Further, and maybe I was making more of it than it was, but, above Seti's head hovered the red disc of the second sun. Was the technology from Nibiru?

Heading in the other direction, at the southern end of the hall, was a second, smaller hall, containing four columns, with three niches on each of the side walls, and three more chapels to the south. There had been considerable restoration work done here, and, for once, it looked well done.

The decorations in this part of the temple were very poor, however, one would presume, they once contained reliefs about the mysteries of the resurrection of Osiris and perhaps an astronomical ceiling. But something didn't add up.

This hall and the shrines were aligned northwest-southeast, as opposed to the main temple being aligned northeast-southwest. So, was *this* the original temple, or at least built before the main temple, or was it tacked on *after* the main temple was built? The poor state of the reliefs seemed to indicate the former, that it existed before the main temple, but the entrance through the Osiris shrine confused me. They weren't built at the same time that was for sure.

Scratching my head, I made my way back through the rear hall and Osiris shrine and joined the others, who were assembling and chatting back in the foyer area of the second hypostyle hall.

'So, are we done?'

Crystal smiled.

'Far from it; we have not even scratched the surface.'

She had that look on her face; the one that led me to believe I was just about to be hit by a thunderbolt from out of nowhere.

'Then let's get digging.'

With Crystal leading the way, we crossed along the front of the shrines towards two doorways in the south-eastern wall. As everyone followed her through the left door, I quickly ducked into the right to check it out. It was a small hall with three columns and two chapels at the far end: the hall of Ptah-Sokar and Nefertem, the northern counterpart to Osiris.

To me, that meant it was either built at a time *before* the 19th Dynasty, when Upper and Lower Egypt were unified, or *after* a period of separation. Given that the rooms seemed 'tacked on' to the main temple, my initial reasoning was they were added after, most probably in the 22nd Dynasty, and possibly by Sheshonq I. But then I considered they may well have been added by Seti as an afterthought to 'cover all the bases' and incorporate the northern gods. There were niches in the southern wall of the hall and, although there was no colour, a few interesting reliefs, particularly in the chapels.

In the Ptah-Sokar chapel was a fascinating image of Isis being impregnated by a dead Osiris, Seti with a hawk-headed depiction of Sokar, and Ptah-Sokar with Sekhmet. In the Nefertum chapel were images of Seti making offerings to the gods of creation of the world, especially Neith who made the sun appear with seven magic words, and both a human and lion-headed Nefertem being crowned with the lotus blossom.

I doubled back, headed through the left door and found the others examining the western wall of the corridor. On it, Seti held a censor while his young son, Ramses II, read from a papyrus scroll. They were making offerings to a long list of cartouches, consisting of three rows of thirty-eight cartouches in each row. The upper two rows contained names of previous pharaohs, while the bottom row merely repeated alternations of Seti I's throne name and personal name.

We were in the Hall of Ancestors and this was the 'Gallery of Lists', a list of cartouches of seventy-six pharaohs beginning with Menes in the 1st Dynasty and ending with Seti I at the start of the 19th Dynasty. I guess this was the famous 'Abydos King List', but it just went to show that not only couldn't you trust what the modern Egyptologists were writing, but even the ancient ones were distorting the truth.

Seti had not only carefully selected those kings whom he considered his legitimate ancestors, but, more importantly, had omitted those he didn't want to be associated with, including Hatshepsut, Akhenaten, Smenkhkare, Tutankhamen and Ay.

Despite that, and besides providing the order of the Old Kingdom pharaohs, albeit with some obvious errors, to date it is the sole source of the names of many of the kings of the 7th and 8th Dynasties, so the list is of great value for many reasons.

It was important to remember that the ancient Egyptians used no consistent system of dating, or of regnal years. As a result, any list of pharaohs compiled today requires conjecture on the length of their reigns and has to adjust for any periods of discontinuity or co-regencies. This leads to further problems, namely, all the ancient

Egyptian king lists are either comprehensive but have significant gaps in their text, such as the Turin King List, or, like the Abydos King List, are textually complete but fail to provide a complete list of rulers. Thus for almost every single ruler of Egypt, we lack accurate details for the length of their reigns.

Add to that altar-loads of religious bias due to the influence of *'The Bible'* and its scholars, the highly questionable date of the biblical flood, now seen as an effect of the last pole shift, Manetho's distorted perception of the age of the Earth, and parallel monarchies due to family disputes and splits between the Upper and Lower regions and rulers of the Nile, and a myriad of chronologies can, and do, easily result.

Egyptologists have tried to resolve some of these discrepancies by using chronological synchronistic events in neighbouring kingdoms such as the Assyrian, Babylonian, Hittite, Palestinian and ancient Greek civilizations. However most evidence only begins to appear around the 15th Century BC, specifically during the Amarna Period between Amenhotep III and Akhenaten and various neighbouring eastern rulers, which is not so surprisingly *after* the Thera tsunami. So, whilst the King List created by Seti I on the wall here at Abydos was impressive, it was definitely not set in concrete.

Continuing on, Crystal led everyone through a door to the right, into and up a wide corridor. There were a couple of other doors leading off the Hall of Ancestors that we hadn't explored, so I decided to give them a quick once over.

First, I ducked into the door at the end of the Hall of Ancestors, entering a court bordered on three sides by a portico with seven columns. On the walls were reliefs of animals being sacrificed, and the floor had a drainage system that supported the images on the walls; this was the Hall of Sacrifices, a butcher shop. There were four rooms, probably storerooms, leading off to the side and rear and a door leading out to the administration area. Apart from that there was nothing of interest.

Returning to the previous hall, I headed into the room to the left, the Sanctuary of Boats, but there was nothing of great interest here either, so I caught up with the others who had paused in the corridor and were chatting to Diane's group, who had just returned from exploring the outside area behind the temple.

We said our customary hellos, and once again we were invited to a circle later that night back at the Nefertiti Hotel. It wasn't so much the circle I was looking forward to, in fact, I noticed I was a little apprehensive about it, understandably so, as it seemed every time I went to one, something weird happened to me. If I went to this one, I wanted to make sure that the only way I was going to pass out on Crystal's bed afterwards was because of several hours of incredibly passionate and perhaps even gymnastically and contortionistically-adventurous sexual revelry. Bidding us adieu, Diane and her group quickly moved on, leaving us to examine the rest of the complex.

On the wall was a clearly defined image of Ramses II, with his young son, Prince Amunherkhopchef, roping a bull. Further on, the animal was offered a sacrifice. I couldn't help but wonder if this symbolized more than simply catching and cooking a cow. Was this also a representation of Ramses II subduing and offering the Age of Taurus up for sacrifice, as a way to show he was the master of the relatively new Age of Aries? Who knows? Bill certainly didn't. He looked more like a stunned mullet; he was looking at the walls, but his mind was miles away.

'What's up, Bill, trying to work out the significance of the bull?'

'Hmm? No, I've been thinking about what Yuko said.'

'Yeah, me too,…and?'

He clicked into another gear.

'Have you read a book called *"Jesus the Man"*, by Barbara Thiering?'

'Never heard of it, why?'

'Thiering puts forward the proposition that Jesus was the leader of a radical faction of Essene priests, that he was not of virgin birth, that he didn't die on the cross, that he married Mary Magdalene, fathered a family, later divorced, and died sometime after 64 AD.'

'Pretty much what Yuko said.'

'Yeah, but Thiering came to that conclusion after decoding the Dead Sea Scrolls.'

'The Dead Sea Scrolls, I know about them, discovered between 1947 to 1956.'

'Yes, I know, we talked a little about it all on the felucca, and I always had my doubts about the Christian version of events, but what Yuko's said about the *"Life of Issa"* and Jesus being Caesarion has really got me thinking.'

'You think it's all true?'

'I'm certainly leaning that way now. You see, Thiering sees Jesus as a prominent member of the Essene movement because of his direct descent from the Davidic kingship. According to Thiering, Jesus' great grandfather, was Hillel the Great....'

'Who was he?'

'He was a famous Jewish religious leader, but *who* he was doesn't seem as important as when he lived, which was during the time of King Herod and, more importantly, Augustus. But then maybe it's just another synchronistic connection.'

'I'm not following.'

'What if the Davidic lineage was a distortion of the lineage from Abraham, or rather, the lineage from Egypt?'

I was all ears.

'Go on.'

Thinking out loud, Bill slowly turned to face the opposing wall, where Ramses II and Amunherkhopchef held four calves.

'Thiering proposes that the biography of Jesus is hidden in the New Testament and shows he was born out of wedlock in Qumran in March, 7 BC.'

'That's not such a big deal, in fact it supports things; Caesar and Cleopatra weren't married, and 7 BC is well within the margin for error.'

'She goes on to say that Jesus' brother, James, was born in wedlock, eight years later in September of 1 AD.'

'No, that's seven years, there was no year zero, it went from 1 BC straight to 1 AD. So how many years between Caesarion and his brothers?'

'Alexander Helios, the twin of Cleopatra Selene II was born on 25th of December 40 BC.'

'If Caesarion was born in 47 BC then that's seven years; it fits perfectly.'

'But it also means Jesus must have had another, younger brother, because Ptolemy Philadelphus was born around four years after that, in August/September 36 BC.'

'If he'd survived; I mean, he would have been, what, eleven years younger, so around eighteen or nineteen when Jesus started preaching. Do you think he was one of the other apostles?'

'It's possible, but not everything matches though. For instance, *"The Bible"* mentions four brothers; James, Joseph, Judas and Simon, as well as several unnamed sisters.'

'Well, we know James was probably Alexander Helios, and Selene was his sister...'

As I said it a shiver went up my spine; if I was Crystal's brother, and she was Cleopatra Selene II, meaning I was Alexander Helios, then that meant I was James, brother of Jesus Christ and one of the twelve apostles. *THAT* really freaked me out. Then I thought, 'Well, shit, I guess someone had to be.'

Taking a moment or two to ground myself, Bill and I meandered further along the wall, pausing before a section where Ramses II and Amunherkhopchef, with animal-headed gods preceding them, caught a net full of birds, then presented the catch to Amun and Mut.

I felt like one of the birds, trapped and being offered up for slaughter like a fully-stuffed turkey at Thanksgiving dinner, with all the trimmings; imagine going public and saying you were not only the reincarnation of Akhenaten, Amenhotep, Imhotep and Apollo, but also the reincarnation of one of Jesus' twelve apostles, in fact Jesus' half-brother, James. Not only would the Catholic Church denounce you, but every fanatical religious zealot in the world would shoot you down in flames, burn you at the stake as a blasphemer and heretic, and the authorities would probably have you comprehensively psychoanalysed, heavily sedated to the eyeballs, and thrown in a padded cell.

But, worse than that, imagine how my ex-mother-in-law would react to the news; it would be open season on ex-son-in-laws. Then again, I don't think that would be a new experience for me either; this 'woman' could break the balls of a raging bull elephant with one ovary tied behind her back, and could make the Spanish Inquisition look like a children's Devon-shire afternoon tea party.

I was slowly coming to grips with the implications, but, if Bill was the reincarnation of Marc Antony, then the ramifications were not showing on him.

'According to the scholars, Simon was born seven years *before* Jesus, and Judas, like Simon, was a son of Clopas, the brother of Jesus' father, Joseph, which means they were cousins rather than brothers.'

'Which leaves James and Joseph as Jesus' actual blood brothers…'

Then I had a thought.

'…Remember how you said Caesarion may have been escorted to India by two of Cleopatra's most trusted servants, probably his wet-nurse and her husband?'

'Yes.'

'Well what if they actually *were* Mary and Joseph, and Simon and Judas were *their* sons, and the other sisters, apart from Selene, were *their* daughters; after all a wet nurse would have to have born children of her own before being a wet-nurse to Caesarion. From his birth, Caesarion would have grown up with the other children around him and definitely considered them his brothers and sisters.'

'Wow! It makes sense. But there are other unresolved issues. What about the fact James was born in wedlock and Jesus wasn't?'

'James wasn't born in wedlock.'

Her offhand interjection revealed Crystal had ears like a hawk, and had been clearly monitoring the conversation.

'What do you mean?'

'It was Ptolemy Philadelphus, or Joseph as he became known, who was the son born in wedlock, not Alexander.'

'How do you figure that?'

I sort of wished I'd let Bill ask the question, because Crystal's disappointed look at me told me I'd jumped the gun yet again and not trusted my inner knowing. She took a slow measured breath and delivered her words in such a way as to ensure the message hit its mark.

'After the birth of Selene and Alexander, Marc Antony married Cleopatra in Egypt and, according to the Egyptian rite and practice, it legitimised *all* her children with him. But really, you are dragging your feet; you must keep up.'

The gauntlet well and truly thrown down, she headed off up the marble staircase that led outside to the rear of the temple. I watched as the sunlight streamed through the doorway and through her white dress, making it totally see through. Man, did this girl have a hot ass.

After spending the previous night in her bed and seeing her this morning wearing nothing more than a smile, I couldn't wait to get back to Luxor this evening and take things to the next level. But, there was something in the way she said what she said that got me thinking, "You are dragging your feet, you must keep up." Crystal wasn't talking about the trip through the temple at all, she meant understanding the full story of Caesarion and Jesus. She had dangled the carrot, and, like Bugs Bunny on his way to Albuquerque, I was champing at the bit.

Exiting the main temple, no more than twenty metres down the path and directly behind the Seti temple, I stopped in awe and amazement; Jesus would have to wait. Bill stopped too, and turned his head.

'Bingo!'

He was right, here was the proof I'd been looking for; dug out of the sand, built and sitting at a level far below the existing Seti temple, was a structure made of massive blocks of red granite; this was it, this was my gold mine.

The Osireion

I instantly dived into my iphone files.

'Half-buried & partly inaccessible due to stagnant water, the Osireion lies immediately behind the Seti Temple on the main axis of Seti's temple but at a subterranean level. It was built in an excavation in the sandy clay stratum of the desert, with almost vertical sides.'

"An excavation"? Dug out? No way! Why the hell would you go to the trouble of digging down into the "sandy clay stratum" *below* the water table?

Wait a minute; stratum, that meant layers, could this be more evidence of my tsunami theory? I looked for more clues, and what better place than the words of Flinders Petrie, the first man to excavate the site in 1904.

'I was told the men had found desert a few feet down. This seemed strange, and on looking at it I saw there was only blown sand. So they were told to go deeper. Again, ... on going there again, the same story of desert at the bottom was repeated; only this time about fifteen feet down. On examining it I found blown sand. So a third time they were told to go down, and soon after they struck some great blocks of limestone. The final result was that we found the pavement of the hall was forty-one feet under the surface.'

So Petrie had found at least three layers, the base layer, of limestone, or limestone blocks, forty-one feet down, then the next layer was at a depth of fifteen feet, the next at three or four feet. But layers of what?

'The earth excavated around the Osireion has been shown to be compacted Nile silt, which has been laid down year after year by the annual inundation of the Nile since time immemorial.'

Nile silt? Perhaps, but that makes no sense of the layers of blown sand that separated the layers, for surely the Nile silt flows every year, as does wind blown sand. The only other explanation was not one, not two, but three tsunamis. The first left a sedimentary layer of twenty-six feet, the second, a layer of ten feet, the third a few feet; it was all consistent with the layers I had seen at Edfu, Esna, and on the West Bank at Luxor. The Nile 'silt' here was not from upstream, but from downstream, from 'topsoil' laid down by previous annual floods. And then there was the 'fact' it was deliberately built *below* the water table.

'The foundations were cut many feet below the current level of the water table and two parallel limestone walls were erected to serve as retaining walls for the sand bed upon which the temple was built.'

That the foundations of the Osireion are much lower than those of the Temple of Seti suggests one of two things, - that it was designed and built deliberately to be below ground level, which would have been unprecedented in Egyptian architecture, and, come on guys, retaining walls of limestone? I couldn't think of anything *worse* to use *below* the level of the water table, it would wash away and dissolve over time; granite, even sandstone, would be far more efficient.

The second option is that the Osireion was designed and built to be above ground, therefore built at a time when the ground level was considerably lower than it is today, indeed lower than the ground level at the time of Seti.

Of course the Osireion sat below the water table *now*, but it didn't *then*. It was only *after* the various tsunamis that the water table rose; I'd seen evidence of that with the temples on Elephantine Island, at el-Kab and Wadi Hillal, as well as the positions of the tombs in the Valley of the Kings and the temples on the West Bank. The evidence was everywhere, how could the Egyptologists be so blind?

'The temple was built by Seti as a cenotaph, or false tomb; a symbol of the closeness of the pharaoh's *ka* to Osiris. It contains a sarcophagus, though Seti was not buried here.'

Of course he wasn't buried here, Seti's tomb is in the Valley of the Kings back in Luxor. Even Flinders Petrie didn't think it was a tomb.

"We expected to find a passage, we found chambers and halls; we expected to find it roofed in, the roof had been completely quarried away; we expected to find a tomb, we found a place of worship."

And it's clear from the sedimentary layers that the Osireion, or at least part of it, had to have been built before the three layers of sediment were laid down. That was at least pre-1600 BC and pre Seti I, so he couldn't have built it. He may have tried to restore it, but he certainly didn't build it. But the experts couldn't see that.

'This was a fairly common practice among many of the pharaohs, having "public" tombs in one location, but actually being buried in another.'

No, I didn't buy that for a minute; where's the sarcophagus?

'It's a complete tomb structure, all ready to receive the mummy of a king, and yet it doesn't appear to have ever been used as a tomb.'

Maybe because it *wasn't* built by Seti, and it wasn't a tomb. Come on, guys, let's at least show some intelligence. Why would Seti build a temple out of marble/alabaster and sandstone, then say, "Hey, I know, let's dig a huge pit in the backyard and build a tomb out of massive blocks of red granite"? If red granite was *that* important, and Seti and Ramses II could cut it and move it, they'd have used it for their temples as well. So, if it wasn't a tomb, what's the alternative? Though it was flooded with water, closer examination was needed.

Measuring about thirty metres long by twenty metres wide, the first thing that struck me about the Osireion was there was something about the mathematical precision of its structure. I wondered if had been designed and constructed to the golden mean ratio of 1:1.6, or perhaps some other geometrical blueprint. Was this what Hesat had said about looking for the sacred geometry?

The only way was to get down and explore the space, but, even if I was able to bribe the guards, it would mean wallowing around in stagnant water, and that didn't appeal to me at all; I'd have to rely quite a bit on my notes.

'The Osireion consisted of a raised rectangular 'island' in the centre about fifteen metres long and seven or eight metres wide. On each of its long sides sat five massive square-cut red granite pillars, each about two-and-a-half metres in diameter, a little over three-and-a-half metres high, and each weighing about a hundred tons apiece. They were linked along the side by equally large red granite lintels that formed four 'doorways' down each side.'

The more I looked at the massive inner red granite parts of the Osireion, the more I was reminded of Stonehenge. Was there a link to the stars here as well?

'Carved into the centre of the floor was a shallow rectangle, most likely there to hold an altar or sarcophagus. A similar square depression was carved in line to the northeast, presumably to hold another altar or massive canopic chest.'

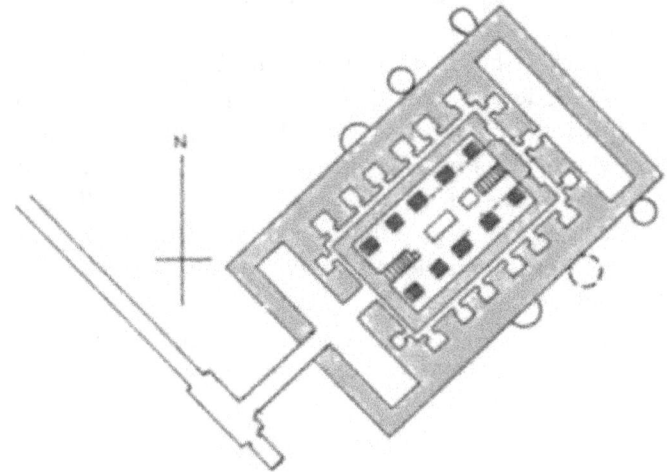

That confused me, and it sent me into a flurry of 'question asking'. Why would such massive pieces of stone, that probably weighed several ton at the least, need a recessed 'holding zone'; they were hardly likely to shift, especially if it were a tomb? Unless of course it wasn't a tomb and the energies generated in the Osireion were such that these altars were rendered 'weightless' and could easily move laterally from their assigned positions. And where were these central objects now? Someone had to have removed them, and removed them *after* the Osireion had outlived its use and been excavated, someone with access to technologies to lift hundred-ton blocks of granite. Were the secrets of the Tat Brotherhood still alive today and being used by the Illuminati to secure important ritualistic objects? There seemed so much to discover here, even in asking questions about why things *weren't* here. The Osireion a tomb? No way.

I suddenly had an image of the inner sanctuary of the Temple of Amun at Karnak, and of the Khepri Plinth nearby. Could the spaces here have contained an altar and a plinth, and someone have reclined here to receive some form of channelled energy from the planet, or even outer space? Although I hadn't read them all, I'd literally compiled hundreds of files on ancient Egypt to bring with me; I had to have something in my notes about that, surely?

I found a file with an analysis of the Osireion by Lucy Lamy, who described how the basic geometry of the Osireion was an edge-on double pentagram, and remembered how witches have used pentagrams for over a thousand years, claiming it's a gateway to other spiritual realms and higher dimensions.

What was a double pentagram all about, an in-door and out-door? As I said it, I instantly saw the false doors in the shrines of the Seti temple. Maybe it was a galactic portal? Further on I read;

> 'The geometry of the Osireion suggests a nest of Third Dimensional generative roots, the square root of 2, 3 and 5, and the Golden Mean ratio of Phi, as well as extending the level of understanding to include the merging of the Cubes of Space, all of which form the connective tissue that holds the collective and the individual worlds together.'

I didn't understand what it all meant, and couldn't see how you could discern it from the diagrams, but I did understand what the Golden Mean was all about, and to me it meant a direct connection to the chambers at Karnak, and thus to their function.

> 'Any pentagon can be employed as the basis for an exercise called "squaring the circle", or in the Third Dimension, "cubing the sphere". The double pentagon of the Osireion allows two such cubed spheres, interpenetrating in the space of the central Osiris island, whose Phi structure allows for the generation of another pentagonal figure. This pentagon pair, unlike the original, interpenetrates to a degree that suggests that the resolution to the whole geometric complex is the dodecahedron, composed of twelve pentagonal faces.'

I think I was lost when I read, "squaring the circle", but I did remember that had something to do with "as above, so below" or "representing the heavens on earth". What I did plug into was the last line.

'Traditionally, this platonic solid is used to represent the spirit.'

At each end of the central island was a staircase, cut into the stone, which descended about three-and-a-half metres to a lower walkway, about three metres across, that surrounded the island. I found an old black-and-white picture of the Osireion in my file, taken after it had been drained of water, showing the staircase.

What was clear was there was a staircase within a staircase and that told me this staircase was originally made for beings much taller than modern man, and that fitted perfectly with the notion this central section was built by the Annunaki.

According to the 'experts', as the Osireion was flooded, it formed a type of moat around the central island.

'The Osireion contains an island surrounded by a moat, symbolizing the primordial mound that arose from the waters of Chaos at the dawn of Creation.'

These geniuses had come to their 'profound' conclusion from a single image, on an Old Kingdom sarcophagus, which had a hemispheric mound, with a chamber deep inside labelled "Osiris lives." Why can't they just say, "I think"…, rather than state it as fact? Simply; they have a piece of paper, and letters after their name, that somehow gives them 'authority' to make such sweeping generalizations and statements, and at the same time condemn any person *without* letters after their name who does the same.

'On the top of the mound are four large and prominent trees, representing the four axis of the celestial sphere, the four Trees of Life.'

Since when have trees been used to represent the four axis of the celestial sphere, and how do they justify and distinguish their use? And since when were there four trees of life? In the end, it all just didn't gel, for two very good reasons: the staircases. If it were meant as a moat, then why the stairs, and if the moat were drained for access then you would only need one staircase.

'The trenches were drained and cleared of debris in 1993 but the bottoms have never been excavated.'

Who knows what they would find!

The more I thought about it, the more I came to the conclusion the 'primordial mound' theory espoused here, was just the 'experts' way of trying to plug the gaps by putting square plugs into round holes. They had bizarrely failed to consider the water table had risen and flooded the current structure; they assumed the original building must have been built deliberately below the water table and ***THAT MAKES ABSOLUTELY NO SENSE WHATSOEVER***.

Radiating out from the central island, I could see there had been some attempts in the past to cover the walkways, but they were incongruent with the original granite pillars and lintels and must have been a later modification.

'There is some evidence in the Osireion that Montuhotep II did some rebuilding of the site in the 11th Dynasty, and hieroglyphs in the antechamber, reveal that Seti I completely rebuilt the structure along the lines of the ruined original temple in the 19th Dynasty, and that the temple may have originally been completely roofed with monolithic slabs.'

There was already significant evidence of alabaster/marble floors in the Seti temple, which now made me think they were more than likely either the roof elements of a temple belonging to Montuhotep II, which was buried by the Thera tsunami and was probably still there below, or the Montuhotep temple was flattened by the tsunami. Given the evidence from Flinders Petrie that there was a limestone floor forty-one feet below the Seti floor level, and that it totally coincided with my theory the limestone and alabaster belonged to the Middle Kingdom or earlier, my money was on an undiscovered subterranean temple still there below the Seti temple.

If Montuhotep had added the roof, then it's possible the Thera tsunami and the twenty-six feet of sediment, caused the ceiling to collapse, leaving it to Seti to repair, however, if it was Seti who added the roof, he would have had to excavate the site first. Looking at the evidence before me, it seemed more consistent that it was Montuhotep who would have added a roof to the complex, but I needed more evidence to be sure.

Under the careful gaze of the guardian, the others made their way down and back the path that ran along the southern side of the Osireion, to a rickety old wooden staircase that descended into the Osireion itself. As they did, I checked out the outer walls of the Osireion.

'Surrounding the walkway were the outside walls of the Osireion, made of red sandstone and about six metres thick, which contained a total of 17 small chambers, six unfinished small chambers on each of the room's long sides, three more on the north-eastern wall adjoining Seti I's temple, three more on the opposite south-western wall, and a ledge forming the outer edge of the walkway about a third of the way up, and around, the walls.'

It struck me as rather strange to build chambers with the entrances halfway up the walls, unless, like the mosque of Abou El-Hagag in the Temple of Luxor, the ground level was much higher. It seems likely then, that when Seti excavated the Osireion, he only dug down as far as the upper level of the central island, then built the sandstone walls and chambers on all four corners; they didn't belong to the original structure at all, the red granite structures were built first.

Beyond the side walls were outer walls made of large blocks of limestone. I scratched my head; they would have been added in or before the Middle Kingdom, which meant the rebuilding done by Seti included constructing most, but not all, of the seventeen inner chambers.

According to the floor-plan in my file, the central doorway on the north eastern wall led to a long transverse chamber that spanned the width of the temple.

'Built of limestone with a vaulted ceiling of sandstone cut in the shape of a pent roof, its decorations, commissioned during the reign of Seti I, consist of finely carved astronomical reliefs on the eastern end, and a splendidly carved representation of the sky-goddess, Nut, supported by Shu, god of the air, with the Decans, on the western end. On the walls at either end of the hall are funerary texts.'

Unfortunately the room was perpetually flooded, apparently even during the dry season, so I had to resort to contemplating an old black-and-white photo in my file. It seemed pretty straight forward though; based on my theories, I could make several assumptions, namely that the walls, being of limestone, dated to at least the Middle

Kingdom, and, though the end walls contained funerary texts, these could well have been added when the ceiling was added, during the reign of Seti. From that I concluded that the rest of the Osireion was probably roofed-in at the same time.

The rest of the group had just been down the wooden staircase and were making their way back. Pieter was radiating, like he had just seen God.

'It's incredible, you have to go and see it.'

Yes, it was incredible, more so for the truths buried within its location and the size of the granite pillars, than its structural complexity or aesthetic beauty. I mean, seriously, it was nothing like Karnak or the alabaster altars and shrines, or the red-granite inner sanctum of Amun. This was just a pile of very very old rocks, nothing I would get so spun out by.

As I reached the bottom section of the stairs, I stopped at the rope that prevented any further access into the central island. Even if you could go further it would have been almost 'impossible' to set foot there because of the pool of green stagnant water that flooded the floor.

I cranked my neck to try and look inside any and all of the chambers in the walls, but the bright sun and dark interiors made the effort fruitless. Similarly, my attempts at squinting and hoping to gaze into the murky water were ineffective. All I could really do was examine the enormous red-granite pillars. Was this what lay below all those other red-granite thresholds in all those other temples?

Smoothly cut, with great precision, at first I was surprised that not one of them had a single hieroglyph or relief, not one! It had to have something to do with the age of them, because this was the most important part of the Osireion, and if all the other temples I had seen in Egypt were anything to go by, if you were a pharaoh, this is where you really would have gone to town and showed your worship of the gods, and your rightful place alongside them.

But there was nothing, not a scratch, not even any graffiti. And if Seti I really did build the Osireion, as the 'experts would have us believe, and his son Ramses II was around to make his mark, then you can bet your bottom dollar Ramses would have been chiselling his monogram all over the place like a rebellious teenager tagging the local neighbourhood. But, there was nothing.

'Can you see them?'

I looked back.

'See what?'

'On the pillar; the flower of life.'

I turned back and looked at the massive pillar before me; what the hell were they talking about, there was just rock.

'Where?'

'On the inside of the next pillar, at the top, just under the ledge, in the shadow.'

I leaned in and took off my sunnies, squinting to try and make out anything other than granite.

'What exactly am I ...'

And then I saw it; the "flower of life", this was the picture Pieter was talking about, the circles he drew in the sand with a stick.

It was beautiful, no, captivating. What had

Bill said about it? '*It describes the structure of all life; the shape of all the geometric solids, the angles and molecular bonds of atoms and molecules, the structure of every element and atomic structure in the universe.*'

But what was it doing here? Perhaps it had something to do with what Lucy Lamy was going on about and Phi? Maybe it was a marker, or a builders' blueprint? Or possibly it had been left as a piece of cryptic graffiti by some enlightened tourist? Not bloody likely. For starters it was right at the top of the pillar, and that was over ten feet from the floor.

I leaned even nearer to examine it more closely, nearly falling over the unstable railing in the process. Suddenly I saw another flower beside it, and then two smaller ones above; there was a little nest of the buggers. The images were faint, but clear. I could see they weren't chiselled into the stone like other reliefs and hieroglyphs, and they weren't painted on either. How the hell were they made?

For a moment I contemplated they were burned into the rock, like a branding iron, but that didn't make sense. Then I thought that maybe they were laser-etched into the rock; it looked almost as if the molecules of the stone had been rearranged so that the darker bits formed the images.

'*Look for the sacred geometry, for it is present in all things; all things exist because of it.*'

It was Hesat, as if she was standing right behind me, in fact when I turned my head, I thought she was. Instead it was Crystal, who had descended the stairs and now stood beside me.

'Feel the stone.'

'Oh oh, here we go again.'

Knowing it had the history of the Osireion within it, I reached out, placed my hand on the nearest pillar, closed my eyes, and took a deep breath. As I exhaled I found myself toning a low 'Ooooh'.

As I continued, the pillar seemed to respond, not in one note, but at a broad range of octaves, causing the other pillars to respond in sympathetic vibration. The whole space felt as if it was shuddering, like I had just turned on a giant electric engine.

Just then, Nemo appeared at the base of the pillar. Initially I felt sorry for him, poor bugger, having to swim his way through the stagnant green water. But, as he made his way towards the centre of the island, towards the large rectangular depression in the floor, the water not only became pure, but it totally disappeared. Nemo was suddenly floundering on a massive red-granite altar that had appeared out of nowhere and sat perfectly within the carved out space in the floor. As he did, the sound of the stones changed, each shifting in pitch and creating a cosmic chord, a subsonic, supersonic, symphonic cluster of acoustic splendour that swelled in a crescendo. The Osireion suddenly filled with brilliant light, shooting out from each of the pillars and into the central altar. Then, about a second later, and just as quickly, the light subsided and Nemo was nowhere to be seen.

Initially I thought he'd been vaporized, that he'd been frazzled by the ultimate backyard BBQ, but no, Nemo was still around, just some *where*, some *place*, and/or some *time* different. The Osireion wasn't a tomb, it seemed it was a star-gate, a portal to travel anywhere on the planet, no, in the galaxy. 'Hey, beam me up, Scotty.'

I had images in my mind of the night sky and I felt the ancients used the Osireion, like a transporter, to connect to other star systems, particularly the part of the sky centred around Orion and Sirius. But it wasn't *just* a star-gate, it was more; the Osireion was an inter-dimensional gateway of, and for, consciousness.

Somehow the flower of life was the key, the map of the universe; all you had to do was plug in the co-ordinates and you could go anywhere, any time. Light seemed to be just the trigger, and then I realized *that*, light, was triggered by sound, and in turn *that* was triggered by matter. And the whole thing was triggered by consciousness, and the intent of that consciousness. And it was the same in the other direction. Matter, sound, light, were just different states of consciousness of the same essential being, just like ice, water and steam were different states of water. And then it hit me; I opened my eyes, and turned to Crystal.

'Consciousness, with Intent, Manifests.'

'Really?…'

She had a look on her face as if I'd just told her that water was wet.

'…and what does that mean?'

I dug into my brain searching for an explanation.

'Consciousness "slows down" to become thought, vibrational energy, which slows down to become light, which slows down to become sound, which slows down to become matter, which at its smallest sub-atomic quantum level is a pea-soup of possibilities and probabilities that modifies consciousness through experience. The whole thing is a cycle of fractals, and the flower of life somehow shows all that.'

'Bravo, you deserve a reward,…'

Then she gave me a congratulatory kiss on the cheek.

'… and I am *sure* it will come your way *very* soon.'

She raised her eyebrows, flicked and tossed her hair like a shampoo model, then, like the Pied Piper of Hamlin, led the way, back up the staircase, and up the path that ran along the Osireion, to join the others. All the way, my gaze was fixed on her magnificent oscillating ass; and even though she had the skimpiest of G-strings on, I knew exactly what that ass looked like under that white skirt, and tonight I was convinced I was going to get myself a piece of it.

Reaching the others, it was obvious Pernille had seen enough, not of Crystal's butt, but of the temple.

'So, shall we call it a day?'

I think she was still pretty overwhelmed and drained from the emotional releases of being at Dendera, and keen to get back to Luxor and process them fully. Bill wasn't so ready.

'Actually, if we have time, I'd like to go and see the Temple of Ramses II.'

As he said it, I got the feeling he'd been a High Priest there at some time, and, despite the fact I was keen to return to Luxor as soon as possible and renew my acquaintance with Crystal's naked body, I felt the urge to join him. So, it seemed, did Pieter.

'There's another Ramses II temple here?'

'I'd be more surprised if there *wasn't* a Temple of Ramses II everywhere we went.'

'Where is it?'

Bill pointed north.

'Supposedly just over those dunes.'

'How far?'

'According to the maps, about four or five-hundred metres.'

That cemented Pernille's thinking.

'Half-a-kilometre! No, I think I'll definitely give it a miss.

The distance didn't bother me, hell, I'd trekked around Karnak yesterday; half-a-kilometre was a doddle.

'Count me in, Bill. Pieter, what about you?

'I'm in as well, after all, you only live once.'

'Yuko?'

'No, I will keep Pernille company.'

That left Crystal to decide, and, before she could be asked, she set the scenario.

'You boys go off on your caravan, we ladies will retire back to the entrance, take a toilet break, and wait for you somewhere that has plenty of shade and cool drinks.'

The sexist divide had finally kicked in; we men, the intrepid butch macho explorers, setting off into the searing heat and endless sand of desert, the ladies on the other hand sipping pina coladas under the shade of a coolabah tree. Who'll come a-waltzing Mathilda, with me?

The three Rhine-maidens disappeared into the temple as we three musketeers, we three stooges, like the three kings visiting Jesus, set off westward towards the desert, the only differences being it was more northwest and we didn't have any gifts, oh, and we weren't kings, at least not in this life anyway.

'Hey, Pieter, you seem to know a fair bit about this "flower of life", right?'

'Yes.'

'What about other sacred geometries?'

'What is it you want to know?'

'I don't know exactly. I was checking out a file on my iphone about the Osireion and it said the Osireion was based on a double, edge-on, pentagon. Does that have any sort of special meaning?'

He took a moment to think, then, fired back the answer.

'Yes, yes it does; the double, edge-on, pentagon structure is also the same pattern as the indole/receptor pattern formed by serotonin and tryptamine alkaloids when they're absorbed by the brain.'

'Ah? In English?'

'An Indole is an aromatic heterocyclic organic compound with a bicyclic structure, that consists of a six-membered benzene ring fused to a five-membered nitrogen-containing pyrrole ring. It is a common component of fragrances and the precursor to many psychodelic pharmaceuticals.'

I looked at Bill to see if he understood.

'I was more of an *in*organic man myself.'

'I'm afraid you'll have to dumb it down for us, Pieter, quite a bit! Better start with Serotonin, at least I've heard of that, it's a hormone right, like melotonin?'

'Yes, serotonin is a monoamine neurotransmitter that's biochemically derived from tryptophan. Ninety percent of it is produced in the gut and regulates appetite. The other ten percent is synthesized in serotonergic neurons of the central nervous system, where it is released into the space between neurons to activate receptors located on the dendrites, cell bodies and presynaptic terminals of adjacent neurons.

Once released, it regulates cognitive functions related to mood, sleep, aging, learning and memory. Modulation of serotonin at the synapses is thought to be a major action of several classes of pharmacological antidepressants and hallucinogenic drugs.'

'So it's an upper?'

'Sort of.'

'And tryptamines?'

'Tryptamines include many biologically active compounds, including neurotransmitters, neuromodulators and psychedelic drugs, that act as serotonin releasing agents and serotonergic activity enhancers.'

'Say again?'

Bill was following and translated into Aussie.

'They fuck with your brain; you know, they create altered states of mind.'

'These compounds are found in certain plants and fungi.'

'Magic mushrooms?'

'Yes, in several mushrooms of the genus *Panaeolus*, but how does all that have anything to do with the Osireion?'

Bill had a thought that said perhaps a little more about his upbringing.

'Maybe the Osireion was a massive trip-out place, a crack house, an ancient hippie drug den. You know, the geometry and architecture mimic the internal process, that sort of thing. Only problem is, as far as I know, there are no mushrooms in Egypt.'

Pieter had the answer.

'I read somewhere about recent revelations concerning the psychotropic qualities of the Blue Lotus of Upper Egypt. It seems the active ingredient in the Blue Lotus is in the Tryptamine family of psychotropic alkaloids, which would explain the geometric link to the Osireion.'

I put all the pieces together.

'So the pharaohs were tripping out on Blue Lotus flowers so they could astral travel, even perform actual physical transportation. Of course, the normal mind would have to let go of its attachment to the body, to its concept of reality, for transportation to take place, but what better way to do it than getting stoned out of your mind.'

We all had a good chuckle as we turned our attentions back to the building itself.

The southwest end of the Osireion had a transverse chamber built of limestone, although this one was not only unearthed and missing its once-vaulted limestone roof, but growing a forest of reeds out of its water-covered floor. Apparently it had images of scenes from the "Book of the Dead" and 'mythical and astronomical scenes', but we certainly weren't going to be able to check them out.

Beyond that, a covered corridor led from the centre of the transverse chamber southwest out into an open pit. This was the first part of the Osireion discovered and unearthed by Flinders Petrie in 1903.

'It is believed to have been constructed by Seti I and decorated later by his grandson Merenptah.'

Given the walls were made of limestone, I personally didn't believe it was built by Seti at all, more likely by Montuhotep II; the decorations done by Merenptah, yes, there was clearly evidence to support that, but the walls built by Seti, no.

This section of the Osireion wasn't flooded, possibly because its floor was slightly higher, but more likely because it had been sealed off, so I started looking for a way to scale down the walls and get into the chambers and passages that opened to either side and check out the decorations.

'No, please, not permitted.'

The guardian had only escorted the ladies as far as the back door of the Seti temple, no doubt flattering them and haggling them for a little extra baksheesh along the way. Pernille had no cash, and Yuko was on a miser's budget, so, unless he smooth-talked Crystal, he would have come up empty-handed, which explained why he had returned to hover over us like an expectant vulture.

I gestured a little 'baksheesh' for him to look the other way, but that wasn't the issue, it was one of access; there had to be another, conventional, access point through one of the two side openings.

'The left hand side of the southwest wall of the pit is decorated with images of Osiris and Horus. In the centre are three registers with chapters 141-143 of the "Book of the Dead" dealing with the names of Osiris; the upper register is a list of deities, the two lower registers concern Osiris, his various epithets and identifications. To the right, Merenptah is represented at a large table of offerings.'

There was the proof Merenptah had done the decorations, but it didn't mean the wall was built in the same era, It would be like me scrawling my name on the Great Wall of China and then saying it was built in my lifetime because my name was on the wall. The 'experts' really needed to think more laterally.

The chamber to the left seemed small and undecorated, whilst the opening to the right appeared to be a long vaulted passage with a limestone roof, now a tunnel, which continued the decorations off into the distance and towards the direction of the Temple of Ramses II.

'Merenptah decorated the right wall of this hall with a complete version of the "Book of Gates" and the left wall with the "Book of Caverns".

I could make out a few of the images, but thankfully had a few more in my files.

'In the 11th hour of the "Book of Gates" the face of Ra is dragged in a boat to the left, while, on the right, the solar boat of Ra, with the cabin, surrounded by the protective snake, *mehen*, is accompanied by the Sia and Heka gods. In the register below is a file of oarsmen for the boat, preceded by the hours' goddesses.

In the long passageway is a scene of the 12th hour in the Book of Gates; a carving of the god, Nun, lifting up the Solar Barque of Ra, represented as Khepri (the rising sun) surrounded by Isis and Nepthys.'

The ancient Egyptians believed that Nun was the primordial waters from which all creation took place, so maybe it was because of this image that the modern Egyptologists concluded the Osireion had something to do with a primordial mound?

'The Egyptians observed that the scarab beetle pushed along a ball of dung, in which it had laid its eggs, and buried it in the sand. From this ball, seemingly by spontaneous generation, emerged baby beetles. Khepri, which means "to become," thus became a potent symbol of rebirth and regeneration.'

The ancient Egyptians were on the right track; regeneration, yes, rebirth, technically no, although it was sort of spiritual rebirthing. But then, to a floundering human race trying to understand their own mortality, the concept of the gods regenerating their bodies would have been incomprehensible, and thus the concept of 'rebirth' would have gained prominence and ultimately legitimacy. It also explained why the modern closed-minded scholars had such difficulty in seeing so much of the obvious evidence that existed at the sites of the ancient temples.

For example, why build a long tunnel when you could build a simple short staircase? Unless the 'tunnel' was not so much a tunnel as a passage, built when the level of the sand was much lower, like perhaps after the first tsunami, the one that left the twenty-six feet of silt, a tsunami millennia *before* the Thera eruption. Hence the need to dig out a part of the sediment, to reconnect the Osireion to some other important structure in the direction of the Ramses II site. The *subsequent* fifteen feet of silt deposited would have been after that time, and that sedimentary layer was probably caused by the Thera eruption and tsunami.

The long passageway was like an arrow of destiny, pointing me into the unknown. It seemed a little symbolic of my whole trip; I thought I knew where I was, but with each step I realized I'd really been in the dark.

Ahead, something was drawing me onwards, a light, an idea, a vision, I really didn't know what it was, but, like a moth to a candle, I couldn't resist. I knew the Temple of Ramses II was in that direction, and knew Ramses II had a habit of building on top of previous temples and sacred sites, so, it was time for me to head out into the unknown and see what lay at the end of the passage.

The light at the end of the tunnel

'No, please, desert.'

The guardian was trying to stop us from following the track that had been cut out of the sedimentary layers above, and which concealed, the passage. I pointed off in the distance.

'Ramses temple.'
'Closed.'

I gestured the universal negotiator.
'Baksheesh?'

Suddenly his face lit up and he looked around to check he was alone.
'Yes, come.'

If this was the way all of Egypt was run, including the present and past governments and the military, then it was no wonder the place was politically such a mess. Money talked, and now it was saying, 'Lead on, Macduff.'.

We followed the guardian as he trekked along the sedimentary 'cliffs' that had been created by Flinders Petrie's excavations, wary not to walk over the actual roofing of the passage on the off chance it may collapse. Bill was almost as excited as I was.

'Well, Alex, here's more evidence for you, right before everyone's eyes.'

'I know, and it's been here for over a hundred years, and yet no one has taken any notice of it; they all walked passed it believing its just layers of sediment from annual floods.'

'Well, as a geologist, I can tell you uncategorically that these sorts of deposits are inconsistent with that conclusion.'

It was good to hear Bill's confirmation, but it didn't answer *all* the questions.

'Do you think we're being just as blind about Jesus and Caesarion?'

'Probably, but that's the point isn't it; how can you see it, if you have been blinded by years of deception, lies and conditioning?'

'You need to take a new perspective.'

'How?'

'To shift your perspective, first you have to let go of the one you are holding on to; completely let go, no frames of reference, no belief structures, nothing.'

'I'm afraid, Alex, that's easier said than done. Look at how vehemently people will defend their beliefs, even if they're shown they're beliefs are based on lies; the Christians, the Muslims, the Jews, they all *say* they see the others' perspective, but in the end they don't, they just play lip-service and then continue to say the other religions are all wrong. Then they go to war with one another, not only to defend their beliefs, but more importantly, to impose and enforce them on any non-believers.'

'Sometimes I think it would be easier if we just dropped in from another planet?'

Bill let out a chuckle.

'Exactly, but you'd still probably have a galactic perspective that humans have it all wrong.'

'Well, looking around at what's happening on earth, I would think I might have hit the nail smack-bang dead-centre on the head.'

'I'm sure billions would find some reason or other to beg to differ.'

'Which leaves us right back where we started.'

'Catch 22.'

We'd reached the remnants of a mud-brick wall that would have formed an enclosure around the complex. It was nowhere near as big as the one at el-Kab or Dendera, and it too had felt the destructive forces of nature; most of it now washed away or buried beneath the shifting sands.

The guardian steered us around it, out into desert, and I started thinking about the journey of Jesus out into the desert for forty days, supposedly to face the devil. Was Jesus really just taking time-out to face his own inner demons, isn't that what he was really doing, especially if he *was* Caesarion and had the option to stake his claim as ruler of most of the known civilized world? It shifted my perspective.

'Hey Bill, what about if, instead of coming from the position of wanting proof about Jesus being Caesarion, and looking for ways to disprove the evidence, right or wrong, we came from the perspective that Jesus *was* Caesarion, and looked for evidence to *support* it?'

'OK, go on.'

'You know Nostradamus wrote about it in one of his quatrains.'

Pieter had caught us both unawares.

'Nostradamus? The dude from the 16th Century who had all the prophecies?'

'Yes, he prophesised that Cleopatra would "be in danger in her eighteenth year, and would be unable to live beyond her thirty-sixth year". Cleopatra was named queen of Egypt at the age of eighteen and committed suicide at the age of thirty-six.'

I wasn't sure where Pieter was heading.

'True, but it's not really prophesy though; Nostradamus was writing, what, nearly sixteen hundred years *after* the time of Cleopatra; he could have read about it.'

'He also wrote she would have three males, and one female, and that two of these would not have the same father.'

'Again, that fits, but again, it's *after* the event. Besides, it doesn't link Caesarion to Jesus.'

'Nostradamus goes on to say that "there will be great differences between the three brothers, but then such great cooperation between them that three quarters of Europe will tremble. That the youngest will continue and expand the Christian religion, and under him sects will be elevated, and suddenly cast down, that Arabs will be driven back, kingdoms united, and new laws promulgated".'

'OK, that sounds more like the religious kafuffle caused by Jesus, it even indicates that it was Joseph, Ptolemy Philadelphus, who was the person we would think of as Peter, or perhaps even Paul, the one responsible for the origins of the Christian faith, but again, it's all *after* the event and hardly prophesy.'

Thankfully, Bill was seeing it from a different perspective.

'I think that's Pieter's point actually; that Nostradamus was writing *after* the event is, in effect, confirmation of the event.'

'Yes, exactly.'

I was a little slow on the uptake.

'Which means?'

'That maybe it's not meant to be a prophecy at all.'

Slow on the uptake, I was positively comatose.

'What do you mean?'

Like a bloodhound after an escaped convict, Bill was closing in on something

'Nostradamus was no fool, if he found out the true story of Jesus, he would hardly have broadcast it to the world; if he did he would've been burned at the stake as a heretic. So maybe he encoded the information deliberately in future tense.'

'OK, I get it, that sounds totally plausible. So let's assume Caesarion went to India in the guardianship of his wet-nurse, her husband who was possibly a carpenter, and their children. His foster parents changed his name to protect his identity, probably changed ALL their names. They fled via Ethiopia, overseas to Sri Lanka, and then, at some time when he was of age, Caesarion left his family in search of the meaning of life, eventually finding his way to the monasteries in India and Nepal and consequently spending years studying the ancient Vedic teachings.

Then, as a man raised to be the pharaoh of Egypt and heir to the Roman empire, when he saw and understood the injustices of the class system in India, he took it upon himself to speak out, to challenge the views of the Brahmins and Kshatriyas, which eventually forced him to flee to save his life and keep his philosophy alive.'

Bill was totally with me, and pushed me for solutions.

'So, what would you do if you were him?

'A good question; I certainly wouldn't give up. By then Jesus was a man on a mission, that's for sure, but I don't think it was so much 'God's' mission, as a personal calling to make the world a better place for everyone.'

'Do you think he intended to use his position and influence as the rightful heir to the thrones of Egypt and Rome?'

'No, the opposite, he wanted all men *and women* to be equal.'

'So, where would you go?'

'I guess I'd take my teachings somewhere else, somewhere it was most needed.'

'The hotbed of Jerusalem?'

'Jerusalem, exactly, I think he would have known about the injustices of the Roman Empire and the Jewish religions, in fact the Pharisees and Sadducees probably reflected the circumstances he found himself with the Brahmins and Kshatriyas.'

'What about the disciples? If the texts say four of them were his brothers, most likely two 'step' brothers, Simon and Judas, and two half-brothers, James and Joseph, who would have had to have been Alexander and Ptolemy Philadelphus, but there's still the question of how Jesus reconnected to his blood siblings.

I can understand him returning from Nepal to India or Sri Lanka, or wherever his foster parents and 'family' where, and influencing them to follow him. After all, he was not only the legal heir to two kingdoms, but now had the profound knowledge of the Vedas, and was a powerful teacher. But how, and more importantly why, did he seek out and reconnect with Alexander and Ptolemy? After all, they had all been taken to Italy and raised by Marc Antony's wife, Octavia.'

'Caesarion wouldn't have known that, unless he learned of it later. And by the time Jesus was ready to return to claim his throne, he wouldn't have known where to find them.'

Yuko had started all this, perhaps Pieter knew more answers.

'Hey, Pieter, you seem pretty clued up on Caesarion being Jesus, do you know what happened to his siblings after they were taken to Italy and raised by Octavia?'

'The only mention of Alexander Helios and Ptolemy Philadelphus comes from Cassius Dio, who states that when their sister, Cleopatra Selene II, was married off by Augustus to King Juba II of Numidia, Augustus spared the lives of the two brothers as a favour to the couple.

After that, there is no mention of them in any military service, political career, involvement in scandals, nothing. So it's believed they died, because if they had survived to adulthood, there would have been some mention of them.'

I was right onto it.

'Unless they went with Selene to Mauretania. Let's see, Selene was how old when her mother committed suicide?

'Ten.'

Bill jumped on board.

'Which means Ptolemy was only five.'

'And how old was she when she was married off?

'Probably around fourteen.'

'Meaning Ptolemy was only nine. So, in the absence of her mother, Selene would have felt she needed to look after her brothers, and probably insisted they go with her. In fact, if Selene was anything like her mother, she probably seduced Octavian into letting them go.'

'A regular Salome.'

'It would explain why there were no more mentions of them in Roman documents, they weren't there.'

'OK, but it makes no sense why Jesus would travel all the way to the kingdom of Mauretania, modern-day Libya, to find a couple of teenagers who were his half-brothers.'

And then it hit me.

'I don't think the brothers were the draw-card at all; I think it was Selene.'

'Why?'

'She was the *sang réal*, the *only living sang réal*, and Caesarion knew that; he was seeking out his half-sister, to marry her.'

We all stopped and looked at each other, even the guardian, by the look on his face, felt something profound had just happened. Bill was the first to speak.

'Alex, do you know what you're saying?'

I felt quite proud of myself as I rolled it all off.

'Sure, Jesus, Caesarion, married his half-sister, Cleopatra Selene II, because she was the *sang réal*, and then she, along with her two brothers, Alexander Helios and Ptolemy Philadelphus, left Mauretania and travelled to Jerusalem, or rather Qumran, where they formed the basis of the Essenes.'

'Alex, you just said that Cleopatra Selene II was Mary Magdalene.'

'I did? … Whoaaa!'

There was a long pregnant pause as we all contemplated the implications of what we'd just stumbled across. It was the guardian who finally snapped us out of it.

'Come, temple, here, yes.'

Ahead, the rear section of the ruins appeared out of the dunes. The temple wasn't very impressive at all, that was for sure, in fact, if the guardian hadn't pointed it out, I'm sure we would have wandered past thinking the walls belonged to a private compound or the foundations of some new local construction.

For the most part, the height of the original walls was only about two metres or less, and barely reached four metres towards the rear. It looked like it had suffered the same fate as most of the other temples in having the upper parts swept away then been restored with either mud-brick or concrete.

And, for me, that was the telltale giveaway sign, the fact the whole wall *wasn't* mud-brick. It drew my attention directly to the lower parts, which not only showed the evidence of reliefs, but that the bottom parts appeared to be constructed from alabaster.

That meant one of two thing; either Ramses II had built yet another of his temples on the site of a previous Middle Kingdom temple, or, he had nicked the alabaster from the temple of his father, Seti I, just down the road. Or maybe it was a bit of both. Given the poor state of the stone, my money was on the latter, that he nicked it. It would certainly explain the missing sections in Seti's temple that had been replaced with sandstone. Maybe my notes had some clues.

'On the edge of the desert, just west of the village of Beni Mansur, the Temple of Ramses II, is smaller than that of his father, Seti I, measuring about seventy metres long and forty wide. Varying in design, and mostly dedicated to Osiris, but containing numerous chapels dedicated to different gods, it is now in ruin, though as recently as Napoleon's time it was reported the temple was almost intact.'

If that were true, then it meant the temple was the victim of a different sort of flood, a flood of local pilferers who scavenged the limestone blocks of the temple to build their own houses.

'On the southern, or rear wall, is the lower part of a calendar of feasts, with a list of offerings. Beneath this, Ramses II describes his temple; a pylon of white limestone, granite doorways and a sanctuary of pure alabaster.'

All that sounded very interesting, but, as we skirted along the eastern wall, emblazoned with reliefs of, you guessed it, Ramses II and his victories at the Battle of Kadesh, and on towards the main entrance, I was more interested in the recent topic of Queen Cleopatra Selene of Mauretania. Truth is, I was pontificating out loud hoping my ravings might trigger some flash of brilliance from Pieter or Bill.

'So Cleopatra Selene II married her half-brother, Caesarion, who was Jesus. That means Cleopatra Selene II was Mary Magdalene, and since we know Crystal was Cleopatra Selene II, that means that Crystal is the reincarnation of Mary Magdalene.'

That amused Bill no end.

'I wonder if she knows?'

Pieter wasn't so convinced.

'Except that Cleopatra Selene II died, and is entombed in the Royal Mausoleum in Mauretania?'

That threw a spanner in the works.

'How did she die, and when?'

'I'm not sure.'

I dived into my iphone and pulled up the files on the Ptolemaic period, particularly Cleopatra. That was the joy of technology; in the months leading up to the trip I'd managed to compile and download on my laptop almost every file on every pharaoh from Menes to Hadrian, and every place from Alexandria to Abu Simbel; I hadn't read most of them mind you, but I'd copied them over to my iphone so I could access them at any time during the visits to the temples, and what a bonus they'd been so far. Once again, I had them at my fingertips.

After a bit of searching, and scrolling through a few paragraphs, eventually I hit pay dirt.

'It seems there's actually a bit of controversy about Cleopatra Selene's exact date of death.'

'A hoard of coins with her head on them was discovered, dated 17 AD, and it's traditionally been believed Cleopatra was alive at the time.'

Bill had it sorted.

'It makes sense to me; if Jesus was seventeen, then Selene was ten when she was taken to Italy. It's only four years later that she was married off to Juba, and they probably commemorated the marriage and her coronation by minting a few coins.

There's only a discrepancy of four years, so I don't see that as such a big problem, but, if Caesarion spent twelve years in the east studying the Vedas, and was back in Jerusalem at the age of twenty-nine, with Selene on his arm, then she would still have had to have been alive around 25-29 AD.'

'But what if she didn't die, what if she just disappeared?'

'What do you mean?'

'What if, just like when she and the boys left Rome and nothing was written about them again, what if they all left Mauretania, nothing was written about them again, and the modern historians have just presumed they died?'

Pieter had another spanner.

'Except that there's an inscription on the mausoleum dedicated to Juba and Cleopatra, it's just a fragment, but it refers to them as the *King and Queen of Mauretania.*

I scanned the file;

'Pieter's right. Listen to this. *"In Mauretania, Cleopatra Selene was called, "The Roman Woman", and the mausoleum is called, "The tomb of the Christian woman"."* So I guess that means the whole theory about Selene being Mary Magdalene is out the window.'

Bill wasn't so quick to give up the ghost.

'Wait a minute, Christianity wasn't even established then.'

'So the inscription must be a later one. Wait, there's more. It goes on to say, *"It can also be translated as, "the tomb of the Feminine Christ"."*

'The plot thickens.'

Rounding the corner, we arrived at a sandy field strewn with shards of pottery; supposedly the first courtyard of the temple. The First Pylon, supposedly once made of polished limestone was nowhere to be seen, nor were the outer walls, or any walls of the courtyard itself, no doubt all harvested to construct homes for the locals. Just off to the side, were the scant remains of a small chapel; basically there was nothing to write home about, not even send an SMS.

The guardian beckoned us towards the temple gates, which were erected in the doorway of the second pylon, which was basically a mish-mash of stones, about four metres high, made out of temple blocks interspersed with concrete, with the top third comprising an extension of mud-bricks. They were nowhere near as impressive as the pylons at Edfu or Karnak.

On the left pylon was a strip of reliefs supposedly representing a list of the eighteen African tribes that Ramses II had 'subdued', from Kush through to Punt.

The state of the pylon had me second-guessing the cause of its demise, because, if it *was* as a result of pilfering by the locals, then surely the dismantling would have started from the top down, and that meant leaving lower sections in place in preference to taking more top stones made no sense. I was back with my tsunami theory, one some time post the era of Ramses II.

Like many of the other temples, the gateway comprised massive blocks of pink granite. Bill raised an eyebrow and flicked his head.
'More granite.'

High on the left upright, Ramses II made offerings of wine to Osiris, whilst, below that, Thoth was seated upon a throne, writing, followed by Iri, the "sight" god. Below that were texts referring to Ramses II and Merenptah. What surprised me a little was the blank rock below the inscriptions; I couldn't believe Ramses II would leave any space free where he had the option of promoting himself.

The damage to the right pylon meant that only fragmentary reliefs remained, but it was the damage itself that drew my attention; it was inconsistent with the granite being 'harvested' and more in keeping with it having been pummelled by other stones tumbling past in the wake of a surging tsunami. Never-the-less, the guardian unlocked the gate and invited us to enter, and, like rolling stones, we tumbled into the inner courtyard.

The second courtyard wasn't in much better state than the outer walls. The remains of a colonnade of sandstone Osirid pillars on its north, east and south sides ran around the perimeter of the courtyard, with the statues of the pharaoh all lacking at least their heads and shoulders. It looked like Darth Vader had come through with a massive light-sabre and cut them all in half with one almighty swish.

Various granite troughs had been lined up on the ground to make a sort of path leading into the temple. Most notable was the alabaster ground. Was this bedrock, or part of an earlier temple?

The walls of the courtyard had faired even worse than the pillars, but again it reinforced my thinking that the blocks weren't pilfered. How could I be so sure? Simple.

Let's say the walls were complete, and that you wanted to remove the blocks. You had two options, knock the wall over completely, which would possibly damage the blocks, or remove them one at a time. The second option was the more logical one, which meant you had to remove them from the top first. The top stones would be the hardest to remove, obviously, with it becoming easier as you moved down the wall. So, why are *all* the top parts of the walls missing and the bottom blocks, the easiest to remove, all still in place?

To the left, on the eastern and southern walls, there was a decorated bull, preceded by servants carrying loaves of bread, cakes, an antelope, various birds and fruit, as well as a gazelle, beer, wine, all being brought for sacrifice.

I had other 'sacrifices' on my mind.
'So, if Jesus is in a tomb in Kashmir, where is Mary Magdalene buried?'

'The official Church version is that she was buried in Ephesus in Turkey.'

'Wait a minute, Ephesus, isn't that where Arsinoe, Cleopatra's sister and Selene's aunt, was killed and entombed?'

'Yes, it is. More than just a synchronicity, hey?'

'Is the Pope a Catholic?'

'Does a bear shit in the woods?'

'Are the Kennedy's gun shy?'

After exchanging quips, Bill focused on the details.

'There's a myth that tells how, after the resurrection, Mary Magdalene visited the Emperor Tiberius in Rome, telling him about "Christ's Resurrection", apparently using an egg as a symbol of the Resurrection, a symbol of new life. With the words "Christ is Risen", she told Tiberius that, in his Province of Judea, Jesus the Nazarene, a holy man, a maker of miracles, powerful before God and all mankind, was executed on the instigation of the Jewish High-Priests, with the sentence affirmed by the procurator, Pontius Pilate.

Tiberius supposedly responded that no one could rise from the dead, anymore than the egg she held could turn red. Miraculously, the egg instantaneously began to turn red as if as testimony to her words, and then, through her urging, Tiberius had Pilate removed from Jerusalem to Gaul, where he later suffered a horrible sickness and agonizing death.

In the meantime, Jesus and Mary Magdalene, using aliases, lived in Rome from 41 AD until 54 AD, filling powerful positions under the emperor Tiberius Claudius, and were responsible for many innovations that improved the lives of Rome's poorest and most vulnerable citizens.'

'Are you serious? There's evidence of all this?'

'It depends what you call evidence. There's "evidence", and then there's how you choose to interpret it.'

'Just like the modern Egyptologists who see a block of worn granite, evidence right under their noses, and can't for the life of them see it's thousands of years older than the sandstone right beside it.'

We crossed over to the northern wall of the courtyard that consisted of reliefs of a procession of animals arriving before four priests. The first priest seemed to be in charge of recording the offerings, the second priest offering incense as thanks before the procession, the third appearing to be the High Priest in charge of the temple, and the fourth yet another scribe of the temple. The procession was followed by scenes of pieces of beef for the sacrifice, soldiers and captives.

I guess it's because of the ancient Egyptian's attention to detail that we have the records we have. It's a pity most of the modern Egyptologists weren't so attentive. As interesting as the reliefs were, they didn't distract me from the topic of conversation.

'So, is Mary buried in Rome?'

'No, well, perhaps, but probably not. There are certain documents by Gregory of Tours, in the late 6th Century, supporting the Byzantium account that Mary Magdalene moved from Rome to Ephesus, where she lived for many years with Jesus's mother, Mary, and the holy Apostle John, whom with she unceasingly laboured to write the first twenty chapters of the Gospel of John. She apparently died there and was buried in Ephesus.'

'Alongside her aunt perhaps, in the Tomb of Ephesus?'

'Perhaps, but they recently only found one skeleton there, and it was of a young girl, most likely Arsinoe IV. But that doesn't mean Mary wasn't originally interred there though. In 899 AD, part of Mary's remains were supposedly transferred

102

from Ephesus to the monastery Church of St Lazarus in Constantinople by Emperor Leo VI, and then, some time after the final Crusade, were moved again, this time to Italy where they were buried beneath the altar of the Lateran Cathedral in Rome.'

'So, she's in Rome.'

'Who knows? There's another tale that says just before she died, Mary was miraculously transported to the chapel of St. Maximin, where she received the last sacraments and died when she was seventy-two. And that's where most of the more modern evidence seems to suggest, that the strongest contender in the burial-probability-stakes comes from Provence in France, where there's a veritable 'Mary Magdalene industry' revolving around other documentation that places at least part of her remains beneath the St Maximum's Basilica near Marseilles.'

'How does that figure?'

'The Byzantine account of Gregory is contradicted somewhat by a legend dating back to 1200 AD, apparently based on a Latin document dating from the 5th to 6th Century, which supposedly refers to an even earlier record, claiming, that fourteen years after the ascension of Jesus, during the persecution of the Christians, Mary Magdalene, along with Mary, mother of James, Lazarus and his other sister, Martha, and several of the seventy-two new disciples who had received baptism, including Maximin, were driven out of Jerusalem by the Jews and set adrift in a small vessel without sails, oars, or rudder.'

'Do you think Martha and Lazarus were the children of Mary and Joseph, Mary Magdalene's step sister and step brother?'

'It would fit in with everything else.'

At the back of the courtyard to the south-western side of the temple, a shallow set of ramp-like stairs, just like the ones I had seen in many of the other temples, led up to the remains of a raised portico with pillars, two narrow chapels to either side, and a magnificent highly polished black granite gateway, five metres tall, in the centre. We headed towards it.

'So the whole family was set adrift on the ocean, just for their religious beliefs?'

'That's quite tame compared to the usual burning at the stake or draw-and-quartering. However, guided by Providence, they safely made their way across the sea and came ashore in a port near Marseilles, in France.

Mary Magdalene then supposedly travelled to Aix-le-Provence with Maximin and they lived there for many years where, in keeping with the mission that Jesus entrusted to Mary Magdalene and the apostles, she and Maximin preached the gospel to the Gauls, before she died at the age of 60 in Aix around the year 75 AD. Maximin supposedly embalmed her body and placed it in a crypt of his chapel in Villalata, later renamed St. Maximin.'

'Embalmed, that's rather a strange way to deal with her body, *unless*, of course, you were familiar with the ancient Egyptian embalming rituals and that Mary was a member of the Egyptian royalty.'

'Exactly.'

I was trying to put the pieces together.

'You think Maximin could have been a member of the Tat Brotherhood?'

'It's a possibility.'

'Then all they need to do is take DNA samples from whoever is in the tomb at Srinagar and who ever is entombed at St.Maxims and compare them.'

'She may not be there.'

'What do you mean?'

'Sometime between the 3rd and 4th Centuries, Mary's body was apparently placed in a magnificent white marble tomb, and had a Basilica built over it to honour and protect it. And there it remained until the Saracen invasion in the year 710 AD, when the Cassian Monks, who had founded their Monastery in St. Maximin in 415 AD and were the guardians of Mary Magdalene's remains, fearing they would be discovered and destroyed, for safety reasons transferred them to a more modest tomb.

Before fleeing, the monks completely buried the tomb and their chapel, and, though many searches were made, by the time the invaders left in 973 AD, nothing could be found of the tomb. Three-hundred years later, on December 9, 1279, Charles, the nephew of King Louis IX of France, finally uncovered the remains of Mary Magdalene and transferred them back to the crypt at St. Maximins on May 5, 1280.'

'So they're there.'

'Not necessarily; rumour has it that, years later, a monk of the Vezelay monastery reputedly found a crypt at the Basilica of St Maximin's in Provence with reference to the Magdalene chiselled into the stone, and that part of the remains were taken to the French monastery of Vezelay in Burgundy which carried Mary Magdalene's name.

Then there's the argument that Mary Magdalene's remains were buried, along with secret documents, on Temple Mount in Jerusalem, and were found when the city was conquered during the First Crusade.'

'What, along with all the other documents that are now under the Rosslyn chapel in Scotland?'

'Maybe that's what they're referring to, that some body was found with the documents.'

'I think they're just confusing the bodies of the Templar Knights at Rosslyn with Mary?'

'It does seem more likely.'

'So was she buried on Temple Mount in Jerusalem, and her remains moved to the west when the crusaders took Jerusalem, is she buried under the Basilica of St Maximin, or are some of her bones hidden in a crypt at Vezelay?...'

And then I had a brainwave.

'...Or, are her remains deliberately buried in more than one place?'

'What do you mean?'

'Well, maybe the Romans, the Catholics, or the Jews, the Illuminati, or even the Tat Brotherhood, knew about the story of Osiris, and if Selene, Mary Magdalene, *was* the *sang réal* and they knew that, then they may have dismembered her body deliberately and scattered the parts all over Europe on purpose.'

Pieter had been mutely listening, but finally he spoke out.

'Why would they do that?'

I wasn't sure, but Bill had it sorted.

'To keep Mary Magdalene well away from "Western Europe" and any theories about the bloodline of Jesus.'

'The *sang réal*?'

'Yes.'

Having made our way up the ramp, we headed to the furthest chapel to the right, dedicated to Ramses II and Osiris. On either side of the door was the pharaoh, wearing, on the left, the white crown of Upper Egypt and, on the right, the red crown of Lower Egypt, inviting visitors to enter. A ridiculous concrete lintel had been put over the doorway. Inside, on the walls, were faded, but exquisitely carved reliefs, including Ramses II on a barque, drinking directly from the teat of the divine cow, Hathor, and, at the front of the barque, on a stand, a sphinx covered by the sun disc with two Osiris feathers on its head, crushing a cobra. Before the barque, Ramses II made a huge pile of offerings to Hathor.

Next along was the chapel to the nine gods of the Ennead. On the north wall of the chapel, Thoth stood before Ramses II on his sacred barque; Ramses seated on his throne, accompanied by a headless goddess, probably Isis, standing behind him. Below the scene, was the beginning of the Litany of the Sun.

We paused briefly at the central five-metre-high gateway at the rear of the portico that led into a hypostyle hall. Only the lower parts of the doorjamb survived, made from highly polished black granite, the rest reconstructed from black concrete. The original pieces were decorated with scenes and inscriptions including, on the right, two scenes of the pharaoh making offerings, and below, on the left, a relief of Thoth probably accompanied by Iri. The image of Thoth triggered a remembrance of other books.

'Hey, Bill, have you read *"The Da Vinci Code"*?'

'By Dan Brown? Sure, who hasn't?'

'Well, me actually, but I have seen the movie. Anyway, doesn't Brown suggest that Da Vinci was a member of some ancient secret society?'

'The "Priory of Sion".'

'That's them: do you think they could have been the Tat Brotherhood?'

'It's possible, they were dedicated to preserving the "truths"; that Jesus and Mary were married and had children, that Jesus nominated Mary Magdalene as his successor, that his message was about celebrating the "sacred feminine", and that the Holy Grail is really Mary Magdalene herself, the "sacred feminine", the "vessel" who carried Jesus' children.'

'The *sang réal*.'

'Yes....'

I followed Bill as he continued his musings, moving on to the two chapels to the left.

'...Interestingly enough, Brown also suggested Mary Magdalene was of royal blood, and that she was Jesus' wife, though Brown proposed she was a descendant of the tribe of Benjamin.'

'The tribe of Benjamin; never heard of them?'

'They're one of the twelve lost tribes of Israel; the one that included King Saul and King David.'

That didn't seem an obstacle to me.

'Couldn't that mean Saul and David could possibly be descended from the Hyksos rulers who invaded Egypt and included Joseph/Moses?'

'I've never thought of that.'

'I wonder if anyone else has; it seems pretty logical.'

'I guess it's possible. Anyway, according to Brown, after the crucifixion, Jesus intended that Mary be the head of his Church, after all she was the celebration of the sacred feminine, but Peter had different ideas and wrested power from her. So, Mary, pregnant with Jesus' child, moved to France. Meanwhile Peter suppressed all the evidence of Jesus' real intentions and set in motion a conspiracy that has demonised Mary Magdalene for around two-thousand years.'

'The Roman Catholic Church.'

'None other.'

We walked to the left, past the bare foundations of the portico wall, and examined the two small chapels, once again decorated with images of Ramses II flanking the doorways, and respectively dedicated to Seti I and the pharaoh's deified ancestors.

The outermost chapel was dedicated to Osiris, and Ramses II's father, Seti I; perhaps in deference to the fact Ramses II had nicked most of the alabaster from Seti's temple down the road. Who knows, the walls may have already had Seti's images on them before Ramses moved them.

That concept was reinforced inside, on the left wall, with a relief of a barque offered by Ramses II in the name of Seti I. At the far end of the chapel, the pharaoh stood before a seated god, given the blue skin, probably Osiris. Only the legs of the pharaoh survived but it was reasonable to assume, given the reliefs in all the other temples and chapels, that it was Seti I and that he was making offerings to Osiris.

The inner of the two left chapels was apparently a shrine of the ancestors and once contained a table of kings, the 'Second Abydos List', on its northern wall, part of which was now in the British Museum.

'Though here it was originally in four registers rather than three, the list mimics the one in the Temple of Seti I, in that it omits the pharaohs of the Amarna period.'

The Brits, senseless bastards that they were, hadn't just 'removed' a part of the wall, in souveniring their prize, they'd smashed it to pieces. Why couldn't they have left it where it was, in one piece, and just taken a few photos, or done a pencil rubbing or something?

It reminded me of World War II, when the Brits mindlessly bombed Dresden, one of the artistic capitals of the world.

Then I suddenly had a thought. Winston Churchill was a Freemason, and more than likely a member of the Illuminati. Did the Illuminati conspire to steal all the great arts works of Dresden and cover it up by obliterating the city, making people believe the art works were lost for all time? Or did they fire-bomb Dresden to prevent them falling into the hands of the Russians who were rapidly advancing on the eastern front?

It was early 1945, the Germans were retreating on all fronts and the end of the war was not that far away, and yet, over three days in February 1945, the RAF and US Army Airforce, dropped nearly four thousand tons of high-explosive bombs and incendiary devices on Dresden, a city filled with museums and historic buildings.

The resulting firestorm destroyed almost forty square kilometres of the city centre, with an estimated death toll of somewhere between twenty-two thousand and twenty-five thousand innocent civilians. And yet, amazingly, the entire art collection had 'fortuitously' been previously evacuated. Was there a secret hidden agenda to almost everything that involved the government? It sure looked that way.

We were about halfway through exploring the temple and, the more I examined it, the more I was convinced that Ramses II had taken limestone/alabaster sections from his father's temple, reconstructed them to form parts of his own temple, then rebuilt sections of his father's temple with sandstone. Perhaps more clues and surprises awaited within?

Pieter had been pretty quiet so far, acting more often than not like a fervid and febrile Chinese tourist snapping one seemingly meaningless photo after another. Although he was listening intently, apart from the occasional aside, he left most of the theological discussion and debate to Bill and me, perhaps because it wasn't his area of expertise. However, somehow I knew it was the calm before the storm and that at any minute I half expected him to erupt like a dormant Professor with some new stream of profound knowledge.

It was Pieter who led the way through a small doorway from the ancestors' chapel into the adjacent hypostyle hall, known as the Hall of Appearances. Like the rest of the temple before it, the top part was missing.

A number of scenes were depicted on the northwest and southern walls, and, overall, they were similar to those in the previous portico and courtyard. They included; scenes of the pharaoh making offerings to Osiris, heading a procession, carrying the cult symbol of Abydos into the temple, and being crowned.

The only discernable difference was, that here in the hypostyle hall, a brightly coloured frieze, depicting the Nile gods as feminine divinities, with the names of the cities they represented on stands before them, ran around the lower part of the walls below the main represented scenes.

'Painted in different colours; red represents the Nile at inundation, blue represents winter, and green, summer.'

Of course it could have meant something else; the red could have represented the sun, or the desert, the blue been water, and the green, the land, or plants, or fertile sections of the Nile, or the whole thing could even just have been a simple pattern that looked nice.

But, who was I to contradict the 'experts'; I was just an uneducated, letter-less, title-less pleb. Clearly my brain was just a water-logged amorphous and vacuous mass that prevented my skull from spontaneously imploding or precluded sounds from pin-balling around in the void created by the very existence of my cranium.

Also in the hall were the remains of eight rectangular pillars, which collectively would have once supported the roof, each pillar containing reliefs of people kneeling in worship. The implication from these reliefs was clearly that ordinary folk were permitted to enter into this first hypostyle hall, with the reliefs acting like signs, or instructions, for the uninitiated – 'Hey, Philistine, this is where you get down on your knees, hand over your offerings, and worship me, Ramses II, as if I were a god.'

No doubt the masses dutifully obeyed.

At the western end of the hall's south wall were the remaining twelve steps of a narrow staircase that ascended to either an upper chamber, or what would have been the roof. To the east, taking up a position directly opposite the staircase, was yet another small chapel, though there was nothing additional of any significance to note.

We moved on and entered the second Hypostyle hall, similarly with eight sandstone pillars, and having three chapels off each of the north, west, and south sides. Suddenly Pieter posed a question.

'I've been thinking about Mary Magdalene and her possible connection to Cleopatra Selene. What if her name was made up to cover up who she really was, like a code to tell you enough about her to work out who she was, but only if you knew the code, just like Caesarion was called Jesus because 'Jesus' means teacher?'

'Go on.'

Pieter shrugged his shoulders.

'That's as far as I've got; what I do know is that in Aramaic, "Magdala" means "great" or "magnificent".'

'So she was Mary the Great.'

Bill laughed.

'I hardly think they would have called her Mary unless it referred to something.'

I already had my iphone out, and though I didn't have a file on Mary Magdalene, I logged online and started searching for a definition. It didn't take long.

'Mary Magdalene: Yes, "Magdala" means "Great" or "Magnificent", and it seems Mary, hey, get this, Mary is a derivation from "Mauro", as is Mauretania, "mauro" meaning *black*, or *dark-skinned*, like in the Moors, and obviously *Mauretania* means 'the place of the blacks.'

'So *Mauro Magdala,* literally means *black greatest.*'

'Which means Mary Magdalene was really Mohammed Ali, Heavyweight Champion of the World; floats like a butterfly, stings like a bee.'

I danced around on the spot; shadow boxing, much to the bewilderment of our guide.

'Actually, Alex, it's probably more likely to mean, "The Great Queen with black skin".'

'Oprah Winfrey?'

Unperturbed by my clownish acts of spontaneous idiocy, Pieter was juggling the pieces.

'But Cleopatra Selene wasn't black, she was the product of Roman and mainly Greek genes; if anything she would have been "Mediterranean".'

I stopped my extraneous antics, preferring verbal quips.

'Perhaps she had a good suntan?'

Thankfully Bill brought some sanity to proceedings.

'Maybe it just meant "Great Queen *from* the land of the blacks", *from* the land of Mauretania.'

'That fits perfectly.'

We briefly explored the chapels to the left, or south-eastern side, which were probably dedicated to the gods of Thebes; Amun-Ra, Mut, and Khonsu, but they were very badly damaged. Opening from the third chapel, in the rear corner of the western and northern walls, was a chamber most likely used as a storage room for statues as it contained nine decorated niches plus a beautiful relief of Ramses II offering to Osiris who is being protected by, of all things, an unusual winged, humanoid, djed pillar.

Bill and I may have had it sorted, but Pieter still saw the loose ends.

'But what about the tomb?'

I quickly mulled it over.

'The way I see it, there's two options. One, the body in the tomb is Cleopatra Selene, but she's not Mary Magdalene, which means we're barking completely up the wrong tree, or, two, the body in the tomb is Cleopatra Selene, and she *is* Mary Magdalene, and she was interred there, or part of her at least, many years after she died.'

Initially that seemed to appease Bill....

'It would account for both titles "The tomb of the Christian woman", and "the tomb of the Feminine Christ"...'

...however it didn't completely satisfy his thinking.

'...but actually there's a third option.'

'There is? What?'

'That the body in the tomb is *not* Cleopatra Selene.'

That threw Pieter a curve ball.

'If the body in the tomb is not Cleopatra Selene, then who could it be?'

Deep in thought, we meandered across to the north-western side of the second hypostyle hall, to the chapels on the right, which were dedicated to the Gods of Abydos; Thoth, Min and Osiris.

The chapels on the western side of the hall were dedicated to Amun-Re, Osiris and most probably Horus. Although only the bottom half of most of them had survived, the scenes were colourful and still in very good condition.

'In the shrine to Horus, on the north wall there is a colourful relief of the goddess Hekat, the 'Mistress of Abydos', usually portrayed as a frog, but in this case showing her human face. Next to her is the god Anubis 'Lord of the Sacred Land' also with the head of a man rather than the usual jackal's head. This is the only known example of Anubis with a human head.'

The reliefs in the three chapels basically included Ramses making various offerings, such as wine, bread, and incense, to various gods, including Horus, Nun, Thoth and Osiris.

In the chapel dedicated to Osiris, Ramses II, attended by Isis, stood before a seated Osiris and was presented the wishes for a long life and much feasting.

Apart from the alabaster and granite finds here, which to me were the real prize, these reliefs were the temple's greatest 'attractions'. In their prime, carved into the alabaster blocks, these brilliantly coloured painted reliefs would have been quite amazing and possibly the finest in any monument built by Ramses II, if not in Egypt itself.

Beyond the third chapel, as there had been on the southern side, in the corner of the western and northern walls, was a second statue chamber, again with nine decorated niches and very colourful reliefs. The remnants of a bench lay along the wall most likely indicating the room was used for storage.

'So if Cleopatra Selene isn't the one in the tomb, who is?'

I dived into my files.

"Juba II's second marriage was to Glaphyra, a princess of Cappadocia, and widow of Alexander, son of Herod the Great. Juba II married Glaphyra in 6 AD or 7 AD."

'Well, that would have pissed Selene off no end. If she was anything like her mother, she wasn't going to play second fiddle to anyone. Did Selene poison her?'

'No, she didn't have a chance.'

"Glaphyra fell in love with her first husband's brother, Herod Archelaus, another son of Herod the Great and Ethnarch of Judea, divorcing Juba to marry Archelaus in 7 AD."

'Short honeymoon, less than a year. I doubt Juba would have been happy to lie next to her for eternity. So, I think it's safe to say the body in the Mausoleum is *not* Glaphyra, so it has to be Selene.'

'So what do you think happened? Do you think Jesus just rocked into Mauretania and said 'Hi, Sis, it's me, Caesarion, dump this geezer and marry me, and you and the boys come with me to Jerusalem where we'll turn the Roman Empire on its ass?'

'It's possible.'

'Come on, the king was hardly going to let it be known publicly that she'd walked out on him to marry her half-brother, he would look like a fool, so he probably made up a story that she died. And if the king says it, then it must be true, right?'

'Unless *he* died first, and their son Ptolemy took over the reign, freeing Selene and her brothers, to do as they wanted.'

I dived back into the iphone.

'It says here,..

"Juba died in 23 AD, and his Roman-educated son Ptolemy of Mauretania

succeeded him on the throne".'

'...23 AD, that's well before Caesarion returned from India, so it's all highly possible; Juba died first. I mean who is going to question the Queen if she says she is going to take a sabbatical in the East?'

'And Mary and the disciples were considered to be very well off financially.'

'She probably travelled back to Egypt with Jesus and then just kept on going.'

'And their mission was to reclaim the thrones that were rightly theirs,...

'... as the *sang réal* and Son of God and King of Kings,..'

'...and to make it the *Holy* Roman Empire.

'Problem solved, case closed, pass the beer nuts.'

'Except, the question still remains; where and when did Mary Magdalene die, and does the body, or parts of the body, in the Mausoleum, belong to Mary Magdalene?'

'Again, simple, if they did a DNA test on the dude at Srinagar, and the chick in Algeria, then we would know one way or the other.'

'Alex, my friend, do you really think, assuming the Illuminati *know* that's in fact the case, they would EVER let anyone perform such a test? NO WAY, JOSE!'

It pissed me off and put a bit of a dampener on my enthusiasm. I mean, think of it, uncovering the greatest lies and deceptions in the history of the world. Where would that leave the millions of people, no, billions of people, in the world who blindly believed in one of the four big religions on the planet? I think it was at that moment I decided to write the book you are now reading and, with renewed vigour, I forged forward, determined to unearth every scrap of evidence I could find.

The three chapels at the rear of the temple, were supposedly the holy of holies, however here they differed slightly from the other temples. Firstly they were tiny, not much bigger than the other chapels to the sides, secondly, well, they just didn't feel *holy*. The chapels to either side, most likely dedicated to Isis and Horus respectively, were not particularly interesting, however the central chapel, dedicated to Osiris, spoke volumes.

This was the 'alabaster' sanctuary of Osiris, and, this room, and this room alone, featured a double false door on its rear wall. Also inside was a really badly restored grey-granite statue of a group of five 'gods', most likely Osiris, Isis, Horus, and the would-be gods of Seti I and Ramses II. It probably didn't even belong here, but had been plonked here because this was the sanctuary and it was as good a place as any.

The walls were indeed made of alabaster, but running around the base of the walls was a foundation of red granite. Here it all was again; the red-granite foundations of the inner sanctuary, the red-granite and black-granite doorways, the alabaster/limestone walls and floors. OK, what was underneath *this* temple?

I knew now from all the layers of sediment covering the Osireion that they had nothing to do with annual flooding of the Nile, that there had been several tsunamis that had swept upstream and swamped over Abydos; the first, deposited twenty-six feet of silt and buried the Osireion, the second, fifteen feet, which buried the Middle Kingdom temples, and the third, five or six feet, had probably flattened everything built before the reconstruction ordered by Alexander in 332 BC.

I'd seen this sort of evidence everywhere I'd gone; I'd seen it at Elephantine Island, at Kom Ombo, and Edfu, at el-Kab, and Esna, at Luxor, at Karnak, at Dendera, and now here at Abydos. If I'd seen all this, how come the 'experts' hadn't? Or had they, and they just weren't speaking up? And if that was the case, why were they keeping silent, who were they afraid of upsetting?

Making our way back out of the temple and towards the main gate, Pieter dropped another bombshell.

'OK, I've been listening closely to what you two have been talking about, and it makes sense. I can see how it's possible Cleopatra Selene II was Mary Magdalene, and that she was the *sang réal,* and that's why Caesarion travelled back to find her, but then why did he go off and preach all that stuff about God if the real focus was Mary Magdalene?

What if the teachings of Jesus were really about the Divine Feminine? What if the *real* Christ was Mary, as the inscription on the tomb of Mauretania would suggest, and Jesus was just the spokesperson? What if Mary Magdalene wasn't the "successor" of Jesus at all, what if it was the other way around, what if Jesus was *her* successor, that *he* worshipped *her,* and everything she represented, I mean, she was the daughter of Isis, and she *was* the *sang réal*?'

It was brilliant, mind-blowing in fact, and a shiver went up my spine.
'Whoa, Pieter, I think you might have hit the mother load.'
'What do you mean?'

My brain kicked into overdrive.
'Jesus had been raised believing his mother, Cleopatra, was the incarnation of Isis, right?'
'Yes.'
'Well, amongst other things, Isis was also known as protector of the dead and goddess of children, worshipped as the ideal mother and wife, the patroness of nature and magic, the friend of slaves, sinners, and artisans, as well as listening to the prayers of the wealthy aristocrats and rulers, all aspects of the Divine Feminine.'

Bill had zeroed straight in.
'All things Jesus spoke of.'
'Exactly. Even the name, "Isis", means "throne", and her headdress is a throne.'
'A direct reference to the throne of heaven.'
'Yes, it must be.'

Pieter wasn't quite following.
'Why is the throne of heaven so important?'

This was right up Bill's alley and I sat back and let him roll with the flow.

'Don't you see, the Throne of God is the focal centre of rule of the sole "one" god of all the Abrahamic-based religions: primarily Judaism, Christianity, and Islam. Imagine this, that the whole concept of the Divine Feminine has been kidnapped and corrupted by the originators of the main religions; by Moses, Paul, and Mohammed, and twisted to serve their own ends.'
'But how?'

Bill dug deep, then had a brainwave.
'Through the teachings of Mary Magdalene. My god, it's so obvious: Mary was the living incarnation of Isis; as she travelled around Europe after the crucifixion, preaching her wisdom, so the religion of Isis spread throughout the Roman Empire.'

We reached the gate and, as expected, the guardian assumed the "baksheesh" position. It seemed to have caught Pieter somewhat unawares and he instantly looked embarrassed. Given the way Yuko ruled the roost, clearly he didn't have much, if any, cash on him. Ever the gentleman, Bill was right on to it.
'I've got it lads.'
'No, Bill, we can all pay our own way.'

He gave me a very direct look, clearly to 'assist me' in understanding the issue.
'No, mate, *my* treat.'

111

And with that he pulled out a wad of hundred-pound notes, peeled off three, and handed them to the wide-eyed guardian, who was most receptive and appreciative. Then Bill peeled off one more.

'This is from us, to your family.'

The guardian almost blessed him and canonized him as a saint on the spot. Eager to minimize the issue, Bill brushed it all aside and gestured around the northern side of the temple.

'Come on, let's go back via the far side of the temple.'

The guardian blessed us all again, then led us off.

'I can't get over how generous you are Bill.'

'It's nothing, hardly anyone would come out this way, maybe three or four people a year, if that; and things are getting worse. Twenty bucks may not be much to us, but our brother here will hopefully be able to feed his family for a month or more on the back of our generosity.'

'I think I'm going to have to start calling you "Saint William of Oz".'

'Oh please, Cardinal Bill, Bill the Bishop, or even Father Bill would be quite sufficient.'

'That Gold Mine Company you work for must pay bloody well.'

'Actually, I don't work for the gold mine any more, I own it, or rather, I used to own it. I sold it off, but kept a position on the board *and* a considerable quantity of shares.'

'Shit, you're a millionaire, aren't you?'

'Hell no, but I was ten years ago. Now? Now, I'm a multi-millionaire.'

A grave state of affairs

Bill laughed away as we headed along the outside of the temple, past more reliefs of Ramses II bragging about his victory at Kadesh; two more opposite extremes of personality couldn't exist; Bill, versus Ramses II, Jacques. Suddenly I was even *more* happy for Pernille, *and* for Bill.

'Now, where were we before the 'evil spectre' of money raised its big ugly head?'

'The spread of the religion of Isis throughout the Roman Empire.'

'Yes! During the early formative centuries of Christianity, temples were built and obelisks erected in honour of Isis. In Greece, the Isis cult was introduced to the traditional centres of worship in Delos, Delphi, and Athens. Harbours of Isis were found on the Arabian Sea and the Black Sea. Isis had followers all over Europe, including Arabia, Asia Minor, Germany, France, Spain, and Portugal. There were even shrines in Britain.'

'Basically everywhere that Mary Magdalene went, an Isis culture emerged.'

'Now that I think of it, the traditional images of Isis from the era of the Roman Empire bear an uncanny resemblance to Cleopatra Selene, even ...

And he paused, like he had just seen a ghost.

'... Shit, even the Statue of Liberty is modelled on her.'

Pieter chipped in.

'I thought it was a symbol of the Babylonian Goddess, Ishtar, or Semiramis?'

Bill shook his head, the pieces falling into place like a temple-load of red-granite blocks.

'The Statue of Liberty is not just a representation of Queen Semiramis *and* Isis *and* Mary Magdalene, with the rays of the Sun around her head representing the Divine Consciousness, exactly the way the ancients did, it is an Illuminati symbol highlighting the lighted torch, but not the torch of liberty, as millions of mindless Americans have been led to believe, but the torch of the illuminated ones, the reptilian Elite. The Statue of Liberty is an Illuminati symbol that says: "We control this country, we're even telling you that, but you're too stupid to see it!"

The guardian stopped at the far corner of the temple and pointed northwards into what looked like more desert.

'Tomb, you see, yes?'

We looked at each other.

'Do we have the time?'

'Not really.'

I was getting itchy feet to get back to Crystal. Bill, on the other hand, was at least open to the option.

'What's there, and how far away is it?'

My handy iphone came to the rescue.

'*To the north-west of the Ramses II temple, in an area known as Kom es-Sultan, are the scant remains of an ancient mud-brick temple dedicated to the god Khenty-Amentiu, possibly an early title of Osiris, but little of the structure survives. Surrounding it is an impressive mud-brick structure dating back to the Middle Kingdom, but little is known about that structure either; a good part of the walls are still standing but only a few blocks now remain to give us a glimpse of the temples they contained.*

It's likely that the area was crowded with temples by the Middle Kingdom with many kings adding to the Temple of Osiris. Recent excavators have found buildings dating back to Predynastic times as well as a residential area to the south-east from the Old Kingdom which contains a street of mud-brick houses with courtyards and a faience workshop with its kilns. Adjoining the enclosure is a recently excavated limestone portal temple, built by Ramses II.'

I showed the guys the image.

'Not really anything there to see.'

'Another Ramses II temple, I'm happy to miss it.'

The mention of limestone had initially attracted me, but I quickly figured it was pretty-much probably the same as the temple here, in fact, by the image, it looked even less, so I was inclined to agree with the others. But it seemed it wasn't the only area of interest in that direction.

'Hang on, there's another area. '*South-west of Kom es-Sultan, is an area called Cemetery U, or Shunet el-Zebib, containing hundreds of graves, offering pits, and several funerary enclosures or "palaces of eternity". Each enclosure is associated with one of the royal tombs of the 1st Dynasty rulers, Djer, Djet and Merneith, and thought to be mud-brick prototypes of the earliest pyramids.*'

Bill wasn't convinced.

'Perhaps a little early in the afternoon to go grave digging, but if the palaces are there...'

I read on.

'*Measuring 122 metres from north to south, 65 metres east to west, with double walls eleven metres high and its massive inner walls 5.5 metres thick, the enclosure of Khasekhemwy, called Shunet el-Zebib, is the only one of seven of these structures clearly visible today.*'

As I showed them the photo, Pieter was finding more reasons to give it a miss.

113

'It sounds very similar to the walls we have already seen at el-Kab and Dendera, but not as big.'

'Recent excavations east of the enclosure revealed fourteen pits containing twelve of the world's oldest seagoing boats, each seventy-two feet long, and dating back to around 3000 BC.'

That re-ignited my interest, for a number of reasons; had they been swamped by the tsunami, or buried there deliberately to assist the Pharaoh in the afterlife?'

'Do you think the boats are still there?'

Bill was quite pragmatic.

'I doubt it. If they were, we would've all heard about it, and it would certainly be part of the local tour. They're probably all tucked away in the dry-docks of the museums of the Illuminati. Anything else?'

I flicked through the file.

'There's the remaining mud-brick walls of another 2nd Dynasty enclosure nearby, and an elaborate brick-lined structure containing twelve chambers, which has been attributed to an important ruler of the Predynastic period, by far the largest of its date found in Egypt.'

'Hmm, interesting...'

Bill scratched his chin.

'...What's it called again?'

'Shunet el-Zebib.'

He turned to the guardian.

'Shunet el-Zebib, how far?'

'Yes, yes, Shunet el-Zebib, this way, one half mile.'

Pieter had another issue.

'Half a mile; that's about seven-hundred-and-fifty metres, which, in this heat, over dunes and desert sands, would take us at least fifteen to twenty minutes each way, plus the time to look around. We've already left the girls alone at the mercy of the hawkers for nearly forty-five minutes, another trek would add on another forty-five at least.'

It was clear Pieter had seen enough, and Bill was quick to placate him.

'You're right; we should head back. Besides, if it was worth seeing, everyone would know about it.'

Mary, Mary, quite contrary

Politely declining the guardian's offer, we set off south, back to the Temple of Seti I. Though we had turned our backs on some of the mysteries of the desert, the true identities of Mary and Jesus were very much in the forefront of our minds, and it was Pieter and Bill who batted it to and fro.

'So, what you were saying before *is,* in the long run, the Isis cult in Rome merely served as a template for the whole Christian Madonna cult?'

'It continued until the suppression of paganism in the Christian era, and, from the 5th Century onward, the Christian Church just absorbed the imagery as their own, for example the image of Isis suckling her son, Horus, was appropriated and adopted as the popular Christian image of Mary suckling the baby Jesus.'

By now, Pieter had a grasp on it all and was asking some great questions.

'So Christianity is really the worship of Isis, but with the focus shifted from the Divine Feminine to the Holy Father.'

'Pieter, I think you nailed it.'

114

'Then why isn't it mentioned somewhere in the religious texts?'

You could almost hear the cogs of Bill's encyclopaedic brain turning and churning.

'The Torah, the Old Testament, was written fifteen-hundred years prior, way *before* then, mostly by Moses, and later Jewish scribes, the *Koran*, over five-hundred years *after* the event, so the only text it could really be in is the New Testament of *The Bible*, which has been censored, edited and manipulated numerous times over the centuries to eliminate anything they don't want you to know.'

'But there must be something still in there, even if it's in code.'

Bill seemed defeated, then suddenly it hit him.

'There is! Sophia!'

Pieter seemed confused.

'Sophia, the goddess of wisdom?'

'Yes.'

'You know, in Aramaic and Hebrew, the word "Spirit", as in The Holy Spirit, is a feminine ending noun that specifically refers to Sophia, Goddess of the All, the Holy Mother.'

'Really? Now that's interesting because in the Book of Proverbs, Sophia was the counsellor Jesus spoke of, who will "*teach all things to those who come to her in purity of intent and service*". Sophia is the "lost key" to entering the heavenly "now" and Jesus taught we are already *in* the "kingdom of heaven", or rather the "queendom of heaven", that the kingdom of the Mother is already here upon the earth, not some unattainable paradise in the sky.

Then there's James 3:17, where he distinguishes between two kinds of wisdom. One is a false wisdom, characterized as "earthly, sensual, and devilish", and associated with strife and contention, which is exactly where the physical Mary, a "free-radical" in a hostile land, would have found herself after the crucifixion, the other is the "wisdom that comes from above": "*first pure, then peaceable, gentle, easy to be entreated, full of mercy and good fruits, without partiality, and without hypocrisy*", the Queen of Mauretania.'

'All those years of bible study finally showing some worth, hey?'

Bill was about as worked up as a frisky dog on a librarian's leg.

'Jesus even mentions her himself in the Gospel of Matthew 11:19, "*Behold a man gluttonous, and a winebibber, a friend of publicans and sinners. But wisdom is justified of her children*." And then there's also the "Sophia of Jesus Christ", one of many Gnostic tracts within the Nag Hammadi codices discovered just down the road from here in 1945.'

I didn't really want to interrupt Bill, he was on a roll, but I felt I had to interject.

'There was a section about Jesus in the Nag Hammadi texts?'

'Oh, yes; a Gnostic text. There's a lot of debate about its age, anywhere between the 1st and 4th Centuries, but in any case, many scholars argue that it reflects the "true, recorded, sayings" of Jesus. According to the text, after he rose from the dead, his twelve disciples and seven women gathered on a mountain in Galilee where Jesus spoke to them. They asked him thirteen questions and Jesus responded.

'Do you remember the questions?'

It was so long ago. The whole tenet of Gnosticism was to discover the "secret wisdom" of God; they didn't believe Jesus was any more the "son of god" than you or I am. In fact, one of the major points of agreement between *all* the early Gnostic movements was that Jesus and the "Christ" were not the same thing, not the same person.

Given that the term Christ, or Christos, means anointed one, and given what we've just figured out, Jesus was Jesus, and the "Christ", the real "anointed one", was Mary Magdalene. You see, to the early Gnostics, Mary Magdalene *was* and *is* Isis; she *is* Sophia, she *is* Wisdom, she *is* the Divine Feminine, she is God-*ess*, the Ess-ence of God, manifest. I remember when I read it, it was one of the things that opened my eyes to the truth about the church, or rather the lies about the church, and the truth about life.'

I could tell Bill was about to go off on an epic narrative, perhaps even have another pow-wow with Sitting Bill, so I gently directed him back to the issue.

'Bill, the questions?'

'Oh, yeah, let me see; I can't remember them all, Christ, it was more than twenty years ago, but, ah,...how the universe began,...... the futility of searching for God,... that to see the truth you have to awaken,...how the spiritual world and the materialistic world are connected, and .....where mankind came from and why its here.'

'Pretty much the very topics we've been discussing since we all met.'

'Shit, do you think we're all reincarnated Gnostics?'

'No, Bill, Essenes!'

He stopped and took a deep breath.

'Whoaaaaaa.'

'Think about it, the disciples surely had to have been composed of both males and females, including Mary's daughter, Drusilla; we know her son, Ptolemy, stayed in Mauretania as ruler, but Drusilla probably went with her mother, as nothing was ever heard of her again. Jesus and Mary's brothers and sisters would also have made up the group.'

Bill's mind was still ticking over at a million miles an hour.

'You know, *The Bible* identifies James and Thomas as whole brothers, while Jesus is identified as their half-brother. There's always been speculation that Jesus had a twin brother, because, well "Thomas" means twin. But Jesus *didn't* have a twin brother at all; he had a half-brother who was a twin, the twin of Selene, Alexander Helios, James.'

I could see Bill was chuffed with his realization; and so he should have been, it was yet another piece of the jigsaw puzzle dropping into place. Pieter was not to be outdone either.

'The group would also have included Jesus and Mary's step-siblings and their most trusted servants, their old wet nurse, Mary of Arthenia, for she surely would have nursed Cleopatra Selene, Alexander and Ptolemy as well, and Mary's wealthy husband, Joseph of Arimathea. Cleopatra Selene would of course have seen everyone in some way as her "children", after all she was their queen, as well as being the daughter of Isis and the spiritual "mother" of them all.'

The only real questions left were, how did it all get so screwed up, and who was responsible?

'Tomb, yes, you come, very old.'

We had arrived back at the mud-brick walls at the rear of the Osireion, and this time the guardian was pointing in the other direction, into the western desert, towards the late afternoon sun shining between a gap in mountains.

'Alex?'

I already had the file open.

"*A few kilometres west of the Temple of Seti I, in an area of the desert known as Cemetery B, or as the locals call it,* Umm el Qa'ab, *are a number of Pre-Dynastic and Early Dynastic royal tombs, the names of whom were found on stelae at the tomb entrances.*"

Pieter knew something about it.

'The Pre-Dynastic kings must be the Thinite kings, who ruled from 5550 BC-3050 BC, and included the "Scorpion" King, who supposedly ruled Upper Egypt just before or during the rule of Menes, first pharaoh of the 1st Dynasty.'

Our guardian was keen for another windfall.

'Umm el Qa'ab, yes, many tomb, you come.'

We held our ground; it would have to be something pretty amazing, and pretty close, for us to make another trek into the wilderness.

"*Other pharaohs buried here include; Djer, Djet, Den, and Queen Mer-Neith from the 1st Dynasty, and Peribsen and Khasekhemwy from the 2nd Dynasty, the latter of which was the largest and latest royal tomb to be built at Abydos.*"

I showed them the images and it seemed clear to Bill...

'They probably all built their tombs here in order to be close to the Osireion, the tomb of Osiris.'

...but there was more to it.

'And to be near the gateway to the Land of the Dead, which is believed to lie under the nearby hills.'

'What do you mean?'

"*The ancient Thinite necropolis is aligned so that the summer solstice sunset shines down on it through the gap in the crescent-shaped limestone mountains to the west, believed by ancient Egyptians to lead directly to the kingdom of the dead, to the underworld. Following this line through the old necropolis brings us to the Osireion and through the western wall of the Hall of the Djed in Seti's temple.*"

'So was the Osireion being associated with Osiris, or was Osiris being associated with the Osireion?'

'Hmm, that's a good question.'

Pieter had some further interesting perspectives to contribute.

'Osiris has always been mysteriously connected with the idea of divine light, either the sun and/or the moon. In the *Book of the Dead*, Thoth, a moon god, announces to Osiris that "*he made the light shine on your inert body, for you he illuminated the dark ways*". However, the clearest description of this idea is in the Gnostic text known as the "Paris Papyrus" in which there is a ritual to attain immortality by inhaling light.

The aspirant is told to perform seven days of rituals, then three days of dark retreat. On the morning of the eleventh day, the aspirant is to face the rising sun and perform an invocation: "*First source of all sources... enlighten my body... that I may participate again in the immortal beginning... that I may be reborn in thought... and that the holy spirit may breathe in me.*"

With this, the aspirant inhales the first rays of the rising sun, then leaves his body behind, rising into the heavens, filled with Light.'

'How do you know all that, are you a closet Gnostic or something?

'Do you think when I sit facing the morning sun I am just trying to get an early start on a sun tan?'

I decided to share a little of my earlier experience.

'So maybe the ancient Egyptians were doing the same thing, using the Osireion in some way to line up with the rays of the sun?'

Bill was way ahead of me.

'Or some other star or planet?'

He was right; it was exactly what I'd experience earlier.

117

'So, should we check it out?'

'Depends what's there.'

"The earliest burial, a pit lined with brick walls, is about three metres by six metres inside, and originally roofed with timber and matting. Other pre-dynastic tombs are around five by eight metres. The probable tomb of Menes is of the latter size, but after that, the tombs increase in size and complexity. With each generation the tombs became more elaborate and were often surrounded by subsidiary burials of wives, servants and pets. Rows of small pits, tombs for the servants of the pharaoh surround the royal chamber, many dozens of such burials being usual.

There's evidence that human sacrifice was practiced as part of the funerary rituals associated with the 1st Dynasty. The tomb of Djer is associated with the burials of 338 individuals, thought to have been sacrificed to assist the pharaoh in the afterlife. It appears that Djer's courtiers were strangled and their tombs all closed at the same time. For unknown reasons, this practice was completely abandoned at the conclusion of the 1st Dynasty, after the last king, Qa'a, with shabtis, taking the place of actual people, to aid the pharaohs in the afterlife."

'Courtier to the pharaoh, hardly a good career move. Once word got out about the superannuation payout they probably found it hard to find good servants, and the incoming pharaoh would suddenly have had to find a complete staff and train them all up.'

'Yeah, just imagine, the Prime Minister dies, or resigns, and suddenly all the politicians and public servants are terminated as well.'

Bill and I looked at each other and laughed.

'Maybe that's the answer we've all been looking for.'

I had other thoughts. Maybe the reason the '338 individuals' all appeared to have died at once was because they were buried alive by a tsunami? Come on, one voluntary sacrifice maybe, but 338 people willing to be buried alive? Unlikely!

Meanwhile, I found a few further references.

'There appears to have been a centre of worship for Thoth here as well. *"Thoth's favourite bird, the ibis, was displayed on several late Pre-Dynastic, and many of the Early Dynastic, commemorative stelae, and also standing atop a strange low-lying shrine-like structure having a dome or mound over it. Archaeologists also discovered a large stone-carved baboon, an animal also sacred to Thoth, inscribed with the name Narmer, another name for Menes.*

Other inscriptions and ivory tablets, from the 1st, 2nd, and 3rd Dynasty tombs, reveal a number of tell-tale symbols and pictographs which reflect on the continued cultural guidance of the rulers, whose chief dedication was to the god Thoth. Curiously, archaeologists have never found any temples to Thoth here at Abydos".'

'It must be somewhere out there, buried under the sand.'

'The truth is buried beneath the grains of sand.'

As I said it, I realized it was just like Dwight leaving the folio beneath the sand on the roof at the Nubian Oasis; it was becoming the theme of my trip to Egypt.

'Anything else buried?'

I quickly scanned the file.

'Not really; *"by the end of the 2nd Dynasty tomb construction changed to a long passage, with chambers to either side and the royal burial in the middle, as in the tomb of Khasekhemwy"*, and *"there are also numerous animal cemeteries in the desert including dogs, falcons and ibis"*, but that's about it.'

'And how far is it?'

'About twice as far as Shunet el-Zebib.'

'Dogs, falcons and ibis, hey, no doubt sacrifices to the Underworld, to Anubis, Horus and Thoth. I don't think we need to act out a re-run of Stephen King's "Pet Semetrey", do you?...'

He kept talking as he set off along the top of the subterranean passage that led to the Osireion. Pieter and I slowly walked alongside him, absorbing every thought as he strung together a myriad of historical beads into a fancy new necklace.

'...Perhaps it's about time we took a leaf out of Jesus' book, and came in *out* of the wilderness.'

I was certainly no expert on *'The Bible'*.

'When was that again?'

'According to the Gospels of Matthew, Mark, and Luke, after being baptised by John the Baptist, around 29 AD, Jesus fasted for forty days and nights in the Judaean Desert.'

'And who exactly was John the Baptist?'

'Not much is known about him other than he was an itinerant preacher, and supposedly Jesus' second cousin....'

As soon as he said it, Bill realized he was on to something.

'...Whoaaa, ... that made him part of the Egyptian royal family, which means he must have been an Egyptian priest.'

'You think John the Baptist was High Priest of Egypt, perhaps even a member of the Tat Brotherhood?'

'He must have been. In the New Testament, John preached that a messianic figure greater than himself was coming, and, Jesus was the one. He wasn't preaching, he knew. He must have known that Caesarion had not only escaped to India, but that one day he would return to claim his throne, and he must have recognized him when he returned, that's why he baptised him. No, that's why he "anointed" him.'

'What's the difference?'

'Baptism literally means "washing"; it's a Christian rite of admission, or adoption, but baptisms didn't exist before Christianity, it would have been ritual cleansing and anointing.'

'Exactly as they would have done with the High Priests and Pharaohs.'

'Yes.'

'The usual form of baptism among the earliest Christians was to be either be totally immersed, submerged in a river for instance, or partially immersed, by standing or kneeling in water while water was poured over them.'

'That's exactly like the images on the walls of the temples, of the pharaohs being anointed by the gods.'

'Yes, it is, isn't it!...'

Bill was glowing, like he'd just won the lotto.

'...*The Bible* even says some of Jesus' early followers had previously been followers of John, which they would have been if they were Caesarion and Selene's "step-siblings", the children of his wet nurse. And other scholars, though it's disputed, have speculated that Jesus was himself a disciple of John for some period of time, which would have been before Caesarion escaped to India, and explains why they knew each other so well...'

He was almost crowing.

'...So, John the Baptist was an Egyptian High Priest, and member of the Egyptian Royal family.'

Pieter showed he had a little biblical knowledge himself, and posed a hiccup to the theory.

'But in the Gospel accounts of John's death, Herod has John imprisoned and later beheaded for denouncing Herod's incestuous marriage to Herodias, Herod's sister-in-law and niece, in violation of Old Testament Law. If John was really part of the Egyptian Royal family, then incestuous marriage was the norm rather than a sin.'

'Good point. Maybe incestuous marriage was restricted to members of the *sang réal* bloodline, or …'

And Bill had clearly just recalled it.

'…according to the 1st Century Jewish historian, Josephus, whose report would have been more contemporary with the actual event and less likely to have been deliberately distorted, gives a slightly different account in his *Antiquities of the Jews*, writing that Herod Antipas had John arrested because John had so many followers that Herod feared they might start a rebellion, and that makes much more sense. After all, religion was really all about politics, it always has been, and it probably always will be.'

We headed back past the Osireion towards the rear of the Seti temple. As we did, I looked into the centre of the red-granite pillars. Out of the blue, a question popped into my head.

'Why go to all the trouble to dismember Osiris?'

The answer was there almost instantaneously.

'Osiris was dismembered so that he couldn't regenerate.'

I tossed off what I thought was a throw-away comment.

'We really *are* coming back out of the wilderness.'

I wasn't really aware I'd said it out loud, but I had, and it opened up even more discussion: it was Pieter that picked up on it and set things off.

'Out of the wilderness of Sin.'

'We're hardly sinning.'

'No, not sin with a small "s", Sin with a capital "S"; Sin was a god.'

'Get out of here, there was a god called, Sin? Are you pulling my leg?'

'Not at all.'

Bill confirmed it.

'Not just Jesus, but Moses as well; he spent thirty-eight of his forty years in the Wilderness of *Sin*, the land where the god, *Sin,* was worshipped. In fact the term "Sinners" originally referred to people devoted to the god, *Sin.*'

That amused me.

'Seriously? I've been practically worshipping a god most of my life and I didn't know it.'

All that talk of Sin, with the capital "S", had aroused my thoughts of committing a few major ones of my own, of the lowercase variety, later that evening. Still, I was curious.

'So, who is this god, Sin?'

Bill couldn't quite remember, but Pieter filled in the blanks.

'Sin was the Akkadian god of the moon, particularly the crescent moon, known as Nanna in the Mesopotamian religion of Sumer, Assyria and Babylonia. He was a wise and unfathomable god represented as an old man with a flowing beard made of lapis lazuli, wearing a headdress of four horns surmounted by a crescent moon, and riding on a winged bull.'

'The old man with the beard sure sounds familiar; I can see where Moses got the image from, from his forty days, or rather forty nights, camped out under the night skies in the "Wilderness of Sin". Just where exactly is this 'Wilderness of Sin'?

'Well, *Sinai* is the feminine form of *Sin*; therefore, *Mount Sinai* can be called "the mountain of the goddess", the feminine counterpart of *Sin*.'

'Jesus, how many times do you need to be slapped in the face before you finally wake up. I mean, there it is again, references to the Divine Feminine. I'm starting to wonder if there's actually anything written in *The Bible* that we can believe; now it all just sounds like a load of macho propaganda; the truth has been completely distorted or fabricated by those who hijacked the teachings of Jesus and Mary Magdalene for their own purpose, that purpose being to control the masses.

Moses was a megalomaniac, Mohammed was as well, so who was the needle-dick who hijacked the wisdom of Selene and Caesarion and created the Frankenstein's monster we now call Christianity, with all it's distorted and deformed appendages?'

Bill gave out one of his chuckles.

'Another insecure megalomaniac; Paul.'

'Just who *was* Paul?'

'Now *that's* a good question.'

It clicked Bill into his contemplative demeanour.

'Paul, or rather Saul as he was originally called, was by birth a Roman citizen, even though he came from a Jewish family and was born in the city of Tarsus in Turkey.'

'Tarsus, isn't that where Cleopatra and Marc Anthony met?'

'Yes, it was.'

'Just a co-incidence? When was Saul born?'

'Around 5AD.'

'And Ptolemy Philadelphus was born around…?'

'…Eleven years after Caesarion. Why, are you suggesting Paul was Ptolemy Philadelphus?'

'Maybe.'

'Pushing it, I think.'

'After all the myths I've had blasted out of the water, I'm not closing the door on *anything* ever again.'

'Well, we'll see then…'

We waved off the guardian, said our thanks, and entered the cool shade of the rear of Seti's temple, our sights set not only on the bus, but more importantly, on the womenfolk. Well, I was, Bill was still thinking of Paul.

"…When he was young, Saul was sent to Jerusalem to receive his education at the school of Gamaliel, a Pharisee doctor of Jewish Law and one of the most noted rabbis in history. Apart from that, nothing else is known about Paul's background until he makes an appearance at the martyrdom of Stephen in Acts 7:58 *"And the witnesses laid down their garments at the feet of a young man named Saul"*.'

'Saul/Paul, it doesn't quite add up, does it? I mean even if Ptolemy was raised by Octavia in Rome, she would hardly have sent an Egyptian Prince to learn Judaism. And if he went to Mauretania with Selene, then it's highly unlikely she shipped him off to Tarsus. OK, I'll concede Paul *probably* wasn't Ptolemy.'

'Alex, you're beginning to sound just like Randy, minus the American accent of course.'

'So what was Saul's big beef with Jesus?'

'I think there's a lot more to it than we have been led to believe, and I think it goes back before Saul was even in the picture.'

'What are you getting at; something to do with the crucifixion?'

'*Everything* to do with the crucifixion.'

Having descended the stairs, and past the image of Ramses II with the bull, we

121

turned left in the Hall of Ancestors. I didn't need to prompt Bill; he was already primed.

'If you believe the story in *The Bible*, Jesus claimed to be the authentic king of the Jews; a claim that was viewed by the Romans as sedition against Rome. It supposedly also threatened Roman Law; because Jesus was teaching that the Law came from God, and not from Rome's Emperor. Therefore, under Roman Law, anyone who claimed to be a king was guilty of rebellion against the emperor, and the usual punishment was crucifixion.

So, because of that, supposedly Jesus was arrested, before being forced to stand trial before the Sanhedrin, Pontius Pilate, and Herod Antipas, then sentenced by Pontius Pilate to be scourged, and finally crucified.'

'You don't buy it?'

'No way, if Jesus *had* claimed to be "King of the Jews", which I now don't think he would have done, because he *wasn't* a Jew, he was half-Roman half-Egyptian, but if he had, then the Pharisee's and Sadducees had no need to involve the Romans, no need to air their dirty linen in public and potentially bring the Romans down on their heads, they would have just sent their henchmen out to incite a mob and have Jesus stoned to death as a blasphemer; which is what they usually did when they wanted someone dead.

Again, if you believe *The Bible*, the Jewish religious leaders saw the crowds that were gathering around Jesus, and knew that many people were calling him the Messiah. Well, many of them would have been Jews, most of them in fact, the people down-trodden by the Roman's, who were looking for, yearning for, a messiah to come and save them. But it doesn't mean Jesus was a Jew, in fact, we now know he wasn't.

And that's probably why the Pharisees and Sadducees feared him even more, because he *wasn't* a Jew and they had no religious "leverage" over him. If they *had* stoned him it would have been murder, and not religiously justifiable. Mark 11:18 says *"they feared him, because the whole crowd was amazed at his teaching"*. Of course they were, he not only did he have the teachings of the Veda's but also the knowledge of the Divine Feminine.

Ultimately the Pharisees and Sadducees' *real* fear was that if growing numbers of *Jews* believed that Jesus *was* the Messiah, then he could eventually become a serious threat to their authority.

'But they could have easily arranged for him to be dispatched in the still of the night with a swift blade. There has to be even more to it, like why did the Roman's get involved, isn't crucifixion a Roman method of punishment?'

'It is, and it's a basic fact that it was Roman soldiers, not Jews, who put Jesus on the cross. In fact, John 18:3 says that it was Roman soldiers who took part in the initial arrest of Jesus, *"So Judas came to the garden, guiding a detachment of soldiers and some officials from the chief priests and the Pharisees"*, which suggests that the Romans were involved almost from the beginning.'

'And I'm sure Judas didn't betray Jesus for just a handful of silver, I've never swallowed that.'

'Judas Iscariot and Simon Magus were part of the Zealots, supposedly a politically active and *re*active faction of Judaism calling for a reform and renewal of religion that would lead to a Jewish empire that would overrule the Roman Empire. But maybe the zealots weren't so much Jewish, as anti-Roman; maybe they supported the Egyptian religion, which had gone to pot under Roman rule?

In any case, Judas was opposed to Jesus' pacifist approach, to Jesus' appeal to reason and morality. Judas probably killed two birds with one stone; by selling out Jesus, Judas not only silenced the pacifist rhetoric, but he though Jesus' followers would be so outraged that he would be able to incite them to rise up against the Romans. After all, to

Judas, Jesus wasn't important, Mary Magdalene, the *sang réal*, was. Jesus was just a spokes person for the Divine Feminine.'

'Now *THAT* makes sense!'

We re-entered the second hypostyle hall, Pieter and I hanging on Bill's every word like two vultures waiting for the last dying breath to pass.

'And yet, despite all this, the gospels put nearly all of the blame for the crucifixion on the Jewish leaders, and would have us believe that Rome supposedly had Jesus crucified merely as a warning to any other Jew who might be so audacious as to challenge the authority of Rome.'

'And that *doesn't* make sense.'

'No, it doesn't. However, the whole thing makes sense if Jesus wasn't a Jewish son of a carpenter, but someone who not only claimed to be the king of Egypt but also the rightful ruler of the Roman Empire.'

'Which, in the case of Caesarion, was true.'

'And it was his claim to the Roman Empire, not to being "King of the Jews", that got him into trouble.'

'But how?'

'Caiaphas.'

'The Pharisee?'

'Actually he was a Sadducee, but, yes, he's the key. According to Josephus, it was Rome that appointed Caiaphas as the chief priest in Jerusalem. Caiaphas must have recognized Jesus as Caesarion and reported back to Emperor Tiberius, the adoptive son of Augustus.

'I get it. Augustus wasn't even a blood relative of Caesar, and his step-son, Tiberius, was even further from the bloodline. Caesarion, on the other hand, was the rightful heir to the Roman throne and therefore a huge threat to Tiberius.'

'Once Caiaphas reported the arrival of Caesarion in Jerusalem to Rome, and to Tiberius, the order would have come back down the line to eliminate "Jesus" any way you see fit. Under Caiaphas' orders, Jesus was arrested and tried before the Sanhedrin, where they tried to beat a confession out of him, but he remained silent.

Mark 14:61 states that the high priest then asked Jesus: *"Art thou the Christ, the Son of the Blessed? And Jesus said, I am"*, which would have been true; Jesus was the son of Isis. And, if we take the actual Greek meaning of Christos as "anointed", then yes he was the "Christ", he was the anointed one, anointed by John the Baptist as the rightful ruler of Egypt, the Son of God.

In Matthew 26:63 the high priest asks: *"tell us whether you are the Christ, the Son of God."* And what does Jesus reply? *"You have said it"*. The Sanhedrin took that as a confession of blasphemy and hauled him off to Rome's appointed Governor, Pontius Pilate.'

'So why didn't Jesus speak up at his trial?'

'It's quite obviously really, if he said he wasn't who he was, the rightful ruler of the Roman Empire, then he would be lying. If he admitted who he was, then he signed his own death warrant.'

'So he was damned if he did, and damned if he didn't.'

'Exactly.'

'But the charge of blasphemy wouldn't have mattered to Pilate; the Romans wouldn't execute someone because the Jew's were pissed off.'

'That's right, so Caiaphas had to shift his legal position to establish that Jesus was guilty, not only of blasphemy, but also of proclaiming himself the messiah, which was understood as the return of the Davidic king, because this *would* have been an act of sedition under Roman Law, and punishable by crucifixion. Once that was established,

Caiaphas, with a guard of Roman soldiers, seized Jesus and handed him over to Pontius Pilate for trial on the charge of sedition against Rome.'

'So, was Jesus crucified, or not?'

'I think it's fair to say he was.'

'So why was he crucified with a thief to either side if crucifixion was "reserved" for such crimes as sedition?'

'I don't think they were thieves at all; I never have, rather, "rebels" as a more proper translation. I think Simon Zealots and Judas Iscariot were the ones beside him, that they were both arrested at Gethsemane as well, and crucified alongside Jesus as a political stunt.'

'It was all about politics?'

'It always has been, and it always will be.'

'So they double-crossed Judas?'

'Give a man enough rope …'

'…and he'll hang himself. It's a metaphor, Judas' hanging is an allegory, a parable.'

'And what better way for Caiaphas to eliminate his competition and for the Romans to make the statement, "Don't fuck with Rome".'

'So the question is not so much whether Jesus was crucified or not, but, whether he died on the cross, or, if he survived?'

'Well, clearly, if he's buried in Srinagar, he survived.'

'But how?'

'Jesus was nailed to the cross just before Passover, and, so that the dying bodies wouldn't remain on the cross on the Sabbath, the Jews asked Pilate if the bodies could be taken down. Pilate agreed, on condition their legs were broken; presumably so they couldn't run away, and no doubt they would have been nailed back up after the Sabbath.'

'But Jesus had supposedly died, so the Roman soldiers didn't bother breaking his legs, as they did to the other two, and they were taken down and put into a sealed cave, perhaps as a tomb, or maybe as a makeshift prison.'

'Or maybe the whole tomb thing was made up?'

'What?"

'The records show Jesus was crucified, but not that he died or was buried; in fact his body was removed from the cross by Joseph of Arimathea.

'Wait a minute, Joseph knew exactly who Jesus really was, he wouldn't have put him in a tomb, at least not without taking him back to Egypt and embalming him first.'

'My thinking exactly.'

Pieter was curious about other details.

'What about the body? What about the spear, and the sponge soaked in vinegar?'

'The sponge was probably laced with some sort of poison to put Jesus out of his misery, to put him to death quickly, to avoid his suffering. He would have lapsed into unconsciousness and his heart probably slowed right down, but, when he was speared, they missed his organs and arteries and he didn't bleed, so they thought he was dead. Then, once Joseph had taken him down, he was probably given some sort of potion or antidote, to make him throw up.'

I was right with it.

'It would have taken him at least several days to recover enough to walk, but even then he must have looked like a ghost, like death warmed up.'

'He "rose from the dead".'

'Yes, especially if everybody assumed he was dead. Only Joseph and those close to him, like Mary and James, would have known the truth, and they were hardly going to make it public knowledge and broadcast it across the Temple Mount.'

'So if he didn't die on the cross, what happened to him, and to the disciples?'

'You're asking the wrong person.'

'What do you mean?'

'Well, If Pernille was Cleopatra…'

'Yes?'

'And Crystal was her daughter, Cleopatra Selene, Mary Magdalene,..'

'Yes?'

'And you were her twin brother, Alexander Helios, James the Just…'

And then I got it.

'Shit! We left Jerusalem and headed …'

'Straight to the lion's den…'

'…to Rome!'

'…to speak directly to the Senate.'

'Yes, But we didn't sail there directly; it was too dangerous. We went by land first, and no doubt had to pass through Ephesus.'

'Exactly.'

'Shit, it all makes sense.'

We made our way out of the temple and back into the heat of the second courtyard. After listening intently while Bill and I played "Passover ping pong", Pieter finally opened his mouth and summed the whole thing up.

'So what you're saying is that the Romans were the ones really responsible for the crucifixion?'

'Yes, and no: Caiaphas was no fool, he was a Sadducee and was able to use the Romans as his instruments, eliminating all his main factional opponents in one masterstroke; I mean if Jesus was guilty, then so were Simon and Judas, the "Pharisee" zealots, they all posed a threat to his nice cushy little position. The Romans may well have crucified Jesus, but it was Caiaphas who handed them the hammer and nails.'

'So the Romans did it, but they were manipulated by Caiaphas?'

'Yep.'

'And the gospel writers have tried to cover it all up by blaming the Pharisees and Sadducees instead?'

'I don't think they've covered it up, I just think they've only told part of the story and glossed over other parts.'

'Why?'

'The gospels were written during a period when the Christians were trying to avoid trouble with the Romans, and putting the blame on the Romans would not have been a wise career move. So, it would have been much safer, and make perfect sense, to just do what everyone did, and blame the Jews.'

'But in a way they were right.'

'Yes they were, but it wasn't the full picture.'

'So who's the one responsible for all the distortions of truth?'

'I guess the finger points fair and square back at Paul; almost half of the books of the New Testament are credited to him, and he was the one responsible for spreading the gospel of Christianity across the Roman Empire.'

Pieter wasn't satisfied.

'But why, why would he distort the truth?'

'Some religious scholars have suggested there was a rift between the disciples, a split, and I think that's highly likely, I mean, no matter where in the world you are today, there are factions in all religions and political parties.'

I got the picture.

'You think it was political.'

'Of course; it's always been that way, and it always will.'

'History repeats itself.'

'Paul, or Saul as he was initially, was a Pharisee, possibly even aligned with the Zealots, but he was also a Roman citizen, which means he was probably appointed by the Romans, a fact that afforded him a certain privileged legal status. The crucifixion of Jesus, Simon and Judas didn't bring the opposing Jewish factions together, because Jesus wasn't Jewish. If anything, the crucifixion drove them further apart, polarized them, and Saul would have been livid, not only at the Romans, but more so at both the Essenes and the Sadducees. He could hardly vent his anger at Caiaphas, or he may have received the same treatment, so I think he blamed Jesus, and he took it out on the pacifists for the death of Simon. And a safe bet too, they were hardly going to fight back.'

'You think Paul was a bully.'

'Without doubt, of the worst kind, he admits it himself. Before becoming a "follower of Christianity", Saul zealously persecuted the followers of Jesus and the newly-forming Church, trying to destroy it.'

Pieter was slightly confused.

'But they weren't responsible for Simon's death.'

'As a Zealot, I think Saul already had a bee in his bonnet with the Essenes, *and* with Mary being the Divine Feminine, the real Christ.'

'What makes you think that?'

'There's a phrase in 1 Corinthians 1:20 where Paul makes an obscure reference to "wisdom", to the concept of the Divine Feminine; *"Where is the wise? where is the scribe? where is the disputer of this world? Hath not God made foolish the wisdom of this world?"* I think he is questioning the validity of Mary as the *sang réal*, as the Divine Feminine. You see, Saul was not only a scholar, he was also a Stoic.'

Now it was my turn to be confused.

'A Stoic?'

'Yes, Stoicism is a school of Hellenistic philosophy founded in the early 3rd Century BC, which provided a unified account of the world consisting of formal logic, non-dualistic physics, and naturalistic ethics; all masculine principals. The Stoics thought the best indication of an individual's philosophy was not what a person said, but how they behaved. They taught that destructive emotions resulted from errors in judgment, and that a person of "moral and intellectual perfection", wouldn't suffer such emotions.

Clearly, Mary was a women of great emotion and passion, and Saul saw this as an imperfection, in fact he must have seen the whole Divine Feminine, the whole Essene movement, as imperfect, illogical, and lacking in ethics.

After the "crucifixion", Mary, Jesus, and several of the others, set off for Rome, most probably to put his case to the Senate. Jesus left his younger half-brother, and Mary's twin, James, in charge of the pacifist "Essenes", and, over the next twenty years or so James slowly built the movement.'

Passing back through the gateway of the second pylon, I was still trying to find answers.

'So what was the trigger that caused Saul to go from being such a zealous persecutor, to Paul, an avid supporter? I don't understand why he just jumped ships?'

126

'According to *The Bible*, Acts 9:3-9, Paul was on his way from Jerusalem to Damascus to arrest followers of Jesus, with the intention of returning them to Jerusalem for questioning and possible execution. But his journey was interrupted. *"suddenly a light from heaven flashed around him. He fell to the ground and heard a voice say to him, "Saul, Saul, why do you persecute me?" "Who are you, Lord?" Saul asked. "I am Jesus, whom you are persecuting," he replied. "Now get up and go into the city, and you will be told what you must do."*

Saul got up from the ground, but when he opened his eyes, he couldn't see, he was blind. So they led him by the hand into Damascus. For three days he was blind, and did not eat or drink anything."

'He could have just had sun stroke, or a seizure.'

'That's true, some theorists have even suggested he had an attack of temporal lobe epilepsy, perhaps ending in a convulsion.'

'So how can we believe it, it could all be bullshit, all made up. After all, it wasn't someone else writing about it, it was Paul writing about it, that's about as reliable as Moses writing about Joseph and the Exodus, or Bernie Madoff saying "The money's in the bank", or "The cheque's in the mail".'

'Or Jack the Ripper saying "Trust me, I'm a doctor".'

'Or Bill Clinton saying that getting a blow-job from Monica was not sexual relations, or the champion High school quarterback saying to the virgin cheerleader, "It's OK, you won't get pregnant".

Having allowed me my humorous, yet irreverent rant, Bill continued where he had left off.

'According to *The Bible*, Paul's "dramatic" conversion on the road to Damascus was sometime around 36 AD, but I think it was later, more like 49 or 50 AD?'

'What's your thinking?

'I think the change of name is a clue; Saul is a very Jewish name, Paul, a very Roman one. If it happened around 36 AD then it may have coincided with the death of Tiberius and the investiture of Caligula, as many of Caligula's first acts were said to be very generous, if somewhat political. But I think that's too early, just a few years after the crucifixion.'

'You think there's another reason?'

'Caligula hardly even took notice of the Christians, except perhaps to feed them to the lions, after all Christianity was hardly distinguishable from Judaism at that point, so he just treated them the same way he treated the Jews.'

'As a problem.'

'Yep. It's also worth considering that Caligula invited Ptolemy, Mary's son, and ruler of Mauretania, to Rome, and then had him suddenly executed. Perhaps that's part of the reason Mary and the others fled Rome? Interestingly enough, Christianity had found its way "home" to Alexandria by the death of Caligula in 41 AD, perhaps because Mary and Jesus made a trip back there after leaving Rome. Anyway, I think, like Tiberius and Augustus, Caligula's real concern was the bloodline of Julius Caesar and Cleopatra.'

'Makes total sense to me, but how did that affect Paul?'

'I don't think it did, it had to be later.'

'How much later?'

'The next change of ruler was in 41 AD when Claudius took the throne. He spoke of the Jews as "a general plague which infests the whole world", and he ordered all the Jews to leave Rome in 49 AD. Apart from that, there's no real evidence of any systematic persecution of Christians during the reign of Claudius.'

Pieter wasn't quite following.

'But, by then, Mary and the others had already fled Rome.'

'I don't think it had anything to do with Mary and the others anyway, I think it was something between James and Saul.'

I was intrigued.

'Go on, Bill.'

'Claudius was followed by Nero in 54 AD, who blamed the Christians for the burning of Rome in 64 AD. I'm figuring by then it wouldn't have been cool to switch sides and call yourself a Christian. So I think it must have happened some time around 49 AD, with the expulsion of the Jews. Up until then, I think Saul had continued on with the Zealot faction of Judaism, but, with the Roman edict of Claudius, I think he saw his opportunity to wipe out the "Essene" opposition, jump ship as you called it, or rather ambushed it and usurped power from James.'

'If you can't fight them, join them.'

'I think so.'

As we arrived back at the first pylon, and started descending the ramp, Bill continued with his dissection of the Gospels.

'It was all about circumcision.'

'Say again?'

'The Old Testament says in Genesis 17: 10-14 *"This is my covenant with you and your descendants after you, the covenant you are to keep: Every male among you shall be circumcised. You are to undergo circumcision, and it will be the sign of the covenant between me and you"*. God had offered a covenant to Abraham to sign, saying it would be everlasting or eternal, and that the way it was to be signed was by circumcision.'

'Are you serious? That's the basis, that's the foundation stone of the Jewish religion?'

'Pretty much.'

'Out of all the possibilities, prayer, sacrifice, temple building, etcetera, you're saying that not only did God pick chopping off the tip of your dick as the way to go, but some weirdo thousands of years ago took it upon himself to agree that every guy from that moment on should have his dick doctored if he wanted to go to heaven?'

'Yep.'

'What sort of perverted God is that?'

'I'm with you on that one; it makes absolutely no sense. Anyway, Abraham agreed, and, according to the Jewish Scriptures, that's how Judaism, and the obedience to God's laws, started.'

'Is that why the Jews go around wearing those silly little hats, to advertise the fact they've had their cocks cut?...'

I couldn't resist the chance for another cheap dick joke.

'...Hey, Pieter, do you know what a lesbian-feminist calls the useless piece of flesh attached to a penis?'

'The foreskin?'

'No, a man.'

Bill had a little chuckle, then got back to his line of thinking.

'In any case, it was this signature commandment, that *"No uncircumcised man will be one of my people"*, that was the central conflict between Saul and James.'

'Between the Zealots, led by Saul, and the Essenes, led by James?'

'Yes, and, according to Acts 21:21, there were so many uncircumcised men calling themselves followers of Jesus, *"that thou teachest all the Jews which are among the Gentiles to forsake Moses, saying that they ought not to circumcise their children, neither to walk after the customs",* that Saul was fearful everyone was flocking to the other side, and he was losing not only his "flock", but the very crook to control them.'

'So James' Jews didn't have to go under the knife?'

'No.'

And then it hit me.

'No, of course they didn't; if Jesus was Caesarion, then he was Egyptian, not Jewish, so Jesus wasn't circumcised, and James and Joseph weren't circumcised either. To them, circumcision was a sign of slavery. The Egyptians had forced circumcision on the Jews and captives as a sign of slavery centuries ago. It's not as if you could argue you weren't a slave; "OK, just drop your toga and show us your tackle".

When Moses started creating his grand fiction, he turned circumcision into a symbol of unity, of belonging, an initiation rite. In fact he probably invented the whole Abraham story.'

'Alex, I think you're spot on. Although some scholars have argued that the reason James hadn't demanded circumcision for the seventeen years he was leading the new sect, was because of the high risk of death from infection.'

'Well that would be a good argument if James was also a microbiologist and had known anything about bacteria and infections in 50 AD, I mean, you wouldn't want to kill off your "members", if you'll excuse the pun, while you were still trying to build your numbers. But, come on, Bill, circumcision, it's all bullshit.

It's not hard to understand why a whole lot of grown men, given the choice to follow one religion that, despite the high probability you may die from infection, says "you have to have your foreskin hacked off to commune with God", or follow another, very similar if not identical religion, saying, "no way Jose, the fan-belt stays in place", would opt for the latter; it's a no-brainer.

No wonder Paul jumped ship; he was never going to win that argument. Jesus wanted to set all men free, so he abolished "slavery", he abolished the symbol of slavery, he abolished the ritual of circumcision for Jews, for all people.'

'In *'The Bible'*, it says it was the other way around.'

'Are you serious?'

'Yep, it says that Jews were rioting against Paul, demanding him to have his men circumcised. According to Acts 15:1, the council in Jerusalem had been called by James precisely to consider this highly contentious circumcision issue.'

'Personally I wouldn't believe a single word Paul said. I think he and his cronies of gospel writers were making it up to suit themselves.'

'Funny you should say that. Coincidently, in Galatians 2:11-21 it says it was in 49 AD that Paul publicly stood against his own teacher, Peter, and against the other representatives sent by James, announcing in Galatians 2:16 that God no longer required obedience to God's laws, that from now on, mere Christ-faith was all that God required in order to send a person to heaven instead of to hell after death.'

'So he'd done a complete back-flip.'

'Yep.'

'It says it all.'

Finally arriving at the entrance of the complex, we looked around and saw the girls sitting some distance away, under a tree, along from the temple. Actually, we didn't spot them straight off; initially we saw the swarm of kids, shop-owners and hawkers that were hovering around them like blowflies on a freshly laid cow turd.

I suppose when referring to the girls I should have said, "like a swarm of honey-bees around a blossom of roses", but the truth was, the hawkers were persistent and annoying. I couldn't really blame them though; the girls would have been like three angelic goddesses, worthy of awe and reverence. Slowly heading in their direction, I still had a piece missing.

'But how did Paul wrestle control from James?'

'I think he used his position, as well as his superior education as a Stoic, to manipulate the people. He probably created a hybrid product that had all the best features, and was just a better self-promoter; most megalomaniacs are. After that, there would have been a short period where there were two streams of "Christianity", there had to be; the "Jesus/James" stream, and the "Paul" stream. But, eventually, Paul took over effective control of what originally had been the Jewish/Egyptian sect which Jesus had started and which James had inherited.'

'So what happened to the rest of the zealots?'

'I think they died in the siege at Masada around 73 AD.'

'And James and the Essenes?'

'The pacifists they were, I think they went underground and passively morphed into the Gnostics.'

'So it was Paul's coup d'etat against James in 49 AD that constituted the real break with Judaism, and the start of Christianity?'

'Yep, and I think Paul did it in order to save his career from collapse, and to avoid having almost all of the men he had converted to Judaism leave him.'

'And he succeeded.'

'He sure did. If you believe *The Bible*, Paul saw himself as an ambassador who was merely carrying out the directives and teachings of his "religious mentor", Jesus. Paul supposedly taught of the life and works of Jesus Christ and his teaching of a New Covenant, or New Testament, that was established through Jesus' death and resurrection.

But the reality appears to be that the New Testament was written by the "enemies" of the Jewish/Egyptian sect that Jesus had started; they were written by Paul and *his* followers, not those of Jesus, they're the ones responsible for the four canonical Gospel accounts of Jesus, and of what he supposedly said; Matthew, Mark, Luke, and John.'

'You don't think they were true apostles?'

'Not for one minute. I think they were either written by Paul himself, or by those Paul had told the stories to. I don't think for one millisecond that Matthew, Mark, Luke or John, ever spent any time with Jesus, Mary and the Essenes; I think they were originally zealots, and as zealots they may have witnessed some of the proceedings leading up to, and including, the crucifixion, but nothing else outside of what Paul told them.'

'How can you be so sure?'

'How can I be so sure? Because Paul retroactively identified Peter, rather than James, as the leader appointed by Jesus, because Peter was Paul's teacher, and the emerging Roman Catholic Church needed *someone* to serve as the "historical" link back to Jesus, since Paul had probably never even met Jesus. Conveniently Peter was put to death during the reign of Nero, so he couldn't dispute Paul's claim.

If Matthew, Mark, Luke and John *had* been part of the original "inner circle" there is no way they would have said Peter was the chosen one, they would have known James was; instead they either deliberately ignored the fact, which would mean they were zealots, or they just didn't know, which again suggests they were aligned with Paul, and probably zealots.

'So you think Paul just invented the "conversion" story on the way to Damascus to give himself some street cred.'

'Precisely. Before then, his contemporaries probably didn't hold him in the same high esteem as they held Peter and James, and he was probably forced to struggle to validate his own worth and authority. In the end, Paul was probably never even a real "apostle" but rather a zealot, the "arch-enemy" of Jesus and all he attempted to teach and to do, and the best way for Paul to defeat Jesus was to hijack Jesus' teachings by hijacking the group and then distorting the teachings to suit his own agenda.'

'You mean just like Moses did, and Mohammed did?'

Bill laughed.

'Maybe they were all the same soul reincarnating.'

Out of the frypan and into the fire

'Look at who has finally returned from the desert; the three amigos.'

Making our way through the perimeter of locals, all of whom were trying to flog us water, soft drinks, postcards or some sculptured treasure, we approached the table where the three girls sat, calm and cool, several empty and half-full drink bottles spread across the table.

Pernille was the most pleased to see us, well, Bill, and had risen to her feet to greet him and give him a huge kiss and a hug. I wondered if she knew he was loaded? She had to know by now, surely. But then, knowing Bill, he wouldn't have felt the need to tell her.

'What took you so long? We thought you'd got yourselves lost in the desert?'

As Pernille had spoken to Bill, it somewhat made him the initial spokesperson.

'No, we got talking and spent a little longer at the Temple of Ramses II than we expected.'

'How was it?'

'Good, interesting.'

Crystal flicked back her hair and licked her lips.

'I can't wait to hear what your little chats were all about.'

'Gee, where do we start...?'

Just then a speeding taxi came to a sudden halt next to the minibus and Saeed jumped out. Pernille was the first to say anything.

'Here's a pleasant surprise.'

He hustled up towards us with a concerned look on his face.

'Indy, quick come, we must go.'

'What? Where? Why?'

'I don't have it the time to tell you now, I will tell you on the way, come, quickly.'

The others froze like stunned statues as Saeed grabbed me by the arm and literally dragged me to my feet.

'Where are they the paper?'

'In my backpack, in the minibus.'

Saeed called out to Saleem, who instantly jumped to his feet and ran to the bus. A chill rippled all over me. Over the past few hours I'd forgotten about Kareem's papers, about the events in Luxor. All of a sudden they flooded back, and the fact Saeed was here in Abydos asking for them, and clearly agitated, meant that the shit had well and truly hit the fan.

'What's going on?'

'We must go.'

Saleem unlocked the bus and retrieved my backpack, handing it to me as Saeed pushed me into the back of the taxi. I looked back through the window at the others, most of whom had risen to their feet and were slowly gravitating towards us. Only Crystal remained seated, calm as usual; I hadn't even said goodbye. Within a minute we were tearing off down the road away from Abydos like a bat out of hell. I wondered, would I ever see her again?

CHAPTER 23 – WE'RE ON THE ROAD TO NOWHERE

'OK, Saeed, what's going on?'

The taxi sped along the road, swerving around several fully-laden donkeys.

'We have to get it you out of Egypt.'

'Why; is it the papers?'

I grabbed my backpack tightly.

'Yes, but now it is worse; they are wait for you back in Luxor.'

'Who are?'

'The Secret Police; they know you have seen it the paper, they are think you must be still are having them.'

'But, I do.'

'Yes.'

We snaked our way down the road, swerving again to the other side of the road as we passed a slow moving truck, nearly wiping out a couple of tok toks heading towards us in the other direction. The only time we came to a virtual standstill was to negotiate the random but regular speed bumps that stopped cars from doing exactly what we were now doing.

'Where the hell are we going?'

'To it the train station; I will be take you to Mohammed in Fayoum. You will be safe there until we can make the arrangement to get it you and the paper of Kareem safe out of Egypt.'

I thought about Crystal back in Luxor.

'Can't I just give the papers to you to give back to Kareem?'

'It is too late, Kareem he is dead.'

It hit me like a runaway steam train.

'What? How?'

'Murdered, they cut his throat.'

'Who did?'

'The Secret Police.'

'Shit!...'

I didn't know what to say.

'...I'm sorry, I'm ...so sorry.'

'Do not be; my uncle, he has lived a good life, he was know he did not have it much time left to be live. He know what he was do, he know the risk, and he understand how important it is for the world to know it the truth. This is why he chose you, he believe in you, that you are honest man, the right man to entrust it his life work to. But he does not deserve to leave like the old goat.'

'What happened, who was it?'

'It was the Secret Police of course, they follow him home, stop him at a road block, then slit his throat and toss his body in it the canal like old street dog.'

'Can't anyone do anything?'

'No, the Secret Police they have said it he was attacked by a foreigner, who steal some very important government document from him.'

'What would anyone....foreigner? You mean *ME*?'

'Yes, they take it the copy of your passport from Nubian Oasis and they have put it out the picture of you. This it is why we must be get you *and* the paper safe out of Egypt.'

'When did it happen?

'Last night.'

'But I have an alibi.'

'Do you think it they will be listen to your alibi? Do you think it they will allow for you to say anything, to give you the fair trial? Do you think it you will even *get it* a trial?'

'What do you mean?'

'I am sorry to say, Indy, you will be made silent as soon as they are finding you.'

'They'll kill me?'

'Oh, no, you will just be the unlucky tourist that happened to suffer it the unfortunate "accident".'

I swallowed a bowling ball; the dryness in my throat not just because of the heat.

'Jesus, these guys mean business.'

'Of course, I do not think it you are realize just what it is in that file.'

I stared at the backpack; it might as well have been crammed with C4 explosives, strapped to my chest, with a massive neon target on it

'I've got a fair idea, for starters it has the real details of the Luxor massacre, that alone would implicate Zahi Hawass in fifty-plus cases of premeditated murder.'

'That it is just tip of the iceberg, a flea on the back of the camel. My uncle he had made it into their confidence, into the inner circle as you would say it, he made many many note on Zahi Hawass, every move he make, what site they are discover and when, all the site that have been looted, who it was take the bribe, who it was the statue and content of the tomb go to, everything and everyone.'

Despite the obvious corruption all around me, I still clung to the vague notion that justice would prevail.

'But I didn't do it; I was with Crystal at the Nefertiti Hotel, she can vouch for me.'

'If you tell it them you are with anyone, then you will put it their life in danger as well. So far the only person they are know is connect to you and the paper it is Saeed, and they will catch it up with me soon enough.'

I started thinking about who else had seen the papers.

'What about Dwight?'

'Mister Dwight, he know it about the file?'

'Yes, I left them with him to look at while I visited Karnak.'

Saeed frowned.

'Mister Dwight he is in Cairo, yes?'

'Yes.'

'Then I can visit him there, I am doubt it the Secret Police they will have figure it out yet. Anyone else.'

'Well, I guess Dwight would have told Randy at some stage, but I think Randy is back in the States by now, and I don't think he was in much of a state to see the nose on his face, let alone comprehend any papers in Arabic.'

'But he is know about them.'

'True.'

'This I can sort it out when I speak with Mister Dwight. Anyone else?'

'Pieter and Yuko saw Dwight with them as well, and Bill, and he told Crystal, but they've all be questioned by the police already, and said they don't know anything about it.'

'I shall still have to call him Saleem and talk to them before they are get back to Luxor.'

That made me think of the Nubian Oasis, and the scene at breakfast.

'Oh, and Seleh, from the Nubian Oasis, he saw them too, that's why he helped Dwight and Randy get to the airport.'

'This it is not good, I may have to be go back to Luxor.'

'But it's too dangerous.'

'It may be more dangerous if I do not.'

Suddenly the taxi pulled to a stop; ahead, a long stream of traffic led to an intersection crammed with all sorts of vehicles. Rather than patiently wait their turn, the Egyptians had just picked any path, even setting a new path on the other side of the road, consequently clogging the intersection within seconds.

Instinctively, the driver started blasting on the horn, in an unconducted symphony of car horns. Saeed said something to the driver in Arabic, who stopped blasting his horn, then reached to the front of the car and grabbed a bundle of black clothes from the front seat.

'Here, put this on.'

It was another set of women's clothing; a large black dress and headdress, another burqa, the full kit and kaboodle.

'Not again! What for this time?'

'There is it the road block ahead; we can not be take the chance that you are recognized.'

I put the backpack on backwards, as a sort of breast pack/stomach pack, and, as I ventured into another episode of trans-gender, trans-cultural dress-ups, I couldn't help but try to sort out how the hell I'd got into this mess.

'How did the Secret Police find out about Kareem's file in the first place?'

'They had been watch my uncle for some time, they watch everyone, but, while he was do nothing, then he was not the threat. However, when he meet with you at Medinet Habu they become more interested.'

I instantly remembered.

'The soldier!'

'He was just it one testicle of the octopus; even the wall of the temple it have it the ear. We are followed to it the restaurant, and then, afterward, to the bazaar. The thing, they are still so bad in Egypt now, that for enough money, the son he would sell his own mother rather than to be held in it the prison and to be tortured.'

'And what about me?'

'As soon as they are realize Kareem he no longer have it the file, that you must be have them, they are set Kareem free, then kill him and are set you up as the killer. They go to your hotel around midday, and hope to arrest you, but find out from Seleh that you have taken it the tour to Dendera and Abydos.

They will be wait for you when you are get back, and it most like they will pass the information on to all the checkpoint between Luxor, Dendera and Abydos. The Secret Police they will not stop until they get them the file back. If we cannot be get you out of Egypt, then they will find you, arrest you, and you will meet it with the fatal accident.'

'Couldn't I just post the file to myself, or to someone else?'

'They are not stupid; they would have be anticipate this, and be watch all the foreign mail out of Luxor and Cairo. I do not think this is it the good idea.'

'Perhaps not. But if we made a copy...'

'It might protect the paper, but it will not save you. No, the best option it is to get you and the paper out of Egypt together.'

As we crossed a canal and passed through a little township, I took off my akubra and slipped the headdress over my head.

'What about the Australian Embassy?'

'You really are think they can help you now, they may well take it the interest in your case, but they would be need to know where you are, and, as I have said it, even the temple wall they have it the ear. Your Embassy it cannot protect you now, not even once you are in it the custody, you would have to actual be enter the embassy and to seek it the asylum. Even then, it is much easier for the Secret Police to explain it an accident than allow for you to be heard, or even to go free.'

The driver said something to Saeed and pointed ahead, where several uniformed militia had set up a road-block at an intersection before another canal, moving from car to car.

'Come, we must go.'

'What?'

Saeed paid the driver fifty pounds then dragged me out of the taxi.

'Do not say anything, just keep it your head down and follow me.'

Outside the taxi, I suddenly felt extremely vulnerable and exposed, even though I was covered from head to toe in black. Ooops, not quite head to toe, my shoes were poking out from under the hem of the dress. I quickly stooped to cover them and my butt in one fell swoop.

'Come.'

'Are you crazy?'

Saeed was leading us straight forward towards the roadblock.

'Indy, if you are want to be live, keep it your mouth shut, your head down, and follow me.'

Not much of a choice really. I cowered down and did as he said, fixing my eyes on his heels. I must have held my breath for nearly two minutes as we weaved our way through cars, carts, buses, bikes, tok toks and finally to the other side of the road block. Several times I brushed past officers who were looking into cars, taxis or buses. All the time, Saeed was talking away in Arabic to me as if I was his subordinate wife. But it worked, we made it, unassailed, to the other side of the checkpoint; or had we?

'Laww Smaht, Istanna,...'

It was coming from behind us, from one of the officers.

'Keep walking, do not look back.'

'Istanna,...Qef! Qef!'

We'd been spotted. I think the dress had lifted to show the back of my shoes and that they didn't match the whole package.

'Quick, get into the tok tok.'

Saeed pushed me into the back of a vacant tok tok parked at the side of the road, jumped in the driver's seat, and took off like the clappers. Now anyone who doesn't know what a tok tok is, or hasn't ridden in one, I can assure you it's like riding a runaway toboggan down an avalanche.

Tok toks are trikes, three-wheeled motorized rickshaws, about as stable as a toddler on a tightrope. It's like sitting in the back of a tiny toaster-oven while it plays Russian roulette dodging in and out of a convoy of Mack trucks. I later discovered, about six thousand people died and thirty-five thousand people were injured in road accidents each year in Egypt. I couldn't help but feel that most of those were in tok toks, and I was about to contribute to the toll. I would have tapped Saeed on the shoulder to tell him I'd rather take my chances with the Secret Police, but my knuckles had turned white due to the tightness of my grip on the framework of the tok tok.

Saeed tooted the squeaky little horn as we dodged cars, buses, other tok toks, pedestrians, cows, dogs, crossed over the railway line, turned right along the track, then left over a canal and continued further into the city. All the way, the threat of capture pursued us.

'I thought we were going to catch the train?'

'This we will do, but we are need to lose them first, and to make them think we are head back to Luxor.'

We ducked and weaved through the traffic, through street stalls, and down a myriad of alleyways I'm sure must have been no wider than the tok tok itself. At one point I was convinced we went through someone's living room and a little later we took out someone else's washing line; it was a scene straight out of a James Bond movie and I had no idea where we were. I didn't have a chance to look behind to see if we were still being followed, I was too preoccupied with what we were going to run into, over, or through. Was this where it was all going to end, splattered under a truck in a back alley of … hell, I didn't even know what town we were in.

Thankfully, almost as soon as it had started, Saeed pulled to a halt, prized my fingers from the frame, dragged me out of the back, and into a sleazy back-alley cafe. From there it was down this alley, into this shop, out the back door into another alley, through a crowded market, down another alley, another shop, another back door, I even remember going through a barber shop, much to the stunned faces of the men getting their hair cut. We came to a stop in a small general store.

'Saeed, I have to get something to drink, I'm as dry as a dead dingos donger.'

The shopkeeper stared in disbelief at the rather large Muslim woman before him who was suddenly speaking in a rather deep broad Australian language. Never the less, we gathered several large bottles of water, some buns, a few packets of chips, and a large bottle of lemon soft drink. I cracked the top on the soft drink, stuck it under my headdress, and swallowed almost half the bottle in one go. 'Hell, I needed that!' Next thing I heard was a distant train horn amid the cacophony of bike horns, car horns and truck horns.

'Saeed, the train, let's go.'

'Not to be in such a hurry, Indy, remember, we are on it Egyptian time. Wait here.'

He headed out of the shop, leaving me standing in my black tent, with all the locals thinking I was his Arabic mama. Thank god he returned less than thirty seconds later.

'Let us go, …slowly.'

Out the door, down the street around the corner and within a minute we were at the railway station: el Balyana; Saeed had done a big circle and landed us back at the station, without a tail.

'Where's the train?'

'Patience, my friend, it will be here presently.'

As we walked onto the platform and mingled with the locals, I looked back down the track for the approaching train. The 'station' was little more than a run down shack, and the 'station-master', for want of a better word, was bashing a signal switch with a sledgehammer trying to make a change of tracks. Oh, that instilled me with confidence – NOT!

The crossing itself was a single length of chain raised to form a makeshift barrier; that nobody took any regard for. It didn't matter that the train was bearing down, people, bikes, anyone who could negotiate the chain, was crossing from one side to the other. There were even people back down the line, trying to board the train as it was moving, and there were *no* platforms back down the line; that was plain crazy.

The last few crazy daredevils streaked in front of the train before it hit the crossing, including a little old lady that I was sure was going to be sliced, diced and pureed. If you think that was mayhem, you should have seen the pandemonium as the train pulled into the platform. Even before it stopped, people were jumping off, while others were launching themselves into quasi-vacant doorways. Others were running alongside throwing bags and boxes to people waiting at other doors or windows, I even saw one young guy dive into an open window. There were a couple of uniformed officers walking up the platform trying to find the proverbial needle in the haystack, but fortunately, with all that going on, Saeed and I had managed to blend and disappear into the background.

Once the train pulled to a stop, the bulk of the locals remaining started to push and shove their way onto the train; that was before those trying to get off had even taken a step. It was total and utter uneducated, inconsiderate, and ignorant chaos; every man and woman for themselves! 'When in Rome...', as they say. I used a few old football moves, a quick shift of the hips, an elbow or two into the ribs, and within a minute Saeed and I had jostled ourselves into the middle of the carriage.

This train ain't bound for glory

This wasn't first class, not even second, third or fourth class, this was cattle class, third-world travel at its 'best'. Windows were cracked, even completely missing, seats were ripped, patched, broken, missing, and the whole carriage hadn't seen a cleaner since it was commissioned, which was probably back when the first railway was built in Egypt back in 1853.

The carriage was chockers, standing room only; like peak hour on the trams back in Melbourne, only twenty degrees hotter, ninety percent humidity, and with the acrid smell of cheap high-tar cigarettes smudged into everything. Saeed said something to a few young men crammed into one of the seats and they reluctantly relinquished their prized possession. I was hot; it was like living in my own personal body sauna, how did the Muslim women do it? As we settled in to our newly gained territory, I leaned over to whisper in Saeed's ear.

'How long until we reach Mohammed's place.'
'About twelve maybe thirteen hour, Inshallah.'

My whisper turned to a mild roar.
'Thirteen hours!'
'Shhh!'

Curious looks and scowls emanated from the crowd of similarly burqa-clad women and rebellious youths that surrounded us. I pulled my head in.
'Thir-teen hours! If you think I'm going to sit here in this poor excuse for a

bunch of gothic glad-rags, then you need your head read, Fred.'

I stood up, my pathetic act of defiance put in its place by the uniformed officer that passed the open window beside me. Having thrown my mini tantrum and drawn undue attention to myself, I quickly and quietly sat back down, my tail firmly plastered between my legs.

'I can't sit here for thirteen hours in this get up, I'll die.'

'Look around you, Indy, all of these women here they will not only do that, and survive, but they will be grateful that they can.'

'What if someone talks to me?'

'It *was* my plan to tell them you are deaf and mute, however given your display it will now be most difficult to convince them of that. I shall have to be tell them you are my Australian wife and still are learn to adjust it to your new life in Egypt.'

A series of clunks and jolts signalled we were underway, creeping past the officers on the platform who seemed to have lost all interest. I breathed a sigh of relief.

'How come they gave up so quickly?'

'These they are just the local police, they do not really have it the interest in the matter of the Secret Police; they may not have even been look for us.'

My hopes lifted.

'Do you think so?

'No. So you had better to sit quiet and try not to draw it any *more* attention to yourself.'

I sat like a frozen pack of peas, just my eyes darting around the carriage. My mind was in paranoia overdrive as I scanned the other people in the train. 'Is *he* secret police?' Can *she* see through my disguise?' 'Will that six-year-old child sudden betray me and pull the emergency breaks, if there are any?' My head riveted in place, my eyes scanned the walls for emergency breaks. No! Then, I don't know why it came into my head, but it did.

'What about my stuff back at the Nubian Oasis?'

'What there is there?'

'A shirt, a pair of trousers, my tooth brush.'

Saeed gave me a look like he was about to burst out laughing at any second.

'Your toothbrush! You are really want to go back to Luxor and to get it?'

I realised the ridiculousness of what I had just said.

'Actually, I think I can live without them?'

Saeed's look of warped amusement turned to one of deadpan consternation.

'Given your present circumstance, it may be your only choice if you are wish to live.'

Saeed took out his mobile.

'Saleem, Saeed. *blah blah blah....*'

Actually it sounded more like he was gargling a fur-ball made of dry and dread-locked camel hair, but it was enough that I was able to deduce he was calling the minibus, that much I understood, the rest ran past me at a million miles an hour until....

'.....Mister Bill, ...shukran!'

He paused as if waiting, giving me a wink and a grin.

'Mister Bill, ...yes, very good, thank you. Please, you all are get safe away from Abydos then?......Good, good, yes, very good. Be aware, you will have it the very unwelcome welcome party when are you arrive back to Luxor. You must please to tell everyone to say nothing, that they have not seen it any paper or document, that they are have no idea what the police they are talk about, and that Mister Alex he is just a stranger to them, that they meet him on the felucca and that is all......yes, he is here, he is fine. He is blend in to the background very well......It is best I do not tell you, the less you are know, the more safe and better for all. I will see him safe to Mohammed and from there out of Egypt, but I will be come back in it a day or two to Luxor. ...you are? Very well, then I shall be speak to you then. ...No, it is not really possible for him to speak at the moment....Yes, yes, I will tell him. ...Very well, yes, ma'assalama, Inshallah.'

'What did he say?'

'They were all stop at the roadblock and the police they searched the bus, but they did not find anything and are let them pass.'

'Is that all?'

'No, he is go back to Aswan with Miss Pernille, but he will make it a point of catch up with you.'

'And Crystal?'

'This I do not know, but Allah he work in strange ways, my friend, I am sure you will be see her again.'

'I hope so.'

Apart from when the conductor came around and Saeed purchased our tickets, I think I sat there stunned, like a statue, hugging my backpack, for the best part of maybe half-an-hour, recalling every image I could of her; the first time as she approached the felucca, lying beside me at the campfire, dropping her sarong and playing naked in the water, walking out of the shower. I made a decision then and there, that if I survived this, no matter what it took, I was going to find her.

Some holiday this was, it was more like an adventure; that was it, I was in my own personal Indiana Jones movie, 'Indiana Alex and the Temples of Deception'. Hell, an adventure, that was an understatement, an experience, a life changing experience, that's what it was; that was if I could survive long enough to make any changes.

The whole trip was running through my mind like a rerun of a 'greatest hits'; the plane trip from Cairo, the bus trip from Abu Simbel through the desert, the taxi around Aswan with Monty, the most amazing felucca trip down to Esna, the magical mystery tour to Luxor, the bike trip across the Nile on the ferry and on to the Valley of the Kings and the West Bank, the took tok ride from hell, and now, a sardine-packed train carriage held together with decades-old layers of grime, cigarette smoke and human sweat. It was surreal to say the least. I had to remind myself, it could have been worse; millions of Jews were transported to Auschwitz, Treblinka and other concentration camps in cattle cars far worse than this.

Various beggars, vendors and street urchins passed through the carriage flogging everything from cha to fruit, nuts, tissues, anything that they could. Each of them had a distinctive short, repetitive, 'melodic' catch phrase that cut through the incessant rattle of the train and hubbub of chatter. It reminded me of a cross between the opening scenes of 'My Fair Lady' and 'Kismet' blended with the back alleys of the Aswan Bazaar and staged in a decrepit railway carriage.

All of a sudden there was a stirring within, a hive-like movement in the carriage, as several people started picking up bags and making their way towards the ends of the carriage. Then the train slowed to a stop: we had arrived at 'Girga'. As it had done at el Balyana, the same scenario of people pushing and shoving played itself out once more; the only difference being Saeed and I were not an active part in it, rather, we were dispassionate spectators.

I looked around, especially outside the windows, to see if there were any signs of police or militia; thankfully there were none. I was feeling a lot more comfortable; it seemed we had made our escape. Partly in celebration, and partly to quench my interminable thirst, I grabbed hold of the soft drink, tucked it under my headdress, and guzzled down the remainder of the contents, much to the amusement and whispered asides of the women opposite me.

Once underway again, I realized there was no way I was going to last another hour in this get-up, let alone a further twelve or more.

'Saeed, I can't do it, I have to take this outfit off.'

'Very well, but wait here while I am go and check it the rest of the train.'

He handed me one of the tickets, then climbed his way over a few bags and bodies before disappearing up the aisle and into the next carriage. I put the bags of provisions on his seat, claiming the territory, then resumed my seated foetal position. If I felt vulnerable before, now I felt totally naked and exposed. I dared not move a muscle or say a word for fear someone might engage in conversation. So staring out the window was the best option, and that's what I did.

Ten minutes later we pulled up again: 'el Osirat'; Christ, no wonder it was going to take twelve hours, if we stopped at every local village over the next six or seven hundred kilometres we were going to get nowhere fast.

I kept an eye out for uniforms but there were none to be seen; hell, I could hardly make out the station. I was feeling even better and starting to relax. Within a minute the cattle were offloaded and loaded and we were off again. I sat in my own little bubble and spent the next half-an-hour or so watching the landscape roll on repetitively outside the window as we rambled alongside the canal, polluted to the hilt with all sorts of rubbish. Despite this, women were washing the family's clothes and dishes in it, whilst nearby children were happily swimming. Beyond that were green fields, banana plantations, date palms, ramshackle dwellings, and the occasional glimpse of the Nile.

Several miles further out, the ever-present desert snaked along both sides as a reminder of the fragility of this third-world country where the majority of the population lived on the edge of life.

As the sun sunk lower in the western sky, shining directly into the carriage, I was getting even hotter, more uncomfortable, and considerably concerned that Saeed had been away for so long. To add to my angst, several of the 'natives' had been eyeing the seat opposite me with wanton lust; I felt a mutiny coming on.

Much to my relief, as the train slowed and pulled to a halt at its next scheduled stop, Saeed appeared from the front carriages. I picked up the bags for him to sit, then leaned in close.

'Thank God you're back, I'm about to melt through the floor.'

'Be patient, my friend, this it is el Monshaa, the next stop it is Sohag. If we are get past Sohag without we see any police on the train, then I think perhaps it might be safe for you to remove your burqa.'

'How long will that be?'

He grinned and chuckled under his breath.

'In Egyptian time, or western time?'

'Give me a break!'

'About another twenty minute or so.'

I took a deep breath and opened a bottle of water. To my shock, rather than keep his large frame parked firmly on the disintegrating leather, Saeed got to his feet and took off again.

'Where are you going?'

'I have still to check it the rear carriage.'

'Shit!...'

I took a few deep gulps of water, slammed the top back on, and resumed my embryonic holding pattern.

'...here we go again.'

The next twenty minutes was déjà vu, just like the previous; street sellers singing out as they carved a path through the smoke-filled train, their nicotine-and-tar-damaged voices scraping across my eardrums like fingernails on the blackboard. Thankfully the open or missing windows helped keep the disgusting stench of rancid cigarette smoke from asphyxiating me. The only difference was the ever-increasing intensity of the late afternoon sun as it seared its way into the sausage-shaped pressure-cooker that was to be my 'home' for the next twelve hours. Wearing black certainly didn't help either; it made me feel like a solar panel or a solar oven.

Just as we pulled into Sohag, Saeed returned from the rear carriages and sat in his seat, which was just as well because the crowd waiting to board the train would have rivalled the MCG on Grand Final day, game seven of the World Series, and the World Cup final, all rolled into one; I don't think I'd have been able to save the seat much longer. If the previous stops were frantic, this was a bun-fight bigger than a bakers' feud on Good Friday; voices were raised in anger, confrontations abounded, and there was much blustering of egos. That was something about the Egyptians though, whilst they vented their emotions and displeasure with 'mucho gusto', seldom if ever did it escalate to physical violence, and if it looked like it was going to, bystanders would interject and keep the squabbling parties separated.

By the time the dust had settled and we were underway once again, everyone had flexed their egos sufficiently enough to feel validated and noticed and had found the most 'comfortable' spot for the trip ahead.

'Any sign of the police?'

'No, it seem we might have fooled them.'

'And about time too!'

As the cabin was packed tighter than a peak-hour train in Tokyo and the sun was finally setting, I decided to disrobe where I was, standing up and reaching for my headdress. Saeed grabbed my leg.

'May I suggest that, rather than cause it a scene and to do it here, you are go to it the toilet and are make your transformation there.'

It made sense, so I sat back down, waited a minute or two until everyone had completely settled down, then casually got up and started to negotiate my way through the carriage to the toilet. I should have asked Saeed what the Arabic words for 'excuse me' were, as my Australian accent was bringing looks of confusion and very little parting of the ways. Never the less, I navigated my way around the obstacle course of people and bags and into the toilet, which fortunately was unoccupied.

Christ, the 'toilet' was just a hole in the floor, and it stank to high heaven. For a second I contemplated leaving the headdress on to act as a gas mask, but then I just gritted my teeth, blocked my nose, and breathed in through my mouth. As I disrobed, I would have loved to have left my disguise behind, even stuffed it through the hole in the floor, but, given there was the possibility I might have had need of it down the track, I folded and rolled it up, and stuffed it into my backpack. Then, slinging the backpack over my shoulder, I plonked my akubra back on my sconce, and headed back out of the toilet.

The teenage boys standing outside the door didn't take much notice when I entered the toilet, but they sure did a double-take or two when I opened the door and walked out; one of them even stuck his head back inside, no doubt half-expecting to see the fully-clad mama that had gone in, still inside.

It was a lot easier making my way back to my seat, as the sight of a tall, bronzed Aussie the size of an outdoor dunny, with an akubra on his head and a swag over his shoulder, was clearly a sight that invoked a reaction. As I sat back down, Saeed leaned across, a grin on his face.

'I think you might have been noticed.'

It seemed like everyone in the train was looking at me.

'I don't get it; what's the deal? Surely they've all seen foreigners before?'

'Oh, yes, of course, but foreigner it is not usual for them to take it the local train, it is not allowed.'

'Why not? I mean I can see *why* foreigners would have second thoughts about travelling on them, but why isn't it allowed?'

'It is not safe; there are no police to protect you.'

'Then, that's a good thing. But who exactly is it the police have to protect foreigners from?'

'The terrorist.'

I looked around the carriage, the twilight creating an eerie atmosphere within the carriage.

'Well, if you believe all the propaganda, then the whole train is full of terrorists.'

'Then do not say I did not warn you, you never know who it is hiding under the burqa.'

Clearly those who had been sitting beside us, or standing nearby, were putting two and two together, they knew it must have been me who was sitting there previously, and dressed in complete Muslim attire. The thoughts and questions running through their heads probably ran along the lines of; 'Why?', 'Is he some sort of western weirdo?', 'He is the ugliest woman I have ever seen.', 'Boy, those western women are butch.', and 'He married *her*?'.

I had to do something to keep my mind occupied or else it was going to explode in a lethal cocktail of boredom and paranoia. Unzipping my backpack, I took out my notebook and fired it up; at least I could use the time to bring my diary up to date.

Music first. I was tempted to play Talking Heads' 'We're on the road to nowhere' but, though it kept running through my head, I didn't have it. I decided on some Renaissance Choral Music, starting with Miserere by Tallis; it was about the furthest from where I currently found myself and I thought it might calm me down and help me get through at least part of the next twelve hours.

No music for the masses this time, hardly their cup of tea in any case, so it was out with the earphones and off into an old English Cathedral.

I started making notes on the discussions over breakfast, the White and Black Deserts, the Valley of the Golden Mummies, on the size of the Thera tsunami, Albert Slosman and the mechanics and timings of the pole shifts. Then there was the Hyksos princess, Scota, or Herit, and her escape from Egypt and ultimate journey to Ireland. It was a breakfast that gave me more to chew over and digest than a dozen bowls of hi-fibre bran.

So much had unfolded during the day; as we stopped at El Maragha, and I watched the circus, I didn't know where to start. Then, as we set off again, I realized it would be much easier to remember things if I grouped them into categories. First, the structural things, the tangible evidence, because I had found even more evidence supporting my theories, both at Dendera and Abydos.

At Dendera;

- the massive mud-brick outer walls,
- the scarab on the underside of the lintel at the Domitian entrance gate,
- the red and black granite columns in and around the Coptic Church,
- the worn red-granite foundation stones of Nectanebo's birth house,
- the orientation of the Iseum,
- the red granite at both the Domitian and Eastern gates and scattered around the site,
- at the threshold to the Hathor temple and at numerous doorways within the temple,
- the alabaster poking through the floor and underground in the crypt.
- The tunnels leading down to…?

Then, at Abydos;

- at both the temples of Seti I and Ramses II, the alabaster, limestone and marble floors and walls,
- the red, and black, granite doorways at the Temple of Ramses II,
- as well as the revelation that was the subterranean Osireion, including,
- the subterranean limestone passageways,
- the massive red-granite pillars and lintels,
- the presence of the 'buried' pre-dynastic and earliest dynasty tombs and structures at Kom es-Sultan, Shunet el-Zebib, and Umm el Qa'ab.

Next I made note of the various images on the walls and ceilings, all revealing pieces of the story, including:

at Dendera;

- the cosmic comic strips of the ceilings, telling the story of the heavens and the journeys of the gods through them,
- the 'festival of the fallen sky' on the rear wall and the zodiac on the ceiling of the Osiris suite, reflecting the pole shift, the world literally turning upside down,
- the image of the man with an anaconda for a penis, that is, the ancient cathode tube, down in the crypt, although I was still somewhat baffled by that,
- the 'insemination' of Isis, looking more like the abdominal harvesting of an ova, fertilization and implantation,
- and the anointing of the pharaoh by pouring drops of holy water over him.

And at Abydos;

- the helicopter hieroglyph,
- the different layers of silt and sand covering Osireion and Merenptah passage.
- and the amazing 'Flowers of Life' on the granite pillar in the Osireion.

By the time we stopped at Tahta, the now familiar human bun-fight hardly drew my attention. I was more focused on recalling the day's events. I didn't quite remember how Pieter's explanation of how the basic geometry of the Osireion, as an edge-on double pentagram, related to the Blue Lotus and to Tryptamines, something about hallucinogens and organic chemistry.

But my experience of the Osireion, touching the stones, and my experience at the false door in the shrine of Amun, sucked off past Mars to the far reaches of the solar system and back, was telling me that either I had a great imagination, I was going crazy, or that something major was shifting within me; my thoughts were drawing me to the latter.

The Osireion wasn't *just* a star-gate, it was more; it was an inter-dimensional gateway of, and for, consciousness. That 'Consciousness, with Intent, Manifests', and that ultimately all matter was just slowed-down consciousness; a pea-soup of possibilities and probabilities that modified, shifted and changed, through experience and the perspective from which you chose to view that experience. The whole thing was and is a cycle of fractals that somehow was represented by and in the 'Flower of Life'.

Hesat, emissary of the Hathors, told me that the night before, *'Look for the sacred geometry, for it is present in all things; all things contain it, all things exist because of it'*, and she was right, I had found it at Abydos, it was like a confirmation, I just had to shift my perspective. My next step was clear, *'Ascension is not a pathway, it's a process of self-awareness and mastery of all levels of the moment that is the Oneness.'*

When we stopped at the village of Tema, I became fully aware of just how far from mastering the moment, and just how far on the pathway to Oneness, the human race had to go, everyone was just looking out for themselves, pushing and shoving without any consideration for anyone else. It was the same scenario about ten minutes down the track at Sidfa; I was glad Saeed had managed to procure seats for us when he did, although the next time the conductor passed he looked quite bemused when it was a westerner who handed him the ticket.

That moment of amusement aside, seeing the other repetitive patterns of human behaviour was a wake up call, I could clearly see it was time for humanity to make a change, and time for me to make a change as well; I'd had enough of English Church music, it was time to bring things back into the 20th Century. I scanned through my library. 'Of course – Jesus Christ Superstar!' As the first guitar notes of the Overture twanged in, I turned my mind to everyone else, and their relationships to each other and to me; especially Bill, Pernille, and Crystal.

My relationship with Bill had taken on a more multi-layered aspect, not just because he was a multi-millionaire, and not just because of him being Roger Mortimer and me being Robert the Bruce. I wondered if I could somehow inspire the scientists to exhume Scota and Robert and do a DNA comparison, and if they did what the outcomes might be. But it was his life as Marc Antony and mine as his son Alexander Helios, that was the most relevant connection in this moment.

'My mind is clearer now, at last all to well, I can see where we all soon will be.
If you strip away, the myth from the man you will see where we all soon will be.'

It was true, I mean, when I jumped on board the White Rose, who'd have thought that Pernille was Cleopatra, Jacques was Ramses II and Julius Caesar, that Bill was Marc Antony, and that Crystal was both Cleopatra's sister, Arsinoe IV, and Cleopatra's daughter, Cleopatra Selene II. As for me, it seemed I was Alexander Helios, the son of Cleopatra and Marc Antony, and that all that was feasible was itself pretty mind-blowing.

The hubbub at the next station, Abu Tig, was mirrored perfectly by the music. Not only that but it was almost begging me to tell what I knew.

'What's the buzz? Tell me what's a happening.
What's the buzz? Tell me what's a happening.'

But, there was also a message, and I grabbed the backpack tightly, thinking about Kareem's murder and the importance of getting his papers out of Egypt.

'Save tomorrow for tomorrow, think about today instead.'

I had to get out of Egypt first, and there was a long way to go before I could say I was safe. Saeed leaned across and got my attention.

'The next stop it is Asyut, if we can get it through there without any police, then I think we may have deceived them.'

It sounded good to me.

'It seems to me a strange thing mystifying that a man like you could waste his time on women of her kind.'

It got me thinking about Crystal, and about Caesarion and Jesus. Many aspects of the Christian Bible saw their origins in ancient Egyptian mythology, the three kings, Jesus' birth, all pointing towards Jesus actually being Caesarion, who had escaped from Egypt in the guardianship of his wet nurse, her husband and their children; if the Romans were looking for a lone child, what better place to hide than as one of many children in a family.

If Caesarion *was* the 'Son of God' and 'King of Kings', and, after studying the Eastern philosophies for around twelve years in India and Nepal, he 'came in' from the wilderness of 'Sin', in from the Sinai, or in from Sumer, and, now known as Jesus, it made perfect sense that he travelled back to Egypt and to Algeria to find his half-sister, Cleopatra Selene II, the *sang réal*, now known as Mary Magdalene.

Having found her, Caesarion then travelled with his 'family', including his half-brother, Alexander Helios, James the Just, namely *me*, to Jerusalem, along the way being baptised, or rather anointed as rightful pharaoh and spiritual leader, by John the Baptist, who was an uncle of Jesus and a High Priest of the Tat Brotherhood, finally arriving in Jerusalem preaching about the Divine Feminine.

If Cleopatra Selene was Mary Magdalene, and the body in Srinagar was Caesarion, then, just like Robert the Bruce and Scota, it could all be confirmed or denied by a simple DNA test on the body at Srinagar, and the woman in the mausoleum in Algeria. And if Crystal was Mary, and I was James, then it would explain perfectly why I was 'wasting' my time on a woman of her kind. Why? because she was the *sang réal*.

The soundtrack was giving me a chronological structure through which I noted the unfolding discussions of the day. When 'Then We Are Decided' started, I listened with great interest to the lyrics.

'Why let him upset us? Caiaphas let him be...
The difference is they call him king; the difference frightens me. What about the Romans, when they see king Jesus crowned, do you think they'll stand around cheering and applauding...
What about our priesthood, don't you see that we could fall, if we are to last at all we cannot be divided.'

But now I know Jesus didn't claim to be the King of the Jews, because he wasn't a Jew, he was King of Egypt *and* Rome, and therefore ruler of all people in those lands. Still, it was a threat to Caiaphas and his authority.

In between typing paragraphs and looking out the window for inspiration, I had been noticing that the closer we got to Asyut, the more Saeed seemed to grow increasingly agitated. Eventually he leaned over and tapped me on the knee.

'Indy, I think perhaps it is best you should be put it your burqa back on, at least until we are get past Asyut.'

We had been on the train for nearly four hours or so, and I was fairly certain we were in the clear. Still, I don't know whether it was false bravado, foolishness, or perhaps the subliminal influence of the music....

> *'Try not to get worried, try not to turn on to problems that upset you.....*
> *Everything's alright, yes Everything's alright yes....*
> *Close your eyes, close your eyes and relax'*

... but I told him everything was fine, not to worry, that we were in the clear, and that he should close his eyes and relax. He wasn't easily convinced, probably because he knew the Secret Police far better than I did, but after a few attempts to get me to change he eventually conceded and sat back in his seat.

> *'We need a more permanent solution to our problem...*
> *Blood and destruction because of one man....*
> *For the sake of the nation this Jesus must die.'*

I saw the parallel straight away, the Secret Police were the Sadducees, the Amun Priests of our times, and they wanted me, and the messages I carried, disposed of, eliminated. Similarly Caiaphas must have used the Romans, used Tiberius and his fear of the true heir, to crucify Jesus as a political enemy and threat to both his and Tiberius's respective positions. Perhaps Saeed was right?

> *'Hosanna, Hey Sanna, Sanna, Sanna Hosanna, Hey Sanna Hosamnna..,'*

The change of song put me back into a more optimistic state of mind and focused me on my notes.

> *'...Tell the mob who sing your song that they are fools and they are wrong,*
> *they are a curse they should disperse.'*

I wish the modern Christians, Jews and Muslims, would get that message; the 'mob' sing the praises of God, Allah, Moses, Jesus, Mohammed (insert your own deity or 'ascended martyr'), not really knowing who Moses, Jesus and Mohammed really were. So the millions of Catholics, Anglicans, Mormons other subdivisions of the Christian faith, along with the various Jewish factions and Islamic streams are all fools, blind sheep, and totally 'wrong', although, as Crystal would say, 'There is no right or wrong, just perspective'.

And she's spot on there; the various religions are just stepping stones to discover the truth. It's just that billions are stranded on their respective stepping stones in the middle of the river of doctrine and dogma. It's just a matter of time before they are swamped and swept away by the river of truth. Until then, to the rest of us, they are indeed a curse and should disperse; I know Bill would be right with me on that one.

The blind adulation was echoed in the next song, Simon Zealotes.

> *'Jesus, I am with you, touch me, touch me, Jesus.*
> *Jesus, I am on your side, kiss me, kiss me Jesus.'*

But it hinted at the real drama going on behind the scenes.

> *'Keep them yelling their devotion, but add a touch of hate at Rome.*
> *You will rise to a greater power, we will win ourselves a home.*
>
> *You'll get the power and the glory.'*

The drive by the Zealots to oust the Romans had clearly concerned Caiaphas, and, once Jesus started gathering a following, Caiaphas used Jesus' real identity as an opportunity to 'keep the peace' by eliminating his major threats, Simon Zealots and Judas Iscariot, the main protagonists of the zealot faction of the Jews/Egyptians, alongside Jesus as a sign against any future political and religious rebellions.

The tempo changed as the album kicked into 'Poor Jerusalem'.

'If you knew all that I knew ...
To conquer death you only have to die.'

I thought about Kareem, he was free now, in many ways he *had* conquered death, and if I could get his papers out of Egypt, then he will not only have conquered death but have defeated his assassins as well. And, as 'Pilate's dream' started, it raised the question of who *really* was responsible for the crucifixion of Jesus.

'And then I heard them mentioning my name,
and leaving me the blame.'

How true was that, Pontius Pilate got the blame for the crucifixion of Jesus, but the reality was he was just a pawn, the real culprits were most probably Caiaphas and possibly Tiberius. It's pretty clear that Judas betrayed the pacifist Essenes, led by Jesus, but in turn was doubled-crossed by Caiaphas, who not only crucified Judas alongside Jesus, but the leader of the Zealots, Simon, as well. Musically we rolled on into the temples of Jerusalem.

'Roll on up, Jerusalem. Come on in, Jerusalem.
Sunday, here we go again.'

Physically, we rolled on to Asyut, and we must have been getting close because Saeed couldn't sit tight any longer. He got to his feet and started to look out the window, down the track towards the station. At the same time the carriage stirred into a hive of activity; Asyut was a major city and then was no doubt going to be considerable traffic on and off the train, just like the moneylenders and merchants in the temple.

'Sunday, here we go again', it suddenly hit me that I had absolutely no idea what day it was, what date it was, or even how long I'd been in Egypt. The past seemed irrelevant, all that mattered was this moment, and getting *out* of Egypt. Saeed had a concerned look on his face.

'Wait here. I really think perhaps you should be put back on your burqa.'

And, with that, he muscled his way up the aisle and towards the door. What had he seen?

'My time is almost through. Little left to do.
After all I've tried for three years, seems like thirty, seems like thirty,'

That didn't help things, hardly the optimistic tune I wanted to hear at this point.

'See my tongue, I can hardly talk.
See my skin, I'm a mass of blood.'

Nor was that; I had images of what the Secret Police would do to me if they caught me. I nervously looked again for Saeed, but he had disappeared amid the masses at the end of the carriage.

'I don't know how to love him. What to do, how to move him. I've been
changed, yes really changed.
In these past few days, when I've seen myself, I seem like someone else.'

This was all getting a bit freaky; it seemed like every time I put on any music, it was almost as if it was commenting on my life, on my journey. Within a few days Saeed had become like a brother to me, in fact more of a brother than my own brother, whom I often felt was more like a stranger that I had shared parents and a house with as

I grew up. My actual brother and I were like chalk and cheese, and if I was different to him before the trip, I was even more so now; I couldn't even remember the person who had climbed aboard a plane ten or eleven days ago, he didn't exist any more. The train pulled to stop just as 'Damned for all time' started, and, as it did, all hell broke loose in the cabin and out on the platform.

'I have no thought at all about my own reward.
I really didn't come here of my own accord.
Just don't say I'm ... damned for all time.'

Wasn't that just the truth, I'd stumbled into the situation I was in, and my only hope was just that, that I wasn't damned.

'Cut the protesting, forget the excuses.
We want information. Get up of the floor.
We have the papers we need to arrest him.
You know his movements. We know the law.
Your help in this matter won't go unrewarded.
We'll pay you in silver, cash on the nail.
We just need to know where the soldiers can find him.
With no crowd around him.
Then we can't fail.'

I had visions that they'd just arrested Saeed on the platform. Yep, and that's what they would do to him, beat him up until they *found* the papers, and, as for their 'reward', I knew from the silver they gave Judas it was quickly sold out for a few rusty nails and a couple of wooden beams. No thanks; these guys were not going to take *me* alive.

What was I saying? I was getting too carried away with the music, with the lyrics, and my imagination was going wild and getting the best of me. The reality was, that at this moment, I was fine; the papers were fine, I was fine, Saeed was fine, and everything was all right! Everyone was settling down but the train still hadn't set off from Asyut.

'Look at all my trials and tribulations,
sinking in a gentle pool of wine.
Don't disturb me now, I can see the answers,
'Til this evening is this morning, life is fine.'

Trials and tribulations was spot on the mark, and forget the pool of wine, what I wouldn't have given for an ice-cold beer or three. In the meantime, until the evening *was* the morning, then life was fine and I could get by on a few bottles of tepid water.

'Always hoped that I'd be an apostle.
Knew that I would make it if I tried
Then when we retire, we can write the Gospels,
so they'll still talk about us when we've died.'

That was ironic, especially considering Matthew, Mark, Luke and John, supposedly the Gospel authors and cornerstones of New Testament of *'The Bible'*, were in fact probably NOT disciples of Jesus at all, rather cronies of Paul's and probably Zealots. That meant that it was their 'split' from the diehard Zealots, their jumping ship, that probably saved them from the Qumran, Masada, massacre in 73 AD.

But there was nothing new about making things up to suit your own agendas. The whole 'Davidic' lineage, the lineage from Abraham cited by Moses, was probably all fabricated by Moses, all an adoption, distortion and corruption of the lineage from

149

Egypt, all just to give himself validity.

And Paul was no different; as a Zealot, because of the popularity of Jesus and his teachings, Paul would have feared losing his power and position, and so around 49 AD with the expulsion of the Jews from Rome, Paul probably invented the 'conversion' story on the way to Damascus to give himself some street cred. He then usurped power from James and used the powerful issue of circumcision to create a new hybrid religion, hijacking the worship of Isis, the divine feminine, and shifting and drastically distorting the focus to the masculine, into the Holy Father.

> *'One of you here dining, one of my twelve chosen,*
> *will leave to betray me.'*

Saeed! He'd left me. Where was he? Had he left, just like Judas had left? When he looked out the window earlier, did he see the Secret Police waiting on the platform and leave to betray me? Was that why we hadn't left Asyut yet? Was this going to be my Last Supper? Suddenly the train clunked and clanked and slowly departed Asyut and I realized I was just getting paranoid; the twilight had disappeared and now it was dark outside, as was my outlook.

> *'I only want to say, if there is a way,*
> *Take this cup away from me*
> *for I don't want to taste its poison.*
> *Feel it burn me, I have changed.*
> *I'm not as sure, as when we started.*
> *Then, I was inspired. Now, I'm sad and tired...'*

I was tired, very tired, and I did want this cup of poison, the file of papers, taken away. And yes, once I *was* inspired, but now, now I *wasn't* as sure as when I'd first been given them. But what could I do? Like Jesus, this was my destiny, and I was resolved to my fate, I had to see it through.

> *'But if I die, See the saga through*
> *and do the things you ask of me,*
> *Let them hate me, hit me, hurt me,*
> *nail me to their tree.'*

Jesus, I had worked myself into quite a state. As we pulled into the next station, Manqabad, I took a few deep breaths and looked at the playlist on my computer. The next track was 'The Arrest'; was it an omen?

I took a chance and stuck my head out the window. Searching through the milling throng, up towards the head of the train, I saw several uniformed police; at least four of them. And who were they talking to? I couldn't believe it, yes, it was, it was Saeed. I sat back down, in stunned disbelief.

> *'Tell me Christ how you feel tonight.*
> *Do you plan to put up a fight*
> *Do you feel that you've had the breaks?*
> *What would you say were your big mistakes?'*

It seemed my biggest mistake was trusting Saeed; he wasn't leading me away from the Secret Police, he was delivering me directly into their grubby little hands. Would I put up a fight? You bet I would. But why would he betray me? What had changed? Careful not to be seen, I cautiously stuck an eyeball back out the window. What was he saying to them? And what were they saying to him?

> '*I think I've seen you somewhere. I remember.*
> *You were with that man they took away.*

I recognize your face.'

Of course, they had recognized him.

'You've got the wrong man, lady. I don't know him,
And I wasn't where he was tonight
Never near the place.'

Just like 'Peter's Denial', Saeed was protecting his butt as well. Of course he was telling them they had the wrong person, that he didn't know what they were talking about, it was a case of history repeating itself; Saeed wasn't Judas, he was Peter, I was Jesus, and the Secret Police were the Roman soldiers and Caiaphas. What next? In someway I could understand it, I mean if Jesus was Caesarion, and Caesarion wasn't owning up to who he was, then Peter would hardly have stuck his head on the chopping block either. But then again, I doubt Jesus expected Judas to turn on him either. The next thing, the officers all got into the second carriage and Saeed walked down the platform, squeezing his way into the third carriage just as the train started to pull out of the station. Was he returning to me, just as Judas had done at the last Supper, to give me the kiss of betrayal?

'Who is this broken man cluttering up my hallway?
Who is this unfortunate?

I'll tell you who, 'Someone, Alex, King of the Patsies'.

'What do you mean by that? That is not an answer.
You're deep in trouble friend,'

Deep in trouble? I was up shit creek without a paddle. But what could I do? I could put the burqa back on and shift to another carriage, hoping to blend in with all the other women. But, no, that would only delay my fate; eventually they would find me. I only had one option, to get off the train and go it alone.

As 'Herod's Song' started up I scanned the carriage, trying to put the pieces of my escape plan together. First, I'd need to get back to the toilet and get back into the burqa. But once I'd made the move, there was no going back; with no one to reserve the seats, they would be snapped up in a blink of an eye and I would not be able to talk my way back.

'Prove to me that you're divine; change my water into wine.'

If only it was that simple! I took a few more huge gulps of water; what I really needed was a stiff drink or two, a little Dutch courage.

'Prove to me that you're no fool; walk across my swimming pool.
If you do that for me, then I'll let you go free.'

Somehow I was starting to think that's what it would take for me to get out of this mess, a bloody miracle. Getting off the train unnoticed was one thing, but that was just the start, somehow I had to get back down and over the Nile to Cairo, and then out of the country. Shit!

'This was unexpected, what do I do now? Could we start again please?'

Oh, if only.

'I've been very hopeful, so far.
Now for the first time, I think we're going wrong.
Hurry up and tell me, this is just a dream.
Oh could we start again please?'

I *think* we're going wrong! Christ, I went way past wrong a few days ago, back in Luxor, when I agreed to take Kareem's papers. And look at the ramifications and

151

repercussions, Kareem got his throat cut and now I'm on the run from probably the most corrupt Secret Police in the world. Good choice – **NOT**!

But it's all a perceived reality, right? It's all a dream, depending of course on where you choose to see things from, and if this *was* happening, and it *was my* dream, then I could change it. What was it again? Yes, 'Consciousness, with Intent, Manifests!'

I closed my eyes and repeated my intention. 'Present me with the solution. Manifest the pathway. Present me with the solution. Manifest the pathway. Present me with the solution. Manifest the pathway. **Christ, how in the hell am I going to get out of this mess**?'

Just the next song, 'Judas' Death', began, and, as if on cue, Saeed appeared at the far end of the carriage, having returned from the front of the train. As he pushed his way through the passengers the following word resounded in my ears.

> *'What you have done will be the saving of everyone.*
> *You'll be remembered forever for this.*
> *And not only that, you've been paid for your efforts.*
> *Pretty good wages for one little kiss.'*

By the time Saeed reached my row, Judas had hung himself and I was in no mood to follow suit. Saeed called to me, gesturing intently whilst checking back up the carriage.

'Come, we must go.'

I held my ground.

'Judas!'

'What?'

'You just want me to come with you so you can betray me to the Secret Police?'

> *'We need him crucified; it's all you have to do.*
> *We need him crucified; it's all you have to do.'*

'Indy, I think it you have been in the sun too long. We must be get off at the next stop, the police they are look for you, they know you are on it the train.'

'Sure they do, you told them.'

'I tell them nothing.'

> *'Crucify him. Crucify him.*
> *He's done no wrong. No, not the slightest thing.'*

'Come on, Saeed, I saw you talking to them.'

'Yes, to find out what it is they were doing. One of them he was a friend from my village. He did not know I was involved, so it was easy for me to find out what it is they are doing. But we do not have it the time to discuss this now, they will come through this carriage very soon, and they are check everyone.'

I paused for a second. 'Present me with the solution. Manifest the pathway.' And here was Saeed, standing with his outstretched hand, almost begging me to follow. Was this the solution I had asked for?

> *'Crucify him. Crucify him.'*

I took a leap of faith.

'OK.'

I grabbed my backpack, the bag of provisions, and my laptop and followed him towards the rear of the carriage, the music to 'the thirty-nine lashes' still playing in my earphones. As we reached the toilet, the train started to pull to a stop at Manfalut.

'Come on, let's jump off.'

Saeed grabbed hold of me.

'No, they will see you; we must wait.'

He was right. As soon as the train stopped, two police quickly jumped out of a carriage two carriages up, to survey the passengers alighting. Saeed pushed me into the toilet.

'Quick, get back into it your disguise.'

Saeed quickly closed the door behind me, the last words I heard before I removed my earphones and shut down the laptop being;

'You've got to be careful. You could be dead soon. Could well be.'

Hardly inspiring, but certainly great motivation to do anything I could to survive. I wasn't sure if I would die at the hands of the Secret Police, or because of the toxic air within the toilet. If I thought it was bad before, now it was a thousand times worse. It was as if a busload of Nullabor truckies had all dumped their loads after a heavy night of beer, and salami, garlic and onion pizzas.

It took me quite a few minutes to get my bearing, partly because the air was making me dizzy and nauseous, but mainly because the light wasn't working in the toilet and, apart from the occasional passing streetlamp, it was virtually pitch black. The irony of that wasn't lost on me either, fumbling around in the dark trying to find my way forward. In fact I felt a bit like those poor souls at Treblinka who had been led into the gas chambers; what a nightmare that must have been.

As I groped around in the dark and finally pulled the burqa out of the backpack and started to put it on, the words of the next song, 'Superstar' came to mind.

'Every time I look at you I don't understand
Why you let the things you did get so out of hand
You'd have managed better if you'd had it planned.
Why'd you choose such a backward time in such a strange land?'

It sort of said it all really. I wondered if it was in fact a bit of a metaphor for my life up until this point; I'd never really followed a plan, I did in a way, in that I always followed my heart, but I never really had a firm and clear direction. My marriages were pretty much the same.

I didn't even have the dress half on when, suddenly, the train lurched forward and we were underway once more. How long to the next stop? Soon, I hoped; I knew exactly where this soundtrack was heading, where this train was heading, and I needed to get off before it reached its destination, the crucifixion. Even though I now knew, according to the Russian aristocrat, Nicolas Notovitch, that Jesus, Yuz Asaf, Isa, or Caesarion, didn't actually die on the cross, but lived to the age of one-hundred-and-twenty and was then buried in a tomb in Srinagar, India, called Roza Bal, I wasn't too thrilled about trying my luck and be nailed to the cross as a martyr.

The up side was that Mary and Jesus were reunited after the crucifixion, travelling to Turkey and Rome, so that gave me hope that I would see Crystal again. Then I wondered if this whole thing with the papers and the train trip was my trial, my crucifixion, to finally kill off the old me and resurrect a newer improved model? Eventually I completed my transformation, stuffed my laptop into the backpack, and went to exit the toilet. I was greeted by Saeed's hand.

'Stay inside.'

And he slammed the door on me.

'Are you serious? It's toxic in here.'

'It is toxic out here too, my friend; lock it the door, the Secret Police they have just entered this carriage. Keep your head down, and no matter what happen, do not say it a word.'

I must have waited, like a condemned man, for nearly half-an-hour; enduring the torture of standing in that gas chamber with my head out the window, waiting for the Secret Police to make their way through the carriage and discover me, or maybe have someone snitch on me and dob me in. I even contemplated climbing out the window at the next station.

Eventually there was a firm knock at the door. I thought it was Saeed and was about to reply, then I hesitated, and just as well, because an Arabic voice said something from the other side, and it sounded very deliberate and authoritative. I quickly put my headdress back on as the next thing I heard was Saeed speaking, I assumed telling the officer I was deaf and mute; so I played along.

Suddenly the moment of truth was upon us as the train slowed to a halt; it was now or never. Unlocking the door, I stooped down, and slowly opened it. Saeed quickly stepped in and grabbed my arm and we made a slow but deliberate break for the carriage door. I almost stopped breathing when a member of the Secret Police grabbed my other arm, but then assisted me down the steps, off the train, and on to the platform.

I spotted the exit, waved my hand in thanks and made a beeline straight for it.
'Istanna, Istanna!'

I knew that meant trouble and went to bolt off, but Saeed held me firmly. From the carriage door the Secret Policeman was holding up not only the bag with the food, but also my backpack; I couldn't believe that in the height off the tension I'd left it behind on the toilet floor. He jumped down and ran over towards us; bags in hand. My god, if he only knew what was inside. Saeed headed him off at the pass and retrieved them.
'Shukran, shukran.'

They exchanged a few more words, embraced, then the officer re-boarded the train and we waited and waved as it headed off on its journey northward to Cairo.

The train safely departed from the platform, I leaned in to Saeed and muttered firmly under my headdress.
'Let's get the hell out of here!'

We made our way off the platform and straight into one of several waiting taxis.
'Where are we?'
'El-Qorgas.'
'And where are we going?'
'Jarf Sarhan.'
'How far away is that?'
'About twenty kilometre.'

I don't know why I was asking; I had no idea where those places were anyway. All I knew was that I was about an hour or so north of Asyut, and a long way from safety.
'And what's there?'
'I have a cousin who live there, I am sure we can stay it with him for the night.'

Within minutes we were out in the countryside passing through small villages. After looking through the rear window to make sure we weren't being followed, I took a few deep breaths; we'd made it.
'I'm sorry I doubted you, I was just getting a little paranoid.'

In the darkness of the back seat, that familiar broad grin returned to Saeed's face.

'Dressing up as the woman can do this to you.'

'Do you think it's safe to take off the outfit now?'

'Perhaps, but, unless you wish to give it our driver the heart attack, I think it may be best you wait until we are safe inside at the house of my cousin.'

'How did you stop the Secret Police from discovering me?'

'I am tell him you are my grandmother; and that you have lost it your mind, that you are deaf and mute, and that you are visit me from Abu Zaabal.'

'Abu Zaabal? Why was that so significant?'

'Abu Zaabal, it is the leper colony.'

We both had a laugh, and it felt great, as the past five hours had been stressful to say the least. Saeed was no fool, and, as he calmly took out his phone, I realized it was stupid of me to underestimate him and doubt him.

'I will just call him my cousin to let him know we will come.'

The call made, and everything confirmed, I spent the rest of the taxi trip filling him in on the discoveries of the day at Dendera and Abydos, and he showed considerable interest, especially in the Osireion.

About half-an-hour after escaping the station, we turned off the main road, into a village, and less than a minute later had pulled up outside a house where we were welcomed by Saeed's cousin, you guessed it, Mohammed, and his family. I couldn't understand the welcome and introduction but they all made a fuss and gave me a huge hug. As we moved inside and I removed the burqa, the looks of shock and stunned disbelief explained why.

'I am tell them you are my wife.'

They were not so much shocked to see me removing my burqa, but rather that I was a westerner, and a man as well. For a minute his cousin must have thought Saeed had gone on the turn. Through hysterical fits of laughter, Saeed explained to them, and then to me, that I was really an Australian friend of his, he met whilst in London, that he was showing me around Egypt, and he couldn't resist the opportunity to play a joke on his cousin.

'It was not wise to be tell them the truth.'

I agreed entirely, no need involving more innocent bystanders in this intrigue. In any case, they didn't speak much English, if any, so conversation wasn't going to be a mainstay of the evening.

Mohammed took great pride in showing me around his home. It was such a culture shock though; the only luxury, if you could call it that, was the television. The 'house' was really a collection of shanty-type mud-brick rooms around the perimeter of a small section of land. There was no glass in the windows and most of the time I couldn't tell if the floors were packed dirt with rugs over them, or whether there was an actual floor.

In contrast, the walls were brightly painted in vivid colours, with patterns not that dissimilar to the friezes on the walls in the tombs. In fact, in many ways, apart from electric light, the rooms were no different from many of the tombs and temple rooms I had visited in the past week; nothing had changed in thirty-five-hundred years.

Mohammed's wife had not just prepared a meal, it was more like a banquet, and I was sure they had dipped into their own pockets to do something special as there was both chicken *and* either goat meat or lamb. I was famished, and more than anything, thirsty.

Saeed spent most of dinner translating to and fro as Mohammed and his wife were very curious about my life, life in Australia, and what I thought of Egypt. Every few minutes they would pick up a bowl or plate of food and offer it towards me. I was conscious that I was probably taking food from their own mouths and the children's mouths, who stared at me as if I had just stepped out of a flying saucer, but having given me the invitation to stuff my face, I have to admit I had my fill and then some.

After dinner Mohammed and Saeed invited me to have some shisha, but I politely declined, indicating my preference to get some sleep; I was knackered and had no idea what tomorrow was going to bring, so I wanted to be as fresh as I could to face it.

I made a point of picking up my backpack and Mohammed escorted me to the 'guest room', which, if the truth be told, was probably one of the children or grandparents' rooms, where I expressed my eternal gratitude as best I could.

'Shukran. Shukran jazeelan.'

'Aafwaan, Itfudul, Ahlan Wa Sahlan.'

'Assalaam Alaikum.'

'Wa Alaikum assalaam.'

As soon as he left the room, I collapsed on the bed and took a huge deep breath…

'What a day!'

…and I was out like a light.

CHAPTER 24 - THE HERETIC KING

Nemo stared back at me, the river streaming passed behind him. He looked dazed, troubled, like the worries of the world were on his shoulders. Over his shoulder, or rather his fins, hundreds of skinny, impoverished fish struggled to hold their ground against the ever-present current that threatened to wash them away, squabbling over the thousands of hooks baited with ten-pound notes. And there, lurking in the shadows behind them all, were the crocodiles. I couldn't see them directly, but I knew they were there; I could feel them, I knew they were all stalking Nemo.

In his fins, Nemo fumbled with something, it looked like scraps of paper, begging me to take them off him. I reached out, only to discover there was an invisible barrier between us; a glass wall. Poor Nemo wasn't in the river at all, but in a goldfish bowl; swimming around in circles unable to escape.

Then I realized the glass wasn't the walls of a goldfish bowl at all, but rather the window of a railway carriage, and the Nile was not flowing along outside, it was flowing through the carriage of the train as it chattered along the track, in fact the whole carriage was a long glass tube. And Nemo wasn't Nemo, Nemo was me; the glass was just acting like a mirror and the fish were all in the carriage with me. That meant, even though I couldn't see them, so were the crocodiles. I could feel their beady little eyes watching me, hear them whispering, muttering, sniggering.

I had to escape, I had to get out of the glass tube, out of the carriage, but I was blocked in, cramped by the myriad of piscatorial figures around me. I writhed, I wriggled, I squirmed, like a netted fish I flapped and floundered, flagged and flailed, I was totally flummoxed.

Not really knowing where I was or which way to turn, I rolled over and half-opened an eye. Two pairs of curious little eyes were watching me like they had never seen a 'white' man, which was probably not far from true.

'Ah, Indy, Sabah al khair, Good morning, I trust you did sleep well.'

'Like a baby.'

'Yes, like a baby water buffalo.'

'My snoring?'

'The children they think it you have swallowed it the cow, or a camel. My cousin, he think it someone was having the sex with an elephant.'

I swung up and sat on the edge of the bed.

'What time is it?'

'Western time or Egyptian time?'

'I guess it doesn't really matter; Western time?'

'A little after 7:00, breakfast it will be ready in five minute.'

'Shukran.'

'Aafwaan.'

Saeed corralled the children out of the room leaving me to rouse myself. I shook the dregs of yesterday out of my head, scrapped the gravel of the night out of my eyes, and fired up the iphone to figure out where the hell we were. I knew we were about an hour or two north of Asyut, about twenty minutes past the last train station, the one we'd left the train at, el-Qorgas. It didn't take long to find – Jarf Sarhan, on the west bank of the Nile about sixty kilometres north of Asyut, just northeast of Dayrout. That meant we still had about a hundred-and-eighty kilometres to go until we reached Beni Suef, and a further one-hundred-and-twenty after that before Cairo. Jesus, I wasn't out of the woods yet, not by a long run.

I found the 'bathroom', which was not much better than the one on the train, and then made my way to join Mohammed and his family for breakfast. This time everyone was there, the grandparents, the brothers, sisters, cousins, aunts, uncles, and a playground full of children; word had obviously spread fast about the unexpected visitor. Once again they had pulled out all the stops, expressing their generosity way beyond their means. It wasn't anything flash, like muesli, cereal, or bacon and eggs, just fresh fruit, freshly baked flat bread, boiled eggs and black tea.

I couldn't believe how basic life was in Egypt, on the surface it appeared like any modern country; cars, mobile phones, cities with glitzy shops, but the truth was it was like an old repainted Holden ute from the seventies; it looked fine on the surface, but under the exterior it was rusted to the hilt and packed with bog. The stark reality was that most of the population lived in abject poverty: no washing machine, no dishwasher, just the local canal, which overflowed with every cause of gastroenteritis known to modern man; it was a trade route to the trots.

'So, what's the plan?'

'We shall take it the train to Beni Suef; Mohammed he will meet us there, and he will be take you to his home.'

The thought of sweating it out in the heat of the day for another six hours as the 'black widow' was not an option. Nor was the possibility of being nabbed on the train.

'I appreciate your cousin putting us up for the night, I really do, and I don't want to put him and his family in any danger, but perhaps we should just stay low for a while?'

'I do not think this is good for us to stay in one place too long; the walls they have the eyes and ears.'

I stole a glance at Mohammed; surely he wouldn't betray us.

'What do you mean?'

Saeed saw my confusion.

'No, no, not Mohammed, the children; if one of them they make talk about the stranger, the foreigner, at their house, then it will not be take long for the police to prick up their ears, for they have their claws everywhere. I think it is best that we get you out of Egypt as soon as we can, and the train it is the only real option.'

I briefly thought about the other options: car, bus, donkey, camel, tok tok; no, Saeed was right.

'OK, but there's no way I can do another six hours in the heat of the day dressed as a black letterbox. Besides, even in my ninja dress, it would be less conspicuous to travel at night than in the light of day.'

'That it is true, but I do not wish it to impose upon my cousin any more.'

'I agree, maybe there are a few sights around here we can see?'

'Are you crazy?'

'No, think about it, they'll be looking for me on the train, or in Luxor or even in Cairo, they would hardly think I would go to a temple or tomb.'

Saeed was reticent.

158

'This it is true, the temple they are only guarded by the Antiquities Police and Tourist Police, but still I think it is very risky.'

'Do you have any other suggestions?'

He took a deep breath and sighed.

'Where is it you wish to go?'

'What is there to see?'

Saeed spoke to Mohammed, who pointed first one way and then in the other.

'There are some tomb about thirty kilometre south west of here, at Meir, if you wish to visit them, they do not get many visitor.'

'Meir? I've never heard of it.'

'It was ancient city here on the west bank, about eight kilometre west of el-Qusiya, at edge of the desert....'

As Saeed continued, I searched through my file notes.

'...There is not much to see of the ancient town, just a few remaining ruin, but the tomb were carved high in the hillside and they are open to the visitor.'

That high position of the tombs in the hillside in itself told me something, that the low-lying city was washed away by the tsunami.

'Do you know what dynasty the tombs belong to?'

Saeed deferred the question to Mohammed, who seemed to have the answer.

'Some they go back to the Old Kingdom.'

'OK, sounds promising, but the question now is, are they worth visiting?'

I was surprised I'd actually found a small section about Meir.

'The necropolis at Meir has many important rock-cut tombs dating to the 6th and 12th Dynasties, including those of the provincial rulers of the 14th nome, but had little archaeological attention since the tombs were excavated by Sayed Pasha Kabasha in 1919 until restoration began in 1997.

Several of the tombs have had the walls consolidated, the reliefs, containing detailed naturalistic painted scenes of daily life, industry and sports, restored to their original bright colours, and new stairways constructed allowing easier access. Currently nine of the planned seventeen tombs have been opened to the public.'

'Would they be anything like the tombs at Wadi Hillal?'

'A little, yes, the main difference it would be that unlike the New Kingdom tomb at Wadi Hillal, the tomb at Meir belonged to the Old and Middle Kingdom.'

'You mean like the Tombs of the Nobles at Aswan?'

'Yes, they would be very much similar.'

I hadn't seen the tombs at Aswan so initially I was highly tempted to go and see them here, but it wasn't resonating with me, something was holding me back, and unless there was anything particularly of added interest, I was leaning towards giving them a miss.

'Meir A-1, the large tomb of Niankh-hpepy, reflects his status as Chancellor of Pepi I during the 6th Dynasty. The tomb contains four chambers, the first and largest of these containing images of Niankh-hpepy and his wife receiving offerings of cattle, birds, animals and food and observing fishing and fowling. On the western wall of the tomb there is a stela with an offering slab in front. There are many shafts in Niankh-hpepy's tomb, for the burials of his family.'

Why would they build 'shafts' within the tomb when they could just add another chamber? Something about that didn't add up.

'Meir A-2, the tomb of Niankh-hpepy's son, Pepyankh, is even larger, and contains many scenes with details of industries and the harvesting of various crops, including grapes, grain and flax. In the western chamber are offering scenes that follow the owner into a long corridor and a room with a large burial shaft. Another small offering chamber to the rear contains a false door.'

There it was again, a burial shaft. If the shaft in the tomb of Niankh-hpepy was supposed to be for his family members, then why did they build a separate tomb for his son, Pepyankh? What if the shafts had a different function altogether? Surely it was easier to cut the rock horizontally, and make a new chamber, than it was to dig a vertical shaft? I was starting to get curious.

'Of the 12th Dynasty tombs, Meir B-1, B-2, and B-4 are perhaps the best-known, belonging to the lineage of Ukhhotep, father of Senbi, Nomarch and 'Overseer of Priests' during the reign of Amenemhet I, and Ukhhotep (II) son of Senbi, 'Great Chief of the Nome', 'Overseer of Priests of Hathor of Cusae' and 'Overseer of Priests of the Lady of All', during the reign of Senwosret I.

The tombs contain many scenes of offerings, as well as agricultural and manufacturing scenes include vase-making. There is also a great variety of wildlife depicted in colourful and lifelike hunting and fishing scenes.'

Nothing in the 12th Dynasty tombs particularly grabbed my attention. The only things that tweaked my curiosity were the 6th Dynasty shafts. But was it enough, to travel thirty kilometres to see a few holes in the ground. I kept thinking about the unfinished obelisk at Aswan and decided to hedge my bets until I found out what there was in the other direction.

'Mohammed said there was something in the other direction?'

'Yes, about eight kilometre north of here, just the other side of Dayr Mawas and over the river, to Tall Bani Umran.'

'Tall Bani Umran?'

'el-Amarna.'

'el-Amarna, as in Tell el-Amarna, the city of Akhenaten?'

'Yes, but actually, Indy, Tell el-Amarna it is not the proper name. In Arabic, the word Tell it mean it the mound or small hill, and the word Amarna, it come from the Bedouin tribe that settle in this village, but, Tel El-Amarna it is a flat piece of land beside the Nile Valley. The new name, it come from the local village called El-Till, so it should really be called Till el-Amarna, village of the Amarna tribe. But in ancient time it was called Akhet-aten, meaning "Horizon of the Aten" or "Horizon of the Solar Disc".'

'Akhet-aten?

'Yes.'

'So why does everyone keep referring to it as Amarna, or Tel el-Amarna?'

'Perhaps because the city it was only discovered just over one-hundred year ago, just before the turn of it the Twentieth Century.'

'Well, from what I already know, the Amarna area, the city and tombs, covers at least ten kilometres long, about five kilometres wide at the centre, and takes at least a half a day to see it, so I think that pretty much decides where we're going.'

'When is it you would like to leave?'

'There's no time like the present.'

'Then, I shall arrange for it the car for the day.'

Saeed had a quick chat with Mohammed, who pulled out his mobile phone and made a brief call. Clearly Saeed understood one-hundred percent more of the conversation than I did.

'The taxi it will be here in about half-an-hour.'

'How much will it cost?'

'How long is it the piece of string? Perhaps one-hundred, one-hundred-fifty Egyptian pound.'

'That reminds me, I haven't paid you for the taxi last night; how much was it?'

'Let us first concern ourself with how to get you out of Egypt.'

Breakfast over, Mohammed and his family started to clear the table. I took out my wad of cash. I didn't want to just thank Saeed's cousin for putting us up, I wanted to repay him for his generosity and somehow make a difference to their lives. I leaned over to whisper in Saeed's ear, why, I don't know, no one else spoke English.

'How much should I offer to Mohammed for his hospitality?'

'Please, no, it was the honour for him to have you stay; you were his guest. To offer him the money it would be considered to be an insult, especially in front of his family.'

I quickly stuffed my hand back in my pocket, I didn't want to offend anyone; I would look for an opportunity later to slip him some cash. In the meantime, I headed back to the room, sat on the bed and took the folio of documents out of my backpack, flicking through the pages. I *had* to get these out of Egypt, for the sake of all the Mohammeds, Saleems, Ahmeds, Selehs, Gomars and Kareems, for all the suppressed and impoverished people of Egypt who had been used and manipulated by the Muburak regime, for all the families of those foreigners murdered by the Egyptian Secret police at Luxor. If Julian Assange had the balls to do it, then so did I. In no time at all, Saeed appeared at the door.

'The taxi it is here.'

With the same reverence given the folding of the American flag at the funeral of JFK, I ceremoniously rewrapped the papers, and slipped them back inside the backpack. How different the world would have been if JFK had been able to expose the truth and lived to change the world. But, instead, it seemed anyone who was outspoken, or in a position to change the world, to make it a better place, John Lennon, Ghandi, JFK, Martin Luther King Jr,, Michael Jackson, they were all eliminated by the cold hand of the Illuminati. It was a wonder the truth ever managed to see the light of day, but, somehow it did, and, it would, thanks to people like Julian Assange; the Tat Brotherhood, the Brotherhood of Thoth, lived on.

Mohammed and his family were all waiting for us outside the house, by the taxi; Saeed and I giving each one a hug in turn. When I came to Mohammed, as we hugged, I shook his hand, five crisp one-hundred-Egyptian-pound notes neatly folded and concealed within it. Pulling out of the embrace I put my left hand to my heart, then put it on his heart.

'From my heart, to your heart, for your family.'

'Shukran, Shukran jazeelan, Assalaam Alaikum.'

Saeed introduced me to the driver, Raashid, yet another of his cousins, and we all climbed aboard the taxi, Saeed in the front, leaving the back seat to me to spread out. And so it was, amid much excitement and waving from the children, that we set off for Amarna.

Homeward bound

We'd hardly gone half a block when, a few minutes later, Saeed indicated for the taxi to pull over at a local shop and he ducked out the door.

'I am just going to get us some water to last the day, it is very hot at Amarna.'

That's all I needed, another day in a bake-oven; I already had a layer or two of sweat and dirt coating my body. No sooner did Saeed settle back into the car, than his phone rang; he had a brief conversation then turned to me.

'You are good man, Mr Indy.'

I presumed it was Mohammed who had called him.

'Just looking after my family, Saeed, *our* family.'

'Ahoya, you are make me cry.'

'Ahoya? What does that mean?'

'It mean, *brother*.'

'Like I said, just looking out for my family, Ahoya.'

As Saeed chatted to Raashid, I decided to save a little time, to refresh my memory before we arrived at our destination, by checking my notes.

'Amarna is roughly halfway between Cairo and Luxor, in the desert, close to the east bank of the Nile, in the province of el-Minya. It sits in a large semicircular arc of almost flat desert hemmed in for much of its perimeter by cliffs that rise approximately 100 metres to a high desert plateau.

The plateau and cliffs are dissected in places by dried valleys and flood beds, or wadis, that lead even further back into the desert. In the south-east, the cliffs fall away to leave a broad flat valley about 3 kilometres wide that begins above a low and very irregular terrace edge that continues the line of the cliffs.

Because much of it lies easily accessible beneath a thin cover of sand and rubble, and because of the excellent preservative properties of the dry desert soil, the ruins of the temples, palaces and houses of Amarna are a prime source of reference for the architecture and layout of ancient Egyptian cities.'

My anticipation was escalating as we passed through a few small villages, lots of plantations, then turned into a road that at ran straight towards the river. Thankfully it was nothing like the experience I'd had at Karnak, but there was a sense of expectation, of going to the city I had especially had built when I had incarnated as Akhenaten.

The river loomed ominously ahead as the road rapidly led towards it. Fortunately we came to a halt before plunging into its watery embrace.

'What's the deal, do we have to swim across?'

'If you wish it, you are more than welcome, but me, I will take it the ferry across to el-Till.'

I looked across the river to the opposite bank, to a flat-topped 'ferry' with a little shack perched atop. It looked like a relic from the Second World War held together by rust and paint; it certainly didn't instil me with confidence. I looked up and down the river looking for a bridge, but they were not to be seen, so, apart from taking Saeed's suggestion to swim across, the ferry was the only option. Talk about a monopoly; I wondered what the fare would be.

'How much is it to cross?'

'Twenty-five pound.'

'I'm guessing that's the tourist price and not the local price.'

'Yes.'

'Twenty-five pounds each way?'

'No, it is for there and back.'

'Five bucks, actually that's pretty reasonable really; provided we don't sink in the process or get swept away to our deaths.'

While we were waiting for the ferry to make its way back across, a bus pulled up beside us.

'Oh, please, not the Chinese tourists *again*.'

But, thankfully, as several of them disembarked to have a cigarette, I figured out from their obvious lack of Asian appearance, but more specifically from their language, it wasn't a busload of Chinese at all, it was a group of Russian tourists. Then I thought, "Wait a minute, this may work to my advantage, I can just blend in with them, one of the crowd, a comrade; the guards wouldn't even notice".

I explained my plan to Saeed, who agreed it was the best way to avoid being noticed at the ticket office, but, unless we wanted to stay with the bus, we would still need a separate guard of our own in the taxi. I figured the bus wouldn't cover the territory I wanted to see, but it would at least get us past the main ticket office. I handed Saeed a hundred pounds.

'Will this cover things?'

'Indy, please.'

'Come on, Saeed, it's one thing to get me out of Egypt, but this is a detour, my detour; I insist.'

'Very well.'

A few minutes later the ferry docked, unloaded, and we were all driving aboard; taxi, bus, donkey and cart, tok toks, a few bikes, a cow and a camel. The captain, who was barely out of diapers, steered us out into the current and we made our convoluted track across the water.

'When we are get to it the ticket office, I will get the taxi to stop near close to the bus. Wait until several people they get off the bus, then go and stand near to them, even to get into it the talk with them if you can. I will go and get the ticket.'

'Sounds like a plan.'

The trip across was routine, in fact it was surprisingly relaxing, it must be something about cruising over water, but as soon as we drove off the ferry we were stopped and hit for another fee - two pounds - as a local fee for the village of el Till. The local kids were right on to it and had it down pat; they swarmed onto the cars and buses like ants at a picnic, flogging everything from reed baskets to carved figures. Being much easier to access than the bus, the majority of them surrounded the taxi like ABBA fans at an airport arrival; even if I'd wanted to buy something, I had nowhere to put it.

Soon enough we were on the move again, sticking closer to the bus than a baby elephant to its mother when surrounded by a pack of hungry hyenas. A hundred metres down the road, a left and a right and we pulled up outside the ticket office. As Saeed took off to buy the tickets, I noticed entrance was thirty Egyptian pounds, plus an additional twenty-five for the Royal Tomb, so I definitely had things covered.

Perfectly to plan, the Russians got off the bus to check things out and have a cigarette. I casually jumped out of the taxi and wandered to the side off the bus, leaning against it just near them. Fortunately I was upwind or I would have been asphyxiated.

'So, whereabouts are you guys from?'

They looked at me, bemused, wondering why I was talking to them and nonchalantly leaning against their bus. Take two: I fanned my face.

'Hot, da?'

'Da.'

That was about it, they weren't too keen to engage in any conversations, especially with someone they not only didn't know, but who they couldn't understand. If the situation had dragged on much longer it would have been very uncomfortable; fortunately Saeed had beaten the Russians to the ticket office and returned, albeit with a machine-gun toting shadow.

As the guard opened the front door of the taxi and slid inside, Saeed whispered in my ear.

'I did not actually say it that you were part of the Russian group, but they are assume it. I explain to them you are the travel agent, and you need it to look at the all the ruin for the other group that you will be bring here.'

I later found out from Saeed that there had been no visitors for several days, that tourism had been so bad in Egypt, and particularly in the less-visited areas, that they were excited when *anyone* turned up.

'So, Indy, where to?'

Akhet-aten

I opened my iphone and examined the map I'd lifted from the net.

'The ruins of the city stretch about eight kilometres from north to south along a "Royal Road", now referred to as "Sikhet es-Sultan". The city is divided into a number of zones, which have been given modern names.

Starting from the south are the residential suburbs. Then comes the Main City, divided into South and North precincts. Beyond that is the Central City, an administrative and religious area including the Small Aten Temple, Great Aten Temple and the Great Palace. To the north of the Central City, after a gap, comes another area of housing, the North Suburb. Further north of that lay the isolated North Palace, and beyond that, nestling on rising ground at the foot of the cliffs, is the North City.

Dotting the outskirts and the perimeter are numerous stelae, tombs, altars and villages.

'I think we should save the best until last, let's head south. First stop, the North Suburb.'

Saeed relayed the location to the guard and he pointed off into the desert to the right, and then for us to do a U-turn. Raashid swung the taxi around and we headed back the way we had come, through the village of Tall Bani Umran.

Less than a minute later, we left the village and headed into desert, turning back to the east for a few hundred metres then coming to a halt.

'North Suburb.'

The guide/guard was pointing off to the right to what looked like a few slightly raised dunes. Since I'd come this far for a reason, I thought I'd best investigate.

As I exited the car, I realized I'd left the backpack behind, exposed on the back seat, sure that the guard would discover it and we would all be busted – BIG time.

'The bag it will be fine…'

Saeed rested his baseball-mitt of a hand on the top.

'…Go.'

'But…'

I tried to surreptitiously eyebrow the 'package'.

'Go!'

I figured, 'if it wasn't safe with Saeed, then who was it safe with', and walked off across the sand, a certain trepidation lingering in my footsteps. It was a good time to check in.

'Completely excavated between 1926 and 1932, the North Suburb, has considerably deteriorated since it was excavated.'

That was an understatement, all I could see were a few low sandy mounds, heaps of loose bricks and the occasional section of wall; quite an anticlimax really.

'In ancient times, the North Suburb was divided in two by a wadi that drained flash floodwaters from the high desert. The ancient houses that lay on the south edge of the wadi seem to have faced towards it, and had with staircases leading down to it, as if the wadi provided a means of access to the river.'

That sounded more like a tributary to me, a permanent course of water like an inlet, the Riviera of Akhet-aten, and if that were so, then not only was the level of the river higher, which was consistent with the location of the ruins, but the climate was very different to what it is now as well.

I stood on one of the sand dunes to get a better look; the modern village of Tall Bani Umran seemed to have been built exactly down the centre of the wadi.

'Numerous objects were found here in the 1933 excavations including; a limestone statuette of a seated official, the head of another small private statuette, a statuette of the god Bes made of steatite, a limestone seat always identified as coming from a lavatory, a sealed pottery jar filled with gold and silver bars and twists, and a tiny silver statuette of what has been identified as a Hittite god.'

Whilst I'm sure the Egyptologists did back-flips over the statuettes, none of the discoveries really inspired me, except perhaps the statuette of the Hittite god, it would have been good to know how, why, and what a Hittite god was doing in the city of the Aten, if it *was* a Hittite god.

Having spent a further five minutes circling around the site, I returned to the taxi.

'Good?'

If I'd paid twenty pound to see it, then no, but, as it had only cost me ten minutes, and was part of an unfolding bigger picture, it was fine.

'Yes, good….'

I settled back in the seat.

'...Lead on Macduff: next stop, the Central City and the Aten Temples.'

Rasshid turned the motor over and we set off down the dusty road to destiny.

The Central City had been completely excavated in the 1930s and was home to the two principal temples to the Aten and the main palace, as well as numerous administrative buildings. It was here, from the palaces to the north, that Akhenaten and the Royal Family would have ridden to on their chariots, making the decisions that changed their world.

'Heading south, beyond the large rectangular space defined by the Great Aten Temple, were the Great Palace, the King's House and several other buildings or groups of buildings including: the house of the High Priest, Panehsy, Chief Servitor of the Aten, store-rooms, barracks, administrative offices such as the Per-Ankh, the "House of Life", domain of the scribes, and the "House of Correspondence of the Pharaoh", the records office where the first of the Amarna letters were found in 1887. They may all have served the temple in its role of provider of foodstuffs via the offerings to the Aten.'

There was a lot to see, and it was only about three or four minutes later, two kilometres further south, that we pulled up again.

'Great Aten Temple.'

Our guard was a man of few words, and, like before, there appeared to be nothing to see. However, in a mock homage to déjà vu, once again I slapped on my akubra and set out on foot.

'The Great Aten Temple consisted of a brick-walled enclosure measuring 800 x 300 metres, with much of the interior left as flat open ground. It did, however, contain two stone buildings, the Long Temple, close to the front, and the Sanctuary, towards the rear.

Commencing with a pair of brick pylons, the Long Temple, or Gem-pa-Aten, had a layer of gypsum as a foundation and measured around 190 x 30 metres; it ran along the central axis of the enclosure. An external portico of monumental columns fronted a succession of six open courtyards, each separated by a huge doorway based on the pylon shape. Each courtyard, in turn, was filled with stone offering-tables, to a total of at least 900.'

I did a double-take; there was nothing, not a wall fragment, a section of pylon, nothing! Thankfully I had a map, because, apart from sand, sand, and more sand, all that was left of the Great Aten Temple were the faint outlines of the structures.

In contrast to the dark, enclosed chambers of the traditional temples, the temples to the Aten were open courtyards filled with altars and platforms. I passed what would have been the location of the ruins of the pylons, and into the area of the six open-air courts.

'There were three important centres of ritual interest and performance situated on the temple's axis. The first was in the outer court, a platform reached by steps, where Akhenaten and his family offered prayers and food-offerings to the Aten.

The other two are a pair of offering tables, that stood on low stepped platforms, in the rear two courts of the temple.'

To the left was a modern cemetery, to the right, the south side, immediately outside the Long Temple, was a field where hundreds of mud-brick offering-tables would have once been laid out in a grid pattern. Fortunately the foundations of a few of the offering-tables had been preserved.

Looking back to the cemetery, I imagined that an identical matching field had once been laid out on the north side of the Long Temple as well. The extraordinary proliferation of offering-tables within the temple implied that the temple was the focal point of a major food cycle, serving not only the priests and priestesses of the temple, but perhaps even a significant portion of the city's population. Alas, the truth may never be known as the offering tables, all nine-hundred of them, on each side of the Long Temple, and possibly representing both Upper and Lower Egypt, were all gone, their footprints barely visible, if at all, beneath the quickly shifting sands of the desert.

I continued deeper in to the desert, into the depths of the Great Aten Temple, to a square enclosed by the remains of a brick wall. According to my map, it had been identified by those who excavated it as a slaughtering-court or butcher's yard. Nothing remained. There was also apparently a stone construction a short distance to the north.

'The foundations suggest a square pedestal or platform reached by a ramp. Many fragments from a purple quartzite stela inscribed with a list of offerings were found in the vicinity. It can be matched with pictures in some of the tombs showing a round-topped stela on a pedestal, accompanied by a seated statue of Akhenaten.'

According to my notes, most of the information about the Great Aten Temple seemed to come from the reliefs on the tombs to the north rather than evidence from the actual site, which was a fair reflection of the level of decimation that I saw before my eyes, of the city, Akhet-aten, and more so of Akhenaten's legacy.

To the north of that, straddling the enclosure wall, was supposedly once another square brick building called the 'House of Foreign Tribute'. I wandered over to check it out.

'The building is in an advanced state of ruin, but once consisted of four separate suites of rooms adorned with stone lustration slabs. The rooms were perhaps used as robing or purification chambers, perhaps for the priests, priestesses, or even members of the Royal Family, about to enter the temple enclosure.'

Looking at the bigger map, the 'entrance' led directly to the North Suburbs and possibly beyond, so it was probably the VIP entrance. Now, there was nothing, it was access all areas.

Moving on, towards the rear of the main enclosure, was the site of the Sanctuary;

'... a rectangular stone building, 48 x 32 metres, subdivided by a stone pylon into two sectors, each open to the sky and filled with perhaps over 150 additional offering-tables.'

Now, it was about as barren as a bare-assed baboon; no limestone or marble, no alabaster, no red-granite pillars, no thresholds, no nothing, full stop. Surely Akhenaten, Amenhotep I, would have built his temple on the site of some importance? I couldn't believe it, this was once the most progressive centre for the development of human consciousness on the planet. What had happened?

It was a sad reflection of the general state of humanity, the state of spiritual integrity; pilfered, stripped bare, decimated, inhospitable and abandoned. Like the stones that once formed the Sanctuary, the building blocks of truth were now scattered and buried in the foundations of other religions. Even the Christian signing off for prayers, "Amen", was in deference to the Egyptian god, Amun. As far as I was concerned the priests of the modern day Catholic Church were just the descendants of the ancient Amun Priests; the corruption was the same, the withholding and distortion of truth was just the same, all covered up in the smoke and mirrors of dogma, doctrine and ritual.

'The sanctuary replaced an earlier layout that included a plantation of trees in mud-filled tree pits, and a square base, either an altar or pedestal for a standing object, that was also made of mud-bricks. Now all that remains is the foundation layer of gypsum at the rear of the Sanctuary.'

Gypsum? Wasn't gypsum just another form of alabaster? Besides, I was pretty sure gypsum wasn't native to Egypt, the closest reserves I could think of were in Spain or Italy, or perhaps it was imported from Iran? Where was Bill when you needed him? I did know gypsum wasn't common to Egypt, but *alabaster*, now that was another matter altogether!

I scratched around in the sand at the rear of the Sanctuary, soon discovering the remains of the 'foundation' layer, made of 'gypsum'; or rather, alabaster! Bingo, pay-dirt! Was the granite I was looking for buried far beneath? Had it too, like everything else along the Nile, been deeply buried by up to forty-odd feet of tsunami silt, sand and mud? It had to have been; if the layers from the tsunamis were over forty feet at Abydos, then they must have at least been that, or possibly even more, here at Akhet-aten.

It made me think Akhenaten had not just randomly picked a spot on the Nile at all, as the Egyptologists have all suggested, but rather had built his temples and city specifically on top of the site of a pre-existing, but now buried, Middle Kingdom temple and city. How could we find out? Dig deeper. How much deeper? If Abydos was any indication, maybe up to forty feet. Had anyone done that here? I don't think so; I think, like me kicking away the sand, they had just scratched the surface. But maybe there was another way to discover what lay deep beneath the sand.

I stood in the centre of the 'Sanctuary', closed my eyes, and in my mind called out to Nemo. He was nowhere to be found, just the images of hundreds of other fish, filleted and hung out to dry on a nearby rock. I had no idea what that meant, but I didn't like it and quickly decided to move on.

Having explored the grounds of the temple for well over half-a-mile into the desert, I couldn't help but feel a little disappointed; I'd come here with high hopes of finding something I could connect to, but all I got so far was a patch of alabaster, a fish market, and a dry throat. I wandered southwards, past the 'house' of Panehsy, Chief Servitor of the Aten', about three hundred metres on to the 'police barracks', a further one-hundred-and fifty metres through the 'military quarters' and a further hundred metres west through the 'clerks office' and the 'Bureau of Correspondence of Pharaoh'.

'It was here in 1887 that a local woman, digging for sebakh, decomposed organic material used as both fertilizer and as a fuel for fires...'

Read.. "dried camel shit".

'...uncovered a cache of over 300 cuneiform tablets now commonly known as the Amarna Letters.'

It was that quirk of fate, that discovery, that led to the recognition of the importance of Akhet-aten, and led to an increase in exploration here. Ironic really; without an old woman looking for dried camel shit Akhenaten may never have been remembered.

'The 382 tablets, predominantly written in Akkadian, the writing system of ancient Mesopotamia, span a period of at most thirty years, from the final decade of the reign of Amenhotep III to the second year of the reign of Tutankhamen, recording select diplomatic correspondences between the Egyptian administration and its corresponding representatives in Canaan and Amurru during the 18th Dynasty.'

Why would Amenhotep III and Akhenaten know and use Akkadian? Well, it wasn't so much why did they use it, but why didn't all the others? It was poles apart from Hieroglyphs. I wondered if there were other cuneiform tablets found from other periods of Egyptian history? If there weren't, then that raised some very interesting questions about the Amenhotep lineage.

Did the 'Bureau of Correspondence of Pharaoh' get its name and 'function' purely because the tablets were located here? Looking at the nearly non-existent buildings submerged by football fields of sand, I wondered how anyone could make any definite conclusions as to what these structures were used for, it could have been a bloody library.

My next port of call was the Small Aten Temple. Many of the bricks discovered here were stamped with the name 'The Mansion', matching the name of a building listed in one of the Boundary Stelae, 'The Mansion of the Aten'.

It was surrounded by the foundations of a brick enclosure measuring about one-hundred-and-ninety metres by one-hundred-and-ten metres; at first I contemplated it seemed very close to the ratio of psi, the golden mean. The outside of the walls showed signs they were once strengthened by regularly spaced buttresses.

'Inside, it was subdivided into three courts, each one entered through a pair of thick, brick pylons with unusually wide stone thresholds unlikely to have contained doors. Each of the pylons was provided with two niches where wooden flagpoles would have stood, and the first and second pairs had small outer chambers that could have been the foundations for staircases rising through the thickness of the pylons.

The first court contained the foundations for a large rectangular platform of mud-brick reached by a staircase and once apparently flanked by one-hundred-and-six mud-brick offering-tables arranged in rows on either side. The second court, shorter than the others, contained a small house-like structure on the south side of the temple axis. It was provided with a very small mud-brick dais reached by steps, as if perhaps a throne base. The third court was dominated by the all-stone Sanctuary, and very similar in design to that at the rear of the Great Aten Temple. It, too, had been filled with offering-tables. A double line of trees in tree-pits had surrounded the Sanctuary on three sides with a number of small brick buildings dotted across the ground outside.'

Apparently in recent years there'd been a great deal of reconstruction and consolidation carried out here. Looking around that seemed a little hard to believe. All they had done was consolidate the foundations of the walls and erect a replica column, the only thing over a few feet high for miles around. It looked impressive, and one could only wonder at what the small and Great Temples would have looked like in their hey day.

'We can be confident in knowing the plans of the stone buildings because each had been built upon an artificial surface of gypsum. The gypsum retained impressions from the lowest course of stone blocks, and other marks related to the planning of the building, and large areas of this gypsum layer survived to modern times.'

'Artificial surface of gypsum', 'Large areas of gypsum', or should that all read 'alabaster'? The plot was thickening.

Though the remaining walls of the sanctuary area at the rear of the temple had been re-covered with sand and modern walls constructed over them to denote the outline, as I made my way towards the road, out of the temple, the floor plan of the temple was still clearly visible, thanks to the work done on the foundations of the mud-brick enclosure walls and remains of the entrance pylons. Again the question was, 'what lay beneath the sands'?

It seemed almost incredulous that, despite being able to label all the other smaller structures surrounding it, the 'police barracks', the 'military quarters', the 'clerks office', and the 'Bureau of Correspondence of Pharaoh', the 'experts' had no idea what the smaller Aten temple, the 'Mansion of the Aten', was actually used for.

'It may have been a mortuary temple for the king as it contained a sanctuary which is oriented in line with the royal wadi.'

Or, if the larger temple was dedicated to the Aten, to the sun, then the smaller temple could have been dedicated to the moon? Or,...and it hit me suddenly,... to the *second* sun, the brown dwarf. If that were so, then it would really turn the understanding of Akhenaten and his city on its head, and possibly explain why the 'experts' were clueless.

I walked back along the western side of the Sikhet es-Sultan, where the royal apartments, the magnificent Great Palace, once stood on the banks of the river Nile. I took particular note of the poor state of restoration, the encroachment of the modern cultivated fields, and the ever-present sand.

'The Great Palace consisted of an open court surrounded by a colonnade and colossal statues of the king. A "Window of Appearances", shown in the tomb reliefs, was probably situated in a bridge that connected the Great Palace to the King's House on the eastern side of the road, from which the royal family bestowed gold collars and other gifts to their loyal courtiers. Built from mud-brick, it has long gone, but when Flinders Petrie excavated the area in 1891 he uncovered beautiful painted pavements which were later destroyed.'

Destroyed? Stolen more likely, or 'relocated' to a museum basement for further examination. And what about those colossal statues of Akhenaten, what happened to them? Surely they weren't made of mud-brick? And what about the columns too, like the one left replicated and standing on its 'pat malone' at the smaller Aten temple, they weren't made of talatats? My guess is they were all made of granite.

So, had they been washed away by a later tsunami, and were now at the bottom of the Nile, or buried somewhere nearby? If not, then they were either smashed to pieces, which means the pieces are somewhere to be found, or they are in someone's private collection. I was sure Kareem's papers had something to say about all that. In the meanwhile, like everyone else, all I had was the 'speculations' and reports of the 'experts'.

'The King's House, on the eastern side of the road was a more practical residence containing a small palace with a courtyard and magazines. Here Petrie found fragments of a superb fresco painting depicting the image of the youngest royal princesses.'

Now, there was just sand.

I reached a point just before where the bridge once crossed the road, the foundations of the bridge still visible, where I was met by Raashid and the others in the taxi; Saeed and the guard had been 'tracking' me as I trekked through the desert like Lawrence of Arabia.

I grabbed a bottle of water and washed down a ton or two of desert sand.

'Where to now, Indy?'

I revisited the map.

'The Main City, the House of Thutmoses, then the South Suburbs and Kom El-Nana.'

Divided into two sections by a wadi, the Main City itself was an area of housing that extended southwards from the Central City for about two-and-a-half kilometres.

'The Main City was arranged along three north-south thoroughfares that connected to the Central City. Though generally keeping a parallel course to the riverbank, the roads themselves weren't straight or parallel, rather they probably represented pathways that spontaneously developed as the city grew.'

No sooner were we underway again than, at the direction of our guard, Raashid pulled off the sealed road to the left and headed back onto the sand and out into the desert. It looked like we had turned right into the wadi that separated the two sections of the Main City.

Most of the extensive archaeological excavations in the early part of the 20th Century were conducted here, in the eastern part of the main city, because this site was the least disturbed by modern digging for bricks and treasure.

The majority of the open area east of the sealed road seemed to consist of the scant remains of closely packed houses, though most of it was covered with sand or badly eroded. None of the stonework had survived, just occasional walls of sun-dried mud-brick, and what *had* survived had suffered badly from the ravages of time, wind, and occasional rainfall.

I jumped out and wandered amongst the ruins, which seldom reached beyond shoulder height. They looked very similar to some of the ruins on Elephantine Island, at Apollonopolis Magna at Edfu, and the Sanatorium at Dendera. The houses differed in structure and size, probably the result of court officials choosing to locate their residences in one place, then filling in the adjacent areas with houses of their offspring and dependents.

One of the larger houses before me belonged to Panehsy, though the reality was I had no idea of knowing which ruin belonged to which official. It was apparently..

'...the source of a well-known carved limestone shrine now
on display in the Egyptian Museum in Cairo'.

I didn't know which one, I didn't even remember seeing it. But then again I was in a bit of a stupor for most of my visit there; I could have walked straight past it, even looked straight at it, and it didn't register for a second.

'Originally, the larger houses announced the name of their
owner on carved limestone doorframes, though very few of these
have been found.'

Limestone, hey! Did that smack of Middle Kingdom, or even Old Kingdom? It did to me. Were the doorframes remnants of a Middle Kingdom city that was obliterated by the Thera tsunami, then reused to build the important parts of the city of Akhet-aten? It sounded very plausible. Oh, I'm sure they have been found, either by the locals and reused, or pilfered by the 'archaeologists' of the past.

One of the other larger houses belonged to a sculptor by the name of Thutmoses, not one of the pharaohs, but who knows, possibly a descendant; I mean why else would a mere 'sculptor' have such an auspicious name and such a large house, unless he held a position of prominence. The main reason, in fact the only reason I wanted to see the house, was because it was there, in 1912, that the famous painted bust of queen Nefertiti, the one now in the Berlin Museum, was discovered.

After kicking around the sand in a few of the 'houses' like a disinterested spectator at the auction of a neighbour's place, I made my way back to the car; what a disappointment that all was. It was clear I wasn't an archaeologist.

Back in the car we headed back to the sealed road and continued south, opting to bypass the ruins to the west between the road and the river.

'West of the road south lie huge heavily stripped rectangular
blocks that progressively disappear beneath the modern fields as
they head towards the river. Situated so close to the river, they were
clearly used for the large-scale storage of commodities brought to
Akhet-aten by river.'

Further on, we passed a large house at the southern end of the Main City which was apparently rebuilt, repaired, and enlarged, and was now the field station and house for the Egypt Exploration Society expedition. Beyond that was the South Suburb; a slight depression in the desert characterized by a reduction in the density of housing.

'The southern suburb of Akhet-aten is known to have been a dormitory settlement containing many large houses belonging to some of the richest and highest officials in the city.'

I don't know how they figured that, very little of it had been excavated, in fact, most of it had been destroyed by the modern cemetery attached to the local village of el-Hagg Qandil. It might have been a dormitory then, but now it was full of bodies in eternal sleep.

We turned eastward, off the sealed road, away from el-Hagg Qandil, and made our way through the cemetery, through a small section of cultivated land and entered another enclosed area of sandy desert; this was Kom el-Nana.

We pulled up at the far end of the enclosure and I climbed out of the car. Nothing; there was absolute nothing to see. What the hell was going on? As I wandered around the site, I double-checked my notes.

'Built by Akhenaten, probably as a sun temple, Kom el-Nana was originally thought to have been a Roman camp. Unknown until 1988, it was excavated between 1988 and 2000 by the Egypt Exploration Society as part of an attempt to prevent the site falling under cultivation.'

Well, they'd achieved that result.

'What they discovered first was a large brick enclosure, 228 x 213 metres, reinforced with thick external buttresses, and entered by pylon-flanked gateways on all four sides. It was divided into two unequal sections by an east–west dividing wall, the northern portion containing a set of parallel brick chambers provided with ovens.'

None of that was visible; just sand. Thankfully there was a photo in the file.

'Inside the northern section were the remains of a Christian monastery dating to the 5th or 6th Century AD, including both the church and domestic/industrial quarters, built over the top of the Akhenaten temple, in part, re-using the earlier walls, and so disguising or destroying the nature of the original buildings. However, traces were also found of a gypsum foundation for a stone building, the North Shrine.'

Ah ha, gypsum! Did they really mean alabaster? Was there a previous Middle Kingdom or earlier temple here? It was common knowledge the Catholic Church claimed sacred sites by building churches on top of them, partly to claim their energy, but mostly to obliterate the existence of the other religion. Had Akhenaten done the same thing?

'The southern section of the Akhenaten temple had survived better, mainly because it remained largely outside the monastery perimeter, although it still suffered significantly from the scavenging of bricks. Within it was the South Pavilion, a narrow rectangular building with stepped entrances to the south, west and east. After that, a central columned building opened on to sunken gardens, set in cubit-sized grids, on the east and west sides. Lastly, the South Shrine, its position and outline defined by a foundation platform of gypsum, which contained markings from the lowest course of blocks. It appears to have consisted of a series of chambers on the east side and a portico of columns to the west.'

There it was again, that 'gypsum' foundation. But that set up seemed strange, 'a series of chambers on the east side and a portico of columns to the west', it reminded me of the axis shift of the Iseum at Dendera, the Osiris suite at the rear of the Seti I Temple at Abydos. Was this an indication this is where the original Middle Kingdom or Old Kingdom was situated. Had the sun temple of Akhenaten been erected smack bang on top of an earlier temple? If that was the case, and it would mean further and deeper excavation to confirm it, then it would mean there was a definite reason why Akhenaten built the city here, not just on a whim as the Egyptologists claim and would have us believe.

'Most of the excavations have been filled in.'

What? Of course they'd been filled in; it makes real sense doesn't it, you go to all the trouble to excavate a site, spend hundreds-of-thousands of philanthropic dollars and thousands of man-hours digging it up, and then you fill it back in with sand? Why? The only logical reason is that you don't want people to visit it, you don't want people to see what you discovered, what is really there? And what could that be? The truth perhaps! The Amun Priests strike again.

As soon as I was back in the car I wanted to ask Saeed if there were any of Kareem's papers that dealt with the 'goings on' at Amarna, but obviously that wasn't possible with the guard in the front seat.

'Where to now, Indy?'

I checked the map.

'The South Tombs.'

We headed out of the enclosure, up north past the eastern side of the cemetery, then right, and back onto the sealed road. I couldn't stop thinking, 'How could the Egyptologists not have put the pieces together?' I'd only been in Egypt for what, ten days, and hadn't shifted a single shovel-load of sand, and yet there it all was right under their noses. Were they so conditioned by their university educations that they had stopped thinking for themselves? It seemed that way.

We travelled southeast for another five minutes, through cultivated fields, until, yep, you guessed it, we hit the desert yet again. This time we headed towards the mountains and, about a hundred metres later, we did a left hand turn and drove alongside the South Tombs, nineteen rock tombs, numbered 7-25, cut into the sides of a low plateau in front of a major break in the cliffs, that belonged to Akhenaten's courtiers and high officials. Eight hundred metres later, at the end of the road, we came to a stop.

'Raashid will drop us here, and meet us back at the other end of the path.'

I grabbed a bottle of water, then Saeed, the guard and I disembarked, leaving my backpack on the back seat in the 'safe' keeping of Raashid.

The tombs here belonged to a broad range of officials, from a chief of police, Tomb No. 9, to the tomb of the future pharaoh, Ay, Tomb No. 25. I ran through the list of tombs;

- 'Tomb no. 7. PARENNEFER, "Royal craftsman, Washer of hands of His Majesty".'

I had to laugh, what a cushy job. It reminded me of the royal ass-wiper of King Henry VIII.

'The internal design of the tomb is simple and unpretentious, but outside there is a fully-decorated facade. No burial chamber is known for this tomb.'

No burial chamber? That said a lot; maybe it wasn't a tomb after all?

- 'Tomb no. 8. TUTU, "Chamberlain, Chief servitor of Neferkheperura-waenra (Akhenaten), Overseer of all works of His Majesty, Overseer of silver and gold of the Lord of the Two Lands". The titles of Tutu and the number, content and length of inscriptions identify him as one of the most prominent men at Akhenaten's court.'

- 'Tomb no. 9. MAHU, "Chief of police of Akhet-aten". This small and inconspicuous tomb is the most finished of the southern group of tombs, and contains scenes of unusual content, reflecting much more than is usual the life of the tomb owner.'

- 'Tomb no. 10. IPY, "Royal scribe, Steward". A small, unfinished tomb, notable only for the decoration within the entrance of the Royal Family worshipping the Aten, which contains some of the best-preserved portraits of the Royal Family.'

- 'Tomb no. 11. RAMOSE, "Royal scribe, Commander of troops of the Lord of the Two Lands, Steward of Nebmaatra (Amenhotep III)".'

- 'Tomb no. 12. NAKHTPA-ATEN, "Prince, Chancellor, Vizier".'

Prince? Nakhtpaaten's house was apparently one of the large mansions I had seen in the southern city, and it included reception halls, bedrooms, a bathroom, a lavatory and offices; quite befitting a prince. But, that would mean he had to be a son of the king, however Akhenaten supposedly only had one son, Tutankhamen, or possibly, if you believe other Egyptologists, two, including Smenkhkare as well.

So who was Nakhtpa-aten? He had to be old enough to warrant a home of his own. So was he another adult son of Amenhotep III and Tiye, a brother to Nefertiti? That would make sense and he would surely have warranted 'Prince' status. Or maybe he was a son of Amenhotep IV?

- 'Tomb no. 13. NEFERKHEPERU-HER-SEKHEPER, "Mayor

of Akhet-aten".'

- 'Tomb no. 14. MAY, "Fan-bearer on the right hand of the King, Royal scribe, scribe of recruits, Steward of the house of Sehetep-Aten, Steward of the house of Waenra in Heliopolis, Overseer of cattle of the estate of Ra in Heliopolis, Overseer of all the works of the King, General of the Lord of the Two Lands". This small and simple tomb has two features of interest: decoration on the sides of the entrance, and the remains of carved statues at the back.'

- 'Tomb no. 15. SUTI, "Standard-bearer of the guild of Neferkheperura (Akhenaten)".'

- 'Tomb no. 16. It has no decoration and thus no indication as to who owned it. Nonetheless it contains a handsome and finely carved columned hall brought almost to completion.'

- 'Tomb nos. 17 and 18. Owners unknown.'

- 'Tomb no. 19. SUTAU, "Overseer of the treasury of the Lord of the Two Lands".'

- 'Tomb nos. 20, 21, and 22. Owners unknown.'

- 'Tomb no. 23. ANY, "Royal scribe, Scribe of the offering-table of the Aten, Steward of the estate of Aakheperura (Amenhotep II)". In its simple corridor design this tomb resembles nos. 3 and 5 in the northern group.'

- 'Tomb no. 24. PA-ATENEMHEB, "Royal scribe, Overseer of soldiery of the Lord of the Two Lands, Steward of the Lord of the Two Lands".'

- 'Tomb no. 25. AY, "God's father, Fan-bearer on the right hand of the King, Overseer of horses of His Majesty".'

Even if I wanted to, there was no way I was going to have time to investigate all the tombs, so I decided I could examine the outside of 7, then enter 8 and 9, on to the outside of 10, maybe visit 12 and 16, but finish with tomb 25, the tomb of Ay.

As we made our way up the slope towards the first tomb, I noticed the area was littered with thousands of pottery fragments, most apparently dating from the period between the 25th and 30th Dynasties. That was very telling; it meant people were still living here, and thus the city must have still been in existence, between the 25th and 30th Dynasties, and possibly not destroyed at the end of Akhenaten's reign as the Egyptologists would have us believe.

I thought about it a little more: Akhenaten may have taken back power from the Amun Priests, but when he moved the capital to Akhet-aten, the Amun priests would still have plotted, planned and schemed away from the relative safety of their power-base back in Karnak. When the opportunity arose due to the untimely death of Tutankhamen, Ay and the Amun Priests seized control of Egypt, and may well have ordered the demolition of the Aten temples and palaces. But the people would hardly have demolished the very houses they were living in, or allowed the priests to do so.

When the 'court' eventually moved back to Karnak holus-bolas, the officials and members of the court would have done so as well, leaving their homes behind them. Those who remained behind, or moved into the area, would hardly have deconstructed the mansions to build new houses, especially houses of mud-brick, they would have just moved in.

The fact it was three hundred years between the end of the New Kingdom, the disappearance of Akhenaten, and the beginning of the 25th Dynasty, seemed to belie the belief that the city of Akhet-aten had been abandoned.

We arrived at the façade of Tomb No. 7, both sides of the doorway having the remains of scenes of the Royal Family worshipping the Aten. Below the scene on the left was a narrow register depicting chariots and, at the right end, Parennefer kneeling in adoration to the Pharaoh. Between both sides, on a lintel above the door was another scene of the Royal Family worshipping, and, below that on each doorjamb, the disc of the Aten with cartouches beneath. I did a double-check to make sure there was nothing else of interest inside.

'The short entrance hall is decorated with images of the Pharaoh and his Queen, shaded by shade-bearers and followed by three daughters, Meritaten, Ankhsenpa-aten, and Meketaten, depicted as if entering the tomb. The transverse hall that followed contained two additional chambers leading off the left end. The interior was unfinished, with images partly carved and partly sketched of everyday events.'

Interesting: Not one funeral text; no Book of Gates, no Book of the Dead, no Book of Caverns, no Amduat, nothing.

Immediately in front of the 'tomb' was the trace of an ancient roadway that had survived and traversed across the cliff face in front of the South Tombs. Then it hit me, the tombs were situated exactly like those at Aswan and Wadi Hillal, high on a cliff face overlooking the city, hardly the ideal location to rest undisturbed for an eternity.

If the Valley of the Kings, the Valley of the Queens, and the cemeteries at Abydos were anything to go by, then all the 'real' tombs were situated on the *west* bank, in a hidden location, far from the prying eyes and invasions of tomb robbers. Why would the courtiers of the Amarna period suddenly have done any different and built in the southeast?

Maybe they didn't. Maybe they weren't tombs at all. Sure, they may well have been used for as tombs in later times, but that didn't mean they were originally intended as burial sites. To me they looked like the 'summer-houses' of the rich, high in the cliffs overlooking the estuaries and inlets. Maybe this was the Riviera of ancient Egypt?

We reached Tomb No. 8, belonging to Tutu, 'Chief servitor of the King'. There wasn't much to see on the exterior, just a few faded reliefs on the doorjambs and lintel. This time I decided to enter the 'tomb' and the guard gladly unlocked the entrance.

Inside, on the left wall of the short entrance corridor, was a damaged scene of the Royal Family worshipping the Aten. Below that, Tutu was offering a prayer of the shorter Hymn to the Aten. I had a short extract from it.

'You rise with beauty in the horizon of the sky, O living Aten, creator of life. When you rise in the eastern horizon, You fill every land with your beauty. You are beautiful, great, gleaming, high above every land.

> Your rays, they embrace the lands To the limits of all that you have made. You are the sun-god (Ra) and conquer them all; You subdue them for your beloved son. You are distant, yet your rays are upon the land. You are in the faces (of mankind), yet your ways are not known.
>
> All flocks gambol on their feet, The whole winged creation lives when you have risen for them. Boats sail downstream and upstream. Every path is opened at your shining. The fish in the river leap in your presence. Your rays are in the midst of the sea.'

And then I started thinking; there was something in the hymn that I needed to note. I thought it might have been the reference to fish, so I called on Nemo, but he wasn't forth-coming, there was no 'leaping into my presence'. All I could see was the sun.

I read it again, slowly line by line, then I saw it as clear as day.

'You are distant, yet your rays are upon the land.'

How did the ancient Egyptians know the sun was so distant, *and* that it gave out rays? Unless of course the message came from off-planet; the Annunaki.

Apparently a further long prayer originally occupied the right side of the entrance corridor, but this was largely destroyed sometime late in the last century along with many other parts of the tombs, so I moved on and stepped into the main hall.

Wow! Two rows of six columns divided the hall it into three transverse aisles, the columns of the rear row linked together into two groups of three by intervening low screen walls just like the outer walls of the Mammasi at Dendera.

Much of the chamber was unfinished, including, at the end of each of the six aisles, niches cut into the rock, most likely to contain statues of Tutu and/or members of the Royal Family, and a rear gallery. The rear wall and northern wall were undecorated, but the remaining walls contained numerous varied images, such as; Tutu before the 'Window of Appearance' of the Great Aten Temple, and detailed images of the Pharaoh's House, including a separate house for girls, shown relaxing. There were rows of figures in the courtyard outside the Pharaoh's House including; foreign emissaries at the top, soldiers in the centre, and then scribes below, and on the opposite side, sacrificial oxen with decorated horns, and female musicians at the bottom. Tutu was also present, emerging on foot from the courtyard of the Pharaoh's House, then driving to the temple in a chariot. There was also a much-simplified depiction of one of the Aten temples, surrounded by trees.

On the shaft of a column in the rear row, the Pharaoh and his Queen appeared on a panel, the rest of the shaft and capital decorated with various motifs including ducks. Finally, in the floor of the northeast part of the hall, were three flights of steps cut out of the rock that led down to nowhere, or rather where the Egyptologists probably believe the burial chamber would have been located. Who knows, it could have been intended to be a wine cellar.

The next tomb was that of Mahu, 'Chief of Police'. It was not as grandiose in design, but far more complete in terms of decoration. Not much to see on the façade due to weathering, but inside, on the walls of the entrance hall, were similar images to those in the previous tomb. The Royal Family, this time with only their eldest daughter, Meritaten, were making offerings to the Aten; Akhenaten pouring incense and oil into three flaming bowls. Below that, a depiction of Mahu in adoration; in front of him a short hymn to the Aten being spoken by the Pharaoh. On the right wall, the decoration consisted of a similar figure of Mahu and a duplicate of the hymn.

Once again there was a transverse outer hall, this time with a stela at each end, one with a false-door and depicting the Royal Family offering trays of food to the Aten, the other with the Royal Family worshipping the Aten.

The decorations were unfinished, covering every stage from ink sketches to the finished relief, and covered Mahu and his daily tasks such as overseeing weapons stores, the transport and storage of produce via person and donkey, and riding in his chariot, as well as images of the Royal Family driving in a chariot from a temple depicted only as a pylon with a columned portico and fluttering flags, to a fortified building, possibly a palace. Other images were similar to those in the previous tomb of people, such as bowing courtiers, waiting in the courtyards outside the Pharaoh's House. This didn't look like a tomb either, a place of worship, perhaps.

At the centre rear of the outer hall, a doorway led to an unfinished and undecorated longitudinal hall containing an unfinished door at the rear, an uncompleted false-door to the left, and a doorway to the right that led down a winding staircase of nearly fifty steps to the right to an empty chamber. The Egyptologists would suggest it was a burial chamber, but, really, what Police Chief worth his salt wouldn't have a well-stocked wine cellar or basement armoury?

Coming back into the open air I was like walking into a furnace oven; it was really starting to get hot. As we walked to the next ridge of the plateau, I reviewed my options.

'Tomb No. 10, belonging to Ipy, "Royal scribe", is small, unfinished and only has a few scenes of the Royal Family; namely Akhenaten, Nefertiti, Meritaten, Meketaten, and Ankhsenpa-aten, possibly the best-preserved portraits in the tombs at Amarna.'

It was tempting, but in the end I decided to skip on past. It wasn't that I wasn't interested in the images, but I figured I could see pictures of them anywhere on the net. What I was really interested in was the evidence; I was looking for granite, alabaster, the sediment.

Just to be sure, on the way past, I double-checked Tomb No. 11, the tomb of Ramose, "Royal scribe", as well.

'Tomb 11 is small and simple, with two features of interest; the decoration on the sides of the entrance, and the remains of carved statues at the back. On the left side of the entrance is a damaged scene of Akhenaten offering incense to the Aten, followed by Nefertiti offering ointment, and Princess Meritaten. On the right side is a kneeling figure of Ramose accompanied by a prayer addressed to the King, praising his generosity.

At the back of the undecorated hall is a niche surrounded by a decorated frame. Inside, is a pair of seated statues carved from the rock and finished in plaster, depicting Ramose and his sister Nebet-iunet.'

The guard was standing, keys poised.

'Tomb eleven, yes?'

'Nope, let's head on to tomb number twelve.'

'Tomb twelve, it closed.'

Well, that put an end to that plan.

'Tomb sixteen?'

'Closed.'

Moving on, I quickly scanned the rest of the tombs on the list, most of which seemed to be of little interest.

'How about the tomb of Ay, Tomb twenty-five?'

'Twenty-five, yes, come, tomb of Ay.'

It was quite a hike to Ay's tomb, at least five hundred metres, so I did a little brainstorming as we walked the track because something didn't add up.

One of Ay's titles was that of 'God's father', which implies he must have been related to either Akhenaten or Nefertiti in some way. It was a fair assumption that the father of Amenhotep IV was Amenhotep III, but was it possible Ay was the father of Akhenaten? It didn't seem likely as Ay was one of Akhenaten's main objectors and Akhenaten had removed all power from the Amun Priests. That didn't ring true, so, was Ay the father of Nefertiti? I checked my notes on Ay's tomb a little closer.

'Some scholars have argued, that in this context, the title "God's father" means "Father-in-law of the king", implying that Nefertiti would have been his daughter. If this is true, then the wife who appears so prominently in the tomb, the lady Tiye, is not likely to have been Nefertiti's mother since she has the title "Nurse of the Queen". Ay would thus have been married at least twice. Tiye, however, is the only wife who appears in the tomb scenes, and she does so with a degree of prominence unusual in the Amarna tombs.'

It raised a few questions. Firstly, 'if Ay was Nefertiti's father, then who was her mother if Tiye wasn't?' If Tiye *was* Nefertiti's mother, which seems the case, then it means Ay would have been married to his sister, Tiye, which is not unusual, except for the fact Tiye was married to Amenhotep III. So, was he Nefertiti's uncle, then at some point did Amenhotep III die and Ay marry Tiye, becoming Nefertiti's step-father? That would make sense. And was the mysterious wife of Ay thus Tiye, who then gave birth to Mutnodjnet? It would mean Mutnodjnet was not Nefertiti's full sister, but rather her maternal half-sister. And if that were the case it would totally support why Horemheb married Mutnodjnet.

We arrived at the entrance to the tomb, again the decorations on the façade were very worn. Inside, on the left wall of the entrance hall, as there was in the other tombs, was a depiction of Akhenaten and his Queen worshipping the Aten in front of a table of offerings. On the bottom register behind them were Meritaten, Meketaten, and Ankhsenpa-aten, and, in the register above, Nefertiti's half-sister, Mutnodjnet, accompanied by two dwarfs.

On the lower part of the left wall was a section of text and images of Ay and his wife, probably Tiye, kneeling in prayer, respect, or honour, to Akhenaten and the rest of the Royal Family. If this *was* Tiye, and I had good reason to believe it was, and Ay had married his sister upon the death of Amenhotep III, then it raised the issue of whether Ay was a power-hungry ass-licking, back-stabbing scheming habitual ladder-climber, seizing the opportunity whenever it presented to marry the *sang réal,* or as close to it as he could get.

He certainly seized the opportunity to marry his Great-niece, and widow of the pharaoh, Ankhsenpa-aten, when Tutankhamen died. Forget Moses, Ramses II, Julius Caesar, how no one had made a Hollywood movie about this guy, Ay, was beyond belief.

The opposite wall, the wall to the right, although partially destroyed, was completely taken up with the most complete and correct version of the Hymn to the Aten in all of Egypt. I took a moment to stand before it and read a translation from my files, why, probably because it was the first profound writing about monotheism, in the form of Atenism, that the world had seen.

'A Hymn of praise of Her-aakhuti, the living one exalted in the Eastern Horizon in his name of Shu who is in the Aten, who liveth for ever and ever, the living and great Aten, he who is in the Set-Festival, the lord of the Circle, the Lord of the Disc, the Lord of heaven, the Lord of earth, the lord of the House of the Aten in Aakhut-Aten, [of] the King of the South and the North, who liveth in Truth, lord of the Two Lands, NEFER-KHEPERU-RA UA-EN-RA, the son of Ra, who liveth in Truth, Lord of Crowns, AAKHUN-ATEN, great in the period of his life, [and of] the great royal woman (or wife) whom he loveth, Lady of the Two Lands, NEFER-NEFERU-ATEN NEFERTITI, who liveth in health and youth for ever and ever.'

I briefly paused, 'AAKHUN-ATEN', which meant 'Aakhun' was his real name, 'Aakhun of the Aten', and what exactly did 'great in the period of his life' mean? Was it a reference to him having already lived a long time, far beyond the normal life span of a human? And then there was the phrase 'Her-aakhuti,... in his name of Shu who is in the Aten', that implied a separate being, a separate consciousness *within* the Aten; that Aakhun didn't worship the physical sun itself, but rather a 'being' or consciousness *within* the sun.

'He saith: Thy rising [is] beautiful in the horizon of heaven, O Aten, ordainer of life. Thou dost shoot up in the horizon of the East, thou fillest every land with thy beneficence. Thou art beautiful and great and sparkling, and exalted above every land.. Thy arrows envelop everywhere all the lands which thou hast made.

Thou art as Ra. Thou bringest [them] according to their number, thou subduest them for thy beloved son. Thou thyself art afar off, but thy beams are upon the earth; thou art in their faces, they [admire] thy goings. Thou settest in the horizon of the west, the earth is in darkness, the form of death. Men lie down in a booth wrapped up in cloths, one eye cannot see its fellow. If all their possessions, which are

181

under their heads, be carried away they perceive it not.'

Moving into the tomb itself, less than half of the outer hall had been completed. As it stood, three transverse rows, each of eight columns, were intended, set close together except for the central aisle leading to the door of what would have been the inner hall. It was probably incomplete because when Akhenaten left Akhet-aten, and the Amarna period came to an end, Ay returned to Karnak where he eventually became pharaoh and constructed a tomb in the Valley of the Kings.

The left hand side of the outer hall had been fully carved out, but, apart from one complete and three incomplete columns, most of the right-hand, or southwest, side of the hall remained to be carved from the rock. As I explored the chamber I kept reading the Hymn to Aten.

'Every lion emergeth from his lair, all the creeping things bite, darkness [is] a warm retreat. The land is in silence. He who made them hath set in his horizon. The earth becometh light, thou shootest up in the horizon, shining in the Aten in the day, thou scatterest the darkness. Thou sendest out thine arrows, the Two Lands make festival, [men] wake up, stand upon their feet, it is thou who raisest them up. [They] wash their members, they take [their apparel] and array themselves therein, their hands are [stretched out] in praise at thy rising, throughout the land they do their works.'

I couldn't believe it, here was this profound document from the one of the earliest periods of civilization and it makes a point of saying that the men wake up in the morning and wash their dicks. It reminded me of a joke.

'Why do men scratch their balls when they wake up in the morning?'

'I don't know, why *do* men scratch their balls when they wake up in the morning?'

'Because they can.'

'Why do women rub their eyes when they wake up in the morning?'

'Because they can?'

'No, because they have no balls to scratch.'

'Beasts and cattle of all kinds settle down upon the pastures, shrubs and vegetables flourish, the feathered fowl fly about over their marshes, their feathers praising thy Ka. All the cattle rise up on their legs, creatures that fly and insects of all kinds spring into life, when thou risest up on them. The boats drop down and sail up the river, likewise every road openeth at thy rising, the fish in the river swim towards thy face, thy beams are in the depths of the Great Green.

Thou makest offspring to take form in women, creating seed in men. Thou makest the son to live in the womb of his mother, making him to be quiet that he crieth not; thou art a nurse in the womb, giving breath to vivify that which he hath made. [When] he droppeth from the womb ... on the day of his birth [he] openeth his mouth in the [ordinary]

182

manner, thou providest his sustenance.

The young bird in the egg speaketh in the shell, thou givest breath to him inside it to make him to live. Thou makest for him his mature form so that he can crack the shell [being] inside the egg. He cometh forth from the egg, he chirpeth with all his might, when he hath come forth from it, he walketh on his two feet. O how many are the things which thou hast made! They are hidden from the face, O thou One God, like whom there is no other.'

In contrast to the extensive detail given in the hymn, only four of the central columns flanking the central aisle had been fully carved in detail, with raised panels depicting Ay and his wife adoring several cartouches.

'Thou didst create the earth by thy heart, thou alone existing, men and women, cattle, beasts of every kind that are upon the earth, and that move upon feet, all the creatures that are in the sky and that fly with their wings, [and] the deserts of Syria and Kesh, and the Land of Egypt. Thou settest every person in his place. Thou providest their daily food, every man having the portion allotted to him, [thou] dost compute the duration of his life. Their tongues are different in speech, their characteristics, and likewise their skins [in colour], giving distinguishing marks to the dwellers in foreign lands.

Thou makest Hapi in the Tuat, thou bringest it when thou wishest to make mortals to live, inasmuch as thou hast made them for thyself, their Lord who dost support them to the uttermost, O thou Lord of every land, thou shinest upon them, O ATEN of the day, thou great one of majesty. Thou makest the life of all remote lands. Thou settest a Nile in heaven, which cometh down to them.'

Circling to the left, in the back corner of the hall, a staircase descended about thirty steps cut into the floor in two flights. It led down to the rear, then to the right, ending in a rough-cut shallow hole, the beginnings of what would have presumably been the burial chamber, or to my irreverent thinking, the wine cellar.

It maketh a flood on the mountains like the Great Green Sea, it maketh to be watered their fields in their villages. How beneficent are thy plans, O Lord of Eternity! A Nile in heaven art thou for the dwellers in the foreign lands (or deserts), and for all the beasts of the desert that go upon feet. Hapi cometh from the Tuat for the land of Egypt. Thy beams nourish every field; thou risest up [and] they live, they germinate for thee.

Thou makest the Seasons to develop everything that thou hast made: The season of Pert so that they may refresh themselves, and the season Heh in order to taste thee. Thou hast made the heaven which is remote that thou mayest shine therein and look upon everything that thou hast made. Thy being is one, thou shinest among thy creatures as the LIVING ATEN, rising, shining, departing afar off, returning. Thou hast made millions of creations from thy one self, towns and cities, villages, fields, roads and river. Every eye beholdeth thee confronting it. Thou art the Aten of the day at its zenith.

Making my way back towards the entrance, in the northern corner, I passed another doorway, this one to an intended statue niche that was never completed. Beyond that, on the inner 'front left' wall of the chamber, was a wall full of reliefs. I stood back a bit so as to take it all in.

The only 'completed' scene in the tomb was the standard reward scene present in the other tombs, that of the Window of Appearances, although the upper parts of the scene had been cut away by treasure seekers and sold on the black market, or by archaeological vandals. That said, what was particularly notable about what was left, was the quality of the carving and the relative lack of mutilation of the figures of the Royal Family, especially as they were basically naked; Meritaten was throwing a collar to Ay, Meketaten standing above her, and Ankhsenpa-aten between Akhenaten and Nefertiti. How the ancient fundamentalist Muslims and/or Christians hadn't hacked the images to pieces was beyond my guess.

Behind the 'Window', stretching over the entrance doorway, was a detailed picture of the Pharaoh's House, including Nefertiti's half-sister Mutnodjmet, the Pharaoh's bedroom, a servants' house, and a separate house for girl musicians doing their hair, eating, and playing instruments. To the right of the 'Window' was the courtyard of the Pharaoh's House where Ay and his wife stood at the bottom receiving their gifts; gold collars, dishes made of precious metal, and, at the top of the pile of gifts, a pair of gloves, whatever they signified.

Then there was that big chunk of the scene missing at the top. I found out from Saeed, who translated for the guard, that it's apparently in the Cairo Museum; fat load of good it's doing there. What a load of fucking vandals: criminals! Forget the damage done by the ancient fundamentalists, what about the mindless hacking done by the modern 'men of science'. For god's sake, put the damn things back where they belong.

Beyond that were five registers of figures filling the courtyard: two royal chariots at the top, then scribes, below that, two rows of officials and soldiers, and, at the bottom, behind Ay and Tiye, a group of dancers. Further to the right was the scene *outside* the courtyard; a group of soldiers at the top, below that, chariots and servants, then, just outside the gateway, Ay wearing his gold collar and 'the gloves', painted in solid red.

I wondered what the gloves represented. Were they purely ceremonial, or was there some practical necessity attached? What was it that Ay had to wear the red gloves to handle - the fan that waved over Akhenaten? I don't think so. Did it have something to do with washing Akhenaten's 'member' every morning in deference to the Aten? I am sure most guys could relate to the one-eyed purple-helmeted spitting cobra that arose with the dawn each morning, surely it couldn't have been related to that? Could it?

'At thy departure thine eye ... thou didst create their faces so that thou mightest not see. ... ONE thou didst make ... Thou art in my heart. There is no other who knoweth thee except thy son Nefer-kheperu-Ra Ua-en-Ra. Thou hast made him wise to understand thy plans [and] thy power. The earth came into being by thy hand, even as thou hast created them. Thou risest, they live; thou settest, they die. As for thee, there is duration of life in thy members, life is in thee.

[All] eyes [gaze upon] thy beauties until thou settest, [when] all labours are relinquished. Thou settest in the West, thou risest, making to flourish ... for the King. Every man who [standeth on his] foot, since thou didst lay the foundation of the earth, thou hast raised up for thy son who came forth from thy body, the King of the South and the North, Living in Truth, Lord of Crowns, Aakhun-Aten, great in the duration of his life [and for] the Royal Wife, great of majesty, Lady of the Two Lands, Nefer-neferu-Aten Nefertiti, living [and] young for ever and ever.'

I instantly zeroed in on 'thou hast raised up for thy son who came forth from thy body', it could have been a quote straight from *'The Bible'*; so much else had been borrowed from ancient Egypt, it was hardly surprising. Or was it a reference to cloning? In any case, I was thankful it wasn't *'The Iliad'* or Homer's epic *'The Odyssey'*, but it was long enough; I could see why they used a shorter version; imagine having to chisel that tome out every time somebody important snuffed it.

But why was the long version only in the tomb of Ay and not in the other tombs? Perhaps because he was 'related', but perhaps because the tomb wasn't a tomb but rather a shrine, and it was Ay's way of brown-nosing to Akhenaten.

As we left the tomb and headed down the slope to Raashid and the awaiting taxi, I turned my mind even more to Ay. Not only was he possibly Nefertiti's uncle and step-father, he was also once an important military general, *and* he was also a priest in the Amun Priesthood, possibly even the High Priest; this guy had some 'push'. Akhenaten removing all power from the priests would have infuriated Ay, but nothing more so than being made 'Fan-bearer on the right hand of the King', unless it was Royal Wanker of the Pharaoh's Serpent'.

No matter what, I'm sure Akhenaten was no fool and he kept Ay as close to him as he could. That said, I don't think that would have stopped Ay from doing what he wanted, plotting and planning behind Akhenaten's back and keeping alive the cult and practices of the Amun Priests, who probably met in secret, or Ay organized regular trips back to Karnak, which was no doubt their stronghold.

'You are happy, Indy?'

'Yes, and no; it seems like everywhere we go I get more questions than I do answers.'

'And why is it that?'

'See, another question.'

Saeed chuckled away.

185

'Very good; and I have it even one more for you.'

'Which is?'

'Where are we to go to next?'

'I think it's time to hit the Royal Tomb.'

'Very good, yes, but may I suggest we take it a break first and have it some lunch?'

'Lunch?'

I looked at my iphone, shit it was nearly11:30 already.

'Lunch it is, what did you have in mind, a *sand*wich or *des*sert.'

Either Saeed didn't get it, or the pun was so bad he totally ignored it; I think it was the latter.

'There is it the café for the visitor just down the road from here, we shall stop there, it is quite a drive to the Royal Tomb, and from there nowhere else to stop until we are getting back to Tall Bani Umran?'

'I'm in your hands, Ahoya.'

The café literally was just down the road, a quick left and there it sat, in the middle of nowhere. It wasn't hard to figure out that they saw as many visitors here each year as I saw smiles on my ex-mother-in-law's face; Amarna was not part of the usual tourist destinations, only the dedicated explorer ventured out here, and even then, most of those only came to see the Royal Tomb, the North Tombs and the North Palace. They just had to sit there all day every day on the off chance someone like me would stumble along.

'Tea?'

'Not for me thanks, Saeed, I think I'll stick to the bottled water.'

The truth was I'd started to feel a little dodgy in the gut since breakfast. I'd been careful all trip to only to eat cooked foods, to not to eat anything that might have been washed in the water, but then I realized I hadn't taken into account the glasses and plates had been washed in the river water. One mouthful of water and I was off to the kazi to take a load off my mind.

Even here they had scams running; if you wanted toilet paper, you had to pay for it. I guess they knew only too well the westerners' weak stomachs would eventually succumb to the local Nile 'nasties', and the attendant was ready with the roll like she was dolling out tickets to the fairground rides; she knew I just *had* to have some. I pulled out ten pounds.

'You better give me the whole roll, ma'am, it could be quite a roller-coaster.'

Of course she didn't understand, and tried to hand me three sheets. Hell, that wasn't even going to clean the seat, if there *was* one! Eventually we sorted things out and, trying to maintain a modicum of dignity, I duck-walked as fast as I could into the loo. And not a second to late, as the full effects of the diminutive denizen of the Nile drained my intestines and did their worst. I needn't go into any details, but god help anyone who had to go in there within half-an-hour after me.

Returning to the table, I noticed Raashid and the driver were talking to the local café 'proprietor', so I took the opportunity to ask Saeed a little more about Kareem's papers.

'Did your uncle have any papers in his folder about Amarna?'

'Kareem he have it the document about everywhere and everyone, I think it is one of the reason the Secret Police they watch him so close.'

'Anything particularly about Amarna?'

Saeed leaned in.

'There was it the great feeling to keep hidden the truth about Amarna. Once Amarna it was found, they could no longer ignore Akhenaten or the city, but they do not want the people to know the truth.'

'And what was that?'

'This I do not know, I have not read them the document.'

I was severely tempted to go back to the taxi and retrieve the backpack, hoping Saeed would be able to flick through the file and find the relevant documents, but that wasn't a realistic option. Saeed had a different suggestion.

'Perhaps it is that you need to find out the truth about Akhenaten for yourself.'

Saeed was right. I took a deep breath, but, before I could do anything else, the Mummy's curse, Montezuma's revenge, the crappy of Hapi, kicked in again, and I was off for another session of the ancient art of ceramic bowl decoration.

By the time I returned it was time to hit the road again. I knew it was important to keep the fluids up, so I kept sipping at the bottled water as we headed to the taxi, as well as, once inside, munching on a packet of potato chips.

'Royal Tomb, yes?'

'Yes.'

As the car took off, I started thinking about what I actually *knew* about Akhenaten, as opposed to what I had *read* about him. As far as I was concerned, the 'history' of Akhenaten had been largely fabricated by Egyptologists based on conjecture and piecing together the scant evidence that had surfaced primarily in the last one hundred years.

The first major difference was that I believed, no, that I knew, that Amenhotep IV and Akhenaten, or rather Aakhun, were two separate people. And the numerous inconsistencies I discovered in the Egyptologists versions of the 'story' seemed to support that.

'Akhenaten, or Amenhotep IV, was invested as king, not in the Amun temple at Karnak as custom dictated, but at Hermonthis, 12 km south of Thebes, where his uncle, Inen, was High Priest of Re, and immediately began building a roofless temple to the Aten, the Disc of the rising sun. He soon forbade the worship of other gods, especially Amun.'

As I saw it, there were several problems with that statement. Firstly, only one off them could have been invested, either it was Amenhotep IV, *or* it was Akhenaten, because Akhenaten technically didn't exist when Amenhotep IV was invested as pharaoh. If it *was* Amenhotep IV, then to be invested at anywhere other than Thebes would have been totally uncalled for, and not been consistent with him later outlawing the worship of Amun.

If, however, the investiture was for Akhenaten, and he was totally aware of the corruption of the Amun Priests, then it would make total sense for him to hold the ceremony away from Thebes, at Hermonthis, which would have been closer to the old capital of Seqenenre at el-Kab, and totally consistent with him outlawing the worship of Amun and all the other gods.

So, it must have been Akhenaten who was the one invested at Hermonthis, and more than likely because the Amun Priests were the ones responsible, because they knew of Akhenaten's background and beliefs, and they refused to invest him in the Amun temple at Karnak. But, of course, the Amun Priests were the scribes of the time so they would hardly make themselves out to be the bad guys.

187

'It was during his 5th year of Amenhotep IV's reign that he changed his names and titles, becoming the king we now know as Akhenaten.'

The experts kept claiming that, but, was there actually any concrete evidence? Other experts claimed it was in his 6th year.

'In the 6th year of his reign Amenhotep IV, meaning "Amun is satisfied", changed his name to Akhenaten, "beneficial to Aten", and left Thebes for a new capital at Akhet-aten.'

If they couldn't agree on a simple thing like the year it happened, how could they agree on anything? Had they based their assumptions purely on the fact there was no record of the 'death' of Amenhotep IV at that time? And what if that wasn't true. What if Akhenaten was what I knew him to be, a member of the Annunaki, and when he suddenly arrived in town, Amenhotep IV had no choice but to surrender the crown?

Wasn't it just as plausible that Amenhotep IV had stepped aside when a twelve-foot-tall actual god turned up and seized power? Was this the truth Kareem's papers were holding? But wait, there's more.

'There is evidence that the sage, Amenhotep, Son of Habu, lived well into the reign of Akhenaten, and both sage and parents had direct hands in guiding and training the son in his revolutionary thinking and policies.'

Wait a minute, what's this, there was an Amenhotep who lived well into the reign of Akhenaten? Surely Amenhotep, Son of Habu, could have been Amenhotep IV, or possibly even Amenhotep III or II? But if he *was* Amenhotep IV then surely that shows Amenhotep IV stepped aside and assumed another title, that of Sage.

And it would seem, in total contrast to the tripe the Egyptologists feed us, that Akhenaten *wasn't* the origin of this revolutionary thinking at all.

'The concept of Atenism was not created by Akhenaten, he was influenced by his predecessors who, as members of the Followers, had actually been preparing the way beforehand for introducing the new religious thought.'

His predecessors, hey, and who were these "Followers", were they the Tat Brotherhood, the Followers of Thoth, the keepers of truth? It would seem so.

'As early as the reign of Amenhotep I we find funerary inscriptions which depicted the Pharaoh as "ascended into the sky to become one with the Aten Disc".'

That made total sense. If Amenhotep I was an Annunaki 'god' who arrived shortly after the passing of Nibiru and the Thera tsunami, then he would have brought Higher awarenesses of consciousness with him, and perhaps ascended into the sky in a spaceship, leaving the knowledge with the Egyptians to implement.

But, by the time of Akhenaten, the Amun Priests were going to have none of that, the confiscation of the wealth of the Amun temples would have wreaked havoc upon its priesthood. Amenhotep IV would have known about the corruption and power of the Amun Priests, and would have known that to cross them would be a dangerous past-time, even as pharaoh, but he did nothing, perhaps he didn't have the balls, but then again he wasn't a twelve-foot tall member of the god race. It wasn't until Amenhotep I returned as Akhenaten that things started to change.

Akhenaten's ultimate goal, like that of the Followers, was to replace the complex, colourful and crowded theology of the past two thousand years with the cult of a single sun-god, the Aten, the universal creator of all life, whose image was the disc from which many rays descended, each one ending in a little hand, and institute principles for the development of higher consciousness among the Egyptian people. But it didn't start out that way. In the earliest years of Akhenaten's religious reform his object of worship took the form of Ra-Harakhty, the rising sun of the Sphinx.

'A Hymn of praise of Her-aakhuti.'

But the shit really didn't hit the fan until Akhenaten took charge and kicked the Amun Priests to the Kybosh, closing the Amun temples at Karnak, hacking the name and image of the former king of the gods out of tombs and monuments all over Egypt, even forcing those people close to him, who had names comprising 'Amun', to change their names.

Akhenaten then outlawed the worship of other gods completely and issued a royal decree that the name "Aten" was no longer to be simply depicted as a solar disc with rays emanating from it, but, instead, had to be spelled out phonetically, reinforcing the belief that Aten was not just the sun, but a universal spiritual presence.

I found that highly significant, that Akhenaten, heretic Pharaoh that he supposedly was, in his apparent zeal to destroy the statues and images of all other gods save his own, didn't touch the Sphinx. What did Akhenaten know it about the Sphinx that was so special?

'Before he disappeared from the historical scene, legends record that Akhenaten entered the Hall of Records beneath the Sphinx leaving a full account of his philosophy as well as a special greeting to the "Children of the West," from where he prophesied would come those to someday open the Hall to all the world.'

That raised several issues. Firstly, that Akhenaten *knew* there was a Hall of Records beneath the Sphinx, second, that he must have been depositing information *before* leaving Egypt, which meant Akhenaten didn't die, and wasn't buried in the tomb I was heading towards. Finally, just who were these "Children of the West"?

In the ultimate act of sovereignty, so the experts would have us believe, Akhenaten built his first temple to the Aten at Karnak and then, in the fifth year of his reign, chose a new site for the new city of Akhet-aten, with most of the work at Akhet-aten underway within a few years and the building work hastily done using mud-brick, sandstone talatats and a limestone plaster, or gypsum, into which were cut reliefs. But, if the new city coincided with Amenhotep IV's name change, then that meant the Aten temple at Karnak and the building of Akhet-aten happened at the same time, which would not only make sense, but it would be supported by the evidence of the use of talatats at both Karnak and Akhet-aten.

The Royal Tomb

After bypassing an area near the base of the southern cliffs known as the 'Workers' Village', a settlement of sixty-four houses for the craftsmen who supposedly worked on the more important of the tombs, including the Royal Tombs in the wadi, we travelled through the dry desert plain of Amarna and on for about another fifteen minutes into the Royal Wadi that snaked its way into the eastern cliffs and plateau.

On the south side of the main Royal Wadi were several large unfinished tombs, none of which were open or, for that matter, of any real interest to me. Apparently,

189

because of their size and location, the Egyptologists had concluded they were also intended for members of the Royal Family.

'One of the tombs in the Royal Wadi, no. 27, has a steep entrance staircase similar to that of the Royal Tomb. It leads to a corridor of impressive dimensions however it does not descend very far.'

A little further into the wadi, to the east, in a side wadi, were two more unfinished and undecorated tombs, Nos. 28 and 29, the latter apparently consisting of a long straight corridor passing down through four doorways, but nothing else of interest. Then we ran out of road and came to a stop, the guard leading Saeed and I up a side wadi.

On the right hand side was a shallow rock-cut chamber, Tomb No. 30.

'Tomb No. 30 was either a tomb abandoned shortly after it was begun, or a chamber for embalming materials.'

Either way, it didn't grab my attention. However, almost opposite it was our prime objective, the Royal Tomb, No. 26.

'The Royal Tomb was discovered in the 1880s by local people in a narrow side valley 6 kms from the mouth of the Royal Wadi, the Darb el-Hamzawi or Darb el-Melek; a valley running east from the plain of Akhet-aten. The rock is of such poor quality that much of the decoration was wholly or partly cut into a thin layer of gypsum plaster spread on the walls. However, much of this has been destroyed, the tomb has been plundered and damaged in ancient times, and has been even further damaged since its discovery.'

That didn't sound too promising.

'Despite this, the impressive dimensions and dramatic atmosphere of the tomb make it well worth a visit.'

I stood for a moment before the entrance to the tomb, which had been covered by a modern construction, intended to prevent the tomb from being flooded by the occasional heavy rains that sent water sweeping down the wadi.

'Its basic design and proportions are similar to those of the royal tombs in the Valley of Kings at Thebes, except that, as it was intended for several persons, there are additional burial chambers.'

According to the Egyptologists, this was supposedly not just the tomb of Akhenaten, but also apparently intended for his daughter, princess Meketaten, possibly his mother, Queen Tiye, and an additional person, most likely Nefertiti. If there was one tomb in Egypt I had to see, for many reasons, it was this one.

'Well, I've come this far; no time like the present.'

A steep flight of twenty steps, with a smooth central ramp running the length of it, led down to the entrance. Beyond that, a long sloping undecorated corridor led down past a doorway on the right about half way down, and then a second doorway, again on the right just near the end, to a second descending flight of sixteen steps. Already the design of the tomb was massively different to the South Tombs; this *was* a tomb, confirming my thoughts the South Tombs weren't.

The corridor led down to an antechamber with a well shaft, filled in, but apparently once about three-and-a-half metres deep. I was still perplexed by the function of these shafts, I didn't believe they were simply there to stop tomb robbers, and there was a physical limit to how much water they could hold to prevent the burial chamber from being flooded. Was there another function?

On the walls above the shaft were the first surviving decorations in the tomb; scant remains of badly damaged reliefs of Akhenaten and Nefertiti making offerings to the Aten, as well as a couple of Meketaten on the end walls. That in itself was hardly proof the tomb belonged to the Royal Family, as there were images of Akhenaten, Nefertiti and Meketaten on the walls of the South Tombs.

Beyond the shaft was the tomb's original burial chamber, recently restored: there were the two square pillars, a raised platform on the left probably to hold some of the pharaoh's prized possessions, a 'rectangular' plinth in a slight dip in the centre of the floor presumably to accommodate the sarcophagus and a small niche in the far corner of the right wall perhaps to hold the Canopic chest. And, throughout the chamber, a modern wooden floor, and modern floor-set recessed lighting to illuminate the walls and thus the tomb. Saeed translated for the guide.

'Some most important object they are found here in the tomb include; the fragment of two granite sarcophagus and the lid, they belong to Akhenaten and to his daughter, Meketaten.'

'Where are the fragments now?'

'The sarcophagus of Akhenaten it has been restored and it is now in the garden of the museum in Cairo.'

'Naturally!'

Fortunately I found an image in my file.

'The sarcophagus of Akhenaten was decorated with carvings of Nefertiti acting as a protective goddess, and by the ever present sun-Discs of the Aten.'

'There were also many alabaster fragment from the Canopic chest of Akhenaten. This, it has also been restored and it is in the museum in Cairo...'

'Collecting dust in the basement no doubt.'

'...and over two-hundred shabti-figure of Akhenaten. It is from this material that it is we can be sure that Akhenaten he was buried in this tomb.'

I wasn't so easily convinced, the sarcophagus was barely recognizable, probably ninety-percent of it was missing. How they even managed to reconstruct it was a miracle in itself. If it wasn't for the Aten image and rays then it would probably have been nigh on impossible to connect it to Akhenaten in any way.

'Did the sarcophagi actually bear the name Akhenaten, or was it the name Amenhotep IV?'

Saeed asked the question.

'The guard, he is not sure.'

'Perhaps it was Amenhotep IV who was buried here?...'

Though I doubted it.

'...Or perhaps it was someone closely related to Akhenaten?...'

I could understand how Akhenaten's daughter, Meketaten, was buried here, so maybe the sarcophagus and Canopic chest were for her or another of his offspring? I used Saeed as a sounding board.

'...Or maybe it was for Tiye, Nefertiti's mother?'

'The tomb was later so thoroughly desecrated that the fate of the king's body is not known. His body was probably removed after the court returned to Thebes, and reburied somewhere in the Valley of the Kings.'

'Maybe Akhenaten's body wasn't ever here at all, *or* in the Valley of the Kings?'

Of course I could have been wrong, this may well have been the final resting place of the body of Akhenaten, but I needed more proof before I could be convinced of that, a lot more.

It looked like I wasn't going to get it from the decoration, little survived. The best-preserved reliefs were on fragile patches of stucco at ceiling level on the left hand entrance wall where Akhenaten and Nefertiti were praying to the Aten.

'On the left side of the wall here there were once the image of Akhenaten, Nefertiti, a princess and the women mourner at it the funeral bier.'

'Well, that seems a major piece of evidence the experts have somehow managed to overlook.'

'Why is this, Indy?'

'Because Akhenaten would hardly have been depicted standing over his own funeral bier now would he?'

'This it is a good point, my friend.'

'It had to be the chamber of someone different, someone related to, but very close to, the Royal Family, and my money's on Nefertiti's mother, Tiye, or one of Nefertiti's children.'

I scoured my notes for clues.

'Around the same time Akhenaten's second wife, Kiya, disappeared, his second daughter, Meketaten, died. Queen Tiye, two other daughters, and perhaps even Nefertiti died in the next few years. All those deaths in such a short time suggest to some scholars that Egypt was racked by plague.'

I think they were right, the plague seemed about as common as fleas on a camel.

'The chamber could of course have been for Kiya, though I doubt it, unless Kiya was Meketaten, which is possible. Nefertiti would hardly have allowed her daughter to be entombed with someone other than her own blood, and if I know anything about women, which is a big question indeed, then Nefertiti would not have allowed her image to be depicted over the bier of a 'rival' wife, a daughter yes, a commoner, no.'

That brought forth a chuckle or two from Saeed, and it made me ponder why there was the need for several tombs in the Royal Wadi in the first place if, as the Egyptologists suggest, the Royal Tomb itself was not just for Akhenaten, but several others as well. If the courtiers and officials were 'buried' in the North and South Tombs, and I'm not so convinced they were, then the Royal Wadi was reserved for 'family', and the only logical list of potential occupants, apart from Nefertiti's children, were the siblings of Nefertiti, and the 'family' of Akhenaten's other wives, particularly Kiya. Perhaps the other chambers had some answers.

Returning across the well shaft, up the stairs and towards the entrance, we made a left turn at the top of the stairs into the first of several chambers.

'To the left of the steps were three rooms, perhaps the funerary chapel of Princess Meketaten, the second of Akhenaten's daughters, the first and third chambers with reliefs and inscriptions.'

Circling clockwise, I followed what was left of the scenes, badly damaged by flooding, as our guard pointed them out, relying for confirmation on my notes; the remains of seven registers of foreign people with arms raised in worship of the Aten, then, on the left side wall, Akhenaten, Nefertiti, and four princesses in a temple, worshipping the Aten as the sun set on the horizon.

To the left of the back wall, containing two doorways into the next chamber, were nine registers of soldiers, including Negroes and Asians, and chariots. In the centre of the two doors were the scant remains of a further seven registers of soldiers worshipping the Aten, and on the wall to the right, a similar scene to the opposite wall, of the Royal Family worshipping the Aten as it rises in the east, birds and animals rejoicing at the dawn.

The final, damaged scene, with all the names hacked out, involved Akhenaten and Nefertiti in the lower register, bent over the dead princess lying on a bier, weeping and gripping each other's arms for support. In the upper row, Akhenaten and Nefertiti mourned with a group of women, a nurse standing nearby, a baby in her arms.

Moving through the second room, bizarrely bereft of images, the only point of interest was that the room had two levels. Was it just a store-room, an antechamber?

The final chamber was more in keeping with the first room, though the flooding had taken its toll of the decorations in here as well. To the left, beside the doorway, were the remains of images of furnishings, mirrors, spoons, caskets; perhaps the objects once stored in the second chamber.

On the next wall was another scene of mourning for the dead princess lying on a bier. Further around, Princess Meketaten, identified by hieroglyphs, stood on a pedestal beneath a canopy decorated with leaves, a symbol of both childbirth and the rebirth of the princess. In front of her, amongst courtiers, stood Akhenaten, Nefertiti and their three remaining daughters, Meritaten, Ankhesenpaaten and Neferneferuaten Tasherit.

Further to the right was yet another image of a wet nurse with an infant at her breast. Overall, the scenes conveyed a depth of emotion unique in Egyptian art and suggested that Meketaten may have died in childbirth, and, as I headed out, that *really* got me thinking.

It was highly likely that Akhenaten married his daughter, Meketaten, so I could only shudder at the genetics that were at work, because, if Akhenaten was Annunaki, and let's consider a little more evidence to support that proposal, that he was, then Meketaten may well have had major complication giving birth.

As we headed out of the triplet of chambers, back up the main corridor, then into the second doorway half way along, I mulled over the evidence that the Egyptologists had either overlooked, or been completely blind to.

Akhenaten fostered new styles in art and literature and encouraged his artists to depict, with realistic detail and animation, scenes of the life surrounding the pharaoh and his family. And that's just what they did, realistic images of plants, horses, ducks, geese, and most of all, people. They represented the members of the Royal Family with degrees of elongated skulls. Why? Well, because they *had* elongated skulls. They depicted Akhenaten with a bizarrely-shaped figure. Why? Because he *had* a bizarrely-shaped figure. They depicted Akhenaten as around twelve to fourteen feet tall. Why? Because he *was* twelve to fourteen feet tall. Folks, Akhenaten was Annunaki.

After having decreed everything should be depicted naturally, why would he then chose to be depicted in such bizarre ways, that exaggerated or deformed certain characteristics of his face and body? The 'experts' tell us that he was deformed because of some genetic disease; a regressive disease that just happened to affect his wife and children. I don't think so; Akhenaten was Annunaki.

Others have suggested it was to emphasize his 'separateness from common humanity', because he was the pharaoh. Why would he need to do that, he *was* the pharaoh, no one was questioning his right to rule.

Akhenaten was Annunaki, and the implications to Meketaten were almost too horrific to consider. If she was barely in her teens, barely past puberty when her father married her, and she was impregnated, then her body would not have been prepared to carry an Annunaki foetus. It was probably oversized, certainly had a large elongated head, and Meketaten's pelvis and birth canal just could not distend enough to give birth. They may have had to perform a caesarean to remove the baby, or, if somehow she did manage to birth the child, she may simply have bled to death.

The doorway had led to a string of unfinished and undecorated corridors and chambers that snaked first to the right, then back on itself to the left, culminating in an unfinished 'burial' chamber that several Egyptologists have suggested was intended for Nefertiti. I disagreed, it could just as easily have been intended for one of her daughters, or even several of them.

As we returned to the main corridor, up the steps to the heat of the outside world and down the wadi to the taxi, I discussed my ideas with Saeed about the true 'ownership' of the Royal Tomb.

'I don't think this was Akhenaten's tomb at all.'

'No?'

'It required a little detective work, but I think I've narrowed it down and figured it out.'

'How is this?'

'By considering who was represented on the walls of the tomb, and, more importantly, who was *not* depicted.'

'I do not understand this; it is not Akhenaten on the wall?'

'Of course Akhenaten is represented, but I ruled him out as the owner of the tomb because of the image of him looking over the bier in the main burial chamber.'

'Then was it the tomb of Nefertiti?'

'No, for the same reasons.'

'Then who it is?'

'Well, the other Royal Family members depicted include their eldest daughter, Meritaten, Meketaten, who occupied the secondary burial chamber, Ankhsenpa-aten, and Nefernefruaten the Younger. The youngest daughters, Nefernefrura; and Setepenra, don't appear to have been mentioned anywhere.'

'Why is this?'

'Probably because they hadn't been born yet. But the other important person who *is* depicted is Nefertiti's half-sister, Mutnodjnet, and that's a major clue.'

'In what way, I am most eager to here this?'

'Well, why would Mutnodjnet be depicted on the walls of Akhenaten's tomb, she was no relation to him by blood? But she *was* related to Nefertiti, she was her half-sister, and, more so, because she was the daughter of Tiye.'

'So Mutnodjnet she was the sister-in-law of Akhenaten; this would seem acceptable in the tomb of Akhenaten.'

'Yes, but if it were Akhenaten's tomb, why are there no depictions of Tutankhamen? If Tutankhamen was really Akhenaten's son, then he would have been the

194

only male heir to the throne, he surely would have been depicted, especially as he assumed the throne supposedly when Akhenaten died, when Tutankhamen was around nine years old.'

'This it is again the very good point indeed, Indy.'

'And why aren't there any depictions of Akhenaten's other wives, including Kiya. Why not? Simple, it wasn't Akhenaten's tomb, and the other wives were not blood related to Tiye, or Kiya was Meketaten. This had to be the original tomb of Nefertiti's mother, Queen Tiye.'

'But, Queen Tiye, she was buried in the Valley of the King.'

'Yes, she was, but her brother was Ay, and their daughter was Mutnodjnet, who was married by Horemheb. Ay may have despised Akhenaten, and destroyed everything about him, but he would have loved his sister and built a new tomb for her in the Valley of the Kings as soon as the Amarna period was over.'

'What about it the sarcophagus of Akhenaten discovered here, it has on it the image of Nefertiti, protecting it?'

'Of course it did, Nefertiti would have been protecting the soul of her mother, the *sang réal*, and, they only found fragments of the sarcophagus, they may have just assumed it was Akhenaten's because of the Aten images.'

Saeed was catching on.

'But, Ay, he still would have smashed it the sarcophagus into many piece because it was covered in the image of the Aten.'

'Exactly. He would have commissioned a new sarcophagus for Tiye and, as soon as the tomb and sarcophagus were completed, transferred her body, and possibly that of Meketaten, though I doubt it, to the new tomb, K55, in the Valley of the Kings.'

'What about it the mummy of Akhenaten, they have found it in the tomb in Deir el Bahri?'

'No, they found the mummy of Amenhotep IV not Akhenaten, they were different people; Amenhotep IV was Tiye's son and deposed by Akhenaten, Ay would have relocated his mummy to the Valley of the Kings as well.'

'So who is it you think the Royal Tomb is belong to?'

'I think this was the original tomb of Nefertiti's mother, Queen Tiye.'

'And you think the reason she was moved to the Valley of the King was because she was the mother of Amenhotep IV?'

'Partly, but more so because she was the sister and wife of Ay.'

We climbed aboard Rasshid's rocket.

'Perhaps this is what Kareem he was talk about; the hidden truth of Amarna?'

'You may be right, Saeed, but I think it's just the tip of the iceberg.'

'So where to now?'

'We go stela, yes?'

The guard had turned around and chipped in, showing he had a better understanding of English than I had given him credit for, which reminded me I had to be a lot more mindful of what I talked to Saeed about when the guard was around.

'North tombs?'

'Yes, we go stela first.'

I think the guard felt I may have been somewhat disappointed by the Royal Tomb, and believed it was going to impact upon his tip at the end of the day, so he wanted to make amends. I gladly appeased his concerns.

'OK, yes we go stela.'

Raashid fired up the Titanic and we headed back down the road in search of our iceberg, out of the Royal Wadi and back into Akhet-aten, and the dangerous unknown that awaited beneath the surface.

Stela!!

The current territory of Akhet-aten comprised an arc of desert bounded by tall cliffs on the east of the Nile, a broad tract of agricultural land with villages across the river on the west, and a narrower strip of western desert in front of a low escarpment. According to the Egyptologists, the whole expanse of land, around twenty-five kilometres across the valley by thirteen kilometres from south to north, including the fields and villages on the west bank as well as the city on the east, was occupied by a substantial population, estimated at around 30,000, perhaps more.

The area was delineated by copies of Akhenaten's decrees carved on a series of stelae, known as the Amarna Boundary Stelae, set into the limestone cliffs and escarpment on both sides of the Nile.

Forgotten for the best part of two-thousand years, once the city had been discovered in modern times, and with it the first of the stelae, the remainder of the stelae, most of which were accompanied by statues of Akhenaten and Nefertiti and some of their daughters, also carved from the rock, were systematically sought out, plotted, and recorded by Flinders Petrie in 1891 and 1892. Petrie 'tagged' each one with a capital letter, leaving gaps in the sequence to allow for future discoveries.

'Petrie's sequence ran: A, B, F for the west bank; with J, K, L, M, N, and P, Q, R, S, as well as U and V for the east bank. Two further stelae were discovered; Stela X was added to the list by N. de G. Davis in 1901, and H by H. Fenwick in 2006.'

Given my situation, it was highly unlikely I was going to be able to extend my 'visit' to Amarna and head back across the river to view stelae A, B, and F, on the west bank, which was a pity because the most northerly of the stelae, stela A, at Tuna el-Gebel, was apparently well-preserved, with the remains of statues of Akhenaten and Nefertiti.

Fortunately I found a photo in my files that showed the text and image above, with the statues of the Royal Family to the left.

It seems there were broad paths running up to several of the Stelae, indicating they were meant to be visited, however, as a consequence many of the other stelae had not fared so well. Unfortunately, most of them, and their accompanying statues, have suffered various degrees of natural erosion and human damage over the years.

'Stela H, with its accompanying statue group, which is currently not open to visitors, was carved into rock of such poor quality that any hieroglyphic text would have to have been cut into an added layer of gypsum plaster, which is now vanished. At the other extreme, Stela P was blown to pieces by gunpowder in the early 1900's by Copts, who expected, as all Egyptians did, to find the stela was a door to a hidden treasure-chamber.'

I found a photo of Stela R from the turn of the last century that showed Akhenaten, Nefertiti and what appeared to be four offspring. What was particularly striking was the elongated heads of not only the pharaoh and his queen, but also of the children; they were not human, part human, possibly, fully human, no way.

'By 2006, the figures of Akhenaten and Nefertiti on the left side of the stela had been destroyed by thieves attempting to cut

196

them out as a single block in order to sell them.

However, subsequent spiteful attacks on the stelae, involving cutting deep and wide grooves across them to assist in the removal of irregular slabs, meant the stela was basically destroyed so that pieces could then be sold to collectors and museums. In was as a result of this very process that pieces of Stela R were bought in the 1940s by the Louvre in Paris.'

It was heartbreaking to think of the level to which 'humanity' would stoop in the name of greed. Apparently, even lower.

Around the time of its discovery, in the early 1900's, the best preserved of all the stelae was Stela S.

'The sculptors had chanced upon a vein of limestone as hard as alabaster, which means the greater part of the monument was marvellously preserved.'

However, early in 2004, the entire stela and its statues, which had stood for three-and-a-half thousand years, were blown out of the hillside with quarry explosives, and it's now just a hole in the hillside.

'Many of the pieces were subsequently collected by the local inspectorate of the Supreme Council of Antiquities with a view to restoring it.'

Were they serious? I didn't know who was more stupid, the vandals who blew the stela up thinking they would have anything left to salvage and sell on the black market, or all the King's horses and all the king's men of the Supreme Council who believed they could put Humpty Dumpty back together again.

Most of the boundary stelae at Akhet-aten are difficult to get to, the most accessible one worth seeing being stela U, cut into the cliff face in a little bay to the north of the entrance to the Royal Wadi. We'd exited the wadi and travelled back into the desert before looping back up towards the cliffs to the north, towards Stela U. The car was like a travelling sauna, even with the windows open to create some breeze, it was still like sitting in a mobile bake-oven.

We came to a halt at the foot of the cliff face, staggered out of the car and back into the afternoon heat; out of the frying pan and into the fire. The guard pointed to the cliffs.

'Stela.'

I looked up into the rock formations of the cliff before finally spotting it; if you didn't know where to look, you would probably have missed it, which explained why the stelae went unnoticed for so long.

Like the stelae I had seen almost everywhere I'd visited, Kalabsha, Philae, Silsila, Wadi Hillal, on the West Bank at Luxor, Karnak, Dendera, and Abydos, it seemed each stela here at Akhet-aten took the usual form of a rectangle with a rounded top, sculpted from, or into, the rock.

'At Akhet-aten, the main rectangular part of the stela was carved with many horizontal lines of hieroglyphic text, and the rounded top panel filled with images of the royal family worshipping the Aten. Most of the stelae were accompanied by statues of Akhenaten and Nefertiti and some of their daughters,

197

also carved from the rock.'

The main text on each of the stelae apparently contained one or other of two proclamations made by Akhenaten, the texts being long, repetitive and damaged, which made them partially untranslatable, especially towards the end, no doubt because the latter parts of the text were closest to the ground and therefore subject to greater risk of damage, be it natural or inflicted by humans.

'The first proclamation, in the 5th year of Akhenaten's reign, dated to his regnal year 5, 4th month of winter, day 13, is found on stelae K, M and X, set at the northern and southern extremities of Akhet-aten, and sets out his intentions.'

'On this day, when One was in Akhet-aten, His Majesty [appeared] on the great chariot of electrum... Setting [off] on a good road [toward] Akhet-aten, His place of creation, which He made for Himself that He might set within it every day... There was presented a great offering to the Father, The Aten, consisting of bread, beer, long- and short-horned cattle, calves, fowl, wine, fruits, incense, all kinds of fresh green plants, and everything good, in front of the mountain of Akhet-aten...'

Now, I know there will always be issues to do with translations, especially since Champollion was probably not the definitive translator of Egyptian Hieroglyphs, so there are bound to be errors, but certain things caught my attention. "great offering to the Father,", did the text actual say 'father' or had Champollion translated it in the masculine gender because of his religious conditioning?

Then, the first line, 'One was in Akhet-aten,' would imply that Akhet-aten already existed. 'His Majesty [appeared] on the great chariot of electrum... Setting [off] on a good road [toward] Akhet-aten, also suggested Akhet-aten already existed. Why? Because good roads only go *to* places that have been established for some time, and this road was good enough for a gilt chariot to travel on. Further, 'His place of creation, which He made for Himself', is in the past tense, 'made', not future tense, will make', would suggest strongly the city already existed. Did he just rename and rebuild a city that had been obliterated by the Thera tsunami two hundred years earlier? It was possible; given the location of Akhet-aten, and the vast number of cities up and down the Nile, it is incomprehensible to think this perfect, fertile location had never been 'colonized' until Akhenaten came along.

'The king addresses his gathered courtiers:

"As the Aten is beheld, the Aten desires that there be made for him [...] as a monument with an eternal and everlasting name. Now, it is the Aten, my father, who advised me concerning it, [namely] Akhet-aten. No official has ever advised me concerning it, not any of the people who are in the entire land has ever advised me concerning it, to

198

suggest making Akhet-aten in this distant place. It was the Aten, my fath[er, who advised me] concerning it, so that it might be made for Him as Akhet-aten... Behold, it is Pharaoh who has discovered it: not being the property of a god, not being the property of a goddess, not being the property of a ruler, not being the property of a female ruler, not being the property of any people to lay claim to it...."

How could the experts have missed so obvious a reference? 'Behold, it is Pharaoh who has discovered it:' How clear could that be; Akhenaten had *discovered* the city! So how is it that he 'discovered' it? Because not only was it there already, but Akhenaten *knew* it was there in the first place *before* the tsunami. How? Because Akhenaten was Amenhotep I, Imhotep, was Annunaki.

'I shall make Akhet-aten for the Aten, my father, in this place. I shall not make Akhet-aten for him to the south of it, to the north of it, to the west of it, to the east of it. I shall not expand beyond the southern stela of Akhet-aten toward the south, nor shall I expand beyond the northern stela of Akhet-aten toward the north, in order to make Akhet-aten for him there. Nor shall I make (it) for him on the western side of Akhet-aten, but I shall make Akhet-aten for the Aten, my father, on the east of Akhet-aten, the place which He Himself made to be enclosed for Him by the mountain...'

OK, surely the only reason you make 'longitudinal' and 'latitudinal' boundaries are if there is something geographically important about the location. Was Akhet-aten the location where two ley lines crossed; I knew the location of Giza had some special significance? According to my iphone we were at 27.6617° N 30.9056 ° E; I'm sure Crystal or even Pieter would have known something about it, but me, I drew a complete blank. Undeterred, I quickly scanned the rest of the translation.

'I shall make the "House of the Aten" for the Aten, my father, in Akhet-aten in this place. I shall make the "Mansion of the Aten" for the Aten, my father, in Akhet-aten in this place. I shall make the Sun Temple of the [Great King's] Wife [Nefernefruaten-Nefertiti] for the Aten, my father, in Akhet-aten in this place. I shall make the "House of Rejoicing" for the Aten, my father, in the "Island of the Aten, Distinguished in Jubilees" in Akhet-aten in this place... I shall make for myself the apartments of Pharaoh, I shall make the apartments of the Great King's Wife in Akhet-aten in this place.'

OK, so he wanted to build a few temples, that was nothing new for a pharaoh, although the reference to the "House of Rejoicing"...in the "Island of the Aten," got me thinking; what exactly is a house of rejoicing? In modern times we might refer to it as a pub, or a brothel perhaps, or maybe even a church or ashram. And what about the "Island of the sun"? an "Island of consciousness"? Maybe it was like the shrines of

Amenhotep and Hatshepsut at the outdoor museum in the grounds of the Karnak Temple? Eventually I came up blank, OK, 'Move on, nothing to see here'.

'Let a tomb be made for me in the eastern mountain of Akhet-aten. Let my burial be made in it, in the millions of jubilees which the Aten, my father, has decreed for me. Let the burial of the Great King's Wife, Nefertiti, be made in it, in the millions of yea[rs which the Aten, my father, decreed for her. Let the burial of] the King's Daughter, Meritaten, [be made] in it, in these millions of years.]f I die in any town downstream, to the south, to the west, to the east in these millions of years, let me be brought back, that I may be buried in Akhet-aten. If the Great King's Wife, Nefertiti, dies in any town downstream, to the south, to the west, to the east in these millions of years, let her be brought back, that she may be buried in Akhet-aten. If the King's Daughter, Meritaten, dies in any town downstream, to the south, to the west, to the east in the millions of years, let her be brought back, that she may be buried in Akhet-aten. Let a cemetery for the Mnevis Bull [be made] in the eastern mountain of Akhet-aten, that he may be buried in it. Let the tombs of the Chief of Seers, of the God's Fathers of the [Aten.......] be made in the eastern mountain of Akhet-aten, that they may be buried in it. Let [the tombs] of the priests of the [Aten] be [made in the eastern mountain of Akhet-aten] that they may b[e bur]ied in it'.

So Akhenaten intended for a tomb to be built for him? OK, that all seemed to totally contradict my thinking. Unless, of course, the Royal Tomb belonged to Tiye, and the 'tomb' of Akhenaten was still to be discovered? And that would make total sense as well; the minute Akhenaten 'died' his body would have been placed in the hands of the priests, the priests secretly still supporting Amun. If they then treated Akhenaten the same way they had treated Hatshepsut, then his body was probably sliced, diced, drawn and quartered, then scattered to the far corners of the globe. But what of the reference to "millions of years", was thus an indication of their lifespans? Or, was the translation completely fucked up? My money was on the latter.

I surveyed the 'path' to the stela.

'Well, I guess if the mountain won't come to Mohammed, then it's time to climb the mountain and have a closer look for myself.'

'Stela S, along with stelae A, B, F, J, N, P, Q, R, U and V, all contained Akhenaten's second proclamation, made in his 6th year, and were mainly concerned with fixing even more securely the boundaries of Akhet-aten and with dedicating all the enclosed land to the Aten.'

As I made my way up the cliff face towards the stela, I remembered that the lower parts of the stela were the most susceptible to damage and therefore the most susceptible to mistranslation and misinterpretation. And that got me thinking; 'was it a "tomb" Akhenaten was referring to, or something different? What if the actual translation intended by Akhenaten was not 'tomb' but 'resting place', meaning a place for him to regenerate? That gave the stela a completely different interpretation, and possibly one in line with the importance of the location. Maybe there were more clues in the text?

Yes, there were; 'the millions of jubilees which the Aten, my father, has decreed for me'. Was this more than just a reference to how long the body would lay interred? It would imply not only a very long period of time, but also a purpose in which to incarnate over that period of time. Was it perhaps a reference to how long they had already lived, or a reference to their understanding of the soul being eternal? It was all possible. And what I was doing, pontificating, was no different to what the university-educated Egyptologists were doing, speculating based on the available evidence AND within the limitations of their own conditioned perspective of reality.

It was a bit of a hike, especially in the heat, but soon we arrived at the foot of Stela S. It was impressive, measuring over seven metres tall and two metres wide; I could instantly see the extent of the damage done to the lower third of the stela.

My guess was the only way Egyptologists could completely decipher the hieroglyphs was to compare all the stelae and make a composite copy. Even then, there would still have to be a lot of conjecture and assumption, even then, there was still the issue of translation.

Speaking of translations, Saeed translated for the guard.

'Akhenaten, he used it the more common type of the hieroglyph, the one for the people, that everyone they could read, not for just the priest and official.'

'That sounds familiar, or rather the opposite sounds familiar.'

'Yes?'

'I'm sure there was a time in the past when *'The Bible'* was only read in Latin, and versions in common Italian or even English, were banned.'

'And why was this?'

'To keep the power with the priests.'

'So Akhenaten, he did this to take it the power away *from* the priest?'

'Probably.'

I read Saeed something in my files.

'The High Priests of Amun at Thebes were such a power and influence that they were effectively the rulers of Upper Egypt from 1080 BC to around 943 BC. By the time Herihor was proclaimed the first ruling High Priest of Amun in 1080 BC—in the 19th year of Ramses XI—the Amun priesthood exercised an effective stranglehold on Egypt's economy. The Amun priests owned two-thirds of all the temple lands in Egypt and 90 percent of her ships plus many other resources.'

'But Akhenaten he was over three-hundred year before Herihor and Dynasty Twenty-One.'

'That's true, but just because the Amun Priests didn't seize the throne, doesn't mean they weren't the constant power-base behind it.'

'Ah, this it is very true.'

On either side of the base of the stela were the badly damaged remains of groups of carved statues of the Royal Family. Despite the considerable damage I could still make out the large elongated head and distorted body of Akhenaten. He and Nefertiti seemed to be looking out over the expanse of the desert, over where the city would have once stood, like sentinels…just like, …just like the Hathors did at Dendera.

OK, now I was really pushing the limits of credibility and plausibility, but I had an excuse, it was hot, scorching, the afternoon sun was beating down directly into and onto the face of the cliff; and it wasn't even summer. The air was dry, sucking every drop of moisture out of my mouth, and I felt like the soles of my shoes were going to melt away from under me. Here I was, probably no more than a few kilometres from the river and yet I could quite easily imagine how easily it would be to die of thirst and dehydration within a few hours.

Visit completed, we scuttled our way back down the slope to the taxi and the awaiting bottles of water. By the time we quenched our thirst, climbed aboard and set off for the North Tombs it was almost 2:00pm. But something was still niggling away at me, so I went back to my notes to try and figure out what it was.

And there it was again, the issue of time, 'If I die in any town ... in these millions of years, let me be brought back, that I may be buried in Akhet-aten', and it became even more relevant. Why? Because modern man, even in ancient times, would hardly have had the conception of thousands of years, let alone *millions* of years. For a simple human of 1500 BC to not only have that concept, but incorporate it into a stela, would be highly unlikely, *unless* that person was familiar with, and had experience of, life spans of four-hundred to five-hundred thousand years or more, which the Annunaki would have had. So, was there something Akhenaten had specifically built here at Akhet-aten, that he knew would be needed to regenerate his body should anything happen to it, that was the question?

And why was it that Akhenaten insisted the "tombs" be specifically located in the east rather than the west, surely the Aten was visible on both horizons? Was it to align and focus on the rebirth or regeneration of the individual rather than on death, or was there something particularly energetic about the hills in the east as opposed to the ground on the west bank? Or maybe it was a purely political move, a direct conflict and challenge to the Amun Priests? Or perhaps there was some other potent reason. Who knows? Perhaps the North Tombs had some answers?

Chugging northwards, parallel to the cliffs, it didn't take long for us to arrive at the North Tombs; pulling up in the car park at the foot of the cliffs that rose about eighty-five metres above the desert plain.

A ravine divided the tombs into two groups, the more important group being Nos. 3 to 6 to the south. As we were not likely to extend the visit to include the tombs north of the ravine, I dived into my notes to check them out.

The North Tombs

- 'Tomb no. 1. HUYA, "Overseer of the Royal Harim and of the Treasuries, and Steward of the Great Royal Wife, Tiye".'

- 'Tomb no. 2. MERYRA (II), "Royal scribe, Steward, Overseer of the Two Treasuries, Overseer of the Royal Harim of Nefertiti".'

'The tomb of Huya, 'Steward of Queen Tiye', consists of a short entrance corridor, with images of Huya in prayer to the Aten. It leads to an outer hall, squarish in shape, with one remaining column. On the walls are as well as numerous royal banquet scenes, images of several altars and temples in the city off Akhet-aten, and presentations from the Window of appearances, all involving

202

various members of the Royal Family; Akhenaten, Nefertiti, Meritaten, Meketaten, Ankhsenpa-aten, Nefernefruaten the Younger, Amenhotep III, Queen Tiye, and their daughter, Nefertiti's sister, Baketaten.'

I wondered why Baketaten was depicted and not Mutnodjnet; surely all the members of the Royal Family would have been represented in the banquets. I considered the possibility that Huya had an issue with Ay, and didn't acknowledge his offspring, but quickly dismissed that theory, as it would be an insult to Queen Tiye. It was fairly certain to assume that Amenhotep III would have been well and truly dead and buried by now, so is it possible that Baketaten was the daughter of Ay and Tiye? Possible, it was highly probable. The only other option was that Baketaten and Mutnodjnet were the same person. There certainly seemed to be a lot of confusion created by the use of different names for different times in people's lives.

'Beyond the outer hall is a transverse rectangular inner hall, unfinished and undecorated, with, to the right, a square shaft in the floor descending over ten metres, leading to the burial chamber. In the centre of the rear wall is a small, decorated shrine containing a badly damaged seated statue of Huya and images of Huya's funeral.'

I found it very strange that a vertical shaft was created in the floor, ten metres straight into the floor, rather than a staircase. And there was no description of the size of the shaft or the 'burial chamber'; the question I had was if there was a sarcophagus lowered down there, and if so, how big was the hole, and how big was the sarcophagus. In fact, was there really a burial chamber at all, or did the shaft have some other function that the Egyptologists don't want us to know about?

What else was significant about the tomb were the scenes on the walls in that they confirmed that Queen Tiye, the Great Royal Wife of Amenhotep III, was at least at some point a resident of Akhet-aten, and thus probably buried here when she died of plague, and that meant it was likely the Royal Tomb was intended for her. I wondered if the other tomb had any clues.

'Tomb No. 2, the tomb of Meryra II, superintendent of Nefertiti's palace, has the same general floor-plan of Huya's tomb, with an outer hall, unfinished and undecorated inner hall, and shrine, though here it is unfinished and undecorated. The main structural differences are; the two outer hall columns are intact, formed from a bundle of eight papyrus stems, and the beginnings of the "pit" is in the outer hall.'

To me, that was even more evidence the 'pit' had some other function.

'In terms of decoration, the images are generally more detailed, but they are also more damaged. They include images of adoration to the Aten, plus celebrations, offerings, and life in and around Nefertiti's palace. Notably, six princesses are represented, the additional ones being Nefernefrura and Setepenra, and a unique drawing featuring a celebration to honour envoys from other countries, in their native dresses, presenting exotic gifts to the

Queen.

This unique scene, different in its execution from the others in the tomb, shows that the Queen was Meritaten, and the King, Smenkhkare, Akhenaten's young and short-reigning successor.'

That meant the tomb had to date to after the end of Akhenaten's reign, and there was that mysterious figure again, Smenkhkare. Who was he really?

What exactly happened immediately after Akhenaten's 'death' is extremely obscure; the Egyptologists can't even say with one-hundred-percent certainty that Akhenaten actually died, or rather if he left Egypt, as I believed, leaving Nefertiti to rule in his place? In any case, when Nefertiti 'departed the scene', the throne passed to Meritaten, or rather Smenkhkare, her consort. Now some Egyptologists have bizarrely suggested Meritaten *was* Smenkhkare, which, given the evidence in Meryre's tomb, makes little sense, or that Smenkhkare was Akhenaten's younger brother, which I also doubted. Meritaten was Akhenaten and Nefertiti's eldest daughter, so custom would normally have dictated Meritaten marry her father. However, that seems not to have happened. So who would have been of such a position that Akhenaten would relinquish his 'rights'?

The finger pointed to Amenhotep IV, and him being offered Meritaten as a wife by Akhenaten was probably a 'peace' offering, or an acknowledgment of Amenhotep IV's distant lineage to Amenhotep I, his Great Great Great Great Great Grandfather, so I was even more convinced Smenkhkare was Amenhotep IV. But, whoever Smenkhkare was, he didn't rule for long as his reign was quickly followed by that of Tutankhamen.

So, what happened to Smenkhkare and Meritaten that caused Tutankhamen to be thrust onto the throne? Maybe the answer lay in one of the four tombs above me in the cliffs.

A modern stepped path led up the steep slope of loose rock to Tombs 3 to 5, and further along to Tomb 6. I did a quick check.

- 'Tomb no. 3. AHMES, "True Scribe of the King, Fan-bearer on the King's Right Hand, Steward of the Estate of Akhenaten".'

- 'Tomb no. 4. MERYRA, "High priest of the Aten in Akhet-aten, Fanbearer on the Right Hand of the King".'

- 'Tomb no. 5. PENTHU, "Royal scribe, First under the King, Chief servitor of the Aten in the Estate of the Aten in Akhet-aten, chief of physicians".'

- 'Tomb no. 6. PANEHSY, "Chief servitor of the Aten in the temple of Aten in Akhet-aten".'

I considered myself fairly fit, but all this cliff climbing in the heat was taking its toll. So much so, that, when I reached the top of the path, I needed a little breather. And I was glad I did, because, as I looked back out over the Amarna plain, I was captivated by its stark, silent beauty.

I took a few deep breaths soaking it all in; it all felt so …peaceful, familiar. I could see the faint trails of a network of ancient paths criss-crossing the desert, linking the outlying areas of the northern part of the vast expanse that was Akhet-aten. I looked back south, past the Royal Wadi, along the cliffs as they curved around the horizon, to where the South Tombs probably were, then towards the river.

Then I followed the river, up passed Kom el Nana, the South Suburbs, Main

City, Central City with the Great Palace and Aten temples, to where I'd started earlier at the Northern Suburbs. Beyond that, in the distance, I could even make out the desert on the far west side of the river. Continuing on I scanned up to the area of the North Palace, North City and back around to where, a short distance away to the northwest, the remains of three large mud-brick altars to the sun sat in the footprints of the cliffs. I'd visit them next, in the meantime, it was time to hit the tombs.

I could see several other unnumbered rock tombs north of Tomb 3 that were apparently open, but I figured they were probably not important. There were also, along the track, on the hillside below the tombs, the remains of groups of stone huts that belonged to a community of Coptic Christians who lived in and around these tombs in the Late Roman Period at the end of the 5th and beginning of the 6th Centuries AD.

Many of the huts were located in front of the unnumbered and unfinished tombs north of tomb No. 3. I decided to skip them all and start with North Tomb No. 3, the tomb of Ahmes, "True Scribe of the King, Fan-bearer on the King's Right Hand, Steward of the Estate of Akhenaten".

After entering through the iron gates that protected the tomb, I passed through the short entrance hall, decorated with images of Ahmes in adoration and hymns to the Aten, and into the outer hall. What a surprise; it was more of a long narrow corridor without columns than a hall, the decorations were unfinished and the stucco was quite damaged in some areas. Some of the scenes to the left, were carved, others, like the figures of Akhenaten, Nefertiti and three princesses beneath the Aten on the right wall, and other images from the temples and altars, were drafted in red outline.

Beyond the outer hall a short corridor led to an undecorated transverse inner hall containing two vertical 'burial' shafts, one unfinished, at either end of the hall, with imitation doors carved into the wall standing over them. Both shafts were squarish and definitely not big enough to lower a sarcophagus down; so was Ahmes expecting to be buried without a sarcophagus? That didn't seem right. And where did the finished 'burial' shaft actually lead? And what was the purpose of the second, unfinished shaft?

Carved into the centre of the rear wall, as there was in the other two tombs, was an undecorated statue shrine containing a badly-damaged seated statue of the 'tomb's' owner. And that, apart from lots of Greek graffiti throughout the tomb, most probably from the Ptolemaic period, was that.

The next tomb along, Tomb No. 4, belonged to Meryra, "High priest of the Aten in Akhet-aten, Fanbearer on the Right Hand of the King". As usual, the entrance hall had images of its owner worshiping the Aten. It opened, not into an outer hall, but into a small antechamber with roughly cut false doors to either side, one carved and decorated with tall floral bouquets, the other with the Aten and cartouches of the King and Queen.

Another elaborately decorated doorway, depicting Meryre and his wife, Tenre, both adoring the Aten, led into the outer hall that originally had four columns supporting the roof, each one in the form of a bundle of eight papyrus stems. Only the two on the right remained, the others had been removed, perhaps in Christian times. You had to scratch your head at that logic; 'let's remove the very things that are preventing tons of rock from caving in on top of us'. It wouldn't have been the first stupid decision made by religious fanatics, but, then again, they probably trusted that God would keep them safe, that 'he' wouldn't bring the heavens down upon their heads and entomb them for eternity, and if he did, then it was 'God's will'. I always shook my head and chuckled away at that sort of religious 'logic'.

I headed to the right, possibly because of the ever-so-slight chance the unsupported roof to the left might choose that moment to collapse. Running across the entire right wall in two registers, and continuing on to the back wall, was a massive scene of Akhet-aten, the numerous buildings and elements included; a depiction of the King's House in the Central City, with the Window of Appearance in the middle, and the Great Aten temple, with its main entrance between two pylons fitted with flagpoles and streamers, the following courtyards and altars with columns and statues of Akhenaten, as well as a depiction of the Akhet-aten harbour, the palaces and the gardens of the ancient city. This must have been where the Egyptologists got their ideas about what Akhet-aten and all its buildings looked like.

On the opposite side of the chamber, below a beautiful representation of a colourful rainbow, Akhenaten and Nefertiti, with two of their daughters, Meritaten and Meketaten, presented a fully-laden offering table to the Aten. The western wall also had similar scenes to those on the eastern wall, including, in the centre, Akhenaten and Nefertiti, in separate chariots, driving to the Great Aten Temple, four princesses following behind in two smaller chariots. In particular, Akhenaten's horse and chariot had been depicted in great detail and colour, including an ornamental case for an archer's bow on the side. In keeping with the erasure of Akhenaten's memory, the images and cartouches of Akhenaten, Nefertiti, and their daughters had been chiselled out.

A doorway in the centre of rear wall, depicting Meryre adoring the Aten, led to the inner hall. Clearly there were meant to be a further four columns in here as well, however the tomb had been abandoned at such an early stage in its excavation only three of the four pillars, and the beginnings of the shrine, had been roughly cut from the rock. What I could see was how the stone-cutters had removed the stone in a series of blocks.

The 'tomb' was unfinished, which was a shame, because, if it had been, it may have been obvious to everyone, including the Egyptologists, that it was a place of worship rather than a tomb. I hadn't seen *anything*, either here or at the South Tombs, that convinced me that these rock-cut chambers were tombs. Perhaps the next tomb had something new to make me think otherwise.

Thank god Tomb No. 5 was only around the bend because it was so hot on the cliff face if I'd been an egg I would have been fried sunny-side up. The tomb belonged to Pentu, "Royal scribe, First under the King, Chief servitor of the Aten in the Estate of the Aten in Akhet-aten, chief of physicians". The entrance hall had what I presumed were the usual adoration scenes of the owner to the Aten, though they were very badly damaged. The outer hall that followed was similar to that of Tomb No. 3, more like a long corridor, and with very badly damaged decorations. To the left I made out two registers, including one scene of Akhenaten, Nefertiti and three of their daughters in chariots heading towards the Great Aten Temple, where there were many offering tables, as well as a scene of Pentu receiving the gift of a gold collar from Akhenaten. The right wall had similarly been lain out in two registers, however there were only traces of red outline drawings at the right end showing Akhenaten and Nefertiti seated at a meal.

The transverse inner hall that followed was totally undecorated, the central rock-cut statue in the shrine at the rear, destroyed; the only point of interest was the twelve-metre-deep, square-shaped 'burial' shaft at the right end, surrounded by a raised rampart, that led to an apparent burial chamber. One tomb to go, perhaps that could shed some light on things.

Situated at the far southern end of the North group of Tombs, Tomb No. 6, the tomb of Panehsy, "Chief servitor of the Aten in the temple of Aten in Akhet-aten", was a fair walks distance south along a narrow track that clung to the cliff face. The tombs were cool, the track was torture, the taxi was *very* tempting; I should have brought a bottle of water with me. But, yay, as I walk through the valley of death, I shall fear no evil, nor heatstroke, nor falling a hundred metres to my death; and I set off for the last tomb.

Along the track, on the hillside below the tombs, were more stone huts from the Coptic Christian community of the Late Roman Period.

'The spiritual centre for the Coptic community was a church, created by modifying Tomb No. 6, the tomb of Panehsy, by enlarging the outer hall on the north-west side, and adding an apse at the end.'

That sounded interesting and I couldn't wait to see it, because it reinforced my belief that these 'tombs' were in fact places of worship; the Copts had 'co-opted' and occupied the temples at various places, Philae, Luxor, Dendera, it didn't make sense they would occupy a tomb, especially if the city below had been 'dismantled' over a thousand years earlier. Why would they travel to a field of ruins and then set up their church in a tomb on the hill when there was a monastery 'just down the road' at Kom el-Nana? I was sure the true story either hadn't been discovered, or it was being suppressed.

Behind the iron gates, the façade of the tomb was still preserved, decorated with scenes of the Royal Family worshipping the Aten. Inside, each side of the entrance hall was similarly decorated with images of the Royal Family, Akhenaten and Nefertiti wearing elaborate crowns, and including a damaged depiction of Nefertiti's half-sister, Mutnodjnet, all worshiping the Aten. In addition was the now familiar scene of the tomb's owner, in this case Panehsy, offering prayers to the Aten and to the Pharaoh. Above the doorway to the following outer hall, were some very clear cartouches of the Aten, Akhenaten and Nefertiti, which somehow had escaped the vandalistic eye and attention of the Amun Priests.

The outer hall itself, like that of Meryre I, once contained four supporting columns in the bundled papyrus format, although here only two were reasonably preserved. Similar scenes, with superb reliefs and considerable remaining colour, decorated most of the walls. To the right, the Royal Family worshiped the Aten, drove in chariots, and presented gifts to Panehsy from the Window of Appearances in the King's House in the Central City.

Below that, a flight of steps had been carved out of the floor that led down to a small, undecorated chamber. There was no way of knowing if this had been excavated contemporary with Panehsy or by the Copts; if you believed the Egyptologists it was an unfinished burial chamber, it could just as easily have been a storage room.

The western wall had the lower half cut away, presumably by the Copts, while on the upper half of the wall survived a depiction of the Royal Family visiting the Great Aten Temple, its main pylon, complete with flagpoles, leading to the slaughter court and Akhenaten on an altar, and, at the rear of the temple, several columned courts with statues of Akhenaten. In the northern wall the Copts had cut out a niche to be used for baptisms. To the right, partly covered by plaster with Coptic decorations, were also images of Panehsy in prayer and adoration, and Akhenaten and Nefertiti making offerings to the Aten.

The inner hall that followed was undecorated except for the left side of the entrance where Panehsy, portrayed as an obese elderly man, sat beside his daughter, adoring the Aten. On the right hand side of the hall a flight of over forty rough-hewn steps led down to the rear, then left, and back on itself to a second unfinished and undecorated chamber. Here were major differences in structure between the 'tombs' of Huya, Ahmes and Pentu, all of which had shafts leading to 'burial chambers', whereas here we had the 'traditional' and conventional descending steps. In both cases I could see no way the ancient Egyptians could have negotiate a ten-ton sarcophagus down and into place; that's if there were granite sarcophagi, they may well have just been gilt wooden coffins.

As with the other 'tombs', in the centre of the rear wall was a rock-hewn shrine, although all that remained was a 'scar' where the statue had been removed or destroyed. On the wall to the right was a family scene of Panehsy, seated at a table of offerings, with his daughter, his sister, and her two daughters.

OK, I was all tombed-out, I'd seen pretty-much all there was to see and I still wasn't convinced these were tombs. Why would you build your tomb high on a hill in plain site of the whole city? Unless,…and the idea hit me almost as suddenly as the sun and heat when I stepped out of the tomb and into the blazing illumination of the Aten, unless you *wanted* them to see it.

Perhaps the 'tombs' were deliberate decoys and the real tombs were still back in the Royal Wadi somewhere, waiting to be discovered? That would make sense why the statues were carved at the rear in the shrines, as a visual substitute for the sarcophagus and the mummy. I couldn't recall seeing any statues or shrines in any of the 18th Dynasty tombs at Luxor, which both pre-dated and post-dated the Amarna period, and, if the officials and courtiers *knew* the Amun Priests were corrupt, and were most likely to rob any and all tombs, then ensuring you rested eternally must have been quite a clandestine operation; as far as I was aware, no mummies or sarcophagi had ever been discovered in these tombs, nor the ones to the south.

It would also explain the deviation from the structure of tombs from those at Luxor, and the artwork on the walls. Previously the tomb construction and decoration would have been done, or at the very least overseen, by the Amun Priests, now, here at Amarna, the Amun Priests had been kicked to the Kybosh and new engineers and artists employed who would have had no idea what the 'usual' tomb plan would have been, nor the subject matter for the decorations.

And that would also explain why there were no sacred texts on the walls, such as the Book of the Dead, the Book of Gates, or Amduat; they were the religious domain of the Amun Priests. In fact the striking difference between these 'tombs' and the Theban tombs of the 18th Dynasty is that the Royal Family and the Aten take precedence here, replacing the more religious themes of the Theban tombs.

As I looked out over the Amarna plain, even the faint trails of the ancient roads seem to make a bee-line straight from the North City, past the Desert Altars, and directly to the tombs. It all started to make sense, and it was a very different picture to that painted in all the 'authoritative' books by the 'experts'.

I headed down the side-track that descended diagonally back to my oasis in the desert, Raashid, the taxi, and, most importantly, my water. Somehow the altars seemed connected to the 'tombs'; perhaps the officials sat up here on deck chairs overlooking sacrificial ceremonies? Perhaps the sacrifices were brought up here to the shrines? I needed to check them out for myself.

No sooner did I reach the taxi than I gulped down almost a full litre-and-a-half bottle of water.

'How are we doing for time, Saeed?'

'We will all die eventually, Indy; I suggest you take it the opportunity to see everything you can, if we get you safe out of Egypt, you may not get it the second chance to come back here again.'

He was joking, but there was a certain message in his words. A lump manifested in my throat and I swallowed like I hadn't had a drink in three weeks.

'True.'

'So, what is it you now wish to see?'

'The Desert Altars.'

Our guard was trying to make sure I was happy, and not be disappointed.

'Desert Altar, nothing to see.'

I directed my response to Saeed.

'No offence, but he doesn't know what I'm looking for.'

Saeed did a quick explanation and the guard nodded his head.

'OK, we go Desert Altar.'

It was only a few minutes down the road towards the river and Raashid came to a halt. The guard pointed northwards into the desert to a few mounds.

'Altar.'

He certainly wasn't going to waste his time wandering out in the heat to look at nothing, so I had the 'pleasure' of slapping on my akubra and doing a 'Lawrence of Arabia' solo.

'The Desert Altars are a group of mud-brick buildings, excavated by the Egypt Exploration Society in 1931–2, which were possibly constructed for the reception of foreign tribute during the great celebrations in year 12 of the king's reign. Alternatively, the altars may have been an adjunct of the North Tombs and of their high officials, including two priests, Meryre, the owner of Tomb 4, and Panehsy, owner of Tomb 6. At the same time, they might also be examples of sun temples that belonged to some of the women of members of Akhenaten's family.'

So, what they were saying is - basically, pick a number between 1 and 10, any number; if you can think of a function or purpose, then that's just as plausible as any of the others.

A hundred metres or so into the desert I reached the remains of the first of the altars; the whole group apparent stood on ground that had been cleared of stones. The guard was right, there was nothing to see.

Well there was, sand. But there were also odd squares and rectangles that seemed to be emerging from the sand. If I was going to make any sense of it, I needed to refer to the photo in the file.

The altars consisted of three separate elements, built along a common alignment running approximately south-south-west to north-north-east. I took of my akubra, wiped the sweat from my brow, then scratched my head; that alignment didn't seem to have any reason, and that didn't make sense. The ancient Egyptians were always methodically pedantic and particular about the alignment of their temples and monuments. If these temples were dedicated to the Aten, then there must have been some alignment with the rising and setting sun, and probably the seasons, or possibly they were used for stargazing.

I stood in the middle of the first altar picking out the features: a large rectangular platform, reached by ramps in the centre of each of the four sides. The four ramps seemed superfluous and must have had some ceremonial function rather than just functioning as practical entrances.

'The complex pattern of its foundations suggests that several columned rooms stood on top, surrounded by an open colonnade.'

Who knows, it may even have been an astronomical observatory of some sort, possibly even a launching pad or landing site.

Moving northwards to the second altar, there was more evidence of structure.

'The second altar consisted of three platforms reached by ramps, two of them flanking the approach to the ramp to the largest one, rebuilt in stone during the Amarna Period.'

What was that? 'Rebuilt in stone *during* the Amarna Period'? How obvious; that there was something here *before* Akhenaten arrived? I looked back at the first altar; it reminded me of the platforms at Deir el Bahri, of the Temple of Montuhotep I. And that might account for the strange alignment; if the passing of Nibiru around 1600 BC caused the eruption of Thera, and earthquakes, then it could easily have caused the earth's crust to have shifted as well.

I looked back up to the North Tombs and a thought hit me; the altars weren't built in alignment with the tombs, the 'tombs' were built so that they overlooked the altars.

I hurried on to the final altar, a square platform reached by a long ramp on each of the four sides.

'There is a deep hole in the middle of the platform that might point to the original existence of a standing stone.'

Or to some sort of marker, perhaps even an obelisk, used to measure and observe the night sky; the altars may not have just been to the Aten, the observing of the motions of the sun, like a giant sundial, but also to the moon and stars.

'To the west lay a rectangular enclosure surrounded by a mud-brick wall reinforced with external buttresses. A small stone building had stood in the middle of the south side, its position marked by a foundation layer of gypsum concrete on which were the impressions of blocks.'

I made a beeline for the remains of the western building, kicking away the sand until I saw and felt the 'gypsum' beneath my feet; it was just like the 'foundations' at the Great Aten Temple and at Kom el-Nana. There was suddenly a real spring in my step; I was convinced, Akhet-aten was not the original city on this part of the Nile.

Back in the taxi we quickly set off for the North City, where, according to the learned scholars, Akhenaten most likely resided with his queen, Nefertiti, six daughters, and, if you believed some of the Egyptologists, possibly even several sons.

Skirting to the east of the cultivated area, by the time I had downed the best part of another half-a-bottle of water, we arrived at ruins of our penultimate destination.

The North City

Sitting in a triangular piece of ground, squeezed between the river and the lower slopes of the cliffs, that eventually met the river and defined the northern boundary of the Amarna plain, the greater part of the North City remained unexcavated by archaeologists, though one quick look at the general state of the ground was enough to see it had been thoroughly dug over in the past by people looking for antiquities.

But how deep had they gone, they may have only scratched the surface? If my theory about the tsunami was correct, which seemed to be the case, then the real treasure may have been anything up to forty feet below the surface and was probably still awaiting discovery; the very ignorance of the true history of Akhet-aten may well have protected much of its history.

The remains of the ancient city extended northwards about eight hundred metres, and measured around two-hundred-and-fifty metres at its widest point along the southern margin. Parts of it were under excavation and off limits, but other sections were easily accessible, so I wandered amongst the ruins.

It didn't take long before I spotted the badly damaged walls of a massive mud-brick double-walled enclosure, with a gateway, running parallel to the river. Buttresses against the eastern face indicated to me that this was the outer wall and that this was most likely the site of the main residence for the Royal Family in Akhet-aten, the Northern Riverside Palace.

'Known locally as the 'Qasr', the North Riverside Palace stood at the northern end of the "Sikhet es-Sultan", the Royal Road that ran through the Central City.'

It was probably the same route Akhenaten and his family took in their chariots; the subject of many of the reliefs in the North and South Tombs of the officials and courtiers.

The whole North City was in a pretty crap condition, even considering the restoration work that had been done. It even had an old disused 'excavation' house, built in 1924 over the site of a large house opposite the palace, that dated back to the first 'organized' excavations here by John Pendlebury and the Egypt Exploration Society during the 1930s.

Amongst the scattered blocks and column bases that dotted the ruins, I focused on the gateway. In particular the northern niche, once lined with limestone blocks sculpted with a frieze of cobras, which had been quasi-restored. I wondered if the limestone came from some other, much older, original building, or if it had been quarried and sculptured especially for the Northern Riverside Palace? There was no real way of knowing.

'When the gateway was excavated in 1930–2 many painted mud plaster fragments were found in the rubble that filled the gateway. The fragments depicted floral patterns, wooden stands with pendant flowers, and a scene of a royal chariot drive. Several of the fragments contained parts of cartouches including the name of Akhenaten and that of a consort: "Ankhkheperura beloved of Neferkheperura" and "Nefernefruaten-beloved of her husband".'

I tried to tune in, to see if I could feel anything, but, maybe because of the heat, there was nothing, Nemo certainly wasn't leaping out of the water, nor did I blame him, it was stifling. I was well and truly on my own.

Oh, how I wished Crystal was here now; I know it was hardly a romantic setting, one-hundred-and-ten in the shade and me being hot and sweaty and probably smelling like the rear end of a camel, but this is possibly where we would have once lived as man and wife. I wondered where she was now, back in Luxor, or had she journeyed with Diane and Pernille back up the Nile to Philae? Would I ever see her again? I didn't even have her contact details, hell, I didn't even know her last name. But I did have Bill's details, and, so long as he stayed with Pernille, I was sure Pernille would stay in contact with Crystal and I could track her down once I was safely out of Egypt. If seeing Kareem's papers safely into the hands of a whistle-blower wasn't enough, it gave me the motivation I needed to do what I had to do to get out of Egypt alive.

I skirted around the rest of the city, heading up towards its northern end where the widening strip of desert behind the palace wall had preserved the foundations of a large group of storerooms and other service buildings.

'At the far northern end of the city, a single major building, excavated in 1924-5 by T. Whittemore and known as the North Administrative Building, ran down the slope on a series of terraces, effectively blocking land access from the north. Used for storage and administration, at its centre was a large courtyard cut back into the slope.'

Nothing of interest there.

Making my way back to the taxi down the 'Sikhet es-Sultan', I briefly explored the large houses and compounds on the eastern side of the road. Much to my surprise, I stumbled upon the 'gypsum' foundations of what was apparently a private stone chapel within one of the houses. Akhet-aten really needed some major exploration, and not just on the surface.

'Last stop, North Palace!'

'Originally thought to be a residence for Akhenaten's queen, Nefertiti, recent inscriptions found in the North Palace show that it was the home of the pharaoh's lesser wife, Kiya. Other altered inscriptions show that the palace was later usurped by Akhenaten's eldest daughter Meritaten.'

The years following Akhenaten's 'death', or disappearance, already provoked enormous argument; my thoughts would provoke even more, especially about who he really was and what really happened while he was ruling. As for Kiya, some Egyptologists have suggested there was an attempt by her to usurp the throne. But was Kiya a lesser wife of Akhenaten, was she his daughter, Meritaten, or was she a wife of Amenhotep IV?

If Kiya was Akhenaten's lesser wife, and the mother of Tutankhamen, there would have been little need for her to usurp the throne as it would automatically have passed to Tutankhamen and not to his 'sister', Meritaten. But, it didn't. When Akhenaten and Nefertiti left, the throne followed the bloodline and went to Meritaten, who could possibly have changed her name to Kiya, and her consort, the 'mysterious' Smenkhkare, Amenhotep IV, which means Tutankhamen could *not* have been Akhenaten's son. So who was Kiya married to if she wasn't Meritaten and wasn't married to Akhenaten? And let's be clear, there are no images of Kiya on the 'tombs' as part of the immediate Akhenaten Royal Family. Kiya would not have dared try to usurp the throne from Nefertiti, even Mutnodjnet would have had a greater claim, so she must have tried to usurp it from her 'co-wife', Meritaten.; after all, hell hath no fury like a woman scorned. Obviously Kiya was married to Amenhotep IV, his mummy was even found buried in her coffin.

Ultimately the mummies of both Amenhotep IV and Tiye were transferred to the tomb of Amenhotep III in the Valley of the Kings during the reign of Tutankhamen, probably by Ay. If Akhenaten and Amenhotep IV were the same person, it doesn't make sense that Ay would have preserved and protected the body of Akhenaten; in fact it was more evidence that they weren't.

The Egyptologist tote the belief Tutankhamen was the son of Akhenaten, who married his sister, Ankhsenpa-aten, that it was all a patriarchal lineage of the throne. But none of that added up. The way I saw it, the *sang réal* was the key, and that went: Tiye, Nefertiti, Meritaten, who was married off to Amenhotep IV, Meketaten, who had been married by her father Akhenaten and died in childbirth, most probably birthing a daughter, and then Ankhsenpa-aten.

Upon Nefertiti leaving Egypt, the throne would logically and rightfully have passed to Meritaten but, as far as we know, Meritaten did not produce a male offspring, possibly something to do with the mix of genetics between Annunaki and 'human' genes. Kiya, on the other hand, was fully 'human' and Amenhotep IV's minor wife. She obviously believed Amenhotep IV should have been reinstated as pharaoh, which would have made her a Queen, and not reduced Amenhotep IV, Smenkhkare, to a mere consort of Meritaten, which in turn left Kiya almost without status.

Given Kiya was more than likely a foreigner, probably a Hittite princess married off to Amenhotep IV some time before the arrival of Akhenaten as a way off ensuring a harmonious relationship between the Hittites and the Egyptians, she would not have taken kindly to being relegated from Queen, to being the minor wife of a deposed king. Her options limited, and her initial overthrow attempt thwarted, Kiya did the next best thing and married off her son, Tutankhamen, who was the only eligible male even vaguely related to the bloodline, to the next in line of the *sang réal*, Ankhsenpa-aten.

The question then has to asked of what happened to Meritaten, did she die of the plague, or was she the victim of foul play, thus thrusting Tutankhamen, or rather Ankhsenpa-aten, onto the throne, which would have catapulted Kiya into the revered positioned once held by Tiye? Or, did Meritaten change her name to Kiya? The permutations and combinations were giving me a headache, or was it dehydration.

The North Palace

It had only been a few minutes on the road and once again Raashid pulled the taxi up at the direction of our guard.

'North Palace.'

Facing the river, on the west side of the Royal Road, the North Palace was an isolated, self-contained, rectangular structure comprised of apartments built around an open court and garden that also incorporated a throne room. Although it was first excavated in 1924, there had been considerable reconstruction and consolidation undertaken in the area in recent years, so, even though there was nothing remaining above waist high, the floor-plan of the various structural elements was clearly visible beyond the flimsy thigh-high barbed-wire fence surrounding it. No entrance fee here, I just climbed through the fence and, using the floor plan from my files, started systematically wandering around.

The palace was built in a 'U' shape, or horseshoe, along three sides of a long open space that was divided into two parts by a wall and pylon. I started in the northwest corner where the foundations of two lines of narrow storerooms, or possibly stables, fronted an altar court.

'North of the first courtyard is a wide space leading up to a group of three stepped platforms originally built of stone upon a gypsum base. The central and largest was flanked with two rows of four offering-tables.'

I briefly scratched around in the centre of the courtyard, scuffing at the gypsum, before crossing to the opposite side of the courtyard where a narrower courtyard was surrounded by the brick foundations of building and colonnades.

'Unusually the palace included a courtyard for cattle, and aviaries with nesting niches, and friezes found here show spectacular paintings of birds diving among marsh plants. It has been suggested the building was a kind of zoological garden where the king could keep animals and birds and satisfy his love of nature.'

Totally plausible, and it may well have started out that way, but my guess is that after Akhenaten left Egypt it was modified to become the palace for Kiya or Meritaten.

Entrance into the inner courtyard was through the remains of a monumental pylon-like entrance consisting of two masses of brickwork.

'The entrance pylon flanked a wide area of gypsum foundation that originally supported columns and a stone pavement. One interpretation is that it formed a Window of Appearance directed towards the west.'

That made sense. There were also two narrower entrances, one to either side, also with stone pavements flanking the outer ends of the pylons. In front of each of these was a pair of square gypsum foundations most likely used as the bases for statues of Akhenaten.

The main inner court was dominated by a large rectangular depression, surrounded by column bases on three sides, that took the form of a traditional 'Hollywood' pool.

'Filled with debris, excavation and drilling have failed to establish how deep the depression goes, although a depth of eight metres below the present ground level has been reached.'

Eight metres, that's around twenty-four feet, still nowhere near deep enough to get down to the pre-tsunami level. But, why would you create a pool over eight metres deep, unless there was something down there you needed to connect with, like a source of water from an underground water table. And what sort of 'debris' still waited to be unearthed?

To the north of the pool the area was divided into three similarly sized units apparently used to house different kinds of animals.

'The easternmost of the three spaces had additional features in the form of two sets of limestone feeding-troughs for various animals combined with tethering-stones. Those in the inner compartment were larger and decorated with carvings of oxen. The smaller troughs, in the outer compartment, were decorated with horned desert animals.'

The rooms to the south of the pool were much more irregularly arranged.

'The equivalent space on the south side was filled with what look like service buildings: houses, probably a bakery, and kilns where perhaps faience jewellery was produced.'

At the rear part of the palace a continuous series of buildings spanned the back wall. The northeast corner consisted of a central sunken garden surrounded by numerous rooms. When it was excavated, the walls of the surrounding chambers still bore areas of painted plaster.

'The central room on the north side, the 'Green Room', was painted with a continuous frieze depicting the natural life of the marshes.'

A corridor led southward to a transverse hall of columns at the centre rear of the palace; the column bases actually being the original bases. To the left, at the very rear of the palace, was a tiny throne room, probably for official private audiences with the 'Queen'. To the right was a much larger many-columned hall, which would have been the central feature of the palace. The positions of the column bases were marked in modern cement but had an unusual arrangement in that the outer row of columns were more closely spaced than those in the centre, presumably indicating that, like the Hypostyle Hall at Karnak, the central part of the roof was probably raised up taller on broader and more widely spaced columns to allow light to enter the space.

'Reconstruction of one of the limestone columns from the eastern part of the palace revealed the texts named the king's daughter Meritaten after the name of Akhenaten.'

It was pretty strong confirmation the palace was once occupied by Meritaten.

In front of the hypostyle hall was a stone terrace reached by a staircase that extended back into the hall, both marked with modern stone blocks that follow the lines of the original foundations.

'The terrace supported a canopy on stone columns.'

It would have been here that the 'Queen' came to chill-out and gaze over the swimming pool. It appeared there were several staircases built into the rear of the palace, which raised the possibility that, apart from the central terrace, there may well have been a second story over the rooms surrounding the garden court and to the final section to the south.

The final section of the palace was the southeast corner, no doubt the private quarters of the palace's owner: the principal bedroom and the bathroom, complete with limestone floor, sandstone tank, and gypsum covering of the walls, as well as other spaces used as storerooms and perhaps accommodation for attendants.

'The south-east corner, a large roofed space supported on brick pillars, was at first filled with storerooms however, during the life of the building, the storerooms were converted into houses and the pillared hall subdivided by partition walls.'

Then I noticed a rather curious pile of stones about thirty or forty metres off to the side of the palace. Normally I wouldn't have bothered, but these were different, they looked like talatats.

They were old, really old, worn, and many of them didn't exactly adhere to the dimensions usually attributed to talatats. Instead of 1/2 x 1/2 x 1 they were more like 1/4 x 1/3 x 1; maybe the talatats weren't as uniform as the Egyptologists would have us believe.

There'd been over sixteen-thousand of them recovered from Karnak, but the whole city of Akhet-aten was supposedly built from talatats, and that got me thinking, 'what if the talatats weren't shipped from Karnak to Amarna, what if it was the other way around, from Akhet-aten to Karnak?'

And that made me think even deeper, 'What if the talatats weren't a new concept at all, what if they were an old idea, an idea left over from the remains of the previous city that sat here before Akhenaten rebuilt it?' Because, if Akhenaten rebuilt it, which is what the stelae indicated, then surely he rebuilt it using the remains of the materials that were here. So, what was the truth, and was it lying somewhere deep beneath the sand? And with those questions running around in my head, my day at Akhet-aten came to an end. I took one last look around, headed back to the taxi and collapsed into the back seat; I had a lot to digest.

No one knows exactly how or why Akhenaten disappeared from the historical record, but, in the midst of growing chaos, with the military forces of the Hittites toppling Egypt's allies, just like Akhet-aten, the city he rebuilt, Akhenaten disappeared beneath the sands of Egypt; all the Egyptologists had were a few inscriptions indicating that his 17th year as pharaoh was his last.

Subsequently, Akhenaten has been referred to by many titles; 'a tormented visionary', a 'misunderstood poet', 'a visual artist of genius whose mission went unheeded', a 'political disaster', 'an incestuous child-abuser', even 'an insane bisexual pope or ayatollah suffering from pathological endocrine disorder'. I related to them all, well, all except the last two, but it was not who Akhenaten *was* that was important, it was what he represented, what he did.

After only seventeen years, Akhenaten and most of his work simply 'disappeared', buried by ignorance and fear beneath the shifting sands of Egypt. Unfortunately his religious reforms did not survive past his reign; rather they were kidnapped, twisted and corrupted by future megalomaniacs. His Aten temples were demolished, and Akhenaten came to be called "the Enemy" or the 'criminal of Akhet-aten'. It seems the revolution that would have raised the spiritual awareness of Egypt, and the world, to a new level, was premature, the land of the Nile was clearly not ready to receive his wisdom.

Akhenaten was ahead of his time, but his mission to guide humanity on an upward pathway has served for many centuries as an inspiration to many Initiates and Teachers who have chosen the same purpose in their lives. So maybe Akhenaten just planted a seed, a seed that has taken a long time to germinate, and may take an even longer time to blossom and bear fruit.

We dropped the guard back at the ticket office and I gave him a *very* healthy tip; he'd spent the best part of six hours with us and we were both grateful for it. I just hoped he wouldn't go inside and talk too much to the others about his day in the desert. After another dodgy purging session at the café toilet, I stuffed the rest of the bog-roll in my pocket, you never know when you're going to get caught short out here in the desert, and sauntered back to the cab.

Minutes later we were driving on to the ferry, and, as we returned back across the Nile, I felt a strange feeling of déjà vu; it was more than likely I would never return to Akhet-aten again.

CHAPTER 25 – THE MUMMY'S CURSE

There was something grounding, something 'secure' about landing back on the west bank; it was if I'd been up in a hot air balloon and come back to earth from another world.

'Tel el-Amarna it was what you expected?'

Saeed was back in the front seat and had turned around to check I was OK.

'No, far from it; at first I was pretty disappointed, I can't believe it's all gone, *but*, as we started digging a little deeper, Akhet-aten started to reveal its secrets.'

Saeed pointed to the backpack beside me.

'And you think this it might be written in the paper of my uncle?'

'Probably, there could even be more; I think I only began to scratch the surface.'

'This it is all the more reason to get you safe out of Egypt.'

'You won't get any arguments from me about *that*! Where are we headed now?'

'Dayr Mawas, to the train station.'

That caught me off guard.

'Not to Mallawi?'

'No, it is too big; there is more chance of the police being there and of being noticed.'

'Fair enough. Do we have time to get something to eat.'

'But of course, the condemned man he always have it the right to have his final meal.'

The town of Dayr Mawas was only five or ten minutes away at the most, and no sooner did we hit the railway station than Saeed indicated for Raashid to pull over.

'We can eat here.'

'Let me guess, it's your uncle's restaurant.'

He laughed.

'No, this it is my cousin.'

'Mohammed?'

'Ah, you have eaten here before?'

Saeed and I climbed out of the taxi but Raashid didn't move a muscle, rather he had a brief conversation with Saeed through the front window. I'd expected Raashid would have joined us for dinner, but apparently he was keen to get home; and I didn't blame him, eight hours chauffeuring an irreverent Aussie around the ruins and tombs of the hot desert would be more than enough for any mere mortal. I dragged the diminishing wad of notes from my pocket.

'Saeed, how much do I owe Raashid?'

'It depend how grateful you are for his time.'

'Jesus,…eight hours at say… thirty pounds an hour,…three hundred?'

Saeed gave a non-committal groan.

'Well, if that is what you think is fair.'

I thought to myself, 'what would Bill give?' then pulled out five 'C'-bills and thrust them into Raashid' grateful hot sweaty little hand.

'Shukran, Mister Alex, Shukran jazeelan.'

'Aafwaan.'

'Maasalaamah, Assalaam Alaikum.'

'Cheers.'

As Raashid took off into the crowded streets, Saeed wrapped his arm around my shoulder.

'Come, Ahoya, let us eat.'

We swaggered inside, picked a table in the corner and, feeling somewhat relaxed and perhaps a little *too* overconfident, I plonked the backpack on the table and went to pull out Kareem's papers.

'Perhaps, Saeed, you can have a quick look through the papers and see what there is about Amarna?'

Saeed purposefully rested his hand on the bag, halting me in my tracks.

'I do not think this it is such a good idea, the less of a risk you take, the better the chance we have to get you out of Egypt alive; the paper, they have waited this long to speak, they can wait for another few days until they can speak without being silenced.'

I looked around the room, suddenly becoming aware that everyone was taking particular note of my presence; it was probably because very few foreigners visited Dayr Mawass, let alone sat down in this restaurant to dine on the local cuisine, but to my rapidly accelerating rampant paranoia it looked like everyone in the place was a snitch for the Secret Police.

To change the mood, we ordered our food; my guts were still a little on the dangerous side of rancid, but the thought and aroma of Egyptian roasted chicken with lime and pepper-salt was too tempting to pass up. I took the opportunity to check in on the rest of the Minnow crew.

'Any news from the others back in Luxor?'

'Not since last night.'

'What happened?'

'When, they are arrive back in Luxor, Saleem he was stopped by the police, they go through the bus and take every one to one side.'

'Just as well I wasn't on it, I would have been history, thanks for saving me, but what happened to the others?'

'It seem they were all asked about you, and about the paper. They are say they have only met you a few days before: that they really did not know you, and know nothing about any paper. They are say you have decide not to return to Luxor, and Mister Bill, he say he is think you are head off to Hurghada.'

'Good old Bill, giving them a red herring to chase.'

'Then they are let go.'

'I hope I get to see them all someday to thank them.'

'Miss Crystal in particular, yes?'

'Yes, that would be good.'

The reality was it was highly unlikely I would see her in Egypt again, which most likely meant a trip to Germany, and that was a country of what ... maybe only a hundred million people or so ... sure, I'd be able to find her, no problems. Hell, I didn't even know her last name. I could just see myself wandering down the streets of Berlin, 'Guten Tag, Sprechen Sie English? Do you know Crystal?' Yeah, no problems! As dinner was served, I put two and two together.

'Hey, Saeed, your second wife is German, right? I don't suppose you have put her and Crystal in touch with each other?'

Saeed grinned like a Cheshire Cat on catnip, he knew exactly what my agenda was.

'But of course, Miss Crystal she does not live that far from my wife. She is live in Heidelberg, and my wife, she is live in Frankfurt.'

'It must be tough being a Muslim in Germany?'

'Oh, my wife, she is not the Muslim.'

'I meant you, anyway, I didn't think Muslims were allowed to marry non-Muslims?'

'What is it make you think I am Muslim?'

'I guess I just assumed you were; all that talk about Allah. And you do have two wives, I mean, you're not a Mormon are you?'

Saeed chuckled away.

'No.'

'OK, I'm confused, are you Muslim or Christian?'

'This it is a very good question; I am neither, and I am both, I am a felucca captain.'

'How does that work?'

'Indy, my friend, religion, it is a coat of many colour; one is wise not to wear snow shoes in the summer.'

I knew about 'Joseph' and his 'coat of many colours', a disguise of many half-truths, deceptions and lies.

'Do you mean, when in Rome do as the Romans do?'

'Yes, when I am in Egypt I am *Muslim*, when I am in Germany I am *Christian*.'

'And when you are in a felucca?'

'I am felucca captain, yes.'

I was starting to get it.

'Meaning you go with the flow and navigate your way around the boulders?'

'Exactly, there is no point in trying to sail through the boulder when there is room enough in the river for both the immovable boulder of religion and the free flowing water of the mind. Why let some other steer your felucca and smash it upon the rock just to prove their point?'

'So you don't believe in religion?'

'Oh, no, I believe in it, religion it is very real. But many people they wear the religion like it was the gold necklace of the pharaoh, parade around as if it give them some sense of importance. It glitter and shine and they wear it because they think it is of value when it is just the image, a concept, an illusion. But it is just a metal, 'worth' nothing. It 'does' nothing; it serve no real function, other than to define what it already is. Would the pharaoh he be any less the pharaoh were he not to wear it? Or it is the symbol of power and submission, to be feared by those who do not bow down to it. And then, when those do not bow down to it rebel, it become the target, or the yoke that bind you to its perceived function. I choose not to wear it *or* be weighed down by it.'

'But you do practice some sort of religion some times?'

'Religion, it is the anchor, there are the time when, for whatever reason, it is good to have something to slow you down, to save you from being swept away by the current of life.'

'Like anchoring at night rather than sailing in the darkness?'

'Yes, very good, but, if you never pull it up the anchor, then it cause you to forever sail in the circle; you convince yourself you are get somewhere, but in fact you are not, your life it revolve around the anchor.'

It was a brilliant analogy; I could instantly picture the billions of people riveted to the spot, like hamsters on a wheel, their lives totally revolving around their religion. And the term 'religion' suddenly had an even broader context; cultural conditioning, intellect, science, job, football team, ego, they were all attachments that anchored you to a perspective, to a boulder in the river of life. Thankfully, Saeed was on a bit of a roll.

'Indy, my brother, religion, it is the heavy burden to bear and yet many they wear it like the badge of honour, but, when you are in the deep water, this badge it can become the stone around your neck, it drag you down and it drown you. This is why many people of the religion they do not swim in the river of life; they prefer to sit on the boulder in the middle of the surging water and pretend it they are more powerful than the river, because the river it cannot move their faith. But the river it has no interest in them and it is not held back in its journey; it merely wash over them or pass them by.

And yet, from their *most exalted* position, they are preach to all about the danger that await beneath it the surface of the water, *"Do not swim, stand firm with me and be saved"*.' But God, Allah, whatever you wish to be call him...'

'Or her,'

'Yes..., if he or she was it the boulder, then they are also the water as well. My parent, they are raise me as the Muslim, I follow the Islamic teaching and I am marry my cousin, I am stand firm on the boulder, but on the felucca you see it life very different, and many people they come and go, and it make you start to ask it many question.'

'Was that when you met your second wife?'

'Yes, I am start to read, *'The Bible'*, the *Gita*, the *Vedas*, I discover the *true* history of Islam and that make me question the origin of *all* the other religion, that is when the boulder it become the stepping-stone and quick is it I learn to jump from one boulder to the next, and finally into the very water that surge all around.'

He'd done it again, given a beautifully poetic explanation.

'Are you sure you're not the reincarnation of Rumi?'

A wry grin crept across Saeed's face.

'I don't know, was he the rock jumper?'

'Nah, I think he was a felucca captain. In any case, it must have been some journey, just leaving the Islamic faith must have been tough.'

'But I did not leave it, there is much to admire about it the Islamic faith, I just did not stay stuck within it.'

'What do you mean?'

As we tucked into our dinner, little did I know we were about to get into another meaty subject.

'Ancient belief they belong to ancient time, modern time they call for the more modern view.'

'So you know Islam came from *'The Bible'*?'

'On the felucca I listen with great interest to your talk with Mr Bill and the other about Moses and Islam, but Islam it did not come from *'The Bible'*.'

'It didn't?'

'Many of the teaching of Jesus, yes, but not Allah; Islam it is the starnge mix of Christianity, Judaism, and the pagan worship of the Assyrian, Babylonian, and Akkadian Moon-god, Suen.'

'Suen? The Akkadian Moon-god? You mean "Sin"?'

'"Sin", yes.'

I started thinking out loud.

'So it was adopted by the Semites, by the Habiru?'

'The Assyrian, the Babylonian, and the Akkadian, they all take it the name "Suen" and transform it into the name "Sin" as the favourite name for their Moon-God, who he is the judge of men and the gods.'

'So where does Allah come in?'

'The Muslim they believe that, before there was the Islamic time, Allah he was the biblical God of the prophet, and of the apostle, but this it is not so, Allah he was the pagan Moon-god, "Sin". But while the name of the Moon-god it was "Sin", his title it was al-ilah, which mean "the god", which was made short to become Al-Ilah, The God, or Allah, the Supreme Being, meaning he was the chief or high god among all of the god.'

'So before Islam, the Arabs had more than one god?'

'Oh, yes, at the Kabah in Mecca they did worship three-hundred-sixty god.'

'I thought Mecca was where Allah was worshipped?'

'It was, it is, but before Islam, Allah, he was the main god and Mecca it was build as the shrine special for the Moon-god.'

'Really?'

'Yes, this is why it was the most sacred site of the pagan Arab. They are worship the Moon-god, Allah, by to pray toward Mecca several time during the day.'

'So what's the deal with the big pilgrimage to Mecca, with kissing the black stone inside the rectangular building?'

'The black stone inside it the Kabah it has been worship for many century before Mohammed he claim it for his new religion.'

'What's so special about the black stone?'

'It was a piece of the moon, a gift from Sin, from Allah.'

'A moon-rock?'

'The meteorite, that it must have fall to earth during the crescent moon, which the ancient pagan Arab believe it was some sort of gift or message from the Moon-god.'

I knew that there were Meteorite-cults that were quite common in Greco-Roman civilizations, and so what Saeed was saying made total sense.

'And that explains why the symbol of Islam is the crescent moon, why it sits on top of their mosques and minarets, and why the crescent moon is found on the flags of Islamic nations?'

'And why the Muslim they fast during Ramadan, which it begin and it end with the crescent moon in the sky?'

'I wondered why I'd never seen you praying, not like the others.'

'Get on my knee and pray to a piece of rock that it has fall from space, I do not think so.'

'So Islam has simply taken the symbols, the rituals, and even the name of its god from the ancient pagan religion of the Moon-god?'

'Exactly.'

'Is that why you left?'

'In some part, yes; it was certain not a very good reason to convince me to stay. I had always wonder who Allah was and why he was never described in the Qur'an.'

'What do you mean?'

'The first teaching of the Muslim faith it is not, "Allah is great" but "Allah he is the great-est", meaning he is the greatest of all the god. I think Mohammed he was raised in the pagan religion of the Moon-god, Allah, and he knows it that the Arab they already know who Allah is, the greatest of all the god. But Mohammed he decide that Allah was not just the greatest god, but the only god.'

'You think Mohammed pulled a double bluff?'

'This it is one way to look at it. Mohammed he believe in the Moon-god, Allah, but to the Jew and the Christian, he say that Allah he is also their God.'

'Yeah, but the Jews and the Christians didn't buy it and I guess that's why they rejected Allah as a false god.'

'And they still do…'

Saeed checked his watch.

'…Come, we must finish up, it is time to go to catch it the train.'

I finished off the rest of the chicken, gulped down the remainder of my Pepsi, and made my way to my feet. Feeding the hunger was one thing, but unfortunately the gravitational alignment of my intestinal tract caused by standing also triggered the peristaltic convulsions of the remnants of the mummy's curse within my colon. I quickly tossed a hundred on the table in front of Saeed.

'Hang five, I've just got to go to the loo.'

Saeed picked up the backpack off the floor and held it out to me.

'Indy, you had better be take this with you.'

'What for?'

'I think you will need to get it back into your disguise.'

'No way!'

'Until we get to Beni Suef, we cannot take it any chance.'

I wasn't about to stand there arguing, the mounting pressure in my bowel was taking immediate precedent. I grabbed the bag and headed out the back. No health regulations here, or mandatory dunnies for the clientele, this was bare-necessity plumbing; thank god I had the wad of poo-paper in my pocket, because there was not a sheet to be found. But I was in no position to argue, I had more runs on the board than Don Bradman on a tour of England, or, if you're a yank, a bigger dose of the runs than the stats of Babe Ruth, Willie Mays, Barry Bonds, Mark McGwire, and Sammy Sosa put together.

The pipes purged, and a toxic catastrophe avoided, I donned the black pillar box, the widow's tent, tucked the backpack underneath, returned to the 'dining room', and, much to the bewilderment of the diners, followed the ever-increasing grin and chuckles of Saeed into the street.

The station was only a few minutes walk away and wasn't anywhere near as busy as I'd expected, and, more importantly, there wasn't a single uniform in sight. When I pointed it out to Saeed, and suggested I ditch the Godmother outfit, he casually nodded towards a well-dressed man half way up the platform.

'Secret Police.'

'Shit!

This train still ain't bound for glory

I stood there like a stunned mullet until the train arrived, just before 6 pm, and we made our way onboard as inconspicuously as possible. Saeed somehow managed to use his magic to secure us a couple of seats from some youngsters and, as the sun was setting in the west, we were off and running, next stop, Beni Suef.

Well, not really, the next stop was a few minutes down the track at Mallawi, and what a bun-fight that was; I was glad Saeed had insisted we went to Dayr Mawas. I stuck my head briefly out the window; the place was crawling with uniforms.

'Shit, the guard at Amarna must have said something.'

'Relax, Indy, if he did, we do not want to draw it any attention to ourself.'

I was sweating; no, I was sweating on top of sweating, it was like Niagara Falls cascading under an electric blanket. As the police checked everyone getting on the train,

222

I sat there like a fat Buddha in a sauna, *wishing* the train onwards. When it did eventually pull out of the station I instantly transmuted into an obsessed accountant, meticulously counting the uniforms as they passed by the window; four, five, six, eight, and then we were free of the platform and I let out a deep sigh of relief. I had a quick scan around the carriage; it seems none of the police had boarded the carriage.

'How far to Beni Suef again?'

'It is about forty kilometre to el-Minya, and another one-hundred-and-twenty to Beni Suef.'

That added up to at least four hours. I buried my hands under the dress and fished and fumbled around for my laptop in the backpack. Saeed leaned forward and whispered to me with a rather intent questioning tone.

'Indy, what is it are you doing?'

'Just going to settle in for the journey, make a few notes, and listen to some music.'

'What about the police?'

'I think we've fooled them. The police would've expected us to get on at Mallawi, that's why they were there, checking everyone on the platform who was getting *on* the train. But they didn't think that we could already have *been* on the train. You're a genius.'

'I thank you, but until we are in Beni Suef we must still be very careful.'

I ran through the list of music on my laptop, no 'Jesus Christ Superstar' this time, and settled on 'Journey's Greatest Hits', and why not, after all I was on a hell of a journey myself. It had always been one of my favourite albums, ever since my first divorce when I used to play it getting ready to go out with my mates to Charlton's nightclub and billiards hall where their band played. It always made me feel great hearing that first song crank out.

'*Another night in any town, You can hear the thunder of their cry...*'

It instantly took me back to those days, to good times.

'*In the shadows of a golden age, A generation waits for dawn.*
Brave carry on, Bold and the strong.'

I'd been through more than my fair share of roller-coasters thank you; halcyon days and some dark days, two failed marriages, lots of water under the bridge that's for sure, but I'd survived, and, as they say, what you survive makes you stronger. The question was whether my golden age was ahead of me, or in the past?

I used the time to make notes about Akhet-aten; the tributaries than ran through the Northern Suburbs into the Nile, indications of higher water levels. Then there was the 'gypsum' limestone 'foundations' in the Aten temples of the Central City and at Kom el-Nana; were they the roofs of even older temples?

'*Just a city boy, born and raised in South Detroit*
He took the midnight train goin' anywhere
A singer in a smoky room, A smell of wine and cheap perfume
For a smile they can share the night,
It goes on and on and on and on.'

How true was that, well apart from the South Detroit bit, South Oakleigh more like it. However, although the sun was setting, it wasn't anywhere near midnight, and we weren't going anywhere, we were headed to Beni Suef, which, the more I thought about it, was the middle of nowhere.

The smoke-filled carriage was also regularly drilled with the raspy tones of local venders flogging their various nibbles to the passengers. I wouldn't have described the 'aroma' as that of wine and cheap perfume, more like rancid sweat, and, embarrassingly, most of it was emanating from under my apparel. But, generally, we were a happy-go-lucky lot, and we certainly were going on and on and on and on.

'Strangers waiting, up and down the boulevard,
Their shadows searching in the night
Don't stop believin', Hold on to your feelings.'

If there was one thing I wasn't going to do, that was stop believing.

I focussed back on Amarna, on the South Tombs and the questions they threw up; 'who was Prince Nakhtpa-aten, why were there no funerary texts on the walls, were they even tombs, or were they shrines of worship poised high in the cliffs for the elite?' Also, 'if Ay was Nefertiti's uncle, then, at some point when Amenhotep III died, did Ay marry Tiye, becoming Nefertiti's step-father?' It would mean Mutnodjnet was Nefertiti's maternal half-sister and again totally support why Horemheb married Mutnodjnet. As for the 'tomb' of Ay, what was the significance of the red gloves?

Yet another stop rolled along, El Roda, and it was good news, there were no police on the platform; another deep sigh of release. A minute later, on cue, as we pulled out from the station, 'Wheel in the Sky' began.

'Winter is here again oh Lord, Haven't been home in a year or more
I hope she holds on a little longer

Sent a letter on a long summer day, Made of silver, not of clay
I've been runnin' down this dusty road.'

It was coming out of winter back in Australia, and though I'd only been gone less that two weeks, it felt like a lifetime ago when I was back in the rat-race of Melbourne, contemplating where my life was headed. Since arriving in Egypt it had been one dusty, or rather, sandy road after another, one path, one journey, and I held on to the hope it somehow led back to Crystal.

'Wheel in the sky keeps on turnin', I don't know where I'll be tomorrow.
Wheel in the sky keeps on turnin''

Like the wheels of the train, my life was turning, onwards, changing, I didn't know where I was going to be tomorrow, but I hoped it was going to be Hawarra.

'I've been trying to make it home, Got to make it before too long
I can't take this very much longer'

It made me stop, I didn't know if I *could* take this very much longer, or if I could, whether I would have to. One way or another, I was either going to escape from Egypt, or I would be caught and probably never seen again.

'Wheel in the sky keeps on turnin', I don't know where I'll be tomorrow
Wheel in the sky keeps on turnin''

My thoughts turned to the Royal Tomb, which ALL the Egyptologists presume to be the final resting place of Akhenaten, but I was of the belief it was more than likely to be that of Nefertiti's mother, Queen Tiye.

'Highway run, Into the midnight sun,
Wheels go round and round, You're on my mind'

And she was, she always was, since the day she walked down the dock and onto the White Rose, Crystal had captivated my heart and soul.

'Restless hearts, Sleep alone tonight, Sending all my love Along the wire
And being apart Ain't easy on this love affair,

Two strangers learn to fall in love again
I get the joy of rediscovering you,
Oh, girl, you stand by me, I'm forever yours, Faithfully'

Love is such a strange beast, no matter how much you think you can tame it, the reality is that Love tames you. How did I know? I'd been there before.

'I'll be alright without you, There'll be someone else,
I keep tellin' myself
I'll be alright without you, Love's an empty face...
Oh I've got to replace'

I was drawn into its spell, distracted from my original thoughts and engrossed in the songs.

'I was alone, I never knew what good love could do
Ooh, then we touched, Then we sang about the lovin' things
Ooh, all night, all night, Oh, every night,
So hold tight, hold tight, Ooh baby, hold tight

Oh, she said, Any way you want it, that's the way you need it,
Any way you want it
She said, Any way you want it, that's the way you need it,
Any way you want it'

It took me back to the morning on the bank of the Nile and then to the night in Crystal's room at the Nefertiti hotel, or rather the morning. What a fool I'd been, I'd missed all my opportunities and blown the chances I'd had. Shit, was that a metaphor for my life?

'You've got some fascination, With you high expectations
This love is your obsession, Your heart, your past possession
Let down your defences, Won't be up to the one who cares
As you search the embers, Think what you've had, remember

Hang on, don't you let go now,
You know, with every heartbeat,
we love, Nothing comes easy, Hang on, ask the lonely'

Without her, my heart felt like Akhenaten's sarcophagus, smashed into a thousand pieces. But was Akhenaten's sarcophagus really his, or did it belong to Queen Tiye? There were so few fragments of it recovered to reassemble, did it have any identifying cartouche, or had the Egyptologists guessed it was Akhenaten's because it had the image of the Aten, or, because they *wanted* to find his sarcophagus? And then there were the depictions of Mutnodjnet in the tomb, but not Tutankhamen, the elongated heads on the stelae, and the evidence that the city of Akhet-aten existed before Akhenaten came along and 'rediscovered' it.

'One love feeds the fire, One heart burns desire,
Wonder who's cryin' now
Two hearts born to run, Who'll be the lonely one,
Wonder who's cryin' now'

Crystal would know, she was Nefertiti, she would remember. I had to see her again. And then one of my most favourite songs, one of the most powerful rock ballads ever written started – 'Separate Ways'. I closed my eyes and lived every word.

Here we stand, Worlds apart, Hearts broken in two, two, two
Sleepless nights, Losing ground, I'm reaching for you, you, you
Feelin' that it's gone, Can't change your mind

If we can't go on, To survive the tide, Love divides

Someday love will find you, Break those chains that bind you
One night will remind you, How we touched and went our separate ways
If he ever hurts you, True love won't desert you,
You know I still love you, Though we touched and went our separate ways

Troubled times, Caught between confusions and pain, pain, pain
Distant eyes, Promises we made were in vain, In vain, vain
If you must go, I wish you love, You'll never walk alone,
Take care my love, Miss you love

Someday love will find you, Break those chains that bind you
One night will remind you, How we touched and went our separate ways
If he ever hurts you, True love won't desert you,
You know I still love you, Though we touched and went our separate ways'

The train slowed as it pulled into the next station, jolting me back to my notes. Who was Baketaten on the walls of the North Tombs, was she Mutnodjnet? And what were the vertical shafts really for? Then there were the desert altars, were they the remnants of previous Middle or Old Kingdom structures? Were they observatories, plotting the course of the sun, moon, and the stars, or galactic launch pads?

And then, at the North Palace, there was the unusual depth of the 'pool', over eight metres, and, finally, was there a power struggle between Kiya and Meritaten for the throne, or were they the same person? My trip there had raised even more questions about the politics of the post-Akhenaten period.

'So you think you're lonely, Well my friend I'm lonely too
I want to get back to my City by the bay, Ooh, ooh'

We'd come to a stop at a place called Abu Qorgas, about twenty kilometres south of Minya and the words triggered me to see what sites we were passing in the night. I pulled out the iphone and scrolled through my notes.

'Several kilometres east of Abu Qorgas, carved into the high limestone cliffs on the east bank of the Nile, are the rock-cut tombs at Beni Hasan El Shorouk. The tombs are reached via a long steep flight of stone steps leading up the hillside and date mostly to 11th and 12th Dynasties, although there are a few smaller and less elaborate ones belonging to the 6th Dynasty.'

Going by the previous 'tomb' sites, the stairs were no doubt a modern construction. The fact they were high up in the cliffs, like those at Aswan, Wadi Hillal, and Amarna gave further support to theory they weren't 'tombs' but rather 'shrines' or possibly some sort of 'summer houses'. What I needed to find was similar sort of evidence consistent with my observations at the other locations.

'There are thirty-nine tombs on the upper part of the cliff, of which twelve are decorated, and four are currently open to visitors. They offer a rare chance to see the distinctive early Middle Kingdom art, with colourfully painted scenes of daily life, recreation and military activities.

Of the open tombs, the 11th Dynasty tomb of Baqet III (BH15) is the earliest. A plain tomb façade with two slender lotus columns leads to a large rectangular chapel at the rear. Inside, there are numerous painted scenes including; a desert hunt, scenes of weaving and spinning, goldsmiths and sculptors mingled with scenes of country living, hunting and fishing in the marshes, catching birds and gathering papyrus, battle scenes, along with wrestlers, a common feature in tombs from this period, and more traditional funerary scenes, and scenes of sports and playing senet. There is also a small L-shaped statue chamber in the eastern side of the south wall.'

Nothing out of the ordinary there, nor in the tomb of Baqet's son, Khety (BH17).

'The tomb of Amenemhet (BH2), dates to the 12th Dynasty and the reign of Senwroset I. It is a little more elaborate than the earlier tombs in that its architecture differs from the earlier style by having a courtyard and a portico with two columns before the entrance to the tomb-chapel.

The tomb chapel is large and rectangular and contains four wide polygonal pillars and two burial shafts...'

There they were again, those 'burial' shafts, two of them in fact, they had to have some other function.

'...The elaborately decorated ceiling is divided into three naves, each with a vaulted roof. The wall-paintings contain themes similar to earlier tombs, with agriculture and industries, hunting in the desert, military activities and funeral rites with offering-bringers.'

In many ways they were sounding very similar to the North Tombs at Akhet-aten and the Tombs of the Nobles at Aswan.

'The tomb of Khnumhotep II (BH3), a successor of Amenemhet, is one of the latest of the Middle Kingdom tombs built at Beni Hasan and follows the architectural style of Amenemhet's, with an impressive façade and portico followed by four polygonal columns in the tomb-chapel behind. The scenes are more colourful and lively than in the other tombs and make this perhaps the most interesting and distinctive of the Beni Hasan tombs.

These later tombs also contain a small statue chamber, to the east beyond the tomb-chapel, the tomb of Khnumhotep II still containing the lower part of a statue of him.'

It would have been nice to see them, but, in some way, I felt as if I already had. But it did raise more questions about the 'burial shafts' in the 'tombs'. These ones dated to the 12th Dynasty so the shafts in the 18th and 19th Dynasty tombs in the Valley of the Kings, and the North Tombs at Akhet-aten were clearly not 'innovations' as the Egyptologists would have us believe.

'You make me weep and wanna die,
Just when you said we'd try
Lovin', touchin', squeezin' each other'

Give me a break, talk about tugging at the heartstrings. I wondered where Crystal was now, whether she was in Luxor, Aswan, or maybe on her way back to Germany. And where was I, we must have been close to el-Minya by now. I checked again in my iphone, this time under Minya.

'About seven kilometres south of Minya, on the east bank at Zawya Sultan Basha, is the Zawiyet el-Meiyitin Pyramid, one of seven small step pyramids scattered along the Nile from Seila to Elephantine Island, all dating from the second half of the 3rd Dynasty to the early 4th Dynasty.'

I'd seen the one on Elephantine, and the one just north of Edfu, I wondered if there was anything significant about this one.

'Originally with three steps and about 17 metres high, with a base length of 22.5 metres, the pyramid was investigated in 1911 by the French Egyptologist Raymond Weill, who described the inner layers of the walls as having a slight incline towards the centre with a progressively decreasing height.'

Was that deliberate, or due to deterioration over time?

'Possibly attributable to Huni, last pharaoh of the 3rd Dynasty, who also built the pyramid on Elephantine Island, and built with small limestone blocks bound by mortar made of mud, sand and lime, the pyramid has no internal chambers, nor any underground structures, and has suffered over time, its remains now only five metres high.'

So, they couldn't possibly have been true tombs.

'Some Egyptologists believe the seven pyramids might have been centotaphs; fake tombs of queens. Others, that they were shrines connected with the myth of Horus and Seth, or perhaps predecessors of later sun temples, while still others believe they represented the primeval mound on which life was created.'

Off they went again, speculating; so much of 'Egyptology' was speculation. And if *they* could do it, so could I. It was pretty clear to me that the pyramids had nothing to do with being tombs for the pharaoh, and that meant there had to be some other 'communal' purpose that warranted them being built, and, in that respect, I think Christopher Dunne, with his book *'The Giza Power Plant'*, hit the nail right on the head, they were some sort of power stations. But why were some so big, so complex and brilliantly constructed, while others were small and of inferior construction? It didn't make sense they would reach the apex of their knowledge so quickly in the Old Kingdom, in the 4th Dynasty with the Great Pyramid at Giza, then go backwards; something didn't add up.

> '*Lying beside you here in the dark, feeling your heart beat with mine*
> *Softly you whisper love so sincere, how could our love be so blind*
> *We sailed on together but drifted apart and here you are by my side*
>
> *So now I'll come to you with open arms, nothing to hide, believe what I say*
> *So here I am with open arms, hoping you'll see what your love means to me,*
> *Open arms.*'

I drifted off into the song within seconds, and was lost in visions of Crystal and

I making mad passionate love in a huge bed at the Nefertiti Hotel, then in the shallows of the Nile, churning in the water like two electric eels on heat. Next, we were like Heathcliffe and Kathy in *'Wuthering Heights'*, running towards each other across the moors, as happy as Julie Andrews twirling around the alpine fields of Salzburg in *'The Sound of Music'*. That was until Saeed nonchalantly leaned forward and slowly but deliberately grabbed my knee.

'Ahoya, I suggest that you put your toy away; we will soon be at el-Minya. If the police they were at Mallawi, you can be sure they will be also at el-Minya.'

I started shutting down the computer, leaving the song to finish and starting with my trip notes.

'Wouldn't want to be caught; not even a good lawyer could get me out of that pit of vipers.'

And then it hit me, like an adrenaline rush.

'Of course, Mark.'

A light at the end of the tunnel

I dived back into my laptop, much to Saeed's concern.

'What is it you are doing? We do not have it much time.'

'You remember, on the felucca, I told you I was hoping to meet up at Hawarra with a couple of guys who are part of an organization called The Horus Foundation?'

'The one who were doing there some scan of the ground?'

'Yes. Well one of them is an Aussie lawyer, he's the one who was telling me all about the Labyrinth. If I could contact him, he might be my salvation. I've got his email here in my laptop, I can't send him an email directly, but, if I can get reception on my iphone, I can send him a message that way.'

Saeed looked around, then out the window.

'You have it about one minute.'

I found his email and quickly set about composing a missive.

'Hi Mark, Alex here. Finally got to Egypt & will be around Hawarra tomorrow and then on to Cairo. Not sure where you are, or what your plans are, but I may have got myself in a spot of bother with the Secret Police about some stuff the Egyptians don't want the world to know, and may need a little help. Here's my number 0478 368 083. Looking forward to hearing from you. Cheers, Alex.'

I hit send just as the train pulled in to the station, stuffed the laptop and phone quickly under my dress and into the backpack, gleaning a few strange looks from several of the locals in the carriage in the process, then sat still and tried to look as inconspicuous as possible.

Saeed was right; the platform was crawling with fuzz; not just police, but heaps of military as well. I guess the level of corruption in Kareem's papers was so comprehensive it infiltrated all aspects of Egyptian politics, including the military. Hell, I was really in deep shit!

'What are we going to do?'

'Nothing.'

'Shouldn't we make a run for it?'

'If you wish to draw it the attention to yourself and to volunteer for the target practice, then yes, but for me, I will just sit and wait.'

'Shit!'

Within seconds the carriage was chock-a-block with soldiers; I was convinced that any second they were going to jump on top of me and drag me off into the desert night never to be seen or heard from again, my body buried up to the next in a pit of sand. But they didn't. Instead, the train slowly pulled out of the station.

I sat motionless for the best part of fifteen minutes, maybe more, my eyes darting from insignia to insignia in an attempt to ascertain their plan; the tension was driving me crazy. My life was passing before me, but not as I expected, you know, your childhood, then your first kiss, first girlfriend, first cold beer, university days, first marriage, second marriage, none of that.

The only things going through my head stemmed from the moment Crystal stepped aboard the felucca; Moses and Joseph, the Reptilians, the brown dwarf, Nibiru and the Annunaki, Caesarion and Jesus, Akhenaten, Nefertiti, alabaster temples, red granite pillars, and, most of all, what the hell was in Kareem's papers, all of it interspersed with images of Crystal, naked and dripping wet.

I wondered if the soldiers were waiting for me to betray myself, reveal myself, give myself up? Then the train started to slow down; that's it, they were waiting until we pulled into the next station?

We came to a halt at Samalut; nothing, not a move, what a torture. Were they waiting for a signal from some Secret Police agent, the guy with the moustache standing in the corridor perhaps? Nothing. I couldn't take it any longer so, as the train stumbled away from the platform, I slowly leaned forward to Saeed.

'What's the deal with all the soldiers?'

'There is it the base for the army and also the airport in el-Minya.'

I sat back and eventually figured they weren't there to arrest me, rather they must just have been heading home on furlough, they probably weren't even aware I was there, which was good. I didn't want to think about it too much, if at all, so I decided to use the time to focus on other subjects, in particular the tsunamis and the timelines relating to the different civilizations beneath the sand.

Starting with the obvious one, the Thera eruption in 1600 BC, and moving backwards, I tried to retrace the catastrophes and align them with the civilizations. The Thera eruption sent a tsunami over six hundred feet high across the Mediterranean that obliterated almost everything before the 18th Dynasty, leaving a layer of at least twelve feet of sand and mud. This deposit would have formed the 'base' of the 18th Dynasty forward, upon which all the New Kingdom through to the 30th Dynasty temples were built and, more importantly, what was beneath or formed the foundations of those temples. It made sense; I'd seen the evidence for my own eyes, at Karnak, at Amarna, everywhere.

Before that, dating back to at least the 4th Dynasty, possibly earlier, many of the temples were probably built of limestone. But, before that, below that, was an even older civilization, the Red Granite civilization, that was another twenty-six feet below, all up, about forty feet!

If the Thera eruption coincided with a passing of Nibiru, then the previous passing, around 5,200 BC, which interestingly enough is around the date the 'experts' claim civilization suddenly appeared out of nowhere, could have caused the previous tsunami, which, going by the depth of the deposited silt on top of the Osireion, was at least twice as devastating as the Thera tsunami would have been. And if 5,200 BC coincided with the return of Nibiru, and the return of the Annunaki, then it made perfect sense that the Annunaki bought 'civilization' back to the primitive humans.

Someone built temples using massive blocks of red granite, particularly the Osireion, possibly the same guys built the Great Pyramid, it made sense, after all, you needed the same technology to cut and move such enormous blocks of stone for both the temples and the pyramids. The questions were 'who' and 'when'. The 'who' part seemed obvious, the Annunaki, the 'when' was harder to nail down.

Going back another thirty six hundred years, another orbit of Nibiru, took us to 8,800 BC, which was around 10,800 years ago, or exactly the time the scientist say we had our last pole-shift and the ice age ended. Coincidence? Hardly. More likely co–incidents; it made sense to me *that* was when the twenty-six feet were deposited, and that meant the 'Red Granite' temples and civilization pre-dated the last pole-shift, meaning it was before 8,800 BC, and that meant we were getting into the realms of the stories of Atlantis.

And if Atlantis was real, which seemed to be the case, and it existed before the pole-shift, then that meant that Atlantis wasn't occupied by humans, well not as the ruling race, but by the Annunaki. Suddenly all sorts of myths, legends and evidence started dropping in to place; the massive submerged ruins off Japan, the Bermuda pyramids, the Bosnian pyramids, the pyramids in China, the ancient cities high in the mountains in Peru, crystal technology.

As the train pulled in and out of the next station, Matai, I wondered if it was possible the Great Pyramids at Giza were built by the same race, and before the last pole-shift? And what about the Sphinx, what if it wasn't built *in* the age of Leo, as is suggested by Bauval and West, but rather way before then? But, why?

According to that Slosman guy Pieter was going on about, a catastrophe came from heaven during the age of Leo, caused the Earth's magnetic poles to reverse and the core to disconnected from the mantle, causing crustal slip, massive earthquakes, volcanic eruptions and tidal waves. Leo was the clearly the clue, but not necessarily the answer; it wouldn't be much good building a giant lion *after* the event. And then I got it.
'Of course!'

Just like you put a circle around an important date coming *up* on your calendar, perhaps the Sphinx was built to indicate an important upcoming event, an event when Leo was rising on the horizon, not *because* Leo was rising, but *as* Leo was rising, something important like the return of Nibiru and a pole-shift perhaps?

And that would explain why there was a Hall of Records under the paw of the sphinx; it probably contains all the calculations and indications of the date. And if it has the key to that date, the last pole shift, then it must contain all the calculations for the *next* pole-shift! Now, *that* all made sense, it was just a matter of finding more proof, after all, unless something concrete and irrefutable turned up, everything was just speculation.

That was pretty much all I could figure out going backwards in time; going forward from 1600 BC should have been a cakewalk, right? Wrong! I'd used the layers of dirt and sand at the rear of Abydos as my 'marker' and that helped me to discern the origin of the 'Red Granite' civilization, the 'Alabaster' civilization, the Thera eruption, but, the pre-Ptolemaic catastrophe that caused Alexander the Great to order the reconstruction of the temples, and the post-Ptolemaic catastrophe or catastrophes, that covered Tutankhamen's tomb and wiped out Akhet-aten and caused the ultimate demise of numerous temples, were still a mystery. By the time we'd pulled out of the next station, Bani Mazar, my curiosity had well and truly over-ridden my caution and I pulled out my iphone to search out and download some info on possible causes of catastrophes before Alexander the Great, and after.

So, what was I looking for? Ruling out meteorite strikes and other 'acts of god', it seemed I was looking for two or more tsunamis, one, some time between 400 BC and 1000 AD, which wiped out the 'Stone' Kingdom, and another one between 1000-1300 AD which wiped out the 'Mud-brick' Kingdom. And to find tsunamis meant finding what caused them, and, in that respect, earthquakes and volcanic eruptions in and around the Mediterranean were the obvious candidates.

So far I had earthquakes around 224 BC, in 27 BC, 1003 AD, and 1303 AD, but there was also the famous eruption of Mount Vesuvius that buried Pompeii, and that was my first suspect.

'The eruption of Vesuvius in 79 AD was one of the most catastrophic eruptions in history. It spewed a deadly cloud of stones, ash and fumes over 20 miles into the air, expelling molten rock and pulverized pumice at the rate of 1.5 million tons per second, ultimately releasing a hundred thousand times the thermal energy released by the Hiroshima bombing.'

I was on to something; surely it would have generated a number of tsunamis as well.

'The eruption was devastating, producing a huge pyroclastic flows that swept through Pompeii and Herculaneum killing tens of thousands of people, burying Herculaneum under twenty metres of tephra and Pompeii under 4 metres, and preserving them perfectly for posterity.

As devastating as it was, the eruption pales in comparison to the Thera eruption 1700 years earlier in that it only produced 4 cubic kilometres of ejecta and had a Volcanic Explosivity Index (VEI) of 6 compared to the Thera eruption that produced about 60 cubic kilometres of ejecta and a VEI of 7. In other words, the Thera eruption was 20 times more powerful.'

And if Thera produced a tsunami six hundred metres high, then, using simple mathematics, surely Vesuvius would have produced one at least thirty metres high, and, although it may have inundated Alexandria and the Nile Delta, I don't think it would have reached up the Nile any more than a hundred miles at the most, probably not even as far as Cairo.

'The 79 AD eruption was preceded by a powerful earthquake 17 years beforehand on February 5, AD 62, which caused widespread destruction around the Bay of Naples, and particularly to Pompeii.'

It probably produced a tsunami as well; clearly there was a lot of geological activity at the time, tsunamis may have been regular events, sweeping across the Mediterranean and constantly changing the face of Southern Europe. And Vesuvius wasn't the only active volcano in the region.

'Around eight thousand years ago, the eastern flank of Mount Etna experienced a catastrophic collapse, generating an enormous landslide, similar to the 1980 eruption of Mount St. Helens, and caused a huge tsunami, which left its mark in several places in the eastern Mediterranean. The most recent collapse event at Etna is thought to have occurred about 2,000 years ago, forming what is known as the Piano Caldera.'

That made Etna a possible candidate as well.

'In 396 BC, an eruption of Etna reportedly thwarted the Carthaginians in their attempt to advance on Syracuse during the Second Sicilian War.'

Eureka, 396 BC; that could have been the eruption that caused the tsunami ultimately responsible for Alexander's edict to rebuild the temples.

'Another particularly violent eruption occurred in 122 BC, and caused heavy tephra falls to the southeast.'

Nothing particularly peaked my interest about that eruption, however, as I was investigating more details on Herculaneum, I discovered another city, with a similar name, that had also been obliterated by a natural catastrophe, and this one fitted the bill even better.

'Around 300 AD, the Egyptian city of Herculion disappeared when an earthquake struck the Mediterranean and a subsequent tsunami wiped out the eastern port of Alexandria, felling massive columns and statues west-northwestard and leaving the ruins 6-8 metres underwater. A possible candidate for the earthquake was a documented earthquake in 365 AD centred in Turkey or Crete.'

I was pretty confident I'd found my smoking gun, or guns; earthquakes were certainly part of the picture, but the main culprit appeared to be tsunamis, because they not only swept everything away, but, more importantly, buried it under metres of silt and sand.

As the next station, Maghagha, came and went without incident, so, despite the proliferation of military men in the carriage, I was feeling pretty confident on most levels. However, reality is never more than a moment away and I was quickly brought down to earth. I may have been feeling confident from the neck up, but, from the stomach down, Ramses' Revenge was gurgling away in the underground corridors of my labyrinth; I was on the verge of a catastrophic tsunami of my own.

I stuffed the iphone in my pocket, pulled the backpack out from under my dress, and, with a certain sense of urgency handed it, and my akubra, to Saeed.

'Hang on to these for a sec will you while I go to the toilet.'

By the expressions on the faces of the locals, as I briskly clambered my way through the uniformed guard of honour to the end of the carriage, it must have looked like I'd just given birth to a brace of albino camels.

Thankfully the toilet was vacant; I didn't want to contemplate what would have eventuated should I've had to wait for even a few seconds longer than I could. There was no delicate way to say or do what I had to do; before I'd even removed my headdress, my strides and jocks were off in a jiffy and I held them to my chest in one hand as I picked up my dress with the other, squatted over the abyss in the floor, and spray-painted the contents of my intestines in an apocalyptical expression of the ultimate relief; it was one of those times when it felt appalling and amazing at the same time.

However, ten minutes and several episodes later, totally expunged, I faced another dilemma, there was no toilet paper, and believe me, I was in dire need of at least a few reams. My salvation was the half-a-roll of bog paper, left over from my visit to Amarna, stuffed in the pocket of my pants. It was a bit of a juggling exercise but I managed to extradite the roll and rectify the rectal Rembrandt.

I donned my jocks but decided to forego my strides for the sake of a little much-needed below-the-waist ventilation, then removed my headdress for a breath of fresh air. Whoa, bad move; boy, did I pong, but not as much as the train's dunny; thank God there was no glass in the window, but God help whoever had to come in here next.

It was tempting to put my pants back on and instead remove the whole disguise, as I'd done on the last train, but something told me that wouldn't be the best option, so, reluctantly, I rolled up my pants, put the headdress back on, emerged from the loo, and slowly made my way to my seat.

'How much further?'

'Maybe fifty kilometre, there are two more stop before Beni Suef, if we are get there.'

Taking the backpack back from Saeed, I quickly stuffed my pants inside, then slipped it and my akubra back under my dress.

'What do you mean?'

'As I have tell you, the hydra it has many head, the vulture it has great eye; your behaviour it has been noticed.'

I quickly scanned the carriage; most of the occupants were looking in my direction, conversing discretely amongst themselves. Concerned I'd blown my disguise, I turned to Saeed.

'Was it the iphone?'

'Perhaps, but maybe that I do not think that it was such a good idea to suddenly make appear a backpack and foreigner hat from under your dress, this it is not the usual thing for the Arabic woman to do. It is even stranger to be put them back again.'

'Do you think we'll be OK?'

'Inshallah.'

'Oh, that's great, coming from someone who's only a part-time Muslim, that doesn't fill me with a world full of confidence.'

'Then we shall just have to wait and see.'

It was probably my paranoid imagination running riot, but, for the next twenty minutes, as we stopped, then set off from the next station, El Fashn, I didn't dare move a muscle. I was certain there was more activity on the platform, more soldiers, more police, more activity within our carriage, but, as the dust settled in the fading early-evening light, nothing changed; we were fine.

The kiss of Judas

Everything back on track, I turned my thoughts to how everything was just like the stations on a railway track; everything was connected, whether you could see it or not, one moment led to the next. I'd even found a 'linear' chronological connection of the essential teachings of the Divine Feminine, the *sang réal,* from ancient Egypt through the Tat Brotherhood, the Essenes, the Gnostics, the Zealots, even the Druids, into the Judaic, Hindu, Christian and Islamic religions; it was like a big family tree.

I'd discovered the true identity of Jesus and Mary Magdalene and how Paul had hijacked Jesus' teachings. In many ways Paul was more of a Judas than Judas, but that got me thinking, 'who really *was* Judas?'

Before I'd come to Egypt and met Bill, all I initially knew was what most people did, that Judas was one of the apostles and that he betrayed Jesus with a kiss. But now, according to my earlier discussions with Bill at Abydos, it appeared that Judas was probably an older 'step-brother' of Jesus, a son of Mary and Joseph, and forced to escape Egypt with Caesarion because of the assassination of Caesar and the imminent Roman invasion.

There is no doubt Judas hated the Romans, but perhaps not as much as he held a deep long-term jealousy and resentment of 'Jesus'; the cause of his displacement from the cushy life he once led in the royal palaces of Alexandria. When he arrived in Jerusalem, along with the rest of the 'apostle' family group, Judas' Egyptian religious upbringing would have clashed with the predominant 'political' religions teachings of the Pharisees and Sadducees, the Jews, the 'slave race'.

So, in contrast to the passive pathway taken by Jesus, Judas, along with his actual blood brother, Simon Magus, formed the core of the Zealots, supposedly a very politically *re*active faction of Judaism, and *very* anti-Roman. But Judas and Simon weren't Jewish at all; they weren't trying to modify the Judaic dogma of the Pharisees and Sadducees, which they knew drew it's roots from the Egyptian religious teachings, they had seen the way the 'truth' had been corrupted and they were trying to *return* it to the teachings of their Egyptian upbringing.

The difference was, that unlike Jesus who believed the path was passive, Judas and Simon believed in fighting fire with fire. But they weren't fighting the Romans, they were fighting the Pharisees and Sadducees, and Caiaphas knew that, and he used the Romans to eliminate Simon and Judas; Jesus probably wasn't even a threat, just a convenient excuse and justification.

As for Paul, he was an opportunist, he used the issue of circumcision to seize control of the masses, then, around thirty years later when he wrote is 'memoirs', he twisted the actual events to suit his own agenda and make himself look good, just as Joseph, or rather Moses, had done.

'It was all about politics, it always has been, and it always will be.'

I couldn't wait to catch up with Bill, fill him in, and listen to him ripping into the clergy.

'*But "The Bible" says…*'

I could just hear the defensive rhetoric rolling off the tongues of the narrow-minded and religiously-conditioned 'pillars of Christianity', but, knowing what I knew about the true origins of the Old and New Testaments, believing what *'The Bible'* says, was like trusting a little boy with chocolate smeared all over his face telling you he didn't put his hand in the cookie jar.

Without thinking, I delved back into my iphone to try and find further evidence on the net. Saeed just looked at me with a raised eyebrow and shook his head. I brushed him off.

'Don't worry, everything's fine.'

I had a sniff of blood and not even the slowing down of the train as it approached the next station, was going to distract me from my quest.

From what I could remember, Judas was only mentioned in the New Testament, in Acts, a text assumed to be written by Paul, so I was pretty confident that any historical reliability of the details and events concerning Judas were highly disputable.

Stopping at Biba, by my calculations the last stop before Beni Suef, I briefly became aware of a bit of a commotion on the platform, raised voices, that sort of thing. Saeed leaned out the window to check it out, then got up and went off to investigate. Thinking Saeed had things well and truly under control, I plugged back in to the net and soon found a quote that recaptured my undivided attention.

'Judas, along with Zadok the Pharisee, had founded the Zealots, the "fourth sect" of 1st Century Judaism (the first three being the Sadducees, the Pharisees, and the Essenes), a group of theocratical-nationalists who preached that God alone was the ruler of Israel and that no taxes should be paid to Rome.'

That was consistent with another grab I found.

'In *"Antiquities of the Jews"* the Jewish-turned-Roman scholar and scribe, Josephus, states that *"around 6 CE, during the administration of Coponius, first Prefect of the Iudaea province, occurred the revolt of Judas the Galilean, who led a violent resistance to the census imposed for Roman tax purposes by Quirinius.* The revolt was brutally crushed by the Romans.'

As we got underway again, fortunately on the last leg of our trip, I found yet another phrase in support of my thoughts, this one referring directly back to *'The Bible'*.

'In Acts, Paul has Gamaliel, a member of the Sanhedrin, refer to Judas as an example of a failed Messianic leader.'

Could this be the same Judas, 'brother' of Jesus, leader of the Zealots? It seemed highly possible. But what happened to him, did he hang himself, was he crucified alongside Jesus or, as another part of *'The Bible'* said, was he thrown down a cliff? I'd already dealt with the 'hanged himself' inference; it was metaphorical - give a man enough rope and he will hang himself. But what about the reference to being crucified, was there any evidence to support it? Yes, there was.

Josephus didn't actually say anything about the death of Judas, but he did report the following:

'Judas' sons, James and Simon, were executed by procurator Tiberius in about 46 CE.'

Now Josephus was not reporting the events as a witness, he was writing almost a hundred years after the event, so he could easily have had dodgy source documents, especially if he was reading the early texts of Paul. Or he may simply have confused names and dates, for, as we now know, Judas and Simon were 'executed' first, by crucifixion, and James, twenty years later.

As for being thrown down a cliff, I didn't need to find anything new to figure that out; if Judas had been crucified alongside Jesus and Simon, and, when Passover came along, all three were taken down, it doesn't take a genius to work out that Judas wasn't put in the 'tomb', or rather rock-cave temporary prison, along with Jesus and Simon. Instead, the 'apostles' loyal to Jesus took matters into their own hands and tossed Judas over a cliff as there own form of 'divine retribution'. All of the pieces fitted and made perfect sense, especially when you consider it in relation to the political situation that was apparent at the time. It was totally different to the version of events in *'The Bible'*, but just as plausible, in fact, more so.

Suddenly I became aware of someone standing in front of me. At first I thought it was Saeed, or perhaps the conductor checking for tickets, wishful thinking, but, when I glanced slightly up, and saw he was wearing trousers and not a galabeya, I quickly realized that it was definitely *not* Saeed, and a chill went up my spine; the jig was up.

He said something to me in Arabic, which I didn't understand, so I stayed in character and pretended to ignore him, focusing on the iphone screen, as if I was deaf and dumb, hoping he would fall for my ruse. Alas, when he tapped me on the shoulder and said it again, I had to look up. Once again I feigned deafness, this time nodding and indicating for him to take Saeed's vacated seat, as if I believed he was asking me for permission to occupy it. He wasn't buying it.

'Passport, please.'

I looked around him, past the uniformed police accompanying him, praying that Saeed would suddenly emerge from the milling throng to save the day and claim me as his leprous grandmother. But Saeed was nowhere to be seen; it appeared he had seen the impending conflagration and abandoned me, left me to fend for myself.

'Passport!'

His demeanour was rapidly changing and I was in no position to make a run for it. I shut down my iphone, slipped it under my dress and into my pocket, removed my passport from the front flap of my backpack, and apprehensively handed it to him, hoping that it was just a random check.

'Please to take off the burqa.'

I reluctantly removed my headdress, which, as you can imagine, in itself caused quite a stir within the carriage. He took a piece of paper from his shirt pocket, unfolded it, and compared it to the photo in the passport then with my face.

'It's a shocker, I know, but you should see the one on my driver's license.'

He failed to be amused.
'Where is your friend?'
'What friend?'
'The man who was with you.'
'I don't know what you mean; I'm travelling alone.'

He held up the headdress.
'Dressed as the woman?'

'It's safer than travelling as a westerner, and I don't get hassled by every passing kalash and taxi driver, or hustled by every street-vendor or hawker trying to flog me anything and everything from used dental floss to original hand-carved statuettes from the tomb of Tutankhamen.'

'Where is your guide?'

'Guide? I don't understand. Oh, you mean the guy who was sitting opposite me. He wasn't with me; I just asked him a few questions; I think he got off at the last stop.'

'Where is the bag?'

'Bag?'

'The backpack, please.'

Shit, it was crunch time; he'd pointed directly to my lap, he knew exactly where it was, there was no point resisting any longer. I slowly took the backpack from under my dress and surrendered it, then took my akubra out, plonked it on my head, and buried my head in my hands, shattered, resigned to my fate, as he unzipped my backpack.

There was an eternal pause as I waited for the words that would seal my fate. When he final spoke, he took me completely by surprise.

'Where are the papers?'

'What?'

I looked up, I was stunned, they weren't there? What the...? Saeed must have taken them out earlier, when I went to the toilet.

'Where are the papers?'

'What papers?'

He motioned for me to stand.

'You will please to come with me.'

With Saeed removing Kareem's file, I'd been given a reprieve, but for how long? There was little I could do but follow his instructions and keep playing dumb, which wasn't hard because it was just plain stupid that I'd got myself into this mess in the first place, still, I held my ground.

'Am I being arrested? What for?'

'We would like for you to come with us; we are looking for the westerner who he kill him the Antiquity supervisor and steal some very important government papers.'

'And you think that's me?'

He held out the unfolded paper before my face; a photocopy of my passport that they must have 'acquired' from Seleh at the Nubian Oasis, then lifted my akubra.

'This it is you?'

'Well,...yes, but all us westerners, we look alike; a bulging wallet with a person attached. I can assure you, I swear to Allah, I didn't kill anyone, and I *don't* have any government papers. I don't know anything about what you're talking about; you've got the wrong person.'

'We will see.'

He indicated again for me to stand.

'Please to take off the dress.'

'We've only just met; not even a bunch of flowers, not even a first a kiss?'

'The dress!'

I pulled the hem up to reveal my bare thighs.

'I.. er... I haven't got anything on underneath; my pants are in the backpack. I need to go to the toilet and get changed.'

He wasn't amused, just handed me the backpack and my akubra.

'Come.'

The passengers in the carriage parted like the waters before Moses, all looking on like spectators at a train wreck, as we made our way down the aisle to the toilet at end. What the hell was I going to do; if I let them take me off the train I doubted if I would get out of this alive. My only chance was to make a run for it, but how?

I closed the door behind me, slowly and silently locking it; I had a minute, two at the most, to come up with a plan. The window! Shit I'd seen it in heaps of movies but I never thought I'd actually be doing it. I threw off the burqa, quickly pulled on my pants, followed by my backpack, and started clambering out the window; what the hell was I doing, I was no stuntman.

'Please to hurry up.'

I'd managed to straddle the windowsill and was about to climb out and onto the roof, but I needed more time to make my escape. I stuck my head back inside the train.

'Just a minute, I need to go to the toilet as well, I have a terrible stomach bug and a really bad case of the runs.'

'You have two minute.'

There's something about being told how long you have to live that changes your life; some folk with cancer get told they have six months, others a few weeks. I had less time than it takes to boil an egg.

Probably due to the adrenaline rush, I suddenly discovered rock-climbing skills I thought I never had, and, within a few seconds, found myself perched precariously on top of a moving train. I looked in both directions; up ahead we were approaching the city of Minya, it seemed logical to head towards the rear.

Clasping my akubra tightly in my hand, I scrambled along the roof of the train as fast as I could. For some reason I had visions of the river crabs, too scared to let go of the riverbed for fear of being swept away to their deaths. Well, in this case, if I stayed where I was, death was a foregone conclusion. As I reached the end of the train, it started to slow; we were pulling into the station.

'Stop!'

An angry head had emerged from the source of my escape route and its owner was slowly climbing out with the intention, no doubt, to pursue me and boil me in oil. My eggs were about to be scrambled; I'd run out of options.

I laid flat, stuck my head over the side to locate the door, which thankfully was open, then grabbed hold of whatever I could, slid down over the side, and into the doorway. Thankfully a few friendly hands grabbed hold of me and guided me inside to temporary safety.

'Saeed!'

He stood there, holding me, as usual grinning like a Cheshire cat.

'Indy, it is so nice of you to drop in.'

'I was wondering what happened to you. Thanks for leaving me holding the bag.'

'The bag, yes, but not the paper.'

'Where are they?'

'Here!'

He pulled them out from under his galabeya, turned me around, and stuffed them once again into my backpack. I naturally started to resist.

'Whoa! I don't know if that's such a good idea, I've got the police on my tail.'

'This I know.'

He zipped the backpack up; Kareem's papers once again becoming a target on my back.

'Are you crazy?'

'Totally, but let us discuss this later, we need to be get out of here, fast.'

'No shit, Sherlock!'

The train continued slowing down, pulling in to the platform, enough for us to take a leap of faith as soon as the platform was underfoot.

'Follow me.'

The train still moving, we literally leapt into the arms of the awaiting crowd, knocking a few folk to the ground in the process; it looked more like strike time at the local bowling alley. As I struggled to my feet, I glanced up and saw the copper on the roof of the train had nearly crawled his way to the end. He stood up and pointed in our direction.

'Stop, police.'

No chance of that, we scampered away like two rats up a drainpipe. Thankfully the whole platform was chockers, blocking and delaying the police as, way up ahead, they tried to push their way first off the train, and then make their pursuit along the platform and through the crowd. It was probably even worse, nigh impossible, within the train.

'This way!'

I followed Saeed as we jumped off the platform, cut behind the train, and across to the other side of the station.

'Stop, police.'

A shot rang out! Shit, the cop on the roof had taken a pot shot at us. It was followed quickly by a second. Thankfully they both missed their mark and we ducked behind the buildings and out into the hustle and bustle of the city; I figured we had maybe a few hundred metres head start at best.

Thankfully the streets were really busy, cars, taxis, carts, buses, hundreds of people shuffling to and fro; it was the perfect cover for us to disappear, although we did dodge a few collisions as we crossed the street, at one stage leaping over a taxi bonnet and sideswiping a kid on a bike before we ducked into an alley. We cut into a shoe shop and straight out the back into an adjacent alley, as, in the process, Saeed pulled out his phone and barked out instructions to the person on the other end. That done, we continued to weave our way through the maze that was the back streets and shops of el-Minya; there was no way anyone could have followed us, even I was having trouble keeping up with Saeed.

We must have been running for about five minutes when, all of a sudden, we emerged from a clothing shop and I saw Mohammed's familiar, but concerned, face. He was standing beside a taxi that was waiting in the street, the rear door and boot both open. Saeed grabbed my arm and shoved me towards the rear of the taxi.

'Quick, get in.'

I tossed my backpack in the boot and went to get in the rear door following Mohammed. Saeed grabbed me again.

'No, you must be get in the trunk as well.'

'Are you serious?'

'There is no time to argue. If you want to live, do as I say!'

My heart was pumping a million miles an hour as I did what he said and crammed into the trunk of the taxi.

'What about you?'

'I will be fine, I will be talk to you tomorrow, Ahoya.'

And he slammed the trunk closed. I yelled out from the darkness.

'You're not coming with us?'

'This it is too dangerous, beside someone have to lead them off the trail, and I have to get back to Luxor.'

He pounded on the trunk, said something to Mohammed in Arabic, and the taxi took off like a bat out of hell. "Too dangerous", that was encouraging, **NOT!** The only other people I knew who spent time in the trunks of cars also finished up dismembered and buried in shallow graves out in the state forests. Shit, I suddenly realized I didn't even have my passport, the cops did; I was really screwed, even if I want to try and fly out, now it was impossible.

How in hell's name did I finish up here, in the trunk of a beaten up taxi driven by someone I've never met, with my life in the hands of a guy who I hardly know, who hardly speaks English, travelling through the poverty-stricken back roads of rural Egypt with half the Egyptian Secret Police and Army on my tail; some holiday!

I lay there, in foetal position for the best part of twenty minutes. Every single one of those speed bumps along the road I'd previously been over in the relative comfort of a minibus, now felt like I was crossing the Himalayas strapped to the back of a malnourished yak. Every time we stopped, or slowed to a crawl, I held my breath and listened intently to see if we were at a roadblock and about to be caught.

'Mister Alex, you are OK?'

'Shaken, not stirred. How much longer, Mohammed?'

'A little more.'

I endured another ten minutes before the taxi came to a halt, I heard the door open and seconds later the trunk opened.

'It is safe now.'

I clambered out of the trunk, looked around in the darkness and stretched the kinks out of my back. We were in the middle of nowhere, a back road of a back road, surrounded by fields and plantations; for a second I half-expected them to hand me a shovel and lead me off to dig my own grave. Instead, I grabbed my akubra and backpack, slid into the back seat, and we were quickly on our way again.

'How much further?'

'Maybe twenty minute, not long.'

I nervously pawed my akubra.

'What the .. ?'

There was hole in it.

'..Shit, that's,…that's a bullet hole.'

It was all just a little too much. I slumped back in the seat, exhausted; I'd well and truly dodged a bullet. I knew it was impolite not to talk, but, truth be told, there wasn't much else to say, besides, whilst Mohammed could understand English fairly well, his vocab was somewhat limited; anything that we had to talk about could surely wait until morning. Consequently, I sat there mindlessly trying to comprehend not only how what had happened had happened, but what was going to happen next.

'Mister Alex, you are hungry?'

'No thanks, Mohammed, I think I just need to get some sleep.'

'Yes, very good, sleep.'

Five minutes later we arrived at Mohammed's family home. In contrast to his namesake's welcome the night before, the welcome at *this* Mohammed's was very low-key, rather hush-hush. I gave the driver my last two hundred pounds and Mohammed surreptitiously led me inside.

After showing me to the toilet, which was a rather urgent blessing, he asked once more if there was anything else I wanted, then led me to the 'guest' room. I didn't even bother taking it in; I just threw the backpack on the bed and sat down beside it.

Ready to collapse, I took out my laptop, thinking there might be a power point to recharge both it, and my iphone. Then I noticed a short groove carved across the lid of the laptop that wasn't there before. Checking the backpack I found a hole in one side and one in the other; the second bullet had missed me by inches, but left its mark as it fizzled by, it had even gone through part of Kareem's file. I lay back on the bed, my hands over my face.

'Fuck!'

CHAPTER 26 – THE MYSTERIES OF HAWARRA

'Wake up, we must go.'

I was startled, disoriented. In the dim light, Saeed stood over me like a protective umbrella.

'Come on, they're right behind us.'

Within seconds Saeed and I were running down a dark corridor, the same dimly-lit, man-made, and heavily-decorated tunnel we'd been running down a few nights ago.

'Who is it?

'The Amun Priests.'

'What do they want?'

'The scroll, Dummy, and if we get caught with it they will feed us to the crocodiles.'

'What scroll?'

'The truth.'

'Where is it?'

'On your back.'

'What?'

Suddenly I stopped, shocked, as Saeed continued on and disappeared into the darkness. I reached around with my arms trying to find it.

'Where? Where is it?'

It was there all right, in the middle of my back, but I couldn't grab it; it was like it had been tattooed into my skin, and now it was a target, a neon sign. From the shadows I heard the caws and shrieks as a kettle of hungry vultures zeroed in on me. Then I felt their razor-sharp talons ripping into my flesh, clawing into my stomach.

It jolted me into the now, and I woke up to the cawing of crows and Mohammed's pet cat kneading at my stomach as if to turn it into a pillow. Where the hell was I? It took a few seconds to wipe the sand from my eyes and look around the basic furnishings and bright blue paint of the room, but eventually my memory staggered into operation and I figured out I was still stuck between a rock and a hard place. I sat up and checked my iphone: 6:58.

Supposedly Mohammed had brought me to his house in Hawarra, around nine kilometres southeast of El Fayoum, but, as far as I knew, he could have taken me anywhere; half-an-hour in the trunk of a taxi travelling through the desert in the night, bullet holes in my hat and backpack, now *that* was a highlight of my life, NOT! I didn't have a choice; I had to trust him. I still did, as Fayoum was about a hundred kilometres south-south-west of Cairo and I still had plenty of work to do to get out of Egypt alive. I weighed my options.

This was day…what?…twelve, of my trip, I think, so my scheduled flight was four days from now. But the stark reality was there was no way I could fly out of Egypt; the police had my passport and they would've checked with the airlines and know exactly when my booked flight out left.

Following the Nile upstream, south, into Sudan, wasn't a realistic option either, it was thousands of miles, and it would have meant backtracking through the lion's den, through Luxor. Nor was heading west across the Sahara Desert and into strife-torn Libya. After recalling Bill's comments and photos about the Black and White Deserts, I briefly contemplated going that way west, but it was thousands of miles of exposed desert, with nowhere to hide; in several ways that would not just be like jumping out of the frying pan into the fire, it would be into a raging bushfire more like it.

Eastwards was either via Qena and Hurghada and a boat to Israel, Saudi Arabia, Eritrea or Somalia, which sounded like even more problems, especially without a passport. In any case, Bill had given Hurghada as a red herring, so it would have been madness to bait the hook and impale it on my own mouth. Or, there was the eastern route across the Sinai Peninsula to Israel, but more and more westerners were giving that route a miss because of kidnappings, and there was no guarantee I would be able to get into Israel, not without a passport.

The only real option left was northward out of Egypt via a fishing boat, or some other vessel, to one of Italy, Greece or Turkey, although Greece and particularly Turkey were seemingly more and more unstable. But they were safer than here, all I had to do was get through Cairo.

To my surprise the phone rang; it was Saeed.

'Ahoya, thank God you're safe. Where are you?'

'I am back in Luxor.'

'You took the train?'

'Yes.'

'So it's safe?'

'For me, perhaps, I can blend in, but for you, no, you would stand out like the pregnant camel in a lady shoe shop.'

'But you made it back to Luxor OK?'

'The Secret Police, they are know you are try to get it to Cairo, they search every train from Beni Suef to Cairo. We shall have to get it you to Cairo some other way.'

'And from there?'

'I have arrange it for a boat to pick you up off the shore and take it you to Greece, but it will not be there for three day.'

'And how am I supposed to get out to it, swim?'

'It is possible, you Aussie are good swimmer, yes?'

'What about the crocodiles?'

'There are no crocodile in the sea off Alexandria, the shark they eat them all.'

'Very funny, I meant the Secret Police.'

'The crocodile it is most dangerous when you cannot see it, when it is under the water and near to the edge of the water.'

'What do you mean?'

'To swim across the river and to be safe, it is best you must have all the crocodile look somewhere else.'

'Meaning?'

'While they are look on the train, we must get you to Cairo some other way.'

'Is Cairo safer than here in Hawarra?'

'A westerner in Hawarra, he is the pregnant camel in the lady shoe shop, in Cairo pregnant camel there are many, no one is look even once.'

'True. So how do I get to Cairo?'

'This I am not sure. But we have to get you past the checkpoint as fast as we can.'

'No more being dressed as a woman, OK?'

'But, Indy, you look so pretty.'

'And no more trips in the trunk of any cars or taxis either.'

'Very well, leave it all to me, I will be think about it and will call you back later today.'

'Great, and Saeed, thanks for saving me at the station, thanks for everything.'

'You are most welcome, Ahoya.'

Mohammed and his family were already up by the time I emerged from the room.

'Good morning, Mister Alex, yes, please come, breakfast.'

Around the table were Mohammed, his wife and three kids, his parents, his grandmother, an uncle, aunt, little brother and a sister. They all sat quietly, the fully-stocked breakfast table untouched, waiting for me to join them.

You wouldn't have known it to look at the sumptuous spread laid out on the table, but I knew they must have been doing it tough. As the eldest son, I'd figured out that Mohammed was probably the chief bread-winner, and that, as there weren't that many tourists around these days compared to before the revolution, there were not many people taking felucca trips, and, yet, here was his family presenting what amounted to a banquet fit for a king before me, a total stranger; there was no end to the generosity of the Egyptian people.

Exchanging pleasantries was awkward; they barely understood a few words of English, so most communication and expressions of gratitude consisted of simple gestures and nods. Resigned to the inevitable, I directed my conversation to Mohammed.

'Mohammed, where exactly are we, Hawarra?'

'Ezbet Saad Abou Diab.'

'What? I thought we were in Hawarra?'

'Yes, Hawarra. My village, Ezbet Saad Abou Diab. Hawwarat al Maqta two mile south, on other side of canal.'

'OK, how far is it to the pyramid?'

He gestured out the window.

'Five minute.'

'Seriously!'

'Yes, very close.'

'If the pyramid is close, so is the Labyrinth.'

I remembered Saeed had said something about Mohammed and his family talking about the Labyrinth, so I tried again to instigate a conversation with his parents and grandmother.

'Labyrinth?'

They either shook their head or looked at each other with a bewildered expression; The kids weren't much better, they knew certain words and phrases, such as "what is your name?" and "where are you from?", but not what they actually meant; another case of parrot learning.

'Under pyramid, big building, many rooms.'

Mohammed came to the rescue.

'There not much to speak, grandfather he talk it of many room under ground, many turn, very hard to know it the way. He say he play as small boy, down hole in ground, find it many strange room, strange stone. But friend he have it very bad thing happen to him, very evil place, so hole they fill in.'

'Where is it?'

'Grandfather he never say, say it too much danger.'

'Where is your grandfather now?'

'Grandfather, he die many year ago.'

'And with him the secret of a possible entrance to the Labyrinth.'

'Can we go see it, the pyramid I mean?'

He shook his head with considerable consternation.

'I do not think this is good idea.'

He was probably right, but this was the site of the Labyrinth, one of the main reasons I was drawn to coming to Egypt, and ever since my conversations on the felucca, and my theories about the tsunamis, I was even more determined to explore it for myself, so much so that I rationalized away the dangers.

'Nonsense, sitting around the house just creates more opportunities to be noticed, and it puts you and your family in danger. But the pyramid is a logical place for a tourist to be and I'll blend right in. Besides, they're looking for me on the trains, not at the temple sites; I was safe at Amarna, I think I'll be safe, especially with other tourists around.'

'Inshallah.'

Breakfast over, I was keen to get going. I contemplated leaving the backpack and papers with Mohammed's parents, but realized that would have been unfair on them; this was my burden and I had to bare it.

Just after 8:00, to the waves of his family, Mohammed led me off on foot, heading out of the village and southward along the canal. It was quiet, peaceful, farmers were out tending to their crops, a donkey half raised his head and twitched an ear in our direction; this was rural Egypt. I was eager to see the pyramid, the one at Edfu was pretty uninspiring, but this one was the real McCoy. Not only that, it was the gateway to one of the world's most mysterious buildings, the Labyrinth.

I didn't have to wait long; we crossed the canal, followed the road as it curved around to the left into the desert, and there it was.

Just under sixty metres high with each side of the base around a hundred metres long, the pyramid was positioned on a long spit of low desert. According to the 'textbooks', it was supposedly constructed around 1850 BC during the Middle Kingdom by Amenemhat III, sixth Pharaoh of the 12th Dynasty.

'Built of mud-brick round a core of limestone passages and burial chambers, it was once faced with a casing of fine white limestone.'

Little more than an eroded, vaguely pyramidal mountain of mud-brick, the casing had long gone, supposedly pillaged by the locals for use in other buildings. However, its absence revealed an obvious and distinct midline down the face that was clearly a structural aspect of its internal construction; what was that all about? But were the casing stones pilfered directly from the pyramid, or after they had been dislodged and/or washed away by the Thera tsunami. Time to find some evidence.

Walking across the sands, we negotiated our way around the small mounds probably created by the locals trying their luck digging for any artefacts; the place resembled a miniature lunar landscape or minefield from the gold-rush days. I stopped for a moment to examine the mixture of sand and rubble. In amongst it all I spotted seashells; as we were at least a hundred-and-fifty miles from the coast, they could only have arrived here during the last tsunami.

If my tsunami theory was true, and the Osireion at Abydos was a guide, then my guesstimate was the sand here would be in an initial layer of maybe five feet from the catastrophe around the turn of the millennia, followed by another layer about fifteen to eighteen feet deep caused by the Thera eruption, and then another layer about twenty-six to thirty feet thick down to the foundations of the Labyrinth.

Looking at the small size of the mounds, it appeared the locals had probably only dug down at most to the base of the top layers, so most of the stuff they would have found would date to the Greco-Roman period. Even the early archaeologists hadn't progressed much further, although they had unearthed just under a hundred-and-fifty fantastic Roman portraits here in Hawarra, "the Portraits of Fayoum", that dated from the 1st to 3rd Centuries AD. I had a few images in my files.

How striking they were, so full of expression; you could almost tell from the anguish and sadness in their eyes about their lives, about the hardships they'd had to face. Many of them were young by our thoughts, in their thirties or forties, perhaps they were the victims of one of the many plagues that had ravaged Egypt over the centuries. The images had a regal sense about them, certainly the owners would have to have been reasonably affluent to warrant and afford a personal portrait affixed to the outside of their mummy.

For a moment I wondered if this was the sort of look of Caesarion and Cleopatra Selene II; a mixture of Roman, Greek and Egyptian characteristics, it was certainly contemporary with them, maybe they were even somehow related. But that was just scratching the surface; I needed to go deeper, and further back in time.

Following the canal, Bahr el-Yusuf, or Joseph's Canal, which passed within thirty metres of the pyramid, we circled around the ruins of the pyramid to the southern side where, tucked into the western corner of the southern face, about ten to fifteen feet below the current ground level, was a small doorway; the entrance to the pyramid. There was something that didn't quite gel about it.

The entrance itself was actually well within what would have been the outer demarcation of the sloping pyramid wall, which meant that clearly there'd been significant excavation done to locate it.

'In 1843, the Lepsius expedition attempted to enter the pyramid, then about 1883, Luigi Vassalli tried again, but it was not until 1889 that Petrie reached the interior and investigated the substructure.'

Given the actual entrance was in the south wall, not the conventional north wall, and that it was tucked into the western corner of the face, then it must have taken some time to locate, which means that, between Lepsius, Vassalli, and Petrie, they must have been the ones responsible for pulling down most of the exterior of the pyramid, not the locals; the stones may well have been carried away by the locals, to use as building blocks for their houses, but they weren't the ones responsible for the destruction. Besides, the locals wouldn't have had the technology to 'dismantle' the massive blocks; they didn't have dynamite! How convenient to simply shift the blame with a stroke of the pen. But, that said, maybe Petrie and Co. had a head start.

There were other things that got me thinking about the entrance. First, if the entrances to pyramids were usually some distance up the face, not at ground level or ten feet below. That meant the pyramid was much bigger than it appeared; that the lower section had been covered by at least twelve to fifteen feet of the Thera tsunami as well as five or so feet of either the tsunami from the 396 BC Etna eruption or the Turkey quake of 365 AD; that is if the pyramid was really built by Amenemhat III in the 12th Dynasty.

What if it was older; the name of the pyramid had never been discovered, only assumed to have been "Amenemhat-Ankh", or "Amenemhat Lives", based on rock inscription in Wadi Hammamat that speak of statues quarried for a building of that name.

Second, if the entrance *had* originally been created facing north, then that meant it had to have been built *before* the last pole shift, around 8,800 BC, or before the last passing of Nibiru in 1600 BC, and that was looking highly possible. And if that were so, then it meant the whole geographical orientation of Egypt before 1600 BC may have been totally different.

I suddenly remembered reading somewhere in the past that NASA had done some sort of satellite survey of Africa using all this whiz-bang technology, infrared, that sort of thing, and from it they concluded that the Nile once flowed westward into lake Chaoh, halfway between the present Nile and the Atlantic. I'd fobbed it off at the time, thinking 'So what?' but now it was far more interesting. And there was more evidence.

I knew the subterranean structure of the pyramid, including the entrance, was constructed from massive blocks of stone, and yet above that was simple mud-brick, it didn't compute! Surely if you had the technology to cut and transport hundreds of blocks of limestone and granite that weighed over fifty or sixty ton each, and positioned them with incredible precision, you wouldn't 'fill up' the rest of the structure with mud bricks?

However, if the upper sections had been washed away by a massive tsunami, and somehow the survivors lost or forgot how to use the technology to rebuild it as it was, you would use whatever technology you had to try and reconstruct it. And surely you wouldn't bother to try and reconstruct a simple tomb to someone in the distant past. You would, however, try to rebuild a power station, or, if that failed, convert it into a tomb or shrine. I was on to something!

Mohammed led me down the incline and in through the entrance; this was it, my first time entering a pyramid. The narrow, stepped corridor was sheathed in fine white limestone, totally bereft of any decoration. However, within a few steps, anticipation turned to disappointment; the corridor was flooded. Shit!

Now, in 1899, when Petrie investigated the interior of the pyramid, it had taken him two long and difficult seasons to finally reach the burial chamber, no doubt bulldogging his way through the limestone, and all without a single mention of flooding. So, either the corridor was flooded now because the water table has risen in the last hundred years, or, and my money was on the latter, there was some underground connection between it, and the canal that ran alongside. However, since I couldn't investigate for myself, I reluctantly returned to the outside and sat down, resigned to refer to my notes.

> 'The descending corridor leads northwards to a first chamber, from where it appears to continue on into a second smaller chamber, then north, leading to a dead end.'

I wasn't so easily convinced.

> 'The northern passage was difficult to explore and could possibly lead to a "Southern Tomb". The corridor was filled with mud, probably the remains of mud bricks used to fill the corridor and seal it.'

Nah, I didn't buy it, just because they hadn't found a secret door that led downwards didn't mean there wasn't one.

> 'A short second passage, running east, is hidden within the

ceiling of the smaller chamber. Once closed by a wooden door, it was originally meant to be blocked by a 20-ton quartzite slab.'

Were the Egyptologists seriously suggesting that, after building this complex structure, the ancient engineers forgot to close a twenty-ton quartzite door, and instead built a wooden door in its place? Oh, please!

I didn't believe the pyramid was built as a tomb, and if it wasn't built as a tomb, then there wasn't any need to create false corridors and hide rooms; every room and chamber must have had a purpose. Why did I believe this? Because there were absolutely no hieroglyphs or texts on any of the walls or chambers, and that was incongruent with the burial practices of the Middle Kingdom, especially for pharaohs, and all that didn't make sense if it was a tomb.

'After heading east and arriving at another small chamber, with another hidden ceiling corridor that was suppose to be blocked by another 20 ton barrier portcullis, the passage does another 90 degree turn, this time to the left, back to the north, through a short corridor that leads to a final 20 ton barrier with the same design, which was in place.'

Guys, please, they built all these barriers but forgot to close some of them? Then it hit me. 'Wait a minute, if some of these "barriers" were open and some closed, there must have been a reason. If they were made of granite, then maybe some vibrational signal caused them to open and close in keeping with the function of the pyramid', acting something like …regulators. Who knows, it may even have been that there was some correlation between the ratio of the length of each of the corridors and the frequency of the signal that went down them.

My thinking was, that if this was the location of the Labyrinth, then the pyramid here would have to have had a specific function as well; I didn't know what that function was yet, but I was ready to find out.

'After a final 90 degree left turn back to the west the passage eventually leads to the northern side of first a wide, shallow antechamber and finally the burial chamber, carefully concealed and set just off the central vertical axis of the pyramid.'

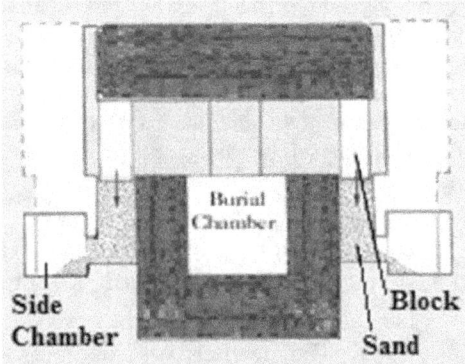

The burial chamber was made out of a single quartzite monolith that was lowered into a larger chamber lined with limestone. This monolithic slab weighed an estimated 110 tons according to Petrie. A course of brick was placed on the chamber to raise the ceiling then the chamber was covered with 3 quartzite slabs (estimated weight 45 tons each). Above the burial chamber were 2 relieving chambers. This was topped with 50-ton limestone slabs forming a pointed roof. Then an enormous arch of brick 3 feet thick was built over the pointed roof to support the core of the pyramid. The first part of the answer would probably lie there.

'The burial chamber is often rightly described as a technical marvel. Firstly a rectangular hole was excavated out of the rock subsoil, decorated with niches on either side, then it was lined with limestone blocks. After that, a single large monolith of quartzite, weighing some 110 tons, was lowered into the chamber of what was to be the burial chamber. It was then carved out, leaving an unroofed room with walls half-a-metre thick, measuring 7 by 2.5 metres and a height of 1.83 metres, with niches in either side to hold two canopic chests.'

Where is the common sense? Surely you would carve it out and reduce the weight of it by around a third, around thirty ton, *before* lowering it into place, unless you had the sort of technology where the weight of something wasn't an issue, which clearly was the case given the massive size and weight of these blocks.

'Before the chamber was sealed, the king's quartzite sarcophagus, a second, smaller sarcophagus and two canopic chests were lowered into it. The quartzite burial chamber was then sealed with three more massive limestone slabs, one of which was propped up on smaller blocks leaving a space so as to introduce the pharaoh's mummy and coffins. So this slab could be lowered, it rested on small pillars, in turn resting on sand-filled shafts on either side of the vault. When the sand drained out into the side galleries, the pillars descended and along with them the ceiling slab.'

I'd never seen any images of any sarcophagi belonging to Amenemhat III, nor was there any mummy attributable to him, so were the Egyptologists just guessing, presuming that is what would have been done if it were a tomb, and not actually referred to any evidence? It seemed the case. Were there really two sarcophagi in the chamber? If so, why do we have no images of them? And what about the mechanism to release the sand; what about that, it surely could only be done from somewhere 'inside' the excavation? And what if it got stuck half way? And how did the Egyptologists know what the internal structure was really used for, in fact, how did they even know what it *was*, how did they examine it, did they pull the whole pyramid apart to find out, or were they once again, just guessing?

'In order to reduce the weight on the burial vault, these three huge slabs extended beyond the sides of the vault and rested on sides of the bedrock trench that dug for the burial chamber.'

They may well have done that, but it didn't make sense. If the blocks rested on the sand, then there may well have been a gap between the ceiling blocks and the walls of the chamber. Besides, the granite walls of the chamber would easily support the weight of the ceiling blocks.

It seemed to me more that it made it virtually impossible to get any leverage from underneath, or, and the idea suddenly hit me, that the ceiling blocks could act independently without being able to move laterally. It also raised the question of how Petrie got into the chamber in the first place; did he smash one of the blocks? There's little doubt he would not have had the technology to lift a ten-ton block. And, as far as I know, the last serious excavation done inside the pyramid was done by Petrie over a hundred years ago!

'In spite of all the innovative precautions carried out by Amenemhat III to secure the structural integrity of the subterranean chambers, to mislead any thieves and protect his tomb at Hawarra, the thieves were still able to enter the burial chamber through an opening in the ceiling, plunder all the valuable and important items inside and burn the pharaoh's wooden coffin.

By the time Petrie reached the antechamber of the burial chamber, all that remained were a few bone fragments inside a coffin, a duck-shaped bowl, and an alabaster offering table inscribed with the name of Amenemhat III's daughter, Neferuptah.'

I was a little confused, was this Amenemhat's 'tomb, or that of his daughter?

'For some time it was thought that Princess Neferuptah had been interred with her father, but that was later shown to be inaccurate when, in 1956, her tomb was discovered two kilometres southeast of the Hawarra pyramid by Naquib Farag in the ruins of another completely destroyed pyramid.'

If it was so completely destroyed, how did they know it was a pyramid, couldn't it just as easily, in fact more easily, have been a mud-brick mastaba?

'Constructed out of limestone, and badly flooded, the tomb contained a pink-granite sarcophagus, within it the decayed remains of two wooden coffins and fragments of mummy linen, as well as her jewellery, three silver vases and an offering table.

The outer of the two decayed coffins was decorated with inscribed gold foil, the inscriptions identical to those found on the sarcophagus of Queen Hatshepsut, 300 years later.'

It was pretty obvious to me that Petrie's discoveries had led early Egyptologists to believe that Neferuptah must have died before her father, and initially been buried at Hawarra in her father's pyramid, then, when Neferuptah's tomb was actually discovered they had to change their thinking and decided that she must have been moved to her own pyramid on it's completion. Interesting how the Egyptologists can make completely wrong conclusions, that they then present as being fact, and are then forced to rethink everything. It seemed to me that was the norm with ancient Egyptian history rather than the exception, and that was not surprising given the 'science' was only about a hundred years old and heavily influenced by the original thinking. And what if that was the case here?

In fact, what if it was totally the other way around? What if Neferuptah's tomb had flooded and some of the artefacts were shifted to the Hawarra 'pyramid', but what if they only got as far as the antechamber and couldn't get into the burial chamber, wasn't that just as plausible? What if there was nothing originally inside the internal structure of the Hawarra pyramid at all, as seemed the case with most pyramids. I returned my thoughts to the pyramid before me.

'Above the ceiling they added a saddle vault, also of enormous limestone monoliths, each weighing more than 50 tons, leaning against each other. Over them, was another massive brick vault about seven metres high, capable of supporting the enormous pressure of the pyramid's mass. In addition Amenemhat III had the pyramid constructed with a less radical slope so as to reduce the mass atop the burial chamber.'

I stepped back up and out onto the sandy surrounds where Mohammed was waiting, and looked up at the pyramid; what a load of crap that was, the rest of the pyramid was mud-brick, a corbelled ceiling would only make sense if there were heavy stones about it. But there was even more.

According to the 'experts', the pyramid here was supposedly built by Amenemhat III as a reaction to the 'failure' of his Dahshur pyramid, the 'Black Pyramid'. He supposedly built it at a shallower angle however, the small pyramidion that sat atop the Hawarra pyramid, interestingly made of black granite and which is now in the Cairo Museum, has a steeper angle than the angle ascribed to the current pyramid.

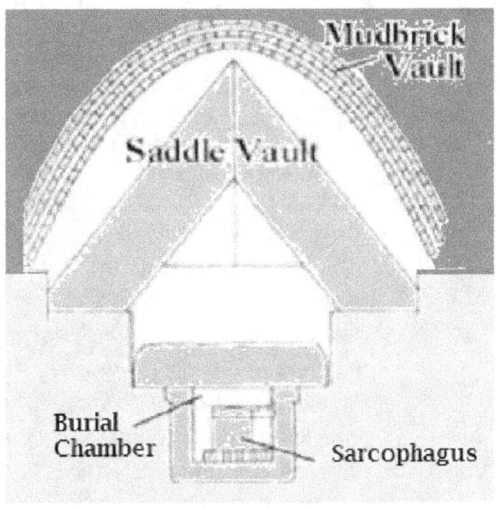

So, if you had the genius, skill and technology to construct such a complex substructure and 'burial chamber' why build a pyramid on top of it out of mud-brick at a particular angle and then top it with a pyramidion of black granite with a totally different angle; that was all a total mismatch! Egyptologists, time for a rethink!

And that's when it hit me; this was a repair job, it had to be, the technology of the mud-brick construction above was vastly inferior to that of the substructure and chambers. I pontificated.

Sometime in the past, the top section of the structure, if it was a pyramid, was swept away by a massive tsunami. But this was Middle Kingdom; this was before the Thera eruption, so that meant the original structure had to date back to at least the tsunami that buried the Osireion for the repair work to have been done in the reign of Amenemhat III, if in fact it was done then, and that would be consistent with the pyramid being much bigger. But if that were so, I needed concrete evidence; actually I needed 'alabaster' and more importantly 'red granite' evidence.

About twenty metres away, towards the centre of the southern face, I started to find it. At some fairly recent time, someone, probably a foreign university, had done a rectangular excavation about twenty metres or so south of the southern face of the pyramid. I'm not sure what they were looking for, but, as they had excavated, they'd revealed gold. Well, it was gold to me as right before my eyes were the layers of the tsunami deposits.

The upper layer was about three to four feet thick consisting of silt, sand and rubble; this would have been the Greco-Roman era tsunami from either 396 BC or 365AD, or possibly it was both, as there seemed to be a central layer of rubble within the layer. So, the top eighteen inches was probably the result of the 'Turkey' tsunami, and from eighteen inches down to four feet down belonged to the pre-Ptolemaic tsunami. I walked closer to see how deep the excavation went.

The hole was partially filled in, so the excavation most likely dated back a few 'digging seasons' at the least, however, I could see it originally went down about twenty feet, which was consistent with the evidence at Abydos, that the sixteen feet of the second layer belonged to the Thera tsunami. Wow! That was impressive; here we were hundreds of miles away and the evidence corroborated one hundred percent! I didn't know if the university had found anything significant in the dig, such as columns, statues, etcetera, or if they had even detailed the different strata and contents of the 'rubble', or if they had even noticed the seashells. Had they reached the barrier to the next layer? If they had, what did they find? Did they reach the labyrinth? Had they done exactly what Petrie had done a hundred years early, reached the ceiling of the labyrinth and assumed it was the foundation?

Petrie had investigated the pyramid as thoroughly as he could, and apparently also closely examined what he believed was the huge mortuary complex of Amenemhat III associated with the pyramid. I turned southward and looked out over the undulating piles of sand; if this was the Labyrinth, there wasn't much to see.

The Labyrinth

The ancient historians, Herodotus, Diodorus Siculus, Strabo, and Pliny, all made reference to the Labyrinth. The first recorded mention was by the Greek historian, Herodotus, who visited Egypt in the 5th Century BC, well before the 396 BC Etna eruption. In Book II of his Histories, he was amazed at what he saw, describing the Labyrinth as the administrative and astronomical centre of Egypt, surpassing the pyramids in its astonishing ambition.

'I saw it myself and it is indeed a wonder past words... surpassing that of the pyramids. It has twelve roofed courts…Inside, the building is of two stories and contains three thousand rooms, of which half are underground, and the other half directly above them. I was taken through the rooms in the upper story, … but the underground ones I can speak of only from report, because the Egyptians in charge refused to let me see them, as they contain the tombs of the kings who built the labyrinth at the beginning, and also the tombs of the sacred crocodiles.'

So, were the twelve roofed courts in addition to the two stories? It was possible, and it would make sense if they were added at a later stage after the initial building had been buried to some degree by several tsunamis.

I also wondered if the tombs mentioned in the lower level were the tombs of the Annunaki, or, if not, of their direct descendants, and, were the tombs of the 'sacred crocodiles' the tombs of the Dracos who had provided the genetic technology to create the human form? This place could be the gold mine of the true history of the origins of the human race.

'The upper rooms, on the contrary, I did actually see, and it is hard to believe that they are the work of men; the baffling and intricate passages from room to room and from court to court were an endless wonder to me. The roof of every chamber, courtyard, and gallery is, like the walls, of stone. The walls are covered with carved figures, and each court is exquisitely built of white marble and surrounded by a colonnade of white pillars.'

So the upper levels at least seemed to be consistent with the 'Alabaster Kingdom', meaning it was built any time up to and including the Middle Kingdoms, which would be consistent with an association to the 12th Dynasty and Amenemhat III.

'At the corner where the labyrinth ends there is, nearby, a pyramid 240 feet high and engraved with great animals. The road to this is made underground.'

Did Herodotus mean there was a tunnel that connected the lower level of the labyrinth directly to the pyramid? Could it be possible this tunnel connected to the end of the 'blind' passage leading north from the first chamber? It certainly sounded that way. And if there was a connecting tunnel, and the pyramid was a tomb, the question had to be asked, why? It reinforced my belief that the pyramid was never intended to be a tomb.

Strabo was the next to write about the Labyrinth, in the 1st Century BC, long after Herodotus.

'In front of the entrances are crypts, as it were, which are long and numerous and have winding passages communicating with one another, so that no stranger can find his way either into any court or out of it without a guide. But the marvellous thing is that the roof of each of the chambers consists of a single stone, and that the breadths of the crypts are likewise roofed with single slabs of surpassing size, with no intermixture anywhere of timber or of any other material.

And, on ascending to the roof, which is at no great height, inasmuch as the Labyrinth has only one story, one can see a plain of stone, consisting of stones of that great size; and thence, descending out into the courts again, one can see that they lie in a row and are each supported by 27 monolithic pillars; and their walls, also, are composed of stones that are no smaller in size.'

Strabo had described it similarly to Herodotus, perhaps he'd even read Herodotus' work, although somewhat surprisingly Strabo didn't make any mention at all of the Labyrinth's lower level or underground chambers. Perhaps Strabo was unknowingly a witness to the after-effects of the Etna tsunami three-hundred years earlier, which had most likely buried any residual visual appearance of the lower level, and, as was the case with Herodotus nearly five-hundred years before him, had not been permitted to view the lower level, nor even told of its existence.

By the time Pliny the Elder was writing in the 1st Century AD, he believed the Labyrinth was already at least three-thousand-six-hundred years old.

'This, the first ever to be constructed, was built, according to tradition, 3,600 years ago by King Petesuchis or King Tithoes, although Herodotus attributes the whole work to the ' twelve kings,' the last of whom was Psammetichus.'

Around 3600 BC, that was Pre-dynastic. I wondered if by the 'twelve kings' it was a reference to the Thinite kings, and did that mean it was a reference to the Annunaki, or to their demi-god offspring? But the real curve ball was 'Psammetichus', that was the term used to refer to the crocodile god, Sobek. Was that again a reference to the Dracos, did they have a hand, or rather claw, in the construction of the lower level of the Labyrinth?

'There is a feature of the Egyptian labyrinth which I for my part find surprising, namely an entrance and columns made of Parian marble [white limestone]. The rest of the structure is of Aswan granite, the great

blocks of which have been laid in such a way that even the lapse of centuries cannot destroy them.'

Oh, that was a major signpost, an *'entrance and columns of limestone'*, which would have implied the upper level, and that correlated with the 'Alabaster Kingdom'. And then there was the *'Aswan granite'*, to me that meant red granite, and *'great blocks of which have been laid in such a way that even the lapse of centuries cannot destroy them'*, that sounded exactly like the massive pillars at Abydos.

'Inside are columns of imperial porphyry, images of gods, statues of kings and figures of monsters. Some of the halls are laid out in such a way that when the doors open there is a terrifying rumble of thunder within: incidentally, most of the building has to be traversed in darkness. The few repairs that have been made there were carried out by one man alone, Chaeremon, the eunuch of King Necthebis [Nectanebo II], 50 years before the time of Alexander the Great.'

'Images of Gods'; now that would be interesting. *'Figures of monsters'*; that would be even more interesting. But, *'repairs'*? Bingo! Nectanebo II ruled around 360-343 BC, which would have been around thirty-to-forty years *after* the Etna eruption and tsunami of 396 BC. Why would a building made of granite and limestone need repairing unless it had been subjected to some major calamity? It all fitted perfectly into place. This was the place, this was the 'plain of stone' referred to by Starbo. This was where Petrie believed the Labyrinth was supposedly once located, south of the pyramid, in the largest 'funerary complex' of the Middle Kingdom.

'The mortuary temple precinct was enclosed by a wall measuring 385 by 158 metres, a few trace foundations of which have been found, one bisecting its width and another at the south end where a causeway in the southeast corner led to what would have been a valley temple, neither of which have been seriously investigated. Apart from that, all that has been found are a few bits of walls and doorjambs, along with parts of columns, two granite shrines, a statue of Amenemhat III, fragments of statues of Hathor and Sobek, and the local palm goddess, Roheshotep.'

Petrie made two attempts to excavate here, one in 1888 the other in 1910, but basically all he found was an enormous artificial stone plateau of limestone several metres below the surface.

"When I began to excavate the result was soon plain, that the brick chambers were built on the top of the ruins of a great stone structure; and hence they were only the houses of a village.... But beneath them, and far away over a vast area, the layers of stone chips were found; and so great was the mass that it was difficult to persuade visitors that the stratum was artificial, and not a natural formation."

That sounded like the layer of rubble deposited by either the Etna or Turkey tsunami.

"Beneath all these fragments was a uniform smooth bed of beton or plaster, on which the pavement of the building had been laid: while on the south side, where the canal had cut across the site, it could be seen how the

chip stratum, about six feet thick, suddenly ceased, at what had been the limits of the building. We know from Pliny and others, how for centuries the labyrinth had been a great quarry for the whole district."

Petrie interpreted the 'plaster bed' as the foundation of the Labyrinth, coming to what I believe was the erroneous conclusion that the building had been totally demolished during the Ptolemaic period and the stone used to build other structures.

Despite that, he still made a floor plan of what he believed the site would have looked like. Not only was that totally unscientific and lacking in any actual archaeological evidence to support the diagram, but it was totally based on his own imagination and the influence of the writings of early historians; the Greek, Diodorus, writing in the 1st Century BC, and the Roman, Pliny the Elder, writing in the 1st Century AD, both of whom had probably never even been to Egypt, let alone visited the Labyrinth itself, and the Greek, Strabo also writing in the 1st Century BC, who, if he did visit the Labyrinth, only mentioned it having one level.

In any case, it seems that Flinders Petrie, the 'father of modern Egyptology', had taught his 'children' well, and they have all been coming up with diagrams and postulating theories as if they were facts ever since.

What was stunningly stupefying to me was that, despite all the evidence to the contrary, most 'qualified' Egyptologists were comfortably content believing Petrie, and in equating the Labyrinth with the Mortuary Temple of Amenemhat III. Further, that Petrie had discovered the floor of the structure, that the ancient Romans had razed it to the ground, and that there was nothing left to discover. They'd even created spectacular 'reconstructions' of what they believed the pyramid, and the accompanying internal structure of the complex, looked like.

But me, I wasn't so easily convinced; I was certain he'd dug down only as far as the roof and then abandoned the dig, especially since I'd stumbled over the overwhelming evidence of the tsunamis. There was something familiar about the reconstruction, familiar but not quite right. And then I got it; it looked like the set up of the Temple of Montuhotep II at Deir el Bahri on the West Bank at Luxor. Similarly with Hatshepsut's temple, only with Amenhotep's pyramid still in place on the terrace. The only difference was the pyramids sat atop the lower layer, not beside it; I bet that was the situation here.

I had an image in my mind of how it all looked, a cross-section of the land that included the different tsunami deposits, the various stages of the pyramid, and its location relative to the two layers of the Labyrinth.

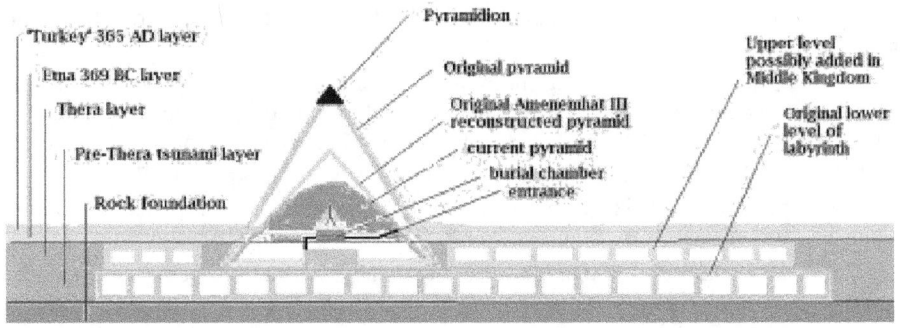

I now believed that, as Amenhotep IV and Akhenaten were separate beings, the mortuary Temple of Amenemhat III and the Labyrinth were different structures, erroneously presumed to be one and the same structure because of the 'lack' of archaeological evidence and, more importantly, the lack of archaeological investigation. Had the Egyptologists merely scratched the surface and come to a shallow conclusion and walked away? Had they just not dug deep enough? Was it possible, just like the Osireion and Seti I's temple at Abydos, that the Labyrinth was built before the tsunami that preceded the Thera tsunami, before the 'alabaster' era, and that the mortuary temple of Amenemhat III was built on top of it? Then, were both subsequently buried by the Thera tsunami, with mainly mud-brick walls and structures later built on top of them? There was evidence for that in almost every single temple site I'd visited so far, so surely that was a high probability of being the case here.

Sure, there was the possibility that the entire upper and lower levels of the Labyrinth had been carted away to build the local villages, but it would have to have been a feat of Herculean proportions considering the size and the mass of the stones used to build it. And, if that *was* the case, then, given the enormous quantity of stone, there would be numerous examples of it in the local villages, but, as far as I knew, no one had made any reference to that being the case.

If this was indeed the location of the Labyrinth described in antiquity, and I believed it was, then no amount of pillaging could match the total annihilation that the Egyptologists say supposedly occurred here. It was time to do some more exploring of my own.

Because of the undulating ground, I couldn't really see anything south of the pyramid other than the tops of the small piles of sand, so I set off to get a closer look at the area. I wasn't really interested in finding sandstone, but, if I could stumbled across a few fragments of columns, or bits of walls or even statues, made either of alabaster, or, more importantly, red granite, then it would totally support my belief that the Labyrinth was possibly still here, forty to fifty feet beneath my feet. I didn't have to wait long.

I'd only gone about twenty feet, over the crest of a mound, when I spotted a few pieces of 'rock' jutting out of the sand in the trough between mounds. They weren't sandstone; they were limestone, alabaster, pieces of a temple. One piece in particular took my attention, it looked like part of the top capitol of an ornately carved pillar, and if the arc was any indication, it was a column with quite a large diameter.

What had Herodotus said, *'a colonnade of white pillars'*, and Strabo, *'each supported by 27 monolithic pillars',* and finally Pliny, *'columns of imperial porphyry, ...columns made of Parian marble [white limestone]'*? Was this fragment once part of the upper level of the Labyrinth mentioned by the ancient historians? It certainly fitted the bill. Had it been discovered during the recent excavation done in front of the south face of the pyramid and simply cast aside? It seemed totally congruent with my theory concerning the tsunami.

I kept walking, searching the miniature valleys created between the mounds, discovering several more fragments of alabaster columns and confirming my thoughts, but what I really wanted to find was red granite. Then, over the next rise, I hit the jackpot; numerous large fragments of red granite lay strewn across the sand.

I ran over to it like a lovelorn puppy-dog; the first piece part of a column, exquisitely carved, but worn, far older than the alabaster column I'd just examined.

It was beautiful. I couldn't control my delight; here was exactly the evidence I needed to prove my theory, two pieces of column, virtually side by side, one of carved alabaster, the other of carved red granite, the granite, a much harder stone, far more worn than the softer alabaster, time worn. It had to belong to the lower level, the original level. This proved the Labyrinth was still here, I could feel it, I could smell it, I could taste it. But how did it get here, it couldn't have come from the university's excavation, they hadn't gone deep enough.

I knelt down, put my hand on it, took a few deep, relaxing breaths, and called on Nemo. Within seconds he was swimming towards me through a dark tunnel.

'Come on, they're right behind me.'

Within seconds Nemo and I were swimming down a dark, flooded corridor, the same dimly-lit, man-made, and heavily-decorated tunnel I'd been dreaming about the last couple of nights, although now I could tell it was all made of red granite.

'Who is it?

'The crocodiles.'

'What do they want?'

'The scrolls, Dummy.'

'Where are they?'

'On your back.'

Suddenly I heard loud Arabic voices in the distance and looked up to see a group of men striding towards me, three soldiers in uniform, each brandishing a kalashnikov, the barrels glistening in the morning sunlight; I noticed them first of course. A fourth man in a grey galabeya, who was obviously the guardian here, led the way. He was the one postulating and carrying on.

'Oh shit!'

One minute I'm flying as high as a kite, the next I'm about to be shot down, about to crash and burn in a ball of fire. I'd been oblivious to the backpack I'd been carrying for the whole morning, but now suddenly it felt like I'd been fitted with a pair of cement shoes by Al Capone himself.

'What are we going to do?'

Mohammed, who had been my silent shadow for the whole morning, calmly came to life and sprung into action, yelling back and waving his hand.

'It all OK, this my friend.'

'What are you going to tell him?'

'I say you friend of my nephew, you visit.'

He started walking towards the approaching posse, leaving me to wallow up to the eyeballs in a quagmire of anxiety.

'Oh, like he's going to believe that! Yeah, this is my nephew Ahkmed's best buddy, Alex, they went to camel-training school together.'

Further back behind the posse, slowly bringing up the rear, was an officer flanked by two other men in shirts and trousers; no doubt the Secret Police. I was crocodile fodder. There was no way I could run, so, instead, my paranoia took off like the clappers: 'Do they know Saeed, or worse, do they know Kareem? Do they know about Kareem's murder? Do they know Saeed brought me to Mohammed? Is that why he's walking towards me escorted by three fully-armed soldiers?'

With every step they drew closer, the more my paranoia escalated. 'Do they know I have Kareem's papers in my backpack? Will they shoot first and ask questions later? Was Mohammed a part of the whole thing, and had he set the whole thing up to dispose of the body here in the canal, or better still, buried at the location of the Labyrinth because they believe that no one will bother digging here again?'

Still gripped in angst, my guts churned as the lead man and Mohammed greeted each other, as good friends who had not seen each other for some time often do here, lots of embraces and kisses on the cheek. Ominously, the three soldiers continued on, fanning out across the mounds of sand as if to cut off all possible avenues of escape.

After a brief exchange in which there were clear and obvious looks and gestured in my direction, Mohammed and his pal turned and walked to me.

'He ask it if you have it the ticket?'

'What? A ticket? What for?'

'To see pyramid.'

'Are you serious? …'

This had to be a scam, seven bucks to walk around the desert, nothing to see, no temple, no entrance inside the pyramid.

'…It's nothing but a collapsed pile of mud bricks, a few little mounds of sand and the odd fragment of a column, so what is it exactly I'm paying for?'

'Pyramid.'

'But it's flooded, and I can see it from the road for free.'

'You must have ticket.'

More trouble was the last thing I needed.

'Can't you pull a few strings?'

Mohammed shook his head.

'He say he must have pay the ticket because the Colonel he is here.'

It must have been the Colonel drawing nearer; Al Capone, with his heavies to either side. Eager to escape, I reached into my pocket, pulled out my wallet, then suddenly remembered I'd given my last two-hundred away last night.

'I'm skint, I gave my last two-hundred pounds to the driver last night. Don't suppose they have EFTpos?'

Mohammed understandably looked bemused, but it didn't last long as the judge, jury and execution arrived to join our little confab.

'Alex?'

'Mark! Boy, am I glad to see you.'

Mark was about my age, born and bred in Melbourne, so we had a lot in common already. He was about five-foot-ten brown hair and had a certain relaxed composure. Even though I'd only physically met him once before, I gave him a huge hug, the sort of hug you give someone who has just saved your life!

'This is my associate, Frank Clark.'

'Pleased to meet you, Frank.'

'Likewise.'

Frank was much older, in his late sixties, early seventies, a wiry-looking American with, from memory, some sort of history in the aviation industry. They made a strange pair.

'And this is Colonel Nasar Mamood of the Antiquities Police.'

'Antiquities Police! Pleased to meet you.'

I shook his hand with a certain gusto; at first I was totally relieved he wasn't the Secret Police, but the Antiquities Police were the ones probably most implicated in the documents concealed in my backpack, so just his presence was enough to keep me on edge. Mark could tell I was uneasy and quickly cut to the chase.

'I got your message. I tried to ring, but your number wouldn't connect, don't you have international roaming?'

'What?'

'Did you get your phone switched to international roaming?'

I felt a right twat.

'I'm sure I did, but maybe in the excitement of leaving for the trip, I didn't think of it. But you can't begin to know how grateful I am you're here.'

'Maybe you were just out of range. So, you're in a spot of bother with the local police?'

'Well, it's a long story, but at the moment I owe them thirty-five pounds to look at a pile of mud bricks, and, for reasons I'll explain later, I haven't got any cash on me; you couldn't lend it to me, could you?'

'Thirty-five Egyptian pounds, a king's ransom, but I think I can cover it…'

He pulled out a fifty and handed it to me.

'…Don't leave the country.'

If only he knew. I gratefully took the note and handed it to the guardian who reciprocated with a ticket and the change, which I offered back to Mark.

'Keep it, you never know, you might need it to retain a good lawyer.'

'I can get a good lawyer for fifteen Egyptian pounds?'

'Maybe a shonky Egyptian one.'

I think Frank was finding the Aussie sense of humour hard to follow and switched the topic.

'Have you had a good look around?'

'I think so, I came in from the north, checked out the pyramid and entrance, which is unfortunately flooded, then I started looking out here and found some very interesting stone fragments.'

'You know this is the location of the Labyrinth?'

'Sure do, and I think I've found evidence to prove it.'

'Such as?'

I took a few minutes and filled Frank and Mark in on my theory about the tsunamis, about the red-granite blocks at most of the sites. At the end, Frank nodded.

'That's fascinating, and it makes perfect sense; I'd never thought that each of the levels of the Labyrinth could have been built at different times out of different materials. And your theory about the use of the red granite is fascinating. Have you looked over by the canal yet?'

'Not yet, why?'

'Then let me show you something.'

Frank led the way as our little trio of explorers headed west, closely shadowed by the Colonel, Mohammed and the guardian, with the armed escort guarding the perimeter. I wondered what they were really here to protect; was it the tourists, or what was really under the sand? My thoughts went to the latter. Meanwhile, Mark stepped in a little closer, talking under his breath.

'So what's really up; I don't think you sent me an email because you were being hassled for a few bucks? Didn't get caught looting, did you, and not pay your cut?'

'No, worse; it's big shit, mate, BIG, but best not to talk here, I've learned that even the fragments of walls have ears. Let's wait until we're somewhere safe.'

'Fair enough. Where are you staying in Cairo?'

'That's part of the problem, I don't know. I need to get there ASAP, but I haven't got anything arranged until tomorrow night when I'm booked back in to the Cairo Palace.'

'I'm sure they'd have a room for you tonight; tourists are as scarce as hen's teeth at the moment. If not, I'm sure they can put you up at our hotel.'

'True, but I still have to get there.'

'We can take you back to Cairo in the car with us if you want.'

'Seriously, that would be awesome, then I could tell you all about it.'

'No problems.'

I turned back to Mohammed, who was following behind with the Colonel and the guardian.

'Mohammed!'

He shuffled up beside me.

'Yes, mister Alex?'

I spoke softly, not wanting the others behind to hear.

'I found a way to get to Cairo, Mark and Frank are going to give me a list.'

'In car?'

'Yes.'

'You are sure?'

'Yes, I'll be fine, safety in numbers, that sort of thing.'

I explained it to Mohammed in more detail, Mark being a lawyer and such, and promised I would get some money to him and his family via Saeed as soon as I got safely out of Egypt. He was very grateful, shook my hand, we embraced, and he walked back to his friend, the guardian.

'Well, there it is.'

Frank was standing on top of a ridge of sand and dried mud that ran along the canal. We climbed the face to join him.

'What exactly am I looking for?'

All I could see was the canal, a palm tree, and, on the other side of the canal, more piles of desert sand.

'Over there, on the other side, that's where Petrie did his excavation.'

I followed Frank's pointing finger to a pile of rubble on the opposite bank.

'There doesn't seem to be much to see, especially from here.'

'Hang on, I've got a few photos on my phone that we took the other day...'

He fumbled around, as we all do when trying to find anything on our phone.

'Here you go.'

I could clearly see the foundations of a structure.

'Is that alabaster, limestone?'

'Further down, underneath, yes, the base.'

'And the stones on top, are they the foundations of other buildings?'

'Yes, from the Roman and Ptolemaic Periods.'

'So that's the pretty much the roof of the Labyrinth, that the Greeks and Romans built on top of, that Petrie thought was the actual floor of the Labyrinth.'

'Basically, yes.'

I was excited, but only to a point.

'I can see why he made his mistake, but how can you be so sure?'

Frank leaned in and muttered under his voice.

'We've got the scans.'

'Scans? What do you mean you've got the scans? ...'

I turned to Mark and stifled my enthusiasm.

'...You mean you managed to get them done?'

'Yeah, a few years ago.'

'Get outta here! What did you find?'

'Not here, let's wait until we get in the car.'

'Then let's go.'

Frank was grinning from ear to ear.

'What's your hurry, there's more.'

'Such as?'

'Red granite; after hearing what you had to say before, I think you'll find what else there is to see very interesting.'

'Then lead on Macduff.'

Frank led us down the other side of the ridge and along the canal about twenty feet or so. I saw it way before Frank even pointed it out, radiating its rosy welcome against the duller background of the sand and mud.

Going by the headdress, the image of Amun was carved into what was most probably a section of wall.

'Oh, it's stunning, perfect!'

It looked almost brand new, pristine, which was more than I could say for the rest of the rock.

'OK, this is a major piece of evidence.'

'Well, firstly, look at the image; it's almost untouched, the face is still intact, it hasn't been vandalized in any way, which means it must have been in a very protected area for a very long time. Next, look at the fragment itself; none of these irregular sides look like the sort of fractures that would occur from the effects of an earthquake, so how did the fragment become a fragment? Thirdly, where are all the accompanying parts of the wall? Carted away? Perhaps, but then why leave this one?' So the question beckons, "where did it come from?"'

Mark pointed to the canal.

'Obviously they dredged it up when they were making the canal; it must have been under the ground.'

'Of course it was; it had to have been, but was it a loose rock, or was it part of the original structure?'

'I think I see where you're heading.'

'You see, the descending corridor that leads from the entrance of the pyramid to the substructure and so-called 'burial chamber' is flooded now, but it wasn't when Petrie excavated here only a hundred years ago.'

'I bet that when they dug the canal, they first broke into the upper level...'

'That would be the alabaster level.'

'...and then they hit the lower level, the real Labyrinth, and merely discarded the pieces to the side as they went, thinking they were just random fragments of a temple long destroyed.'

'Which explains why this part of the ridge had several large pieces within and around it.'

'Not only that, but also that when they broke into the structure they allowed the water from the canal to flood into the Labyrinth.'

'This part of it at the very least, and the connecting passage that led to the pyramid and its inner chambers.'

'There's another piece over here.'

I eagerly scuttled over to where Frank was standing.

'Oh, this is old, this is *really* old.'

It wasn't just that the carvings were faded, but the very style was ancient, so much so I couldn't define what they really represented. And the stone was somehow different; where had I seen it before?

It was similar to the stone altars at Philae and on Elephantine Island, which was not surprising as most of the red granite came from Aswan, but it most resembled the stone used in making some of the sarcophagi in the Valley of the Kings. In any case, it reinforced my belief it came from the bottom of the canal.

'Any other surprises?'

'Just the scans.'

'Well then, what are we waiting for? Let's go.'

Frank took off over the ridge and I was after him like a hungry ferret after a rabbit; Mark and the Colonel bringing up the rear as we all headed east across the piles of sand, over the roof of the Labyrinth, to where Mohammed and the guardian were waiting beside a small mud-brick 'enclosure' that looked more like a decrepit graveyard from the old wild west.

Random pieces of red granite and alabaster had been lined up like tombstones in a sort of makeshift outdoor museum. Unlike most of the large pieces still scattered near the canal, these were small enough to have been carried here by one or two guys. I suppose they had to create some sort of 'reason' to justify the entrance fee. Geez, if I didn't know the truth, the real significance about the site, I would have dumped it in with the unfinished obelisk as one of the biggest rip-offs in Egypt.

With permission from the guardian I stepped over the token wall of the enclosure and, like a general inspecting an official line-up or parade, checked out all the pieces, just on the off chance there might be something significant.

There was a fractured torso, a section of an alabaster statue, that caught my eye, plus a few other pieces of red-granite columns, but then I saw a small piece of alabaster on the ground. It was the hand of a statue, or at first I thought it was a hand, mainly because of what I thought were long slender fingers. But it could just have easily been the foot of a rather strangely formed humanoid.

It got me thinking about the Annunaki again; had they built the original Lower level of the Labyrinth? According to Herodotus, their coffins and, one would presume, the bodies within them, were in crypts either in the lower level or below that.

I imagined excavating here; sealing off the canal, pumping out the water, digging down to the lowest level, and discovering a row of sarcophagi with the bodies of alien life forms within. I couldn't wait to see the scans.

My tour of the graveyard complete, Mark slipped the guardian a few notes, a few more to the Colonel, and I gave Mohammed a huge hug.

'Shukran! Shukran!

'I talk to Saeed. He happy you go with Australian friend. He say he give you call tonight.'

'OK, cool. Again, shukran jazeelan.'

'Aafwaan.'

We bid the locals farewell, jumped in the car, Frank in the front with the driver, me in the back with Mark, and set off. To be honest it was a relief to see the kalashnikovs fade into the distance.

'OK, so, show me the money!'

My Tom Cruise impersonation was pretty pathetic but enough for Frank to decipher my desires and have his ipad fired up in seconds.

'This is a schematic of the locations the scans were done; two sites, the first about a hundred-and-fifty metres by a hundred metres to the east of the Bahr Wahbi canal, which is the area where we walked across the ground, and on the other side of the canal, in an area about eighty metres by a hundred metres, roughly near where Petrie did his excavations.'

'How did you scan it?'

'GPR.'

'What's that?'

'Ground Penetrating Radar. Until very recently GPR techniques were only used by the military and the oil industry, and totally new to the field of archaeology., so archaeologists were doubtful about its usefulness, they'd rather get their hands dirty and take forever to dig it up one trowel load at a time.'

'I presume the twenty-two-point-five is the angle of the scan relative to magnetic north?'

'Then you would presume incorrectly; it's the angle of the structures under the ground relative to the angle of the pyramid.'

'Seriously?...'

It opened a can of worms.

'...That means the pyramid and the lower levels were probably not built at the same time.'

Mark was right on top of it.

'I would seem that way.'

I handed the ipad back to Frank.

'But why?'

'We think it's something to do with the lower level being built before the last pole shift.'

'But wasn't the last pole shift like ten thousand years ago, and didn't the poles do a complete one-eighty?'

That was Frank's department.

'Actually you're half right. The last complete one-hundred-eighty degree pole shift was about ten-thousand-eight-hundred years ago, but there have been two others since then, one of around fifteen degrees, the other about ten degrees, which is consistent with the most recent passings of Nibiru.'

'You know about Nibiru?'

'The second sun, the winged destroyer; we sure do. That's why we're so interested in the Labyrinth, we believe it contains all the data to tell us when the next passing is.'

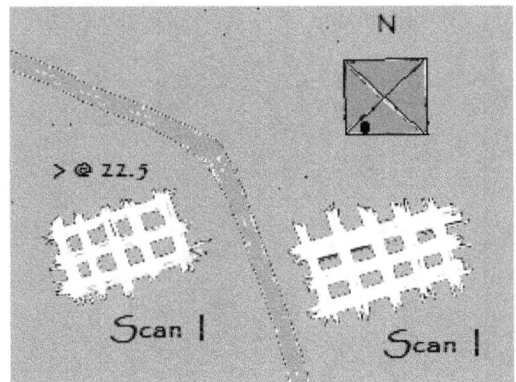

'Boy would Pieter love talking to you guys.'

Mark was curious.

'Who's he?'

'A Belgian guy I met on the felucca a few days ago, he was right into all this stuff.'

Frank scoffed and raised his eyebrows.

'We already know a Belgian, Patrick Geryl.'

'Never heard of him.'

Mark salvaged the situation.

'He's done a lot of work deciphering the Mayan Dresden codex about the next pole shift. He was part of getting the scans done here at Hawarra.'

'In what way?'

'He brought in a Belgian artist called Louis De Cordier to fund the scans.'

'But I thought only universities were allowed to dig in Egypt. How did you get permission?'

'They got Ghent University on board as well, but actually the scans were done by Dr. Abbas Abbas of the National Research Institute of Astronomy and Geophysics here in Cairo.'

'So the whole thing was set up by these Belgian guys?'

Frank couldn't hold back.

'Yes, and they also nearly blew they whole thing as well.'

'How?'

'They pissed off Zahi Hawass.'

'In what way?'

Mark to the rescue.

'It was called the "Mataha-expedition" and its mission was to research Flinders Petrie's finding of a "great artificial stone surface" around three-hundred metres by two-hundred-and-fifty metres. According to the rules that were set down by Hawass and the SCA, only the Egyptians could release the first results. But Louis set up a website and let the cat out of the bag, which pissed Hawass off completely.'

Frank scoffed again.

'That's an understatement.'

I was all ears.

'But the results *were* released, right?'

'Not publicly; the first results of the scans were officially released by the N.R.I.A.G. at a workshop in Cairo on 11th of August 2008.'

'Who was there?'

'Zahi Hawass of course, plus other members of the Supreme Council of Antiquities, a representative of UNESCO, several professors from international Universities and researchers of Cairo based archaeological institutes.'

'So it was closed shop?'

'Exactly.'

'And UNESCO? They're the Illuminati.'

'You know about them?'

'I do now!'

'Then you can understand why they were pissed off when Louis released the information on his website.'

'He's lucky he's still alive. What happened next.'

'Classic disinformation; they held a "public lecture" at Ghent university in October 2008 where Hawass dismissed the results. He said, "*If I will go and excavate at Hawarra I will not discover ANYTHING!*".'

Frank handed me back the Ipad.

'Have a look at that.'

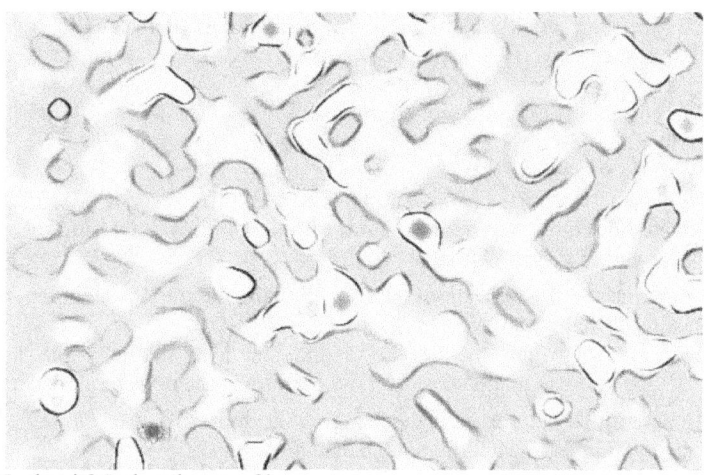

'Is that it? It that the scan?'

'It's one of them. *"Nothing to see folks; only a fucking Labyrinth of corridors and rooms."* The results clearly confirm the presence of the sort of archaeological features consistent with the Labyrinth, exactly where Herodotus said it was, in an area south of the pyramid of Amenemhat III.'

'I'm no geological expert, but clearly there's something here that's not just rock, although it is a little blurry.'

'That's because of the high salinity of the shallow subsurface groundwater; it affected the consistency of the survey.'

'The water from the canal?'

'Exactly.'

'So you think the remains of the labyrinth run underneath the canal.'

'Sure do, the two scanned sections, on both sides of the Bahr Wahbi canal, have similar parallel grids at around twenty-two-and-a-half degrees, so they must be connected.'

'That would make a hell of a lot of sense, but twenty-two-and-a-half degrees, you realize what that means don't you?'

They looked at each other for an answer, before Mark replied for them.

'No, we've just thought the pyramid was built at the corner of the Labyrinth as Herodotus said, but built after the pole shift. We're not really interested in the pyramid, more in the Labyrinth'

'Twenty-two-and-a-half degrees? Let's say twenty-three degrees!'

Frank got it straight away, sparking up like a rattrap.

'The tilt of the earth! Of course, how could I not have seen it.'

Mark quickly followed.

'If the whole Labyrinth was built in alignment with the tilted axis of the earth, that meant the builders had advanced astronomical knowledge, which totally correlates with…'

And he looked at Frank, them completing the sentence in Unison.

'…the Annunaki.'

'You guys know about them?'

'We sure do, that's why we're here. We think that not only are their bodies buried in crypts in the lower levels, but also their technologies. That's what we think those blue and red spots are, some sort of energy devices.'

'So divert the canal, drain the Labyrinth and do another scan?'

'Perhaps, or maybe just start excavating.'

'Did you do any scans to the north?'

'No, Herodotus only mentioned the south.'

'I think Herodotus only got half the picture.'

'What do you mean?'

'Herodotus was there a thousand years *after* the lower level and part of the upper level were buried by the Thera tsunami; I think there's more of it to the north.'

'What makes you think that?'

I explained my observations at Deir el-Bahri, about Montuhotep II's temple and Hatshepsut's Temple. Mark nodded.

'You may be right, the total size and shape of the labyrinth hasn't been concluded. All we know is that it covers an underground area of several hectares.'

Frank chipped in, momentarily changing the subject.

'Have you been to Meidum and Dahshur?'

'Not yet, I started at Abu Simbel and I've been working my way down the Nile.'

'So you haven't really been inside a pyramid yet?'

'Only the first few feet at Hawarra.'

Mark let out a little chuckle.

'That doesn't count.'

'Are you interested in getting right inside one?'

'Does a camel spit!'

Frank indicated to the driver....

'Meidum.'

...and I handed him back the ipad.

'Do you have any other scans, Frank?'

'Lots, and they all show basically the same thing. But have a look at this.'

Having flicked a few files, Frank handed me back the ipad, but, to tell you the truth, I wasn't sure what I was looking at.

'What is it?'

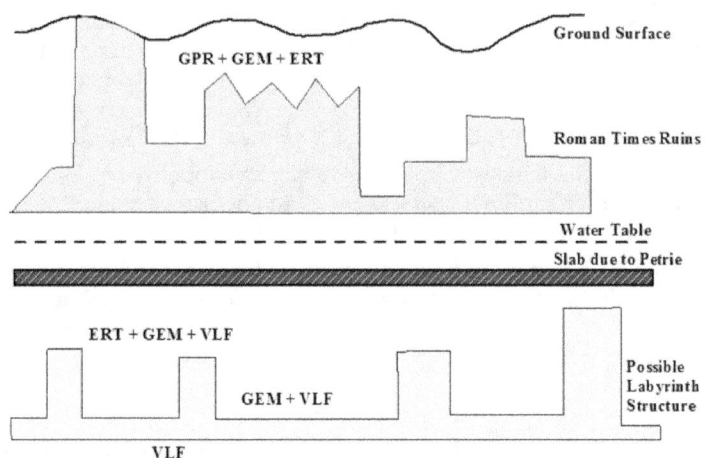

'It's a speculated cross-section of the ground using the accumulated results of the scans. It shows the prominent signature of vertical walls with an average thickness of

266

several metres, connected to form nearly closed rooms. The green section is the Roman layer, which goes down about four metres.'

'I think only the top metre or so is Ptolemaic and Roman.'

'Why?'

'Did you see the excavation just south of the pyramid, the rectangular pit?'

'Of course, it was done by a Polish University a few years ago.'

'Did you take any note of the layers of sand, mud and rubble?'

'Not really, no, we were more focused on the deeper layers.'

'Well, they didn't dig deep enough. Anyway, it shows exactly the layers associated with the Etna eruption of 396BC and the Turkey earthquake of 365AD. I think the bottom part of that green layer, from about four feet deep, belongs to the post Thera eruption, from the 18th Dynasty onwards.'

'And below that?'

'Below that is the current level of the water table, and below that, in blue, is the alabaster slab discovered by Flinders Petrie The depth of Petrie's slab is totally consistent with the evidence he found at Abydos; I can't believe he didn't put it together, but then again, he probably didn't know about the Thera eruption or the tsunami. I'm sure, if he did, he would've worked out that the level you have here in yellow, was the upper level, the alabaster level, and that there's at least another level below, going down to fifteen metres, that is made of red granite.'

'It's funny you should say that, read the text on the next page.'

As we turned off the main road, the image of the Meidum pyramid appeared in the distance.

'Now that's impressive.'

Mark laughed.

'I thought you'd like it. Wait until you get inside.'

As we headed down the approach road, I flipped the file.

'In the upper ground zone above the water level, walls appear at the shallow depth ranging between 1.5 to 2.5 metres. These decayed mud-brick features are very chaotic and show no consistent grid structure and can be comfortably related with the historic period of the Ptolemaic and Roman times.'

'What's this from?'

It was Mark who filled me in.

'It's from the report of Dr Abbass Abbass of the N.R.I.A.G.; the expert who did the scan.'

I read the next bit out loud.

'*"The upper part appear at a depth ranging between 5 & 6 metre below surface."* I think he's referring to the post Thera section, from the 18th Dynasty onwards. *"Underneath this upper zone, below the artificial stone surface appears (in spite of the turbid effect of the groundwater) at the depth of 8 to 12 metres a grid structure of gigantic size made of a very high resistivity material like granite stone."* Ah, there's the red granite. *"This states the presence of a colossal archaeological feature below the labyrinth "foundation" zone of Petrie, which has to be reconsidered as the roof of the still existing labyrinth."* It's pretty conclusive.'

'It sure is, but it's still not been "officially" released by the Supreme Council of Antiquities. Initially we couldn't understand why they didn't act on it, especially since the water level has risen dramatically in the last few decades, drowning the whole site in corrosive salty water.'

'Are you sure it's really salt water, ground-water, or is it fresh water from the canal?'

'That's a good point, although you couldn't really call the canal water 'fresh', but I suppose we won't really know until we get in there. In either case, after the official release of the research at the workshop in Cairo, members of the UNESCO committee publicly recommended listing the whole Hawarra site "world heritage", making environmental protection of the utmost necessity.'

I was stunned.

'Well, that speaks volumes. Firstly that UNESCO agreed the Labyrinth was there, despite what Zahi Hawass said, and, secondly, and perhaps more importantly, that they were going to seal it off from the general public while they 'rescued and restored' it.'

'An archaeological rescue operation as never seen before will therefore have to be organized, to raise the necessary media attention, experts, technology and funds to start the drainage, protection and the total excavation of the Labyrinth of Egypt. The Egyptian Supreme Council of Antiquities expressed their great devotion and responsibility by announcing the start of the actual renovate master plan for the site.'

'It looks like they were planning to do exactly what they did with Abu Simbel, Philae and the Aswan dam, rob them blind, right in front of the world. I wonder what stopped them?'

'They were too busy robbing the Giza Plateau.'
'What?…'

Frank had taken me completely by surprise.
'…do tell.'

The tip of the iceberg

'Dr Abbass did scans of Giza as well. Here, let me show you.'

He took the ipad, flicked a few files, and passed it back.

'Take a look at that; it's a schematic of the Giza Plateau. The areas in red are the areas scanned by Abbass.'

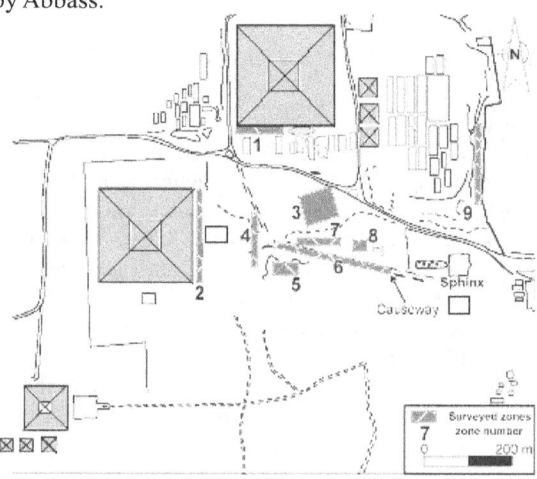

'It's pretty comprehensive, when was it done?'

'The early part of 2008, before the Hawarra scans; they did it more as a test because the GPR had never really been used in archaeological research before.'

'They're pretty specifically defined areas, who chose them?'

'Now that's a good question; we're not really sure, although we do know that Abbass was constantly under the direction and supervision of Zahi Hawass.'

'I think I smell a rat.'

'A very big greedy one.'

'Did they find anything?'

'Flick to the next image…'

It was an aerial shot of the Giza Plateau exactly corresponding to the schematic.

'…You see those red dots, that's where they found anomalies beneath the surface.'

'Anomalies? What do you mean?'

'Voids; inconsistencies in the rock strata, in several cases, large chambers?'

I compared the two images.

'But they're nearly everywhere the scans are.'

'Which means there's lots more under Giza than we know about, or are being told about.'

Mark took up the lead.

'Do you remember a few years back Zahi Hawass was announcing the discovery of the Tomb of Osiris?'

'Yeah, they had a big documentary on it, going down these shafts in the Giza Plateau.'

'Where do you think he found out about it?'

'From the scans?'

Frank followed up.

'Exactly. Flick to the next page, it shows the Osiris shaft as seen in photographs and as defined from the GPR data.'

'Wow!'

'But Hawass went down first and cleaned it out before letting anyone else in to film.'

'Clean it out, you mean pump out the water and make it secure?'

'Sure, he did that, but he also removed anything of value.'

'Like what?'

It was Mark's turn at bat.

'We may never know. We were there in March 2010 and we saw a massive hole dug in the area right in front of the Sphinx. It was supposedly for the erection of something to do with the Red Bull games, but that was just a cover-up, they were really digging down to access discoveries and chambers under Sphinx and under the Giza Plateau itself.'

'The Hall of Records?'

'What else?'

'How do you know?'

'Just over a month later, on the 28th April 2010, we had some associates staying at the Sphinx Guest House, overlooking the Giza Plateau. They were out on the roof in the evening when they heard several muffled explosions come from under the plateau. Later they saw front-end loaders removing sarcophagi and statues from underneath the plateau.'

'You're kidding? No way!'

'Oh yeah, they took a video of it.'

'Seriously? Have you got a copy?'

'Not on here, but I do have a few stills from the video.'

He took the ipad back and flicked a few files.

'Here you go, I've made a few notes on it to make it easier to define what's what.'

'Is that a sarcophagus being carried on a tractor?'

'Sure is.'

'This is dynamite! Did they post the video on Youtube, or contact the media?'

'All of the above, they even put it up on a website, but the website and the video have mysteriously disappeared from the web and they're in hiding. However there is a video containing photos of the excavation that were taken about a week later, that's the link on the next page.'

I flicked over.

"Giza Plateau Excavation Photos 2010"

http://www.youtube.com/watch?v=S0ea6R_oABo

I made a note to check it out if, or rather when, I got home.

'All we can hope, is that Nostradamus was right.'

Frank had caught me on the hop.

'Nostradamus, the 16th Century prophet? He wrote about it?'

'Sure did, Century six, Quatrain ninety-nine, and Century eight, Quatrain thirty.'

He took the ipad and flicked through a few files.

'The prophecy basically outlines a major archaeological project at Giza to find the Hall of Records, headed by someone of great learning but possessing none of the Ancient Wisdom. The failed attempt will uncover very little of actual worth, the real treasure being secretly protected by the Guardians of the Giza Plateau.'

He handed me back the ipad.

'Here you go.'

> 'L'ennemy docte se trouuera confus,
>
> Grand camp malade, det défaict par embusches,
>
> Môts Pyrenees et Poenus luy serôt faicts refus,
>
> Proche du fleuue desouurant antiques roches.'

'My French isn't that crash hot, you'll have to fill me in.'

'It's actually a mixture of old French and Latin.'

'Might as well be Double-Dutch to me now-a-days.'

'OK then, line one, *"L'ennemy docte se trouuera confus"* translates as *"The enemy who is learned,.."* or, *"The enemy of learning, will be found confused."* It refers to someone who is either well educated, or an enemy of wisdom, or both; *"docte"* could even refer to someone with a doctoral degree, who is opposed to esoteric wisdom.'

'Well, Zahi Hawass would fit the bill there.'

'The second line reads, *"Grand camp malade, et défaict par embusches"*. One variant of *"embusches"* is "ambushes", meaning to be under cover, to lie in wait, to be hidden and unexpected. So it translates as, *"The great encampment sick, and defeated by ambushes."* I think it means, the secret Guardians of the Hall of Records, recruited and planted amongst the local workmen and acting like incompetent and clumsy morons, will act to undermine the work by means of a series of careless mistakes, false leads, and well-placed accidents, subtly sabotaging every effort to find or penetrate the entrance.'

My High-school French kicked in.

'Doesn't "*embuche*" mean a trap or pitfall?'

'It does.'

'And doesn't malade also mean "mad", as in "crazy"?'

'True.'

'So it could read, "*The mad group, defeated by a trap*"?'

Frank was impressed.

'Yes, possibly, and it's a better fit.'

'But doesn't the third line, '*Môts Pyrenees et Poenus luy serôt faicts refus*' refer to the Pyrenees Mountains between France and Spain as the location?'

'It may appear that way on the surface, but "*Pyrenees*" can be broken down to "*Pyre née*", meaning the "fire's birth".'

'A volcano? Thera perhaps?'

'No, it's an esoteric reference to the Pyramids, the very name, "pyramiddim", means "Fire in the Centre", thus, "*Mountains where the Spiritual Fire of Rebirth or Initiation took place*".

'I'm not convinced.'

'OK, take, "*Poenus*"; it's derived from the Latin words penes, penus and poena, which together describe a location of great power, a storehouse, or where challenges are overcome. As it's related to the Pyramids, it can only be the Hall of Records.'

'Or it could mean a power station; with a central reactor in the centre; the birth of fire.'

'Alex, you're a genius.'

'Thanks.'

'But it could still be a reference to the excavations under Giza; "*luy serôt faicts refus*', "*to him will be refused*", meaning he will be refused entrance to the area under the Giza Plateau.'

'What does the last line, "*Proche du fleuue desouurant antiques roches*", translate as?'

'There's actually some confusion, as "*roches*" is more often recorded as "*cruches*", and thus it is often translated as, "*Near the flow, discovering antique jugs*", or urns.'

'So, if it *is* an urn of some type, that the "*enemy of learning*" is involved with stealing it?'

'Well, that *would* be up Hawass's alley.'

'But doesn't "roche" mean "rocks"?'

'It does indeed.'

'So, "*Near the flow*", could mean, "*Near the river*", but it could also refer to an underground stream, and "*discovering antique jugs*", could really mean "*discovering ancient stones*", as in stone walls or doorways? And the only way you could determine that they were "ancient" would be if they had ancient markings on them.'

'I like it.'

'So how come the media weren't all over it like ants on a jam sandwich?'

'Because the same people who control Zahi Hawass, control the media.'

'The Illuminati!'

'Yep.'

'But didn't all that change when the people's revolution happened? In fact, couldn't the crazy group have been the people's revolution?'

Frank was not so easily duped.

'It could, but nothing's changed. I think the revolution was all a front to get the

271

foreigners out of Egypt, confine the media to their hotels and get everyone looking in the wrong direction. Then they put the military around the Giza Plateau, supposedly to protect it from thieves, but the reality was they had even bigger objects to remove.'

'So why is Muburak in jail and not Hawass?'

Frank scoffed.

'Muburak was expendable, he was the fall guy, but Hawass was the man on the ground, in control of all the sites.'

'But didn't they try to put Hawass in jail.'

'And the verdict was squashed the next day; so what does that tell you?'

'But they've had proper elections.'

'You wait and see; you really think the Muslim Brotherhood will stay in power long? Egypt is run by the Illuminati through the military; nothing's changed.'

Meidum

We pulled up, about eighty kilometres south of Cairo, on the western bank of the Nile at the edge of the cultivated area where it becomes desert. I got out of the car, and looked up at the pyramid.

'That's awesome.'

I stood looking at it while Frank went off to get the tickets.

'You can leave your backpack in the car if you want, Alex, it'll be safe.'

'No thanks, Mark, I think I'd better keep it with me.'

'OK.'

I couldn't think of anything better than getting the target off my back, but the reality would have been if I'd left it in the car I would have worried about it so much I would have expected the entire weight of the pyramid to come crashing down upon my head. No, at this point it was best to keep it with me at all times.

The pyramid consisted of a number of steps, three visible, towering out of the rubble.

'It looks like a ziggurat, like the ones in ancient Sumer.'

'Yeah, interesting isn't it. According to the Egyptologists, it was built by Snefru, first pharaoh of the 4th Dynasty, although some of them believe it was Snefru's father, Huni, who laid the foundations, even though there's actually no record of Huni at all in the structure.'

'Sounds to me more like another case of academic guesswork.'

'You think it's older?'

'Possibly. No, probably!'

I fired up the iphone; the battery was getting low, but I was sure I could get through the day. Quickly finding the Meidum file, I picked out some interesting notes, which I shared with Mark.

The only references to Snefru are several blocks found by Flinders Petrie that contain graffiti with the date of Snefru's 17th year of reign, and some 18th Dynasty graffiti in a passage and chamber of the mortuary temple.'

That started Mark thinking.

'It's hardly conclusive evidence, is it?'

'The structure could just as easily have been built by anyone at any time before Snefru; it may not have even been a pyramid.'

'What do you mean?'

'Well, look at it, it could have been just what it looks like, a ziggurat.'

'That would put it at least a thousand years earlier.'

'At least.'

'But according to most Egyptologists, the Meidum pyramid is the transition point between the early step pyramids and the pyramids at Giza. Supposedly it was built in three phases, the first consisting of the building of a seven-stepped structure, which, in the second phase was enlarged and amended to eight steps, then, during the later years of Snefru's reign, it was filled in with packing and regular courses of better quality stone to create the smooth surface of its final casing.'

I wandered over to the pyramid, to the western side, where some limestone casing blocks were still visible at ground level, my mind ticking over a million miles an hour.

'But what if it wasn't, what if that's all wrong? What if it's a totally different history? I mean, if there were smooth outer casing blocks, what happened to them all?'

'They collapsed.'

'So where are they?'

'The most likely explanation is that they were carted away by the locals to use in building their houses.'

'I don't buy it.'

'Even Petrie recorded that the stone was being quarried at the time he investigated it in the late 19th Century.'

'You're starting to sound like an Egyptologist. What, all of them were carted away, even the massive ones? Not one left behind? I mean, look around, we're in the middle of nowhere, there isn't a house for miles.'

'I've never thought of that.'

'It's just like the outer casing of the Hawarra pyramid, where are all those pieces?'

'Are you suggesting there may be a ziggurat under the mud-bricks at Hawarra?'

'It's possible. What if the only "quarrying" being done was being done by Petrie himself, because he was blasting into this lower level and then getting the locals to cart away the debris, or rather the evidence?'

'I guess it's possible.'

I pointed back up to the top of the pyramid.

'If we assume there *were* casing stones and they were right up there, what caused them to collapse?'

'The consensus of opinion is poor construction techniques.'

'Well, that makes sense, doesn't it; they create a brilliant ziggurat interior, then sudden lose their skills and build a substandard outer casing? Hardly!'

'Good point. Others have speculated it was probably an earthquake, or a series of earthquakes.'

'This is great, Mark, you're doing exactly what successive Egyptologists have done, made "educated" guesses. A series of earthquakes might be plausible if it weren't for the fact the earthquakes supposedly totally fractured the outer casing, causing it to collapse to the ground, but left the ziggurat itself almost completely intact? Earthquakes? No, I don't think so.'

'You think it was washed away by one of your tsunamis?'

'If it was even there to begin with, and I don't think it was. Think about it, no one has ever seen it as an actual pyramid, and there are no records of it actually having a pyramidal shape.'

'That's true.'

As we made our way around the perimeter of the pyramid to the north face, Mark was playing the devil's advocate.

'Various so-called "experts" have argued that the upper cladding stones collapsed and were stolen.'

'But they base their argument, not on any actual stones that have fallen, rather, totally on the lower stones still in place. What if there were only lower stones to begin with, what if they were part of the ziggurat structure, or even added at a later date.'

'Possibly during the reign of Snefru.'

'Exactly my thinking.'

'Which accounts for all the graffiti.'

'That it does.'

'But what about the piles of rubble around the base?'

I picked up a handful of it.

'The Egyptologists seems seem to be of the opinion that the structure didn't collapse until at least the New Kingdom, and I think they're on the right track. But take a look at it, it's made of the sort of small stones that form the type of strata always associated with eroded and deposited materials, not chunks of a major collapse.'

'You think it was left here by one of the tsunamis?'

'I'd bet my life on it, most probably the Thera tsunami.'

'If you're right, you might have to rewrite the history of ancient Egypt.'

'I've already started, Mark, already started.'

Unlike at Hawarra where he and Mark had an armed escort, Frank had sorted out the tickets and strolled up on his own to join us.

'Right, let's go.'

'They're not going to escort us?'

Frank laughed.

'No, they've been there before.'

It was a relief.

'How much do I owe you?'

'A pint of blood and your first-born child.'

'Seriously, how much?'

'Would it matter, at the moment you couldn't buy your way out of trouble with a "Get out of Jail free" card.'

Frank was right, I was in deep shit way past my eyeballs, but that didn't mean I wasn't going to cover my debts.

'Seriously, what's the damage?'

'It's thirty-five Egyptian pound, you can fix us up when we get to Cairo.'

Frank led the way as we made our way along the makeshift 'staircase' that angled about twenty metres up the mound of debris to the entrance.

'So, you're in a bit of strife with the police.'

'That's an understatement. But it's not just the police, it's the Secret Police.'

'Why, what did you do, burn down a mosque, steal Tutankhamen's golden death mask, make love to the Chief of Police's daughter?'

'I should be so lucky. The police say I murdered an Antiquities Superintendent and stole a folder of top secret government documents.'

'Well, did you?'

We reached the entrance, a no-frills rectangular hole in the northern side of the pyramid, protected by a modern metal door.

'No!'

'So why are they chasing you?'

Talk about paranoid, I looked around as if to check no one was listening; hell, we were twenty metres above the ground and about to enter a pyramid. Despite that, I was still cautious.

'Let's get inside.'

Once again Frank led the way, this time single-file into the darkness, down a low rough-cut passage that sloped from the entrance into the heart of the pyramid; this was it, *this* was the real McCoy. It was incredible, if a tad ominous, even claustrophobic, but it didn't feel like the sort of passageway befitting that of a pharaoh's tomb.

There were no hieroglyphs, no decorations of any kind; it was more like a workman's access tunnel for maintenance. If it weren't for the modern handrails, footholds, and lighting, the descent would have been like a descent into the pits of hell; terrifying.

As we made our way slowly down the passage I explained how I met Saeed, then his uncle, and how Kareem had given me the folio of papers to take out of Egypt, and how later he was found with his throat cut. I told them of my escape from Abydos in the tok tok, and then again from the train station at Beni Suef. Frank was all ears.

'You're a regular Indiana Jones.'

'Yeah, so long as it all works out in the final reel.'

We reached the end of the descent and entered a short horizontal passage with a small antechamber and a niche on the right-hand side, all dug into the bedrock running beneath the base of the structure.

'What's so special about these papers?'

'I'm not sure, they're all in Arabic, but I do know some of them are official documents that go way back to the building of the Aswan Dam and that others implicate Zahi Hawass in heaps of things, including the Luxor massacre.'

Mark was astonished.

'Wow! No wonder they're after you, especially given all the current unrest and uncertainly with the political situation here in Egypt. If Hawass *is* mentioned, then others may be as well, and the public disclosure of the contents could prove major obstacles to the political aspirations of many of Hawass's cohorts.'

The antechamber led to a vertical shaft barely wide enough for a man to get through, with a rickety pair of ladders that gave access up through the bedrock to the 'burial chamber', which sat at the original ground level. That seemed bizarre: why cut out the antechamber from the bedrock, but not the tomb? And the access shaft was barely big enough for me to climb through let alone a granite sarcophagus weighing several ton; it was more evidence the structure was never a tomb but had some other function.

As I followed Frank up the second ladder, he reached the chamber then briefly turned back and down to lend me a hand.

'So where are these papers?'

'In my backpack.'

'The one you're wearing?'

'Yep'

Behind me, Mark let out a slight gasp.

'No wonder you didn't want to leave them in the car.'

Meanwhile Frank had reached the 'burial chamber'.

'That's a hell of a burden to be carrying around, more like a target on your back.'

As I reached the burial chamber, I took off the backpack and fingered one of the bullet holes.

'Tell me about; I've got the bullet holes to prove it.'
'It sounds like you've got a price on your head.'

Joining us in the tomb, Mark was straight to the point.
'Do you mind if we take a look?'
'Be my guest.'

I took out the folder and handed it to them.
'Do you read Arabic?'
'Frank does, a little.'

While they flicked through the pages I explored the confines of the chamber, its corbelled walls and roof of limestone projecting above the bedrock to form a sort of 'A' shaped chamber; in many ways it reminded me of a potters' kiln, an oven.

There were traces of an ancient wooden beam near the apex, which no doubt the Egyptologists would propose was used to lift the sarcophagus. But a wooden beam could hardly support a sarcophagus weighing several ton, even if wood had been readily available in Egypt, which it wasn't, and the corbelling of the walls would reduce the area into which a sarcophagus could be lifted and negotiated, so I think that theory didn't have legs.

Also, when it was discovered, the chamber was empty; there was no trace of a sarcophagus, no pharaoh's remains, nothing. However...

'Petrie reported finding remains of a plain wooden coffin in the entry corridor which he considered to possibly date to the Old Kingdom.'

Who knows what happened to it?

If there was a coffin found in the outer corridor, and it *was* from the Old Kingdom, it could have been placed there hundreds or even thousands of years after the original ziggurat was constructed. The coffin may have been introduced with the intention of placing it in the corbelled chamber, but, once the priests realized they couldn't navigate it through the narrow vertical shaft, it was left abandoned in the outer corridor.

A few minutes examining the walls and floor and there wasn't anything else to see. I turned my attention back to Mark and Frank who were engrossed in the folio like two prepubescent boys ogling a copy of playboy.
'Found anything interesting?'
'Heaps. I'm just looking for any documents on Hawarra, or on the Labyrinth. It looks like there's a copy of Abbass's report here and several other pages attached to it signed by Hawass, but my Arabic is only basic and I can't really tell. But if what you said about this guy Kareem being a Superintendent is true, and there's stuff in here about Hawass and the Luxor massacre, then there's probably stuff about the Labyrinth as well.'

He handed back the papers and I stuffed them back in the backpack.
'So, what do I do?'

He pointed back down the vertical shaft.
'You get your ass out of Egypt as fast as you can, and you take the papers with you.'
'Easier said than done!'

I headed down the ladder and out through the antechamber, Frank and Mark right behind me. As Mark reached the bottom of the ladder, he called after me.

'When are you booked to fly out?'

'A few days from today, but that's no good, they have my passport.'

'Which means they will have checked with the airlines and know when your flight is, so, even if you had your passport, they would arrest you at the airport.'

'Right.'

Being the lawyer he was, Mark was quickly putting it all together.

'Then we need to find you another exit strategy.'

'Saeed's trying to organize a boat to take me to Greece.'

'It's a long shot, but it might work; you can always get a new passport there.'

As we started to ascend the passage, Frank had an idea.

'Have you thought of posting the papers out?'

'Sure, but my guess is they're watching any foreign mail out of the major cities. Besides, do you really think it's worth the risk?'

'You're right. In any case, I think you need to make a copy, or several copies.'

'I haven't had a chance.'

Mark was taking a different tack.

'I think we need to get you to the Aussie Embassy in Cairo.'

'Won't the Secret Police be watching there as well?'

'Probably, but unless you can get that boat to Greece, it's probably your safest bet.'

Emerging back into the desert heat, I took a moment as I waited for Frank and Mark to exit, to take in the view, noticing several large mounds, two to the north and one closer to the northeast.

'The Meidum pyramid is surrounded by several mastabas dating to the 4th Dynasty. The large mastaba to the north, Mastaba 16, the tomb of Nefermaat, probably a son of Snefru, was built with mud-bricks, with inner walls lined with limestone blocks decorated with painted scenes of daily life. Northeast of Nefermaat's tomb is Mastaba 6, the mastaba of Rahotep and his wife Nofret, son and daughter-in-law of Snefru. Its outer walls are decorated with the 'palace façade' motif, whilst scenes inside include scenes of everyday life.

The largest mastaba, Mastaba 17, located just outside the enclosure walls on the north-east corner of the pyramid, is thought to belong to an unknown son of Snefru, as inside the tomb sits an uninscribed sarcophagus.'

'Do you want to go and have a look?'

Frank had joined me on the path.

'It depends, is there anything worth seeing?'

'What are you looking for?'

'Red granite?'

Frank shook his head.

'Save your legs.'

Mark chipped in.

'Although there is something I think you should have a look at on the east side of the pyramid.'

'What is it?'

'A small chapel, although it's not so much *what* it is, but *where* it is.'

'I'm right behind you!'

We made our way down the 'staircase' of debris, then Frank gave it a miss and headed back to the car as Mark and I scooted around the corner and down a slope into an excavated area that fronted the eastern face of the pyramid.

'Now that's interesting; *very* interesting.'

It was a partially excavated small limestone offerings chapel, possibly a forerunner to the later and much larger 'mortuary' temples that 'fronted' the pyramids and led to the Nile. Examining it closer, it consisted of a courtyard and a vestibule with a central altar and two tall, very worn, granite stelae.

'What do you think?'

I started thinking out loud.

'Well, firstly, they're made of granite, but unfortunately the stelae lack any inscriptions, but that in itself raises a few interesting questions. Was it the norm to erect a stela, *then* do the inscriptions? If it was, then what event happened to prevent these from being inscribed?'

'A tsunami?'

'Possibly. But if it *wasn't* the norm to inscribe them once in situ, then what was the significance of erecting two blank stelae? Then there's their positioning relative to the vestibule that follows; they seem too close, surely any inscriptions could have been added to the walls? Unless the stelae were in situ way before the vestibule was added, which raises even more questions.'

Mark threw in his thoughts.

'They remind me of the monolith found on the moon at the beginning of the movie *"2001 A Space Odyssey"*.'

'Mmm; blank, but full of meaning.'

'But what's the meaning?'

'The big 'hello' to me is that it all sits on the bedrock, and that's at least twenty feet below the 'ground level' of the surrounding debris mounds. That means the stelae are at least contemporary with the original ziggurat.

The rest of the chapel may well have been added after the pre-Thera tsunami, with the whole lot then buried by the Thera tsunami in 1600 BC. And that all adds up to it being built way before the reign of Snefru.'

'It all makes sense to me.'

Having seen all that I needed to see, we turned around and started back for the car.

'You know, there would also have been a causeway here, maybe two-hundred metres long, which would have led to a valley temple close to what would have once been the western bank of the Nile.'

'Both of which haven't as yet been discovered?'

'They're probably out there, east of the pyramid, about fifteen to twenty feet below the surface.'

'And if your theory about the tsunamis is correct, then that means the exploration of ancient Egypt has barely scratched the surface.'

'My thoughts exactly.'

We made our way back to the car, completing our circumnavigation via the southern side of the pyramid.

'So what's the story with you and Frank? You aren't a couple are you?'

'Hardly. Frank's a bit of a genius actually; strangely enough, as a kid, he originally wanted to be an archaeologist but his father worked at Lockheed so he finished up being an aeronautical designer for Aerospace Lines and was involved with McDonnell Douglas on modifications to the DC-10. You know he came up with the concept of the Megalifter?'

'What's that, a protein powder for weightlifters and bodybuilders?'

'No, it's quite famous in aeronautical design. It's a hybrid airship that uses helium.'

'You mean a blimp.'

'Don't let Frank hear you call it that; it had wings and used helium to offset weight. The concept was taken on and was being developed by Howard Hughes before his death.'

'The tycoon Howard Hughes, maker of the spruce goose, Frank worked with him?'

'Yep.'

'That's impressive.'

'That's not the half of it; he's been to Patterson Air Force base, Andrews Air Force base, secret naval offices, he was involved with NASA and the development of the Space Shuttle.'

'Frank worked at NASA?'

'Yeah, I think he even worked with Werner Von Braun. But NASA stole his designs and used them for military black ops.'

'So how did he finish up in Egypt digging sandcastles?'

'He heard a few things over the years that got him thinking, and eventually his interest turned to discovering the truth about the human race, god and religion, and that led ultimately back to archaeology, which in turn led him to the Labyrinth.'

As we approached the car, Frank spotted us and made his way from the ticket office to join us.

'So how did a lawyer from Melbourne hook up with a geriatric aeronautics designer from California?'

'We met at the Santa Barbara Yacht Club and got talking about life. I can't remember how we got on to the subject of Egypt, but before we knew it we'd set up The Horus Foundation.'

'As in, "the search for truth"?'

'Exactly.'

'And how did you get connected with the Belgians and Dr. Abbass?'

'Actually we were the ones originally in contact with Abbass and working to get the scans done. Then Frank read Patrick's books on 2012 and the Labyrinth, and we got in contact with him to see if we could all work together.'

'It sounds like that was a story in itself.'

'More like a melodrama.'

Arriving at the car, Frank was keen to get underway.

'So, are you ready to see the pyramids at Dahshur?'

'Sure am; I just need a quick pit-stop.'

Frank pointed to the ticket office and I headed off.

'Won't be long.'

Thankfully the effects of my "Ramses' Revenge" had subsided considerably and my internal ramifications were almost back to normal, so a few minutes later I was climbing back into the car.

'Right, let's hit Dahshur.'

Frank had a serious look on his face.

'We have an important stop before then.'

'What?'

'Lunch.'

As the car pulled out and away from the Medium ziggurat, a thought crossed my mind; almost everyone I'd met on this trip had some past-life connection to ancient Egypt; so who were Frank and Mark?

CHAPTER 27 - DAHSHUR

Turning back onto the main road north, I was curious to find out more about this unlikely Dynamic Duo.

'Hey Frank, Mark was telling me you used to work for NASA?'

'Thieving assholes; I didn't so much work *for* them, as was engaged *with* them on certain projects.'

'The Apollo program?'

'No, that was a cover up anyway.'

'What for?'

'NASA has been on the moon since the late fifties.'

'That's what Randy said.'

'Who's Randy?'

'He was one of the guys I met on the felucca. He said that the Apollo program was all about covering up that they were mining on the moon, that the broadcast landings were all shot in studios here on earth.'

'Then your friend, Randy, is a smart kid.'

I was starting to think Frank might have been right about Randy; never judge a book by its cover.

'Were you involved in the Space Shuttle program?'

'Yeah, another cover-up?'

'What for; don't tell me, they only built the shuttle so they could retrieve alien satellites from orbit?'

I was half kidding, but Frank looked at me stunned.

'How do you know about that?'

'You mean it's true?'

Frank hesitated, before opening up, although he spoke softly, as if the car was bugged.

'NASA had seen them through telescopes then confirmed their presence during the Gemini missions. But how do you know about them, it's one of NASA's closest kept secrets.'

I wasn't sure what to say, I mean I didn't want to sound like a nutcase, but, in the end, I just told it as it was.

'Well, I was at Karnak and I'd been putting my hands on various alabaster and granite altars, and then some of the obelisks, tuning in so to speak, and the images just came into my head.'

'I would suggest you keep them there, NASA has a nasty habit of eliminating any loose canons.'

'Is that why they stopped the shuttle program, because the truth had leaked out?'

'No, they've managed to still keep the lid on that one.'

'So why did they stop?'

'Wouldn't you call it off if the aliens got fed up with you stealing their property and started shooting your toys out of the skies.'

'Columbia?'

'Yep.'

Shit, it was one thing to have abstract thoughts of alien beings in the universe, quite another to know they were sitting outside your backdoor blasting you to smithereens for nicking one of their satellites.

'So is that the mission of The Horus Foundation, to expose the truth about aliens?'

It was Mark who answered.

'It's more than that; it's to discover the true origins of the human race. However, in doing that, it *will* reveal the truth about the alien intervention on this planet. Frank's been researching and writing a book about it, not just about the origins of modern humans but also about their religions.'

'What's it called?'

Understandably, it was Frank who replied.

'The Story of Sibyl.'

'Who was Sibyl?'

'In ancient texts, the name, Sibyl, has generally been applied to the priestesses, but it's not really who, it's what; a sibyl is an object from the different emerging cultures of the pre-ancient world that had many names associated with it.'

'Such as?'

'Stones which produced the Light, Ark, Oracle, and the like.'

'Stones?'

I was initially thinking it may have been a reference to the *sang réal*, but when Frank said "stones" I immediately started thinking of red granite. However, I was a little off the mark.

'The Sibyl were devices of high technology with the perceived ability to talk with the priests in any human tongue. From the ancient texts it's clear the power of these devices covers everything from communication to awesome and fearful super-destructive capabilities.'

'And you think one of these Sibyls might be in the Labyrinth, one of those blue spots on the scan?'

'Exactly.'

'And with one of these stones in your possession you could talk with god, or rather *the* gods who created mankind?'

'Most probably; or at least they could communicate with you.'

'You should have been on the felucca with me.'

'Why's that?'

'I had the most amazing discussions with the other guys on the boat; Bill, Pieter, Dwight and even Randy.'

'What was so significant about them?'

'Bill was an ex-priest, Pieter was a masseur from Belgium, and Dwight and Randy were a couple of college kids from Philadelphia, Dwight's actually studying here in Cairo to be an Egyptologist. You would have fitted right in.'

'And why's that?'

'We talked about the Apollo stuff, the assassination of JFK and others by the Illuminati...'

'You know the driver did it.'

'...yeah, so Randy said.'

'William Greer; blew JFK's head apart with a gas-fired gun containing a pellet of cone-shell toxin, so that if the blast didn't kill him the shell toxin would; that's why they confiscated his brain.'

'Randy didn't say anything about that.'

'There's knowing, and then there's KNOWING.'

I got the impression Frank knew more about most conspiracy theories than most people, possibly because he'd been inside the dragon's den. And yet he was the one pressing me for information, possibly to 'sus' me out.

'What else did you talk about?'

'God, heaps of stuff; the Amun Priests, the Tat Brotherhood, who Jesus Christ and Mary Magdalene really were...'

'And who do you think they were?'

'Well, now I'm positive they were Caesarion and Cleopatra Selene II.'

'Interesting!...'

It was like Frank was cross-referencing against sections of his own book.

'...What else?'

'Who Moses really was,...'

'And who was he?'

'He was the vizier of the northern pharaoh, Apopi, at the end of the 15th Dynasty, whom we also know as Joseph of the "Technicolour Dreamcoat" fame.'

'You're saying they were one and the same person?'

'Yes. He was responsible for the murder of the 17th Dynasty southern pharaoh, Seqenenre Tao II, which caused a civil war between the north and south, ending with Joseph being chased out of Egypt by Kamose, Seqenenre's eldest son.'

'The Exodus?'

'Yes.'

Mark was also interested.

'So it wasn't Ramses II as most experts presume?'

'No. And that gives a totally different perspective on the Torah, the origins of 'The Bible', the ten commandments, the ten plagues, Islam and the Koran.'

'I've never heard that, but I like your thinking...'

The car had entered a village and pulled up outside a shop.

'...We should talk more about it later, but first let's have some lunch.'

I took my backpack with me as we sat at a table near the entrance of the open air 'restaurant'. Frank was still eager to discover what I knew.

'It sounds like you've had an amazing trip.'

'A trip of a lifetime, that's if I get to finish it and get out of Egypt in one piece.'

Thankfully Mark was confident.

'I'm sure the Embassy will help.'

Feeling unusually relaxed, over lunch I explained in detail to Frank and Mark the discussions on the felucca about Joseph, the passing of Nibiru and the early eruption of Thera, and how it caused the ten plagues, how it signalled civil war and "The Exodus", how the waters were really parted by the tsunami that wiped out the 17th Dynasty, about Mt Sinai being in Saudi Arabia, which Frank was aware of, and how Joseph changed his name to Moses, created first the seven, then ten, commandments by carving Egyptian hieroglyphs on stone, and how it all led to the original 'Old Testament', and the torah.

That took up all of our meal and, as we got up to leave and headed to the car, Frank summed it all up from his perspective.

'You know, the record we have of ancient human history and its beliefs has primarily been handed down by oral traditions, word of mouth. Over the millennia, like

Chinese whispers, these stories and histories have been added to and modified from the original, mostly through the "priesthoods" who managed and controlled the information and interpreted everything from myths, legends and god's laws to the management of crops and how to scratch your butt.

Then, influenced by various groups within societies whose mission was to control and manage human behaviour, the '"priests" interpreted and reinterpreted "history" to fit the understanding and "hidden social agendas" of the day. It wasn't until the invention of the written word, and materials like papyrus and parchment with which to collect the earlier human stories and myths, that man was able to document his earlier beginnings, and with it, all the distortions, both intentional and unintentional.

And with that, as writing was reserved for the educated and privileged, the written word and laws for human conduct were conceived, perceived and perpetuated to have always had a sense of coming from the gods. But, during the last century, that started to shift as giant leaps in technology led to an enormous amount of new data about our world and its earlier inhabitants, and we've started to question those written records.'

By the time Frank had finished, we were back in the car and on our way to Dahshur.

'Was there anything else you talked about on the boat?'

'Heaps more; Nibiru and the Annunaki, pole-shifts and the eruption of Thera, the Dracos, the origins of the human species,...'

'And what direction did that discussion take?'

'That, just as Zeccharia Sitchin has suggested, we were the product of genetic engineering by aliens.'

Frank had a little chuckle to himself.

'Did you know there's a professor of genetic research at Oxford University, Dr. Richard Dawkins, who has concluded that the modern human female, with two "X" chromosomes, XX, showed up around a hundred-forty-thousand years ago, whereas the modern human male, with his XY chromosomes, shows up eighty-thousand years later, which modern science can't seem to explain if they stick to the theory, or rather "story", of evolution.'

'That's sort of what we worked out, that women would have been created first.'

Mark gave another perspective.

'The legend of the Amazons perhaps.'

'It fits.'

'And how they would have interbred with the gods who created them, the Annunaki, to produce a hybrid species...'

It sparked me to fine tune my understanding.

'Or a bloodline, a *sang réal*, a royal lineage of rulership through the maternal bloodline, that was reinstated with the return of Nibiru, the return of the Annunaki, and the pharaonic lineage of the 18th Dynasty.'

Mark and Frank were unfamiliar with the term *sang réal*, so I briefly explained how it was a mistranslation of the original French term "san greal", or holy grail. As soon as I did, Frank had an almost instantaneous epiphany.

'Of course, the Templars weren't after an object, they were searching for the genetic clues to the origins of the human race, the bloodline.'

'We had a big discussion about them, the Knights of Templar, about the crusades, and what they found under Solomon's Temple and reburied under the Rosslyn Chapel in Scotland.'

'And what was that?'

'The original scrolls of the Essenes, of Jesus.'

'Is that all?'

'Well, they also found gold, which they used to become the richest merchants and moneylenders in the world. But, when Philip IV of France betrayed them to the Catholic Church in 1307, they were persecuted and fled France west to the east coast of America, or la Merica as it was known then, including the Caribbean, and north to Scotland. I don't know what they left in the Americas, but they buried the scrolls and the bodies of the Templars under the chapel in Scotland.'

'Oh, there's more to it than that.'

'There is?'

'Are you aware that the Templars became wealthy with what was termed "green gold"?'

'No, never heard of it; I've heard of mono-atomic gold, but that's a white powder.'

'No mono-atomic gold is a different issue all together; this is "green gold".'

'What's that?'

'Scientists have stated that gold would only turn a blue-green colour due to radiation over an extended period.'

'Solomon's temple was radioactive?'

'No, but what it was built *over* was.'

'What?'

'A nuclear reactor.'

'Seriously?'

'Sure, there is even evidence, scant though it my be, that the Templars who discovered the underground chambers beneath Solomon's Temple all became very sick, many, like Godfrey de Bouillon, dying not long after the crusade, supposedly of some unknown illness.'

'Radiation poisoning?'

'Exactly.'

'But a nuclear reactor?'

'With the shape of a labyrinth.'

That had me really confused.

'You mean like the Labyrinth at Hawarra?'

'No, this has a different, specific shape; a winding six-pathed image. The labyrinth design is almost identical to a cross-section of a six-chamber, rod-less, reflector-type, Russian designed reactor used in one of their spacecraft.'...'

He turned on the ipad.

'...I've got an image of it in here. The dimensions may have been about forty feet across, exactly what would be required for such a reactor to provide sufficient power to an Earth base as described by Zeccariah Sitchin....'

He handed me the ipad.

'...Here you go.'

'I've seen this image before, in backyard mazes at amusement parks, and marked out on the ground in stone pathways; New Age 'feather-wavers' think it has some sort of magical power, that if you walk it you go on some sort of meditative journey into the depth of your true self.'

'What do *you* think?'

'Whatever you think is your reality, right, so if you think it works, you'll create the outcome you desire, or maybe just convince yourself you have.'

'It's not the only place you'll find the image, flick to the next photo.'

'Where's that?'

'France; it's the floor of the Cathedral in Chartres, South France, a stronghold of the Knights of Templar.'

'So you think the Templars copied the image from a nuclear reactor underneath Solomon's Temple?'

'Where else?'

'In 1110 AD?'

'It all adds up that way.'

'A nuclear reactor underneath the present day Islamic Dome of the Rock?'

'Yes. Obviously it wasn't from then, but from an era way way before then. If you believe Zeccariah Sitchin, there was a nuclear war in Egypt in 2,024 BC.'

I was having my doubts, but then I remembered the Colossi back on the west bank at Luxor.

'Have you ever heard about the Colossi of Memnon, and how the quartzite on the northern side had transformed into tiny glass spheres?'

'Ah yes, the Colossi.'

I tried to remember what Bill had said.

'Bill, from the felucca, he's a geologist, he said something about the glass spheres being one thing or another depending on what caused their creation.'

'You mean impactite from a comet impact, or trinitite from a nuclear explosion?'

'That's it; do you know what's in the Colossi?'

'I do believe it's trinitite; and I think that's part of the evidence Sitchin based his claim on, that, and a housing project in India outside Deli where workers dug down a few feet and discovered a white ash with human bones.'

'Why is that significant?'

'The search area was expanded and it revealed an area of radioactive ash that covered three miles across, slightly less than the diameter of the blast area of Hiroshima.'

'Shit! That's a real Pandora's box.'

'Sure is.'

'But if the ground under Solomon's Temple was radioactive, why did the Essenes hide their scrolls and gold there?'

Mark had a thought.

'Maybe they weren't aware of the dangers?'

So did Frank.

'Or maybe they did; they knew the location was significant, but thought no one would go there.'

'Maybe both?'

In the meantime, I was thinking, given Christopher Dunne's suggestion the Great Pyramid was a power-plant generating free energy, why there would be a need for atomic power at all.

'In either case, the implication *is*, that given the Annunaki had advanced technologies and no need for nuclear power, sometime in the past, mankind had atomic power and we managed to blow each other to kingdom come.'

'It would appear that way.'

'Then, given Hiroshima and Nagasaki and the plethora of nuclear warheads aimed at just about everyone on the planet, we haven't learned much.'

Frank was more to the point.

'My biggest fear is that History has a big habit of repeating itself.'

The ominous atmosphere was broken by the distant appearance in the desert to the left of several pyramids, including the remarkable ruins of Amenemhat III's Black Pyramid and the distinctive shape of the Bent Pyramid; we were about to arrive at our destination.

Dahshur

'We're now about twenty miles south of the Giza Plateau, in the southern part of Saqqara. The Dahshur pyramids sit in the desert about two miles west of the actual village of Dahshur in an area of desert that up until 1996 was a military area.'

Frank wasn't telling me anything I didn't already know, but I guess he felt he had to assume the role of tour guide, as this was what might turn out to be my only visit. What it did do was get me thinking. Why would the Egyptian Military set up an 'off-limits' military zone in an area of desert that just happened to include numerous pyramids and tombs? I smelled a rat, or rather a venue of vultures, led by your friend and mine, the "saviour" and "protector" of the pharaohs, Zahi Hawass. Were they there to protect the pyramids, or rob them? I thought of the backpack on the seat beside me, and the wad of papers crammed inside; no doubt there were pages documenting what had happened here.

But maybe the vultures weren't as smart as they thought; maybe they didn't know what I knew, about the tsunamis, about needing to dig down more than forty-five to fifty feet. Maybe, just like at Hawarra back up the Nile, they'd believed the early Egyptologists and only scratched the surface. Maybe there were hidden treasures, buried deep below the sand, waiting to be unearthed?

As we turned off the road and headed towards them, Frank continued to fill me in on the 'official rhetoric' whereas I couldn't wait to look for real evidence.

'The area of Dahshur is one of the most important sites in Egypt, not just because it belonged to the vast necropolis of the ancient capital of Memphis, but more because of its importance in representing the various evolutionary phases in pyramid building, beginning with the 4th Dynasty pyramids of Snefru and ending with the 12th Dynasty monuments of Senwroset III, Amenemhat II and Amenemhat III.'

'That is if they really built them, and didn't just appropriate them or claim them as their own. Or worse still, they were assigned to them by the Egyptologists on some scant piece of evidence, just like at Medium and at Hawarra. For instance, I know there are 6th Dynasty pyramids down the road at Saqqara, but why aren't there any here, or are there?'

'I like your thinking, Alex. Well, we've got time to check them all out, so let's do it...'

The car pulled up at the ticket office and Frank handed me the ipad.

'...Here's a map so you can get your bearings. I'll get the tickets and be back in a minute.'

The first thing I noticed was really obvious, and I wondered why the so-called "experts" hadn't noticed it as well; all the 12th Dynasty pyramids were almost in a straight line and closer to the Nile, all approximately the same distance from what would have been the bank of the Nile during the 12th Dynasty.

On the other hand, the 4th Dynasty pyramids were further inland; suggesting the level of the Nile may well have been higher during the 4th Dynasty. As far as I knew, there were no tsunamis between 2650 BC and 1880 BC, and that added weight to the possibility the Red and Bent Pyramids weren't from the 4th Dynasty at all, but dated to a much earlier pre-tsunami era, perhaps that associated with the tsunami that buried the Osireion and the Labyrinth.

By the time Frank returned I was in full-on explorer mode.

'So, where to first?'

'How about the pyramid of Senwroset III?'

Frank was a little surprised.

'I'm pretty sure the inside won't be open, but we can have a look around.'

'Great. After that, let's go to Amenemhat II, the Red Pyramid, Bent Pyramid, and finish up with the Black Pyramid?'

Mark was nodding his head.

'Sounds interesting; Frank and I've never actually been to any of the 12th Dynasty pyramids here, so it'll be a first for all of us. Senwroset, here we come.'

The Pyramid of Senwroset III

The 5th pharaoh of the 12th Dynasty, of the Middle Kingdom, Khakhaure Senwroset III is considered to be perhaps the most powerful and important rulers of ancient Egyptian, one of the few pharaohs deified and honoured with a cult during their own lifetime. He ruled from 1878 BC to 1839 BC, although a papyrus in the Berlin Museum indicates Senwroset III initiated a co-regency with his son, Amenemhat III, in the twentieth year of his reign.

Located in the northeast corner of the Dahshur region, from a distance, the pyramid of Senwroset III was little more than a twenty-metre high mound of mud-brick, much like the pyramid at Hawarra, though this one had a hollowed-out centre that gave it the overall appearance of a miniature volcanic crater more than a pyramid.

We drove back down the access road from the ticket office, pulled off into the car park on the left, and hiked the remaining hundred metres or so across the desert to the site. Since we were all somewhat in the dark about what was before us, as we approached the complex I referred to the notes on my iphone, reading them out for the benefit of the others.

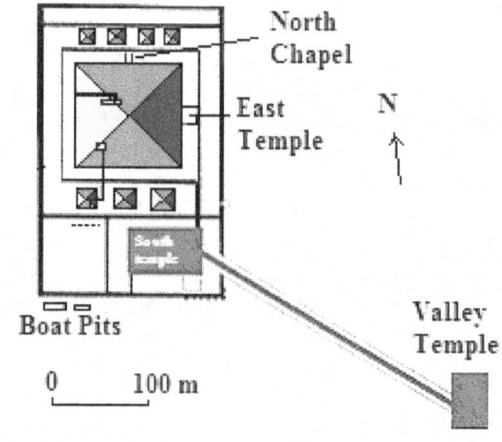

'The pyramid complex of Senwroset III was constructed in several phases. The original complex, which closely followed Old Kingdom prototypes, included the pyramid, a small mortuary temple to the east, and a stone inner enclosure wall.

A second, outer enclosure wall, made of brick, was added next. It surrounded six smaller pyramids, one for each of six royal women, with and an underground gallery with further burials for the royal women, and a seventh pyramid that served as the pharaoh's subsidiary or ka pyramid.

Later in Senwroset's reign, the pyramid complex was enlarged to the north and south with the addition of niched walls, transforming the originally square ground plan into an elongated rectangle. The larger southern extension contained the South Temple, which has since been destroyed, though it seems to have marked the appearance of a new building type in a royal pyramid complex, perhaps replacing or broadening the function of the traditional pyramid temple.'

Arriving at the site, the first thing we noticed was that there were clearly excavations still going on here, although it wasn't the digging season so no one was around. Despite that, there seemed to have been very little actual restoration of the site. We thought there was no one around until the local guardian magically appeared out of nowhere.

'Closed.'

I pretty much knew that was just an opening bid to negotiate a deal, but as I had no cash I was in no position to open the bidding. Frank and Mark had an even better strategy.

'Professor. Doctor Frank from University of Santa Barbara, USA, Doctor Alex and Doctor Mark from University of Melbourne, Australia.'

It was a little white lie, as we weren't professors, though each of us did have university qualifications. The guardian didn't care, he probably hadn't seen a foreigner in months, he simply brought his hands together in homage and did a small bow in our honour.

'Yes, Doctor, come.'

He led us to the southwest corner of the site.

'Boat, yes? In ground, yes?'

Before us were the almost completely filled in excavations of a few boat-pits.

'Near the southwest corner of the complex six wooded funerary boats were found buried in the sand, each of which was six metres long.'

Frank pondered the implications.

'Strange place to bury boats.'

On the other hand, Mark saw the correlation.

'Not really, six boats, six small pyramids, six princesses.'

I had other thoughts.

'What if they didn't bury them, what if this was a dock, or a mooring outside the complex, and the boats weren't buried by Senwroset III in the 12th Dynasty but buried by the tsunami at the end of the 17th Dynasty?'

Mark just raised an eyebrow.

'Buried by the tsunami,…in neat little arrangements? Alex, I think you've been out in the sun too long; you're starting to sound like an Egyptologist, ignoring the actual evidence and stating, as fact, wild assumptions based on your theories? Besides, wouldn't it depend how deep they found them buried?'

Mark was right, I was doing exactly what I was critical of the "experts" doing. On the other hand, Frank was still pondering.

'Still, it's a strange place to bury boats.'

'Not as strange as northern England.'

'What?'

Frank suddenly had a quizzical look all over his face.

'You don't know about the ancient Egyptian sea-going boats buried in a bog somewhere in Northern England?'

'No.'

'What about Scota?'

'Scotland? There are boats there as well?'

'Not Scotland, Scota; she was the daughter of a 15th Dynasty Hyksos pharaoh, married to a Minoan prince called Milesius, and supposedly a contemporary of Moses. Bill and I figured out that Scota must have been Herit, daughter of Apopi, and forced to flee the advancing armies of Seqenenre's son, Kamose. Somehow she survived the Thera eruption and subsequent tsunami that obliterated Egypt, and made her way first to Spain and then on to Ireland. From there it's not hard to see how the boats finished up in northern England.'

The look on Mark's face said it all.
'That's fascinating! It sounds like the script for a Hollywood movie.'
'Truth is stranger than fiction, that's for sure.'

Frank was more pragmatic.
'Shall we dig deeper, or sail on?'
'Hoist the mainsail.'

We went to move on, beyond the line of the exterior wall, the base of which had been partially reconstructed, but something struck me as unusual.
'That's bizarre, it's nothing like the outer, niched walls at El-Kab or Dendera.'
'What do you mean?'
'Well, these are more …stylised; the others are made of mud-brick and far less formally designed and structured.'

Frank gave the answer…
'They're almost identical to the wall designs just up the road at Saqqara.'

…but that raised even more questions.
'But isn't Saqqara Old Kingdom; 5th and 6th Dynasties? '
'And earlier.'
'So what's an Old Kingdom wall doing surrounding a Middle Kingdom pyramid?'

Frank got it straight away.
'Well, either they're reconstructing it incorrectly, or, the dating of the pyramid or central part of the site is wrong.'
'I think that's what's happened at Hawarra and Meidum, and I think it may be possible here as well.'
'Then let's move on and see what else we can find to support it.'

To the right, were the partially reconstructed remains of the outline of a temple that once stood to the south of the pyramid. This would once probably have consisted of a forecourt with papyrus-stemmed columns followed by a covered, possibly hypostyle hall containing the actual sanctuary. However, there was no way of identifying the temple, let alone to what Dynasty it belonged.

There would also have been a causeway connecting the south temple to what would have been a Valley Temple or maybe even a dock on the Nile, but it has not been explored and, like at Medium, probably still lay there in ruin fifteen to twenty feet below the surface, waiting to reveal its secrets.

The foundations of a second, interior enclosure wall, a square one that surrounded the pyramid, also embraced the bases of what were once three small pyramids that ran along the south wall of the pyramid, and several shaft tombs supposedly for the women of the royal family.
'Tomb of queen, Weret.'

The guardian was pointing towards the westernmost of what remained of the three small pyramids, then underground and towards the main pyramid. I checked the notes.

'In 1994 a shaft was found in the western most of these tombs that led to a tunnel which in turn led to an antechamber, burial chamber and canopic chamber, all located under the southwest corner of the king's pyramid. A granite sarcophagus filled the western end of the burial chamber, as well as fragments of a canopic jar found bearing the name of Khnumetneferhedjetweret (Weret), who was the wife of Senwroset II and the mother of Senwroset III.'

Frank was looking back and forward between the two pyramids.

'Sounds to me like the tomb may have been built first, with the pyramid built on top later.'

'Maybe the pyramid was built by Senwroset II.'

'Makes sense.'

'But still Middle Kingdom.'

'True.'

The seeds of doubt planted in all our minds, the guardian led us around to the eastern side of the pyramid, where, according to my notes, there was originally a small mortuary temple. There was nothing; it was in such a state of ruin we couldn't make out anything of the floorplan, except sand. That didn't mean there was nothing there, just that we couldn't see anything. There was always the possibility there was something beneath the surface. How far, that was the question.

'The temple may have comprised an offering hall with a granite false door, storage magazines and an entrance chamber. Wall fragments show the decorations were executed in high relief, bearing the royal name and titles, with scenes of deities moving towards the king, the king enthroned before an offering table with rows of offering bearers, officials and the slaughter of cattle.'

The mention of a granite false door gave me an indication the temple may even have been a reconstruction of an earlier structure. Optimistically, Mark was looking for some trace of it.

'You'd think there'd be something left.'

'Not if it was swept away by a tsunami.'

'True.'

The northern side of the pyramid had a similar arrangement of small pyramids to the southern side, although there were four of them here, and they were in slightly better shape. There were also the ruins of a small chapel.

'Tomb of many princess.'

The guardian was again pointing to the opening of a shaft in the ground near the first small pyramid. Thankfully, my notes were quite detailed.

'North of the pyramid are more shaft tombs for some of the women of the royal family. The gallery of tombs located here is more complex, arranged in two galleries.

At least four of the tombs in the upper gallery probably had superstructures in the form of a pyramid. Under these galleries, a principal shaft provided access to a long vaulted corridor connecting four sets of chambers, each built to hold a sarcophagus and canopic chest. There were also one or two niches in the walls.

Below this was a second level where a corridor connected with eight niches containing sarcophagi, two of which were inscribed. One carried the name of a woman named Merit, perhaps both his daughter and wife, and the other Senet-senebti, who may have been princesses. In addition, archaeologist also found some splendid jewellery, as well as other items of the women's burial equipment, belonging to a princess Sit-Hathor, probably a sister and wife of Senwroset III.'

291

By now, possibly because of his legal background, Mark had a far more questioning attitude.

'What if all these women weren't so much related to Senwroset III, as to his father, Senwroset II?'

'What do you mean?'

'Well, as far as I can see, the only evidence linking Senwroset III to *this* pyramid is a few fragmentary reliefs from the remains of the eastern temple. But if that temple was built after the pyramid, then the pyramid could have belonged to his father, Senwroset II.'

'Especially as the Egyptologists believe there is a sophisticated funerary complex for Senwroset III at Abydos.'

'That would make the royal women in the tombs, daughters and wives of Senwroset II, which would make sense if Weret was a wife of Senwroset II, and Senwroset III's mother.'

'So Senwroset III could just have added a temple to his father's pyramid?'

'It wouldn't be the first time.'

Frank took it a step, or rather a giant leap, further.

'What if all these women weren't directly related to either of the Senwrosets?'

'How do you figure that, Frank?'

'Well, we have the names, Weret, Merit, Senet-senebti, and Sit-Hathor, from the tombs below the ground, and we have the name Senwroset III from a fragment on the east temple above the ground, but what do we have linking the two? Isn't is possible the Egyptologists found the name of Senwroset III on a fragment of the temple, assigned the pyramid to him, then assigned each subsequent name discovered below the ground to him as well?'

'It's possible.'

'Then isn't it just as possible they made a mistake and the names under the ground belong to another Dynasty, possibly even the Old Kingdom?'

'It sure is.'

'My guess the answer lies below ground level and possibly in the main burial chamber.'

We made our way around to the western side and for the first time turned our attention to the main pyramid itself.

'*The pyramid of Senwroset III measures one-hundred-five metres at the base and, from the angle of 56°18'35" determined from some of the original casing blocks that were found, once rose to a height of some 78 metres.*

Built with a bottom course on a foundation of three courses of mud-bricks and directly on the desert gravel, which contributed to the instability of the monument, Senwroset had abandoned the structural framework of earlier 12th Dynasty pyramids, and instead constructed his pyramid with an inner core of mud-bricks of inconsistent sizes, laid in stepped horizontal courses and without mortar to hold them together. The whole core was then encased in limestone blocks joined together with dovetail-shaped cramps.'

I knew Frank would be on to it.

'That doesn't sound like a step forward, it sounds more consistent with an 11th Dynasty structure, or even an Old Kingdom approach.'

It didn't take long before the guardian was pointing out another tomb.

'Tomb of King, enter here, go under ground into pyramid.'

The entrance to the pyramid was located in front of the western face, near the northern corner. That in itself was an anomaly, the entrances were usually *in* the wall of the pyramid, not before and under it, and usually in the northern wall. It lent support to the possibility the tomb predated the pyramid that sat above it.

'The entrance was found hidden under the courtyard pavement west of the pyramid, near the northwest corner. From there, a vertical shaft dropped to a descending corridor that led off to the east and under the pyramid, finally turning south and arriving first at an antechamber, with a small annex to the east, called a serdab, reminiscent of many Old Kingdom pyramids, and then on to the burial chamber to the west. Interestingly, the tomb had no corridor barriers.'

Once again Frank was a step ahead.

'That definitely sounds like the tomb and passageways were here before the pyramid; first a descending passage, the burial chamber must sit below ground level. And no barriers?'

Mark and I agreed. All that was left was to explore the chamber itself to confirm our thoughts. Alas, not even the almighty power of the baksheesh god could gain us entry and we were forced to rely on my notes.

'Apart from the burial chamber, which was made of granite and covered in a thin layer of white stucco, or gypsum, elsewhere in the substructure, the floors, ceiling walls and false door are covered in cheaper limestone and painted with red and black dots to resemble the more expensive and durable pink granite.'

Was that a clue that the burial chamber was built even earlier than the antechamber and passages, and not as a tomb? It did appear that may have been the case. The appearance of the antechamber concerned me as well, sure there had been some restoration work done, but it was the absence of any barriers and any funerary texts or hieroglyphs that had me doubting it was a passageway in a tomb. I'd seen numerous Middle Kingdom 'tombs' now, and they had plenty of reliefs. This was bare.

Could the antechamber and passages be Old Kingdom or even pre-Dynastic? It was certainly a possibility. Perhaps the 'burial' chamber had all the answers?

My first thoughts when I looked at the image of the 'burial' chamber were that is was remarkably *un*impressive. Then I had a thought; why would you go to the trouble of building a passageway and antechamber of limestone, then paint it to look like red granite, when you have just built a main chamber of red granite and covered it in gypsum; that doesn't add up?

Mark added to the mystery.

'Why would you cover a chamber made of polished red granite in the first place, and if you did cover it in gypsum, why wouldn't you decorate it?'

'Something doesn't add up, that's for sure.'

'The burial chamber is some distance from the vertical axes of the pyramid, and was found as good as empty, raising the question of whether the king was actually buried here. Despite that, a marvellous, yet empty, red granite sarcophagus stood against the west wall.

Like those of a number of future 12th Dynasty rulers, it had fifteen niches along its side, often referred to as a palace façade, in imitation of the Djoser Step Pyramid enclosure wall at Saqqara. In the south wall was a niche for a canopic chest while the north wall had a blocked opening that once led back into the antechamber.'

Frank had first crack at it.

'You know, I think it's Old Kingdom; the pattern is the give away, same with the outer enclosure wall, they match perfectly with the designs at Saqqara.'

Mark agreed.

'I don't think the sarcophagus original sat against the wall either, I think it once sat around the other way, longways, in the centre of the room, I think that's what the room was made for, and that way the canopic niche is perfectly in line with the sarcophagus.'

I was still contemplating the gypsum.

'But why cover the room with gypsum and then not decorate it?'

'Maybe they did it to cover images that were already there?'

Mark had opened a Pandora's box.

'And maybe it wasn't done millennia ago, maybe it was done as part of the "restoration"?'

'What are you getting at, Alex?'

'What if it had something to do with why they declared this a military zone for so long?'

'Now *that's* interesting.'

Being the engineer he was, Frank had another answer.

'Maybe they covered the room with gypsum to seal it.'

'Seal it?'

'If it wasn't to paint it, it maybe it was to seal it. I can't tell from your photo, but the only logical reason could be that the granite was somehow cracked and they used the gypsum to seal the surface.'

It was Mark who asked the obvious.

'Why would they need it sealed?'

'Good question; functionality, if it was filled with water, or was a resonance chamber of some sort.'

'Either of which could be relevant if it was a power station.'

'Yep.'

'What about the antechamber and passage?'

'I think, like the gypsum, they were probably added later, most likely during the Middle Kingdom. Is there any more information?'

'*Above the false vaulted ceiling of the burial chamber was a second, stress-relieving chamber with a gabled roof built of five pairs of limestone beams each weighing 30 tons. Above this was a third mud-brick vault.*'

'Five pairs of limestone beams each weighing thirty tons? And they built the rest with mud-brick? I don't think so.'

'So what do you reckon?'

'I think the original chamber and the gabled roof above it was built first, the limestone passage later, and the pyramid was built on top even later, probably during the early Middle Kingdom, with the final addition being the east temple of Senwroset III in the 12th Dynasty.'

It all made sense, but I had even more questions.

'What about the other tombs? It says here, "*The plan of the apartments under Senwroset III's pyramid closely follows those built by the pharaohs of late 5th and early 6th Dynasties*".'

'I think that confirms it; the other tombs must belong to the Old Kingdom, and all those names must belong to the royal woman of a 5th or 6th Dynasty pharaoh.'

'And the whole kit and kaboodle was washed away by the Thera tsunami.'

'So it would appear.'

OK. So much for an obscure and "unimportant" pyramid.

'I wonder if we'll find a similar story at the White Pyramid, which supposedly belongs to Senwroset III's grandfather, Amenemhat II?'

Mark laughed.

'Why not, I think we've totally deconstructed this pyramid.'

He gave the guardian a rather generous thank you and we returned to the car, where we all paused for a drink of water.

'If the pyramid of Amenemhat II is anything like the one we've just seen, then it should give us even more evidence to set the cat amongst the pigeons.'

Our thirsts replenished, we followed the map south, crossing the road and looking out over the desert.

'It may not be as easy as we think.'

The Pyramid of Amenemhat II

As the others looked at the ruins before us, I read from my notes.

'*The son of Senwroset I, Nubkhaure Amenemhat II was the third pharaoh of the 12th Dynasty. He ruled for thirty-five years, from 1929 BC to 1895 BC, but, apart from that, not much is known of his reign, nor of his pyramid, which is very badly documented and has had almost no research done at the site. Not even the base of the pyramid has been cleared for a proper measuring, therefore we are not sure of its size, the angle of its slope, or its height.*'

'That doesn't sound very promising.'

'We might as well do a lap and have a look around.'

As we did I scanned my notes for more information.

'*In its time, the pyramid was most likely called "Amenemhat is well cared for", or "Amenemhat Provides", though now it is called the "White Pyramid", a name derived from the many white Tura limestone chips left behind from when stone thieves stole the casing stones.*'

We headed west, looking to circumnavigate the site, hoping to find something relevant, something other than sand and mounds of limestone chips, to speculate on, though it seemed the greatest source of information was proving to be my notes.

'*All that exists is a very crude map, which is very likely incomplete and inaccurate. From it, the entire complex was surrounded by a rectangular enclosure wall running east-west, reminiscent of the enclosure wall surrounding the complex of Netjerikhet at Saqqara.*'

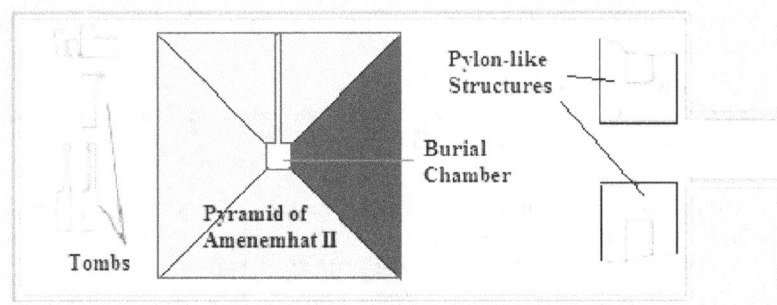

Frank was looking for the slightest clue.

'Now if the wall was the same as the one we just saw across the road, then that would strongly link it to the Old Kingdom.'

Alas, the problem was, everything was covered in sand. Any exploration that had been done here was over a hundred years ago, and the sands of time had well-and-truly reclaimed the site.

Mark started looking for depressions in the sand that could be tomb shafts filled with sand.

'Do you think the Egyptologists could have made the same mistake here?'

'It's possible.'

We weren't having much success and quickly wandered behind the pyramid, around to the east side where the mortuary temple, most probably called "Lighted is the place of Amenemhat's pleasures", was located. It was almost completely destroyed, though it was yet to be closely examined. Scratching and scuffing around in the sand, looking for clues, we found numerous fragments of buildings, some of which included relief decorations.

Of even more interest were the remnants of the massive, tower-like structures, possibly the foundations of a pylon, in the temple's east facade.

'What do you think, Frank, 18th Dynasty?'

'Noooo, it looks more like the 5th Dynasty structures at Saqqara; Old Kingdom definitely.'

Beyond the pylon, it was possible to make out the broad, steep slope of the causeway that would have led down to a Valley temple or a dock, but the cultivated area adjacent to the Nile had encroached significantly and the ruins of any temple was now buried beneath it, probably at least fifteen feet below it.

We completed our lap and turned to the pyramid, artistically framed with the Bent Pyramid in the background.

As it stood, the pyramid's base measured roughly fifty metres by fifty metres, but, as no casing stones have ever been found, and without knowing the angle of the faces, it was impossible to estimate what its original height would have been. It was highly possible, as there hadn't been any serious exploration done here, that there were some casing stones perhaps two or three metres below the surface, but, as it stood, the pyramid was little more than a scattered pile of rubble.

Despite the lack of investigation here, the 'experts' still claimed they knew all about it; were they just speculating as usual and claiming it as fact?

'*The building technique of the pyramid is fairly typical for the Middle Kingdom: the core was made with a framework of horizontal lines of white limestone blocks to form a grid, a skeleton of walls, with corners radiating out. The compartments between the walls were then filled with sand and the entire pyramid encased in white limestone.*'

Frank said it succinctly.

'That's possible, but without excavating and confirming it as fact, it's really just a guess. Anyway, I'm more interested in what's inside.'

So were Mark and I.

'"*Little research has been done on the pyramid, so we only have a very sketchy idea of its internal structure. The entrance is in the middle of the north face and was covered by a north chapel.*" There's not even a north chapel on the map!'

We walked right up to the base of the north face; not only couldn't we make out the semblance of a north chapel, couldn't spot the entrance either.

'*From the entrance a descending corridor built of limestone blocks leads into the pyramid. The corridor has a false, flat ceiling, atop which is a gabled ceiling made of limestone slabs leaning one against the other. The corridor levels out, before arriving first at a barrier made of two granite portcullis slabs, one of which slid vertically in to place, and the other sideways, before reaching the burial chamber.*'

As Mark and I examined the cross-section, Frank started musing.

'The gabled corridor is interesting.'

It jogged my memory as well.

'I don't know how big the corridor is, but I've seen a similar gabled limestone passage leading to the Osireion at Abydos, and that had to be from the Old or Middle Kingdom at least.'

'Yeah, but the granite doors would indicate it's inconsistent with the corridors in Senwroset III's pyramid, and yet this is supposed to pre-date it by maybe forty or fifty years; no matter what way you look at it, that doesn't add up.'

'Just after the second barrier, but before the entrance to the burial chamber itself, there is a square shaft about 2 metres deep that leads to a corridor that returns back underneath the entrance corridor beyond the two granite barriers above. There is a pit at the end of this lower corridor, which was probably intended for the canopic chest…'

Mark was dubious.

'That doesn't sound right?'

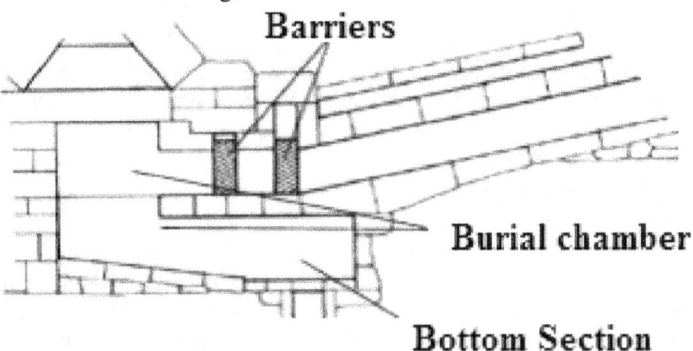

Barriers

Burial chamber

Bottom Section

'…It is not known if the burial chamber and subterranean corridor are located inside the core of the pyramid, or below the ground, although what is known is the burial chamber is oriented east-west and located on the vertical axis of the pyramid. Within the walls are four niches, including one on either short wall and two on the wall opposite the entrance, but it is not known if these niches were used for statues, or offerings. There was also a large quartzite sarcophagus found set in the floor against the west wall of the burial chamber.'

Mark followed up on his doubts.

'See, why put the canopic chest in a drain when there are niches in the walls, like the one in Senwroset's chamber? The pit must have been for something else.'

Frank had other thoughts.

'There *are* certain similarities between the two main chambers of the two pyramids, especially if this one is below the ground level of the pyramid, It might lend support to them being built independently before the pyramid. As to the sarcophagus being against the west wall, for all we know it may have been shifted. Without a proper investigation, we're really just guessing.'

Although Frank was eager to find the truth, thankfully his pragmatic analytical attitude prevented him from running off and turning assumptions and guesses into facts, which also kept Mark and I from becoming the latest graduates of the Speculative University of Egyptologists.

'Anything else?'

'The burial chamber, like the entrance corridor, also has a false flat ceiling topped by a more structurally-sound gabled ceiling made of huge limestone slabs that lean against one another to spread the weight of the masonry above.'

Frank looked at the pile of rubble before him.

'It hasn't been investigated properly, how do they know that? But, if it is the case, then it again raises the question of if the gabled ceiling was functional in terms of supporting and diverting the weight of the mud-bricks above it, which I doubt, or if the gabled stones had some other functional purpose relative to what was occurring in the chamber below it.'

'What are you getting at?'

'If the gabled ceiling had another space above it, with either another gabled ceiling, or a mud-brick ceiling, then only the top ceiling would actually bare any weight, so it's a mockery to think the lower ceiling had any structural purpose related to supporting what was above them. So, what if the gabled stones were designed not to relieve pressure from above, but from within?'

'Like a safety valve?'

'Exactly.'

'How?'

'Pressure builds up inside the chamber, maybe because of a chemical reaction, or water pressure, steam, even sonic vibration, when it reaches a certain pressure it forces the gabled stones to lift, thus creating a space between the centre of them allowing the pressure to dissipate.'

'Fuck, that's brilliant.'

'Rudimental actually, at least for an engineer; I'm surprised I didn't think of it earlier. Actually, I'm surprised anyone hasn't thought of it earlier.'

Frank was justifiably pleased with himself; he had the sort of look on his face that you'd see from a cat who'd just licked the cream off the top of the cow's milk. In fact, I got the impression Frank considered this discovery topped his achievements with Howard Hughes and NASA, or it at least ranked up there with them. But Frank was not one to dwell on his achievements; he wanted to see where they led.

'Right then, let's see how that impacts on the other pyramids.'

That said, Frank started striding off through the desert sands back to the car. Mark and I looked at each other.

'That one concept may turn the history of Egyptology on its head.'

'Or see it decapitated.'

We both knew the implications and, quickly putting them on the backburner, set off to catch up with Frank. A few minutes later we were motoring back up the road to the Red Pyramid.

'So Frank, what's your thinking? Power station?'

'If it looks like a duck, walks like a duck and quacks like a duck...'

'Then it's a vulture.'

'Huh.'

They both looked at me, totally bemused.

'It's a long story! But, given this was once a military zone, I bet Muburak and Zahi Hawass are somehow involved...'

Having just removed the backpack from my back, and placed it on the seat beside me, I picked it back up again; with every location I visited, the contents seemed to gain in weight.

'...And I bet there's something about it in these papers.'

'Then we'd better get them safely to Cairo, and out of the country.'
'What about me?'
'Let's let the Embassy deal with that....'

Suddenly I felt like Julian Assange, seeking sanctuary wherever I could find it.
'...Relax, Alex, you'll be fine.'

Relax? How could I relax when the target on my back was growing bigger every second? Not only that, I was deliberately heading further into a military zone. Well, what, until seventeen years ago, *was* a military zone.

Minutes later we pulled up beside the next stop on our itinerary.

The Red Pyramid

'Now *that's* a pyramid.'

Supposedly built by Snefru (2575-2551 BC), founder of the 4th Dynasty, the pyramid, whose ancient name was probably 'Snefru Shines', apparently derived its modern name from the colour of the special kind of rosette limestone used in constructing the pyramid's inner burial chamber. That made no sense at all because most of the pyramids had red-granite inner chambers. For me, it was because the original white limestone casing blocks were gone, and the high iron-stone content of the rough-hewn sandstone core blocks that adorned the surface now, formed a tough oxidized ruddy layer on the surface of the pyramid.

Though he'd obviously been here before, Mark had a different perspective and was keen to investigate.
'Well lads, in, or around?'

I had a quick check of the schematic.
'Let's do a lap of honour first.'
'Clockwise or anticlockwise?'
'Western time or Egyptian time?'
'Huh?'
'Never mind; private joke. Let's head right.'

As we headed off, Frank continued with his role of tour guide.
'The Red Pyramid is the third largest pyramid in Egypt; each side of the base being just over seven-hundred-twenty feet. It was built at an angle of forty-three degrees; that gave it an original height of about three-hundred-forty-five feet, although it's lost around nineteen feet, partly because of the loss of the outer casing of limestone, and partly because of the missing pyramidion that once sat on top, which now sits restored in the ruins of the mortuary temple to the east. What's of particular interest is that each of

the faces is not flat, they are all concave.'

I'd actually done my research, but having someone spell it out to you as you were taking it in with your own eyes in person was a different matter; it gave me a chance to look, listen, and more importantly, think.

'Concave? Usually when surfaces are curved, like a parabola, it's to focus the energy or vibration to a particular focal point. But concave, that would work the other way within the internal structure, dissipating the energy?'

'Any answers?'

'No, but maybe we'll find some when we head inside.'

I kicked the sand and looked at the western face.

'Do you think there's anything below us?'

'Apart from Hell?'

'Yeah, something more concrete.'

'Or granite?'

'Exactly.'

Mark chimed in.

'Your tsunami theory?'

'I was just wondering how far the pyramid really goes down: where the base really is? That would give an indication what period it was built.'

Frank continued.

'Dates found in builders' marks on some of the blocks indicate it took ten years and seven months to build, and, once completed, it supposedly became the "blueprint" for all the pyramids that appeared during the 4th, 5th, and 6th Dynasties.'

'But what if the marks only represent when the blocks were quarried; they could have sat around for years? And what if those blocks weren't used to build the pyramid at all, but rather to repair it thousands of years after it was first built? Who knows, maybe it took ten years to repair?'

Mark coined it succinctly with a poignant Australian colloquialism.

'If that's the case, then the dating is all up the creek.'

'We might find some answers on the east side, at the mortuary temple.'

For a septuagenarian Frank was as fit as a fiddle and Mark and I raced to catch up as he motored around the south side, the Bent Pyramid beckoning in the distance.

'Frank, you were saying in your book that a sibyl was a stone with super-destructive capabilities and the power to communicate. Would that include crystals?'

'Of course, I used to have a crystal radio in the 50's; every kid on the block did. Why?'

'When I was talking on the felucca, Randy came up with the idea that Joseph, or Moses, stole a sacred source of power or something, and then fled Egypt with it in the Ark of the Covenant. Do you think that could have been a sibyl?'

'I'm sure of it.'

'Do you think it could have been stolen from inside one of the pyramids, the Great Pyramid for instance?'

Like he'd suddenly been turned into a pillar of salt, Frank stopped in his tracks.

'Brilliant! Christopher Dunne talks of the very thing in *'The Giza Powerplant'*; of a massive crystal sitting inside the sarcophagus inside the King's Chamber. But the sarcophagus wasn't a sarcophagus at all, never was, it was a resonating box, a chamber within a chamber, used to concentrate and amplify the resonance. Somehow the crystal was tuned to that frequency and would vibrate in sympathy emanating charge, or power, and god knows what else.

But Dunne didn't connect it to Moses and the Ark of the Covenant though. In fact it's more than just coincidental that, if the Ark were placed inside the granite box inside the King's Chamber of the Great Pyramid, it would fit perfectly.

Of course Moses stole it; if Moses was Joseph, and Apopi's vizier, he would have known exactly what was in the pyramid, it's power, and known how to get in, and had access. He simply wandered in and stole it, taking it with him on his so-called Exodus; it all fits perfectly.'

'And then?'

'If he took it back to Jerusalem he may have tried to use it in the nuclear reactor as some sort of control rod, or focusing element; hence why you build a sacred temple over the top.'

'Do you think it's still there, the crystal, I mean?'

'Who knows, according to reports in 983 BC Pharaoh Sheshonq attacked Jerusalem and removed the Ark back to the land of the Nile.'

'To Elephantine Island, the city of Yebu, and then it supposedly went to Ethiopia.'

Mark chipped in the final piece of the puzzle.

'Until it reappeared in *"Indiana Jones and the Temple of Doom"* and is now locked away in a CIA warehouse.'

We all had a good chuckle as we turned the corner to the east side.

This was the apparent site of Snefru's mortuary temple. It appeared to have been totally ruined, not dismantled, which was consistent with my tsunami theory, although I wasn't sure about the layers of sediment, so the bulk of the temple could have still been fifteen to twenty feet under the sand.

'Snefru's mortuary temple seems likely to have been hastily completed after the king's death. A plan of the temple has been reconstructed from the scant remains, which included a fragment of a pink granite false door stela, fragments of a sed-festival relief and remains of mud-brick store-rooms.'

A pink-granite false door? Was that borrowed from an earlier, flattened temple? And mud-brick store rooms, they seemed more in keeping with the post Thera tsunami and the possibly the New Kingdom, or even Ptolemaic era. In any case, it was from the fragments of the temple found here that they had 'tagged' the pyramid as belonging to Snefru, however, as was becoming all to evident, the temple could have been added hundreds, even thousands, of years after the pyramid was first constructed.

There'd been some restoration work done, but had they simply taken a few surviving fragments and reconstructed them based on what they 'thought' the floor plan would have been based on other temples, but fifteen to twenty feet *above* where it would have once been?

Looking around, as with the other pyramids, though it was almost impossible to define, were the remains of what would once have been a rectangular perimeter wall that enclosed the whole complex. To the east, there were also faint indications of a sloped causeway that would have led down to a valley temple.

Turning back towards the pyramid, situated on a modern plinth in the middle of the 'restoration', was a reconstructed pyramidion, or capstone, uncovered nearby, and supposedly belonging to the Red Pyramid. Mark joined me in contemplating it.

'The problem is, it's got a different angle of slope to that of the pyramid, which to me suggests it wasn't originally meant for this pyramid.'

'Me too; just like at Hawarra. It seems to be a common oversight by the majority of Egyptologists.'

'Any thoughts?'

'It's possible that when the tsunamis struck the pyramids the capstones were dislodged and tumbled across the landscape for who knows how far, perhaps up to hundreds of miles? Maybe if the experts do a simple comparison of pyramidion angles to pyramid angles, irrespective of their respective location, they may come to different conclusions, and if that evidence is forthcoming, it may give great weight not only to the tsunami theory, but to the extent of its impact.'

Mark was running it through his mind, nodding in agreement.

'That's an interesting concept.'

'And look at that!...'

I pointed at some of the original fine, Tura limestone, casing stones that were still present along the base of the pyramid.

'...That's consistent with the effects of the tsunami, or tsunamis; impacting from the north and removing all of the north face but leaving lower parts of the sides and back.'

Frank and Mark took a second look, before Frank nodded his head.

'I've never thought of that before; you may well be right.'

We made our way back around to the north side and I stood for a moment at ground level, taking in the entrance, hacked out of the face. There was a layer of rubble measuring about fifteen metres that was built up in front of the pyramid; clearly that indicated the actual base of the pyramid was way below the surface.

I walked up the sandy path and then started climbing the pyramid itself up to the entrance; at least another twenty metres up the face. No freebies here; the guardian was waiting at the entrance, ripped the corners of our tickets, and we took our first steps into the pyramid.

Just like at Meidum, the passage was narrow, low, and steep, about three feet in height, four feet wide, and about sloping downwards at an angle of around twenty-seven degrees. And it was long, very long, over sixty metres long. That may not seem that far to most people, but to someone over six foot tall it was a challenge to the back and hamstrings, not to mention avoiding cracking your head on the ceiling every few steps. To anyone with claustrophobia, it would have been a nightmare.

At the bottom of the passage was a short, low corridor that we had to hunch over and scuttle along. If these pyramids were tombs then they must have been built by a wayward tribe of pygmies, or maybe Snow White's dwarves on steroids. And anyone who had just been where I'd been, and honestly believed the ancient Egyptians built this as a tomb and then moved a ten-ton sarcophagus down the steep entrance passage and along this claustrophobic corridor, needed their head read.

Thankfully we arrived at the first antechamber, so I could discard my atrocious rendition of the Hunchback of Notre Dame. The place reeked of ammonia.

'Christ, what a pong!'

'It's from the bat shit, that or the stuff they used to get rid of the bats.'

The chamber was about forty feet high, with a corbel-vaulted ceiling of eleven courses.

'It's the same as at Medium, just bigger and better finished; there must've been some functional reasoning for this design?'

'Of course, to support the weight of the pyramid.'

Frank was being totally sarcastic, he knew as well as I did that that explanation was lame to say the least, and inconsistent with the evidence in other pyramids.

In the corner was a narrow low rectangular passage that led to the second antechamber, 'tagged' with graffiti of the names of 19th and early 20th Century explorers. The second antechamber was very similar in size and construction to the first, with another high, corbelled ceiling made of large blocks of fine white limestone.

'This chamber is in line with the vertical axis and lies directly beneath the apex of the pyramid.'

'There must be something to it.'

'You would think so.'

At the southern end of the second chamber was a modern wooden staircase that rose about eight metres above the floor level.

'After you.'

Frank and Mark were standing back allowing me to take the lead. Maybe they were using me as a guinea pig to see if the rickety structure was stable enough to support us all at once. As they slowly followed, forming a sort of reverent procession, I felt like I was walking up the stairs to the gallows.

Arriving at the top, I could see our objective; the stairs led to another entrance, this one high up in the southern wall of the chamber.

'This makes absolutely no sense if this is supposed to be a tomb.'

Frank just laughed.

'None at all. Keep going.'

The entrance led into another short, low corridor and finally a modern wooden bridge that spanned a third chamber, the burial chamber. The burial chamber was oriented east to west, with another high vaulted ceiling rising about forty-five feet above the floor. It certain places, treasure hunters, who had obviously made their way to the 'burial' chamber only to find it empty, had obviously blasted away parts of the walls and floor hoping to find some hidden passage or chamber. Apart from the three of us standing on the bridge, there was nothing, no sarcophagus, nothing.

For some reason I thought of Crystal, and what she would do in here. Then I realized she *wouldn't* be in here, it wasn't part of her purpose; she was focused on the temples and altars. But, if she were here, what would she suggest to me?

'*Feel the stone.*'

I placed my hands on the wall and closed my eyes; it was a long shot, but I tried to hook up with Nemo. At first he was nowhere to be seen, although I got the feeling that not only was the rock old, but so was the pyramid, just like the Osireion. Maybe it was just the effect of the ammonia, but there was a weird feeling here, like something had gone wrong. Eventually Nemo appeared in the distance, shaking his head, not venturing to come close. He reminded me of the fish in the water near the Fukushima nuclear disaster; this was not a good place to be. I opened my eyes and took my hands off the rock.

'Hey, Frank, has anyone done any tests in here for residual radioactivity?'

'Radioactivity? I don't think so. I know they've done all sorts of tests inside the Great Pyramid, though I'm not sure if they've tested it for radioactivity; but I don't think they've done any tests in here. Why? Do you think a Geiger counter might be in order?'

'Who knows? What I do know, is I think I'm done in here.'

Lots of stuff was going through my mind as we made our way out of the chamber, down the staircase, out through the second chamber, and up the descending passage. With each step I yearned for the sweet smell of fresh air.

It was like hitting an oven as we stepped out of the pyramid, but at least the air was fresh. A few deep breaths cleared my lungs and cleared my thinking. That is, until Mark dropped a bombshell.

'Well, so much for the Draco pyramid.'

I couldn't believe what I'd heard him say.

'Did you say Draco?'

'Yep, there's some thought that the Red Pyramid corresponds to Thuban in the constellation of Draco, and, as you may or may not know, 'thuban' in Arabic means snake.'

There had to be a connection.

'I don't suppose you know about a reptilian race from there, the Dracos?'

Mark laughed.

'Now you've done it!'

As we set off down the north face of the pyramid and back to the car, Frank started musing, and it was clear this was something Frank loved to do.

'You're talking about the Alpha Draconians; now I've never actually had an encounter with them, but when I was at NASA I heard lots of whispers about them being in the lower levels of the DUMBS.'

'Dumbs?'

'Deep Underground Military Bases; the reptilians have a major presence on the lower levels there.'

'I've never heard of them.'

'They're all over the planet, mainly in the US, and connected by a vast tunnel system using high velocity magnetic transports that can take you from one side of the country to the other, or to another continent in an hour or so.'

'No way!'

'You don't know the half of it.'

'And these DUMBS are run by reptilians, by the Dracos?'

'I wouldn't say "run" by them, but certainly they dictate many of the agendas.'

'So they've been cooperating with NASA and the Military?'

'They don't cooperate with anyone; they're just using humans like lab animals.'

'If they're so advanced, why don't they just take over?'

'They already have.'

'What do you mean?'

'Well, have you ever seen a scientist jump into the cage with his own experiments?'

We reached the car, climbed in, and quenched our thirsts.

'What do these reptilians look like, Frank?'

'The Alpha Draconians are about nine foot tall, with a skinny, humanoid morphology, but it seems the reptilians come in many different manifestations, most of which are bipedal, such as the crocodile humanoids, lizard humanoids, snake humanoids and other various reptilian beings.'

'I've seen them, on the walls of the temples and tombs; Sobek for instance, and all the winged-snakes and multi-headed snakes on the walls of the New Kingdom tombs.'

As we rattled along down the sandy track towards our next objective, so did Frank.

'From what I've been able to research, the reptilians were created at least thirty-five million years ago on a planet that orbits Alpha Draconis by some sort of bird-beings who ruled the constellation of Draco.'

'Bird beings?...'

Suddenly my mind was filled with images of the bird creatures on the columns at Esna and Dendera, and the images in the Sumerian tablets of the god-creatures with eagle beaks.

'...But I thought the birds were a later evolutionary offshoot?'

'I wouldn't be putting my faith in "evolution", certainly not as science has defined it.'

'So you're a creationist.'

Frank burst into laughter.

'Sure am, but not in the sense of the religious perspective, by an old white-bearded omnipotent man sitting up in the clouds directing traffic. I'm convinced man was created all right, but by genetic intervention.'

'By the reptilians?'

'Or the bird beings.'

'Why them?'

'The bird people were clearly very intellectual beings, and very militaristic, traits they would have passed on to the reptilians. And when you look at the images of Thoth, as the Ibis, as the wise scribe, and of Horus, as the falcon, as the keeper of truth, it makes you wonder if they were both bird creatures.'

'Shit, I've never thought of that.'

We came to a halt as I contemplated the possibility that Thoth and Horus were descendants of a race of bird creatures that went back in excess of thirty-five million years; the weird was getting weirder. Anyway, time to contemplate that later, it was time to explore the unique structure before us.

The Bent Pyramid

The Bent Pyramid obviously gets its modern name from its unusual bent angle half way up, where the initial fifty-four degree angle changes to forty-three degrees. It is 618 ft on each side, with an 'original' height of 344 ft and a 'planned' height of 421 feet. It was supposedly built by Snefru, the ancient formal name of the Bent Pyramid was apparently either "The Southern Shining Pyramid" or "Snefru is Shining in the South". However, the core of the Bent Pyramid, despite being right next to the Red pyramid, is made from a different material; rough limestone instead of sandstone blocks, with a mud mortar in between to form the basic shape.

The mortar between the casing stones is different as well, here replaced by a fine pink mastic; apparently so strong that many of the casing blocks have split into two before the mortar itself gave way. "Maybe different builders, maybe different techniques?" I hear you say. Well, obviously that's the case, but it doesn't necessarily mean Snefru built either the Red *or* Bent Pyramids, just that he had claimed them as his own; there are no inscriptions within them to confirm this proposal, and here there are just a few of his cartouches on the outer casing and on the stele of the mortuary temple.

As we walked the relatively short distance from the car park to the pyramid, I took out my iphone and revisited my notes.

"Evidence suggests the Bent Pyramid was actually started as a smaller pyramid with an angle of about 60°."

That sounded to me more like the mastaba-type construction of the interior structure of the pyramid at Meidum, which made the connection between them even stronger.

"At a height of about 112 ft signs of structural instability and cracks appeared in the casing and in the chambers, so a supporting girdle was added to the bottom courses, resulting in a new base length of around 618 ft and a new angle of 54° 27'44"."

OK, that was exactly like Meidum, and possibly even Hawarra. But were the cracks a later occurence?

"The pyramid was then built up to about a height of about 162 ft and then a curious change occurred; the angle of the pyramid was reduced to 43º 21'."

If you believe the self-appointed experts, the Egyptologists, then the architect for Snefru's second attempt at building a pyramid made a 'mistake' when building the pyramid, but didn't realize it until they'd already reached a height just under fifty metres. Mind you, they didn't get it wrong just once; they made the *same* 'mistake' on all four faces. Or maybe it wasn't the architect's fault at all; maybe it was the builders who screwed up the blueprint. Maybe they were dyslexic and read the 'original' angle of 45, as 54?

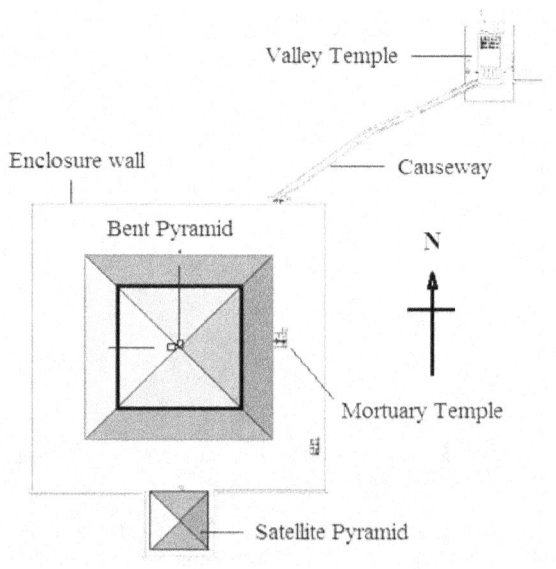

Seriously, do the 'experts' really believe we would swallow the notion that the ancient Egyptians, masters of design and construction, built it forty-eight metres high *before* they noticed something was wrong? Surely it would make more sense to look for a reason *why* the design was deliberately the way it was?

In any case, once the 'mistake' was discovered, the angle was supposedly 'changed' to make the pyramid safer and avoid it collapsing, as the Meidum pyramid

306

had apparently done. So why bother finishing it? Why not just level it off as a mastaba, or use the blocks to build the supposed new pyramid? It would have saved quarrying and transporting millions of blocks.

We stopped briefly before the massive structure, thinking we must have looked like the Three Wise Men from the east, three eminent professors of the university of common sense, though to the Archaeological establishment we were more akin to the Three Stooges. Frank looked like Yul Brynner in 'The King and I', confident and defiant, with his fists on his hips.

'Well, what do you think?'

We were standing before the north face, before one of the two entrances that led within the pyramid, this one, on the north face, about twelve metres above the ground.

'Pretty damn impressive for the greatest "mistake" in architectural history.'

'Sure is.'

'So, which way; left, right, or straight in?'

I checked out the map on my iphone.

It was tempting to head straight inside, especially considering the heat, but I was somewhat of a creature of habit.

'Let's do a lap again before heading in.'

So, once again, we set off to the right. I looked around to see where we were in relation to the outer enclosure wall but it was barely discernable.

"Like many other pyramids, Snefru's Bent Pyramid was surrounded by a huge enclosure wall made of yellow limestone."

I wondered if it was exactly like the one we had seen earlier, that they were reconstructing at the pyramid of Senwroset III, and, if it was, it was possible evidence it had been added sometime during the 'alabaster period' of the Middle Kingdom.

It wasn't hard to figure out why the wall was gone; the Thera tsunami would have made short work of it. However, it also possibly explained why much of the outer limestone casing of the pyramid itself had actually survived, the wall had afforded the pyramid a certain amount of protection from the surging waters. In fact, although it is damaged, the Bent Pyramid is the only Egyptian pyramid that retains a major portion of its original limestone casing.

As we skirted the northwest corner of the pyramid, I examined the way in which the corners had been 'knocked off'. It was clearly the sort of damage that would be caused by surging rubble-filled water making its way around the pyramid; the pieces of outer wall and other debris would crash into the corners, eventually damaging them and causing them to become loose and carried away with the surge.

It was all making perfect sense, and there it was, right before my eyes. How could the Egyptologists have been so blind, or stupid?

I turned my thoughts back to Mark's comments about each pyramid being related to a star.

'So, Mark, which star is this pyramid named after?'

'Vega.'

'Suzanne Vega?...'

Frank had a bemused blank look on his face.

'...You know, the Canadian singer, "My name is Luca", "Marlene on the wall'?'

Thankfully Mark saved the day.

'Frank's more of a Dionne Warwick fan.'

'Damn good singer. *Walk on by. Walk on by.*'

And with that, as we traversed the western face, Frank launched into a medley of her greatest hits, 'I just don't know what to do with myself', 'Anyone who had a heart', and 'Do you know the way to San Jose?' He sounded like a cross between Willie Nelson and Marlon Brando with a little William Shatner thrown in for good measure. If I didn't change the subject fast, Mark and I would have had the extremes and tolerances of our tastes pushed to their limits.

'So, Frank, what's your theory on the change of angle?'

'One thing's for sure, it weren't no accident; it was deliberate.'

'How can you tell?'

He stopped just before the western entrance, pointing up at the edges of the pyramid.

'Well, you know if you extend the forty-three degree plane of the upper outer casing down to the ground, that the shape, size and volume created is exactly the same as the Red Pyramid.'

'Really?'

'That's not the half of it. The sides of the pyramid measure 200, 210 and 290 cubits respectively, which means it is formed directly from the Pythagorean 20-21-29 triangle.'

'Hell of a "mistake". So why the change of angle, what does it all mean?'

'Your guess is as good as mine; if we could figure out who actually built the pyramid, and when, then we might get some clues as to why.'

I gazed back up at the western face, the second entrance, discovered by Professor Ahmed Fakhry in 1951, about thirty metres up.

'Do you think the two entrances are related to the different angles and the inner chambers?'

'I'm sure of it, but what that relationship is, well, that's the sixty-four-thousand-dollar question.'

Access to the western entrance was restricted, and I had no intention of climbing the equivalent of about a ten story building up the precarious sheer face of the pyramid on the off chance they had left it open.

"The gentler slope of the two entrances, the passage on the western side of the pyramid leads down into the centre of the pyramid, where it continues horizontally just above what would be ground level, through a passage blocked by two portcullis slabs, the most elaborate such system in any pyramid yet, a system that lowers the blocks diagonally rather than vertically or horizontally. This then leads to an upper burial chamber also with a high-corbelled roof and evidence of it having possibly been shored up by huge beams of cedar wood. It was on the roughly hewn blocks in this chamber that Snefru's name was first found, in a crude inscription written in red pigment and including his cartouche. This passageway, the blocking system and chamber are all located within the body of the pyramid."

It was yet another case of the 'experts' designating the construction of the pyramid to someone based on scant evidence of that name being scratched on at some later stage. Surely there had been an attempt to repair the chamber, hence the cedar beams, and that repair had occurred during the reign of Snefru, but that didn't mean the original pyramid was built at the same time as when the repairs were made. There had to be more to find.

The Egyptologists have put forward several possible reasons as to why there are two sets of chambers in this pyramid.

"The western passages and chamber represent something similar to the South Tomb of the Djoser Step Pyramid Complex at Saqqara, and were built to correct the contradictory orientation of the substructure."

I didn't buy that for a second; it just didn't ring true, especially since there is a smaller pyramid south of this pyramid that could fulfil that purpose. Then there was this one:

"One set of chambers is a decoy to discourage looters from looking for other chambers within the pyramid."

Really? What if they find the other chamber first? And, if the western chamber was a decoy, why put two portcullis doors in it, and none in the actual north chamber?

The third possibility was predictable, that this pyramid was intended for the burial of Snefru and his wife, Queen Heterpheres. The problem with that theory is, there is absolutely no evidence to support it, but, if you believe the pyramids were tombs, which I don't, then it's plausible.

The final theory the 'experts' trot out is that the two chambers had some sort of religious significance related to the pharaoh's journey in the afterlife. They don't explain their theory, just throw it out in the academic wilderness. Talk about a stab in the dark! I wanted hard evidence and I was sure there were concrete, or possibly even granite, answers within.

Heading around to the southern side of the Bent Pyramid, were the remains of the much smaller 'satellite' pyramid. This was not particularly surprising as there had been numerous smaller pyramids alongside the pyramid of Senwroset III. What was surprising was its position relative to the outer limestone wall, which did a 'detour' to encompass the pyramid.

That had me scratching my head; if the smaller pyramid was built first, then the whole southern part of the exterior wall could simply have been extended further south. This way it looked like the smaller pyramid had been added after the outer wall. In the end I couldn't make sense of it either way. The other question it proposed was, 'Was the smaller pyramid contemporary with the main pyramid, or a much later addition?'

"The smaller pyramid was cleared in 1947 by the Egyptologist Abd El-Salam Hussein. In it he discovered an undecorated single chamber, reached first by a short descending passage, followed by a short horizontal passage, and then by an interesting feature, what may be described as a precursor to the Grand Gallery of the Great Pyramid, an ascending passage. "

It was certainly a possible chronological link to the Great Pyramid, but it was by no means a confirmation they were built during the 4th Dynasty. On the contrary, it suggested they weren't.

"It appears that the configuration of this passage was for the purpose of storing the portcullis plugging blocks, supported by the presence a piece of wood fitted into a notch that appears to have been involved in the lowering of the plugs."

Surely someone would be quasi-intelligent enough to do a carbon-dating on the wood? It wouldn't confirm the date of the pyramid but it would be a pretty good start.

"The burial chamber is too small to fit a burial and so it is thought that this might have been ceremonial tomb containing the king's statue, or perhaps was intended for jars that contained the king's viscera."

All that to bury a fucking statue, get real! Or maybe it was *never* a tomb of *any* sort?

On its eastern side, the satellite pyramid had the remains of a small chapel, which once contained two stelae "bearing the names and titles of Snefru", and a small altar.

There was no suggestion as to whom the satellite pyramid belonged, but I'm guessing the natural presumptions of the Egyptologists would have ascribed it to Snefru's wife, or one of his children. That said, if the pyramid *wasn't* built by Snefru, then, although the stele beside it may have carried his name, maybe the satellite pyramid wasn't his either.

Moving around to the eastern side of the Bent Pyramid, we came upon the scant remains of a small mortuary temple, built of mud-brick and very similar to, but smaller than, the one at Meidum, even to them both being located on the eastern side.

"Within the mortuary temple were the remnants of a small shrine, consisting of a limestone offering table; two limestone blocks with a slab roof in the shape of the 'hetep' symbol, that meant "offering". This table was flanked by two round-topped monolithic stelae, which would once have been around 9 feet high, and on which Snefru's names and titles were inscribed. Remains of the upper part of one of the stelae can be seen in Cairo Museum, while the lower thirds of both remain in situ. The simple chapel was then extended with mud-brick walls."

The more I immersed myself in these temples the more I found myself lost in all things ancient Egyptian. So, as Mark and Frank examined the casing stones, I put my hands on the limestone offering table, trying not to look too much like a New-Age feather-waver, and closed my eyes. A few breaths later I had tuned into the stone, the sun dawning over ancient Egypt with Nemo leaping in and out of the Nile like a freshly-landed barramundi on a hot frying pan. I think he was trying to get my attention and tell me something so I took another deep breath and focused in.

Suddenly, from beneath Nemo, the figure of a naked woman emerged from the water and picked up Nemo in her hands. It was Crystal, just as she had been when we were on the felucca trip and she had emerged from her morning swim, dripping with sensuality. I zeroed in; yes, it was Crystal, but it wasn't her, it was a past incarnation of her, as a high priestess. Slowly she sauntered towards me then gently put Nemo down on the offering table. What did it mean?

Clearly Nemo was me, and I was definitely feeling I was out of the flow of life, out of the Nile, and somewhat floundering, jumping out of my skin. Was I about to be offered up as a sacrifice to the Egyptians? And was Crystal my deliverer? Why Crystal? She seemed so ritualistic in the way she cradled me and gently laid me down. Did it mean I had to sacrifice my old me for the purpose of finding some Higher Self?

Before I could shift my focus beyond the image of Crystal's exquisite breasts and down to Nemo, Frank pulled me back to the Now.

'Who knows what they laid out as an offering?'

'Ah, fish I suppose.'

'Fish?'

'And food and wine, too I guess.'

'Maybe the occasional sacrificial virgin.'

The image of Crystal's naked body spread over the offering table flooded my mind, but certainly not as a sacrificial virgin, although the thought of her sacrificing her 'virginity' was definitely a pleasing possibility that rippled through my mind; though it was hardly the image to be sharing with Frank.

'Nah, I think sacrificing virgins was strictly the domain of the Aztecs and the Mayans.'

'Not necessarily, you know that before the 1st Dynasty, after the pharaoh died, they used to bury his servants alive so that he had them in the Afterworld.'

My connection with the altar interrupted, I approached the base of the pyramid to join them.

'Yeah, I know, they found evidence of it at Abydos, at Umm el Qa'ab.'

'That's right.'

'Maybe they were all buried alive by a tsunami.'

'It's possible, but, were they virgins?'

'Who knows if they were "virgins" before pharaoh's death or not? One things for sure, they were well and truly fucked afterwards.'

We all laughed and made our way back around to the north face.

'Tough gig, and we complain about today's superannuation schemes.'

Frank scoffed.

'At least you have them.'

'True, we should be thankful for small mercies…'

I turned my attention to what Frank and Mark had been looking at.

'…What were you looking at?'

Mark eagerly rejoined the discussion.

'The casing stones, if your theory about the tsunami is correct, it might explain why the rest of the casing stones are damaged while the stones behind the eastern mortuary temple are virtually intact.'

'What do you mean?'

'Well, it's funny you should have mentioned the tsunami, because I've just finished reading an online article by Ralph Ellis.'

'Who's he?'

'Another truth-seeker I do believe, pretty astute guy actually; he also wrote 'Thoth, Architect of the Universe', a book well worth reading. Winters puts forward the proposition that, over the years of its existence, the Bent Pyramid had become "pockmarked" because of thousands and thousands of small areas of erosion in the limestone casing stones all over the pyramid, from top to bottom.'

We stopped back before the northern face; the fine workmanship of the massive casing blocks easy to see, as were the many irregularities.

'It looks like the casing stones have been patched up?'

311

Mark laughed.

'They have. Ellis suggests that some of the damaged areas were minuscule, only a few centimetres across, and only required minor repairs, but others needed the whole face of the stone stripped back.'

'And he thinks the original damage was caused by erosion? What about the foundation, beneath the pyramid, how does explain the damage there? Does he follow the thinking of the Egyptologists that they accidentally built it on an unstable foundation? And what about the signs of collapse in the internal chambers?...'

Yes, I was very interested in the damage to the casing stones, but not because of "erosion".

'...It doesn't make sense to me. Is Ellis seriously suggesting that wind, water and sand were responsible for damaging the entire surface of the pyramid?'

'Except for the section of the eastern face behind the mortuary temple, yes. Ellis says it was because the temple provided protection from the elements, but it could just have easily provided protection from the surging waters of a tsunami.'

'Or it could mean the surge could have come more from the west.'

We made our way towards the entrance, Frank now firmly in my camp.

'So you think it was the tsunami?'

'I'd bet my house on it; if I owned one that is. Just imagine all the debris, bits of granite statues, walls, temples, all tumbling around and crashing into the pyramid. They would have chipped and bashed out pieces as they crashed into the casing stones. And look at the corners, that's exactly what would happen as the pieces tumble passed the edges.'

'And the missing top parts?'

'If you believe the Egyptologists, which I don't, they were pilfered by locals to build houses. Well, first of all, why scale a hundred metres, all the way to the top, to take stones from there, when it would be much easier to take the ones at the base. Secondly, I don't see any houses made of limestone casing blocks in the near vicinity, do you?...'

We all looked around; it was miles of desert to the nearest village.

'...To me, the missing stones at the top indicate how high the Thera tsunami must at least have been. And that's consistent with all the other evidence I've seen at Meidum, Hawarra, Amarna, Abydos, in fact right up the Nile as far as Aswan.'

Mark still had some doubts.

'It all sounds totally plausible except for the fact Ellis suggests the repairs were done *before* the New Kingdom, around the time of Snefru.'

'How does he figure that?'

'Firstly, Winters thinks that if the repairs were done in the New Kingdom, a period that was relatively well documented, then we would have heard about it.'

'Not necessarily.'

'Really? There are records documenting the repairs made to the Sphinx by Thutmoses IV, and the repairs to the surface of the pyramid would have been much bigger than that, and yet there is no mention of it? I don't think so.'

'Which means?'

'That the pyramid wasn't built by Snefru at all, that he just made the repairs to it. And, to record his 'great achievement', Snefru carved his cartouche in the lower casing blocks of the pyramid and within the mortuary temple, which also must have been there before him.'

'Unless he rebuilt the mortuary temple as well?'

'It's possible.'

'And erected the stele beside both pyramids, as a sign of his achievements; not of building the pyramids, but of repairing them.'

'Well, it's still possible he built the smaller one to the south.'

'True.'

'But no matter what, it means it wasn't the Thera tsunami that caused the surface damage.'

'Well, maybe not to the casing stones, it must have been the one before that, the tsunami that buried the Osireion at Abydos.'

'And when was that?'

'If it was because of a passing of Nibiru, then around 5200 BC at the latest, possibly 8,800 BC or even 12,400 BC.'

'In either case, way before the Egyptologists say.'

'Way WAY before.'

As Frank made his way up the rickety staircase that led up to the entrance, he put an interesting twist on the matter.

'The corners of the pyramid *could still* have been knocked away during the Thera tsunami.'

It was a good point, so I started summarizing the discussion, Mark and Frank throwing in their two cents.

'Let's say the pyramid was built anywhere from seven to fourteen thousand years ago,..'

'Maybe more.'

'Maybe fifty thousand.'

'...Then a first catastrophe, maybe an earthquake...'

'Or a crustal shift.'

'A pole shift.'

'...destabilized the foundation and caused collapses in the inner chambers,...'

'And a tsunami extensively damaged the surface casing stones.'

'...Then, during the 4th Dynasty, Snefru decides to repair not just the exterior, but also sure up the inner chambers with cedar beams,...'

'Scrawling his name on the lower casing stones.'

'And erecting stele in praise of himself.'

'...Finally, the Thera tsunami around 1600 BC smashed the casing stones off the corners and away at the top.'

Mark was nodding his head.

'It's all possible.'

Frank was now champing on the bit.

'Maybe we'll find more answers inside.'

'After you, Kemosabi.'

Mark was in the dark about my reference to Kemosabi, but Frank clearly had memories of The Lone Ranger and appreciated my askew metaphor of being led into the dark interior. When we reached the top of the staircase, we found the entrance protected by a padlocked metal door, probably a relic of when the area was designated as a military zone, and the guardian waiting for us, keys in hand.

Why they would need to put a locked door on it was anybodies guess; anything of value would have been stolen decades ago. It probably was, by Zahi Hawass and his kettle of vultures. Maybe it was left here to stop tourists sneaking through the desert in the middle of the night and entering the pyramid to perform bizarre rituals?

I later found out the interior of the Bent Pyramid was usually off-limits to visitors but that Frank had pulled a few aces from up his sleeve; the old 'three professors' card, as well as a healthy wad of baksheesh. The reality was, these guys hadn't seen any tourists for over a week and were so desperate for money, my guess was, that for the right price, they would willingly have unlocked the chastity belt to their own wife or daughter.

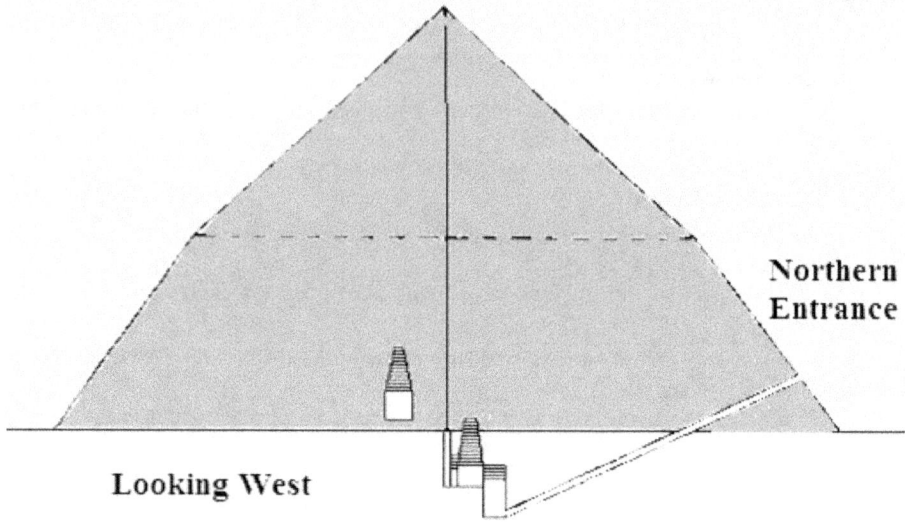

Northern Entrance

Looking West

As the guardian opened the door I took a quick look at my iphone and the layout of the northern passage. It all seemed pretty straight-forward; a long descending passage led to an antechamber, which was followed by a supposed secondary "burial" chamber.

But suddenly I was having different thoughts and images running through my head. They took me back to the original notes I had made on the Bent Pyramid.

"Evidence suggests the Bent Pyramid was actually started as a smaller pyramid with an angle of about 60°."

It wasn't started as a smaller pyramid, it *was* a smaller pyramid, possibly a ziggurat, and this entrance and the chambers that were in the bedrock, were a part of that structure.

"At a height of about 112 ft signs of structural instability and cracks appeared in the casing and in the chambers, so a supporting girdle was added to the bottom courses, resulting in a new base length of around 618 ft and a new angle of 54° 27′44″."

OK, it was exactly like Meidum; I'd figured it out. What had happened was, the original, smaller pyramid, which was probably a ziggurat, was built maybe ten thousand years ago, or more, and had been structurally compromised because of some catastrophe, probably the earthquakes caused by a pole shift. At some time later, a first repair job was done, not Snefru's, but an even earlier one, in which the "supporting girdle" was added, along with the modified top section. Perhaps there was some mathematical harmonic relationship between the three angles: 60, 54, 43. I though about Frank's Pythagorean triangle: 29-21-20, which would be 58-42-40 if doubled. It was close, but no cigar. But, was I on to something? Perhaps the answers lay within?

The door swung back and we got our first look inside. There were no lights and

314

the passage descended into the darkness.

'Shit, that's steep and deep! It's more like a mine-shaft!'

The guardian held out three small torches for us to use. I looked at them with some considerable trepidation, visualizing the batteries dying exactly as we arrived in the deepest part of the pyramid. It was clear that the descending passage was never intended for human traversing. In addition to there being no lights, there were no modern footholds or railings either to make it any easier.

'Having second thoughts?'

'Yep, but not about heading in, just about how the hell we're going to get out.'

The guardian gestured for us to enter so I grabbed a torch and followed Frank into Hades, Mark bringing up the rear. As we climbed over a few leather buckets, obviously used to remove sand and other debris, I took particular note of several massive blocks lining the wall and ceiling which had been displaced from being flush; these were part of the "supporting girdle' of rocks added after the first catastrophe. The fact they were dispersed was an indication of a second major shake up, most probably the Thera event. If I could find a second definite change in the compositional structure of this passage, the 54°/60° boundary, before it then descended into the bedrock, then it would confirm my thinking even more about the history of the pyramid.

The decent was tough, especially for someone my size. The footings weren't always secure and several times I hit my head on the ceiling, forcing me to remove my akubra to give myself a better view of what lay ahead. So, one hand holding my akubra and the torch, the other pressing against the wall or ceiling for guidance and some scant misguided sense of stability, we scrambled/crab-walked/duck-walked down. Now I knew why the guardian had left us to it, it was bloody hard going.

There wasn't any talking; everyone was too busy concentrating and I was sweating like a Greek wrestler in a steam bath. Despite my obvious discomfort, I did find my 54°/60° boundary, which brought me momentary delight. But it wasn't really the place to stop and have a chat with the guys about it, that could wait until we were at least supine, or even better, reclining in the pool bar and savouring an ice-cold beer.

Reaching the bottom of the descending passageway, there was some brief momentary relief and a chance to stretch my aching back before moving on into the next low passage, a short horizontal section over a shallow depression covered with several wooden planks. I really did feel like I was in an Indiana Jones movie, or 'The Great Escape'. Were there treasures at the end of the passage, maybe a golden sarcophagus inscribed with hidden secrets; the clues to answering some great mystery? Highly unlikely, probably just an empty room, but, until you go, you'll never know.

The horizontal passage led to the 'antechamber', a narrow room about forty feet high, with a corbelled ceiling made of large limestone slabs. The walls were unpolished, undecorated, and the corbelled ceiling had a roughened appearance, giving the overall impression that the chamber was unfinished. It would have been 'unfinished' if it was intended to be the lavish antechamber to a tomb, however, if the chamber *was* finished, then that would mean it had a totally different function altogether, a function related to the chamber that followed.

The only thing in the room was a long modern wooden ladder set against the southern wall. I followed it up with my torch, high into the ceiling space, where a small hole in the southern wall of the 'antechamber' gave access to the next chamber. It lent weight to the fact the chambers were definitely *not* part of a tomb.

'Well, the ladder must lead somewhere important, and, since the only way is up, shall we continue?'

315

'Ever onward, ever upward!'

It's not that we didn't trust the local engineers, and that the ladder might collapse, it's just 'we didn't trust the local engineers'. So Mark and I footed the ladder as Frank led the way. I was next to ascend, squeezing through the narrow gap into the second chamber.

'A tomb? No frickin' way! No smoothly finished walls, no decorations.'

As I turned back to hold the top of the ladder with Frank so that Mark could join us, I took in the significance of the miniscule gap I had just squeezed through. It seemed sculptured to align exactly with the dimensions of the corbelled ceiling in the antechamber. I shared my thoughts with Frank.

'This opening may have been made deliberately to let through something, but it wasn't men.'

'No arguments from me on that one.'

Moments later, Mark reached the top of the ladder, we pulled him inside, and all stood looking at the chamber.

'What a train wreck.'

Mark was right, the chamber looked like something very 'wrong' had happened here. In the southeast corner was an opening that led to a separate shaft that rose behind the southern wall of the chamber.

At the top, this 'chimney' shaft had a small, corbelled niche in its southern wall, probably some outlet from the passage. There was no way of exploring it, so I returned my attention to the main space of the second chamber.

'Jesus, what a bun-fight.'

There were pieces of wood, braced between the walls, connected to vertical beams to form a make-shift scaffolding. It was as if the whole shoddy structure was in place to prevent the chamber from total collapse.

A wooden ladder, at least fifty feet long, speared up through the mayhem to the now-familiar structure of a corbelled ceiling above. In the shifting torchlight it created quite an ominous atmosphere; it looked like another set of ghostly gallows.

'You know this chamber sits directly beneath the central axis of the pyramid.'

I double-checked the image on my iphone.

'Actually, Frank, it's set just off centre…'

I pointed to the blind shaft to the southeast.

'…the centre actually seems to line up perfectly with that shaft.'

Frank stepped over to look at my iphone.

'So it does. Now that's interesting, and look, both this chamber and the antechamber we just came through are located within the bedrock, below ground level; only the top part of the corbelled ceiling of this chamber projects into the body of the pyramid above. It has to mean something.'

'Well, let's go up and have a look. My guess is, that's what the ladder is for.'

And with that, his torch in his mouth lighting the way, Mark set off up the ladder.

"Better him, than me", I thought, as Mark, step by tenuous step, carefully made his way to the top. I was certain the whole thing was going to collapse on top of us at any second.

'Hey, there's another tunnel up here.'

'It must be the connecting passage that leads to the western passage and the main burial chamber.'

'OK, I'm clear, come on up.'

As I footed the ladder, Frank started his ascent and I examined another image I had on my iphone, this one of the connecting passage and its relationship to the two chambers. It didn't look too far, maybe twenty metres or so.

> "The upper and lower chambers were linked by a tunnel, hacked through the masonry at some time after the chambers were built by people who were somehow aware of the exact locations of the separate sets of chambers.
>
> The connecting passageway leads from the upper part of the north chamber to the east-west passageway, intersecting it between two portcullis blocks built to seal the main chamber after the burial of the king."

Hacked through? Interesting! But were they tunnelling from north to west, or west to north?

> "The blocking system here is unique because the blocks slide down diagonally, as opposed to vertically as in other pyramids. The first block is in place, but has a rectangular hole cut through it. The other portcullis block, looking east toward the burial chamber, is held up and open by a wooden brace."

That posed several questions: Firstly, were they tunnelling from the western passage to access the north chamber, or from the north chamber to access the east-west passage? Second, why?

'Come on, Alex.'

I guessed I could figure it out along the way and made my way very carefully for fifty feet up the rickety ladder.

Mark had already scouted way ahead, and, because of the restricted space, I was forced to follow Frank's backside, pretty much on hands and knees, torch in my mouth, through the narrow low passage. It was considerably smaller than the entrance passage; a little bit too 'cosy' for my liking, and, if I'd stopped to think about it, I would probably have been overcome with claustrophobia. God forbid if the batteries should suddenly decide to die. This sort of adventure was definitely not for the faint hearted. I just kept saying, 'It's only twenty metres, now fifteen, ten metres tops, five". Well, it felt like fifty, at least!

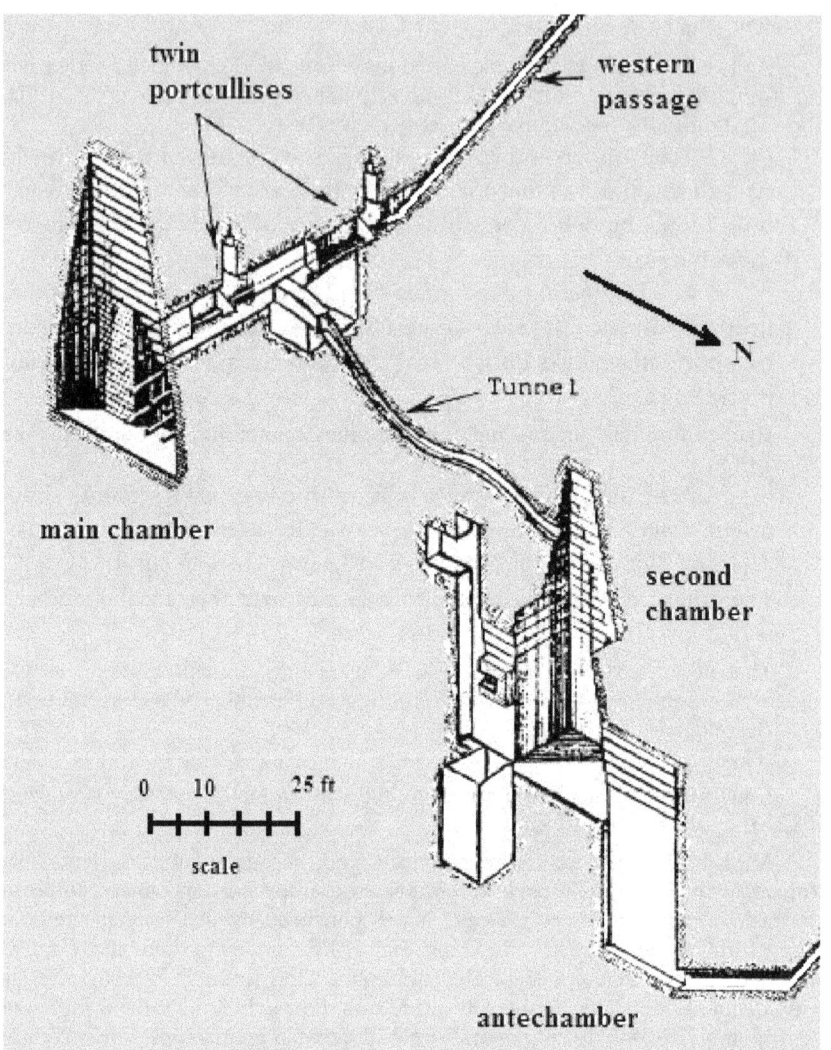

twin
portcullises

western
passage

N

Tunnel

main chamber

second
chamber

0   10   25 ft
scale

antechamber

Despite my discomfort, I did notice that whoever created the tunnel had gone to considerable effort to smooth all four walls. That seemed strange. Why? If it was a simple access tunnel, then it could be left fairly rough-cut, but this was deliberately smoothed out, not perfect, but obviously made the way it was for some reason. To me, that meant it had some other ongoing functionality other than just an access tunnel.

Finally I made it to the east-west passageway and was able to stretch out, partly thanks to a shallow pit in the floor, which was more than just a simple pit as there was a section cut out of the passage floor leading up to it that contained a block of stone for no apparent logical reason.

Beyond the floor stone, to the west, was the first portcullis, with the rectangular opening cut out of it. Even if I'd wanted to travel further up the descending passage, which I didn't, there was no way I was going to be able to squeeze through the narrow opening cut in the portcullis. But what I did notice was, that the lower point of the portcullis sat directly on the floor block.

Now that was either a coincidence, or a deliberate functional aspect of the reason why the portcullis was designed the way it was, on an angle. Given the design and ingenuity of the pyramid, my money was one hundred percent on the latter. But why, what was the functionality?

The floor block had 'freedom' to move laterally towards me, towards the east, or upwards. I had no idea how, but if it moved upwards, it would cause the portcullis to lift, thus partly opening the 'door' by creating a small triangular wedge of space near the floor.

So was this some sort of simple, but advanced, pressure valve? If it were, then it would totally support Christopher Dunne's theory that the pyramids were power stations. The questions then would be: 'What was the fuel?' 'What sort of power did it produce?' and 'How did it operate?'

By the intermittent flashes of torchlight from the end of the passageway to the left, it was clear that Mark and Frank had also passed on the option to squeeze through the first portcullis, and, instead, had headed into the main chamber to the east. That meant passing through and beyond the second portcullis, wedged open by a length of wood in the top left corner, possibly over four or even five thousand years old.

I very VERY carefully made my way past the 'doorway', ensuring that I didn't risk dislodging the brace with my backpack. One false move and the narrow beam might snap like a toothpick and I could be trapped, crushed, or even worse, left entombed indefinitely with Frank and Mark, who, I am sure, would not be very amused.

Safely beyond the second portcullis I briefly pondered it's function, as there was no visible mechanism for raising the stone once it was closed. I was positive this wasn't a tomb, so the door couldn't have been there to protect the pharaoh's tomb from being robbed. So, was it a safety door, that would seal the contents of the main chamber should anything go amiss? What else could it be?

There were a further two shallow shafts beyond the portcullis before the passageway terminated at a ledge which led into the main 'burial' chamber. Frank and Mark had already made there way to the chamber floor and assisted me down.

There was absolutely nothing particular of interest to see that we hadn't seen before; a narrow room, high corbelled ceiling, with a few cedar beams high up, seemingly keeping the ceiling from crashing in on our heads. My shirt absolutely saturated, I took off my backpack and took out a bottle of water for us all to share.

'That was crazy.'

'To say the least.'

'Still, here we are, inside the main chamber.'

'You know, I don't think this actually *was* the original main chamber.'

Mark was all ears.

'What makes you say that, Alex?'

'I think the original pyramid was a much smaller ziggurat, with an entrance from the north, and the lower chambers, cut into the bedrock, were the original ones.'

'Just like at Meidum?'

'Yep.'

He crossed his arms and started scratching his chin.

'Hmm, which means there may still be an as yet undiscovered entrance in the western face of the Meidum Pyramid that leads down to another separate chamber; very interesting, go on.'

Frank added his thoughts.

'What about the Red Pyramid, it has the same sort of three-chambered structure, and it's only got one entrance?'

'That we know about. Besides, the chambers there were clearly intended to be joined from the beginning.'

It triggered Mark into an interesting thought.

'Maybe the Red Pyramid is a later model, an improved model.'

Frank wasn't convinced, but certainly open to the concept.

'OK, it's possible; go on.'

I took another mouthful of water, before continuing.

'I was thinking about whether the connecting tunnel was cut out from the north chamber to here, or whether it was cut from the east-west passage to the lower chamber.'

'I hadn't considered that, what's your reckoning?'

'It depends on their objective. If they tunnelled from the second chamber to the west, then the western chamber was their objective. But, it would have been easier to use the western entrance and cut through the first portcullis than thirty metres of rock.'

'But they did cut through the first portcullis.'

'Well, someone did. But was it done at the same time, by the same people, or earlier, or much later? In any case, why cut through the first portcullis and then wedge open the second? That doesn't make sense.'

'Maybe they couldn't get under the first one to wedge it open.'

'That's highly probable, the mechanism certainly would have made it almost impossible to get under it from the outer side of the passage.'

'So they cut through.'

'No, I think cutting through the first portcullis may well have compromised its function, and that of the pyramid.'

'As what?'

'I think Christopher Dunne was right, the pyramid was a power plant, and the first portcullis was some sort of pressure valve.'

'Interesting! So you think they'd have entered through the northern entrance, as we did?'

'It's certainly easier; it might be a bit steeper but there are no portcullis to negotiate.'

'Unless the northern entrance was buried in sand and silt from the after-effects of a tsunami and they entered from the west?'

'Possible, but unlikely, as we would probably see evidence of it. Also, it would be much easier to dig out twenty feet of silt and sand than twenty metres of solid rock.'

'So you think they entered through the north, and that the main chamber was their objective?'

'Yes. I think that's why the connecting tunnel comes out where it does, between the two portcullis; it wasn't an accident, they finished exactly where they intended, because there was a functional reason for it?'

'What?'

'I'm not sure yet...'

Frank was looking agitated and impatient, as if he had something important to say.

'...What do you think, Frank?'

'Maybe their objective wasn't just to fix *both* chambers, but to connect them together so they *could* work?...'

I hadn't thought of that.

'… Anyway, I think it's a conversation better suited to a hotel bar and a long island tea; I'm starting to feel a bit like those three guys trapped inside the Great Pyramid in '76.'

I had no idea what he was referring to, but I had visions of the wooden beam holding up the second portcullis suddenly snapping and entombing us.

'There were people trapped inside the Great Pyramid?'

'Only for twenty-four hours or so.'

'What happened, was there a collapse, or did some secret door close and entomb them?'

I was half laughing as I'd said the latter remark, but, as Frank made his way to the ledge, his raised eyebrows and the look on his face told me there was a lot more to it.

'Come on, let's get going, I'll tell you about it on the way out.'

We scrambled back up to the east-west passage and started our return trip, Mark once again leading the way. This time I went second so that Frank could talk and I could hear him.

'There was a group of guys from an esoteric mystery school who apparently found a series of ancient scrolls in an underground tomb somewhere outside of Athens, Greece, in 1936.'

I immediately started putting two and two together; these could have been part of the stash of the Essenes. But then I thought, "Greece? They could be even earlier, from the times of Alexander the Great". I had to contain my enthusiasm as, at that point, I was passing through the second portcullis and had to be especially careful that I didn't dislodge the beam with my backpack and seal Frank inside.

Safely negotiated, I paused before re-entering the connecting tunnel.

'Do you know where the scrolls were found?'

'Not the exact location, no, just that it was outside Athens.'

I crawled into the tunnel, my mind shifting into overdrive. The scrolls could easily have been found at Delphi, or any location the Tat Brotherhood had occupied. They could have been written by Socrates or Plato, even Manetho or Herodotus. They could even be from Akhenaten's trip to Greece, and the establishment of the ancient Greek civilization.

Frank continued.

'Apparently it took about forty years to translate and decipher them, but, once they were translated, they revealed instructions about the location of a secret entrance, four-hundred-and-seventy feet up, in the southern face of the Great Pyramid, and intricate codes about how to open it. There is supposedly one particular stone, weighing about fifteen ton, that when you tone a particular key word at a particular frequency, will slide back into the pyramid, revealing a steep, rough-cut staircase only twenty-nine inches wide, barely six feet high, that zigzags down over nine-hundred-and-eight feet, to a metal door five-hundred-and-ten feet below the Giza Plateau.'

I had a thousand questions springing into my mind, but it was impossible to stop and turn around in the small confines of the tunnel to ask them. It wasn't until we'd reached the end of the passage, and I started down the first ladder, that I let fly.

'Did they find it, Frank, did they locate the stone?'

'Yep, in June 1976. They were part of a California university expedition officially there to scan the pyramid with some sort of cosmic and gamma X-ray device, but at night they would sneak away, climb up the southern face of the pyramid, and search for it. And eventually, they found the right spot.'

'Did they manage to open it?'

321

I stood there footing the ladder as Frank made his descent.

'Sure did, but it took them thirty-seven attempts, and even then it was a bit of an accident.'

'How did they do it?'

'Following the instructions in the scrolls, they'd practiced a whole series of key words spoken at different pitches; they'd even recorded them to listen back. Apparently it wasn't just the words, they had to be at a particular frequency, and said by someone whose own energy was in tune with the structure.'

'Like a sonic fingerprint.'

'That's a good way of putting it. Anyway, after trying to say them directly without any success, one night the recorder accidental switched on, and 'Open Sesame", the stone started to shift.'

'"Open sesame", were they really the words?'

I thought maybe for a moment, there may have been some actual connection and truth to the origin of the term, like 'open says-a-me', but, when Frank reached the bottom of the ladder and gave me an "Are you being serious?" glare, I quickly realized how stupid I must have sounded. And, if his glare didn't register, his words sure did.

'Yeah, and then the genie of the lamp rolled out a magic carpet to greet them and offer them three wishes.'

I felt like an idiot; but maybe Frank was just pulling my leg. As he headed straight across the chamber, I followed him like an adulating puppy snapping at his heels.

'Is this all true, Frank, or are you just having a lend of me? Or is it all a hoax, just a story you've heard about, or read on the Internet?'

'Oh, it's real all right.'

And he started down the next ladder.

'I first heard about it when I was working with NASA, from someone who'd been a part of the original expedition, but at the time it was all very hush hush. They didn't want the Egyptian authorities finding out about it.'

I remembered something Kareem had told me.

'You say this was 1976?'

'Yep.'

'That's exactly in the middle of the time Zahi Hawass was First Inspector of the Giza Pyramids; 1974 to 1979. I bet Hawass knew all about it.'

'Possibly, he may have found out about it, but he couldn't get inside.'

'Why not?'

'He didn't know the key words or tones; I doubt he even knew which stone it was, and I doubt the others were about to tell him.'

'It didn't seem to stop him. Kareem told me that from about 1980, when Hawass became Chief Inspector at Giza, that he discovered all sorts of things beneath the Giza Plateau, and didn't reveal any of them to the world.'

'Maybe it's all in that backpack of yours, including the actions by Hawass to ridicule and dismiss the discoveries under the plateau so that he could have complete uninterrupted access to them.'

I turned my thoughts once again to my backpack and its contents. That, in turn, made me think of my predicament; one way or another, I *had* to get these papers out of Egypt.

'Come on, it's not really the best place to contemplate the meaning of life.'

I snapped out of it and commenced my descent.

'So what was the magic word?'

'What?'

'What was the secret password?'

'Something like "Urim".'

'Urim? What does that mean?'

'My guess is, "open".'

As I made my way down the ladder, Frank must have been wondering if I was really just an epsilon semi-moron masquerading as a free-thinker. And yet, with each rung on the ladder, I was running it all through my mind. This was confirmation that there was some significance to toning, to the use of sound as a major functional form of energy.

The red granite, black granite, they reacted to sound, to frequency; it made sense that an advanced civilization would use something like voice activation and recognition as the opening mechanism for doors, even if they were made of stone.

Mark was waiting in the antechamber, at the entrance to the final northern passage up to the surface. He motioned for me to lead the way out, but, before I took the lead, I rapidly fired a few more questions at Frank.

'So they got in. What did they find?'

'They didn't just *get in*, the stone apparently only opens at certain specific times of day that have something to do with multiples of the number seven, like 7:07, 14:14, 21:21 that sort of thing. As soon as the three guys scrambled into the opening, it closed behind them, and despite trying for an hour or so to reopen it, the stone wouldn't budge, potentially entombing them forever.'

'You said they were trapped in there for around twenty-four hours, so, what did they do, what did they find?'

Frank slapped me on the shoulder,...

'Let's get out of here first, I'll tell you more about it then.'

...then he gave me a shove into the entrance passage.

As I clambered up the passage, my mind was running riot over all the possible contents they discovered. Did they find a tomb filled with the missing treasure of the pharaohs; gold, silver, jewels, maybe a solid gold sarcophagus? Maybe they found the bodies of Osiris and Isis, or other alien bodies? Perhaps they found an alien spaceship buried tens of thousands of years ago by a massive tsunami? With each step, each thought, up ahead, the pinpoint light at the end of the tunnel was slowly getting bigger, drawing thankfully nearer.

When I reached the exit, I crawled out onto the platform, stretched my limbs and took a deep lung-full of air. It was hot, damn hot, and dry, and my shirt was soaking wet. It was absolutely amazing to be out of the depths of the pyramid, the hot breeze drying my shirt and creating a much-needed cooling effect.

The guardian was nowhere to be seen, but the view out over Dahshur was impressive. To the left, beyond the car park, was endless desert, virtually straight ahead, in the near distance, was the Red Pyramid. Around sixty degrees further to the right, the causeway from the Bent Pyramid led to what looked like the remains of a valley temple. Continuing along, at almost ninety degrees to the right, were the alluring remains of the Black Pyramid.

Frank and Mark quickly joined me and we made our way down the staircase, discovering the guardian chilling out in the shadows beneath the platforms. We handed him back the torches, Mark giving him and additional 'helping hand' of baksheesh.

'Had enough yet, Alex?'

'Assuming I get out of Egypt alive, then this could probably my one and only trip here, so what do you think?'

'OK, so off to the Black Pyramid.'

'Actually, can we go via the causeway and Valley Temple?'

'It's your pilgrimage.'

Mark turned to the guardian and pointed off into the desert.

'Temple, then pyramid.'

'Yes, please to come.'

And the guardian led us off down the causeway.

How green is my valley: not!

The open limestone causeway, that would also once have had limestone walls, ran about half-a-kilometre from the north-eastern corner of the enclosure in a roughly north-easterly direction towards what would once have been an imposing valley temple.

'So, Frank, what did they find?'

'Well, eventually they gave up trying to reopen the entrance and headed down the staircase, descending around nine-hundred-eighty feet into the depths of the pyramid and far beyond.

At the end of the staircase, the path was blocked by a plain metal door that had no doorjamb, no hinges, no handle or locks, and, to all appearances, slid upwards in hidden side grooves provided in the limestone walls. They spent another two hours trying to open it, they even tried saying the magic words backwards and playing the tape backwards, but without success. Then for some reason, maybe because they thought that their number was up, one of them muttered the word "Genesis", and, lo and behold, the door slid open.'

'Seriously? Genesis?'

'So they say, though I doubt "Genesis" was actually the word, being pupils and adepts of the mystery school themselves, they would hardly have publicised the real words. It was more than likely their own code to remember it.'

'And what did they find?'

'A massive complex of rooms and alcoves spread over four levels and totalling around one-hundred-twenty square feet, which was apparently constructed thousands of years before the Pyramid.'

'And inside?'

'No jewels, no piles of precious stones, no gold or silver statues; the real treasure was tens-of-thousands of mysterious metal discs, tissue-paper thin, made of an unknown metal that was totally heat resistant, couldn't be mutilated, cut, or scratched by the cutting edge of a diamond, and that were stored in shelved containers.'

'Like a library; the Hall of Records.'

'So it would seem, everything in perfect condition, as if it was put there yesterday. They also found a book, encased in some sort of translucent case, opened midway, which revealed all the previous civilizations on the planet, including when man first set foot on earth five-hundred-seventy-six thousand years ago.'

I stopped in my tracks.

'Get out of here!'

Frank paused, waiting for me to start walking again.

'Oh, that's not the half of it; they also found all sorts of strange machines; levitation machines, a giant metallic ring, like a tunnel, twenty-five feet in diameter, and twelve feet deep.'

He took off again, and I was right behind him.

'You think it's some sort of teleportation device, even a star gate?'

'That, or a time machine.'

As I pulled alongside, I couldn't believe the directions conversations were going in.

'I didn't think time machines were possible.'

'Everything is possible. Something may be highly improbably, but that doesn't mean it's impossible. There was a time when man thought it was impossible to fly, impossible to break the four-minute mile.'

'So, with time, everything is possible.'

'With time, everything is not only possible, it's eventual.'

'But an actual time machine! That's the stuff of Jules Verne.'

'If you enjoy reading, then you need to read up about the Philadelphia Project, and the Montauk Project.'

'The Philadelphia Project; isn't that where the US Navy made a battleship disappear in the early 1940's?'

'Yep, but it wasn't a battleship, it was a destroyer, the Eldridge, and it didn't just disappear.'

'No?'

'No, There was much more to it. The original project, Project Rainbow, was headed by Nickola Tesla, and designed to make ships invisible to radar. But Tesla quickly realized the implications of the project, that the military had unscrupulous agendas, sabotaged the experiment by de-tuning the equipment so nothing would work, and resigned in December 1942. A few weeks later, on 7th January 1943, he was found dead in his New York hotel room.'

'Murdered?'

'Well, "officially" he died of a coronary thrombosis.'

'A heart attack; how old was he?'

'Eighty-six.'

'That's not really an unlikely cause of death.'

'Except the assistant medical officer who was called to the scene made his ruling on the cause of death just by a "preliminary" examination of the body, *before* any autopsy had been performed, ruling that there were no suspicious circumstances.'

'You think he was injected with something to cause a heart attack.'

'Most likely poisoned. Then the body was quickly cremated to destroy the evidence.'

Now, I may have been becoming a conspiracy theorist, but I still needed more information.

'Without an autopsy, that would be hard to confirm; you'd need more evidence.'

'How about the fact that two days later the FBI ordered the Alien Property Custodian to seize all of Tesla's belongings, even though he was an American citizen?'

'OK, now I smell a rat.'

'Tesla's entire estate, from the New Yorker and other New York City hotels, was seized and transported to the Manhattan Storage and Warehouse Company under an official OAP seal.'

'OAP? Order of the American President?'

'No, nothing that grandiose, it's Old Age Pension. But it shows he was no "alien".'

'So what happened to the Project?'

'A German doctor by the name of Von Neumann took over, made changes in some of the equipment, which was built into the Eldridge, and, on 12th August 1943, they flicked the switch.'

'And?'

'Everything was fine for about a minute, with just the outline of the ship visible in the water, but suddenly there was a blue flash and the ship completely vanished into hyperspace. About three hours later, it reappeared, two of its transmitter cabinets and a generator missing, and one of the masts was broken. But the real damage was to the crew of thirty-three volunteer seamen, who'd only graduated the year before; they had no idea what they were volunteering for.'

'What happened to them?'

'Some of them were partially imbedded in the steel deck, others were fading in and out of this reality, some had simply disappeared. One poor guy was apparently on fire and burned for four days; there was nothing they could do to extinguish the flames. Most of those who survived went insane. But some of the crew who'd disappeared had apparently jumped overboard when things started to go haywire and finished up in a time tunnel that ended at Montauk Air Force base in New Jersey, exactly forty years later, August 12th 1983. Imagine the surprise on the sailors' faces when one minute they're in 1943, and then they're greeted by Von Neumann as an old man and its 1983.'

'My guess is you'd be a tad pissed off. What did he tell them?'

'That they'd created a hyperspace lockup and that they had to go back and shut off the generators on the ship or the hyperspace rift would keep increasing and possibly engulf the whole planet. What he didn't tell them was that several UFOs had been seen hovering around the Eldridge before the switches were flicked and that one of them had been sucked up into hyperspace along with the Eldridge and they feared an alien attack as a possible repercussion.'

'And...?'

'What choice did they have? The sailors returned and smashed the equipment with axes and the Eldridge returned to its original point in space but about three hours later in time.'

'And the UFO?'

'It ended up in an underground facility in Montauk in 1983 where they pulled it apart for analysis.'

'And those on board the UFO, what happened to them?'

'I don't know. For their sake, I hope they died in the time jump. Anyway, in 1953, the Navy pulled the pin on Project Rainbow and Von Neumann started Project Phoenix, which eventually became the Montauk Project around 1969.'

'And was that about time travel too?'

'No, the Phoenix and Montauk Projects were about mind-control.'

'Mind-control? I don't see the connection.'

'Von Neumann was in charge of them all. He was one of a group of "ex" Nazi's who came from Germany both before and after the end of the Second World War. They took over the derelict Montauk Air Force base in New Jersey.'

'They? The Nazis?'

'Basically, yes, but in the guise of a private corporation. Of course, the various US intelligence agencies knew what was going on, and the CIA monitored everything, but who knows half of what they got up to.'

'So who funded it, who was really behind it?'

'The same people who were behind the Nazis, and who are behind everything, the Illuminati; they run the military, they run NASA, they run the CIA, they run the Federal Reserve, they run the US Government.'

'So they used taxpayers money to fund their projects?'

'Now they do, but not then; they didn't need to. In 1944 there was an American troop train carrying ten billion dollars of 'captured' Nazi gold, which they had supposedly "found"; that's ten billion at the *1944* price, at twenty dollars an ounce.'

I did some quick math.

'Shit, that's like… five trillion dollars in today's market! What happened to it?'

'It "disappeared".'

'No way!'

'The train was going through a French railroad tunnel when it was supposedly "blown up", killing around fifty American soldiers.'

'Blown up by who; the war had been over in Europe for two years?'

'Exactly. Then, ten years later, the gold magically turned up at Montauk and they used the money to finance their projects for years to come. Not just the Montauk project though; they had a total of twenty-five bases around the United States. But, even though the value of gold went up, they ran out of money, and the last of the bases shut down on August 12, 1983.'

'The same day the sailors from the Philadelphia Project arrived?'

'Yeah, quite a coincidence, don't you think?'

'What's the significance?'

'Part of the mind-control experiments involved people sitting in chairs they had obtained from aliens, that amplified thoughts to such an extent that they would actually materialize. The government would have specially trained individuals sit in the chair and generate thought-forms, which would be amplified and transmitted.

But a lot of people thought the project had gone too far and, in an effort to sabotage it, someone planted the thought of a "monster from the ID" type creature in the mind of the operator in the chair.'

'What happened?'

'Well, it manifested; the creature materialized. It went wild; it ate people, equipment, and everyone went into a panic. They shut the transmitter off, but the monster wouldn't disappear, they had to send the sailors back to 1943 and shut down the unit in Philadelphia in order to shut off the unit in the future and stop the creature in 1983. After that, the whole project was shut down.'

'What about the UFO?'

'They moved it.'

'Area 51?'

'Probably.'

Like sands through the hourglass

We arrived at the Valley Temple, or rather the remnants of it. There wasn't much to see, just the scant remains of the limestone walls slowly being swallowed by the desert sands. To me it was more evidence that the whole temple had been swept away by a tsunami.

As hard as it was, I made a point of putting any other thoughts out of my mind as much as possible so that I wouldn't miss anything that might be here. It was my turn to be tour guide.

"The remains of the Valley Temple were excavated by the Egyptian archaeologist Ahmed Fakhry in 1951; the floor plan revealing a simple rectangular building surrounded by a mud-brick wall. The entrance was from the south, the southern wall flanked by two large stelae bearing the name and titles of Snefru."

The stelae were gone, most of the southern wall was gone, hell, most of the temple was gone. The entrance led to an entrance hall flanked by two long storerooms to either side.

"The walls were carved in bold relief with scenes depicting royal estates of the nomes of Upper Egypt on the west wall and the nomes of Lower Egypt on the east wall."

'That's interesting...'

Frank was scratching his chin.

'...It confirms the importance of the location.'

'How's that?'

Frank made his way along the remnants of the walls, looking for possible reliefs, for something recognizable.

'Well, as you travel down the Nile, the names and order of the patron gods of the nomes closely parallels the names and order of the Forty-two Assessors of Initiation in the subterranean "Hall of Truth" as written in the Egyptian 'Book of the Dead'', which was thought to have been written by the great teacher Tehuty, or Thoth, who arrived in Egypt just over fifty-thousand years ago. The fact that the entire land was deliberately organized into forty-two nomes reflects that long ago someone very knowledgeable about the secret Initiations of Thoth-Hermes was responsible.'

'Weren't the nomes created first, and the religious Initiations created in line with them?'

'No, I don't think so. The religious system must have existed first, and then the political economic and geographical patterns came later.'

'So why are the nomes so significant?'

'Primarily, they divided Egypt into a series of forty-two religious centres, where neophytes would travel down the Nile from centre to centre, studying the specific wisdom of each nome along the way, in preparation for their entrance into the final initiations at Giza.'

Apart from the scant remnants of a partial image or two on the lower part of the walls, there was nothing discernable. "Move along, nothing to see here".

Next was an open court, bounded by plain walls, leading to a ten-pillared portico. I returned to reading out my notes:

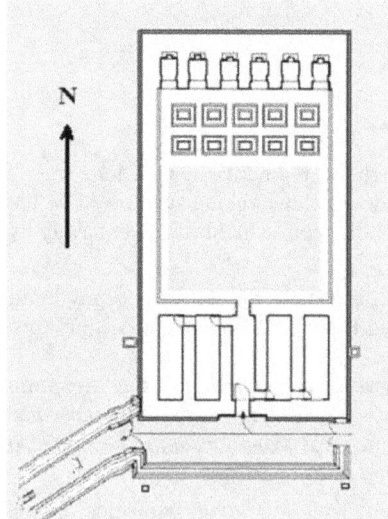

"The walls of the portico were carved with scenes of the royal estates. Scenes were carved on the columns on at least two sides – these included depictions of the Snefru's Sed Festival and the ceremonial visit to the shrines of Buto. Another fragment was found showing Snefru being embraced by a lion goddess."

At the rear of the temple, located in the north inner wall, were six niches, or shrines.

"Above the opening of the 6 niches the names of the king were carved, flanked by emblems and topped by a band of five-pointed stars. In the niches were life-size, or larger, statues of Snefru in different poses and costumes, actually carved from the same huge limestone slabs that comprised the back walls, therefore interestingly these statues were attached and not free standing."

The only additional 'evidence' I gained from the temple, apart from its *not* being there, was it being constructed of limestone; that just confirmed my thoughts that the Old and Middle Kingdoms were dominated by limestone constructions and alabaster statues.

That done, I was ready not only to move on to the Black Pyramid, but to return to our previous discussions. That was until Mark pointed to the east and threw in a curve ball.

'There appears to be some ruins over there suggesting that there might have been a second causeway, running from the temple to the Nile. That means, if the Bent Pyramid *was* a power station, then the Valley Temple could well have been a pumping station, pumping water from the Nile to the pyramid.'

'What?'

I looked eastwards towards the Nile, and yes there did seem to be some sort of abnormality that looked like another possible causeway. As we all made our way off towards the Black Pyramid, about half-a-kilometre to the southeast, Mark continued on with his thoughts.

'Well, I was thinking about what you said about the first portcullis being a pressure valve, and about what Frank said about the connecting tunnel being dug to fix both chambers. Any lighter-than-air gas produced in the lower chamber would rise up to the corbelled ceiling, then travel through the connecting tunnel and into the western chamber. Maybe the lower chamber was too damaged to function properly. The questions are, how, and when?'

I had some ideas.

'Let's say the original ziggurat was built sometime around 10,000 BC, maybe earlier. Then, there was a catastrophe, maybe a pole shift, around 8,800 BC which somehow damaged the chambers to such an extent that they ceased to function. So the pyramid was rebuilt and expanded, to the shape we see today, and a new chamber built, this one with a new entrance from the west.

Then there was another catastrophe, maybe another pole shift, say around 5,200 BC, which damaged the new chamber as well as creating a tsunami that damaged the exterior, and further damaged the original lower chambers.'

Mark was right with me, and filled in the rest.

'And then, in the 4th Dynasty, Snefru decides to try and repair it. They dig a tunnel from the original chamber, connecting it to the new chamber, and prop up the walls here and in the lower chamber with cedar beams.'

'Exactly.'

'And he builds a few temples and erects a few stelae to brag about it.'

'Precisely. Then around 1600 BC there's a massive eruption of Thera, which not only shakes the earth, but it sends a tsunami, over six-hundred feet high, that crashes in to Egypt and flattens everything in its path all the way up the Nile, at least as far as Aswan.'

Frank was smirking.

'You want to be careful, Alex; you sound like you're rewriting the history of Egypt, and there's a lot of people who wouldn't be too happy about that.'

'Look who's talking! I bet you've done heaps of research for your book, Frank, I doubt you're just going to regurgitate the current beliefs.'

He slapped me on the shoulder.

'You pegged me in one, Alex.'

'So, do you think the Bent Pyramid belongs to Snefru, or, if not, how old do you think the pyramid really is?'

'Oh, I like your thinking, son; you've certainly got me thinking of things I hadn't even been aware of. You've raised the bar and filled in a few blanks for me, that's for sure.'

'And these sibyls, you think there's some beneath the Giza Plateau as well?'

'More than ever.'

'Why didn't the mystery school guys bring one back with them?'

'I don't think they're the sort of thing you can just stick in your pocket or carry nearly a thousand feet up a staircase only twenty-nine inches wide.'

'Good point!'

'Besides, they were only able to make a total of six visits down into the chambers before the Egyptians got suspicious, and they had to abandon their plans. BUT... what they *did* manage to do was to take twenty-seven-hundred microfilms of the records; things that prove far distant ET visitations, underground civilizations and advanced societies here on earth.'

'Two-thousand-seven-hundred microfilms!...'

It reminded me of the conspiratorial withholding of the Dead Sea Scrolls from examination.

'...Where are they, why haven't we even seen them?'

'They took them to a laboratory set up in Germany, somewhere on the remote outskirts of Bonn, where the films were developed and translated.'

'And...?'

'According to an Air Force contact of mine, they were moved to Kirtland Air Force Base in New Mexico, and are locked away in a safe.'

'And...?'

'That's it. These guys were from an esoteric mystery school, they didn't want the public to know; and they were hardly going to publish their findings in 'The Scientific Journal' or 'Archaeology's Latest and Greatest Digs'.

'And that's what Hawass was after when he dug the big hole in the Giza Plateau, the one that was supposedly for the Red Bull games?'

'Of course.'

'That was in 2010, right, and they discovered the chambers way back in 1976?'

'Yep.'

'So it took Hawass over thirty years to get there.'

Mark corrected me.

'If he *did* get there; he may only have looted the first layer, remember, the chamber is over a-hundred-and-fifty metres below the surface.'

Frank changed the subject, pointing to the impressive feature that loomed about another two hundred metres ahead of us.

'Speaking of "below the surface", I bet there's heaps more to be discovered there.'

The Black Pyramid

In many ways, the Black Pyramid looked very similar to the Meidum Pyramid, just black, almost sinister; I wondered if it was built around the same time, with the same additions, and whether it looked the way it did because of the same fate, the tsunami. It certainly looked that way.

In ancient times it was apparently known as "Amenemhat is Mighty", despite the fact that rather than being buried here, Amenemhat III supposedly abandoned this pyramid and chose to build a second pyramid to be interred, the one at Hawarra, which I'd seen earlier in the day and ruled out as *not* belonging to Amenemhat III. So, did this pyramid belong to him, or, like all the others, was it from a much earlier time?

I half expected Frank to resume his role as tour guide and gave him a prompt.

'Hey Frank, given that the pyramid at Hawarra and the Black Pyramid both supposedly belong to Amenemhat III, I guess you know quite a bit about the Black Pyramid.'

Not really, I've primarily been focused on things at Hawarra and Giza.'

It was Mark who was the one forthcoming with more information.

'The first references to the Black Pyramid in the modern "archaeological" era date to around the 1850's, with Perring, and, after him, Lepsius, who both made note of it. But it wasn't until 1894-1895 that Jacques de Morgan, assisted by George Legrain, became the first to really investigate the area. They carried out extensive excavations, but were understandably more interested in searching for buried treasure, and excavated the tombs of the royal ladies and high officials surrounding the pyramid, rather than explore the pyramid itself...'

He scuffed his way through the sand.

'...As you can imagine, at the time, the excavation methods were pretty crude, and so many questions about the pyramid remained unanswered. For instance, because the footings of the structure have never been properly cleared, its base length is only estimated, at around fifty metres, and its angle, and thus its height, have never been properly determined.

It wasn't until 1976 that a team from the German Archaeological Institute of Cairo, lead by a guy called Arnold, spent the next seven years carrying out a modern, extensive examination.'

'There's that year again, 1976, and a German connection as well. It must have been an interesting time in Egyptian exploration!'

It made Mark consider the possibilities.

'I would normally have thought it was just a coincidence, but, given Dahshur was a military zone until the late '90s, and everything else we now know was going on, well, now I'm not so sure.'

'What did they discover?'

'Who knows what they actually found, only what they reported.'

'Which was?'

'That even though the nearby Bent Pyramid was built upon compacted gravel, Amenemhat III chose to build his pyramid on hard clay, which later became unstable subsoil, and that the weight of the pyramid was pushing down on the ceiling with such force that the walls sank in places up to three centimetres into the floor.'

'Which could just as easily be as a result of an earthquake and the liquefaction of the clay, which would have given an actual reason for the walls to sink, and not that the pyramid was originally built on an unstable base at all.'

'A good point! They also proposed that the builders compounded the mistake by constructing the pyramid in one of the lowest locations of any pyramid in Egypt, only thirty-three feet above sea level.'

'That's based on where it is now, but who knows what the sea level was when it was built, or the level of the land in relation to it, or where it was in relation to the river bank.'

'All viable hypotheses. They also claim the pyramid took fifteen years to build, and that soon after the pyramid was completed, ground water from the nearby Nile seeped into the pyramid's substructure, causing structural damage and menacing cracks to appear in the corridor and chamber walls because of the shear number of corridors and chambers within the substructure, and the reliance that the builders had placed on their ceilings, which had no real stress-relieving devices above the king's burial chamber.

331

Some ceiling and wall tiles have fallen in some places up to three centimetres.'

'Or, once the earthquakes and pole shifts caused the ground to liquefy and the walls to shift and crack, it allowed ground water to seep in. That it didn't take fifteen years to build, rather fifteen years to repair.'

'Just as plausible.'

'So, where does that leave us now? When *was* the pyramid actually built, and by whom? And was it built on top of pre-existing tombs, or were the tombs built under the pyramid sometime after?'

Frank was eager to do some exploring.

'Let's see if we can find out. Left or right?'

We'd arrived at the northwest 'corner' of the structure. There wasn't much recognizable so I checked my notes and the diagram, then looked around to get my bearings.

'Let's head left; there doesn't seem to be anything to the right. *"The whole complex was once surrounded by two plastered, whitewashed mud-brick enclosure walls, with, to the north, a row of ten shaft-tombs between the two of them.'*

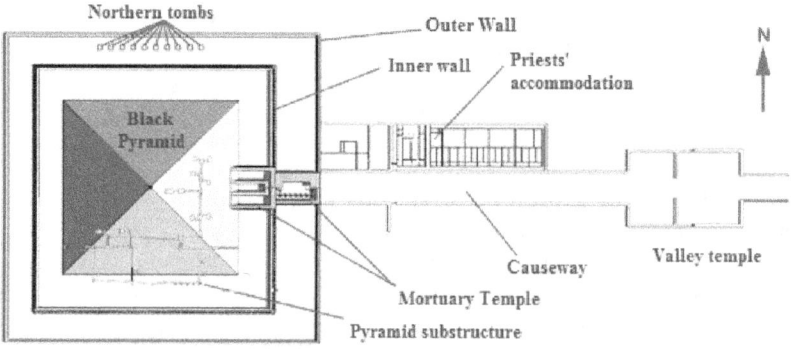

There was virtually nothing to see, but my thinking was, that as the walls were made of mud-brick, rather than limestone, it suggested the walls were not constructed during the Middle Kingdom, but a much later addition, possibly the New Kingdom or after. And what about the tombs?

Heading east, the tombs were almost undetectable, all closed off, and, despite our urgings, the guardian was unwilling to open them, gesturing with his hand, two fingers like fangs.

'No, not go in; cobra.'

I had visions of the Indiana Jones' movie where he gets trapped in the tomb with all the snakes; I wasn't quite ready to meet my maker, and neither were Mark and Frank. Besides, having just extracted myself from the bowels of the Bent Pyramid, the unstable nature of the subterranean corridors and chambers here didn't really fill me with the urge to 'baksheesh' my way in to check them out. Instead I simply referred to my trusty notes, again reading them out loud for the others.

"North of the pyramid, in the courtyard between the inner and outer perimeter walls, is a row of ten shaft tombs that belonged to the members of Amenemhat III's royal family.

The first tomb from the east was later usurped by one of the rulers of the 13th Dynasty, King Auibre Hor I, an insignificant ruler of the 13th Dynasty, whose mummy was discovered within a wooden coffin in the tomb along with a wooden Ka statue, one of the most valuable objects in the Egyptian Antiquities Museum, and a wooden canopic chest that bore the name of Nimaatre, a name for Amenemhat III. However, the view these days among Egyptologists seems to be that the name actually refers to a Khendjer, a successor of Hor's. The second tomb from the east belongs to the Amenemhat III's daughter, Princess Nebheteptikhered."

As we reached the location of the penultimate tomb, Mark, paused; clearly he had doubts.

'What if the tomb of Nebheteptikhered was usurped as well?'

Frank was even more sceptical.

'Who's to say that the whole row of tombs wasn't usurped from some earlier Dynasty; I mean, they appear very basic shaft tombs. If the evidence we discovered at the pyramids of Senwroset III and Amenemhat II is anything to go by, then these tombs may have originally belonged to the Old Kingdom, or even earlier.'

Mark had taken another tack.

'Why would Amenemhat bury one of his daughters here, and another, Neferuptah, at Hawarra?'

Frank and I each had a few thoughts.

'Maybe they had different mothers?'

'Maybe they didn't get along; you know sibling rivalry.'

'Maybe Amenemhat didn't bury them at all, because he was already dead?'

Then I thought back to Hawarra.

'What if Neferuptah's original tomb at Hawarra had flooded, and some of the artefacts were shifted to the Hawarra pyramid, and Nebheteptikhered's original burial place, which they probably haven't found, was flooded as well, but she was moved here?'

'You think flooding from the Thera tsunami?'

'It's possible; it's only about two-hundred years between the burials and the tsunami. Which means it's also possible that most of the pre-Thera tombs were flooded by the tsunami as well; especially the 12th, 13th, and 17th Dynasties.'

'It's worth considering.'

As he scratched around the tomb of Hor, Frank added another interesting tit-bit.

'You know, I don't think they've found many 13th Dynasty tombs, and I don't think they've found any tombs dating from the 17th Dynasty.'

We moved on; Mark still pondering the 'evidence'.

'I'm starting to think that the "usurping" and relocations that the modern Egyptologists ascribe to, may well have been a case of the early 18th Dynasty rebuilding after the tsunami, discovering and relocating any tombs they could get to. And if they couldn't find them, or get to them…'

I was way ahead of him, looking out over the desert.

'…then they're probably still out there somewhere, buried under twenty feet of sand and silt. I bet the 12th and 13th Dynasty tombs are all around here somewhere.'

'Which would explain why Dahshur was a military zone until the late '90s, they were looking for the original tombs.'

'And the 17th Dynasty ones are all somewhere under the ground in and around El Kab, south of Luxor, but the vultures either haven't got around to them yet, or they haven't figured out where they are.'

'And what about the dynasties in between; the 14th, 15th, and 16th Dynasties?'

By now Frank was on the same train of thought.

'They're up north, in Lower Egypt: but they were Hyksos rulers and may not even have buried their kings the same way. But, if they did, then they would've borne the full brunt of the tsunami, and so could well be under thirty, forty, maybe fifty feet of sediment.'

I looked back towards the row of tombs behind us.

'So the north tombs may have actually been dug during the 18th Dynasty.'

'It's possible, very possible. Anyway, I think it's fair to say, that as they're outside the inner wall, they must post-date the pyramid and are not a true indication of when the pyramid was built, or who built it. Otherwise the tombs would surely have been under or in the main body of the pyramid.'

And if that was the case, then, like the Hawarra Pyramid, the Black Pyramid was also built before the tsunami that buried the Osireion. And if that were so, I needed to find some evidence, 'red granite' evidence.

Beyond the tombs, the 'collapsed' mass of the pyramid made it difficult to assess whether there had been a northern chapel, or whether there was a northern entrance in the centre of its northern side, which would have been the norm. If there was, did it lead to a main chamber, or a series of chambers, each with a high-corbelled ceiling?

'Hey Mark, do you know much about the pyramid's structure?'

Looking at the remains of the dark grey structure seemed to further trigger his memory.

'The Egyptologists say the east-west orientation is similar to Old Kingdom pyramids, but structurally they say it's just like the other, earlier 12th Dynasty pyramids, with a core of mud-brick, and built in step form.'

'A ziggurat?'

'Sounds like it.'

'Which would make it much older, Old Kingdom at least, and in keeping with what we found at Meidum and with the Bent Pyramid.'

'That it would.'

'And the outer layers?'

'Next was a filler layer of Tura limestone, with the outer mantle, five metres thick, made of blocks of fine white limestone held together with a system of wooden dovetail joining pegs.'

'A later addition; after the first tsunami?'

'Could be!'

The use of limestone had me again thinking that this particular part of the pyramid was contemporary with the Old or Middle Kingdom, but could it have been even later, after Thera perhaps?

'I've seen dovetail joins at Kom Ombo and Dendera, and other temples reconstructed during the Ptolemaic period, and there were dovetails apparently used at the pyramid of Senwroset III we looked at earlier. Why use wooden pegs to join the stones, unless you wanted to hold the whole structure together, to stop it "spreading" from the inside?'

As ever, Frank had an insightful aside.

'Maybe they just "forgot" how to join them with mortar?'

Maybe, but it was more evidence the pyramid had been built in stages, possibly thousands of years apart, each 'stage' primarily a repair and reconstruction job. Meanwhile, Mark continued.

'In any case, the cladding stones formed a convex surface on each of the four faces.'

'Convex or concave?'

'It depends whether you're looking from the inside or the outside; curving in.'

Anyway, there it was again. What was the significance of the curved faces? It would be much easier to make straight faces, there had to be some functional reason for it.

'Could the additions here, the outer parts of the pyramid, actually be repairs done as late as 200 BC?'

Mark put a damper on that theory straight away.

'I doubt it, there's apparently some builder's graffiti on the casing stones that dates to year two of the reign of Amenemhat III; I think that's why they ascribe the Black Pyramid to him.'

'That just means the extensions, or even just the repairs to the extensions, were done during the 12th Dynasty, and that they were most possibly instigated by Amenemhat III, but that doesn't mean the mud-brick ziggurat at the core of the pyramid dates from that period.'

'They also found an inscribed dark-grey granite pyramidion in the rubble here in 1990, that's now in the museum in Cairo.'

'Granite! Yes, I remember seeing it at the museum; one face had a winged-disc flanked by two cobras.'

'Nibiru.'

'That's right.'

'And under the disc were two wadjet eyes. Under the eyes were three lutes, and under them was another large sun disc.'

'Presumably our sun.'

'That's how I see it.'

'Do you know what it all means?'

'No, Frank's the expert in that area.'

It sure didn't take any prompting for Frank to fill in the blanks.

'At the base of each of the four faces are two lines of hieroglyphs. They say something like: *"May the face of the king be opened so that he may see the Lord of the Horizon when he crosses the sky; may he cause the king to rise as a god, lord of eternity and indestructible. Horakhty has said, I have given to the king of Upper and Lower Egypt the beautiful horizon who takes the inheritance of the two lands...so that you may unite with the horizon...the horizon has said that you rest upon it, which pleases me."* Although, Horakhty is replaced on the South face by Anubis; on the West face by Ptah-Sokar-Osiris; and on the North face by Sah-Orion.'

'Horakhty? Isn't that another name for Ra, for the sun?'

'Yep.'

'So, what does it mean?'

Frank shrugged his shoulders.

'Who knows?'

'Maybe the translation is crap? I've got all sorts of doubts about Champollion's translations; they're weak, short, non-scientific, and full of incorrect assumptions. You know there's a guy who thinks it's all based on Meroitic hieroglyphics.'

Mark was in the dark.

'Meroitic hieroglyphs?'

'It's a language from Sudan, very similar to ancient Egyptian hieroglyphs, and supposedly very close to a star language.'

'Well, that would explain things better.'

The whole subject had set Frank off on a bit of a roll.

335

'Another curious aspect is that one of the inscriptions, the one containing the name of Amun, had been deliberately destroyed, one would presume during the reign of Akhenaten.'

'That pretty much proves the pyramidion must have been on the ground by the 18th Dynasty, which is *after* the Thera tsunami would have demolished the pyramid.'

Frank hadn't finished.

'But, and here's the clincher, on each side of the sun-disc were royal cartouches bearing the names of Amenemhat III.'

'Couldn't the inscriptions have been added later, just like Ramses II claimed all the temples and statues for himself?'

'It's possible.'

I had it sorted!

'What if the pyramidion was on the ground way before that? What if original pyramidion was totally bereft of inscriptions, or maybe just had the winged-disc on it? Then the pole shift, around 8,800 BC or 5,200 BC, caused an earthquake or tsunami that dislodged the pyramidion... '

Mark went to answer, but I was on a bit of a roll.

'What if it lay in the sand and rubble until the Middle Kingdom when Amenemhat III decided to rebuild the pyramid, out of mud-brick? What if the inscriptions to Amenemhat were done while the pyramidion was still on the ground, but, once the Black Pyramid was rebuilt, they didn't have the technology to raise the pyramidion back up to the apex of the pyramid?

Or maybe they did, but the Thera tsunami dislodged it again, as well as decimating the rebuilt pyramid. Then, in the 18th Dynasty, Akhenaten came along and ordered the name of Amun to be chiselled out?'

'It's quite a story, but no more far fetched than the theories the current Egyptologists have trotted out. In fact, it makes a hell-of-a-lot more sense.'

As he scuffed his way through the desert sand, Mark cast a glance back over his shoulder.

'I wonder what other secrets the Black Pyramid has to reveal?'

We'd made our way through the scant ruins of what was the priests' accommodation, situated just north of the causeway, and out as far as the Valley Temple. Beyond it, to the east, a broad, open causeway would have led directly from the Nile, and most likely a quay, through the Valley Temple and on to the mortuary temple adjoining the pyramid.

It was clear that whilst there had been some clearing of the Valley Temple in the past, nothing out this side of the pyramid had be systematically excavated; not the causeway, the Valley Temple, nor the mortuary temple, and the quay had either been washed away, or was now buried under the cultivated bank of the existing Nile.

Although it was almost completely destroyed, the Valley Temple itself, as much as I could make it out by the mounds and ridges of sand, was very simple, with two broad open courts built on ascending terraces.

"The side walls of the first court were thickened to form a huge pylon-like gateway, and Jacques de Morgan found fragments of reliefs indicating the walls were decorated and contained a cartouche of Amenemhat IV..."

Where was it all now? Swept away no doubt!

"...Within these ruins was found a limestone model, of the

subterranean corridors and chambers of a 13th Dynasty pyramid, that has not yet been discovered."

I didn't think it would have been a 13th Dynasty model, probably earlier, perhaps from the Old Kingdom, and who's to say it was a pyramid, it may just as well have been a model of the tombs under a mastaba. Or maybe it was a model of a planned tomb substructure that was never built? Question was, "what was it doing here?" Unless, of course, it had been swept here by the tsunami.

'Hey Mark, are there any other pyramids around here?'

He pointed south.

'The pyramid of Senwroset I is about one-and-a-half kilometres south of here, at Lisht, and Senwroset II's pyramid is beyond that at el-Lahun.'

Frank chipped in as well.

'If you want to go further, about three to five kilometres south of here, there's apparently five more pyramids at Mazghuna. Although I've never been there myself, mainly because they're all apparently really difficult to reach and we'd need a guide to get to them, they all supposedly belong to the end of the Middle Kingdom. Why, do you want to visit them as well?'

I could see Mark was about all pyramided out, so was Frank, and I wasn't far behind them.

'No, no, just curious.'

Checking my notes, I quickly located a brief file on Senwroset I.

"Built on a foundation of stone blocks, the pyramid of Senwroset I was constructed mainly of limestone from the nearby quarries. The core was supported by a stone framework filled with fragments of limestone, sand, and waste. The casing of blocks of Tura limestone was firmly anchored in a flat trench dug around the pyramid's base."

Nothing out of the ordinary so far.

"The pyramid was surrounded by a unique, inner perimeter wall, built of limestone blocks, with narrow panels decorated with images in bas-relief on its inner side at intervals of five metres. Somewhat farther away was the outer perimeter wall, which surrounded the tombs of the members of the royal family."

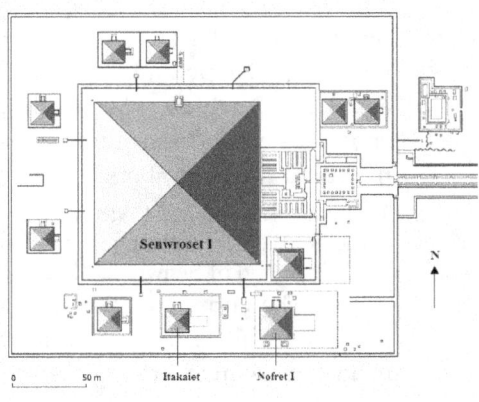

Well, I wasn't so convinced about the last part, as to the smaller pyramids being originally tombs, but the sheer number and specific position of the smaller pyramids here certainly raised the issue of the significance of this pyramid complex.

"In the space between the inner and the outer perimeter

walls, nine small pyramid complexes were discovered, three on the south side and two each on the west, north and east sides of the pyramid. Each small pyramid had a mortuary temples and its own perimeter wall. So far, the pyramid complexes of Nofret I, Amenemhat I's daughter and consort of Senwroset I, and Itakaiet, probably Senwroset 's daughter, have been identified."

Itakaiet could also have been another wife, or third cousin twice removed, or the old lady who lived in the shoe; the truth was the Egyptologists were just guessing and suggested she was a daughter because her pyramid was smaller than the pyramid of Nofret I. In any case, it didn't seem much use to me. Why a 'cult' pyramid separate to the Queen's pyramids, was there any significance?

"The shaft in the centre of the north side of Nofret I's pyramid leads to a gently descending corridor paved with limestone. The corridor in turn leads to a chamber, lined with limestone, under the centre of the pyramid, with a hole for the sarcophagus and an unfinished niche for the canopic chest. Alongside, a 32-sided column, inscribed with name of queen Itakaiet, was found within the ruins of next complex, its burial chamber, barely more than an extension of the entrance corridor, sealed with mortared limestone slabs and lacking a sarcophagus."

That was a bit of a bummer: no granite. Perhaps the chambers were unfinished, or stripped bare, which was unlikely?

"Now in ruin, the cult pyramid, southeast of the pyramid, is the most complicated, with two subterranean chambers and evidence of two or three phases of construction."

Again, nothing. I was about to give up on the complex until I read the last paragraph.

"The entrance to the subterranean chambers of the main pyramid was via the pavement of the courtyard, in front of the middle of the pyramid's north side. A descending corridor, the entrance of which was lined in granite, led past barriers of enormous blocks of the same stone, weighing as much as 20 tons, to the burial chamber, about 24 metres under ground level."

That was the evidence I was looking for, the granite portcullises, the lining. It didn't say whether the burial chamber was made of red granite, but I suspected it did. I wondered if the pyramid of Senwroset II at el-Lahun had similar evidence.

"The entire complex of Senwroset II was surrounded by a perimeter wall, within which the builders used a rock outcropping to anchor the mud-brick core of the pyramid, surrounding it with a framework of stone masonry. The casing is gone, although a few fragments of a black granite pyramidion were discovered."

It sounded promising.

"A small mortuary temple, now almost completely destroyed, once stood before the east side of the pyramid, as well as a small chapel to the north. To the northeast of the main pyramid, was a small queen's pyramid. Though Petrie explored it with tunnels and a deep vertical shaft he never found a single passage or chamber beneath it; part of a name on a vase the only evidence it belonged to a queen."

The vase could have come from anywhere, from any time; it could have been dumped there thousands of years after the 'queen's' pyramid was built. Despite that, the Egyptologists had assigned the main pyramid to Senwroset I, not based on any actual evidence in or on the main pyramid itself, but based on a single fragment of a broken vase found around the "queen's" pyramid. I'm not saying it's not possible, but it's a big stretch, and hardly sound scientific methodology.

"The substructure of the main pyramid contained a labyrinth of shafts, chambers, and passageways surrounding the burial chamber. The burial chamber, oriented east-west, consisted of a vaulted ceiling of granite blocks and a masterfully worked sarcophagus, which stood against the west wall."

The vaulted ceiling of granite blocks confirmed my thinking the subterranean chambers were a pre-Thera tsunami. According to the diagram, there were a number of other subterranean tunnels and chambers that, because of their irregular shape, seemed to be more primitive substructures. That didn't mean they were even earlier than the main 'burial' chamber, in fact, they may well have been much later, post-pole shift, either from the Old Kingdom, or more likely from the 26th Dynasty onwards. Without exploring them personally, or having any detailed notes, it was impossible to tell.

Heading further south, I was surprised when I discovered I didn't have any files on Mazghuna on my iphone, in fact I'd never even heard of it, but, thanks to the marvels of modern technology, I simply went online, punched in 'pyramids of Mazghuna' and pulled up a webpage.

"At Mazghuna, three miles south of the Bent Pyramid at Dahshur, is a field of five mud-brick pyramids dating from the late Middle Kingdom. Two are unidentified, one belongs to Ameny-Qemau, and there are two unfinished pyramids, believed to belong to the last two rulers of the 12th Dynasty, the northern pyramid, ascribed to Amenemhat IV, and the southern pyramid, belonging to Sobeknefru, or Queen Nefrusobek, although there are no inscriptions or finds confirming this identification."

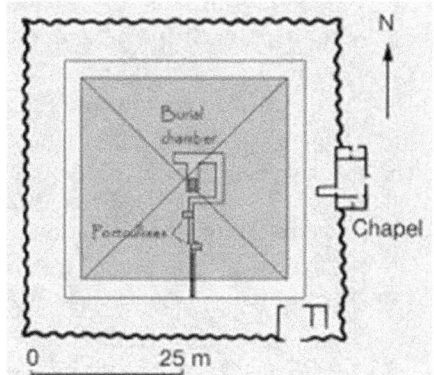

Nefrusobek? I'm sure that was one of the past lives Crystal said she'd been? Initially it made me want to visit Mazghuna, just on the off chance Crystal might be there, but then I thought the Mazghuna pyramids probably dated to an earlier time and the Egyptologists were just guessing, based on their previous incorrect assumptions about the 'ownership' of the pyramids here at Dahshur.

"The southern pyramid of Amenemhat IV was surrounded by an almost square, wavy wall, of the type we typically see at the beginning of the early Middle Kingdom."

Or, is the wall actually attributable to the end of the Old Kingdom?

"The broad entrance in the wall is a vestibule built into the east end of its south side. The area around this entrance was covered in limestone chips. Along the centre of the eastern part of the enclosure wall was a mud-brick mortuary temple, really nothing more than a chapel that consisted of a large central chamber, or court, and several smaller storage annexes to either side of the chamber. Attached to the rear, or southwest corner of the central chamber was an offering hall, which oddly, did not abut the pyramid. No traces of a causeway or valley temple have been found, if they were ever built."

So, was this an earlier prototype of the buildings we find at the other pyramids, or a later modification? Appearance-wise, and from a functional perspective, it would appear to be an earlier structure, supporting a possible Old Kingdom origin.

"The ruins of the pyramid are heavily damaged; whereas the mud-brick core can still be discerned, no trace of the limestone casing has been found. Its superstructure was never finished. Apparently only one or two courses of brick were laid to form the core of this pyramid, and a trench was dug around the outer edge in typical Middle Kingdom fashion to hold the casing securely in place. However, no casing stones have ever been found."

So, was the pyramid washed away, or was it left incomplete? And if it was left incomplete, why, what event caused it to be abandoned?

Arriving at what would have been the mortuary temple, in front of the east side of the Black Pyramid, it was so badly damaged I couldn't make anything out without my notes to guide me.

"Relatively small and simple, the mortuary temple consisted of an entrance, an open courtyard surrounded by eighteen granite columns each in the shape of eight-stemmed papyrus. The inner enclosure wall, decorated with niches, divided the outer open courtyard of the mortuary temple from the inner sanctuary."

How in the hell did they figure all that out from the amorphous mass of grey rubble that lay before me? It reinforced my serious doubts about the authenticity of any of the modern restorations and reconstructions. And what was the significance of the granite columns? Were they, like the ones at Dendera and Elephantine Island; recycled?

Continuing south, around the rest of the pyramid, I turned my thoughts back to the supposed pyramid of Amenemhat IV at Mazghuna.

"The entrance to the substructure is from the middle of its south side and opens into a narrow stairway with shallow steps and side ramps that slope down to a great portcullis block intended to block the passage. At this transition point the passage levels out, the lower part of the passage blocked by a granite slab, so that when the plug was slid into place from its recess, it blocked the continuation of the passage at the higher level. From this higher opening, another stairway ramp descended to a second block. This barrier is similar to the first, but the plug was left open."

This seemed a common aspect the Egyptologists were overlooking, the first portcullis was sealed, or semi-sealed, while the second one was open. A coincidence? I don't think so.

"From here, corridors twisted around the eastern part of the burial chamber in three 90 degree turns, the first to the east, the next two to the left, before arriving at a service chamber to the north of the burial chamber in which were found an alabaster vessel in the form of a trussed duck and three limestone lamps. This small service chamber had a trench dug to assist the introduction of funerary equipment, such as a small alabaster kohl pot and a piece of glazed steatite, into the burial chamber which was located on the pyramid's vertical axis, probably with a ceiling reinforced by a saddle vault of limestone blocks."

There was that saddle ceiling again. I suddenly thought, maybe it was a form of pressure valve as well. The massive blocks of limestone would lean against each other until some upward force caused them to separate, releasing pressure into the space above, possibly into a mud-brick vault. Then the limestone slabs would naturally fall back together due to gravity; simple, but highly effective.

"Similar to the chamber built for Amenemhat III at Hawarra, a single block of red quartzite fills the chamber space with receptacles for the coffin and canopic chest carved into the block's interior. There was a lid to this inner burial chamber that featured two large slabs resting on the rim of the vault, with a gap left between them. Supports, resting on sand filled shafts, held the missing lid piece. Side channels allowed the sand to be removed, so that the missing lid piece would slip down into its slot, however it was never used since no one was ever buried here. These similarities, along with similarities in the passages, are what lead many Egyptologists to believe that this pyramid is attributable to Amenemhat IV."

I would hardly consider that to be concrete evidence. That would be like me building a replica of the Eiffel tower then people claiming me to be Eiffel's son; ludicrous. Thankfully the guardian pulled me back to the 'Now', pointing to an area south of the causeway.

'Palace, home of pharaoh.'

It wasn't on the map, but that didn't mean there was nothing there, and clearly something had once existed there. Now it was just regularly delineated, undulating ridges of sand. He pointed a little further south into the desert.

'Many boat, dig from under sand.'

That seemed a common thing associated with these pyramids as well, but were they really funerary boats for the dead pharaoh to travel to the underworld, or were they simply associated with the normal day-to-day functions of the temples, moored close to the Nile in narrow channels, and subsequently buried by the tsunami? Next, he pointed at the level of the lowest foundation layer, near the southeast corner of the Black Pyramid.

'Enter here, tomb of king, Amenemhat Three.'

A lot of good it did him pointing at the rubble, the entrance was closed off and access was forbidden. No snakes this time, no doubt simply the genuine possibility of the whole pile of sand and stone collapsing on top of us. It was OK for an official university expedition to be buried alive, they would have paid big money for the privilege, but to the three wise monkeys, despite the fact we would 'see' nothing, 'say' nothing, and 'hear' nothing, venturing into the subterranean warren of the Black Pyramid wasn't an option; we would have to rely on my file notes.

Checking my iphone, I quickly flicked to the relevant Black Pyramid documents and read them out for the others.

"The Black Pyramid is more complex, and differs entirely from the underground layout of earlier 12th Dynasty pyramids, in that it accommodates not only the tomb of the king, but also several of his queens, in an system of passageways, shafts, barriers and chambers, at various levels, all of it covered in fine white limestone. In fact, there are more underground chambers and passages here than any other pyramid since the 3rd Dynasty."

Frank wasn't convinced.

'That's of course *if* you assume the substructure is directly chronologically linked to the superstructure; which we don't! The fact the entrance isn't actually *in* what would have been the pyramid's face, but down through the lowest foundation layer would seem to indicate the underground chambers may well have been there *before* the pyramid was built, or tunnelled out *afterwards.*'

'Or, the core, the ziggurat, was built first, then the underground chambers, then the outer layers of the pyramid some time later.'

'Maybe there are some clues below?'

We examined the diagram, noting that although connected by a number of passages, the subterranean area could be 'divided' into three areas: the first, mostly under the eastern quadrant of the pyramid, was for the king, the second, to the south and between the outer edge of the pyramid and the inner enclosure wall, comprised several corridors and tombs of the king's offspring, whilst the third, comprising the tombs of Queen Aat and Queen Neferuptah, was under the south-east corner of the pyramid and had its own entrance from the west.

"From the entrance, a stairway leads down for about twenty metres to a corridor. To the left, a second corridor leads off to the south, eventually arriving at the queen's section of the pyramid. Meanwhile, the original entrance corridor continues on to a chamber, aligned to the north, with a niche high in

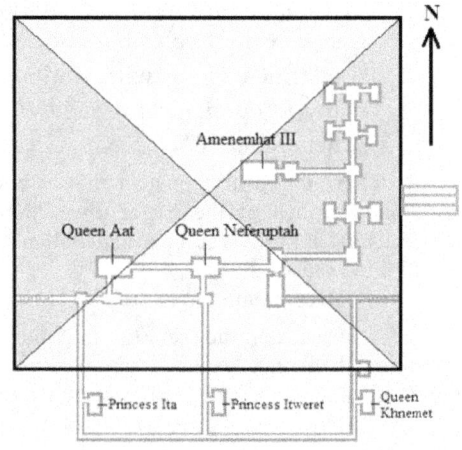

the wall for the king's canopic chest.

At the north end of the chamber a short staircase leads to a second 'chamber', off which a second corridor leads westwards to the queen's chambers. The passage then heads right 90 degrees back in the direction of the pyramid's eastern entrance. Following the corridor another 90 degree left turn leads past a pair of annexes before a final left turn takes us to a small antechamber and then the burial chamber.

The burial chamber is offset from the vertical axis of the pyramid, but was probably suppose to be directly under it; apparently the builders lacked the knowledge that others before them had demonstrated."

Frank scoffed incredulously.

'Well, I don't believe that for a minute, they would have known exactly what they were doing.'

'Maybe the chamber is off-centre because there's a yet-to-be-discovered corbelled chamber under the axis, with its own entrance from the north?'

'It's possible. Now wouldn't that be interesting!'

"Oriented east-west, the burial chamber is covered in a fine poultice of white limestone, but lacks any stress-relieving chamber or a gabled roof above the ceiling."

'That supports the idea there was not meant to be a pyramid on top.'

Frank had continued the brainstorming, but Mark was quick to keep it ticking over.

'They could have added a relief chamber if they'd wanted to, when they were building the pyramid, but they didn't.'

I started thinking way outside the box.

'Maybe they didn't know the chamber was there?'

It was Frank who reeled in my über-exuberance.

'Unlikely. More probable, that, as they were building with mud-brick, they didn't think they needed a relief chamber. Anything else?'

' "Though Amenemhat III wasn't buried in this pyramid, there is a pink granite sarcophagus near the west wall. It has a vaulted top and niches that imitate the perimeter wall of Djoser's Step Pyramid at Saqqara, and a set of wadjet eyes near the north end of its east side for the occupant to look out in the direction of the sunrise and resurrection." It's almost identical to the sarcophagus and chamber in the pyramid of Senwroset III; the gypsum coating, the niched granite sarcophagus. But do the niches imitate Djoser's wall or is it vica versa?'

While I was pondering the granite sarcophagus, Mark put all the pieces together.

'So, the king's chamber here may well belong to the Old Kingdom as well?'

'Or early dynastic, even pre-dynastic.'

We both looked at Frank; the plot was thickening.

'What about the rest of the tombs?'

'One way to find out?'

As we rounded the southern side of the pyramid I continued reading from my notes.

"The second corridor, the more complex corridor leading south off the eastern entrance, leads to the 'South Tomb'. It contains a labyrinth of passageways, side niches and six chapels, underground between the inner enclosure wall and the pyramid.

Excavated by Jacques de Morgan in 1895, he discovered the intact tombs of several of Amenemhat III's relatives: Princesses Ita, Itweret, and Sithathormeret, as well as the tombs of Queen Khnemet and Prince Amenemhatankh. The tombs contained a *variety of funerary furniture such as wooden coffins, alabaster perfume jars, and canopic chests; The burials of Ita and Khnemet especially revealed a large quantity of beautiful jewellery which are now on display in the Cairo Museum."*

Frank was right on to it.

'How do we know they're all related to Amenemhat III? Maybe they're all from a much earlier kingdom and the Egyptologists simply ascribed them to Amenemhat because they believed the pyramid was his? If they think the tomb of Hor was usurped, what's to say all these tombs aren't the same; they could have been placed here much later, or much earlier.'

'Maybe they did the same thing with the tomb of Nebheteptikhered on the north side, maybe she wasn't one of his daughters either?'

'Who knows? But one thing's certain; this Egyptology business is fraught with very dubious assumptions.'

As we continued around to the western side of the pyramid, one particular note on my iphone caught my attention.

"Some Egyptologists have even suggested that Amenemhat IV and Nefrusobek are buried here."

It made me flick back to my notes on Mazghuna, to the northern pyramid, supposedly that of Nefrusobek.

"Though construction of the pyramid's core was never started, and no traces of its casing stones have been found, meaning the precise measurements of the superstructure are not known, the unfinished Northern Mazghuna Pyramid is the largest of the two ruins found in the Mazghuna field. It is attributed to Queen Sobekneferu, assumed to be the daughter of Amenemhat III and the full or half sister and consort of Amenemhat IV, solely on the grounds of a few bits of structural and archaeological evidence."

No casing stones? No core? So, it was really just an underground chamber? If the core wasn't started, then originally maybe there was never meant to be a pyramid on top of it? That seemed to match with my thoughts about the Hawarra pyramid.

"There was no mortuary or valley temple, however two mud-brick walls flanked a causeway from the east, which was probably used for the transport of building materials."

Or, if the underground chamber was simply a power plant, the causeway was used to pump water directly from the Nile. Maybe there was no need for a mortuary temple or valley temple? Maybe the temples were later additions, when the pyramids assumed a more religious function?

"The entrance, on the north side of the

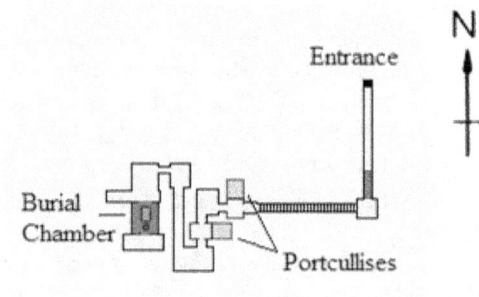

pyramid, leads to a short staircase descending to a square chamber containing another descending staircase to the right. That leads to the first portcullis chamber where a 42-ton quartzite plug lies in a recess to the chamber's north. It would have slid into the chamber over a quartzite slab, forming a wall, but was never closed.

Beyond the portcullis, the corridor continues on, turns south, past a second barrier chamber, then doubles back on itself in a U shape before heading left, arriving at an antechamber to the north of the burial chamber."

The descending turns reminded me a little of the tombs of Thutmoses III & IV and Amenhotep II & III in the Valley of the Kings. It seemed so long ago when I was there, freewheeling down the road on a bike with not a care in the world. That was …what… three, four days ago? Then I met Kareem and my life got turned into an Indiana Jones movie. Anyway, here there was, not one, but two, forty-two ton granite 'plugs'; that was telling.

"The burial chamber is filled with a monolithic quartzite sarcophagus vault that almost completely fills the burial chamber, with just a 2 cm gap between the vault and the chamber walls.…"

This was sounding familiar.

"…There is a void cut in the north of the quartzite block for the coffin and for the canopic chest in its southern end. As there was never a burial, the lid to the sarcophagus was never put in place. It remained in a low chamber, waiting to be slid over the top of the vault and locked by a blocking slab that would have been slid across to lock it in its position was in its recess."

Yes, it was just like the main chamber in the Hawarra pyramid, just without the saddle vault above. Maybe the top was swept away, including the limestone monoliths that formed the saddle vault? No, that was unlikely, they would have been somewhere nearby if they had been there at all. Of course, the top may have been removed, or reused? Possible, but, again unlikely. The most likely explanation is that it was never there in the first place. And there was more evidence, the massive granite 'sarcophagus'; that 'tomb' was much older than the Middle or even Old Kingdom.

"The exposed part of the quartzite sarcophagus was covered in plaster, and, like elsewhere in the pyramid, painted red. On this painted surface are patterns of vertical black strokes bounded by fine horizontal lines."

The plastering and painting was just like at the pyramid of Senwroset III; more repair work to a damaged vibrational chamber? And were these preliminary marks the guidelines for text, like those I had seen in several tombs in the Valley of the Kings? The tomb of Nefrusobek? I doubt it.

I'd hoped the western side of the pyramid might have held a few more answers but I was sadly disillusioned, especially when our guardian pointed to the south corner of the 'face'.

'Here, tomb of queen.'

It was almost a mirror image of the eastern entrance, and just as disappointing to find it in a similar state. Again, like the eastern entrance, it descended from the lowest level of the foundation layer, which immediately suggested they had been created around the same time. According to the diagram, the tombs of the queens' lay mainly under the southern quadrant of the pyramid.

"A second descending stairway, from the west, leads to a chamber with a niche above the doorway for the canopic chest of Queen Aat. Though the canopic chest was broken, all the pieces were found and it contained one canopic jar. From this, the corridor continues east, firstly passing a short corridor on the left that leads to the burial chamber of Queen Aat, who was about 35 when she died. On the west wall of the burial chamber was a sarcophagus very similar to that of the king's, with the bones of the queen also found within the chamber."

'Another granite sarcophagus with niches; more evidence of the Old Kingdom?'

I was with Mark on that.

'Looks like it. Interesting too that they say "the bones", and not "the mummy". Surely if you were going to rob the tomb, you would steal the whole mummy?'

Thankfully Frank wasn't so quick to make wild assumptions.

'Not necessarily, why carry a whole body? More likely you would rip the mummy to pieces to find the jewels wrapped inside it. But it does raise the question as to whether the bones really belonged to Aat, or whether it was someone else? Does it say anything else?'

"Though thieves had long ago broken into the pyramid, a few items of funerary equipment were left behind; two mace heads, seven alabaster cases in the form of ducks, an alabaster unguent jar and scattered pieces of jewellery."

'They could have been placed there after the tomb was robbed, or when it was usurped.'

'Yeah, not really concrete evidence, is it?'

'What does it say about the other chamber?'

"The corridor continues eastwards past a second northern corridor that leads to the second burial chamber, that of the second queen, most probably Neferuptah, who was around 25 when she died, and whose bones were also found within her chamber. Again, on the west wall of the burial chamber was a sarcophagus similar to that of the king's, however, in this case, it lacked the niches found on Amenemhat III's sarcophagus."

'Which means it could be an even earlier design?'

Once again, Frank was quick to put forward an alternative.

'Or, the fact she died young meant they didn't have time to finish it.'

The second queen's chambers contained an obsidian vassal decorated with gold bands, three alabaster duck shaped vessels, granite and alabaster mace heads, and jewellery. There were also parts of this queen's stone shrine, originally encased in gold and containing a ka statue. In addition to the ka statues in the tombs, they also found a mysterious wooden cabinet whose lid contained the cartouche of a monarch named Nimaatre."

'Who's he?'

I quickly scanned the notes.

'No one knows, though apparently *"some Egyptologists believe it's another name of Amenemhat III".'*

The cynicism flowed from Frank's lips like champagne at a wedding reception.

'Oh, I found a sweater with Gary's name on it, but I don't know a Gary, so I'm going to say it belongs to Paul and suggest Gary is another name Paul goes by; great scientific logic in that process. Shit! Morons!'

346

I had a chuckle at Frank's irreverence and obvious lack of respect for 'mainstream archaeology'. Then Mark lobbed another ball back over the net at me.

'So, Alex, do you think all this stuff was put there before your Thera tsunami, or relocated there after it, in the 18th Dynasty?'

I scratched my head.

'Who knows?…'

So much about conventional 'Egyptology' was proving to be conjecture, speculation, and fabrication, based on assumptions, dodgy deductions and plain guesswork. And, all of *that*, was based on the preconceived ideas the supposed 'experts' brought to the table, educated or uneducated.

It reminded me of the story of the five blind men, each holding on to a separate piece of an elephant: one has the trunk, one has an ear, one has the tail, one has a leg, the last one is feeling the side. Then they each try describing the whole animal based on the scant evidence they have in their hands. Were the mainstream Egyptologists any different? Were *we* any different?

Everything we were discovering, and that I had discovered so far in my trip, seemed to fly in the face of the conventional views. Was I totally wrong, or, because I had no preconceptions or misconceptions, was I closer to the truth?

"…The pyramid was presumable sealed in the 20th year of Amenemhat III's 47-year reign. The entrance stairways were filled in with limestone blocks, as well as the king's chamber and antechambers, the queens' burial chambers and the entrance corridors to the ka chapels. Other chambers and corridors were filled with mud-brick."

As usual, Frank was the first to question the 'experts'.

'None of that makes sense; who seals their 'tomb' twenty-seven years *before* they die?'

'Maybe he sealed it after it collapsed, then built a new tomb?'

'What, and sealed his wife and children in as well? I doubt it. Surely he would have moved them to his new pyramid, if there in fact was one.'

The next thought came from Mark.

'Maybe it was to prevent the pyramid's collapse; there were chambers in Amenemhat III's pyramid at Hawara similarly filled with blocks.'

'So why use mud-brick? No, they were used to seal the chambers, but I think it was after the chambers had been usurped from their original owners, or rather their original purpose. Or, that the limestone blocks were put in place some time during the Middle Kingdom, meaning those chambers contained people and belongings from Middle Kingdom or the Old Kingdom, and the mud-brick filling was a much later addition, after rediscovered tombs had been relocated. So Alex may well be right when he suggested it was all done in the 18th Dynasty, after the tsunami.'

I had a few more questions of my own.

'You know, there are a few more questions I still have, namely, if there was the convention that every pharaoh built a pyramid over his tomb, or put his tomb inside a pyramid, then why don't we have over five hundred pyramids in Egypt? Where are the seventh to eleventh Dynasty pyramids? Where are the thirteenth to seventeenth Dynasty pyramids? And what about the New Kingdom, if anyone was going to build pyramids it would have been Ramses II, right? But, nothing! Why? What was the telling factor? Why did they stop building them if they were such a status symbol?

And think about those portcullises, has anyone ever considered how these lowly "tomb robbers" had the knowledge and technology to lift forty-ton blocks of solid granite, in such confined spaces, without being noticed by anyone? And if the tomb robbers *could* open the tombs so easily, why would the builders still persisted in using portcullises to seal them? None of it adds up, not if you go by what the so-called "experts' tell you.'

'I don't know about you, Frank, but I think all those questions are best discussed over a cold beer or two back at the hotel in Cairo.'

Mark was right; it was time to call it a day.

The road trip!

No sooner had we started the long walk back to the car, than we noticed a military vehicle approaching from the west, from the direction of the Bent Pyramid, several armed soldiers seated in the open tray at the back.

'Oh, shit, they've found me.'

Suddenly there was nowhere to hide, nowhere to run, nowhere to dump the backpack. How was I going to talk myself out of it? "Someone must have put the papers there", "I found them", "I didn't kill anyone". Thank god Mark was there, as a solicitor he'd surely be able to look after me.

As soon as the car pulled up, an officer got out of the car and walked towards us. The guardian greeted him, and they had a brief discussion before the officer stepped towards us.

'Doctor, pyramid is good?'

Frank shook his hand.

'Excellent, excellent. Thank you, yes, very good.'

The officer seemed delighted.

'Very good. Yes, please, you would like it to have it the drive back?'

Was that all it was, a lift? Or were they biding their time, not wanting to shoot me in the desert and have to lug the body back through the afternoon heat?

Frank graciously accepted for all of us, and we climbed aboard, Frank in the front with the officer, Mark and I in the tray with the guardian and two kalashnikov-toting teenagers. It seems Frank had arranged it earlier, when he bought the tickets, for them to pick us up later on at the Black Pyramid and give us a lift back.

The trip back to the car park was about a kilometre or so through the desert sand, and only took about two or three minutes, but it was a godsend and saved us what would have been an exhausting fifteen to twenty minute hike through the heat, although, every second I expected one of the soldiers to ask me what was in my backpack. I tried not to make eye contact with anyone, pretending I was worn out, waving my akubra in my face until I remembered the bullet holes through it, which would clearly have been visible. I surreptitiously wrapped my hand over them and tucked my hands and my hat down between my knees, leaving Mark to make small talk with the young soldiers.

As soon as the vehicle came to a halt in the car park, I jumped down, gave everyone a handshake and moved around to the far side of our car, using it as a shield, as a barrier, ready to jump in. Frank gave the officer a 'baksheesh' handshake, Mark did likewise with the guardian, then we all climbed aboard, bid farewell to the locals, and headed off.

It wasn't until we'd past the ticket office and were turning back onto the main road that I glanced behind to check we weren't being followed, then, sure we weren't, collapsed back into the seat and breathed a massive sigh of relief. Mark started chuckling away.

'You looked like any minute you were going to have a coronary.'

'Jesus, Mark, you have no idea!...'

I took the backpack off and put it down on the seat beside us.

'...These papers have taken ten, twenty years off my life; the sooner I'm out of Egypt the better.'

From the front seat, Frank turned his head.

'When's your flight again?'

'Three days from now.'

'By the time we get back to Cairo, it's probably going to be too late today, but I suggest that first thing in the morning you go to the Australian Embassy, at least they should be able to arrange a new passport for you.'

'And what do I do about the papers?'

'Maybe they'll let you claim diplomatic immunity?'

'Seriously?'

'No, I doubt they'll want anything to do with them! Actually, I wouldn't even mention them, or the fact the Secret Police are after you. Just tell them your passport was stolen and you have a flight out in three days?'

'Shit! I don't suppose you could come with me to the Embassy?'

'Sorry, Mark and I are going to Abu Raoush early tomorrow morning.'

'Abu Raoush? Where's that?'

'Just north of Giza.'

'What's there?'

'Abu Raoush is possibly the most important of all the pyramids.'

'It's a pyramid? I've never heard of it.'

'Most people haven't, it's in the middle of a military zone, strictly off-limits to the public.'

'How come *you're* allowed in?'

'We're not, but flash a little baksheesh; money talks.'

'There must be something pretty important there.'

Mark extended an invitation.

'Maybe you'd like to come with us and see for yourself? After that, we're going to Zawiyet el-Aryan, another interesting pyramid. We can drop you at the Embassy on the way.'

'Are you sure?'

Frank chipped in.

'You know we can't guarantee your safety, right?'

'Can anyone? Besides, it's probably the last place they'd expect me to go, so it's probably safer than sitting around in a hotel.'

Frank gestured to the backpack.

'Maybe there's something about Abu Raoush in those papers of yours, do you mind if I have another look?'

'Be my guest.'

I handed him the backpack and turned my mind back to less ominous considerations.

'So, Mark, what are your thoughts now about the dating of the pyramids at Dahshur, Hawarra and Meidum?'

'Well, clearly it's wrong, the actual evidence reinforces that, they've got to at least date to the Old Kingdom, possibly even earlier. And, from what we've seen today, it would appear they were built in stages, perhaps even thousands of years apart.'

'How does that fit with your research on the Labyrinth and Herodotus's

349

observations?'

From the front seat, Frank interjected.
'Oh, I don't think Herodotus was telling us the full story.'
'You don't? Why not? Wasn't he an historian?'

He swung around to face us.
'No, I don't think Herodotus was *just* an historian.'
'What do you mean?'

After taking a moment or too to settle in, it was obvious Frank was about to launch into a tome or two.
'Well if you read what the "text books" tell you, Herodotus went to Egypt in 443 BC to record it's history. But that's not *why* he went there, it's just part of what he *did* once he got there.'
'Why did he go then?'
'To spend several years in its sacred schools, which means he was not only aware of the sacred Mystery Schools there, but more importantly that he had either been invited to study in them, or believed he was eligible to study in them. Think about it, the scholars and "historians" surely came out of the Greek esoteric schools, as they were the centres of education and wisdom.'
'You're saying he was part of the Tat Brotherhood?'
'Maybe not the mainstream core, but an "off-shoot" stream of it for sure.'

I shared my thoughts with the guys about Akhenaten leaving Egypt around 1300 BC and going to Greece after the obliteration of the Mycenaean civilization by the Thera tsunami, of taking with him the teachings of the Tat Brotherhood, and how those teachings became the foundations of the Classical Greece civilization and its theology, and how, if that was the case, then it was extremely plausible that Herodotus was possibly a disciple, a student, of the esoteric teachings, and headed to Egypt for his 'final initiation'. Frank didn't need convincing.
'Oh, I'm sure of it! When Herodotus wrote about the Labyrinth, initially he said, the priests prevented him from entering. However the details he then goes on to outline would suggest that at some later time he was allowed to go in and inspect the Labyrinth, which would only have been permitted if he was "eligible", that is, if he was a "neophyte", and only then after his initiations were completed.'

BUT...the major significance after that is not what he says, but more importantly what he *doesn't* say; his general reticence about revealing any significant details is a sure sign of his vow of silence *not* to divulge the secrets of the Mystery Schools. And that's backed up by his writings about the Sphinx.'
'I didn't know Herodotus wrote about the Sphinx?'
'That's just it; he didn't. If we believe the "historians" and "Egyptologists", Herodotus was apparently "eager to record every foreign and strange wonder his eyes beheld". And yet, even though he visited Giza at a time when the worship of the Sphinx was being revived, he didn't write a single word about it. The Sphinx, one of the largest sculpted pieces in the ancient world; it would have been impossible to miss or ignore it. So, by *not* writing about it at all, Herodotus's silence is mute testimony that he must have had the sort of knowledge about its inner sacred chambers and function that only a true Initiate could possess, and was sworn never to reveal. That said, he did reveal more than Pythagoras.'
'Pythagoras visited Egypt as well?'
'He sure did, about seventy years earlier; Herodotus was just following in Pythagoras's footsteps.'
'What did Pythagoras say?'

'Absolutely nothing. Figure it out for yourself, Pythagoras left Greece in the latter years of the 6th Century BC, which was smack bang in the middle of when Greece was at war with the Persians, who just happened to have invaded and claimed Egypt in 525 BC, establishing the 27th Dynasty, which lasted until around 400 BC. When he left Greece, Pythagoras was supposedly in search of the secrets of the Chaldeans of south-east Mesopotamia, and the Magi, the followers of Zoroaster. But, surprise, surprise, he finishes up in Egypt, learning directly from Oenuphis, High Priest of Heliopolis, despite the fact Greece is supposedly at war with the Persians.'

'How did he do it, unless the Tat Brotherhood infiltrated the Persians once they arrived?'

'I think Pythagoras was invited because his father was a High Priest of Apollo and his mother was one of the Pythia, the high priestesses of the Temple of Delphi…'

It was all making perfect sense; it was like someone was not only handing me all the missing pieces of a gigantic jigsaw, but putting them exactly where they fitted.

'…Then he's initiated and returns to Greece as a greatly respected and wise teacher, but keeps the secrets of the Egyptian Mystery School to the confines of his own esoteric circles.'

'Which is where Herodotus comes into the picture.'

'Exactly. And then, another seventy or eighty years after Herodotus, around 360 BC, another new generation of "neophytes", led by Plato, soon to become one of the classical world's most famous philosophers, similarly "arrives" in Egypt to take part in "the great learnings of the Mysteries along the Nile".'

I was already thinking ahead.

'Plato, who tutored Aristotle, who in turn tutored Alexander the Great. Plato, who spent thirteen years in Egypt, supposedly "consulting the scribes and records in the Library of Alexandria".'

'Exactly! Except for the fact the Library of Alexandria was supposedly built about a hundred years later, during the reign of Ptolemy. However, according to the Roman historian, Lucius, Plato supposedly said he journeyed to Egypt to "make the acquaintance of the prophets of wisdom", and that he "descended into the shrines and temples and learned from the Books of Isis and Horus". Which means he must have studied the original metal discs and books in the sacred underground chambers.'

'The ones discovered by the California university guys in 1976.'

'Most likely.'

'Then, at the age of forty-nine, after three days in the "Great Hall", one of the subterranean halls of the Great Pyramid in Egypt, having passed the three degrees, the three dimensions, he was initiated and received by the Hierophant of the Pyramids who verbally gave Plato the highest esoteric teachings. After a further three months' studying in the underground halls of the Pyramid and the Sphinx, the Initiate, Plato, as Pythagoras had been before him, was sent out into the world to do the work of the "great Order".'

I joined the dots.

'Thoth, Imhotep, Amenhotep I, Akhenaten/Apollo, the Temple of Delphi, Pythagoras, Herodotus, Plato, Aristotle, Alexander the Great, it's like threading beads on a necklace. I wonder who was the next beady little character in line?'

It was Mark's turn to interrupt.

'Manetho, around 300 BC.'

'Manetho, the Greek scholar? That makes sense.'

'No, Manetho the Egyptian; most probably the Chief Priest of the sun-god, Ra, at Heliopolis.'

I was confused.

'A different Manetho?'

'No, the same one; Manetho just solely wrote in Greek, even though he was Egyptian and his topics dealt with Egyptian matters.'

'I'm sorry, but that sounds incongruently bizarre. Isn't it possible that, thanks to the "invasion" of Alexander in 332 BC that expelled the Persians, when Greece *saved*, or rather *occupied* Egypt, that Manetho travelled from Greece, just like all the others before him, but as a much younger neophyte, stayed in Egypt after his initiation, and worked his way up to being a Chief Priest?'

Mark shivered, like someone had just walked over his grave, and suddenly had a look on his face like he'd been hit by a thunderbolt of awakening.

'I hadn't thought of that. Yes, it's possible, not just possible, but highly probably…'

His mind shifted up a gear.

'…We don't know when Manetho was born, or where, or when he died. What we do know is that he was responsible for the building of the Library of Alexandria, and that his works are associated with the reigns of at least two, possibly three pharaohs; Ptolemy I Soter, 323-283 BC, and Ptolemy II Philadelphus, 285-246 BC, and, if the *Hibeh Papyri* of 240 BC is the same Manetho who was the author of *Aegyptiaca*, which is highly probably, then he may well have still been alive and writing into the reign of Ptolemy III Euergetes as well, which was 246-222 BC.'

I did the math.

'323-222 BC, that's about a hundred years!'

'No, he would only have been writing from say 290-240 BC.'

'Which is still fifty years! Even if he became a High Priest at forty, which is nine years earlier than Pythagoras, that would mean Manetho lived until he was ninety.'

'Manetho is probably not even his original name, as the original Egyptian version of Manetho's name was most likely Mai-en-Thoth, which translates as "Beloved of Thoth".'

'Like a pen name, a nom de plume?'

'Yeah. Or…'

I could see the pennies dropping in Mark's head.

'…a title! It was a title! Which might explain why we don't know that much about him other than what we can deduce from what he wrote.'

I thought back to the notes I had read earlier in the trip.

'Manetho wrote about the dynasties, right?'

'Yeah, he laid it all out in *"Aegyptiaca"*, which was written around 250 BC.'

'But that doesn't survive, right, just sections quoted by other writers.'

'No, you're thinking of the *"Book of Sothis"*, an astrological text attributed to Manetho which has been quoted by other, later authors, up to six, even eight hundred years later. Hell, we're still quoting them all today.

In fact, it was from one of those later fragments, from the Roman historian, Syncellus, citing Manetho, who wrote that the Egyptian priests were once in possession of tablets called the "Old Chronicle" that contained a list of thirty dynasties covering a period of around 36,525 years. He also quoted a letter from Manetho to Ptolemy II Philadelphus, that we know the true source of Manetho's thinking. It went something along the lines of: *"We are making calculations about what will happen in the world. According to your command, the sacred books written by our forefather, Thrice-Great Hermes, which I have studied, shall be shown to you."'*

'Now *that's* pretty telling: clearly Manetho not only had access to the Books of Thoth, the "Old Chronicles", but he'd also studied them, and all the knowledge and wisdom in them, including Egypt's true history, and including the idea of there being thirty dynasties. And that would never have been possible unless he was an Initiate.'

'It tells more than that! Manetho called Hermes his "forefather" which means he was a "son" of Hermes.'

'He was a member of the Tat Brotherhood.'

'Exactly. And the fact Ptolemy II requested that he see the books himself, and that Manetho agreed he could, implies that Ptolemy must have been a member as well.'

My mind really started ticking over.

'What do you think Manetho meant about calculating "*what will happen in the world*"?'

'Clearly it's not about day-to-day events. It would have to have been based on secret esoteric knowledge; calculations can only mean one thing, the movements of the sun, moon, eclipses, planets and stars. What will happen in the world can only mean events like earthquakes, eclipses, tsunami's…'

'Or the passing of Nibiru.'

Frank, who had returned to perusing Kareem's papers, briefly tossed his head back over the seat again.

'Possibly, but highly unlikely, especially if Nibiru passed in 1600 BC and isn't due again until, well, now! What were you saying earlier about other tsunamis, around 250 BC?'

I counted them off as I trawled through my memory.

'There was an earthquake around 224 BC. There was also the Etna eruption of 122 BC, as well as earthquakes in 27 BC, 62 AD, and of course Vesuvius erupted in 79 AD wiping out Pompeii and Herculaneum.'

'Well, if any of those could be directly attributable to certain positions of the sun, moon, and/or planets, then they would be impressive calculations to say the least.'

Mark got excited.

'Maybe they're encoded somewhere in *"Aegyptiaca"*.'

I wasn't so sure.

'Does it survive?'

'Three pieces of the original papyrus do; one's in the museum in Turin, Italy, one's in the Cairo Museum, and one's in the Petrie Collection at the University of London.'

'Then it's possible.'

'Maybe it wasn't Manetho who was wrong, just everyone who cited him. If it's been misconstrued, like the thirty dynasties have been, then *"Aegyptiaca"* could hold all sorts of hidden secrets.'

It suddenly seemed obvious!

'You know, I think you're right, I think the whole "modern" dynasty thing is a huge screw up. In fact I've always had doubts about the whole 'official' chronology of ancient Egypt, it's flawed; not so much the events, but more the dating of those events.'

'Why's that?'

'Firstly, it's not a true construction of the ancient Egyptians, they just had long lists, like the Turin Papyrus, and the Abydos Kings' List, which, in themselves, were deliberately incomplete. As far as we know, Manetho created the dynastic system by simply grouping modern pharaohs together based on the evidence he had, and on their lineage. He knew there were thirty dynasties, but what if he discounted the periods of the gods and the demi-gods, the Zep Tepi. What if he was wrong, and what if the modern Egyptologists have simply assumed he was corrected, adopted it as fact?

Clearly, the *fledgling* Egyptologists confused things even more in the 19th Century when they introduced the concepts of Old, Middle, and New Kingdoms, and the Intermediate Periods, which were simply based on their uneducated perceptions of changes in the architecture of the buildings, but what if it was all based on a fallacy?'

'So how do you see it?'

'According to my thinking, the lineage, the *sang réal*, is all about the bloodline from the gods, from the Annunaki. That means the first pharaoh, Menes, or Narmer, must not only have been a High Priest of some description, but more than likely a direct descendant of the gods and demi-gods who ruled during the Zep Tepi, most probably the eldest child.'

'Interesting, because Manetho was one of a number of Egyptian sources who described Menes as having been "guided by the counsels of the gods of long ago", and that he "received his laws directly from Thoth".'

Then a thought hit me.

'Isn't there some speculation that Menes was actually a woman?'

'Wow, I haven't read that, but you may be right. If it were true, and you could prove it, then it would throw a completely different perspective on the question of inheritance on the whole dynastic lineage. The question then becomes, how do you prove it?'

'Through the *sang réal*. From Menes, I think the *sang réal* runs through until the end of the 8th Dynasty pretty much uninterrupted, before it skips the 9th and 10th Dynasties, then continues from the 11th Dynasty to the middle of the 13th Dynasty, when it jumps to the 17th and 18th Dynasties. Then, with the departure of Akhenaten, it headed to Greece for nearly a thousand years, before returning after the 31st Dynasty with Alexander the Great and the Macedonian and Ptolemaic Kings, the initiations of Pythagoras, Herodotus and Plato, paving the way for its return.'

'How do you account for the other "skipped" dynasties?'

'Coups and invasions. In between the "direct-lineage" dynasties, there were several internal and external attempts to take over the sovereignty from the bloodline, from the *sang réal*; the 9th and 10th Dynasties were internal, the 14th to 16th Dynasties, external, the military pharaohs of the 19th and 20th Dynasties, internal, the Amun Priests of the 21st, 25th, 26th, 29th and 30th Dynasties, internal, and the northern invaders such as the Libyans and Persians of the 21st to 24th, 27th, 28th and 31st Dynasties, external.'

As we hit the hustle and bustle of Cairo, I filled in Mark and Frank with the details on my thinking, eliciting many nods of acknowledgment and approval from the two of them along the way. Then I shifted the focus slightly.

'And what if we don't have the full picture, what if the members of the Tat Brotherhood weren't giving us the full picture?'

'What do you mean?'

'Well, if most of our understanding about ancient Egypt comes indirectly from Herodotus and Manetho,…'

'Yes.'

'…and, if like Pythagoras and Plato, they were both initiated members of the secretive Tat Brotherhood,…'

'Yes.'

'…then wouldn't it be highly likely they withheld knowledge from the general populace, even deliberately distorted or encoded information, so that only other initiates would understand it?'

'Yes!'

Frank went one step further.

'Wow, that would give a whole new perspective not only on ancient Egypt, but also on the origins of mathematics, geometry, and the roots of philosophical thinking.'

Suddenly we came to a unexpected halt and I turned to see a soldier standing at the driver's window.

'Yes, please, where is it you are from?'

I couldn't believe it; I was history. They had set their trap and I, unwittingly, had walked right into it. What was I going to do now, make a run for it, leaving Frank holding the evidence? Unperturbed, Frank took the lead and leaned over to address him.

'Dr. Clarke, Dr. Beaver, and Dr. Jones from the University of Santa Barbara in California USA, we've just been visiting the pyramids at Hawarra and Dahshur with Colonel Nasar Mamood.'

'American, yes?'

'As apple pie!'

'Passport please.'

'They're in the safe back at the hotel. Why, what's the problem, we've never been asked for our IDs before?'

Was he crazy? Frank was not only challenging this guy, but waving several of Kareem's papers at him.

'What hotel, please?'

'The Soffitel. Now, can we get on our way, we're late for dinner?'

The soldier looked at what must clearly have been a faxed copy of my passport photo, then at Frank, before looking through the back window, first at Mark, then over to me. I tried to look disinterested, looking out the window the other way, displeased, my head dropped, arms crossed chin in my hand. After scrutinizing the human cargo, the soldier turned his attention back to Frank.

'You have met any man of Australia?'

'Any Aussies? No. You, Mark?'

When Mark stayed mute and shook his head, Frank threw his head back towards me.

'Dr. Jones?'

What the hell was Frank's game? I shook my head and mumbled in my best Yankee accent.

'Nah.'

Frank turned abruptly back to the soldier at the window, this time with a discernibly pissed-off edge to his voice.

'No, no Aussies, so is that all? Can we get on back to our hotel now, or do I have to call Colonel Mamood and ask *him* what the hell this is all about? What was your name again?'

There was a brief pause as the soldier contemplated his options; either Frank's bravado was going to work, or the whole wrath of Seth was about to suddenly befall us; well, me! Thankfully it seemed to work.

'No, it all good. Yes, OK, you go.'

As the car took off, I dared not move, just on the off chance I gave them a second chance to ID me.

'Well, Alex, it's confirmed; it seems you're public enemy number one. I wonder how much the bounty is?'

'Jesus, Frank, what was the deal with waving around Kareem's papers? It was like waving a red flag to a bull.'

'Actually, Alex, bulls are colour-blind; but by waving them around, the guy couldn't really read them if he wanted to, all he could maybe make out was the letterhead, making him think we had official authorization.'

'But what if he'd asked to see it?'

'Relax, Alex, I've been through lots of checkpoints at NASA; believe me, the last thing the guy at the checkpoint wants to do is piss off someone important. You just have to act like you belong, and that being held up is an inconvenience.'

It wasn't until we'd gone several hundred metres down the road, and I felt we were in the clear, that I casually glanced back. Unbelievable; we'd run the gauntlet and I'd made it through relatively unscathed.

'I can't believe he didn't recognize me! It must have been the difference between the clean-shaven, short-hair-cut appearance of my ten-year-old passport photo, and my current, grotty, dishevelled, unshaven and unkempt appearance that got me through. But, Frank, Dr. Jones?'

'Well, Indiana, if you're going to live like him, and get bullet-holes through your hat, then you might as well go by his name.'

Mark was more sympathetic.

'Actually, Dude, you look like the wreck of the Hesperus, like something the cat dragged in.'

Frank, less so.

'And I have to tell you, man, that you're starting to smell a little on the rancid side.'

I took a quick whiff under the old warwick-farms.

'To be expected, but nothing a good shower and a change of clothes won't fix.'

Then I realized the only change of clothes I had, I'd been forced to abandon back in Luxor.

'Can we stop at an ATM; I need to get some cash to pay you guys back and get some new clothes before we arrive at the Cairo Palace.'

No sooner had the message been relayed to the driver than we'd stopped in the main drag, I'd withdrawn a sufficient wad to cover my ass until I made my escape, purchased a new shirt, trousers, jocks and socks, and we were back enroute. I immediately started counting out Egyptian hundred pound notes to Mark.

'How much do I owe you?'

He waved it off.

'Dinner's on you!'

'Are you sure that's enough? The entrance tickets, all the baksheesh thank-yous?'

Frank had other thoughts.

'I know, how about a complete copy of these documents once you've had them translated, and the authorization to use or quote any of the material?'

'Fine by me; are you sure you don't want to take them now, make your own copy, and get them translated yourself?'

'As tempting as it is, I think I'll pass.'

'Mark?'

'I think I'm with Frank on this one, but I do think you should make a copy as soon as possible, maybe several.'

'You think I should mail one back to myself in Australia?'

'You could, but the problem with that is, if they do intercept your mail, then not only will they confiscated and destroy the copy, but they'll come hunting for you in Australia as they'll have your home address. I was thinking more that you scan them as jpgs or pdfs and email them to yourself, that would be almost impossible for them to trace.'

'That could be the best option, then I could lock them safely away in a safe-deposit box in a vault in a bank somewhere.'

Minutes later we pulled up outside the familiar façade of the Cairo Palace in downtown Cairo. Frank looked out the window at the sign above the door, then and screwed up his face.

'*This* is your hotel?'

'Yep, it's on the third floor.'

Mark was already getting out of the car.

'I'll go with you up to reception to make sure there's room at the inn.'

Frank put the papers in the backpack and handed it to me.

'Good luck.'

'Thanks.'

Mark and I made our way through the iron gates, past the sleeping doorman and into the antique lift, which wobbled its way heavenwards.

'Are you sure you don't want to change your mind and risk the luxury of the Sofitel?'

'No, Mark, it's fine; the hotel is perfect.'

Arriving at the third floor, Mark was pleasantly surprised as we exited the lift and entered the Cairo Palace.

'Not what I expected at all.'

It was Magdy who greeted us at reception.

'Mr. Alex, what a pleasure it is to see you again.'

'If it isn't The Famous Magdy! You know, Mark, you only have to open the paper here in Cairo and you will find Magdy's picture, he's very famous, a veritable legend in his own lunchbox.'

'Oh, yes, I am very famous. Mr. Alex, how was it, your adventure? Luxor, yes, Aswan, very good?'

'What can I say; a trip of a lifetime!'

'Very good, yes.'

'Magdy, I know I'm not due until tomorrow night, but I'm a day early and I was wondering if you had a spare bed tonight?'

'Early, no problem, Mr. Alex, of course, of course.'

Mark made one last offer.

'Are you sure?'

'Positive, thanks.'

He gave me a supportive slap on the shoulder.

'Right then, if there's any problems, give me a call, otherwise, we'll meet you downstairs in about an hour or so…'

He checked his watch.

'…Let's say 7.00 pm.'

'Done!'

Mark headed off back down the corridor and I checked in with Magdy. The place was like a ghost town and the political turmoil in Egypt was taking its toll on the people, especially those who relied on the tourist dollar to survive.

'Do you have it your passport, please, Mr. Alex?'

'Ah, no, it was stolen.'

'Oh dear, this it is not good.'

'It's OK, I'm going to the Embassy tomorrow to sort it out.'

He dived under the desk...

'I will see if we still have it, the copy...'

...quickly re-emerging.

'...Yes, yes, it is all good. Come, please, Mr. Alex, I will take you to your room.'

'Where's Abdo?'

It's not that I didn't trust Magdy, but I'd built a bit of a rapport with Abdo and at this point I really couldn't trust anyone new unless I absolutely had to.

'Abdo, he is at his home, with his family. Yes, he will be here at the hotel tomorrow.'

I hesitated slightly before I took Kareem's papers out of the backpack and handed them to him.

'Can you put these in your safe for me?'

'Certainly, Mr. Alex.'

I watched with almost obsessive intensity, as he locked them away, for the first time in days, feeling relief flooding over my body; I was going to sleep tight tonight knowing they were safe under lock and key.

Once in my room, I tossed the backpack and shopping bag on the bed, emptied my pockets, plugged in my iphone and laptop to recharge, turned on the shower, then walked straight under it. Oh my god, it was amazing, even better than when I'd done it after visiting Karnak. I made a point of giving everything a thorough wash, not just my clothes, but my body as well; it seemed over the passed few days I'd accumulated layers of grime on top of layers of dirt, sweat and anguish.

By the time I'd finished, hung everything up to dry, dried myself off and dressed, it was 6.30, meaning I still had about half-an-hour before Mark and Frank were due. I took the opportunity to update my diary notes.

My last entry was on the train to Beni Suef, before my Indiana Jones style escape via the roof, through the streets, and in the boot of Mohammed's taxi. Saeed had gone out on a limb so many times for me, and for his uncle's papers, I hoped he was all right. As for me, I had so many questions, some answered, most unanswered.

Having discovered who Jesus and Mary really were, now I had questions about who Judas really was. Was he the actual son of Joseph and Mary, Jesus's foster-brother, and did he betray Jesus because was he jealous of Jesus, pissed-off at him for being the cause of Judas no longer having the luxuries of the Egyptian Royal Court? The questions were theological nitro-glycerine; the answers could blow most modern religious dogma to smithereens.

On top of that, I had questions about the pole shifts, the tsunamis, whether the Sphinx was some sort of cosmic marker, like on a calendar, whether it was built on top of pre-existing chambers that had been buried by tsunamis, or whether the chambers had been built under the Sphinx. What came first, the chicken or the egg?

In a blink it was 7.00pm, the events of today would have to wait until later. I shut down the laptop, gathered my belongings, and headed off.

As soon as I hit the lounge area, Magdy was flooding me with friendly hospitality.

'Mr. Alex, you are feeling better?'

'Very good thanks Magdy, nothing like a good shower after running around in the desert for a week or so.'

I handed him my laptop.
'Can you put this in the safe for me as well, please?'
'Yes, but of course.'

He took the laptop and headed behind the reception counter.
'And… while you're there…'
'Yes?'

I contemplated whether to ask Magdy to make a copy of the papers for me, that with Saeed back in Luxor, and Mohammed in Hawarra, there became a point when I had to trust someone else local, someone other than Mark and Frank, if I was going to escape Egypt alive *and* with Kareem's papers. In the end I realized that asking him to copy them was too risky, both for me, and also to involve him; the less people who knew of their existence the better. It might be best to ask Abdo if I could scan them personally myself tomorrow afternoon?

'…Nothing. Don't worry about it, I'll take care of it tomorrow.'

I started down the corridor towards the lift.
'You need it the taxi, Mr. Alex?'
'No thanks, I'm just meeting a few colleagues downstairs and we're heading off for a bit of dinner.'
'There is it the very good restaurant in market just around corner, you wish for me to take you?'
'No thanks, I'm sure the others will have it sorted.'
'Very good, enjoy.'

As I pushed the button and waited for the lift, for the first time in days I felt back on top of things. I'd made it safely to Cairo, the papers out of my hands, and the monkey was off my back!

In a city of twenty million people, all I had to do now was wait for Saeed's call tonight with the rest of the escape plan, and, in a day or so, I'd be safely in Greece. I felt a bit like Akhenaten, escaping the corruption of Egypt to enlighten the rest of the world; was history repeating itself?

Digging deeper

Frank and Mark were just getting out of a taxi as I arrived downstairs in the street, Mark wearing a wry grin like a stylish fedora.
'You look like a new man.'
'I feel like one, in more ways than you can imagine. Now all I have to do is down a few cold ales to seal the deal, then get the hell out of Egypt and make the most of it.'
'Then let's go.'
'Where to?'
'Frank and I know a little restaurant near here; great food.'

Formalities dispensed with, I followed Mark and Frank around the corner where the locals were amassing in the market-type atmosphere of al-fresco street dining. It was a smorgasbord for the senses, surrounded by the local culture, musicians, street vendors, families, and all sorts of exotic aromas, so much so that my mouth started salivating like a pack of Pavlov's dogs.

This was a part of Egypt that many tourists, who spent their meals in the hotel restaurants, never got to see. The meal at Saheed's cousin's was great, and I was extremely grateful for it, but the truth was I hadn't had a good meal in days, partly because of my bout of Ramses' Revenge and partly because of my being on the run.

There were plenty of tables to choose from as 7.00pm was still a little early for the main evening trade, several young men were each trying to lure us into their respective establishments.

'How about this one?'

'No good, Alex, we have to go inside.'

'Why?'

'Muslim country, dude! They won't serve alcohol outside; it's disrespectful to their religion for anyone to drink in public. And the last thing *you* need to do is draw unwanted attention to yourself.'

'Ain't that the truth; when in Rome, don't drink the holy water, don't even gargle it.'

'You can bathe in it if you have to.'

'Just don't piss in it.'

They had a way of getting me to laugh, to let go of my worries and just enjoy the moment. Within minutes we'd arrived at the restaurant, were seated at a table, and, finally, had a cold beer in our hands.

'Cheers!'

The first one barely touched the sides on its way down.

'Nectar of the Gods!'

'Not the nectar of Allah though.'

I looked at Frank, not really sure how much he knew about Islam.

'Don't you think it's somewhat ironic that beer was invented by the ancient Egyptians, consumed to worship and celebrate their gods, and yet now the country is beating to the drum of a different god, a 'tea-total' god, the god of Sin, Sin, the Akkadian god of the moon, who I'm sure most Muslims don't even know was the origin of Allah.'

Frank knew enough to bring things more into focus.

'Them's dangerous words, Alex.'

'The truth always is, Frank.'

After that, the discussion quickly returned to the events and discoveries of the day, to the actual history of the Dahshur pyramids and tombs, to Meidum, to Hawarra and the Labyrinth, and, more importantly, to the revelations of the chambers beneath the Great Pyramid. Having ordered our meals and another beer, I politely pressed Frank for more details.

'Tell me, Frank, what else do you know about the chambers under Khufu's Pyramid?'

'Well, for starters, despite what conservative scholars would have us believe, and what they've tried to prove, the pyramid wasn't built by Khufu; I think we all know that. There's plenty of evidence from the ancient records that Khufu did at Giza exactly what Snefru had done at Dahshur and Meidum, he carried out repair work on the Pyramids and monuments.'

'Evidence? What evidence?'

Frank leaned back in his chair.

'First, there's the Inventory Stele, found by Mariette just east of the Pyramid in 1857. Though it dates to around 1500 BC, according to many experts it's a copy of a 4th Dynasty stele in which Khufu details the discoveries he made while clearing away the sands from the Pyramid and Sphinx.'

'That in itself is evidence the pyramid and Sphinx were there *before* Khufu.'

'You think! Pity the majority of Egyptologists can't see that! They prefer to ascribe the pyramid to Khufu based on a single scrawl on a block in one of the upper relieving chambers above the King's Chamber; hardly sound scientific process. They also conveniently ignore that Khufu identified the Great Pyramid as the "House of Isis".'

'Why's that so significant?'

'Because the stele also describes how Khufu gave Isis a new offering, rebuilding her "temple of stone".'

'Couldn't that refer to the mortuary temple beside the pyramid, or maybe the valley temple beside the Sphinx?'

'It's possible, but unlikely. You see, the stele also describes how Khufu inspected the Sphinx after part of the headdress had been knocked off by a bolt of lightning, and how Khufu carefully restored it.'

'You know there's lots of speculation the head was once much bigger, that it was even a lion's head, and that Khufu shaped it to look like him.'

'There's also speculation it was done by Amenemhat III in the 12th Dynasty, but that doesn't mean it's true. Was *is* true, is that when the Sphinx was dug out the sand in the 1930's by Selim Hassan, he observed there was indeed evidence that portions of it had been damaged by lightning, and that it had undergone ancient repairs.'

That surprised me.

'A lightning bolt! Why would it hit the Sphinx, and not the pyramid?'

'Maybe because of what's inside the Sphinx.'

'Which is?'

'Well, if you believe Drunvalo Melchizidek, there's a large golden sphere, a time capsule, which will be discovered when the head falls off.'

'I've heard that name before. Melchizidek? I think Crystal mentioned him. He wrote a book, right, about circles that supposedly describe the structure of every element and atomic structure in the universe.'

'*The Ancient Secret of the Flower of Life.*'

'That's it! And I saw the image at Abydos.'

'On a granite pillar in the Osireion.'

I started getting flashbacks of what had happened when I touched the granite pillars and tuned in to the rock.

'Yeah…Consciousness "slows down", becomes thought, which slows down to become light, which slows down to become sound, which slows down to become matter, which at the sub-atomic level is a pea-soup of possibilities that modifies consciousness through experience. The whole thing is a cycle of fractals, and the flower of life shows all that.'

I'd said it almost by rote; it rolled off the tongue as if I'd memorized it as a monologue for a play I'd performed thousands of times, and yet the idea had only come to me several days earlier. Despite its somewhat deadpan delivery, Frank was suitably impressed, holding up his beer.

'I'll drink to that! Now all we need is the proof.'

As he downed another mouthful, I focused back on the wealth of information others had incredulously overlooked.

'What else does the Inventory Stele say?'

'It ends with how Khufu built small pyramids for himself and his family next to the Great Pyramid.'

'And aren't there the ruins of some small satellite pyramids next to the pyramid?'

'Exactly: four, on the east side; three queen's pyramids and a cult pyramid. The stele says that Khufu erected one of them for Princess Henutsen "beside the temple of

Isis", and archaeologists have confirmed that the southernmost of the three satellite pyramids is indeed dedicated to Henutsen, one of Khufu's wives.

You would think that if that part of the stele proved to be true, then the rest of it must be true as well, including the fact that Khufu described that the Pyramid and Sphinx were already present at Giza during his reign. However, despite that, and the fact the satellite pyramids are unquestionably inferior in design and construction to the Great Pyramid, the "experts" still insist Khufu built them all. I don't even think Khufu was actually a pharaoh.'

'What do you mean, you think he should be called Cheops?'

'No, Cheops was just a later Greek name. In its most mystic terms, "Khu" refers to the higher soul-spirit principle, similar to *ka* but higher. It's also interconnected with the serpentine god Cnubis or Khuphis, having great magical powers; in fact Manetho recorded his "Khufu's name as Suphis.'

'Serpents? You think Khufu was a descendant of the Dracos?'

'No, but it's all significant, because "Khu-fu" is generally translated as "he protects me", and the name appears on various Egyptian monuments, amulets and rings as a powerful magical charm to ward off evil spirits.'

'"He protects me" from *what*?'

'Good question. In Hermetic literature "Khouphis" also had the name "Good Daimon" which was the exact same title bestowed on Hermes.'

'Daimon, demon?'

'Perhaps, but unlikely. However, the characteristics attributed to him, of great wisdom and power, the keeper of books, and the symbol of the serpent, were the same for Thoth and Hermes. Khufu was even recorded as having written the "sacred book", which reduced the whole history of Egypt and their entire system of theology into an organized form.'

'Wait a minute, are you suggesting Khufu was Thoth?'

Frank realized what it was he was actually saying.

'Maybe. Maybe Thoth reincarnated.'

It hit me like a lightning bolt.

'Imhotep!'

'Imhotep, from the 3rd Dynasty?'

'Yes! Imhotep's name is associated with at least four pharaohs, from Djoser around 2700 BC through to Huni around 2650 BC. The next pharaoh was Snefru, supposedly responsible for all the big pyramids we saw at Dahshur and Meidum, and after him was Khufu. Isn't it possible that Khufu was Imhotep, Thoth reincarnated, that Imhotep was the second incarnation of Thoth, of Hermes, the thrice-lived?'

Mark and Frank were momentarily speechless. Then, as the waiter served us dinner, Frank's brain clicked back into gear.

'There's another inscription from the 4th Dynasty, one by Khufu's son, Dedafre, that tells how Khufu found ancient writings in the capstone, the pyramidion, of the Great Pyramid. Surely Khufu didn't find them by accident. I mean, imagine trying to scale the steep, smooth limestone faces hundreds of feet into the air. Why would you do it?'

Mark joined in the speculation.

'Unless Khufu knew the writings were there.'

'The question is, "*How* did Khufu know they were there?"'

'Maybe it was in the ancient writings?'

'If that was the case, then why didn't any of the previous pharaohs recover them?'

'Good point.'

'Obviously they date from a far distant time in the past, a time when the pyramid was actually built. The only way Khufu could know the writings were there was if he was there when the pyramid was built, or if he actually put them there in the capstone?'

'Or if he was the one responsible for building the pyramid.'

'Thoth!'

'Thoth.'

Mark was on a slightly different tack.

'So why remove them?'

Once again Frank was playing Devil's advocate.

'More importantly, why put them there in the first place?'

I had an answer.

'Just like in the Sphinx; as a time capsule; for future reference.'

Meanwhile, Frank was slowly piecing it together.

'Which means whoever put them there must have known about the impending pole shift, as well as the after effects, and placed them there to be recovered afterwards, to rebuild civilization.'

Mark had a good and rather obvious point.

'How do you place a series of writings in a solid granite pyramidion?'

'They wouldn't have been writings on paper; they must have been wafer-thin metal discs just like those in the underground chambers.'

Then the answer hit me like a runaway freight train.

'Actually, no, I don't think it's that either. I think the information was encoded directly into the molecular structure of the stone itself!'

'What?'

'Bill told me that granite is about sixty-something percent silicon dioxide, which is exactly the compound we use in computers to store memory.'

'Which means maybe the information is still there?'

Mark had posed another powerful question, but Frank was as pragmatic as ever.

'If that were the case, the real question is, "where is the capstone?"'

'Do you think it could it be the one sitting in the Cairo Museum?'

It made Frank laugh.

'What an irony that would be, the Egyptian authorities have suppressed the truth for decades and there it is, the key to the whole history of the human race, on blatant display to the world in the Cairo museum, no one knowing what it really contains, or how to retrieve it.'

He leaned back in his chair and took another long drink, clearly running something else through his mind.

'You know, according to the Westcar Papyrus, Khufu's work may have been aided by a mysterious sage by the name of Djeda, who was brought to the royal court at the age of a-hundred-ten, and apparently amazed everyone by performing all sorts of feats of wisdom and magic.'

I wasn't sure where he was heading, but I saw the connections straight away.

'Djeda, that's very similar to Djehuty.'

'Which is another name for Thoth, yes! There's no mention of where he came from, but Djeda was apparently taken to the house of Khufu's son, Dedafre, to live and become his teacher. Shortly after, Djeda disappears and Dedafre emerges as a great sage, one of the "Fathers of Wisdom". In later times he was even deified as a god of learning and medicine, just like Imhotep before him and Thoth before them both.'

'If the texts say he was brought to the court at the age of a-hundred-ten, it would mean in his younger years would have made him a contemporary of Imhotep, and that's just too much of a coincidence. And let's be clear that when we're talking about the ancient texts, we're actually talking about Champollion-inspired translations, right, not necessarily accurate translations? Who knows, it could translate as; "Djeda took charge of the royal court, created a house of protection, even a house of rejuvenation or regeneration, before reappearing in younger form". Djeda may just have been another name for Imhotep.'

The dialogue was setting Frank right off on a roll.

'That's an interesting perspective, because there's another fascinating story in the Westcar Papyrus that relates Dedafre, Khufu and Djeda to the Hall of Records. In the text, Dedafre informs his father, Khufu, that Djeda knows the place of the ipwt and the wnt of Thoth, for which Khufu had long been looking to make his tomb.'

I was momentarily in the dark.

'Ipwt? Wnt? I've never heard of them? But clearly they're some sort of special room.'

'The Egyptologists can't even agree what "ipwt" and "wnt" refer to, anything from a sanctuary or shrine to a large container of books.'

'Or a secret Hall of sacred Records.'

'Exactly. And what's really interesting is that although Dedafre succeeded his "father", "Khufu", as pharaoh, supposedly building the pyramid at Abu Raoush, which we shall see tomorrow, Dedafre also apparently continued to live through the reigns of the next three pharaohs, Khafre, Bakara, and Menkhare.'

'That doesn't make sense, pharaoh's usually ruled until they died. If Dedafre was pharaoh, why would he step aside for not just one, but three subsequent pharaohs?'

'That's a great question. Perhaps they were his offspring, and, as he was a demi-god himself, he intended to leave Egypt to build other civilizations elsewhere?'

'Whoa, whoa, whoa, wait a minute!...'

I remembered what Yuko had said several days ago as we trundled along on the way to the Valley of the Kings.

'...we're talking about say 2600-2500 BC, right?'

'Yep.'

'Which is exactly around the time when three other civilizations began; the Minoan civilization around 2700 BC, the Mayans around 2600 BC. and the Harappon Civilization in the Indus Valley which arose around 2500 BC. If Khufu was Imhotep, and he retrieved the time capsule from the pyramidion of the Great Pyramid, then it makes total sense that he would rebuild the Egyptian civilization first, including repairing the Great Pyramid, leave his offspring in charge, then, knowing the global impacts of a pole shift, go off and rebuild or set up other civilizations around the globe.'

'It also makes sense that he would convince Khafre and Menkhare to repair the Second and Third Pyramids at Giza, because clearly if Khufu didn't build the Great Pyramid, which I think we all agree is the case, then Khafre and Menkhare have similarly been wrongly attributed with having built the Second and Third Pyramids.'

We paused for a moment, taking a drink, taking it all in. I thought we'd literally extracted blood from the stone, but Frank was keen to discover the full extent of my knowledge and thinking.

'What else do you know about the Books of Thoth?'

'The first I ever heard of them was about a week ago on the felucca, when Bill mentioned them; forty-two volumes of knowledge and spells encompassing all the great arts, sciences, philosophies and mysteries of the ancient Egyptians; he called them "a compendium of religious practices, sacred hymns and chants, medical knowledge about diseases and cures, with instructions on surgery and plant extracts for drug use". The words are apparently so powerful that even just reading them gives you the knowledge to understand the movements of the heavens and how to control the weather, as well as the knowledge of how to duplicate the creation of life.

But, according to Bill, they weren't kept beneath the Great Pyramid; they were supposedly locked inside a series of boxes; gold, silver, ivory and ebony, sycamore, bronze then iron.'

Frank was mulling it over.

'I wonder if that's some sort of metaphor for the seven seals of the apocalypse?'

'The whole package was then supposedly placed at the bottom of the Nile just south of Qena, where it's guarded by scorpions, and a serpent that can't be slain...'

I briefly considered if that was a reference to the serpent slain by Apollo, then continued.

'...And to make it even harder to gain access, the keys to each of the boxes were hidden throughout Egypt, either with high priests, or hidden in hard-to-reach secret locations inside temples, or placed under the guard of fearful beasts or enchantments and curses.'

I took a long drink, watching Frank as he mused with his chin, clearly cross-referencing what I had told him with data stored in his own brain. I wanted to know his thoughts.

'What do *you* know about the Book of Thoth?'

'I think there's three things to consider here; firstly, when they found the chamber beneath the Great Pyramid, they found over thirty-thousand recording discs and alien equipment.'

My enthusiasm took over and I cut off Frank almost as soon as he'd begun.

'It all adds up: apparently Manetho counted as many as thirty-six-thousand "texts", which means that someone, possibly him, or others under his direction, had more than likely copied and translated the texts onto papyrus, and set up the Library of Alexandria to house them. However, most, if not all of them were destroyed or lost in the 3rd Century AD when the Roman Emperor, Diocletian, fearing that the secret wisdom of the Egyptians might someday be a threat to the Roman Empire, ordered the destruction of all the Egyptian sacred texts on magic and alchemy. But some of the texts, including the lost "Books of Imhotep" supposedly survived and were buried in ancient underground vaults somewhere in the desert near the Step Pyramid of Saqqara.'

Frank gave me that 'are you finished' look, and, realizing the effects of the beer had set me running off at the mouth, I quickly apologized, shut up, and gestured for Frank to continue.

'There may well be papyrus copies of several books buried there, however the discs they were copied from must have been like an ongoing library that documented the history and culture of ancient Egypt going back tens of thousands of years, I don't think they were specifically the "Book of Thoth". The fact they were referred to as the "Books of Imhotep" and *not* the "Books of Thoth" would tend to indicate they were more than likely papyrus copies of the original either made by Manetho, or Imhotep himself.'

'But if they're the only remaining copies of the books...?'

Frank was being very patient with me, slowly piecing things together in his mind.

'They may not be. Perhaps other copies were made which Imhotep took with him to other countries, like Greece, the Indus Valley and South America.'

I looked at Frank with eager eyes, almost begging him to continue.
'Yes?'
'Well, if you let me finish,...'

I zipped my lip.
'...the second thing to consider is that there is a report about the "Emerald Tablets of Thoth", that date back to around 36,000 BC, written by Thoth, an Atlantean Priest-King, who founded a colony in ancient Egypt after the sinking of Atlantis.'
'The "Emerald Tablets of Thoth"?'

I remembered Pieter had mentioned them over breakfast on the rooftop in Luxor.
'They're supposedly twelve imperishable emerald-green tablets, made through alchemy of a substance with a fixed atomic and cellular structure making them resistant to all elements and substances, bound together by hoops of a gold-coloured alloy suspended from a rod of the same material. The tablets are engraved with ancient Atlantean characters that respond to attuned thought-waves, releasing the associated mental vibration in the mind of the reader.'
'They plant thoughts in your mind?'
'It says something like: *"Read, and the vibration within will awaken a response in your soul"*, and, *"for the one who reads with open eyes and mind, his wisdom shall be increased a hundred-fold".'*
'Like what I said before about the words having power to give you knowledge.'
'Exactly.'
'So they were made during the period of Atlantis?'
'According to the tablets, they must have been made *after* a pole shift, but before the establishment of ancient Egyptian history, which would be consistent with the datings by Manetho and Herodotus concerning the Zepi Tepi, and the passing of Nibiru and a pole shift, all around 34,000 BC.'

Thoth writes something like; "The great waters broke over the world, drowning and sinking the land, changing the earth's balance until only the Temple of Light was left standing on the great mountain on Undal; the Great Temple vanished from the earth, until the appointed time.'
'That sounds to me like a description of a massive tsunami covering the pyramid.'
'No disagreements here.'
'And where are these Emerald Tablets supposed to be now?'
'Apparently they're back inside the Giza Pyramid, perhaps in the chamber discovered in '76. But what's more interesting is where they apparently came from.'
'Which is?'
'South America.'
'No way!'

Pieter hadn't said anything about that!
'The person who discovered, translated, and relocated them says that around 1300 BC Egypt was in turmoil, and numerous delegations of priests were sent to other parts of the world.'
'1300 BC, that's around the time when the military rulers took over and started the 19th Dynasty, when Akhenaten left Egypt to go to Greece, then South America, exactly as Imhotep had done about eight-hundred years earlier, to rebuild civilizations.'
'Yes, apparently a particular group of priests bearing the Emerald Tablets immigrated to South America, where they found the Mayans.'

'The Tat Brotherhood!'

'If the shoe fits! Anyway, by the 10th Century, the Mayans had thoroughly settled the Yucatan, and the tablets were placed beneath the altar of one of the great temples of the Sun God. But after the conquest of the Mayans by the Spaniards, the cities were abandoned and the hidden treasures of the temples all but forgotten.

It wasn't until 1925, that a member of the Great White Lodge, the Tat Brotherhood, after numerous adventures, recovered the tablets and returned them to the Great Pyramid, to the custody of the pyramid priests. But not before he was given permission to translate them and release all but two of the tablets' translations to the public.'

'What do they say?'

I'd been completely useless at keeping my mouth zipped, but, so long as I was asking sensible questions, Frank didn't seem too perturbed, however, just at that moment, my iphone rang.

'Alex speaking.'

'Indy!'

'Ahoya!'

'Mohammed he tell me that you have found it your Australian friend who they take you under their wing.'

'I'm having dinner with them as we speak.'

'You are in Cairo, yes?'

'Yes I arrived safe and sound a couple of hours ago.'

'This it is very good. I am about to catch it the train to Cairo tonight and will take you to Alexandria the day after tomorrow. Where is it you are staying?'

'The Cairo Palace in downtown Cairo, do you know it?'

'I will find it. I will be meet you there tomorrow evening around 7pm, from there we will make it our way to Alexandria to catch it the boat. Do you still have the paper of my uncle?'

'Yes, they're in the hotel's safe.'

'This it is good. What is it you will be do tomorrow, stay in the hotel I trust?'

'No, I'm going off to visit Abu Raoush with Frank and Mark.'

'Abu Raoush! This it is the military zone.'

'I know, but it'll be fine, I'm heading to the Australian Embassy straight after that.'

'I do not think this it is the good idea, Indy, the Secret Police, they will be expect for you to go there, to the Embassy.'

'Maybe you could come with me, what time does your train get in?'

'In the morning, 8:00 am.'

'Why don't you meet me in at the hotel beforehand?'

'This it is not possible, I must be go to Saqqara and Abu Ghurab, and I will not be back until at least 5:00 or 6:00 pm. Please, to think again about going out, especially to it the Embassy.'

'I will, but I'm sure everything will be fine. Have you seen or heard from the others, Bill, Pernille, Crystal?'

'Yes, indeed, I will tell you all about it tomorrow night, now I must get on it the train.'

Knowing what a bunfight that was, I left him to it.

'Alright, have a good trip, I'll see you tomorrow, Inshallah!'

'Ma'asalaamah.'

'Ma'asalaamah Ahoya. Assalaam Alaikum.'

'Wa alaikum assalaam.'

I slipped the phone back in my pocket and turned my attention back to the conversation with Mark and Frank.

'Well, that's sorted. That was Saeed, Kareem's nephew, he's arriving in Cairo tomorrow and will take me to Alexandria the day after to catch a boat to Greece and to safety.'

'Everything OK?'

'He doesn't think it's such a good idea to go to the Embassy, he thinks the Secret Police will be waiting.'

'He may be right; it might be best to get a new passport in Greece.'

'Possibly, I'll think about it more tonight. Let's get back to Thoth, to the Emerald Tablets, what do they say?'

Frank picked up where he left off.

'Ten of the twelve tablets have been translated and released; divided into thirteen parts for the sake of convenience. Apparently the last two tablets are so great and far-reaching in their importance that it's presently forbidden to release them to the world. The ones that *have* been released are at times very cryptic, which means the translations may be poor, or they've been deliberately encoded so only the fully initiated can decipher them.

What is discernable from the translations is that Thoth, who had travelled the stars, ruled ancient Egypt for sixteen-*thousand* years, from approximately 52,000 BC to 36,000 BC. That he was immortal, in that he'd conquered death, passing over only when he willed it, and, even then, not through "death" as we know it.'

'Like the modern yogis who can just leave their bodies?'

'Exactly.'

'Then he appointed guards for his secrets from among the highest of his people.'

'The Tat Brotherhood.'

'Yes.'

'So where did he go?'

'The tablets say that when the time came for him to leave Egypt, Thoth used levitation to build the Great Pyramid, patterning it after the pyramid of Earth force, and then descended into the Halls of Amenti.'

'"*Patterning it after the pyramid of Earth force*", what does that mean? Is it part of the "Flower of Life" pattern?'

Mark, who had been quietly eating his meal and sipping beer, chipped in.

'Yeah, the earth has a tetrahedral energetic pattern, like two interlocking pyramids, one of them inverted, which forms a three-dimensional star form.'

As Mark took out a pen and scrawled the shape on a paper napkin, Frank continued.

'Thoth supposedly built the pyramid over the entrance to the Great Halls of Amenti, secretly secured his records, his knowledge of the ancient wisdom and instruments of ancient Atlantis within it, to be retrieved when he returned from Amenti, then set a crystal in the apex, that sent rays out into "Time-Space", drawing the force from out of the ether.'

'A capstone of crystal; that would make even more sense than granite.'

'Granite has a crystalline structure as well; it may just be confirmation that the information is actually in the stone.'

'And that granite was also used to conduct other frequencies of energy. Do the tablets say what sort of rays it transmitted?'

'No, but clearly they were drawing some force from the ether and converting it or using it for something that could be related to the as yet undiscovered chambers within the pyramid.'

'There are more chambers in the pyramid itself?'

'I'd bet on it. The esoteric expedition of 1976 passed several locked "doors" as they descended the staircase to the lower chamber, and the Emerald Tablets confirm their presence by talking of other supposedly empty chambers that contain hidden keys to Amenti.'

'Amenti? The more I hear it, the more I think it isn't so much a physical place as a state of being, a state of consciousness, like the 4th or 5th Dimension.'

'You may be right, Alex. Thoth apparently says "while I sleep in the Halls of Amenti, my Soul will roam free and incarnate among men in this form or another.'

'So his Annunaki body may lie in stasis, but his consciousness incarnates into human form.'

'That's what it sounds like.'

To Frank's great interest, I related Crystal's thoughts about how the Annunaki, Imhotep in particular, had gone into a state of stasis; of suspended animation, hibernation, to regenerate, and at the same time, incarnate in a human form. Frank was open to it, but Mark was having the same problems conceiving it as I initially had, so I tried to explain it.

'Time is relative, right, an illusion; there is only this moment.'

'Yeah.'

'So all lives, past, present and future, are "simultaneous".'

'I get that, but one soul in more than one body at the same time?'

'It's a question of consciousness versus awareness; the body is just a vehicle, the soul is the driver. The driver parks one car in the garage for repairs and restoration, then gets in another, or a series of other cars, for each additional trip.'

Mark wasn't buying in.

'But it's still one driver in one vehicle: it doesn't explain how the soul can drive more than one car at a time?'

He had a good point and momentarily I was stumped. Then an image popped into my mind.

'Picture this then. An actor makes several movies, let's say five, each with it's own distinctive character specific to the script. At some point, all five movies are being shown somewhere around the world at exactly the same time.'

It wasn't a brilliant analogy, but it was good enough for Mark to grab the concept.

'OK, I see it, although it still comes back to the one actor.'

'Yes, but that one actor is God, Allah, whatever you want to call it.'

'Right, now I get it, and people's egos are the character in the film.'

'Exactly.'

Frank had been on another line of thought.

'Which means there's probably an alien body, anywhere from twelve to fourteen feet tall, laying in stasis somewhere under the Giza Plateau.'

We all took a swig of beer, as if to wash down the concept.

'So, when do you think Thoth will come back, when Hermes the thrice-lived, will return and become Bruce, the four-times-lived?'

Frank chuckled away.

'Who's to say he's not back already, incarnated in human form? Who's to say he's not sitting at this table?'

I looked straight back at Frank.

'Don't look at me, believe me, if I was Thoth, I'd know it.'

'Mark?'

'Count me out.'

It was at that moment I realized who Mark and Frank were the incarnations of; they were members of the Tat Brotherhood, seekers and keepers of truth, most likely Manetho and Herodotus, though I wasn't sure which was which, although I was pretty sure Frank was Herodotus. He threw the question back at me again.

'And you, Alex?'

'To tell you the truth, Frank, so much has happened to me in the last two weeks that I don't know if I'm Arthur or Martha.'

Mark checked his watch.

'Well, it's nearly 9:00 pm, and I don't know about you two, but it's been a long hot day and we've got an early start tomorrow; I'm ready to call it a night.'

We finished our beers and I headed to the counter to pay the bill. Despite the fact I'd hardly noticed it, the meal was almost as sumptuous and satisfying as the conversation, and it only came to three hundred Egyptian pound for the three of us, including the beers, which was about sixty bucks. I took a leaf out of Bill, Mark and Frank's book and gave the headwaiter five hundred, for which he was noticeably grateful.

As we suantered back towards the Cairo Palace, I remembered Frank had mentioned that there were three things that he was going to say about the *'Book of Thoth'*, and we'd only covered two.

'So, Frank, if the discs in the underground chamber aren't the *'Book of Thoth'*, arc they the Emerald Tablets?'

'No, by their own admission, they're a later and far lesser exposition of the ancient mysteries. They were written circa 34,000 BC, the *'Book of Thoth'* supposedly dates to 50,000 BC or even earlier.'

'So, where is it?'

'I think it's in the chamber under the Great Pyramid, the book in the clear case,...'

'That would make sense.'

'...and it's from that "book" that the Emerald Tablets and papyrus copies were made.'

'Is that the real reason why you guys did the scans at the Giza Plateau?'

'Partly. Find the entrances to the subterranean chambers of the Giza Plateau and you find the *'Book of Thoth'*, find the *'Book of Thoth'* and you find the real truthful history of not just the human race, but the "extra"-terrestrial life forms that have had, and most likely will have, an influence on the genetic and cultural development of all life on this planet.'

We arrived outside the Cairo Palace and Mark and Frank thanked me once again for dinner before we bid our farewells.

'We'll pick you up here in the morning.'

'What time?'

'Around 6:00. Are you sure you want to come?'

'I'm sure, I'll see you then.'

They hailed down a cab within seconds and disappeared into the Cairo night. By the time I'd taken the lift up to the hotel I was feeling the effects of the last few days and several beers and looking forward to bed. But my mind was racing with all sorts of thoughts about the contents of the great pyramid, the chambers beneath it, and especially the *'Book of Thoth'*.

'Mr. Alex! Welcome back. How was your dinner?'

'It was a smorgasbord!'

'Zmorga's board?'

'Lots to chew on and digest.'

'Oh, this is good?'

'Brilliant!'

'Very good. Mr. Alex.'

'May I have my laptop please Magdy?'

'But of course.'

He opened the safe and pulled it out.

'Do you wish it to have your paper?'

'No thanks, they can stay there.'

'Very well.'

'Do you have wi-fi?'

'But of course, the password, it is cairopalace, all one word.'

'Thanks.'

'It is my pleasure.'

'Magdy, can I get breakfast early in the morning, say around 5:45?'

'But of course.'

'Great, thanks, Goodnight.'

I headed back to my room and plugged in the computer; it had been a hell of a day but there was too much going through my head not to note it all down.

It'd all started in a little village in the middle of nowhere, before a morning stroll took me along the canal to the pyramid of Hawarra, with its substructure of massive granite blocks and the saddle vault over the granite box they called a burial chamber. That all sat beneath a superstructure of mud-brick. But were the human remains found there, as well as the mud-brick and outer casing, all later additions?

Beneath the pyramid clearly sat the Labyrinth at an angle of around twenty-two degrees. Was that in correlation with tilt of the earth? Was it built in layers and at different times, granite at the bottom, alabaster on top? The red-granite and alabaster fragments alongside the canal and Frank's scans were conclusive evidence it was there, flooded by the water from the canal that had been dredged through it. So why had the Supreme Council of Antiquities covered up the Mataha-expedition results, what was it they didn't want the world to know?

Then there were the other scans, the ones at Giza, that clearly showed there was much more beneath the surface than Zahi Hawass was admitting. And what was the real purpose of the Red Bull games in front of the Sphinx? Were they a diversion, a cover up for the robbing of the plateau in the middle of the night in April 2010?

Was that what was really behind the people's revolution, to get the foreigners out of Egypt, or locked in hotels, to close down the plateau and surround it with the military, to "protect it", all so that Hawass could then use the military to remove large objects from under the plateau without prying eyes observing him? It was almost incredulous to consider it was possible, but if it looks like a duck, walks like a duck and quacks like a duck, maybe it's a vulture in a fedora.

I was totally convinced Meidum was originally a ziggurat, with a pyramid shaped over the top and an eastern chapel added later, during the repairs made by Snefru.

It threw a whole new perspective over the construction and dating of not only this pyramid but also the one at Hawarra. And if it cast doubt on the dating of these pyramids, then it threw doubt over the dating of *all* the pyramids.

Heading inside, into my first pyramid, I was amazed and bemused by the corbelled burial chambers and what would have been their true function, because they clearly weren't burial chambers. If I was bemused by that, I was gob-smacked by Frank's NASA connections and the confirmation of the faked moon landings, the truth about the shuttle program and of alien satellites, and about the nuclear reactor under the Dome of the Rock in Jerusalem. Could all, or *any*, of that actually be true?

By the time we moved on to Dahshur, I was in true sceptic mode, not about the pyramids, but about anything the 'experts' and Egyptian authorities put forward as fact. Why had they *really* set up the military zone here? They could just as easily have set it up a few miles away, it's not as if they didn't have plenty of desert to choose from.

Because of the architecture around it, the repaired granite tomb, and the gypsum "sealing" of the tomb, the pyramid of Senwroset III seemed to date more from the Old Kingdom or even earlier. That then raised the question of when the surrounding tombs were actually built, and why? And there were the ruins of the pyramid of Amenemhat II, and the saddle vault, was it really for pressure relief?

Then we hit the big pyramids. First, the Red Pyramid, the Draco pyramid, with its concave faces, and the distinct possibility of the casing stones being washed away by tsunamis. There was the different angle of the pyramidion to the angle of the pyramid, were they wrongly associated?

Next was the Bent Pyramid, with its mathematical relationship to the Red Pyramid and its internal ziggurat structure. What was the significance of the angle change, of the separate chambers within, and the hacked out connecting tunnel? Why did the damaged casing stones show evidence not only of damage but also repair? Was the original ziggurat built around 10,000 BC, even earlier, then did a pole shift, around 8,800 BC somehow damage the chambers? Was the Bent Pyramid then added around it, and a new chamber built, with an entrance from the west, only to have another catastrophe hit, say around 5,200 BC, which damaged the new chamber and the exterior? Finally, in the 4th Dynasty, did Snefru repair it, digging a tunnel from the original chamber and connecting it to the new chamber, and prop up the walls here and in the lower chamber with cedar beams, then build a few temples and erects a few stelae to brag about it? If it were so, then again the history of *all* the pyramids was questionable.

That doubt was reinforced by the evidence I read about at Lisht, El-Lahuna and Mazghuna, of the granite chambers and portcullises, and the evidence I found at the Black Pyramid, of the usurped tombs, the relocation of tombs from before the Thera tsunami by the 18th Dynasty priests, and the grey pyramidion found in the rubble. Which pyramid was it really from, and did it contain information encoded in the actual stone?

I was still buzzing about the discussion on Herodotus, Plato and Manetho, neophytes of the Tat Brotherhood, coming to Egypt from Greece to be initiated in the chambers under the Great Pyramid, the same chambers discovered in 1976; it all supported my theory about Akhenaten and Apollo. But perhaps the most mind-blowing information was specifically about the guys who discovered the secret entrance in the southern face of the Great Pyramid in 1976 that led to the chambers beneath it, the Hall of Records; thirty-seven-thousand wafer-thin metal discs of information, and a book encased in some sort of translucent case that apparently revealed all the previous civilizations on the planet, including when man first set foot on earth five-hundred-and-seventy-six *thousand* years ago. And there's supposedly also a levitation machine, as

372

well as a time machine or star gate down there. It all tied in with the talk about the Montauk Project, and the Philadelphia Project, Project Rainbow.

By the time we sat down for dinner, the discussion centred on Thoth, who'd arrived in Egypt just over fifty-thousand years ago, and, using levitation, built the Great Pyramid on top of pre-existing ancient chambers, the Halls of Amenti. It was clear from the Inventory Stele that the Great Pyramid wasn't built by Khufu, but rather repaired by him. The evidence of him finding ancient "writings" secreted in the capstone, which would have been secreted at a time when the pyramid was actually built, suggested Khufu was actually Thoth reincarnated as Imhotep.

And if Khufu was Imhotep, and he retrieved the "time capsule" from the pyramidion of the Great Pyramid, then he must have known about the impending pole shift, as well as its after effects, and originally placed the capstone there to be recovered afterwards, using the knowledge within it to rebuild not only Egypt, but other civilizations around the globe, including the Minoan civilization around 2700 BC, the Mayans around 2600 BC, and the Harappon Civilization in the Indus Valley around 2500 BC.

So, the search was on for the *'Book of Thoth'*, and, whilst the 'Emerald Tablets' seemed to have been recovered from South America and returned to an "undiscovered" chamber within or beneath the Great Pyramid by a member of the Tat brotherhood in 1925, they were a later and lesser version of the true *'Book of Thoth'*, which more than likely sits, enclosed in a transparent viewing case, in the Great Halls beneath the Great Pyramid. Find the entrances to the subterranean chambers of the Giza Plateau and you find the *'Book of Thoth'*, find the *'Book of Thoth'* and you find the real history of all life on earth.

That done, I checked the time: 10:25pm; a quick check of my emails and then off to bed. I logged on to the hotel's wifi and to my email. Nothing important, just the usual junk mail on how to purchase cheap viagra, how to make my penis bigger, even a letter from a Ukrainian mail-order bride looking for love, or rather a free pass out of Russia. No point going on facebook, I'd get stuck there for ages, besides, what could I say; "I'm in Egypt on the run from the Secret Police as a murder suspect".

Then a thought struck me; what if I *was* arrested tomorrow? The Secret Police would probably torture me and track down the papers, they'd certainly confiscate my computer, then, once they had all the evidence, I'd suffer an unfortunate and untimely freak fatal accident, like being trampled by a herd of stampeding hormonal camels, and no one would ever find out the truth. I needed a plan B.

First thing was I needed a copy of the papers, not a hard copy, like photocopies, they would be too easy to destroy, and twice as much trouble handling, I needed an electronic copy of them, a set of jpegs or pdfs. I could take photos of all of them with my camera, but that would take hours, or ..., and it was like a light-bulb moment, ... or, tomorrow morning, while I was at Abu Raoush, I could get Abdo to scan Kareem's papers for me and save them as pdfs; brilliant. Then, before going to the Embassy, I could drop back here to the Cairo Palace and email the pdfs to Mark, before taking the originals with me to the Embassy. But that was only part of the solution, part of the story, there were all the things I'd discovered along my trip down the Nile; they needed to get out of Egypt as well.

Mark was the obvious "keeper of secrets", hell, he was a lawyer, not only that, he was probably the incarnation of Manetho; if I could trust anyone to know what to do, it was Mark. I attached a copy of all my diary notes to an email and addressed it to Mark, with a copy to myself.

"Mark,

The next few days are critical in my trip. I'm going to have the 'papers' scanned tomorrow and will email them to you by late tomorrow morning, as insurance, just in case for any reason something happens to me, like with Julian Assange, or worse. If it does, then translate and make public the documents and my story. The truth needs to be told about what is really beneath the sands of Egypt.

Alex."

Then I emailed all the photos that I'd taken with my iphone over the passed two weeks, to myself, and to Mark, just in case they confiscated my phone as well. Had I covered all the bases? I was pretty sure I had. Had I covered my ass? Only time will tell.

I shut everything down, plugged in my iphone to recharge, and hit the sack; tomorrow was going to be a pivotal day in my life and I had a feeling I was going to need my wits about me. Saeed's words still reverberated in my ears, and the question still lingered, "do I go to the Embassy, or not?" Before I could weigh it up, I fell asleep.

Also in this series

RED GRANITE
The Grains of Truth Beneath the Sands of Egypt
I
Abu Simbel - Wadi Hillal

RED GRANITE
The Grains of Truth Beneath the Sands of Egypt
II
Luxor - Karnak

RED GRANITE
The Grains of Truth Beneath the Sands of Egypt
IV
Saqqara - Abusir

RED GRANITE
The Grains of Truth Beneath the Sands of Egypt
V
Giza - Alexandria

Other books by this authhior

PIAHNA'S GIFT

12 FOOT FENCES